Prophecy

Books by Elizabeth Haydon in Gollancz

RHAPSODY

Prophecy
CHILD OF EARTH

Elizabeth Haydon

GOLLANCZ
London

Copyright © 2001 Elizabeth Haydon
All rights reserved

Maps by Ed Gazsi

The right of Elizabeth Haydon to be identified as the author
of this work has been asserted by her in accordance
with the Copyright, Designs and Patents Act 1988.

This edition first published in Great Britain in 2000 by

Gollancz
An imprint of the Orion Publishing Group
Orion House, 5 Upper St Martin's Lane, London WC2H 9EA

A CIP catalogue record for this book is available
from the British Library

Typeset by Deltatype Ltd, Birkenhead, Merseyside

Printed in Great Britain by
Clays Ltd St Ives plc

To the peacemakers and the negotiators
The nightmare chasers and the kissers of knee scrapes
Those who build up the civilization of the world
one child at a time
The legacy creators, the history writers
Those who honor the Past by shaping the Future
To those for whom being a parent is a calling
Particularly the ones I know most intimately
With profound love

Acknowledgments

With gratitude to Simon Spanton and Oisin Murphy-Lawless of Gollancz, for their extraordinary professionalism and good humour. Special thanks to Anthony Cheetham.

With appreciation to my family and friends, for not stuffing me in a crate and sending me over Niagara Falls through this process, and for your endless love and support.

With humble recognition to Anu Garg, a Singer possessing a great personal lexicon, who seeks to share his love of language through his wonderful Web site, www.wordsmith.org, for the perfect words you have provided by serendipity.

With gratitude to Richard Curtis and Amy Meo, for allowing me to watch while you shape the future.

And to the late Mario Puzo.

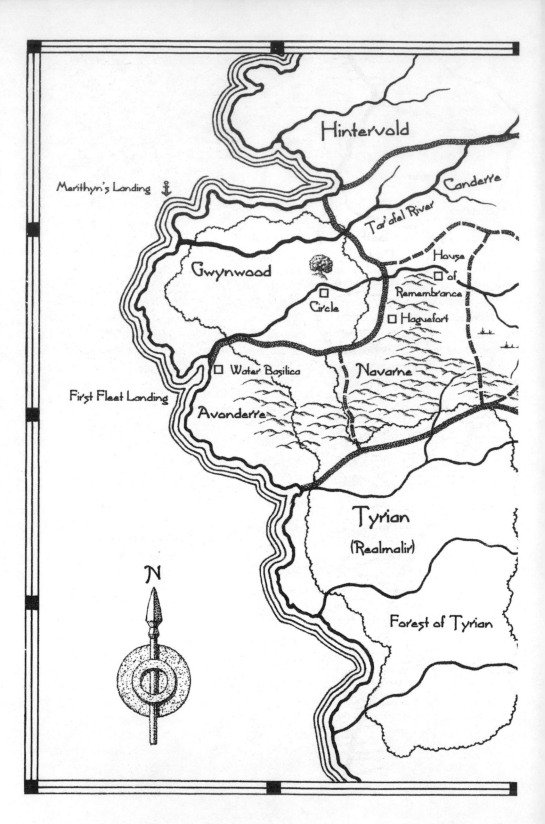

Hintervold

Marithyn's Landing ⚓

Canderre

Ta'afel River

House of Remembrance

Gwynwood

Circle

Haguefort

Water Basilica

Navarne

First Fleet Landing

Avonderre

Tyrian

(Realmalir)

Forest of Tyrian

N

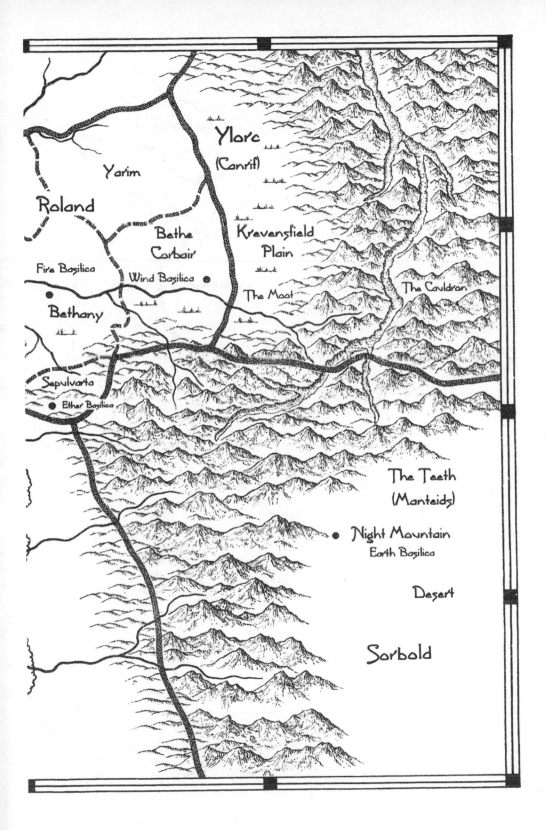

THE PROPHECY OF THE THREE

The Three shall come, leaving early, arriving late,
The lifestages of all men:
Child of Blood, Child of Earth, Child of the Sky.

Each man, formed in blood and born in it,
Walks the Earth and sustained by it,
Reaching to the sky, and sheltered beneath it,
He ascends there only in his ending, becoming part
    of the stars.
Blood gives new beginning, Earth gives sustenance,
The Sky gives dreams in life – eternity in death.
Thus shall the Three be, one to the other.

THE PROPHECY OF THE UNINVITED GUEST

Among the last to leave, among the first to come,
Seeking a new host, uninvited, in a new place.
The power gained being the first,
Was lost in being the last.
Hosts shall nurture it, unknowing,
Like the guest wreathed in smiles
While secretly poisoning the larder.
Jealously guarded of its own power,
Ne'er has, nor ever shall its host bear or sire children,
Yet ever it seeks to procreate.

THE PROPHECY OF THE SLEEPING CHILD

The Sleeping Child, the youngest born
Lives on in dreams, though Death has come
To write her name within his tome
And no one yet has thought to mourn.

The middle child, who sleeping lies,
'Twixt watersky and shifting sands
Sits silent, holding patient hands
Until the day she can arise.

The eldest child rests deep within
The ever-silent vault of earth,
Unborn as yet, but with its birth
The end of Time Itself begins.

THE PROPHECY OF THE LAST GUARDIAN

Within a Circle of Four will stand a Circle of Three
Children of the Wind all, and yet none
The hunter, the sustainer, the healer,
Brought together by fear, held together by love,
To find that which hides from the Wind.

Hear, oh guardian, and look upon your destiny:
The one who hunts also will stand guard
The one who sustains also will abandon,
The one who heals also will kill
To find that which hides from the Wind.

Listen, oh Last One, to the wind:
The wind of the past to beckon her home
The wind of the earth to carry her to safety
The wind of the stars to sing the mother's-song most known to her soul
To hide the Child from the Wind.

From the lips of the Sleeping Child will come the words of ultimate
    wisdom:
Beware the Sleepwalker
For blood will be the means
To find that which hides from the Wind.

Intermezzo

Meridion

Meridion sat in the darkness, lost in thought. The instrument panel of the Time Editor was dark as well; the great machine stood silent for the moment, the gleaming threads of diaphanous film hanging idle on their spools, each reel carefully labeled *Past* or *Future*. The Present, as ever, hung evanescent like silver mist in the air under the Editor's lamp, twisting and changing moment by moment in the half-light.

Draped across his knees was an ancient piece of thread, a lore strand from the Past. It was a film fragment of immeasurable importance, burnt and broken beyond repair on one end. Meridion picked it up gingerly, then turned it over in his hands and sighed.

Time was a fragile thing, especially when manipulated mechanically. He had tried to be gentle with the dry film, but it had cracked and ignited in the press of the Time Editor's gears, burning the image he had needed to see. Now it was too late; the moment was gone forever, along with the information it held. The identity of the demon he was seeking would remain hidden. There was no going back, at least not this way.

Meridion rubbed his eyes and leaned back against the translucent aurelay, the gleaming field of energy tied to his life essence that he had shaped for the moment into a chairlike seat, resting his head within its hum. The prickling melody that surrounded him was invigorating, clearing his thoughts and helping him to concentrate. It was his namesong, his life's own innate tune. A vibration unique in all the world, tied to his true name.

The demon he was seeking had great power over names, too. Meridion had gone back into the Past itself to find it, looking for a way to avert the path of devastation it had carefully constructed over Time, but the demon had eluded him. F'dor were the masters of lies, the fathers of deception. They were without corporeal form, binding themselves to innocent hosts and living through them or using them to do their will, then moving on to another more powerful host when the opportunity presented itself. Even far away, from his vantage point in the Future, there was no real way to see them.

For this reason Meridion had manipulated Time, had sliced and moved around pieces of the Past to bring a Namer of great potential together with those that might help her in the task of finding and destroying the demon. It had been his hope that these three would be able to accomplish this feat on their side of Time before it was too late to prevent what the demon had wrought, the devastation that was now consuming lands on both sides of the world. But the strategy had been a risky one. Just bringing lives together did not guarantee how they would be put to use.

Already he had seen the unfortunate consequences of his actions. The Time Editor had run heatedly with the unspooling of the time strands, fragments of film rending apart and swirling into the air above the machine as the Past destroyed itself in favor of the new. The stench of the burning timefilm was rank and bitter, searing Meridion's nostrils and his lungs, leaving him trembling at the thought of what damage he might inadvertently be doing to the Future by meddling in the Past. But it was too late now.

Meridion waved his hand over the instrument panel of the Time Editor. The enormous machine roared to life, the intricate lenses illuminated by its ferocious internal light source. A warm glow spilled onto the tall panes of glass that formed the walls of the circular room and ascended to the clear ceiling above. The glimmering stars that had been visible from every angle above and below him in the darkness a moment before disappeared in the blaze of reflected brilliance. Meridion held the broken fragment of film up to the light.

The images were still there, but hard to make out. He could see the small, slender woman because of her shining hair, golden and reflecting the sunrise, bound back with a black ribbon, standing on the brink of morning in the vast panorama of the mountains where he had last sighted the two of them. Meridion blew gently on the lore-strand to clear it of dust and smiled as the tiny woman in the frame drew her cloak closer about herself. She stared off into the valley that stretched below her, prickled with spring frost and the patchy light of dawn.

Her traveling companion was harder to find. Had Meridion not known he was there prior to examining the film he never would have seen him, hidden in the shadows cast by the sun. It took him several long moments to find the outline of the man's cloak, designed as it was to hide him from the eyes of the world. A faint trace of mist rose from the cloak and blended with the rising dew burning off in the sunlight.

As he suspected, the lore-strand had burnt at precisely the wrong moment, obliterating the Namer's chance to catch a glimpse of the F'dor's ambassador before he or she reached Ylorc. Meridion had been watching through her eyes, waiting for the moment when she first beheld the henchman, as the Seer had advised. He could make out a thin dark line in the distance; that must have been the ambassadorial caravan. She had already seen it. The opportunity had passed. And he had missed it.

He dimmed the lamp on the Time Editor again and sat back in the dark sphere of his room to think, suspended within his glass globe amid the stars, surrounded by them. There must be another window, another way to get back into her eyes.

Meridion glanced at the endless wall of glass next to him and down at the surface of the Earth miles below. Black molten fire was crawling slowly across the darkened face of the world, withering the continents in its path, burning without smoke in the lifeless atmosphere. At the rim of the horizon another glow was beginning; soon the fire sources would meet and consume what little was left. It took all of Meridion's strength to keep from succumbing to the urge to scream. In his darkest dreams he could never have imagined this.

In his darkest dreams. Meridion sat upright with the thought. The Namer was prescient, she could see the Past and Future in her dreams, or sometimes just by reading the vibrations that events had left behind, hovering in the air or clinging to an object. Dreams gave off vibrational energy; if he could find a trace of one of them, like the dust that hovered in afternoon light, he could follow it back to her, anchor himself behind her eyes again, in the Past. Meridion eyed the spool which had held the brittle lore-strand he had spliced together, hanging listlessly on the Editor's main pinion.

He seized the ancient reel and spun out the film, carefully drawing the edge where it had broken cleanly back under the Time Editor's lens. He adjusted the eyepiece and looked. The film in frame was dark, and at first it was hard to make out anything within the image. Then after a few moments his eyes adjusted, and he caught a flash of gold as the Namer sighed in the darkness of her chamber and rolled over in her sleep. Meridion smiled.

He had found the record of the night before she and Ashe had left on their journey. Meridion had no doubt she had been in the throes of dreaming then.

After a moment's consideration he selected two silver instruments, a gathering tool with a hair-thin point and a tiny sieve basket soldered onto a long slender handle. The mesh of the thumbnail-sized basket was fine enough to hold even the slightest particle of dust. With the greatest of care Meridion blew on the frame of film, and watched under the lens for a reaction. He saw nothing. He blew again, and this time a tiny white spark rose from the strand, too small to be seen without magnification even by his extraordinarily sensitive eyes.

Skillfully Meridion caught the speck with the gathering tool and transferred it to the basket. Then, watching intently, he waited until the lamp of the Time Editor illuminated the whisper-thin thread that connected it to the film. He turned his head and exhaled. He had caught a dream-thread.

Working carefully he drew it out more until it was long enough to position under the most powerful lens. He never averted his eyes as he gestured to one of the cabinets floating in the air above the Editor. The doors opened, and a tiny bottle of oily liquid skittered to the front of the shelf, then leapt into the air, wafting gently down until it came to rest on the gleaming prismatic disc hovering in the air beside him. Keeping his eyes fixed on the thread lest he lose sight of it, Meridion uncorked the bottle with one hand and carefully removed the dropper. Then he held it over the thread and squeezed.

The glass below the lens swirled in a pink-yellow haze, then cleared. Meridion reached over and turned the viewing screen onto the wall. It would take a moment for him to get his bearings, but it was always that way when one was watching from inside someone else's dreams.

Nightmares

Rhapsody did not sleep well the night before she handed herself over to a man she barely knew, a man whose face she had never seen. Having been gifted with prescience, the ability to see visions of the Future and the Past, she was accustomed to restless nights and terrifying dreams, but this was different somehow.

She was awake for much of the long, torturous night, fighting nagging doubts that were very likely the warnings, not of some special foresight, but of ordinary common sense. By morning she was completely unsure as to the wisdom of her decision to go overland with him, beyond the stalwart protection of her strange, formidable friends.

The firecoals in the small, poorly ventilated grate burned silently while she tossed and muttered, neither awake nor really asleep. The mute flames cast bright sheets of pulsing light on the walls and ceiling of her tiny windowless bedchamber deep within the mountain. Upon becoming king of the Firbolg in Ylorc, Achmed had named his seat of power the Cauldron, but tonight the place more closely approximated the Underworld.

Achmed had made no secret of his disapproval at her leaving the mountain with Ashe. From the moment they had met on the streets of Bethe Corbair the two men had exuded a mutual mistrust that was impossible not to notice; the tension in the air made her scalp hum with negative static. But trust was not Achmed's common state. Aside from herself and Grunthor, his giant sergeant-major and long-time friend, as far as she knew he had extended it to no one.

Ashe seemed pleasant enough, and harmless. He had been willing to visit Rhapsody and her companions in Ylorc, their forbidding, mountainous home. He had not appeared uncomfortable with the fact that Ylorc was the lair of the Firbolg, primitive, sometimes brutish people that most humans feared as monsters.

Ashe had exhibited no such prejudices. He had dined agreeably at the same table with the glowering Bolg chieftains, taking no notice of their crude table manners and ignoring their propensity to spit bone fragments onto the floor. And he had taken up arms willingly in defense of the Firbolg realm against an attack by the Hill-Eye, the last holdout clan to swear fealty to Achmed, whose reign as Warlord was still new and sorting itself out. If he was amused or displeased in any way by Rhapsody's obnoxious companion's ascent to monstrous royalty, Ashe did not show it.

But there was little, in fact, that Ashe did show. His face was always carefully covered by the hood of his cloak, a strange garment that seemed to wrap him in mist, making him even harder to discern than he already was.

Rhapsody rolled over in bed and let out a painful sigh. She accepted his right to concealment, understood that the great Cymrian War had left many of its survivors disfigured and maimed, but still could not escape the nagging thought that he might be hiding more than a hideous scar. Men with hidden faces had plagued many different areas of her life.

Rhapsody opened her emerald eyes in the darkness of her cavelike chamber. In response, the coals on the fire glowed more intensely for a moment. The remnants of charred wood, reducing in the heat to white-hot cinders, sent forth wisps of smoke that rose above the coalbed and up the chimney that had been hewn into her chamber centuries before, when Ylorc was still Canrif, the old Cymrian seat of power. She drew a deep breath and watched as more smoke billowed up, forming a thin cloud above the ashes.

She shuddered; the smoke had seeped into her memory, bringing back an unwelcome picture. It was not one of the lingering images from her old life on streets of Serendair, her island homeland, gone now beneath the waves of the sea on the other side of the world. Those days of abuse and prostitution that had haunted her for so long rarely plagued her sleep anymore.

Now she dreamt mostly of the terrors of this new land. Almost every night brought the hideous memories of the House of Remembrance, an ancient library in this new world, and of a curtain of fire that formed a hazy tunnel. At the end of the column of smoke a man had stood, a man in a gray mantled-cloak, much like the one Ashe wore. A man whom the documents they had found identified only as the Rakshas. A man who had stolen children, sacrificing them for their blood. A man whose face she had also not seen. The coincidence was unnerving.

The coals were doing little to dispel the dampness of the room, she thought hazily. Her skin was clammy, causing the blankets to cling to her and scratch. Beads of sweat tangled the hairs at the back of her neck in the chain of the locket she never took off, pulling painfully as she writhed again, struggling to break free of the clutching bedding.

Just as her stomach was beginning to twist in cold worry, a pragmatic thought descended. Achmed was arguably her best friend in this land, the surly other side of her cheerful coin, and he tended to walk the world veiled from sight as well.

It never ceased to amaze her, after all this time, how she could be so close to this assassin-turned-king, a man who seemed to make it a life's goal to annoy anyone with whom he came in contact. The fact that he had dragged her through the Earth itself, against her will, away from Serendair before the Island was consumed in volcanic fire, saving her life in the process, had not inspired gratitude in her. Although she had ceased to resent her kidnapping over time, a tiny corner of her heart would never forgive him for it. She had learned to love him and Grunthor in spite of it.

And she had learned to love the Firbolg as well, largely through the eyes of these two friends, whose blood was half-Bolg. Despite their primitive nature and warlike tendencies, Rhapsody had come to appreciate many aspects of this cave-dwelling culture that she found surprisingly sophisticated, and far more admirable than some of the behavior she had seen exhibited by their human counterparts in the provinces of Roland. They followed leaders out of respect and fear, not arbitrary or dubious family heritage; they spent what meager healing resources they had on bringing forth infants and protecting mothers and their young, a moral tenet Rhapsody shared. The refined social structure Achmed and Grunthor had introduced was just beginning to take root when the need for her journey had become clear.

Rhapsody writhed onto her back, seeking refuge from her dreams and a more comfortable position, but neither was to be had. She succumbed to the rapid whirring of thoughts through her brain again.

Finding the claw had changed everything. From deep within the vaults of Ylorc they had unearthed the talon of a dragon, fitted with a handle for use as a dagger. The claw had rested undisturbed for centuries, even as the Bolg took over the mountains, making the abandoned Cymrian realm their own. Now it was in the air, and the dragon to whom it belonged would feel it, would taste its vibrations on the wind. Rhapsody believed she would come for it eventually. Having heard the tales of the mighty Elynsynos, and seen the fierce and horrific statues of the beast in the Cymrian museum and in village squares across Roland, she had no doubt that the dragon's wrath would be virulent. Images of that wrath had led the parade of nightmares on this last night in Ylorc, causing her to wake for the first of many times, trembling.

It was to spare the Bolg from the devastating consequences of that wrath that she had decided to find the wyrm first and return the dagger, though both Achmed and Grunthor had objected strenuously. Rhapsody had stood firm in her decision to go, her determination fueled by the thought of her adopted Bolg grandchildren withering to ashes beneath the dragon's breath. It was another of the dreams that haunted her, though sometimes the victims changed. Her dreams did not discriminate.

She feared for Jo, the teenaged street child she had found in the House of Remembrance and adopted as her sister. She also feared for Lord Stephen, the pleasant young duke of Navarne, and his children, whom she also had taken into her heart. Each of these loved ones took turns in her nightmares roasting alive before her eyes. This night the honor had belonged to Lord Stephen.

It was within his castle that she had first seen a statue of Elynsynos. He had already suffered the loss of his wife, his best friend, Gwydion of Manosse, and countless people within his duchy to whatever evil was plaguing this land, causing inexplicable outbreaks of violence. The loss of

Rhapsody's world and her family had almost killed her; the Bolg and her friends, this was her family now. To leave that family open to attack would be almost as bad as losing it the first time, in some ways worse. Ashe said he knew how to find the dragon. It was well worth risking herself and her safety to save them. She just couldn't be sure, in this land of deception, that she was not endangering them even more by going with him.

Rhapsody twisted onto her side, entangling herself in the rough woolen blankets again. Nothing made sense anymore. It was impossible to tell whom or what to trust, including her own senses. She could only pray that the dreams of the coming destruction were warnings, not like the foregone premonitions that had told her of the death of Serendair, but either way, it would be impossible to tell until it was too late.

As she drifted off to troubled sleep it seemed to her that the smoke from the fire had thickened and formed a ribbon in the air, a translucent thread that wound around her dreams and settled behind her eyes.

Achmed the Snake, king of the Firbolg, was having nightmares as well, and it irritated him. Sleeping terrors were Rhapsody's personal curse; generally he was immune to them, having lived out more than his share of torments in the waking world, the old world, a life that he was well glad to be rid of.

The inert stone walls of the Cauldron, his seat of power within the mountain, normally provided him with dark and restful sleep, dreamless and undisturbed by the vibrations of the air to which he was especially sensitive. His Dhracian physiology, the burdensome gift granted to him by his mother's race, was both a blessing and a curse. It gave him the ability to read the signals of the world that were indiscernible to the eyes and minds of the rest of the populace, but the toll was great; it left him with little peace, having to daily endure the assault of the myriad invisible signatures that others defined as Life.

He was therefore unintentionally appreciative to find this fortress hewn deeply into the mountainous realm of darkness that was Ylorc. The smoothly polished basalt walls held in the quiet, stagnant air of his royal bedchamber, keeping the noise and tumult of the world at bay. As a result his nights were generally free from disturbance, tranquil and comforting in their silence.

But not this night.

In a flurry of growled curses Achmed spun over in his bed and rose to stand, angry. It was all he could do to keep from striding down the corridor to Rhapsody's room and dragging her out of her own sleep, demanding to know what was wrong with her, why she was so oblivious to the danger in what she was about to undertake. There would be little point in doing that, however; Achmed already knew the answer to that question.

Rhapsody was oblivious to almost everything. For a woman whose brain was keen and mind vibrant with an intelligence he could feel in his skin, she was capable of disregarding even the most obvious facts if she didn't want to believe them.

Initially he had assumed that this was a factor of the cataclysmic transformation they had each undergone, a metamorphosis that occurred when they walked through the inferno that burned at the center of the Earth during their escape from Serendair. Upon exiting the conflagration Rhapsody was vastly different; she had emerged from the fire physically perfect, her natural beauty enhanced to supernatural proportions. He had been fascinated, not only by the potential power that was inherent in her now, but by her utter inability to recognize the change. The open-mouthed gawking that she experienced in the street whenever she put the hood of her cloak down had done nothing to convince her of the magnificence of her visage; rather, it made her feel like a freak.

Achmed gave the bedsheet that had remained wrapped around his foot a savage kick. Over time, as he had gotten to know Rhapsody better, he realized that her self-deceptive tendencies had long preceded their walk through the fire. It was actually her way of protecting the last shred of her innocence, her fierce desire to believe in good where none existed, to trust when there was no reason to do so.

Her life on the street had clearly been one from which innocent belief could not hide easily. She had had commerce with one of his master's servants, Michael, the Wind of Death, and had doubtless been introduced to the harshest of realities by him. Nevertheless, she was always looking for the happy ending, trying to recreate the family she had lost in volcanic fire a thousand years before by adopting every waif and foundling she came across. Up until now this tendency had only served to set her up for heartache, which didn't bother him a bit. Her latest undertaking, however, threatened to compromise more than her life, and that aspect of it disturbed him deeply.

Somewhere out in the vastness of the lands to the west was a human host harboring a demon, he was sure of it; he had seen the work of F'dor before. He had, in fact, been the unwilling servant of one. A twisted race, evil and ancient, born of dark fire, he had hoped that the demise of their Island homeland would have taken the last of the F'dor with it. Had he been there during the Seren War that raged after they left he would have seen to it as his final act of assassination, the trade he had plied in those days.

But he had escaped the Island early. The war had come and gone, Serendair had disappeared beneath the waves a millennium before he emerged from the Root, half a world away, on the other side of Time. And those that had lived through the conflict, had seen the cataclysm coming and had possessed the wisdom to leave before it did, had undoubtedly brought the evil with them to this new place.

It had all the pathos of the World's Cruelest Joke. He had broken the unbreakable chain of the demon, fled from something from which flight was impossible, had made a successful escape from that which could not be escaped only to find it here again, waiting out there somewhere for him, indiscernibly bound to one of the millions of inhabitants of this new land, biding its time. For the moment they were safe from it, it seemed; the evil had not broached the mountains yet, as far as he could tell. But now this brainless harlot was leaving the protection of his realm. If she survived, she would undoubtedly come back as its thrall without even knowing it.

In earlier days, this would actually have been, in a warped way, a good thing. The possibility that the F'dor had bound itself to her would have alleviated the need for him to go in search of it. Upon Rhapsody's return to the Teeth, the Firbolg mountains, Grunthor would have killed her in front of him while he performed the Thrall ritual. It was another racial gift he possessed as half-Dhracian, the strange death dance he had seen but never performed that would prevent the demon from escaping as the host died, destroying it eternally along with its human body, in this case Rhapsody's. If she had not, in fact, been possessed, her needless death would have caused neither of them a second thought.

But that was no longer the case. Grunthor loved Rhapsody fiercely, defended her with ever fiber of his monstrous being. At seven and a half feet, and the same width as a dray horse, that was a lot of ferociously determined protection.

Even he himself had come to acknowledge that she was useful to have around. In addition to her compelling beauty, which frightened the Firbolg or at least made them hold her in awe, there was Rhapsody's music, one of the most useful tools they had in their arsenal aimed at bringing about the conquest of the mountain and the advancement of the Firbolg civilization.

Rhapsody was Liringlas, a Skysinger, proficient in the science of Naming. There were pleasing aesthestics to the music that was inherent in her, part of her physical makeup. She emanated vibrations which soothed the sensitive veins that traced the surface of his skin. Achmed had decided long before that this was one of the reasons that he found her endearingly irritating, rather than a genuine annoyance, as he found most people to be.

The more useful aspects of her musical ability, however, were its powers to persuade and to inspire fear, to heal wounds and cause damage, to discern vibrations that even he could not identify. Rhapsody had been instrumental in their taking the mountain; without her the campaign would certainly have taken much longer and would have been far bloodier. Unfortunately, though these were the talents he valued, Rhapsody did not.

She spent an inordinate amount of time instead using the comforting aspects of her musical healing, singing to the injured to ease their pain, soothing anxiety, ministrations that he felt confused the Bolg and annoyed him beyond belief. But eventually he had come to tolerate her need to alleviate suffering; it secured her assistance in the necessary things.

In addition to helping win the mountain, she had been responsible for negotiating the treaties with Roland and Sorbold, organizing the vineyard plantings and establishing an educational system, all things that were critical to his master plan. So he had come to respect her ideas and rely on her almost as much as he did on Grunthor, which was why her leaving with Ashe felt like betrayal. At least that was the reason he attached to the

11

stabbing sense of frustration he had felt ever since she had announced her plan to go with this interloper, this stranger shrouded in mist and secrets.

Just the prospect of her departing Ylorc in the morning made him feel physically cold. Achmed cursed again, running thin hands through sweaty hair and sitting down angrily in the chair before his uncooperative fire. He stared at the minuscule flames for a moment, remembering the sight of Rhapsody as she came back from her walk through the wall of fire within the belly of the Earth, having unintentionally absorbed its power and lore, purged from even the smallest of physical flaws. From that moment forward any fire, from the flickering flame of a candle to roaring bonfires, responded to her with the same adulation that men did, mirroring her mood, sensing her presence, obeying her commands. It was power that he needed here, within the cold mountain.

The Firbolg king leaned forward, elbows on knees, his folded hands resting on his lips, thinking. Perhaps he was worrying unnecessarily. Rhapsody's initial work was done and progressing nicely. The hospital and hospice were running smoothly, the vineyards tended carefully, even through the winter, by the Firbolg she had trained in agriculture. The Bolg children now were studying the techniques that would make their clans healthier and more long-lived, more prepared to stand their ground against the men of Roland. The lifeless mountain had grown warm under her ministrations. The Cymrian forges constructed by Gwylliam, the fool who had built and ruled Canrif and had started the war that destroyed it, blazed night and day in the fabrication of steel for weapons and tools, the residual heated air circulating within the mountain. The Bolg would barely miss her presence.

And her status as a Namer provided the insurance against her going unnoticed as an unwilling thrall of the demon. F'dor were the masters of lies, deceptive and secretive; Namers were forsworn to the truth. Their powers were deeply tied to it; it was the act of keeping their thinking and speaking honed on the truth as they knew it that allowed them to discern it on deeper levels than most. Rhapsody had demonstrated the ability to manipulate the power of a true name in the moment they had met, though she had done so unintentionally.

A moment before he and Grunthor had come upon her in the old land he was still known by the name given him at birth: the Brother. He was enslaved, breathing air tainted by the sickening smell of burning flesh; the malodor of the F'dor whose mark was upon him, the demon that had possession of his own true name. The invisible chain around his neck was tightening as each second passed. Undoubtedly the F'dor had begun to suspect that he was running, trying to escape its last hideous command.

And in the next moment, he had tripped over Rhapsody, running from her own pursuers in the back streets of Easton, trying to escape the lascivious intentions of Michael, the Waste of Breath. A slight smile crossed his lips and he closed his eyes, turning the memory over in his mind again.

Pardon me, but would you be willing to adopt me for a moment? I'd be grateful.

He had nodded, not having any idea why.

Thank you. She had turned back to the town guards who were chasing her. *What an extraordinary coincidence. You gentlemen are just in time to meet my brother. Brother, these are the town guard. Gentlemen, this is my brother – Achmed – the Snake.*

The crack of the invisible collar had been inaudible, but he had felt it in his soul. For the first time since the F'dor had taken his name the air in his nostrils cleared, dispelling the hideous odor from his nose and mind. He was free, released from his enslavement and the damnation that would eventually follow, and this stranger, this tiny half-Lirin woman, had been his rescuer.

She had, in her own panicked moment, taken his old name, the Brother, and changed it forever into something ridiculous but safe, giving him back the life and soul over which he had lost control. He could see in his memory even now the look of shock in her clear green eyes; she had had no idea what she had done. Even as he and Grunthor had dragged her overland and into the root of Sagia, the immense tree sacred to the Lirin, her mother's people, she was still suffering the notion that in their escape they were trying to save her from the Waste of Breath. To his knowledge she was still under that mistaken impression.

So if the F'dor should come upon her and bind itself to her soul, it would be easy to discern. She would no longer be able to act as a Namer, would lose her powers of truth once she was the host of a demonic spirit that was an innate liar. It was small comfort, given all the other dangers that were lying in wait for her out there somewhere, beyond his lands and his protection.

Achmed shivered and looked at the hearth. The last of the firecoals had burned down, vanishing in a thin wisp of smoke.

Deep within the barracks of the Firbolg mountain guard, Grunthor was dreaming, too, something he did not tend to do. Unlike the Firbolg king, he was a simple man with a simple outlook on life. As a result, he had simple nightmares. His bad dreams, however, tended to cause more collective suffering.

Grunthor, like Achmed, was half-Bolg, but the other half was Bengard, a giant race of grisly featured desert dwellers with oily, hide-like skin that held back the effects of the sun. The Bolg-Bengard combination was as unappealing to the eye as Rhapsody's human-Lirin mix was pleasing, even to the sensibilities of the Bolg, who held Grunthor in high esteem dwarfed only by their utter fear of him. It was an attitude that pleased him.

As Grunthor muttered in his sleep, whispering through the meticulously polished tusks that protruded from his jutting jaw, the elite mountain guard captains and lieutenants who shared his barracks remained still. To a one the Bolg soldiers were afraid that any movement might in some way disturb the Sergeant-Major or set him off, which undoubtedly qualified as the last thing any of them wanted to do. It seemed that neither Grunthor nor any of the Bolg who shared the sleeping corridor with him would be getting any rest that night.

Grunthor dreamt of the dragon. He had never seen one before, except for a rather bad statue of one in the Cymrian museum, so his visions were limited to the scope of his imagination, which had never been vast. His only knowledge of them came from Rhapsody, who had told him dragon tales during their endless journey along the Root, stories of the great beasts' physical might and power over the elements, as well as their ferocious intelligence and tendency to hoard treasure.

It was this last characteristic that was giving him nightmares. He feared that once Rhapsody was within the dragon's lair, it would seek to possess her and never let her return to the mountain. This was a loss he could not contemplate, having never before cared enough about anything to miss it.

Unconsciously he patted the wall next to his bunk, whispering in Bolgish the words of comfort he had imparted to Achmed not long after they had emerged from the Root, seeking to console his longtime friend and leader about the loss of his blood gift. Grunthor had known him in the days when he was the Brother, the most proficient assassin the world had ever known, so called because he was the first of his race born on the Island from which they had come.

Serendair was a unique land, one of the places Time itself was said to have begun. As the Firstborn of his race in that unique land, the Brother had a bond to the blood of all who lived there. He could seek out any individual heartbeat with the skill of a hound on the hunt, matching his own to it and following it with deadly accuracy, relentless in his quest until he found his quarry. Watching him seek and find his prey was a marvel to behold.

All that had changed when they came forth from the Root into this new land on the other side of the world. Achmed's gift was gone; now the only heartbeats he could hear were the ones that had come from the old world of Serendair. Even though Achmed had said nothing, Grunthor had felt his despair, and so knew that there were things in life that brought sorrow when they were no longer there. It was the first time he had ever had this realization.

He was now experiencing the feeling himself. Rhapsody was Lirin; a slight, frail race upon which the Firbolg in the old land had preyed very successfully, though what Lirin lacked in strength they generally made up for by being sly and swift. They were a race he had even consumed a few of himself, though not as many as he had teasingly led her to believe.

In many ways Lirin were as opposite to the Firbolg as he himself was to Rhapsody. Lirin were sharp and angular where Bolg were sinewy and muscular. The Lirin lived outside, in the fields and forests beneath the stars, while the Bolg were born of the caves and mountains, the children of the dark of the earth. In Grunthor's opinion Rhapsody had benefited from being sired by a human; her appearance was still slight but not frail, the sharp angles giving way to slender curves, high cheekbones and softer facial features than her mother undoubtedly had. She was beautiful. No doubt the dragon would think so, too.

At the thought Grunthor roared in his sleep, sending his lieutenants scrambling up the roughhewn walls of their chamber or out of their bunks entirely. The wood of his massive bed screamed and groaned as he thrashed about, snorting and growling, finally settling onto his side in silence again. The only sound in the room for a few moments afterwards was the quickened breathing of his unfortunate bunkmates who huddled against the barracks walls, their eyes glittering and blinking rapidly in the dark.

Unconsciously Grunthor pulled his rough woolen blanket up over his shoulder and sighed as the warmth touched his neck, a sensation similar to being near Rhapsody. He had initially been reluctant to leave the Root once they had arrived here. He had been bound to the Earth by the song of his name that she had sung to lead them through the great Fire. *Grunthor, strong and reliable as the Earth itself*, she had called him in his namesong, among other descriptions. From the moment he had exited the Fire he had felt the beating heart of the world in his blood, a tie to the granite and basalt and all that grew above it. The Earth was like the lover he had never had, warm and comforting in the darkness, a feeling of acceptance he had never known, and it was inextricably linked to Rhapsody.

In a way he did not miss being within the Earth, or the earthsong that still hummed in his ears when he was wrapped in silence, because she was there. He could still see her smile in the dark, her dirty face gleaming in the glow given off by the Axis Mundi, the great Root that bisected the world that had been their path away from Serendair and to this new place.

He had been her protector from the very beginning, had comforted her in her night terrors, let her sleep on his chest in the dank chill of their journey along the Root, kept her from falling into nothingness during the arduous climb. It was a role so far removed from any he had ever played before that he hardly believed himself capable of it. It had taken every resource of self-control that he had to keep from locking her in her chambers now and driving her guide from the mountain. How he would deal with a double first loss – Rhapsody herself, and the memory she kept alive of being within the Earth – was more than he could imagine. If she were to die, or just never come back, Grunthor was not sure he could go on.

And then, as ever, his mind cleared as the thoughts became too complicated, and pragmatism returned. Grunthor was a man of military solutions, and weighed the odds of her survival unconsciously. She carried a credible weapon – Daystar Clarion, a sword from the old world they had found within the earth, for reasons unknown, here on the other side of the world. It, like they, had undergone a significant change; its blade burned with flame now, where in Serendair it had only reflected the light of the

15

stars. He had taught her how to fight with it, and she was a credit to her instructor, performing admirably in their campaigns to subdue the Bolg. She could take care of herself. She would be all right.

Grunthor began to snore, a sound that was music to the ears of his bunkmates. They settled back in for the night quietly, taking care not to disturb the Sergeant-Major's newly found sleep.

Across the hall from Rhapsody's chambers, Jo was having the dreams typical of a sixteen-year-old with an obsession, full of chemical excitement and pictures of hideous deformity. She slept on her back in her grotesquely messy room, the favored sleeping position of street children who had found a comfortable spot in an area of town in which they didn't belong. From time to time she unconsciously dabbed at the beads of perspiration that dotted her chest, or drew her legs more tightly together when the flesh between them began to burn with arousal.

The image in her dream was that of Ashe, and it changed from moment to moment. This was largely because she had never actually seen what Ashe looked like, though she had been closer to doing so than most. From the moment of their awkward introduction in the marketplace in Bethe Corbair she had longed for him. She had no idea why.

Initially he had been nothing more than a pocket to pick, the glint of a sword hilt as he stood, near-invisible, in the street, watching the commotion that Rhapsody was unintentionally causing across the way. Upon slipping her hand into his trousers pocket, however, she had felt a surge of power that had unbalanced her. The mist that enveloped her wrist had caused her to lurch and slip, grasping his testicles instead of his coin purse. The row that had ensued served as an unpleasant but effective introduction, not only between Ashe and herself, but Ashe and Rhapsody as well. It had sorted itself out neatly, as everything seemed to when Rhapsody was involved.

Now Jo dreamed of the image of his eyes, furiously blue and clear within the darkness of his hood, blazing down at her beneath a wave of coppery hair, the only aspects of his face visible from below. She had watched carefully ever since Ashe had come, months later, to visit them in Ylorc, waiting for any glimpse of further features, but it had never happened. Sometimes she wondered if she had actually seen anything at all, if the memory of his eyes and hair was just her mind's way of filling in the desperately desired blanks.

Sometimes Jo would dream of his face, but more often than not it was an unpleasant experience. No matter how nicely the image had begun, it would often resolve itself into something frightening. In her waking moments Jo had come to realize that men who shielded their faces from sight often had good reason to do so, and generally it translated into some form of hideous appearance. Achmed, another man with a hidden face, was ugly as death; uglier, if at all possible.

The first time she had seen Achmed without the benefit of the swath of

16

material that usually veiled his lower face she had gasped aloud at the sight. His skin was pocked and mottled, lined with exposed veins and imbued with an unhealthy pallor. And always above the veil were the eyes, closely set and somewhat mismatched, giving him the appearance of being transfixed in a perennial stare.

She had pulled Rhapsody aside.

How can you stand looking at him?

Who?

Achmed, of course.

Why?

Her adopted older sister had been of little use in making sense of the confusion she felt within the Firbolg mountain. Rhapsody seemed at ease among the ugly and the monstrous. She had stared at Jo as if she had two heads every time Jo made reference to the fact that looking at Achmed was not a pleasant experience. At the same time she seemed utterly unaware of any reason to be attracted to Ashe. Jo was secretly glad; it made the furtive desire that was growing daily within her a little less guilt-ridden.

There was enough guilt to bear about the other thing that secretly gladdened her; she was relieved that Rhapsody seemed ignorant of Ashe's attraction to her as well. Jo's life on the street had made her a keen observer, and even though Ashe tended not to display his interest noticeably, she had picked up on it anyway. Achmed and Grunthor had seen it too, she was certain. But Grunthor was gone most of the time on maneuvers, and Achmed had found other reasons to dislike Ashe, so it was hard to confirm without asking them, something she would rather die than do.

Jo turned onto her stomach and curled her knees and arms under her, trying to shield herself from the missiles of jealousy that rained down on her now in the dim light of her bedchamber. As much as she thought she wanted the attention of this hidden stranger, she found herself shuddering at the brutal thoughts that plagued her about Rhapsody, the only person who had ever loved her; who was now an unintentional obstacle.

Rhapsody and the two Bolg had rescued her from the House of Remembrance, saving her from the blood sacrifice of the other children she had witnessed there. And while Achmed and Grunthor would have turned her over to Lord Stephen, Rhapsody had adopted her instead, bringing her along with them, protecting her, giving her an opportunity to belong, loving her. Jo was just beginning to learn to love her back when Ashe came to visit, complicating things. Life before had been a simple matter of survival, daily brushes with the law and other unsavory types, and the simple challenge of finding food and shelter for the night. Now it was far too complicated.

The last flickering candle in Jo's chamber faltered, then burned out, leaving nothing but the glowing wick and the acrid smell of the liquid wax in the new darkness. Her nose wrinkled, and she pulled the covers over her head. Morning couldn't come soon enough.

★

Ashe's dreams were not of anyone in this world, or in this time. Being neither dead nor really alive, the only comfort Ashe ever found from the agony he carried each waking moment was in his memories of the Past.

Even unconsciousness was not a respite from his torment. What few night visions his hideous half-sleep now granted him were hazy and filled with pain. They were generally nightmares of what his life now was, or even more agonizing memories of what it had once been. It was difficult to say which kind of dream was harder to endure.

The dragon blood within him, his dual nature that was both alien and his own, lay dormant for the moment, allowing him a few seconds' peace in the constant torture of his existence. When it awoke it would begin whispering to him again, nattering away with a thousand stupid insistences, a thousand demands. But now, at least for a little while, the constant drone of it was quiet, crowded into the back recesses of his mind by the sweetness of the dream he was having on this, his last night in the strange realm of Ylorc.

In the silence of the guest chamber he now occupied, Ashe was dreaming of Emily. It had been years, decades, even, since she had graced his dreams, beautiful, innocent Emily, his soulmate, dead a thousand years now. He had met her but once, had passed only one evening in her company, and had known almost from the moment his eyes beheld her that she was the other half that completed him.

She had known it, too, had in that briefest of moments said that she loved him, had gifted him with her heart, her absolute trust and her virtue, had consummated with him what had felt like their marriage, even though they were both barely out of childhood. One night together. And now her ashes blew about somewhere in the winds of Time, on the other side of the world, a lifetime away. The only vestige of her that remained was hidden away in the rusted vault of his memory.

But while Emily was dead, in the Past, Ashe was half-alive in the Present. His existence was a secretive one, hidden from the many who hunted him and dictated by the one who manipulated him. For that reason he walked the world in a cloak powered by the element of water, drawn from Kirsdarke, the sword formed of and dedicated to that element. The cloak wrapped him in mist and shielded him from those who could read his vibrational signature on the wind.

His living shroud obscured him from the eyes of the rest of the world as well. He was only here now, in the realm of the Bolg, on orders to observe the three who ruled the monsters of Ylorc and report back. Ashe hated being used in this way, but had no power to do otherwise. It was one of the drawbacks of his life not being his own, his fate and destiny in the dark hands of another.

The one pleasant thing about this assignment was that it allowed him to be with Rhapsody. From the moment the dragon in his blood had felt her presence for the first time on the Krevensfield Plain he had been involuntarily fascinated with her, drawn like a moth to a flame as intense as the fire that burned in the belly of the world. Upon actually meeting her, both sides of his nature, the dragon and the man, had fallen deeply under her spell. Had he been more a living man than the shell of a man that he was, Ashe might have been able to resist whatever charms she had bound him with. As it was, he feared her almost as much as he was enchanted by her.

Sam. The word echoed in his memory, Emily's soft voice bringing water to the edges of his eyes, even in sleep. She had called him Sam, and he had loved the sound of it. They had parted far too soon; he had not had the chance to correct her.

I can't believe you really came, she had whispered on that night, that one night, so long ago beneath an endless blanket of stars. Her voice still whispered to him now, in his dreams. *Where are you from? You were my wish, weren't you? Have you come to save me from the lottery, to take me away? I wished for you to come last night on my star, right after midnight, and here you are. You don't know where you are, do you? Did I bring you from a long way off?* There was magic in her, he had decided then, and still believed now. It was magic strong enough to have brought him over the waves of Time, back into the Past to find her waiting there for him in Serendair, a land that had disappeared into the sea fourteen centuries before he had been born.

All a dream, his father had insisted, trying to comfort him when he found himself back in his own time, alone, without her. *The sun was bright, and you must have been overcome with the heat.*

Ashe turned on his side and groaned, overcome with heat now. The fire in the small grate twisted and pulsed, casting its warmth over him in waves. The image of Rhapsody rose up in his mind again. It was never far from the edge of his consciousness anyway; the dragon's obsession with her was strong. His fingertips and lips still stung with the unspent desire to touch her that had pooled like acid there since he first beheld her, the consequences of the dragon's unsatisfied longing. Bitterly he struggled to put her out of his mind, reaching back blindly to the sweetness of the memory he had been reliving only a moment before.

'Emily,' he called brokenly, but the dream eluded him, dissipating at the edge of the room beyond his reach.

In his sleep he fumbled in a small pocket of the mist cloak until his fingers brushed it, tiny and hard in its pouch of velvet, worn thin from years of serving as his touchstone. A tiny silver button, heart-shaped, of modest manufacture, given to him by the one woman he had ever loved. It was the only thing he had left of her, that and his memories, each one cherished with the ferocity of a dragon guarding its greatest treasure.

Touching the button worked; it brought her near to him again, if only for a moment. He could still feel the ripping of the lace as he inadvertently tore it from her bodice, his hand trembling with fear and excitement. He could still see the smile in her eyes.

Keep it, Sam, as a memento of the night when I gave you my heart. He had complied, had carried the tiny button heart next to his own scarred one, clinging to the memory of what he had lost.

He had searched for her endlessly, in the museums and the history vaults, in the House of Remembrance, in the face of every woman, young and old, that had hair the color of pale flax on a summer's day, as Emily's hair had seemed in the dark. He had carefully examined any female wrist, looking for the tiny scar that was burned into his memory. Of course he had never found her; the Seer of the Past had assured him that she had not come on any of the ships that escaped Serendair before it was consumed in volcanic fire.

Well, child, I'm sorry to disappoint you, but no one by that name or description was among those to leave on the ships from the Island before its destruction. She did not land; she did not come.

The Seer was his grandmother, and would never have lied to him, both for that reason and because she was unable to do so at the risk of losing her powers. Anwyn would never have hazarded such a loss.

Nor would Rhonwyn, Anwyn's sister, the Seer of the Present. He had begged her to use the compass, one of three ancient artifacts with which Merithyn, her Cymrian explorer father, had first found this land. His hand had trembled as he gave her the copper threepenny piece, a valueless, thirteen-sided coin, which was the mate to the one he had given Emily. *These coins are unique in all the world,* he had told the Seer, his then-young voice wavering, betraying his agony. *If you can find the one that matches this one, you'll have found her.*

The Seer of the Present had held the compass in her fragile hands. He recalled how it had begun to glow, then resonate in a humming echo that stung behind his eyes. Finally Rhonwyn had shaken her head sadly.

Your coin is unlike any in the wide world, child; I am sorry. None other like it exists, except perhaps beneath the waves of the sea. Even I cannot see what treasures are held in the Ocean-Father's vaults. Ashe could not possibly have known that the Seer's powers also did not reach into the Earth itself, where Time had no dominion.

He had given up then, had come to almost believe the awful truth, though he still sought her in the face of anyone he came across who could have even possibly been Emily. She had lingered in his every thought, smiled at him in his dreams, had fulfilled the promise he had unwittingly made in his last words to her.

I'll be thinking about you every moment until I see you again.

It was not until many years that her image deserted him, had left in the face of the horror his life had become. Where once his heart was a holy shrine to her memory, now it was a dark and twisted place, touched by the hand of evil. Emily's memory could no longer remain in such a charnel house. He had no idea why she had been able to return this night, lingering lightly on the smoke that had risen up from the firegrate and wrapped itself behind his eyes.

I'll be thinking about you every moment until I see you again.

The image in the distance grew dimmer. Ashe roiled, grasping again at the mist in his memory as she began to disperse, calling to him as she left.

I love you, Sam. I've been waiting for you for so long. I always knew you would come to me if I wished for you.

Ashe sat up, sweat pouring from his clammy skin, wrapped in the cool vapor of the mist cloak, shaking. If only the same magic had worked for him.

The Firbolg guard standing watch at the hallway's end nodded deferentially to Achmed as he emerged from his chamber and made his way down the corridor to Rhapsody's room. He knocked loudly and swung the door open, part of the morning charade performed for the benefit of the Bolg populace, who believed Rhapsody and Jo to be the king's courtesans and therefore left the women alone. Both Achmed and Grunthor derived great amusement from the smoldering resentment they knew this survival game stoked in Rhapsody's soul, but she had adopted a practical attitude about it, mostly for Jo's sake.

The fire on her hearth was flickering uncertainly, mirroring the look on her face. She did not look up from the scroll she was poring over as he entered.

'Well, good morning to you, too, First Woman. You're going to have to work a little harder at this if you're going to convince the Bolg you're the royal harlot.'

'Shut up,' Rhapsody said automatically, continuing to read.

Achmed smirked. He picked up the teapot from her untouched breakfast tray and poured himself a cup; it was cold. She must have been up even earlier than usual.

'What Scum-rian manuscript are you reading this time?' he asked, holding the tepid tea out to her. Without looking up, Rhapsody touched the cup. A moment later, Achmed felt the heat from the liquid permeate the smooth clay sides of the mug, and took a sip, making sure to blow the steam off first.

'*The Rampage of the Wyrm*. Amazing; it just appeared out of thin air under my door last night. What an extraordinary coincidence.'

Achmed sat down on her neatly made bed, hiding his grin. 'Indeed. Learn anything interesting about Elynsynos?'

Finally a small smile crossed Rhapsody's face, and she looked up at him. 'Well, let's see.' She sat back in the chair, holding the ancient scroll of parchment up to the candlelight.

'Elynsynos was said to be between one and five hundred feet long, with teeth as long and as sharp as finely honed bastard swords,' she read. 'She could assume any form at will, including that of a force of nature, like a tornado, an earthquake, a flood, or the wind. Within her belly were gems of brimstone born in the fires of the Underworld, which allowed her to immolate anything that she breathed on. She was wicked and cruel, and when Merithyn, her sailor lover, didn't come back, she went on a rampage

21

that decimated the western half of the continent up to and including the central province of Bethany. The devastating fire she caused lighted the eternal flame in the basilica that burns there to this day.'

'I detect a note of sarcasm in your voice. Do you reject this historical account?'

'Much of it. You forget, Achmed, I'm a Singer. We're the ones who write these ballads and this legend lore. I'm a little more versed in how it can be exaggerated than you are.'

'Having done so yourself?'

Rhapsody sighed. 'You know better than that. Singers, and especially Namers, can't make up a lie without losing their status and abilities, although we can repeat tales that are apocryphal or outright fiction as long as we present them that way, as stories.'

Achmed nodded. 'So if you reject this story out of hand, why are you worried?'

'Who said I was worried?'

The Firbolg king grinned repulsively. 'The fire,' he said smugly, nodding at the hearth. Rhapsody turned toward the thin flames; they were lapping unsteadily around a heavy log which refused to ignite. She laughed in spite of herself.

'All right, you caught me. And, by the way, I don't reject the story out of hand. I just said there are some parts that I think are exaggerated. Some of it may very well be right.'

'Such as?'

Rhapsody put the manuscript back down on the table and folded her arms. 'Well, despite the disparity in the reports of her actual size, I have no doubt that she was – is – immense.' Achmed thought he detected a slight shudder run through her. 'She may actually have the ability to assume those fire, wind, water, and earth forms; dragons are said to be tied to each of the five elements. And though she may, in fact, be evil and vicious, I don't believe the story about the devastation of the western continent.'

'Oh?'

'Yes, the forests there are virgin in most of the parts we passed through, and the trees are the wrong kind to have sprung up after a fire.'

'I see. Well, I don't doubt your knowledge of forests, or virgins – after all, you've been one twice – '

'Shut up,' Rhapsody said again. This time the fire reacted; the weak flames sprang to violent life, roaring angrily. She pushed her chair back, rose and walked purposely to the coat peg near the door. She snatched down her cape. 'Get out of my room. I have to go meet Jo.' With a savage shrug she donned the garment, then rerolled the scroll and slapped it into Achmed's hand.

'Thanks for the bedtime reading,' she said sarcastically, opening her door. 'I assume I don't need to give you specific anatomical directions as to where you should store it.' Achmed chuckled as the door slammed shut behind her.

Winter was beginning to abate, or so it seemed. It had been hovering indecisively on the threshold of leaving for some time, reluctant to release its icy grip entirely while giving way grudgingly to a fairer wind and sky. The air of early spring was clear and cold, but held the scent of the earth again, a promise of warmth to come.

Rhapsody climbed carefully up the rocky face of the crags that led to the heath at the top of the world, a wide, expansive meadow beyond the canyon that a long-dead river had carved many millennia before. The basket she was lugging had almost spilled twice by the time she reached the flat land; she was off-balance, weighed down by the additional burden of the gear for her impending journey.

Waiting above in the dark meadow, Jo watched in amusement as the basket appeared at the crest of the heath, wobbled a moment, then righted itself. It slid forward a few inches as if under its own power, then finally a golden head surfaced, followed by intense green eyes. A second later Rhapsody's smile emerged over the edge; it was a smaller version of the sunrise that would come in an hour or so.

'Good morning,' she said. Only her head was visible.

Jo rose and came to help her, laughing. 'What's taking you so long? Usually you can make this climb in a dead run. You must be getting old.' She offered her elder, smaller sister a hand and hauled her up over the edge.

'Be nice, or you don't get any breakfast.' Rhapsody smiled as she laid her pack on the ground. Jo had no idea how right she was. By her own calculations she was somewhere in the neighborhood of sixteen hundred twenty years old in actual time, though all but two decades of that had passed while she and the two Bolg were within the Earth, crawling along the Root.

Jo grabbed the basket and unhooked the catch, then dumped its contents unceremoniously onto the frozen meadow grass, ignoring Rhapsody's dismayed expression. 'Did you bring any of those honey muffins?'

'Yes.'

The teenager had already located one and stuffed it into her mouth, then pulled out the sticky mass and looked at it in annoyance. 'Ick. I told you not to put currants in them; it ruins the flavor.'

'I didn't. That must be something from the ground, a beetle, perhaps.' Rhapsody laughed as Jo spat, then hurled the partially masticated muffin into the canyon below.

'So where's Ashe?' Jo asked as she sat cross-legged on the ground, picking up another muffin and brushing it off carefully.

'He should be here in half an hour or so,' Rhapsody answered, sorting through her satchel. 'I wanted to see you alone for a little while before we leave.'

Jo nodded, her mouth full. 'Grnmuthor um Achmmegd are commiddg, too?'

'Yes, I expect them shortly, although I had a hostile exchange with Achmed earlier, so perhaps he won't bother.'

'Why would that stop him? That's normal conversation for Achmed. What was his problem this morning?'

'Oh, we just had an argument over a Cymrian manuscript he slipped under my door last night.'

Jo swallowed and poured herself a mug of tea. 'No wonder; you know how much he hates the Dum-rians.'

Rhapsody hid her smile. Since the Cymrians had come from Serendair, their homeland, she, Grunthor, and even Achmed were technically Cymrians themselves, a fact she had not been allowed to share with Jo. 'Why do you think that?'

'I heard him talking to Grunthor a few nights back.'

'Oh?'

Jo leaned back importantly. 'He said that you had your head wedged up your arse.'

Rhapsody grinned. 'Really?'

'Yes. He said the dragon probably had a Cymrian agenda, because she was the one who invited the arse-rags here in the first place to please her lover – that's what he called them: arse-rags.'

'Yes, I believe I've heard him use that word about them myself.'

'He also said that you were trying to find out more about the Cymrians, to help bring them back into power, and that it was stupid. He thinks the Bolg are much more worthy of your time and attention, not to mention your loyalty. Is that true?'

'About the Bolg?'

'No, about the Cymrians.'

Rhapsody looked off at the eastern horizon. The sky at the very edge of the land was beginning to lighten to the faintest shade of cobalt blue; otherwise the coming of foredawn was still indiscernible. Her face flushed in the darkness as she thought back to Llauron, the gentle, elderly Invoker of the Filids, the religious order of the western forest lands and some of the provinces of Roland.

Llauron had taken her in not long after the three of them had arrived, had made her welcome. He had taught her the history of the land, as well as many useful things that were now helping Achmed build his empire, among them planting lore, herbalism, and the healing of men and animals. His voice nagged in her head now, expecting information and solutions to problems she didn't understand.

Now that you've learned about the Cymrians, and the growing unrest that threatens to sunder this land again, I hope you will agree to help me by being my eyes and ears out in the world, and report back what you see.

I'll be glad to help you, Llauron, but –

Good, good. And remember, Rhapsody, though you are a commoner, you can still be useful in a royal cause.

I don't understand.

24

Llauron's eyes had glinted with impatience, though his voice was soothing. *The reunification of the Cymrians. I thought I had been clear. In my view, nothing is going to spare us from ultimate destruction, with these unexplained uprisings and acts of terror, except to reunite the Cymrian factions, Roland and Sorbold, and possibly even the Bolglands, again, under a new Lord and Lady. The time is almost here. And though you are a peasant – please don't take offense, most of my following are peasants – you have a pretty face and a persuasive voice. You could be of great assistance to me in bringing this about. Now, please, say you will do as I've asked. You do want to see peace come to this land, do you not? And the violence which is presently killing and maiming many innocent women and children; that is something you'd like to see ended?*

Jo was staring at her intently. Rhapsody shook off the memory. 'I'm going to find the dragon to give her back the claw dagger, in the hope she won't come and lay waste to Ylorc, and all the Bolg in the bargain,' she said simply. 'This journey has nothing to do with the Cymrians.'

'Oh.' Jo took another bite of her muffin. 'Does Ashe know that?'

There was a warning note in her sister's voice that Rhapsody heard, a fluctuation to which she, as a Singer, was sensitive. 'I assume so. Why?' An awkward silence took up residence between them. 'What aren't you telling me, Jo?'

'Nothing,' said Jo defensively. 'He just asked if you were Cymrian, that's all. More than once, in fact.'

Rhapsody's stomach turned over in the grip of cold to rival the chill that the land still held. 'Me? He asked you that about me?'

'Well, about the three of you; Achmed and Grunthor, too.'

'But not you?'

A blank look crossed Jo's face as she considered the question. 'No, he never did. I think he assumes I'm not. I wonder why that is.'

Rhapsody rose to a stand and brushed off her trousers and cloak. 'Maybe you're the only one of us he doesn't think is an arse-rag.'

Jo's eyes sparkled wickedly. 'I hope not,' she said, looking innocently up at the sky. 'Grunthor's certainly not an arse-rag, either.' She laughed as a shower of snow and dried leaves flew into her face. 'Seriously, Rhaps, I mean, have you ever even met a Cymrian? I thought they were all long dead.'

The sky was lightening at the horizon to a thin gray-blue. '*You've* met a Cymrian yourself, Jo,' Rhapsody said flatly, beginning to pack up the remains of breakfast. 'Lord Stephen is of Cymrian descent.'

'Well, I guess that proves the arse-rag theory,' said Jo, wiping the crumbs from her mouth with the back of her hand. 'I meant an old one, one of the ones who lived through the War. The kind that lives forever.'

Rhapsody thought for a moment. 'Yes, I think so. I was once almost trampled on the road from Gwynwood to Navarne by the horse of an obnoxious soldier named Anborn. If he is the one mentioned in the history we heard, he was Gwylliam's general in the War. That would make him fairly old. The War ended four hundred years ago, but it went on for seven hundred.'

Jo had been there when they had opened the library vault and found Gwylliam's body. 'Guess the old bastard didn't look that bad, then. He didn't seem dead a day past two hundred.' Rhapsody laughed. 'Was he the one who started the war when he hit his wife?'

'Yes; her name was Anwyn. She was the daughter of the explorer, Merithyn, the first Cymrian, and the dragon Elynsynos – '

'The one you're going to see now?'

'Yes – who fell in love with him and told him the Cymrians could come live in her lands, where no human had ever been allowed before.'

Jo popped the last muffin into her mouth. 'Whyys diggeeay wanddadoo dhat?'

'The king of Serendair, Gwylliam – '

'The same stiff we found?'

Rhapsody laughed. 'The very one. He had foreseen that the Island was about to be destroyed in volcanic fire, so he wanted to relocate the bulk of the population of his kingdom somewhere they could maintain their culture, and where he could remain their king.'

'Power-mad arse-rag.'

'So they say. But he did save most of his people from certain death, brought them safely halfway around the world and built Canrif – '

'Now *there's* an accomplishment. A fancy place with indoor plumbing that the Bolg don't bother to use.'

'Stop interrupting. The Bolg overran it later. He and later Anwyn built an extraordinary civilization out of very little, and reigned in peace over an era of unprecedented advances until the night he hit her. That incident was called the Grievous Blow, because that single slap between the Lord and the Lady started the war that destroyed about a quarter of the population of the continent and much of the Cymrian civilization.'

'Definitely arse-rags,' Jo said resoundingly. 'Is there anything you need me to do while you're away?'

Rhapsody smiled. 'Now that you mention it, yes. Would you keep an eye on my Firbolg grandchildren for me?' Jo made a face and a gagging sound, which her sister ignored. 'And don't forget your studies.'

'Sorry I asked,' Jo muttered.

'And look in on Elysian from time to time, will you? If the new plantings need water, give them a drink.'

Jo rolled her eyes. 'You know I can't *find* Elysian.' Rhapsody's house, a tiny cottage situated on an island in an underground grotto, was virtually impossible to discern by anyone except Achmed or Grunthor. The four companions kept its secret deliberately.

'Get Grunthor to take you. Sorry these tasks seem so odious. What did you have in mind when you offered?'

Jo's pallid face lit up. 'I can keep an eye on Daystar Clarion for you.'

Rhapsody laughed. 'I'm taking my sword with me, Jo.' Jo had long been fascinated with the burning blade, watching the flames as though hypnotized. When they were traveling overland, Rhapsody had kept the sword out at night until Jo had fallen asleep, the starlight that radiated from the blade comforting her in the dark.

'Oh.'

'After all, I might need it. You do want me to come back, don't you?' Rhapsody said, patting Jo's crestfallen face.

'Yes,' said Jo quickly; there was an unintended urgency in her voice. 'If you leave me here alone among the Bolg I'll hunt you down and kill you.'

The sky in the east had faded to a soft pink, with a ribbon of palest yellow touching the edge of the horizon below it. Rhapsody closed her eyes, feeling the coming of the sun. At the edge of her hearing she could feel a musical note sound softly, wafting on the wind; it was *re*, the second note of the scale. In the lore of Singers, *re* was the portent of a peaceful day, a day without incident.

Softly she began her morning aubade, the love song to the sun that her race, the Liringlas, sang to greet the daybreak. It was a song passed from mother to child, like the vespers that bade the sun Godspeed at the end of the day and welcomed the stars as they came forth in the twilight. To Rhapsody, the act of marking these ancient devotions was always a poignant one; it was the only way she had left of feeling close to the mother she missed more than anything else she had lost with the sinking of the Island.

Beside her she could feel Jo begin to tremble as she listened to the song, and Rhapsody took her hand. The primordial song of mother-to-daughter passage was especially poignant to her, too. Jo had never known her mother, having been abandoned to the streets as a child. Rhapsody took the girl into her arms as the song came to its end.

'She loved you, I know she did,' she whispered. She had been trying to convince Jo of it for a long time.

'Right,' Jo muttered sardonically.

'That was beautiful,' said Ashe. Both women jumped. As always, they had not seen him approach. Rhapsody colored in embarrassment, her face taking on the same hue as the edge of the predawn horizon.

'Thank you,' she said, turning hurriedly away. 'Are you ready?'

'Yes. Achmed and Grunthor are right behind me. I assume they want to say goodbye.'

'Don't worry, I'll be back,' Rhapsody said, giving Jo one more hug. 'If we pass through Sepulvarta, the holy city where the Patriarch lives, I'll try to get you some more of those sweets you liked.'

'Thanks,' said Jo, wiping her eyes with her sleeve defensively. 'Now hurry up and leave so I can get out of this fornicating wind; it's stinging my eyes.'

As Grunthor hugged her goodbye, Rhapsody struggled not to gasp, but her face was turning an unhealthy shade of red in the giant's embrace. The panoramic vista of the Orlandan Plateau swam before her eyes, the crags of the Teeth tipping at a sickening angle. In her disconnected thoughts she wondered if this was something like being squeezed to death by a bear.

Finally Grunthor set her down, released her, and patted her shoulder awkwardly. Rhapsody looked up into the great gray-green face and smiled. The Bolg's face was set in a nonchalant expression, but she could see the tightness of his massive jaw, and the faintest hint of glistening liquid at the corners of his amber eyes.

'I really wish you'd reconsider, Duchess,' he said solemnly.

Rhapsody shook her head. 'We've been through this already at great length, Grunthor. I'll be safe. I've haven't had a single bad dream about this trip, and you know how rare that is.'

The giant folded his arms. 'And just who is gonna save you from the dreams you *do* have on the road?' he demanded. 'Last I knew, that was my job.'

The amused expression on the Singer's face softened with his words. 'Indeed, you're the only one who's ever been able to,' she said, running her hand along the enormous muscular arm. 'I guess it's just another small sacrifice I'll have to make to keep the Bolg safe.'

Another thought occurred to her, and Rhapsody dug for a moment in her pack, finally pulling out a large seashell. 'But I have this,' she said, smiling brightly. Grunthor chuckled. He had given it to her not long after they had emerged from the Root, a memento from a journey he and Achmed had made to the seacoast, searching for a way to get her back to Serendair after their long journey through the Earth's belly.

His smile faded with the memory. When finally they had met up again, she had informed them that the Island was gone, swallowed by the sea more than a millennium before. At that moment, he had felt guilt for the first time in his life, knowing that he and Achmed had dragged her away from a home and a family she would now never see again. She slept sometimes with the shell covering her ear, attempting to use the noise of the crashing waves to drown out the torturous nightmares that left her thrashing and sobbing in despair.

'You know I'd take the worst of them dreams for you if I could, Your Ladyship,' he said sincerely.

Rhapsody felt her throat tighten, and a sense of overwhelming loss tugged at the edges of her consciousness. 'I know, I know you would,' she said, and hugged him again. Abruptly she pulled away, trying to regain her composure. A wicked twinkle came into her eye. 'And believe me, if it was within my power, I'd *give* you the worst of them. Where's Achmed? Ashe and I need to be going.'

A sudden lightheadedness washed over her, a sensation that time was expanding all around her. She had felt this way before, but where or when she was uncertain. Grunthor seemed to be feeling it, too; the amber eyes clouded over for a moment, then he blinked rapidly, and smiled.

'Don't forget to say goodbye to His Majesty,' he said merrily, pointing to the cloaked figure standing a little way off.

'Do I have to? Our last exchange was probably about as tender a goodbye as I'm ever going to get out of him. We almost came to blows.'

'Yes, you have to,' Grunthor commanded with mock severity. 'And that's an order, miss.'

Rhapsody saluted, laughing. 'All right. Far be it from me to defy The Ultimate Authority, to Be Obeyed at All Costs," she said. 'Does that ultimate authority apply only to me?'

'Nope,' said Grunthor.

'You have final dominion over everyone in the world?'

'Damn right.' The giant sergeant signaled to the Firbolg king. 'Aw, come on, Duchess. Tell him goodbye. He may not show it, but he's gonna miss you terrible.'

'Sure he is,' she said as Achmed approached. 'I've heard he's already taking bids on my quarters and planning to auction off my worldly goods.'

'Only the clothes, and only if you aren't back in a reasonable amount of time,' the Firbolg king said as pleasantly as he was able. 'I don't want that hrekin cluttering up my mountain.'

'I'll be back, and I'll send word with the guarded mail caravan as often as I am able,' Rhapsody said, shouldering her pack. 'Now that the interprovincial messengers are coming regularly to Ylorc, I should be able to get a message to you if need be.'

'Of course. I'm sure the dragon's cave is a regular stop on the mail caravan's route,' Achmed replied, a note of angry sarcasm creeping into his voice.

'Don't start,' Rhapsody warned, casting an eye over toward Jo, who was chatting with Ashe.

'No,' Achmed agreed. 'I just thought I'd give you a little send-off.' He handed her a scroll of tightly bound parchment. 'Be careful. It's very old and very valuable.'

'If it's another version of *The Rampage of the Wyrm*, I'm going to stow it forcibly in the place I suggested to you earlier this morning.'

'Have a look.'

Carefully Rhapsody unbound the ancient thread of silk that tied the scroll closed. Achmed had made a substantial study of the writings from Gwylliam's library and reliquary vault, but the collection was so vast that it would take him hundreds of years to examine even half of it. The fragile parchment crumbled a bit as she unrolled it. It was a careful rendering of an architectural design.

After a few minutes of staring intently at the plans, she looked back to find the Firbolg king watching her with equal interest. 'What is this?' she asked. 'I don't recognize it. Is this someplace in Ylorc?'

Achmed looked over at Ashe, then back to her, moving slightly nearer. 'Yes, if it exists. It was Gwylliam's masterpiece, the crown jewel of his vision for the mountain. I don't know if he got to build it or not. He called it the Loritorium.'

Rhapsody's palms grew moist. 'Loritorium?'

'Yes, the corresponding documentation describes it as an annex, a deliberately hidden city, a place where ancient lore was housed and the purest forms of elemental power in the Cymrians' possession would one day be stored, along with a vast conservatory in which to study them. I believe the sword you carry might have been one of those exhibits, based on the dimensions of the display cases and some of the notes.'

She turned the scroll over. 'I don't see any words. How do you know this?'

Achmed nodded slightly toward Ashe and lowered his voice even more. 'I'm not an idiot; I left the text safely in the vault. I've told you repeatedly that I do not trust him. Besides, I didn't know if the dew might damage the scrolls.

'From what I have been able to glean, this place was never opened to the Cymrian inhabitants of Canrif. It may never have been started, or if it was, it may never have been finished. But of course, it may have been both, and just known to Gwylliam and a few of his closest advisors. Who knows?

'What is most fascinating is the way the complex is laid out, at least according to these maps. The cases and displays must have been intended to contain something with great care, judging by the detail with which those elements were rendered. Gwylliam devoted a good deal of effort to designing the defenses, both from the outside and the inside. I'm not sure whether he was more intent on protecting his displays, or protecting the Cymrians from them.'

Rhapsody shuddered. 'Any idea what it might have been, besides Daystar Clarion?'

'No, but I plan to find out. While you're gone, Grunthor and I will be checking into some of the Cymrian ruins, the parts of Canrif that were built last and destroyed first when the Bolg overran the mountain. We've already seen some signs that point the way to what might have been the Loritorium. It promises to be a fascinating exploration if we find it. Interested?'

'Of course I'm interested,' Rhapsody whispered fiercely, annoyed by the smirk on his face. 'What Namer wouldn't be interested in a place like that?'

'Then stay,' Achmed suggested with mock innocence. 'It certainly would be better if you were along. Grunthor and I, clumsy oafs that we are, might inadvertently make a mess or destroy something of historical significance, who knows, perhaps even a one-of-a-kind piece of ancient lore.' He laughed as her cheeks reddened with smoldering anger. 'All right, we'll wait for you. We'll locate the place, and give you a reasonable period to return. If you're not back by the time we had discussed, we'll start without you. Agreed?'

30

'Agreed,' she said. 'But you don't need to give me incentive to hurry back, Achmed. Believe it or not, I have plenty of that.'

The Firbolg king nodded. 'Do you still have your dagger from your days on the streets of Serendair?'

Rhapsody looked at him oddly. 'Yes; why?'

Achmed's face lost the last vestige of a smile. 'If you find yourself in a compromising situation with Ashe, use your dagger to cut his balls off, not your sword. Daystar Clarion's fire will cauterize the wound, as you've seen before. If that need arises, you want him to bleed to death rapidly.'

'Thank you,' Rhapsody said sincerely. She knew the grisly comment was an expression of genuine concern, and she opened her arms. Achmed returned her embrace quickly and uncomfortably, then looked down at her.

'What's that in your eyes?' he demanded. 'You're not crying, are you? You know the law.'

Rhapsody wiped her hand across them quickly. 'Shut up,' she said. 'You can stuff the law right in the same cavity behind *The Rampage of the Wyrm*; there's certainly enough room in your case. By your own definition, you should be Lord of the Cymrians.' Achmed smirked as she turned and went over to where Jo and Ashe were standing.

'Are you ready?' Ashe asked, picking up his smoothly carved walking staff.

'Yes,' Rhapsody said, hugging Jo one last time. 'Take care of yourself, sis, and our two big brothers.' The teenager rolled her eyes. Rhapsody turned back to Ashe. 'Now let's be off before I say something else to Achmed. I want the last thing I said to him to be something as obnoxious as what he said to me.'

Ashe chuckled. 'That's a contest you don't want to get into,' he said as he checked the bindings on his gear. 'I believe you will lose every time.'

As she and Ashe reached the summit of the last of the crags before the foothills, Rhapsody turned and stared east into the rising sun, which had just begun to crest the horizon. She shaded her eyes, wondering if the long shadows were really the silhouettes of the three people she loved most dearly in the world, or only the hollow reflections of rock and chasm, reaching ominously skyward. She decided after a moment she had seen one of them wave; whether or not she was right didn't matter, anyway.

'Look,' said Ashe, his pleasant baritone shattering her reverie. Rhapsody turned and let her gaze follow his outstretched finger in the direction of another line of shadows, miles off, at the edge of the steppes where the lowlands and the rockier plains met.

'What is that?' she asked. A sudden gust of wind swirled around her, raising a cloud of dust and whipping her hair into her eyes. She pulled her cloak tighter about her shoulders.

'Looks like a convocation of some sort, humans, undoubtedly,' he said after a moment.

Rhapsody nodded. 'Ambassadors,' she said softly. 'They're coming to pay court to Achmed.'

Ashe shuddered; the tremor was visible, even beneath his cloak of mist. 'I don't envy them,' he said humorously. 'That ought to shake up their notions of protocol. Shall we?' He looked off to the west, over the thawing valley and the wide plain past the foothills below them.

Rhapsody looked back for a moment longer, then turned her eyes toward the west as well. A slice of the sun had risen behind them, casting a shaft of golden light into the gray mist of the world that stretched out below them. By contrast, the distant line of black figures moved through a jagged shadow.

'Yes,' she said, shifting her pack. 'I'm ready.' Without looking back she followed him down the western side of the last crag, beginning the long journey to the dragon's lair.

In the distance, a figure of a man touched by a darker, unseen shadow stopped for a moment, gazed up into the hills, then continued on its way to the realm of the Firbolg.

Second Movement

I

Dawn found them at the crest of the foothills, laying their course for the lands north of the Avonderre-Navarne border. Ashe said the lair of Elynsynos lay within the ancient forest, northwest of Llauron's domain and the vast Lirin forest of Tyrian, so they would be following the sun, then the Tara'fel River northward.

When they reached the conjunction of the foothills and the rocky steppes that those hills became at the mountain's threshold, Ashe suddenly directed her into a thicket of evergreen trees. Rhapsody followed quickly, hiding herself from sight, all but unable to see him.

'What's the matter?' she whispered at the dark branches, thick with fragrant needles beginning to soften with the new growth of early spring.

'There's an armed caravan within sight,' he answered in a low voice. 'They're heading toward Ylorc.'

Rhapsody nodded. 'Yes; it's the fourth-week mail caravan.'

'Mail caravan?'

'Yes, Achmed established an four-week cycle of caravans that travel between Ylorc, Sorbold, Tyrian, and Roland. Now that there is a working trade agreement between the Bolg and Roland, he thought it made sense to make sure that messages and deliveries were escorted by soldiers from Roland to assure that they don't fall prey to the unexplained violence that has been around for so long.

'A contingent arrives on the same day of each week, and if for any reason that were not to happen, whichever post was expecting the caravan would go out in search to make certain they were safe. It takes two cycles, or eight weeks, for each individual caravan to complete the whole circuitous route between Roland, Tyrian, Sorbold, and Ylorc. It has been working very well so far.' *And Llauron has been making excellent use of it to badger me about sending him information,* she thought to herself. So far she had shared very little. She also didn't mention that the most sensitive information was entrusted not to the soldiers of the caravan, but to birds. Achmed had developed a whole squadron of avian messengers who carried the most important missives through the skies to their destinations. Llauron made use of avian messengers as well.

Ashe said nothing. Rhapsody waited for a few moments, then, hearing no further comments, turned to leave the thicket.

'Wait.'

'What's the matter now, Ashe?'

He was still hard to see within the darkness of the branches. 'We'll need to wait here. I thought you understood that if we were going to travel overland together, we would need to remain out of sight.'

Rhapsody drew her cloak a little closer. 'Well, of course, when we're vulnerable in the wide fields, or in unfamiliar territory. But that's just the mail caravan.'

'*Always*. No exceptions. Understood?'

His tone annoyed her; there was a gritty edge to his voice she had not heard before. It served to remind her how little she actually knew him, and underscored why Achmed and Grunthor had objected to her going with him in the first place. Rhapsody sighed, some of her confidence evaporating into the chilly air.

'All right,' she said. 'We'll wait for them to pass. Let me know when they're out of sight.'

They crossed the steppes and the wastelands to the Krevensfield Plain, heading northwest to avoid all but the outskirts of the province of Bethe Corbair and the city itself entirely. The traveling was difficult, the terrain rough and hard to cross in the muck left by the rains of early spring that were falling consistently. Rhapsody found herself stuck in the mud more than once. Ashe had offered his assistance but had been politely refused while she freed herself, muttering under her breath.

The comfortable familiarity that had begun to grow between them in Ylorc seemed to have disappeared now that they were alone together. Rhapsody had no idea why, though much of it seemed to be due to Ashe's unpredictability.

At times he was pleasant enough, joking with her or passing the time when they were encamped in reasonable, if insignificant, conversation. Other times she got the sense he was brooding, angry even; he would snap at her unexpectedly when she spoke to him, as though she was disturbing his concentration. It was as if he were two different people, and there was no way to tell which one was present since his face remained hidden at all times. As a result, most of their time was passed in silence.

It was a little better once they had traversed the wide fields of Bethe Corbair and the southwestern corner of the province of Yarim. They were chasing winter's tail; spring had come to the Bolglands a few weeks before, but the ground was still frozen here, the thaw only just beginning. The terrain was easier to walk and the rains less frequent, which helped their moods somewhat. Still, they were both aware of the lack of cover, and spent a great deal of time hiding when soldiers or travelers came within Ashe's senses. Usually Rhapsody could not see these wayfarers, but had grown accustomed to being grabbed suddenly from behind and pushed into thickets or clumps of weeds. She understood the necessity of these actions, but it did not do much to improve the relationship.

Finally, after several weeks of travel, they reached the province of Canderre, a land with more forests and wooded valleys than either Bethe

Corbair or Yarim. The tension eased up a little; Ashe seemed calmer in woods. Rhapsody assumed this was because they were no longer such obvious targets as they had been on the great wide plains.

They began to talk a little more, though still not often. Ashe was frequently pleasant, even funny, but he was holding her at arm's length. He did not share his thoughts, or any of his history, and, above all, he never took down his hood. Rhapsody was beginning to wonder what had happened to his face that made him feel the need to hide it from sight. She wished he trusted her more. His isolation made it impossible to keep from growing suspicious of him as well.

The one thing that he did not object to, to Rhapsody's surprise, were her daily devotions. Each morning and evening she greeted the sun and the stars with song. When she did she kept her voice low, particularly when they were on the plain, but she knew it made them more vulnerable nonetheless. She was generally sitting watch when dawn came, and so her morning aubade was his call to wakefulness. In the evening, as the twilight took the sky, she excused herself and found an open spot some ways off, to avoid disturbing him. When she returned he never commented, and was still busy with whatever task he had been performing when she left.

The forest thickened, and it became clear that they had passed into the most important and difficult part of the journey. They were now in the Great Forest, an area that covered much of western Canderre and all of northern Navarne and Avonderre to the sea. Their journey had reached the halfway point; Ashe had plotted and achieved the course perfectly. Up until now that had not been very difficult; though there were few landmarks to gauge by, the stars were clear on the plains and the direction simple. They were heading due west, so they had followed the sun. Now came the hard part, the main reason his services as guide were necessary. They were in woods, thick and dark and directionless, with real opportunity for losing their way.

Though Rhapsody had said nothing, Ashe picked up on her increased nervousness.

'You're worried.'

'A little,' she admitted. Their voices broke the stillness of the wood, sounding strange.

'I've been there before; I know where I'm going,' he said. His tone held none of the annoyance it had on occasion before.

'I know,' Rhapsody said with a weak smile. 'But I've never met a dragon before, so I guess it's fair that I'm a little worried. Is she large – for a dragon?'

Ashe chuckled. 'I didn't say I was an expert on dragons. Nor did I say I had met her. I just said I'd been near to her lair.'

'Oh.' Rhapsody dissolved into silence, her questions unvoiced, knowing Ashe wouldn't answer them.

'Perhaps we should stop for supper,' he said. 'Food often calms nerves,

I've found. Besides, it's your turn to cook.' There was a mischievous note in his voice.

Rhapsody smiled. 'I see, it's a ploy. All right, I'll cook. A fire should be safe enough here, don't you think?' They had rarely had one while on the plain, both of them knowing it would act as a beacon in the absolute darkness.

'I suppose so.'

'Good,' she said, her spirits lifting a little. 'I'm going to see what I can find in the immediate vicinity, forage a bit.'

'Don't go far.' Ashe heard her sigh as she walked away into a copse of trees.

She was back a few minutes later, looking excited. 'Wait until you see what I found,' she said, sitting cross-legged on the ground of the clearing they had chosen as camp for the night. She pulled her pack into her lap and began to rummage through it.

Ashe watched as she spread a kerchief on the new shoots of spring grass, mixed a number of ingredients in a battered tin cylinder, then covered it, dug a small hole, and buried it in the ground. Along with it she buried two potatoes she had brought with her, and then built a fire directly on top of it all.

While it burned she cored two small apples she had located in the woods, leftovers from the fall, and spiced them with dried matter from a pouch in her pack. She hung a small pot over the fire into which she had sliced some old leeks and wild horseradish she had found in the forest. When the flames had reduced to coals she pulled the pot off the fire and set the apples into the glowing embers, roasting the fruit in the heat. After a while they began to bubble and send forth an amazing smell that made his mouth begin to water.

Rhapsody pulled the apples from the fire and set them aside to cool, then dug up the cylinder and the potatoes. The latter she set with the apples while she pried open the tin and gave it a good shake. Onto the kerchief slid a small loaf of bread, the aroma of which was slightly nutty and wholesome. She gave the leek soup a brisk stir, releasing an impressive tang into the smoky air.

Ashe felt his appetite increase as she cut the steaming loaf open, then reached back into her pack for a small piece of hard cheese. She sliced this effortlessly, and topped the bread with it. The cheese melted as she set the other elements of the meal before him.

'There. I'm afraid it's simple fare, but it should stave off your hunger for the night.'

'Thank you.' Ashe sat down next to her, pulling the kerchief she offered him closer. 'This looks good.' He watched until she had sampled the food herself, then took a bite of each thing she ate in turn.

'It's not much,' she said apologetically. 'Just a country folk tune.'

Ashe's mouth was filled with the spiced apple. 'Hmmm?'

'I'm afraid you can't do much composing when you only have the ingredients that you can find in the immediate vicinity.'

He swallowed. 'Composing?'

Rhapsody smiled at the hooded figure. 'Yes, well, a truly well-planned meal has all the aromatic elements of a good musical piece.' There was no response, so she continued on with her explanation, hoping he didn't find it as inane as Achmed had. 'You see, if you put enough thought into the way things impact the senses, you can affect the way they are perceived.

'For instance, if you were planning an intimate dinner, you might want it to come off like a minor orchestral concerto. So you have the string bass section be something like a rich soup. Then, to put in an overlay of violins, some flaky biscuits, topped with sweet butter and honey. Perhaps you serve something light and tangy, like crisp vegetables in an orange sauce, for that addition of an impish flute line. So first you decide what you want the meal to be in terms of a musical piece, and then you compose the food to match the mood.'

Ashe took a bite of the bread. 'Interesting. Manipulative, but very interesting.' The nutty flavor melded perfectly with the cheese, making both items seem far more substantial than they would have been separately.

Rhapsody looked at him in surprise. 'Manipulative? I don't understand.' He said nothing. 'Can you explain your meaning?'

Ashe took another bite. 'Is the tea ready?'

Rhapsody rose and went to the fire. Tea was best made from the offerings of summer: strawberry leaves and rose hips, sweet fern and red sumac berries. The herbs she had located were not the best blend, plantain and slippery elm, dandelion roots and yarrow, but they were mild and had only passive, healthy properties. She poured a cup of the steaming liquid and passed it to him, her brow still furrowed, waiting for an explanation.

One was not forthcoming. The cloaked figure raised the cup inside his hood and took a sip. Rhapsody jumped as he spat the tea out violently, spraying some into the fire.

'Bleah. What *is* this?' His tone was rude, and Rhapsody could feel her blood start to steam.

'Well, now it's herbal vapor, but prior to your mature response it was tea.'

'A new and interesting definition for it, I'd say.'

Rhapsody's ire was rising. 'Well, I'm sorry you don't like it, but it was the best grouping of herbs I could find. All the properties are healthy ones.'

'If their taste doesn't kill you first.'

'Well, next time I'll be sure to find licorice just for you. I didn't realize until now what serious need you were in of a laxative.'

She thought she heard a chuckle as the hidden man rose and went to his own pack. He rummaged for a moment; finally he located what he was looking for.

'You could make some of this.' He tossed her a small canvas sack tied with a rawhide cord.

Rhapsody opened the bag and held it to her nose, inhaling its aroma. She recoiled instantly in disgust.

'Gods, what is this?' She held the sack away from her face.

'Coffee. A special blend from Sepulvarta.'

'Ugh. It's repulsive.'

Ashe laughed. 'You know, you're being very close-minded. You should at least try it before you declare it repulsive.'

'No, thank you. It smells like dirt from a skunk's grave.'

'Well, be that as it may, I like it, certainly much more than your odious tea.' Rhapsody's face fell, and he hastened to mitigate the damage. 'Though I'm sure tea you make when you are not in the forest and dependent on the availability of certain plants – '

'Spare me,' she said coldly. 'You are entitled to dislike my tea. No one said it was delicious, just healthy. And if you wish to poison yourself by drinking that bile, please don't let me stop you. But you can make it yourself; I have no desire to inhale the fumes. In fact, I think I'll make a new campsite elsewhere until you're done.' She rose from the fire and walked away into the woods, leaving most of her supper untouched.

Words between them that evening were few. Rhapsody returned after sunset, having sung her vespers, and settled down for the night in her corner of the camp.

Ashe was repairing one of his boots when she walked into the fire circle, and watched her pass by the flames with interest. He had noticed the effect her presence had on fire, and the way it reflected her mood. It was snapping and hissing now with unspoken anger. She obviously had not gotten over the offense he had committed, probably because he had not apologized.

He decided to do so now. 'I'm sorry about earlier,' he said, turning the boot over without looking up in her direction.

'Put it from your mind.'

'All right,' he said, pulling the boot back on, 'I will. I wish more women let me off that easily.'

Rhapsody rolled up her cloak and stuffed it under her head to serve as a pillow. The ground was broken here with tree roots and buried stones, making for uncomfortable sleeping. 'Nonsense,' she said. 'I'm sure your mother let you get away with murder.'

Ashe laughed. 'Gained,' he said; it was the sword-trainer's term indicating a point had been scored and acknowledged. 'I assume my apology was accepted, then?'

'Don't become accustomed to it,' Rhapsody mumbled from inside her bedroll, a hint of humor returning to her voice. 'I rarely forgive spitting. Customarily I'd cut your heart out, although it's fairly obvious someone already has.' She closed her eyes and prepared to go to sleep.

A split-second later she heard a humming next to her upturned ear; even behind her eyelids she could see a blue-white light fill the darkness. The sharp metal point of a sword jabbed her throat just below her chin. She opened her eyes.

Ashe stood above her. Even in the dark, his silhouette showed the signs of unbridled rage. With a vicious twist of the wrist he pressed the sword tip deeper into her neck, just before the point of breaking the skin. Within his hood two points of intense light gleamed furiously.

'Get up,' he said, kicking her boot savagely.

Rhapsody rose, following the lead of the sword. It pulsated with a blue light, a light she had seen out of the corner of her eye in battle, but never up close before. It was a bastard sword, a weapon of broader blade and hilt and greater length than her own. The sword was scrolled in gleaming blue runes that decorated both the hilt and blade, but these patterns were not the most hypnotic aspect of it.

The blade itself appeared to be liquid. It hovered in the air, rippling repeatedly toward the hilt like waves in the sea crashing to the shore. The watery weapon emitted a vaporous mist that rose, like steam from the fires of the Underworld, forming a column of fog before her, a moving tunnel at the end of which was a stranger with murder in his eyes. She knew this without seeing those eyes clearly. He would never have made a weapon of this power known to her unless he expected her sight of it to be momentary.

A deadly calm descended on Rhapsody. She stared into the vaporous tunnel in the direction of the cloaked man at the other end. He was silent, but his anger was palpable, she could feel it around her in the air.

When he didn't speak after another endless moment, she decided to do so.

'Why did I have to get up? Are you too much of a gentleman to kill me in my sleep?'

Ashe said nothing, but pressed the blade even deeper. The world blackened for a moment before her eyes as the blood to her head was stanched. She summoned all the remaining strength she had and glared in his direction.

'Remove your sword immediately, or get on with it and kill me,' she ordered coldly. 'You're interrupting my sleep.'

'Who are you?' Ashe's voice was thick with murderous intent.

Rhapsody's mind leapt at the words; she had heard them before, uttered by another cloaked stranger. Her introduction to Achmed had been much the same. The tone in his voice had been similarly murderous as he rifled through her pack, while Grunthor held her stationary in the shadows of the first of many campfires they had shared.

Who are you?

Hey, put that down.

I wouldn't do that if I were you, miss. Just answer the question.

41

I already told you; my name is Rhapsody. Now put that down before you break something.

I never break anything unless I mean to. Now, try again. Who are you?

She sighed inwardly. 'I seemed destined to repeat this conversation for all of eternity to men who want to harm me. My name is Rhapsody. You know this already, Ashe.'

'I know nothing about you, apparently,' he said in a low, deadly voice. 'Who sent you? Who is your master?'

The last word stung, bringing back a brisk explosion of memories forged in the agony of the streets, of degradation and forced prostitution. Rhapsody's eyes narrowed to gleaming green slits. 'How dare you. I have no master. What are you insinuating?'

'That you're a liar, at best. At worst you are evil incarnate, and about to die for the suffering and woe you have inflicted throughout Time.'

'Whoa! What woe?' Rhapsody asked incredulously. 'And don't you call me a liar, you cowardly ass. You're the liar; you told my friends I'd be safe with you. If you were looking to kill me, I would have fought you in the venue of your choice. You didn't need to lure me out here to the woods so you could do it with impunity, you craven piece of Bolg-dung.'

Ashe stood up a little straighter; the sword did not move. It was as if his anger had tempered a little. Rhapsody was not sure how she knew this, but she was certain of it.

'Confess who sent you and I will spare your life,' he said, a slightly more reasonable tone in his voice. 'Tell me who the host is, and I'll let you go.'

'I have no idea what you are blithering about,' she retorted angrily. 'No one sent me.'

Ashe gave her throat another savage jab. 'Don't lie to me! Who sent you? You have ten seconds to come up with the name if you want to live.'

Rhapsody thought for a moment, knowing he was utterly serious. It would be simple to make up a name in the hope that he would leave her to find whatever host he was babbling about. Living wasn't worth the lie. Time slowed around her, and she thought of the family with which she was about to be reunited.

'Save yourself the time,' she said. 'I don't know what you're talking about, and I won't lie just to live.' She raised her throat to an easier angle of attack to facilitate his strike. 'Go ahead.'

Ashe remained frozen for a moment, then pulled the sword away from her neck with a sweep that spattered drops of water over her face and into the fire, where it hissed angrily. He continued to look at her from beneath the misty hood.

After a few moments of returning his stare, Rhapsody spoke. 'I don't know what's gotten into you. Maybe your brain has been curdled by that skunk urine you call coffee.' She took a deep breath and used her true-speaking lore as a Namer. 'In any case, your behavior is inexcusable. I am not a liar, nor am I evil incarnate. I don't know why you're angry at me, but I have no master, I am no one's whore, and I don't know anything about a host. Now get away from me. I'll find the dragon without you.'

Ashe considered her words. 'What was that comment about my heart supposed to mean?'

Customarily I'd cut your heart out, although it's fairly obvious someone already has.

Rhapsody looked puzzled; it had been a joke. 'That you're heartless, rude. Willing to insult the dinner I made you, to spit my tea out, to be unduly offensive. You're an insufferable pig. You have no respect for anyone. You can't take a joke, but you expect others to. You're cranky. Shall I go on? When I said it I was teasing. I no longer am.'

Ashe's shoulders uncoiled, and Rhapsody heard a deep exhalation of breath from within the hood. They stared at each other for a few moments more. Then the cloaked figure lowered its head.

'I'm very sorry,' he said softly. 'Your assessment of me, in all its parts, is correct.'

'You'll get no argument from me,' Rhapsody said, her heartbeat slowing slightly. 'Now, back away. If you still want to fight, I'd be happy to oblige. Otherwise, be on your way.'

Ashe sheathed his sword. The glen they were standing in became immediately darker in the absence of its light. The fire had been roaring in time with her anger; it had settled down somewhat as well, having expended much of its fuel in its fury.

'If you wanted me to leave, why didn't you just make up a name? I would have left you here, unharmed. You're lucky. You took an awful risk.'

'What risk?' Rhapsody snapped. 'You asked me a question. There was only one possible answer, and it did not consist of making up a name. What if I had and it belonged to some poor innocent whose only crime was being unfortunately titled?'

Ashe sighed. 'You're right. These are bad times, Rhapsody. I know you deserve to hate me forever, but please don't. I thought you were someone you're not, and I beg your forgiveness. Many of my friends and countless other innocent people have died at the hands of something sinister that is causing these raids. For a moment I thought it was you.'

'What a coincidence. Achmed thinks it's you.'

Ashe's words were soft. 'He's wiser than I thought.'

Rhapsody blinked in spite of herself. There was a poignancy in his words she felt in the depths of her soul. 'What do you mean by that?'

'Nothing,' he said quickly, 'nothing at all. This was a misunderstanding.' A wry tone came into his voice. 'Possibly brought on by that skunk urine, as you so charmingly have named it.'

Rhapsody sat back down by the fire. 'You know, Ashe, most people have misunderstandings on a slightly different scale. They argue, they call each other names. My neighbor once threw a plate at her husband. They don't usually draw weapons on each other. Generally I don't think what just happened qualifies as a misunderstanding.'

'I'm very sorry,' he said. 'Please tell me what I can do to make it up to you. I swear it won't happen again. I know you may not believe this, but it was an overreaction to what is happening across the land. War is coming, Rhapsody; I can feel it. And it makes me suspect everyone, even those without any hand in it, like you.'

She could hear the truth in his voice. Rhapsody sighed and considered her options. She could drive him off, refusing to spend another moment in his presence, which would leave her alone and lost in the woods. She could agree to go on with him but remain wary, setting up precautions to avoid further mishap. Or she could take him at his word.

She was too tired to do anything other than the last. 'All right,' she said finally. 'I guess I can get past this, as long as you promise not to draw on me ever again. Swear it, and we'll forget this happened.'

'I do,' he said. There was amazement in his voice, and something else that she couldn't put her finger on.

'And throw away that coffee. It addles your brain.'

In spite of the grimness of the situation, Ashe laughed. He reached into his pack and drew forth the sack.

'Not into the fire,' she said hastily. 'We'll have to evacuate the woods. Bury it in the morning with the waste.'

'All right.'

She tossed another handful of sticks on the fire. It was burning low, apparently tired, too. 'And you take the first sleep rotation.'

'Agreed.' Ashe crossed to his spot within the camp and pulled out his bedroll, slipping into it rapidly, as if to show his trust that she would not retaliate on him in his slumber. 'Good night.'

'Good night.' In spite of everything that had happened, Rhapsody felt a smile come over her face. She sat back and listened to the nightsounds of the forest, the music the wind made and the song of the crickets in the dark.

Shrike cursed and spurred his horse again. The Orlandan ambassadorial caravan was several days ahead, and he was not making any gains in his quest to catch up with it. Shrike had no need of their company nor any desire for it; by and large he considered the ambassadorial class of Roland to be a pathetic collection of doddering old men incapable of forming a direct statement, let alone a coherent thought. *Puppets*, he mused sourly, *every one of them. Off to pay homage to the new Lord of the Monsters.*

His master's words came back to him as he galloped along the muddy pathway that in drier times was the trans-Orlandan thoroughfare, the roadway built in Cymrian times bisecting Roland from the seacoast to the edge of the Manteids. *Anything and everything you can find out about Canrif and what manner of insanity is going on there. Everything, Shrike.* The depth of the voice made the inherent threat in the words even more obvious.

Shrike could feel that threat in the wind as well, despite the sweetness that filled the air at Spring's return. Canrif was a ruin, the rotting carcass of a long-dead age; it should have remained that way, left to the scavenging monsters that roamed the peaks and the wind that had not cleansed the memory of what had happened there, even all this time past. He was uncertain as to what he would find when presented at the skeletal court of Gwylliam the Abuser and Anwyn the Manipulator, but whatever it might be, Shrike was fairly certain he would not like it.

2

Sir Francis Pratt, the emissary from Canderre, blinked several times and swallowed nervously. When this duty had been assigned he had pled rheumatism and an unreliable bladder in the attempt to get out of it, believing that the possible curtailment of his career as an ambassador was preferable to a posting to Ylorc. His attempts had fallen on deaf ears, and now here he was, following a subhuman guide to the head of the jumbled line waiting with grim anticipation to see the new Firbolg king.

His colleagues in the ambassadorial service were as agitated as he was. No chamberlain was present to greet them or to organize their interviews into any semblance of appropriate placement. Instead, emissaries of high-ranking provinces and duchies milled about in confusion, attempting to devise a self-invented pecking order of sorts. This was causing more consternation among the powerful ambassadors than the lesser ones; tempers were running very near the surface as the emissaries from Bethany and Sorbold argued about who should be standing nearer the door. In any civilized court the two men would never have even been invited on the same day, let alone left to sort out their differences themselves.

Canderre, Pratt's homeland, was a region of little political influence. Among the provinces of Roland it was seen by and large as a low-ranking region, populated primarily by gentlemen farmers, craftsman, merchants, and peasants. None of the more famous of the Orlandan lines lived there, although several of the dukes held Canderian estates, and Cedric Canderre, the province's duke, came from a House that was considered a reputable one. Therefore it was a major discomfiture to him when the Firbolg guard had come into the room, demanding to know who was there from Canderre. He had considered stepping behind a tapestry but had determined that such an action would cost him his life, not because of its evasiveness but rather due to the hideous stench of the heavy wall hangings. What lay behind them could not possibly be conducive to one's continued good health.

So he owned up to his role and found, to his horror, that the guard planned to bypass all the waiting emissaries in favor of presenting him now, first, to the Firbolg court. He could feel the astonishment and furor of his colleagues, invisible daggers piercing his back as he followed the grisly man into the Great Hall.

He breathed an initial sigh of relief upon entering the enormous room. Contrary to the whispered rumors, there was no throne of bones, no dais trimmed with human skulls. Instead there were two enormous chairs carved from marble, inlaid with a channel of blue and gold giltwork and padded with cushions of ancient manufacture. His eyes roamed over them in wonder. Undoubtedly they were the legendary thrones of Gwylliam and Anwyn, unchanged from the days when this was the Cymrian seat of power, the place Gwylliam had named Canrif.

In one of these ancient chairs sat the Firbolg king. He was swathed in black robes that covered even his face, all but the eyes. Sir Francis was grateful; judging just by the eyes, if more was visible he would undoubtedly be trembling. The eyes stared piercingly at him, assessing him as though sizing up a brood mare or a harlot.

Standing behind the occupied throne was a giant of immense proportion, a broad-faced, flat-nosed monster with hidelike multitoned skin that was the color of old bruises. His shoulders were as broad as the yoke of a two-ox plow, and he was attired in a dress uniform trimmed with medals and ribbons. Sir Francis felt his head swim. The room was taking on a nightmarish quality that made everything seem surreal.

The only apparently normal person in the room sat on the top stair next to the unoccupied throne. It was a teenage girl with long, straw-colored hair, her face unremarkable. What drew the eye was the game she was playing; she was engaged in a solo round of mumblety-peg, using a long, thin dirk, absently stabbing in between each of her extended fingers that rested on her knee with an astonishing speed and obvious accuracy. The impressive feat of manual dexterity caused Sir Francis to shudder involuntarily.

'What's your name?' demanded the king. His Firbolg blood was not immediately visible, but then nothing was except those unsettling eyes. The emissary decided he was probably of mixed race, as his physical frame did not resemble that of any of the gruesome specimens of the citizenry he had encountered thus far. Obviously standard court etiquette was not going to be the rule of order here.

'Sir Francis Pratt, Your Majesty, emissary from the court of Lord Cedric Canderre. It is an honor to be here.'

'Yes, it is,' said the king. 'I doubt you know it yet, but you will. Before we get to points, do you have something you are supposed to say?'

Sir Francis swallowed his rising ire. 'Yes, Your Majesty.' There was something inherently repulsive about having to address a Bolg by the title that had not been used since the last true king occupied that throne. 'Lord Cedric sends you his congratulations on your ascendancy, and wishes you a long and joyous reign.'

The king smiled; the expression was clear even beneath his cloaked face. 'I'm very glad to hear that. Here's how he can assure that my reign is joyous: I want Canderre to perform an economic experiment for me.'

Sir Francis blinked. He had never been addressed so bluntly before. Generally the art of diplomacy involved a respected, complicated dance full of ritual and intricacy, like a courtship of sorts. In his youth it had been a game he relished, but as he grew older he had tired of it, and tended to place more of a value on plain-spokenness than he had when he was younger. He found the directness of the monstrous king surprisingly refreshing.

'What sort of experiment, Your Majesty?'

The Firbolg king gestured, and two of his minions came forward, one bearing a beautifully carved chair fashioned in a dark wood the color of black walnut but with a deeper, richer luster and an almost blue undertone. The other held a silver tray on which rested a goblet. There was something oddly amusing about the delicacies in hairy Firbolg hands. The chair was placed behind him, the glass before him.

'Sit.'

'Thank you, Sire.' Sir Francis sat and accepted the goblet. He sniffed it surreptitiously, hoping to be subtle, but he could see that the king had noticed what he had done immediately. The wine it contained had an elegant bouquet.

To make up for his rude action he took a deep drink. He had swallowed before the flavor caught up with him; it was surprisingly good, with a rich, full body and a tang that was barely perceptible. Like most nobles in Canderre, Sir Francis knew wine, and he was impressed by the king's choice. He took another sip. It was a young wine, undoubtedly just a spring pressing, one that needed a little time to reach full maturity, but a bellwether of vines that would produce excellent grapes in a year or two.

The king motioned again, and two more guards came in, bearing an enormous nautical net. They dropped it on the floor at Sir Francis's feet. He bent to pick up a corner of it and found that he could lift almost all of it, a feat of which he had never expected to be capable. He knew most nets of that size weighed a tremendous amount, but for some reason this one was only a fraction of standard weight. Instantly the value of it was apparent to him.

'Where did you get this?'

The Firbolg king sighed in annoyance. 'Do not give me the impression that Cedric Canderre sent me an idiot.'

Sir Francis's face flushed. 'I'm sorry.'

The giant's face spread into a wide grin, revealing grotesque teeth. 'Well, yes, we've thought so all along, but we're far too polite to say so.'

'We made it, obviously. What's your opinion of it, Pratt?'

'It's amazing.' Sir Francis turned the rope net over in his hands. 'The workmanship is extraordinary, as is the material.'

The Firbolg king nodded, and signaled once more. A chest was dropped at Sir Francis's feet. The emissary opened it; what he lifted out made him blush. It was a set of lingerie, fashioned from intricately crocheted silk threads, or something that looked like them. It was softer than gossamer, and had a natural sheen to the textile, but what was most appealing about it was the design. It was spare and cut in a scandalous way, but still beautiful and elegant, like the more refined and staid camisoles and undergarments Canderre was famous for producing. The process by which the garment was crafted was totally unknown to him, a situation he would have thought impossible, given his training and background.

'What do you call this?' he asked.

'Underwear, you nitwit,' said the girl without looking up from her game.

'I call mine "Beulah,"' offered the giant Bolg helpfully.

'I meant the fiber, the process,' said the emissary.

'It doesn't matter,' said the Firbolg king. He glanced at Grunthor, and they exchanged a nod. Rhapsody's expertise on such things was borne out; she knew what women felt beautiful in, and in what men wanted to see them. 'Do you like it?'

'Yes, indeed, it's very impressive.'

'What about the wine?'

Sir Francis's eyes opened in amazement. 'That's a Firbolg product as well?' The hooded king nodded. Pratt rubbed his neck, trying to sort out his comments and thoughts. 'What form does this economic experiment take?'

The king leaned forward slightly. 'We wish to test the interest in these things, without revealing their origins as yet.' It was Sir Francis's turn to nod. 'I want you to put them into your trade stream, sell these products through your merchant network. They will be assumed to be Canderian, and their quality will be judged against the high standards that name invokes.'

Sir Francis smiled at the compliment. 'Thank you, Sire.'

'In a year's time you will report back to me accurately about the performance of these products. I warn you, don't ever try to dupe me, Pratt; I don't take well to it. I'd offer to let you question someone who tried, but there are none presently alive.'

The elderly ambassador drew himself up to his full height. 'I assure you, Sire, strictly honorable trade practices are an age-old matter of pride in Canderre.'

'So I've heard. I just want to be sure that is true, even when your suppliers are Firbolg.'

'Of course.'

'Good. If, at the end of the year, there is a demand, as I expect there will be, we will enter into a trade agreement by which Canderre will be granted the exclusive right to sell certain Bolg merchandise, specifically the luxury items. In addition, we will consider selling you the raw materials to use in your own manufacturing, specifically the grapes and the wood.'

Pratt looked confused. 'Wood?'

48

The giant laughed. 'Look under your arse, sonny.'

The emissary checked the chair beneath him. When he looked up the new admiration was apparent on his face. 'Well, well. This certainly has been an interesting day.'

The king smirked. 'You feeling genuinely honored yet, Pratt?'

'Yes, indeed.' Sir Francis smiled. In a strange way, he was.

Centuries had passed since the road to Canrif had seen such traffic as Shrike saw today. Not since the wedding celebration a thousand years earlier had a host of hopeful emissaries trod their way through the waiting front gates as they did now, and as they had apparently been doing for days.

He almost laughed out loud at the high and mighty falling over themselves, pretending to legitimize the reign of a monster over what had at one time been the richest fortress of this world or the last. He stopped himself when he realized he had been sent on the same mission as they had: to discover who this new king was, get a glimpse of what remained of the glory of Canrif, and prevent what happened to two thousand troops of Roland from happening to the armies of each of their homelands.

Shrike was a practical man. He could see them all, the elite of the ambassadorial game: Abercromby and Evans, Gittleson, Bois de Berne, Mateaus and Syn Crote, the favored representatives of all the Orlandan and Sorboldian regents and benisons, each of whom had undoubtedly given their emissaries the same instructions. The representatives from Sorbold and the Nonaligned States were there, a few weeks ahead of the emissaries from the Hintervold and other distant lands. The two religious leaders of the continent, The Invoker of Gwynwood, head of the Filidic order, and the Patriarch of Sepulvarta, the leader of the Patriarchal faith who had dominion over the benisons, had each sent representatives as well.

The news of the Firbolg king had spread far and wide in a very short time. There was some wisdom in hanging back, listening to the scuttlebutt from the ones who had won the shoving match to be the first in. They would be patently unable to refrain from gossiping about the sights they beheld and the deals they made; there were, after all, bragging rights as much among ambassadors as there were among benisons and lords. The game of pecking order and self-importance did not interest Shrike. Information did.

In the end, Shrike knew, it was the entrée into Canrif that mattered. Any king crafty enough to engineer the defeat of a full brigade of Roland's warriors, led by the late great Rosentharn, Knight Marshal, would have already arranged for the emissaries to see what he wanted them to see and take away with them the impression he wanted them to have. A better strategy, perhaps, was to learn these things by word of mouth, and use his time in the chambers of Ylorc to observe what might *not* be on the agenda.

Even the smallest detail might be useful to his master. He did not expect to discover anything consequential, because Shrike was a practical man.

I can't stand this anymore, I am bored out of my gourd. Good night.' Jo stood and slid her dagger back into her wrist sheath.

'Go ahead,' said Achmed, checking the list. 'There are only a few more.' He had entertained twenty-seven representatives from various heads of state and the church, only two of which he had wanted to see; his gourd was numb, too.

'You keep yer 'ands outta those presents, now,' warned Grunthor with a twinkle in his amber eyes. ''Is Majesty gets to look through 'em first.'

Jo scowled. 'You know, I liked it a lot better before you were king, Achmed.' She strode out of the Great Hall and back to her chambers.

Achmed sighed. 'So did I.'

3

The morning following their argument the interaction between the traveling companions was easier, less strained, than it had been in weeks. Rhapsody was at a loss to explain why, finally deciding that what had erupted was mutual suspicion that had been brewing over the course of their journey, unspoken until the night before.

It was odd; he had drawn on her, she had insulted him, and here they were, feeling more comfortable than they had since they had left Ylorc, almost like breaking a fever. *Being around the Bolg is making me strange,* she thought with an amused sigh. The appalling behavior of the men in her acquaintance, over which her brothers would have felt the need to defend her honor, was now routine. All her male friends were rude to her.

Perhaps that was what she liked about Ashe. Unlike the other human men she knew, he treated her like a friend, or even a politely disinterested acquaintance. He was not constantly aroused; the detection of amorous intentions was a skill she had learned from Nana, the proprietor of the brothel in which she had lived in Serendair, and it served her well. She had come to realize that men existed in a state of almost permanent arousal, with a few exceptions. Ashe was one of them. He treated her in a friendly, teasing manner, much the way her brothers had, dropping an occasional flirtation but never pressing it. Whether his platonic attitude toward her was a sign of disinterest or a problem with his physiology did not matter. It made for comfortable companionship, and she appreciated it.

Ashe knew she was under this misconception, and it made him breathe easier. Nothing could be further from the truth. His mist cloak, his hated disguise from the eyes of the world, was a blessing here. It shielded his longing for her, and his less-than-noble desires. Rhapsody's own strange abilities of self-deception played into the situation as well. So they went about their journey – he gave her no reason to be wary of his intentions, and she ignored any sign of them.

The rains caught up with them, and the walking became arduous. The forest grew deeper as they journeyed west, making traveling slower. The snow around the base of the trees had melted, leaving rings of brown grass, the harbingers of warmer, if not better, weather.

One late afternoon, after a day of plodding through overgrown thickets and twisted patches of briars, they stopped at the edge of a bog. Rhapsody found a comfortable-looking pile of leaves within such a circle beneath an elm tree and dropped down into it wearily. Ashe backed away as she jumped up with a squawk, rubbinng her backside, and muttering ugly curses in the Firbolg tongue.

A moment later, when she had regained her composure, she knelt beneath the tree and brushed the leaves away, uncovering a large square stone with runes carved into it. The words were filled with dirt that had hardened with time. Carefully she rubbed the crevices clean, then exhaled when she made out the inscription.

Cyme we inne frid, fram the grip of deap to lif inne dis smylte land

The inscription was one Llauron had shown her long ago, the words Gwylliam had instructed his explorer, Merithyn, to greet anyone he met in his travels with, the words he had carved upon Elynsynos's cave. *Come we in peace from the grip of death to life in this fair land.* 'It's a Cymrian marker,' she murmured, more to herself than aloud.

Ashe bent next to her to examine it. 'Indeed,' he said agreeably. 'Do you recognize it?'

Rhapsody looked at him, puzzled. 'What do you mean? If I knew it was here, do you think I would have injured myself on it?'

Ashe stood up again. 'No,' he said. 'I was just wondering if perhaps you had seen it before.'

'When would I have? If I had been here before, why would I need you to guide me?' She took off her cloak and laid it on the ground.

Ashe unslung his pack. 'I thought perhaps you might have seen it when it was erected.'

Rhapsody exhaled loudly in aggravation. This had become an old saw; he was continually dropping hints, making veiled reference to the First Generation Cymrians. She had determined early on he was trying to trip her up, attempting to make her reveal herself as one. This was the most blatant he had been so far.

'I'm really getting tired of this game,' she said. 'If you want to know if I sailed with the First Fleet, why don't you just ask me?'

Ashe stood up even straighter in evident surprise. 'Did you?'

'No.'

'Oh.' He seemed somewhat taken aback. 'The Second? Third?'

'No. I've never been on any ship, except for rowboats and ferries.'

'So you have never traveled from one land to another on the sea? You've walked everywhere you've traveled?'

Rhapsody thought back to her trek within the Earth along the Root and shuddered slightly. 'Or ridden on horseback. Now, will you please desist?'

Ashe dropped his pack on the ground. 'Desist?'

'You have been quizzing me about the Cymrians since we left, in subtle ways. I don't appreciate it.'

'But you do know who they were?'

'Yes,' she admitted, 'but what I've heard about them I've learned from writings and students of history. So if you don't mind, I would appreciate you ending this cat-and-mouse game.'

Ashe chuckled. 'If I'm not mistaken, the way cat-and-mouse games end is by the cat eating the mouse.' He pulled the cooking utensils out of his pack. 'I assume I don't have to tell you which one of us is which in the analogy.'

Rhapsody was gathering sticks and peat for the campfire she had started. 'Is that something you'd like to do tonight?'

'Are you offering?' His tone was suggestive.

'Well,' she said, bending over and picking up more fallen branches, 'I think it can be arranged. After I get the fire going I'll hunt around and see if I can find you some small rodents for supper.' She went about her gathering chore, and unconsciously began to whistle. A moment later Ashe recognized the tune. It was a hymn to the ancient harvest goddess, a song from the old land.

She was Cymrian; he was virtually certain of it. Ashe decided to try something else. He thought about the languages she would have used in the old world if she really was Cymrian, but his knowledge of Ancient Lirin was limited. He decided to try one comment in the archaic Lirin tongue first, then one in Old Cymrian. He waited until he could see her face on the other side of the fire.

'You know, Rhapsody, I find you extremely attractive,' he said in the dead Lirin language, then shifted into the tongue of the Cymrians. 'I really love to watch you bend over.' She gave him a strange look, but she said nothing, and the dragon did not sense any blood rise to her face in a blush. The furrow in her brow seemed more extreme at his first comment than his second; perhaps she had lived in a Lirin village, or a meadow longhouse, where the only language spoken was the Lirin tongue. He tried again.

'And you have the most incredible backside,' he said, waiting to see the reaction. She turned to gather more peat, and fed it to the fire, seeming to grow annoyed.

'I don't understand you,' she said, glaring at him through the smoke. 'Please stop babbling at me.' She heard him sigh as he returned to unpacking the utensils, waiting until his back was turned to allow the smile to take over her face. *Tahn, Rhapsody, evet marva hidion* – Listen without rancor, Rhapsody, I think you are a beautiful magnet. *Abria jirist hyst ovetis bec* – I love to watch you squat. *Kwelster evet re marya* – you have the most beautiful muffins. It was all she could do to keep from choking with laughter. While his Old Cymrian was not too far off, his knowledge of Ancient Lirin was even more limited than he knew. And she spoke the truth, as always. She didn't understand him at all.

They had taken to sitting shorter, more frequent watches, mostly because of her nightmares. After an hour or so of deep sleep, Rhapsody would invariably begin to toss and turn, muttering under her breath, sometimes crying, sometimes gasping as she woke in shock. Ashe wished he could comfort her when these dreams occurred, and thought often about waking her gently to save her from them, but he knew that she was probably prescient. If she was seeing visions of the Future it might be important to allow her to do so, no matter what it cost her. So he sat in frustrated sorrow and watched her suffer through the nights, sleeping lightly, to wake, trembling.

They spoke little during the day. It was the evening that eased the tensions and facilitated conversation. Darkness cloaked the forest; its sounds increased, along with the crackling of the fire and the whispering of the wind in the trees, so difficult to hear in the daylight. By day words seemed as though they were held up to the light, and so were used very little. The night hid them, made them safer, and so it was then Rhapsody and Ashe were able to exchange them.

They were but a few days out from their destination. Ashe had said they would make Elynsynos's lair by week's end. There was still a wide river to cross, and many more leagues to travel, but they were within reach.

There was a loneliness in the air that night. They had been walking in the forest so long that it was hard to recall when they were not surrounded by trees. Rhapsody's sunset devotions seemed to be swallowed by the forest canopy, as if the songs themselves were suddenly too heavy to soar to the stars. She sat now on the rise of a small forest hill, watching those stars appear in the twilight one by one, to duck again behind the passing clouds that swallowed them intermittently. It put Rhapsody in mind of tiny minnows, their scales twinkling in the water of a dark lake, pursued by misty white predatory fish that consumed them and moved on.

'Rhapsody?' Ashe's voice broke her solitude. She turned in the direction of her shadowy companion. He was sitting at the fire's edge, its light flickering off his misty cloak, wrapping him in haze.

'Yes?'

'Do you feel safe here with me?'

She considered for a moment. 'As safe as I do anywhere, I suppose.'

The hooded figure looked up. 'What does that mean?' His voice was soft, almost gentle.

Rhapsody looked into the sky again. 'I guess I don't remember what feeling safe feels like.'

Ashe nodded, and went back to his thoughts. A moment later he spoke again.

'Is it because of the dreams?'

Rhapsody pulled her knees up to her chest and wrapped her arms around them. 'Partly.'

'Are you afraid of meeting Elynsynos?'

She smiled slightly. 'A little.'

Ashe picked up the kettle and poured himself another mug of tea. As if to make up for his rude behavior earlier in the trip, he was now drinking most of the pot over the course of a night, which she found amusing. 'I could go in with you, if it would help.'

Rhapsody thought about it, then shook her head. 'I don't think that would be wise, but thank you.'

'Have you ever felt safe?' He took a sip from the mug.

'Yes, but not for a long time.'

Ashe thought about asking her what he wanted to know directly, but decided against it. 'When?'

Rhapsody inched a little closer to the fire. She was feeling chilled suddenly and pulled her cloak around her shoulders.

'When I was still a young girl, I guess, before I ran away from home.'

Ashe nodded. 'Why did you run away?'

She looked up at him sharply. 'Why does anyone run away? I was stupid and thoughtless and selfish; especially selfish.'

He knew of other reasons people did. 'And were you beautiful as a young girl?'

Rhapsody laughed. 'Gods, no. And my brothers told me so constantly.'

Ashe laughed too, in spite of himself. 'That's a brother's main job, keeping his sister in line.'

'Do you have sisters?'

There was a long silence. 'No,' he finally answered. 'So you were a late bloomer?'

She blinked. 'Excuse me?'

'Isn't that the term for a girl who was, well, not beautiful as a child but becomes beautiful as a woman?'

Rhapsody looked at him strangely. 'You think I'm beautiful?'

Beneath his hood Ashe smiled. 'Of course. Don't you?'

She shrugged. 'Beauty is a matter of opinion. I suppose I like the way I look, or at least I'm comfortable with it. It never really mattered to me whether other people did or not.'

'That's a very Lirin attitude.'

'Well, in case you hadn't noticed, I'm Lirin.'

Ashe let loose a humorous sigh. 'I suppose this means that telling you you're beautiful is not a way to get into your good graces.'

She ran a hand absently over her hair. 'No, not really. It makes me uncomfortable, especially if you don't mean it.'

'Why would you think I don't mean it?'

'There seem to be quite a few people in these parts that think I'm odd-looking or freakish, but that doesn't really bother me most of the time.'

'What? That's ridiculous.' Ashe put down his empty mug.

'It is not ridiculous. I have to endure strange glances and curious looks more often than you might think. If you saw me walk down a street, you'd see what I mean.'

Ashe wasn't sure whether to be amused or annoyed at her lack of grasp of the obvious. 'Rhapsody, haven't you noticed that men follow you when you're walking down that street?'

'Yes, but that's because I'm a woman.'

'I'll say.'

'Well, men do that – follow women, I mean. It's their nature. They live constantly primed to mate, and they are almost always, well, ready for it. They can't help it. It must be a very uncomfortable way to live.'

Ashe swallowed his amusement. 'And you think any woman has this effect on any man?'

Rhapsody blinked again. 'Well, yes. It's part of nature, the cycle of propagation, of attraction and mating.'

Ashe couldn't refrain from laughing. 'You are sadly misinformed.'

'I don't think so.'

'I do, if you are under the impression that every woman affects men the way you do. You are judging by your own experience, and it is very different from the way it is for most people.'

The conversation was making her uncomfortable; Ashe could tell because Rhapsody reached for her pack and rummaged until she found her lark's flute. She occasionally played the tiny instrument in the woods, as it had a sound that blended into the forest air, complementing the birdsong. That was by day; now the birds were silent, and the only music in the forest now was that of the wind. She settled back against a tree and regarded him with a wry look.

'And you think you have a better perspective on men and women?'

Ashe laughed again. 'Well, not than most, but better than yours.'

Rhapsody began to play, a tripping series of notes that tickled the hairs on the back of his neck. She pulled the flute away from her lips and smiled.

'I think you are as unqualified to judge as I am, maybe more so.'

Ashe sat up in interest. 'Really? Why?'

'Because you're a wanderer.'

'And what does that have to do with anything?'

'In my experience, foresters and other wanderers are very different from the majority of men,' she said lightly. Twilight had faded completely into night; her eyes scanned the sky, but she did not seem to find what she sought.

'How so?'

'They seek different things from women, for one. Women they would have on a temporary basis, that is.'

She couldn't tell if Ashe really was smiling or if she just imagined she heard it in his voice. 'And what might that be?'

Rhapsody returned to playing her lark's flute, lost in thought. The melody was airy but melancholy, and Ashe imagined he could see the colors and textures she was weaving with her notes, patterns of deep, soft swirls in shades of blue and purple, like ocean waves against the darkening sky before a storm. Then the song changed into brighter, longer measures, and the colors lightened and stretched until they wafted like clouds on a warm wind at sunset. Ashe listened, enthralled, until she was done, but held onto the thought she had left unanswered.

'Well?'

She jumped a little. It was obvious her mind was far away. 'Yes?'

'Sorry. What do most men seek from temporary interaction with women?'

Rhapsody smiled. 'Release.'

Ashe nodded. 'And wanderers?'

She thought for a moment. 'Contact.'

'Contact?'

'Yes. People who walk alone in the wide world all their lives sometimes lose perspective on what is real and what is not, what still remains and what is only memory. What men who wander most of their lives want, when they come upon a woman for a short time, is contact, reaffirmation that they really do exist. At least in my experience, anyway.'

Ashe was silent for a moment. When he finally spoke his voice was soft. 'And do they instead find sometimes that they do not exist?'

'I wouldn't know. I'm not a wanderer, at least not by choice. I hope only to be one for a short while. It's not a life I find suits me, and I am growing tired of it.'

They sat in silence until her watch began. Ashe rose slowly and made his gear ready for the night, then slipped into the shadows, disappearing on the other side of the fire. Rhapsody watched him lie down, and thought she heard him sigh deeply. Perhaps she was reading her own feelings into the sound, but she felt its music speak of deep loneliness, not unlike her own. She had been wrong about his feelings before and had been taken aback when she tried to comfort or reassure him, only to find he felt no need for it, and was annoyed by her attempt. Rhapsody weighed her options for a moment, then decided to err on the side of being too kind.

'Ashe?'

'Hmmm?'

'You do exist, even if you are hard to see sometimes.'

The voice from the shadows was noncommittal. 'Thank you so very much for telling me.'

Rhapsody cringed. She had chosen wrong again. She sat her watch, scanning the horizon for signs of life, but saw none. The night was quiet except for the crackling of the flames and the occasional sound of the wind. In the silence she heard him speak softly, as if to himself.

'I'm glad you think so.'

At midnight she woke him for his watch and crawled gratefully into her bedroll, settling down to sleep almost before she was fully reclining. The nightmares came an hour or so later, taking her so violently that Ashe forgot his resolve to stay out of it and shook her awake gently. She sat up abruptly in tears. It took her more than an hour to become calm again.

It was an old dream, a dream that had come to her when she first learned that Serendair was gone, destroyed fourteen centuries before while she and the two Bolg were crawling through the belly of the Earth. In her dream she stood in a village consumed by black fire, while soldiers rode through the streets, slaying everyone in sight. In the distance at the edge of the horizon she saw eyes, tinged in red, laughing at her. And then, as a bloodstained warrior on a black charger with fire in its eyes rode down on her like a man possessed, she was lifted up in the air in the claw of a great copper dragon.

She drew her camp blanket around her shoulders, glancing occasionally out into the darkness beyond the glowing circle of campfire light. Ashe had given her a mug of tea and watched as she held it in both her hands until it was undoubtedly cold, staring into the flames. They sat together in the shadows of the fire, silently. Finally he spoke.

'If the memory of the dream is disturbing to you, I can help you be rid of it.'

Rhapsody barely seemed to hear him. 'Hmmm?'

Ashe rose and dug in the folds of his cloak, a moment later pulling out the coin purse Jo had once tried to steal from him on the street in Bethe Corbair. He untied the drawstring and drew forth a small gleaming sphere which he then put in Rhapsody's hand. Her brows drew together.

'A pearl?'

'Yes. A pearl is layer upon layer of tears from the sea. It is a natural vault of sorts that can hold such ephemeral things as vows and memories – traditionally deals of state or important bargains are sealed in the presence of a large pearl of great value.' Rhapsody nodded vaguely; she knew that brides in the old land wove pearls into their hair or wore them set in jewelry for the same reason. 'You're a Canwr,' Ashe continued. 'If you want to be free of the nightmare, speak the true name of the pearl and will it to hold the memory. When the thought has left your memory and is captured in the pearl, crush the pearl under your heel. It will be gone forever then.'

Rhapsody's eyes narrowed. *Canwr* was the Lirin word for *Namer*. 'How do you know that I'm a Canwr?'

Ashe laughed and crossed his arms. 'Are you saying you're not?'

She swallowed hard. Even his question proved he already knew the answer, since it was phrased in a way that would require her to lie if she were to deny it. 'No,' she answered angrily. 'Actually, I believe I am not saying anything from this moment forward, except to thank you for your offer of the pearl and to decline it.' She lapsed back into silence, staring out into the night once more.

Ashe sat back down by the fire's edge and poured himself more tea. 'Well, my intention was to divert your thoughts from your nightmare. This isn't exactly the way I had hoped to do it, but at least my attempt was successful. I'm not certain why you are angry. I was trying to help you.'

Rhapsody looked up at the sky. The stars were shrouded in mist from the smoke of the fire.

'Perhaps it is because, while I respect your desire not to share details about your life and your past, you seem to be insistent on worming very personal and meaningful information out of me,' she said. 'To Lirin, Naming is not a casual topic of discussion, it is a religious belief.'

There was silence for a moment. When Ashe spoke again, his tone was soft. 'You're right. I'm sorry.'

'You are also relentless about determining whether or not I'm Cymrian. From what Lord Stephen tells me, in many places the fact that you think I am Cymrian would be considered a grave insult.'

'Right again.' He watched for a long while as she stared into the night at nothing in particular. Finally, unwilling to be the cause of her silent consternation, he made one more attempt at friendly conversation. 'Maybe it's best if we try to avoid talking about the Past. Bargain?'

'Agreed,' she said, her eyes still searching for something in the darkness.

'Then why don't we talk about something you enjoy instead. Perhaps that will help drive the memory of the dreams away. You choose the topic, and I may even answer questions.'

Rhapsody snapped out of her reverie. She looked over to him and smiled.

'All right.' She thought for a moment until her mind settled on her adopted grandchildren, Gwydion and Melisande, and the dozen little Firbolg. They were her touchstone, the things she thought about when she was brooding, when her mind was filled with unpleasant thoughts.

'Do you have any children?' she asked.

'No. Why?'

'Well, I am always looking for grandchildren to adopt.'

'Grandchildren?'

'Yes,' Rhapsody answered, ignoring the almost-rude tone in his voice. 'Grandchildren. You see, you can spoil an adopted grandchild while you're around, but you don't have the responsibility of raising it all the time. This works for me because it gives me children to love, even though I don't have the time to be with them always. I have twelve Firbolg grandchildren, and two human, and they are very dear to me.'

'Well, I don't have any children. I'm sorry I couldn't accommodate you. Perhaps we could work something out. How important is it to you, and how long are you willing to wait?' She could almost hear him smirk.

Rhapsody ignored the odd flirtation. 'Are you married?'

Laughter.

'I'm sorry – why is that a funny question?'

'Most women don't like me. In fact, most people don't like me; but that's fine – the feeling's mutual.'

'My, what a cranky attitude. Well, I can tell you confidentially but with absolute certainty that you are not without feminine admirers in Ylorc.'

'You are not talking about one of the Firbolg midwives, are you?'

'Goodness, no. Bbbrrrr.'

'My sentiments exactly.'

'No; my sister is somewhat enamored of you.'

Ashe nodded awkwardly. 'Oh. Yes.'

'Is that a problem?'

'No. But it won't come to anything.'

Rhapsody felt a twinge of sadness. 'Really? I certainly believe you, but do you mind if I ask why?'

'Well, for one thing, I happen to be in love with someone else, if that's all right with you.' His tone was annoyed.

Rhapsody turned crimson with embarrassment. 'I'm very sorry,' she said sheepishly. 'How stupid of me. I didn't mean to be rude.'

Ashe poured himself more tea. 'Why not? I am, and I offer no apologies for it. Another prominent reason is that she is a child.'

'Yes. You're right.'

'She is also a human.'

'Is there something wrong with that?'

'No. But the racial makeup of my blood is much longer lived than that, like your own.'

'You're Lirin, then?' The thought had never occurred to her.

'Partly, like you.'

'I see. Well, that makes sense. But is it really all that important? My parents were Lirin and human, as some in your family obviously were as well. It didn't stop them.'

'Some diverse life expectancies are closer than others. For instance, if you really are Cymrian, as I believe you are but won't admit, you will have a major problem facing you.'

'Why?'

'Because even the extended life span of the Lirin will still be no match for yours.'

'What are you talking about?'

Ashe got up and threw another handful of twigs on the fire, then looked over at her. Rhapsody caught a glimpse of what she thought was a scruffily bearded chin, but in the flickering shadows it was impossible to tell.

'When the First Generation Cymrians came, it was as if time had stopped for them,' he said. 'I'm not sure what caused it to happen. Perhaps it had something to do with completing an arc across the world, across the Prime Meridian; I have no idea. But for whatever reason, the

Cymrians did not seem to be affected by the ravages of time. They didn't age, and as years, then centuries, passed, it became evident that they weren't going to. They had essentially become immortal. And as they reproduced, their offspring, while not completely immortal, were extraordinarily long-lived. Of course, the farther the generations move away from the first, the shorter the life span becomes until it will finally blend into the way it should be. But that doesn't affect the immortals. There are still First Generation Cymrians alive today; mostly in hiding.'

'Why? Why do they hide?'

'Many of them are insane; driven mad by the "blessing" of immortality. You see, Rhapsody, if they had been immortal from the beginning, it probably wouldn't have affected them so much, but they were humans and Lirin and Nain and the like, extraordinary only in the journey they made. They had already embarked on a life cycle that had a certain course, and it was interrupted, wherever they were in it, and frozen there.

'So imagine being a human who had lived seventy or eighty years, and had passed through all the stages of infancy, childhood, youth, adulthood, middle age, and then finally old age, preparing to meet death soon, to discover that you were going to live forever that way, elderly and infirm.' He poured yet another cup of tea and offered the pot to Rhapsody, who had grown quiet in the firelight. She shook her head, lost in thought.

'Children continued to grow and mature, until they reached adulthood, but they never got any older. Some of them are alive still, looking no older than you do. But far more of them died in the war, or at their own hands, just to avoid facing an eternity they couldn't accept, sometimes with powers they didn't understand. Virtually every First Generation Cymrian took at least a small piece of elemental lore away from the Island with him, whether he knew it or not.

'So that's why I say you may have a problem. If you are a later-generation Cymrian, you will be extraordinarily long-lived, and you will undoubtedly face what others did: the prospect of watching those you love grow old and die in what seems like a brief moment in your life. And if you are a First Generation Cymrian, it will be even worse, because unless you are killed outright you will never die. Imagine losing people over and over, your lovers, your spouse, your children – '

'Stop it,' Rhapsody said. Her voice was terse. She rose from the ground and walked to the edge of the firelight, then tossed the remainder of her cold tea out into the darkness. When she came back she took a different seat, farther away from him, so that he did not have as good a view of her face.

They sat in silence for a long time, Rhapsody watching the smoke from the fire crackle with sparks and rise, like that of a Lirin funeral pyre, to the dark sky above, where it wafted among the scattered stars and dissipated. Finally Ashe spoke.

'I'm sorry,' he said, and his voice was uncharacteristically gentle. 'I didn't mean to upset you.'

Rhapsody looked pointedly over at him across the fire. 'I'm not upset,' she said coolly. 'I am not worried about anything like that.'

'Really?' he said, and there was amusement in his tone. 'Not even a little?'

'Not in the least,' she answered softly. 'I doubt I will even live to see the end of what is coming now, let alone forever.'

'Oh?' Ashe's tone had a controlled steadiness. 'What makes you think so?'

'Just a hunch,' she said, reaching for her cloak. She shook the dirt and leaves from it and wrapped it around herself.

'I see. So you would rather die than acknowledge the prospect that you might live forever?'

Rhapsody chuckled. 'You really are persistent, Ashe, but not very subtle. Is there actually a point here, other than just trying to determine whether I am what you think I am?'

Ashe leaned forward and rested his elbows on his knees. 'I'm just explaining why I could never be interested in someone like Jo; that she has a completely different life expectancy than I do. And if you are First Generation, you will have a very limited pool of others as long-lived as yourself to make a life with, who won't die on you before you have even gotten to know them.'

Rhapsody smiled and set about brushing the mud from her boots. 'Well, thank you for your concern, but I wouldn't worry. First, I don't plan to marry anyway; I'll make do with my grandchildren as my family. Second, I'm not afraid of time differences. My mother told me when I was very young that the time you had together was worth the loss because without the acceptance of that pain there would be nothing valuable to lose. And, of course, since you know I am Achmed's contemporary, there's always him. Grunthor, of course, is out of the question.'

Ashe's voice contained a note of horror. 'There's always Achmed for what?'

Rhapsody said nothing, but her smile broadened as she continued to scrape her equipment clean.

'You *have* to be joking. Please tell me you are – that's disgusting.'

'Why?'

'I would think that is obvious.' Even as far away as he was from her, Rhapsody could feel him shudder.

'Well, of course, that really is no concern of yours, since you're already spoken for. By the way,' she said, growing serious, 'does she mind that you're here? You know, for such a long time?'

'Who?'

'Your – well – whatever she is. I assume she's not your wife, since you said you're not married, I think. Actually, you didn't say that, did you?' Receiving no reply, she tried lamely to finish the thought. 'You know, this woman you're in love with? Is this journey causing a problem with her?'

'No.'

Rhapsody exhaled in relief. 'I'm very glad. I do try to make a point of not causing problems with people's relationships, especially married people. I have great respect for the institution.'

'Then why don't you intend to marry?'

Rhapsody got up again and began to spread out her bed roll. 'Well, it isn't really fair to marry someone unless you have a heart to share with them, to love them with. I don't have one, you see. It wouldn't be right.'

'I don't believe that.'

'Suit yourself,' said Rhapsody, crawling into the bedroll. 'Anyway, thank you for being honest about my sister.'

'Just out of curiosity, why do you call her that? Obviously you're not related.'

Rhapsody sighed. 'I can't believe you don't understand that, Ashe. There are different ways to make a family. You can be born into it, or you can choose it. Bonds to family you choose to be a part of are often as strong as those you are born into, because you want to be, rather than have to be, part of each other.'

On the other side of the fire Ashe was unpacking his own gear, settling into his watch. 'I'm not sure that's true.'

'Well,' said Rhapsody, lying down and trying to get comfortable, 'I guess it depends on who you are. They aren't mutually exclusive – your love for both can be equally strong. But that's why I have so much respect for the institution of marriage, because husbands and wives choose each other out of everyone else in the world, and therefore ought to be accorded the acknowledgment that this is the most special relationship of their lives.'

From across the fire came a sound that was half-chuckle, half-sigh. 'You really have led a sheltered life, Rhapsody.'

Rhapsody thought for a moment about answering, then decided against it. 'Good night, Ashe. Wake me when it's my watch.'

'Had you ever thought about just doing it the regular way?'

'Doing what?'

'The grandchildren process?'

'Hhmm?' She was almost asleep already.

'You know, finding a husband, having children, letting them have the grandchildren – is this a concept you're familiar with?'

Deep within the bedroll he heard a musical yawn. 'I already told you,' came the sleepy voice, 'I don't expect I'll live that long.'

In the night he woke her as her watch came due. She felt him shaking her gently.

'Rhapsody?'

'Hmmm? Yes?'

'It's your watch. Do you want to sleep a little longer?'

'No,' she said, pulling herself free from the bedroll. 'But thank you.'

'You didn't mean what you said earlier, did you? About Achmed?'

She looked at him foggily. 'What?'

'You would never, well, mate with Achmed, would you? The thought has been churning my stomach for the last three hours.'

Rhapsody was now awake. 'You know, Ashe, I really don't like your attitude. And frankly, it's none of your concern. Now go to sleep.' She made ready her bow and arrow, and stirred the dying fire, causing it to roar back to life, finding fuel from some unknown source.

Ashe stood above her a moment longer, then the shadows on the other side of the fire took him. If she hadn't been watching, Rhapsody would not even have known where he lay.

4

When dawn came the next day they rose in heavy mist that blanketed the forest. It burned off quickly in the light of the rising sun, and they set out on what they knew was the last leg of the journey.

Midday they came to Tar'afel River, the child of the same waterway that carved the canyons of the Teeth uncounted millennia before. It bisected the forest lands of northern Roland, forming an unofficial boundary between the inhabited and generally uninhabited woodlands.

The Tar'afel was a strong river, wide as a battlefield, its current swift. Rhapsody walked to the edge of the woods and watched it, roaring in fury and swollen with the rains of early spring. She glanced back at Ashe, who had made a quick camp and was preparing the noonday meal over a small campfire.

'How much of this is floodplain?' she asked, pointing to the riverbank and the grassy area between it and the forest.

'Almost all of it,' he replied, not looking up. 'It's over its banks a bit now. By the end of spring the water will be up to where you're standing.'

Rhapsody closed her eyes and listened to the music of the rushing river. Her homeland had been bisected by a great river, too, though she had never seen it. She could tell that the current was uneven, faster in some places than others, and by listening to the variations in tonal quality she could almost plot a map through it, finding the sheltered spots. After the meal was over she would put the theory to the test.

They ate in companionable silence, the noise of the water drowning out the ability to converse in anything but a shout. Rhapsody found herself forgetting several times that Ashe was there. When she remembered to look she could always see him, as he didn't move from his spot, but unless she was concentrating he slipped from her focus, and from her view. Whatever magic was bound up in the cloak he always wore, hooded without exception, it was compelling enough to let him disappear from the mind as well as from the eye.

After they had finished eating they repacked the gear, and Rhapsody set about cleaning up the campsite. She was getting ready to extinguish the fire when Ashe began picking up the equipment in preparation of leaving. Rhapsody was not ready to go yet.

'Stay here.' Ashe shifted his gear onto one shoulder and hoisted her pack onto the other. Before Rhapsody could protest he had crossed the floodplain and entered the river, wading across effortlessly.

Within moments the water was up to his waist, but his body mass seemed to be offering no resistance to the racing flow of the river. In fact, he left no wake or disturbance at all – the water flowed around him as though it was moving through him. Halfway across the river he was almost indistinguishable from the water itself.

Rhapsody was not really surprised, though she made note. *He must be tied to water as I am to fire,* she thought, although she realized a moment later that it might have been an effect of the sword he carried; perhaps the first was true as a result of the second. That explained many things she had not understood until now, particularly the source of the water to replenish the misty cloak.

It also explained his obsession about what he suspected was her Cymrian heritage – he must be one too, and probably one of early origin, given the amount of elemental lore he obviously had access to. She felt a tug at her heart. Perhaps he had lived through the war, and whatever deformity he was hiding behind the cloak was from that time.

And finally, she now understood why they were comfortable around each other and there was no attraction between them – they were comprised of different and opposing elements. She was grateful; with the exception of Achmed and Grunthor, he was the first adult male in her memory she was at ease with. It was much like being around her brothers, and with that realization came a sudden wave of homesickness and grief that she thought she had put long behind her.

Catching her off guard, the heartache doubled her over, and she struggled to hold back sudden tears. Rhapsody pressed her arms against her stomach and took several quick breaths, the technique she had learned ages before to combat the painful memories, and shook her head violently as if to shake loose the thoughts from her mind.

'Rhapsody! Rhapsody, are you all right?' She looked up to see Ashe, mid-river, halfway back from offloading the gear. Though she couldn't see his face, there was alarm in his voice.

She stood erect again, smiled and waved. 'Fine. I'm fine,' she shouted over the roar of the river.

Ashe had quickened his pace, and moments later he was out of the water and crossing the floodplain until he stood beside her again. He was breathing heavily; he put a hand on her shoulder and looked down into her face.

'Are you sure you're all right?'

'Yes, I'm fine,' she said absently. She was staring at his hand. It was as dry as if he had never touched the water at all, as was the rest of him. 'That's an interesting trick.'

'You like that, do you? Well, it does come in handy. Now, let's get going. Here,' he said, and he opened his arms to her.

Rhapsody stared at him, not comprehending. 'What? You want a hug?'

'No, I'm going to carry you.'

'Bugger off.' The words slipped out before she could stop them. She coughed. 'Sorry, that was rude and ungracious. No, thank you. I can make it on my own.'

Ashe laughed. 'Don't be ridiculous. The water's up to my waist – it would be over your head. Now, come.'

Rhapsody's face lost its natural smile. 'First, I may be small of stature, but your waist is not taller than my head. Second, I do not want you to carry me. I said I was capable of making the passage and I meant it. Now, I appreciate your concern and your offer of help, but I can do this on my own. If you want to provide some assistance, you could carry my cloak for me. That would be useful, and I'd be grateful.'

'I'm going to carry all of you. Gods, you don't stand a chance in that current. You don't weigh enough.'

Rhapsody looked at him as directly as she could, hoping she was making eye contact. '*No*. Thank you.' She walked to the campfire, crouched down and extinguished it, then she stood and began to adjust her clothing and belongings for the trip across the river.

The current was growing steadily, and Ashe was tired of waiting. He checked the integrity of the bindings on his gear, then went up behind her and effortlessly swept her off her feet. He began carrying her to the river, picking his way carefully among the rocks on the floodplain.

The blow that snapped his head back felt like it was delivered by a man twice her size. Ashe staggered back a few paces, dropping her to the ground. He watched in detached admiration, and more than a little pain, as she executed a fairly impressive horseman's rollout and came up crouched in defensive position, dagger and sword fully drawn. The intensity of the anger on her face amazed him.

'I'm sorry.' He took a step toward her and stopped as she slashed at the air between them, a murderous look on her face. 'Rhapsody, forgive me, I'm sorry. I'm sorry. I didn't mean to – '

'My refusal wasn't clear to you?'

'No. I mean yes. There's no excuse, except, well, perhaps it's just a natural impulse, you know – I mean – I'm sorry. I was just trying to help.' His words ground to a sheepish halt, under the fury of her eyes. They were blazing, green as the grass, and they held none of the ready forgiveness she had so easily extended for other rudenesses she had suffered in the past.

'Men have used the excuse of natural impulse to justify many things they did and wanted to do to me. Make no mistake, Ashe – I swear by whatever is holy in this unholy place that before you or anyone else takes me anywhere or in any way against my will, one of us will be dead. This time I think it would have been you.'

'I think you're right,' he said, rubbing his chin.

'But it wouldn't matter even if it is me who dies. I'll not be taken in any way against my will. Not by you; not by anyone.'

'I understand,' he said, but he didn't, not fully. The degree to which she was upset flabbergasted him; her face was as red had he had ever seen it, and she was angry to a degree she had never been, even in battle.

'I'm sorry,' he said again. 'Tell me what to do to make amends.'

'Just stay away from me.' Her face began to cool, but still she glared at him as she walked to the water's edge, looking across. He could tell she was calculating something. Then she sheathed her weapons, turned and left the riverbank and began to walk south again in the direction they had just come. She paused at the edge of the floodplain.

'Well, you've cost me some valuable gear.'

'I don't know what you mean,' Ashe said. 'It hasn't been injured – you can see for yourself when we get to the other side.'

'I won't be going on with you. We part company here.'

'Wait – '

'You can sell it when you get back to Bethany, or wherever it is you're going,' she said, walking away. 'Perhaps it will pay for your time serving as guide. Goodbye.'

Ashe was dumbfounded. Surely she was not so offended by this that she would abandon her quest and her musical instruments over it – yet there she was, rapidly disappearing into the forest. He ran after her, struggling to catch up.

'Rhapsody, wait – please, wait.'

She drew her sword again and turned to face him. She no longer looked annoyed, just guarded. And there was a look of resignation on her face that he had never seen before; it twisted his heart, though he had no idea why.

He stopped, leaving a respectable distance between them, and pondered the extremity of her reaction. *Men have used the excuse of natural impulse to justify many things they did and wanted to do to me.* Dismay knotted his stomach as he began to suspect what she might have meant. He felt sick as he contemplated it.

Never in his life before had he been at such a loss for words, so unsure of what to do. She had a way of unbalancing him, and had from the moment he had first met her in Bethe Corbair. He cursed his own stupidity and tried to think of what he could say to win back her trust.

Ashe got down on one knee on the ground before her. 'Rhapsody, please forgive me. What I did was stupid and thoughtless, and you have every right to be angry. If you'll just come back I swear to you that I will never touch you again against your will. Please. What you are looking for is too important to give up just because you have an idiot for a traveling companion.'

Rhapsody looked at him with no real expression on her face, saying nothing. For the first time Ashe could not read her thoughts by looking into her eyes; they were closed to him. Anxiety was beginning to choke him, and though he displayed no outward sign, he felt that if she were to abandon him and her mission that he might die right there for lack of a good reason to go on. He knew that she had no personal investment in this undertaking, that her motives were altruistic, that walking away would be easy; her obnoxious sovereign back in Ylorc would be thrilled. At the edge of his consciousness the dragon in his blood berated him mercilessly, but it was no worse than what he was saying to himself.

Finally she dropped her eyes and sheathed her sword again. She made no gesture toward him, but located a large stick the size of a quarterstaff and walked directly back to the river. She tested the depth of the first area she had guessed was sheltered by the rocks of the riverbed and the pattern of the current, and found that it was, in fact, shallower. She turned and gave Ashe a measured look.

'Don't distract me.'

Ashe nodded.

Rhapsody closed her eyes and spoke the river's name. She began to hum a tune that matched the music of the current. When she finally located the right pitch and note pattern she could see the river in her mind as a tremendous continuous flow of power, racing along the space before her eyes.

She listened for the shallows and could see them as stepping-stones across the rushing flood. She tied her cloak up around her waist and slowly stepped out into the water, eyes still closed, feeling her way along. She sank almost immediately up to her waist and shoulders, but the water did not seem to have the force to unbalance her in the places she forded the river.

When she was a few feet into the river Ashe followed her in slowly. He still believed she was too small to withstand the rush of the current, that her body mass was too slight to keep from being swept away in the torrent. For a moment he considered using his power over water to calm the raging river, but decided it would be unwise to reveal even more to her than he already had. He hoped fervently that when she lost her footing he would be able to reach her in time, given that he knew he had to hang back or risk facing her ire again.

He watched in amazement as she stepped from rock to rock along the river bottom seamlessly, with her eyes closed. She seemed to be able to sense the river's floor and navigate around it, using the intrinsic moraines and dredges to step in places where the water was naturally blocked and the current slower. Somehow she had found a way to determine the underwater topography that was innately clear to him because of his nature and his sword.

Rhapsody had made it two-thirds of the way across the river when she stopped. Ashe knew her dilemma instantly; before her was a large sinkhole, sheltered in a dam of rocks and debris. It was not safe to cross, nor was it easy to get around due to the swiftness of the current that its barricades circumvented. She stood in a swale, puzzling what to do. It seemed the best route might be to climb the dam on its upriver face and then use it to brace herself against the surge of the diverted current. Just as she decided to try it and took the first step, Ashe called out from behind her.

'Watch for the hole in – '

Rhapsody's concentration shattered and the song vanished. With it went the vision of the river's floor; she toppled into the water and was lost in a raging torrent that threatened to pull her down. She struggled to keep from panicking as the current dragged her off the dam and swept her over the sinkhole. Her hand flailed as she grabbed blindly for the place where she had seen the rock outcropping. The water surged over her head, choking her.

Ashe rushed forward, moving effortlessly through the rapids. He was about to reach out and snag her cloak when she emerged, gasping, anchored to a log wedged in the riverbed. He hung back and watched as she dragged herself up over it, steadied herself, and began to hum again. It took her a moment to find the song, but then she was off again slowly, picking her way across the bottom once more. Ashe stood where he was and waited until she had pulled herself, sodden and dripping, from the river and up onto the shore of the floodplain.

She bent over for a moment. Ashe assumed she was catching her breath, but then saw her pick something up from the ground. He climbed up onto the debris dam and headed for shore himself.

He was almost to the edge of the dam when the sizable rock she hurled at him caught him in the forehead. His dragon senses had registered her movements, her intent, even before it had left her hand, but the action shocked him so greatly that he was unable to react. He tried to duck at the last second and succeeded only in stumbling into the water and losing his balance. It was the first time he remembered anything like that happening. The Kirsdarkenvar, master of the element of water, one of the most agile men in all of Roland, tripped and plunged face-first into the Tar'afel.

Ashe stood up, dripping for a moment, then emerged, dry, from the river. He went up behind Rhapsody, who was picking up the gear he had brought across the river previously.

'What was that for?' he demanded.

She stood, hoisted her pack onto her shoulder and glared at him. 'It's the same thing you did to me. Don't ever interrupt me when I'm concentrating, unless something is swooping in from a place I can't know about. For me it's the same as if you had thrown a rock at my head. I can hurl one at yours each time you break my focus, if you'd like, to remind you.'

'That won't be necessary,' said Ashe, annoyed. 'So, now I'm to speak only if spoken to, is that it?'

'That's tempting, but not required,' Rhapsody replied. 'If you want to go back now, I think I can find my way from here.'

'No, you can't,' Ashe said. Before the words had left his lips, he regretted them. Twice already that afternoon he had condescended to her, doubted her ability to do what she said she could, and it only served to infuriate her more each time, as evidenced by the glowering anger that was taking up residence on her exquisite face now. 'Wait; I'm sorry, that's not what I meant. I don't want to give up the journey now. We're almost there. I said I would escort you as far as Elynsynos's lair, and I don't want to break my word. Surely you can respect that.'

The rolling boil tempered to a steaming simmer. 'I suppose,' she said grudgingly. 'But I'm very tired of not being taken seriously because of my size.' She carried the packs to a small clearing in the woods and dropped them on the ground, then stripped off her cloak. She was dripping wet from head to foot, her boots sodden and squishing, her clothes clinging to her body. The sight made Ashe swallow hard and give silent thanks that he could not be seen. To quell his building arousal he challenged her statement.

'You think people don't take you seriously because you're small?'

Rhapsody pulled her soaking shirt over her head and draped it over a tree branch. She was wearing a sleeveless camisole of Sorboldian linen trimmed with lace, the outline of her graceful breasts made obvious by the way it clung to her wet body. Ashe could feel his temperature rise and his hands begin to tremble.

'That, or my hair color. For some reason people seem to equate the darkness of someone's hair with the mental heat their head is generating. I don't understand it at all.' She pulled off her boots and unlaced the ties of her trousers.

Ashe was beginning to fear losing control. 'Well, perhaps it's more a matter of lack of common sense,' he said, hoping to forestall her removing any more clothing and at the same time wishing she would continue.

The rolling boil was back. 'Excuse me? Did you just say I had no common sense?'

'Well, look at you. You're alone in an uninhabited forest glade with a man you barely know, stripping down to your undergarments.'

'My clothes are wet.'

'I understand that, and, believe me, I'm enjoying the sight, but if I were someone else, you could be in considerable hazard at this moment.'

'Why?' She let her trousers fall to the ground and stepped out of them, hanging them on the branch next to her dripping shirt. Her long slender legs were clad in slim knee-length pants of linen that matched her camisole, with similarly clinging tendencies.

'Well, you could be ravaged or worse.'

Rhapsody smiled at him in great amusement. 'Now, Ashe, how intimidated can a woman be by a man whose sword is made of water?' She winked at him and went back to spreading her clothes out evenly on the branch.

Ashe stared at her, then laughed aloud. She really did personify the unpredictability of the type of musical piece whose name she bore; wild, different from moment to moment, full of the unexpected. He had anticipated a longer, more drawn-out argument over his last choice of insult, and instead she was gently mocking him.

'Never underestimate the power of water,' he said teasingly. 'My sword can be icy, and as hard as steel. I can even make it smoke.'

'Ooooo,' she said, her back still turned and sounding unimpressed. 'But what good does that do if it melts when it comes in contact with heat?' She patted the scabbard of Daystar Clarion without turning around.

Ashe couldn't tell if she was flirting with him, but he certainly was hoping that she was. He reached out a hand from behind her over her shoulder and touched the clothing she had hung up, drawing the water from it. She ran a hand over it in surprise to find that her shirt, trousers and stockings were dry.

'Impressive,' she said.

'If I might have permission to touch your shoulder, I can dry the rest of them,' he said.

Rhapsody considered for a moment, then nodded. Ashe's fingers came to rest on her shoulder, and the camisole stiffened in the absence of the water that soaked it the moment before. A moment later the rest of her garments were dry as well.

'Thank you,' she said, pulling her clothes off the tree and donning her shirt. 'Now you can start taking me seriously again.'

'Rhapsody, I do take you seriously,' Ashe said. He was being truthful; he prayed she was what she seemed, not a demonic minion. If she was evil, he knew that when the time came he would hand his soul over to her without a struggle.

She was lacing her trousers back up. 'Most men don't. Most men don't take most women seriously when they are unclothed.'

'Why do you think that is?'

'Well, I think it's because men are uncomfortable with being unclothed themselves by and large. Unlike women, they have an indicator that can betray things about them, that tells what, and if, they're thinking.'

Ashe felt the color rise in his face. 'Excuse me?' He hoped she was not referring to him.

'Well, when he's naked, a man's brain is hanging out for all the world to see.'

'That's ridiculous.'

Rhapsody gave him a thoughtful look as she pulled her boot on. 'No, it's not. From my experience, that's the organ men think with.'

Ashe decided to let the conversation drop then. She was right. He was thinking long and hard at the moment.

The fire burned low that night, smoldering quietly in the wind. Ashe had fed it with twigs and peat several times, but it refused the sustenance, maintaining a steady flame. He smiled at the irony of it; he had never seen a pensive campfire before. Its mood matched Rhapsody's exactly.

She had said little from the time they had made camp, and had gone about checking and repacking the gear while he cooked. She had eaten in silence as well, but it was not a hostile one. She answered questions without rancor but did not seem to initiate any conversation. The depth of her thought was such that it could almost be heard, so Ashe respected her stillness, and by and large left her to her musings.

After she had cleaned and repacked the eating and cooking utensils she slipped away to the edge of the firelight, watching the stars come out, one by one, over the dimming shapes of the hills in the distance. The wind was from the east, and it blew the smoke from the fire across the fields before her, sending occasional sparks drifting over her head and into the night sky where they vanished without a trace.

Ashe sat on the opposite side of the fire, his back to her. She was well within the range of his senses, and he wanted to afford her whatever distance she needed. He listened with interest for the sunset devotions she always sang as the stars came forth, as he did each night, delighting in the beauty of her voice and the purity of the song, but twilight came, then dusk, then darkness, and still she was silent.

From where he sat he sensed a single tear form and fall; her eyes were searching the sky intensely, not finding what they sought. Ashe's heart twisted. He longed to go to her, to take her in his arms and whisper words of comfort, but he knew better. He was condemned to his distance, to her privacy, and to the possibility that it was he who had caused her sadness with his stupidity. He cursed himself and prayed that her pain did not derive from reliving old memories he had stirred up.

Your fault, the dragon muttered. *All your fault.*

Finally he heard her whisper something to herself. The words were imperceptible to the human ear, but the dragon caught them as if she had spoken them next to him.

'Liacor miathmyn evet tana rosha? Evet ria diandaer. Diefi aria.'

He recognized the language immediately; she was speaking in Ancient Lirin. He thought he could translate it fairly closely: *How can I expect you to answer? You don't know me. I have lost the star.*

A jumble of feelings swarmed in his head. Delight – his suspicions had been all but confirmed; she must be Cymrian to know the tongue of the Lirin of Serendair. Uncertainty – was she addressing the stars, or him, or perhaps another altogether? And pain – the despair in her voice was of a depth he recognized; it held a loneliness not unlike his own.

Ashe stood up and walked slowly around the fire until he came up behind her. He could feel her shoulders straighten as he approached, and the tear dissipated as the surface temperature of her skin rose momentarily. She remained otherwise motionless. He smiled to himself, touched by the use of her fire lore, then made his voice as casual as he could.

'Are you looking for any star in particular?' She shook her head in response. 'I have a – well – that is to say, I know something of astronomy,' he continued, groping for the right words, and missing, in the dark.

'Why do you ask?' It really wasn't even a question.

Ashe winced at his inept attempt. 'Well,' he said, trying the honest route, 'I thought I heard you say "diefi aria". Doesn't that mean "I've lost the star"?'

Rhapsody's eyes closed, and she sighed deeply. When she turned to him there was a look of sadness and resignation on her face. He could detect no trace of anger.

' "Diefi" is "I have lost," ' you're right,' she said, looking past him. 'But you have mistranslated "aria." It doesn't mean the "star;" it means "my star." '

Ashe knew better than to claim victory in his quest for her past. 'And what does that mean, if you don't mind my asking? What star have you lost?'

Rhapsody walked back to the fire and sat, resting her forehead on her palm. She was silent. Ashe cursed himself again.

'I'm sorry; that was inexcusable of me. I had no right to pry into things I overheard.'

Rhapsody looked up at him for the first time since supper. 'My mother's family were Liringlas, the people of the woods and meadows, Skysingers. They watched the heavens for guidance, and greeted the passing of the night into morning, and the dusk into night, with song. I believe you've noticed.'

'Yes. Beautiful.' His words had many meanings.

'They also believed that each child was born under a specific guiding star, and that there was a bond between each Lirin soul and its star. "Aria" is the word for "my guiding star," though of course each star had its own name as well. There were many rituals and traditions around it, I guess. My father thought it was nonsense.'

'I think it is a wonderful belief.'

Rhapsody said nothing. She gazed into the fire again, the light reflecting off her face in a somber rhythm.

'So which star is your star? Perhaps I can help you find it again.'

She rose and stirred the fire. 'No, you can't. Thank you, nonetheless. I'll take the first watch. Get some sleep.' She went to the gear and prepared the weapons for the night.

It was not until he was deep within his bedroll that Ashe fully understood her answer. Her star was on the other side of the world, shining over a sea that held the place of her birth in a watery tomb.

He lay back in the silence of his bedchamber and listened to the sound of the warm Spring wind. All around him the noise and distraction of the day had settled into muffled torpidity. How he loved this time of the night, when the mask could come off and he could relish all those things he had put in place without being discovered.

If the wind was clear and the night silent enough he could feel the heat, the friction in the air from violence that was being made by his manipulation, even from a great distance away. This night, it came to him courtesy of the squad of Yarimese guards in his thrall that had turned from their normal duties patroling the water routes outside the crumbling capital city of Yarim Paar, safeguarding the Shanouin, the clan of well diggers and water carriers as they bore their precious burden back to the thirsty town.

The Shanouin had depended upon the protection of the guards for centuries. He chuckled at the thought. Mayhem was always valuable; it brought the electric fervor he craved. It was even better when the victims trusted the thralls. The static from the initial shock added to the amusement value. And the horror of the guards that would result when the thrall wore off and they had to confront their murderous actions was the stuff of delicious anticipation.

His skin tingled at the rush of fear that broke over him in waves as the slaughter began. The water carriers were men of brawn, but worked routinely with their families in tow. He took a deeper breath, stretching his limbs as the warmth of spilling blood coursed over them.

It was friction, the heat of contact, of violence, that roared through his body, that caressed his spirit nature now, the power of heat that so recalled the fire from which he had come. All nature of actions generated it, but the place it was most surely found was the fierce combat of murder, heinous and ferocious and utterly stimulating. He felt arousal building in his human flesh, flesh denied satisfaction in most other ways due to age and the other restraints of dual nature.

The patrol was efficient; too efficient – they weren't taking their time. He grunted in frustration, willing the guards to slow their efforts, to stab more rather than decapitate, to leave the children until the end. His hopes for the heat of the gore building to an invigorating climax grew dim; he had not committed enough of his own essence when he had enthralled the group. A shame, really. A mistake he would not make again.

There was no need to conserve his power anymore. He was now powerful enough to spare more of his life essence, that which would have been a soul if F'dor had such a thing. The next time he had the opportunity to make a group of soldiers into his unwitting temporary servants he would be sure to commit more of himself to the undertaking. That way he would feel more of the misery, soak up more of the agony. It certainly was worth it, given that the only other pleasures his human form allowed him were brandy and rich pastries.

His breathing grew shallow again as the massacre grew to a fever pitch, then settled into the aftermath of keening wails and weakening cries for mercy far too late. It was wonderful to feel the surge of power that accompanied the shedding of the blood of children again. With his toy out wandering the wide world, away from the House of Remembrance that had been the scene of such wonderful carnage, it had been too long, much too long.

When the orgiastic sensations had finally cooled, he covered himself over again with blankets and fell into the comforting darkness of sleep, dreaming of the day when these occasional secret pleasures would be routine, when the agony of another child, one hidden in the mountains of Ylorc, would be at hand. It was coming soon, all in good time.

5

Birdsong and a sudden shaft of sunlight woke Rhapsody the next morning. She had had a difficult night, and as a result had slept in past dawn, something she virtually never did. She sat up in panic, distressed at having missed her sunrise devotions.

'Good morning.' The voice came from the other side of their campsite, where Ashe was sitting, cloaked in his usual misty attire, watching her. 'Did you get any rest at all?'

'Yes; I'm sorry,' she said, embarrassed. Her hair had come down during the night in the midst of her frantic thrashing about. Ashe had a sudden epiphany. With her burnished golden locks falling loose around her perfect face she was without question the most sexually alluring thing he had ever seen. On an unconscious level she must have some inkling of this. Finally he understood why she always bound her hair back in the staid black velvet ribbon – she was downplaying her attractiveness to avoid standing out. Ashe chuckled to himself. Far too little, far too late.

'Don't apologize,' he said, tossing a handful of twigs into the fire. 'It must be awful being unable to pass even a single night in peace.'

Rhapsody looked away. 'Yes, it is.' She rose slowly and pulled herself from the bedroll, brushing the leaves and grass off her clothes. 'Do you think we'll make it there today?'

'To Elynsynos?'

'Yes.'

'I'd say tomorrow. If you were within her realm, you would have slept better.'

Rhapsody finished binding her hair back into its ribbon and looked at him again. 'What do you mean?'

'They say dragons can guard a person's dreams, keep the bad ones at bay. If we had been within her reach, she doubtlessly would have chased your nightmares away.'

'How do you know she'd want to?'

'Because she will be fascinated with you, Rhapsody. Trust me.'

Ashe apparently knew what he was talking about. After an uneventful day of walking through woods that deepened and became ever more quiet with each mile they traveled, Rhapsody and Ashe stopped for the night again. She still had not lost her contemplative mood, and they had traveled mostly in silence through the greenwood, stopping at last in a dark glen

74

surrounded with holly bushes. They made camp, and Ashe took the first watch.

Midnight came, and still Rhapsody slumbered quietly, her rest undisturbed by her nightly terrors except for one moment of hiccoughing whispers, after which she settled down again. Ashe decided to let her sleep as long as she could without interruption, and as a result was still sitting watch when morning came. He saw the slender arms emerge from the bedroll and stretch to the sound of a long, deep sigh; a moment later her head came forth, the golden crown of hair resembling the sun coming over the horizon. The enormous eyes opened wide with panic.

She pulled herself rapidly out of the bedroll and ran for the nearest clearing where she could see the sky. The light of dawn was coming into it, turning the deep blue into azure and touching the east with pink. The daystar began to set just as Rhapsody began her aubade, singing with a sweet clarity that broke the heavy silence of the glen and sent shivers up Ashe's back. He felt a gentle rumble in the ground beneath him and the wind picked up slightly.

Elynsynos had heard her, too.

This is the place,' Ashe said. His voice was a near whisper, and Rhapsody wondered if it was from reverence or fear.

Set in a hollow in the hillside below them was a small woodland lake. Its crystal waters were perfectly calm and reflected the trees that lined it like a mirror. The waters of the lake emptied into the small creek they had followed on and off since the Tar'afel.

The forest itself was quiet, the stillness broken only by occasional birdsong and the sound of the brook. There was a beauty and serenity to it that defied Rhapsody's expectations of what a dragon's lair would look like. There was no sign that a great reptilian beast, or in fact anyone, lived here at all.

They walked around the lake to the far side, and Rhapsody could see its source. A cave was set in the steepest of the hillsides, invisible except from this vantage point, and from it a small stream flowed, emptying silently into the glassy waters of the reflecting pool. The mouth of the cave was perhaps twenty feet high. There was no question that this was the place; she could feel power emanating from the cave that made her shiver internally.

As they walked down the long path Rhapsody thought she heard the sound of whispered voices on the wind, but when she stopped to listen, no words were there; all she heard was the rustling of the budding branches in the early spring breeze. She had the distinct feeling that they were being watched. Ashe did not speak, and she could discern no reaction beneath the hood of his cloak.

Finally they came to the mouth of the cave. A warm breeze flowed from it in rhythmic patterns; *the breath of the dragon*, Rhapsody thought. Doubt rose in her mind as to the wisdom of coming here. She was considering taking hasty leave when the peace of the forest was broken by a voice that could only have been that of Elynsynos.

'You interest me,' the voice said, sounding in multiple tones, at once bass, baritone, tenor, alto and soprano. Its resonance contained an elemental intimacy that even Rhapsody's fireborn heart could not fathom. It spoke to the deepest levels of her soul, and for a moment she could not tell if she had actually heard the words, or merely felt them. 'Come in.'

Rhapsody swallowed hard and started slowly into the mouth of the cave. She stopped to examine a carved rune on the outside edge of the cave wall, brushing away the lichens and overgrown ivy. The words were suddenly familiar.

Cyme we inne friđ, fram the griþ of deaþ to lif inne đis smylte land

A gentle vibration tingled beneath the tips of her fingers as she touched the ancient inscription, the feeling of lore lying dormant for centuries, and she was filled with a sudden wonder, a sense of discovery and more – the sensation of excitement, the heart-squeezing thrill of a first passion. She recognized it instantly, and it was unmistakable, despite having felt it herself only once in her life before.

The lore, old as it was, hung in the very air of the place, was extant in the stone of the cave wall. This must have been where Merithyn had come, where he had first inscribed the pledge of his king. In a way, then, this was the birthplace of the Cymrian people, and as such it held an almost magical air about it. Even more, there had been love here once, great love, and a fragment of it still remained. Rhapsody felt she could stay for a long time, just gazing at the runes.

'Rhapsody.' Ashe's voice rang out from behind her, causing her to jump. 'Don't look into her eyes.'

She shook off her trancelike state and nodded. She checked the integrity of her gear, then turned to him.

'I'll be careful. Goodbye, Ashe,' she said softly. 'Thank you for everything. May your travels home be safe.'

'Rhapsody, tarry a moment.' Ashe reached out his hand to her. She turned around and took it, allowing him to bring her off the rocks and back onto the ground again.

'Yes?' She was standing before him, looking up into the darkness of his hood.

Slowly he reached up and took hold of the hood, then pulled it down suddenly, revealing his face. Rhapsody gasped.

Jo had been right. He was not scarred or deformed. His face was beautiful, and it had an uncertain smile on it as he looked down at her.

Like her sister, the first thing Rhapsody noticed was his hair. It shone like burnished copper, and as it caught the light of the afternoon sun, Rhapsody thought it looked as though it had been crafted by a smith. She had seen nothing like it in this land or that of her birth, and wondered if it was gossamer-soft, as the delicacy of its strands suggested, or hard and wiry, as its metallic sheen insisted. The puzzle fascinated her; she could have spent the rest of the day standing there, staring at it, trying to resist the urge to touch it.

It took a moment for her eyes to note the rest of his face. It was classically handsome, and like her own, showed mixed human and Lirin descent. His skin was fair and smooth, and his chiseled jaw was covered by a scraggly, half-grown beard. In a pure human it would have suggested a month without shaving, but Rhapsody knew that in a half-blood it probably was a year's growth at least. If he was a human, he would have been in his mid-twenties, but as a half-Lirin, possibly of Cymrian ancestry, Rhapsody had no way to judge his real age.

And then she looked into his eyes, eyes that were beautiful and alien. They were startlingly blue, and set about the iris were tiny stars of an amber hue. It took her a moment to discern what seemed so alien about them, until she took a second look. Their humanity was broken by their pupils, which were vertical slits, like that of a serpent, yet they held no reptilian horror; rather they spoke of an antiquity and power that was ancient and enduring. She felt drawn to them as by the power of a flooded river rushing over a waterfall, or the tranquillity of a calm lagoon. Then he closed them, only for a moment, an extended blink, and she caught her breath.

As she began to breathe once more she could feel her cheeks, wet with tears she did not know she had shed. Like a slap across the face she was aware now, understood many things she hadn't before, about why he hid beneath the cloak, why he pushed her away.

He was hunted. It could be the only reason.

She struggled to speak, but the emotion was too strong. Ashe looked down into her eyes, as if dreading her words and needing to hear them despite that dread. Finally she felt them come to her lips.

'Ashe?'

'Yes?'

She took a deep breath.

'You should shave off that beard, it's awful.'

He stared at her blankly as the comment registered, then laughed. Rhapsody exhaled in relief, and as he looked away for a moment, still chuckling, she reached up and hugged him. She didn't want him to see the tears continue to well in her eyes.

Ashe pulled her closer in a warm embrace, holding her gently, but as he did she felt him wince. Somehow her action had caused him pain, and she let go of him, trying to keep from making it worse. It seemed centered in his chest, but she couldn't be sure. He released her as well, with a sigh.

'Thank you,' she said sincerely. 'I know that was a difficult thing for you, and I'm honored that you did it. If you hadn't shown me, I always would have wondered.'

'Be careful in there,' he said, nodding toward the cave.

'You be careful on your way back,' she answered, turning to go. She bent and picked up a stick of dry wood lying at the mouth of the cave. 'Thank you again. Godspeed.' She blew him a kiss, then climbed onto the wet stone and into the cave entrance.

The mouth of the cave widened into a dark tunnel, with a glowing light pulsing deep within it. At the outer edge, starlike lichen grew on the cave walls, reaching out into the light of day, to grow thinner and eventually disappear in the darkness as the tunnel went deeper in.

Rhapsody followed the tunnel slowly, listening for movement. A moment later she could hear it, the splash of something moving through the water in the depths of the cave, followed by the pounding of taloned feet as they trod the rock floor. There was a sound of steel grinding against stone, and the cave filled with the hot wind of the dragon's breath, tainted with the acrid smells that Rhapsody had only encountered before at a smithy, or Achmed's forges, odors that issued forth from smelting fires.

The tunnel twisted as she followed it, opening at the bottom into a large cavern below. The darkness of the cavern was impenetrable, so Rhapsody touched the stick she carried and ignited the end of it, hoping a torch would illuminate the place. It roared to life almost immediately; the leaping flames cast elongated shadows down the tunnel, outlining and exaggerating the movements of the great beast as it pulled itself from the waters that filled the cave floor. The ground trembled with its every step, and the flickering light of the torch danced off the copper scales, gleaming like a million tiny shields of burnished bronze in the darkness.

Elynsynos was immense. In the half-light Rhapsody estimated she was almost one hundred feet long, easily able to fill the entire length of the tunnel she had just traversed. The strength denoted by the enormous musculature was enough to drain the color from the Singer's face.

Then she saw the eyes of the beast, too late to heed Ashe's warning. They appeared in the tunnel like two gigantic lanterns that had suddenly been unhooded. The great orbs shone with prismatic light; they were so intensely beautiful that Rhapsody felt she could easily pass her life there, gazing into them. Long vertical slits bisected each silver iris, rimmed in shimmering rainbow colors. At once Rhapsody felt the fires of her soul leap, as if fed with a sudden breath of air. For a moment she was dizzy, lost inside herself, but the feeling passed in a moment, and she dragged her gaze away from the beast, her soul screaming in protest.

'Pretty,' Elynsynos said. There was a power in the word Rhapsody recognized immediately. Elynsynos was speaking with an elemental music, and the word she had spoken was not a description, but a name. The harmonic sound came not from a voice box – little as she knew of dragon lore, one thing that Rhapsody did know was that wyrms did not have a natural larynx – but from the masterful manipulation of the vibrations of the wind. Rhapsody was tempted to look once more directly at her but did not, watching her only through the corner of her eye.

'Why do you come, Pretty?' There was wisdom in the voice that belied the childlike tone and words.

Rhapsody took a deep breath and turned a little farther away. 'Many reasons,' she answered, looking at the serpentine shadow on the cave wall before her. 'I have dreamt of you. I have come to return something that is yours, and to sing to you, if you will let me.' She could see the shadow move as the head of the dragon came to rest on the ground directly behind her, and she felt its hot breath on her back. The fire inside her drank in the heat and the power it held. The moisture from her clothing evaporated, leaving the fabric hot and on the verge of igniting.

'Turn around, please,' said the multitone voice. Rhapsody closed her eyes and complied, feeling the waves of warmth on her face as though she was turning blindly toward the sun. 'Are you afraid?'

'A little,' Rhapsody answered, still not opening her eyes.

'Why?'

'We fear what we do not know, and do not understand. I hope to remedy both those situations, and then I will not be afraid.'

Once again, as before she entered the cave, she heard what sounded like whispered voices. 'You are wise to be afraid,' said Elynsynos. There was no menace in her tone, but its depth was intimidating. 'You are perfect treasure, Pretty. Your hair is like spun gold, your eyes are emeralds. Even your skin is like fine porcelain, and you are untouched. There is music in you, and fire, and time. Any dragon would covet you to have for its own.'

'I belong only to myself,' Rhapsody said. The dragon chuckled. 'But I came here in the hope that we could be friends. Then I am yours willingly, in a way. A friend is one of the greatest kinds of treasures, isn't it?' She glanced quickly at the dragon, then looked away.

The dragon's enormous face took on a look of curiosity that was oddly endearing, visible even in the glimpse Rhapsody caught out of the corner of her eye.

'I do not know. I do not have any friends.'

'Then I will be a new kind of treasure for you, if you want me to be,' said Rhapsody, her fear beginning to abate. 'First, let me return this to you.' She dug in her pack and pulled out the dragon's claw dagger.

The enormous prismatic eyes blinked. Rhapsody was still not looking at her directly, but could feel the light in the cave dim for a second. Her skin prickled as an electric hum began around her, buzzing in the cavern like a great hive of bees. She saw the shadow on the wall shift, and a huge claw reached over her head and gingerly took the dagger in between nails that resembled it exactly. Then the claw returned to its place behind her once more. Rhapsody let her breath out.

'Where did you get this?'

'In the depths of Gwylliam's lair,' said Rhapsody, trying to couch her words in imagery the dragon would appreciate. 'It was hidden deep, but when we found it we knew it should be returned to you.'

'Gwylliam was a bad man,' said the harmonious voice. It was without rancor; Rhapsody was grateful. She did not want to be within the lair of a dragon who was incensed. 'He hit Anwyn, and he killed so many of the Cymrians. This claw was given to her, and he kept it for spite. Thank you for bringing it back, Pretty.'

'You're welcome, Elynsynos. I'm sorry about what happened to Anwyn.'

The humming sound grew louder. Rhapsody felt the heat in the air around her rise. 'Anwyn is bad as well, as bad as Gwylliam. She destroyed her own hoard. That is something a dragon must never do. I am ashamed she is my hatchling. She is no child of mine. A dragon defends its treasure with everything it has. Anwyn destroyed her own hoard.'

'Her hoard? What hoard?'

'Look at me, Pretty. I will not try to take you.' The multitone voice was warm and sweet. 'If you are my friend, you should trust me, yes?'

Rhapsody, don't look into her eyes.

Rhapsody turned around slowly, staring at the ground. She could feel the glimmering scales reflecting the light from her torch; it undulated in wavelike patterns over her linen shirt, turning the white fabric into a translucent rainbow. The warmth of the voice had captured her heart, even though her brain continued to function for the moment, telling her to be wary of the gigantic serpent. The trickery of dragons was well known, and Ashe's warning was still ringing in her ears.

Rhapsody, don't look into her eyes.

'Her hoard was the Cymrian people,' said Elynsynos. 'They were magic; they had crossed the Earth and made time to stop for themselves by doing so. In them all the elements found a manifestation, even if they did not know how to use it. There were some of races that had never been seen in these parts, Gwadd and Liringlas and Gwenen and Nain, Ancient Seren and Dhracians and Mythlin, a human garden full of many different and beautiful kinds of flowers. They were special, Pretty, a unique people that deserved to be cherished and kept safe. And she turned against them and destroyed many of them, so that Gwylliam could not have them. Ashamed I am.'

Rhapsody felt mist on her face; she looked down and found she was standing in glimmering liquid. She raised her eyes without thinking and found herself staring, entranced, at the great beast. Elynsynos was weeping.

Rhapsody felt her heart break; at that moment she would have gladly given everything she had to comfort the dragon, to ease her pain and wash away her sadness. In the back of her mind she wondered if her deep feelings for the wyrm were a result of enchantment or if, as her heart told her, she just loved her because she was so rare and beautiful. She stepped toward Elynsynos and touched her massive claw tenderly.

'Don't cry, Elynsynos.'

The dragon angled her massive head downward and regarded her intensely, a blinding glint shining in her eyes. 'Then you will stay for a little while?'

'Yes. I will stay.'

6

Grunthor lumbered to a halt for the fourth time that afternoon, too ungainly to stop quickly as Achmed did, and sighed aloud.

'Is she still there, sir?'

'Yes.' The tone of irritation in Achmed's voice had grown darker with each pause. The Firbolg king turned around in the tunnel and shouted back behind them.

'Damn you, Jo, go home or I'll tie you to a stalagmite and leave you until we return.'

The air next to his head whistled, and a small, bronze-backed dirk imbedded itself into the cave wall next to his ear.

'You're a fornicating pig,' Jo's voice answered with an echoing snarl. 'You can't leave me alone with those little brats. I'm coming with you, you bastard, whether you like it or not.'

Achmed hid a smile and strode back up the tunnel, then reached behind an outcropping of rocks and dragged the teenager out of her hiding place.

'A word of advice about fornicating pigs,' he said almost pleasantly. 'They bite. Don't get in their way, or they'll take a piece out of you.'

'Yeah, well, you'd know all about fornicating pigs, Achmed. I'm sure you do it all the time. Gods know nobody else would ever knob you, unless they were blind.'

'Go home, little miss,' said Grunthor severely. 'You don't want to see me lose my temper.'

'Come on, Grunthor,' Jo whined, making an attempt at wide-eyed, innocent pleading and failing utterly. 'I hate those little bastards. I want to go with you. *Please.*'

'Now, is that any way to talk about your grand-nieces and nephews?' asked Achmed disingenuously. 'Your sister would be very distressed to hear you referring to her grandbrats that way.'

'They're little beasts. They try to trip me when we're out on the crags,' Jo said. 'Next time I might just accidentally boot one or two of them into the canyon by mistake. Please don't leave me alone with them. I want to go wherever you're going.'

'No. Now are you going to go back on your own, or will you need to be escorted?'

Jo crossed her arms, her face fixed in a furious expression. Achmed sighed.

'Look, Jo, here's my final offer. If it turns out that we find what we're looking for, and the danger is manageable, we'll bring you back with us the next time. But if you follow us again, I'm going to bind you hand and foot and throw you into the nursery, and Rhapsody's grandbrats can use you as a ball, or play Badger-in-the-Bag with you. Do you understand?' Jo nodded sullenly. 'Good. Now get back to the Cauldron and stop following us.' Grunthor pulled the knife he had given her from the wall and held it out. Jo snatched it from his hand and stuck it back in her boot.

The two Bolg watched as the teenager whirled angrily and stalked back up the ascending tunnel. After a few moments of hearing nothing they returned to their descent, only to stop once more.

Achmed spun about in annoyance. The light from the world above was no longer within sight; they were deep within the tunnel now, too deep to go back without wasting the entire day. It had taken a number of weeks to put aside time when both he and Grunthor could go exploring, searching out the Loritorium, the hidden vault he had shown the maps of to Rhapsody. Unfortunately, the teenaged brat she had adopted as her sister had gotten wind of the expedition, and refused to heed his commands that she stay behind, both before they left the Cauldron, and all along the way. It was evident she still was not complying with his directive.

He could sense her, though her heartbeat was not audible to him as Grunthor's and Rhapsody's were, along with the few thousand others he sometimes heard drumming in the distance. The ability to discern those rhythms was the fragmented remains of his blood-gift from the old world; the only hearts he could hear were ones that had been born there.

Sensing Jo was different. This was his mountain, he was the king, and as a result he knew she was here again, defying his instructions, following behind them just out of sight. He turned to the giant Sergeant-Major.

'Grunthor, do you remember how you once told me you thought you could feel the movement of the earth?'

Grunthor scratched his head and grinned. 'Goodness, sir, I don't ever recall getting that personal with you. In fact, the only sweet talkin' I ever remember doing was with ol' Brenda at Madame Parri's Pleasure Palace all those years ago.'

Achmed chuckled and pointed at the ground beneath their feet. 'Fire responds to Rhapsody, and the more she experiments with it, the more she is able to control it at will. Perhaps since you have a similar bond with earth, the same might be true for you.' He looked up the tunnel again. 'And perhaps your first experiment in manipulating the earth might take a form that would grant us a respite from the recurring nightmare that won't stop following us.'

Grunthor considered for a moment, then closed his eyes. All around him he could feel the heartbeat of the Earth, a subtle thrum whispering in the air he breathed, pulsing in the ground below his feet, bristling across his hidelike skin. It was a vibration that had hummed in his bones and blood since they had traveled through the Earth along the Root that connected the two great trees. It spoke to him now, giving him an insight into the layers of rock around him.

In his mind's eye he could see the paths of the different strata as the Earth sang to him of the birth of this place, a lament recalling the horrific pressure that forced the great sheets of rock upwards, screaming in the pain of its delivery, erupting into the craggy peaks that now formed the Teeth. Through his bond to the Earth his soul whispered wordless consolation in return, gentling down the age-old memory.

He could see each pocket of frailty within the ground, each place where an obsidian river scored the basalt and shale, each crack where the Nain, other earthlovers tied to the lore as he was, had carefully sculpted out the endless passageways of Canrif, the tunnels like the one in which they now stood. He could sense Jo's feet resting on the crust a stone's throw away, and willed the earth to soften there for a moment, to swallow her ankles and solidify again.

Her scream of shock broke his reverie, and Grunthor opened his eyes to a stabbing pain pulsing behind them. A string of vile curses punctuated with screeches of fury reverberated around them, unsettling some of the loose rock and raising a minor storm of dust. Achmed chuckled.

'That ought to hold her, at least until we can make it to the entrance tunnel to the annex. Then you can release her. I doubt even Jo would want to risk having the ground grab her feet again.' His eyes narrowed as he noticed the paling of Grunthor's skin in the half-light of the torch he was carrying, the beads of sweat on his friend's massive brow. 'Are you all right?'

Grunthor wiped his forehead with a neat linen handkerchief. 'Not sure I like the way that felt,' he said. 'Never hurt before when I was just generally aware of things in the ground, or makin' myself look like the rock.'

'It's bound to be somewhat painful the first time,' said Achmed. 'As you become more experienced, more proficient at using your gift, I think you will find the pain subsides.'

'I bet you say that to all the girls,' Grunthor retorted, folding his handkerchief and storing it away again. 'Come to think of it, I think they're the exact words I used on ol' Brenda. Well, shall we be off, then?'

Achmed nodded and the two men walked off into the depths of the Earth, leaving Jo up to her ankles in solid rock, howling with rage behind them.

The deeper Achmed traveled into the lands he now ruled, the more the silence enveloped him. The ancient corridors, half-formed and crumbling, required frequent stopping and intervention from Grunthor, who cleared away the rubble and tore through the stone as if it were aqueous, almost liquid, much as he had once dug them out of the skin of the Earth at the end of their journey along the Root. The clamor of the falling debris was momentary, and each new threshold they crossed revealed an even deeper stillness, heavy air that had been undisturbed for centuries.

83

It had taken Achmed less than a day to determine where the Loritorium had been built, informed by his ferocious study of the manuscripts in Gwylliam's vault, his own innate sense of the mountain and his path lore. Finding it had merely been a matter of a quiet moment's meditation on his throne in the Great Hall, contemplating where he would have built the secret annex if he had been Gwylliam. And then, behind his closed eyes, his mind raced off, speeding along the twists and turns of the meticulously mined tunnels of the inner mountain. It followed the corridors out of the interior city of Canrif and roamed over the wide Heath, past Kraldurge, the Realm of Ghosts, the guardian rocks that formed the hidden barrier above Elysian, Rhapsody's hidden lands.

He had found the entrance to the ancient ruin deep below the villages that had once been settled by the Cymrians, past a second canyon, and guarded by an ominous drop of several thousand feet onto jagged and rocky steppes below. Its entry passage was cleverly disguised as part of the mountain face, a man-made fissure that resembled little more than a mountain-goat trail, and now was traveled only by animals, if at all.

Once he and Grunthor were inside the tunnel he knew they were headed in the right direction, and it had infuriated him that Jo had breached the security of the Loritorium by following them in. Most likely the teenager was only being an annoyance, but Achmed trusted no one, and it was just one more thing that convinced him of Rhapsody's folly in adopting the street wench in the first place. *Mark my words*, he had told her through gritted teeth, *we will regret this*. As with all things she didn't want to believe, Rhapsody had ignored those words.

Now, as Grunthor ripped through the detritus clogging the tunnel before them, Achmed could feel the silence grow even deeper. The sensation was akin to the one he had experienced upon finding a Cymrian wine cellar filled with barrels and glass bottles of ancient cider deep within the desolate ruin that had once been the capital city of Canrif. Much of the liquid had dissipated centuries before, leaving a thick, oozing gel that had at one time been potable but now was almost solid, with a concentrated sweetness. The silence within the newly revealed section of tunnel was almost as palpable.

Grunthor, meanwhile, was not hearing a deafening silence, but a deepening song. With each new revelation, each new break in the strata, the earth music was growing purer, more vibrant, hanging heavy with old magic that carried with it a sense of dread. His fingers tingled, even through his goat-hide gloves, as he moved rocks and boulders to the sides of the tunnels. Finally he stopped and leaned against the rockwall before him, resting his head on his forearm. He breathed deeply, absorbing the music that now surrounded him, filling his ears, drowning out all other sound.

'You all right, Sergeant?'

Grunthor nodded, unable to speak. He ran his hand over the wall again, finally looking up.

'They blew the tunnel when they left, before they was overrun,' he said. 'Didn't crumble on its own. Brought down the whole mountain. Why here, sir? Why not the ramparts, or the feeder tunnels to the Great Hall? They could've held the Bolg off a lot longer, probably cut them off in the Heath canyon and crushed the external attack, at least. Seems odd.'

Achmed handed him a waterskin, and the giant drank deeply. 'There must have been something in there that Gwylliam was willing to sacrifice the mountain in order to keep from falling into the hands of the Bolg, or perhaps someone he feared would wrest it from the Bolg. You still game? We can go back, rest up a bit.'

Grunthor wiped the sweat from his brow and shook his head. 'No. Dug this far; makes no sense givin' up here. There's quite a bit more rock, though; I guess as much as we already dug through.' He rose and brushed off his greatcloak, then ran his hands over the rock again.

As he concentrated the makeup of the stone again became clear to him. In his mind's eye he could see each fissure, each pocket of ancient air trapped within the solidified rubble. He closed his eyes, keeping the image in his mind, then passed his hand through the stone as if it were the air, and felt it give way to him. He held both arms out to his sides, pushed a little farther and felt the solid wall of rock liquefy, then slide away from him like cool molten glass, smooth and slippery.

Achmed watched in amazement as his giant friend's skin grew pale, then ashen, then stone-gray in the waning light of the torch as he blended into the earth around him. A moment later he could no longer see Grunthor, only a moving shadow as the massive mound of granite and shalestone plowed before his eyes into the mountain wall, opening an eight-foot-high tunnel ahead of him. He held the torch inside the hole. The rock at the edges of the new opening glowed red-gold, almost the color of lava for a moment, then cooled immediately into a smooth-hewn tunnel wall. Achmed smiled and stepped into the opening, following the Sergeant's shadow.

'Always knew you were a quick study, Grunthor,' he said. 'Perhaps it's a good thing Rhapsody's not here; this is a lot like being on the Root again. You know how much she enjoyed being underground.'

'Lirin,' Grunthor muttered, the word echoing up the length of the tunnel like the growl of a subterranean wolf. 'Throw a couple 'undred feet of solid rock on top of them, and they get all nervy on you. Pantywaists.'

The farther he burrowed within the Earth, the faster Grunthor moved. Achmed could no longer keep up with him, could no longer even make out his shadow in the inconstant light. It was as if the rocky flesh of the mountain was nothing more than air around the giant, where before it had been as if he was walking waist-deep in the sea.

Suddenly Achmed felt the force of a great rush of air from the belly of the mountain billow over him, a rolling gust both stale and sweet, heavy with magic. His sensitive skin stung with the power of it, thick and undisturbed by time and the wind of the world above. Grunthor must have broken through to the Loritorium.

He lit a new torch from the remnant of the one he had been carrying and tossed the dead one aside. The fire at the torch's head roared with life, leaping to the top of the tunnel as if shouting aloud in celebration.

'Grunthor?' he called. No sound answered him.

Achmed broke into a run. He hurried down the remaining length of the tunnel and through the dark maw at its end, an opening into a place even darker than the tunnel had been, then stopped where he stood.

Above him, higher than even the roaring flames of the torch could fully illuminate, stretched a carved vaulted ceiling, smoothly polished and engraved with intricate designs, fashioned from the most exquisite marble Achmed had ever seen. Each massive slab of the pale stone had been shaped to a precise dimension and fitted perfectly into the vast cavern in which he now stood. The walls of the cavern were of marble as well, though some of them were still unfinished, with large scaffolds, stone blocks, and tools lying abandoned at the edges of the enormous underground cave.

Achmed turned to the tall bank of rock that had plowed out into the cavern in front of Grunthor as he had tunneled into this place. He swung the torch around, looking for the Firbolg sergeant, but saw nothing save for great mounds of stone and earth heaped on the smooth cave floor, with marble fragments scattered around the base of them. 'Grunthor!' he shouted again, shadows flashing over the newly made moraine and the ancient walls in the dark. His voice echoed for a moment, then was swallowed by silence.

A low pile of rubble at his feet stretched and shrugged. Moments later it took on a more distinct outline and shape. What appeared to be a large stone sculpture of a giant man flexed and began to breathe, each moment becoming a little more distinguishable from the rock.

As Achmed watched, color began to return to Grunthor's face. The Sergeant-Major was sitting on the ground, propped against the great pile of stone rubbish left from his burrowing, breathing shallowly as he returned to himself, separating himself from the earth as once he had at the end of their journey along the Root.

'Blimey,' he whispered as Achmed knelt beside him. He shook his head at the waterskin the king offered him, crossing his arms over his knees and lowering his head onto them.

Achmed stood and looked around again. The Loritorium was approximately the size of the town square in what had once been the capital city of Canrif, a city built within the crags and base of the guardian mountains at the western rim of the Teeth. When they had first come to Ylorc he had found the dead city in a desolate state of ruin. Now the Bolg were working feverishly to restore it to the magnificence it once had in the Cymrian heyday. Even in its decay, the genius of its design and the craftsmanship of its construction had been readily apparent.

The design and construction of the Loritorium was even more impressive. It would have stood as Gwylliam's masterpiece, if he had had the chance to complete it. As with most of the structures Gwylliam designed, the Loritorium had been fashioned in the shape of an enormous hexagon, sculpted in precise proportion from within the mountain itself. The marble walls met the vault of the ceiling more than two hundred feet above the floor. The floor was smoothly polished marble inlaid in mosaic patterns whose colors glimmered in the flickering shadows. In the center of the ceiling was a dark hole which Achmed could just barely see in the blazing light of the torch.

The streets of the Loritorium were lined with beautifully sculpted stone benches and bordered with half-walls from which lampposts fashioned of brass and glass emerged every few yards. The capping stones of the half-walls were scored by shallow troughs that ran between each lamppost, channels blackened with ancient stains that appeared to be the residue of a thick oily substance.

Two large buildings loomed in the darkness at the far side of the Loritorium, identical in size and shape, with huge doors, intricately wrought and gilded with rysin, a rare metal, gleaming a metallic blue-green in the torchlight. Achmed recognized them instantly from the plans as the Library and the Prophesory, the repositories Gwylliam designed for the most valuable of his books and manuscripts. The Library was expected to house all forms of writing about ancient lore, while the Prophesory was to contain all records of prophecies and other predictions known to man. Warehouses of ancient knowledge.

Achmed turned back to his friend. 'Are you all right? Are you coming around?' he asked the giant Sergeant.

Grunthor shook his head. 'If it's all the same to you, sir, I'll just take a little rest right here.'

Achmed nodded. 'I'm going to have a look about, not far; I'll be right back.' Grunthor waved a weak hand dismissively, then stretched out on the debris of the marble floor, groaning, and closed his eyes.

The Firbolg king watched his friend a moment longer until he had ascertained that Grunthor was fully separated from the earth and drawing breath without difficulty. Then he reassessed the torch; it had consumed almost none of its fuel, but still burned brightly in the darkness, as if eager to be shining in this place of ancient magic.

Achmed dropped his pack and equipment to the ground, saving out twin daggers Rhapsody had given him as a coronation gift, found on one of her exploratory sojourns within the mountain some months before. He examined them quickly; they were formed from an ancient metal that no one knew the name of, seemingly impervious to rust, that the Cymrians had used in the framework of buildings and to bard the hulls of ships. Achmed sheathed one of them at his wrist, keeping the other drawn, and quietly made his way through the empty city.

His footsteps echoed hollowly up the streets and reverberated to the vaulted ceiling as he walked, even though he was most often able to travel without sound in the world above. Achmed slowed his pace in the vain attempt to pass more quietly, but it did little good. The heavy air of the newly unsealed cavern seized upon each sound and amplified it. Achmed was filled with an unwelcome sense that the place had been without company too long and was now relishing it.

When he reached the center of the hexagonal cavern he stopped. In the Loritorium's central area was what appeared to have been a small garden with an immense dry fountain, its large reflecting pond surrounded by a circle of marble benches. Around the fountain's base in the dry pond was a small puddle of shining liquid, thick as quicksilver. The font from which water once undoubtedly sprayed was capped with a heavy block of volcanic rock.

This central spot afforded an excellent view of the whole Loritorium. Achmed cast a glance around. Here and there in the narrow streets were more pools of the viscous silver liquid, their iridescent surfaces glimmering in the torchlight. He brought his hand nearer to the pool in the fountain and pulled it quickly back, stung by the intense vibration issuing forth from it. It was signature of great power, one that he did not recognize, that made his fingers and skin hum with its concentrated purity. He broke his attention away from the luminous puddles and looked at the rest of the square.

Set at the directional angles north, south, east, and west around the Loritorium's square were four displays, each roughly built in the shape of an altar. Achmed recalled the drawings of each of them from the manuscripts of Gwylliam's plans. They appeared to be cases which were intended to house what Gwylliam had called the August Relics, items of surpassing importance from the old world tied to each of the five elements. Achmed cursed silently. He had not fully understood the manuscript that had recounted the descriptions of each of these relics, and Rhapsody had left before she could study the scroll and explain it to him.

Carefully he circumvented the fountain and approached the first of the cases. It was fashioned in the shape of a marble bowl on top of a pedestal, similar to a birdbath, encased in a great rectangular block of clear stone taller than Grunthor. Achmed's skin prickled as he recognized the deadly shatter trap that had been set within the base of the clear stone block. The other altars also seemed to be similarly rigged with protective devices and other defenses to keep them from being removed.

Under normal circumstances Achmed was an aficionado of well-thought-out defenses. Now he was merely annoyed. Gwylliam's paranoia toward the end of the Loritorium's construction had led him to abandon some of the higher aspirations he had originally held for the complex. Instead of allowing it to be the seat of scholarship where broad, unfettered knowledge was enthusiastically pursued, as he had envisioned in the first records of his plans for the place, Gwylliam had seemed to become jealous of the power he planned to store there. He had ordered his artisans to set aside the craftsmanship that was beautifying the small city into a showplace of architecture and art in favor of building ingenious traps and defenses to protect it from attack. It made Achmed wonder what those cases must have once contained.

His consideration of that question was shattered by Grunthor's bloodcurdling scream.

7

'Would you like to see my hoard, Pretty?'

'Yes,' said Rhapsody. She was still recovering from the initial fear of losing her heart to the dragon. So far everything seemed fine; Elynsynos had made no false moves nor tried to restrict her in any way. The true test would come when it was time to leave. 'I would be honored.'

'Then come.'

The immense beast hoisted herself out of the fetid water in the cavern's basin and began the process of turning around. Rhapsody pressed up against the cave wall in an effort to stay out of the way, but her actions proved unnecessary. Elynsynos was far more agile and fluid than Rhapsody could have imagined; it was as if she had no solid form. She shifted her body with a smooth rolling movement, and within moments her enormous head was pointed toward the depths of the cave. She waited as Rhapsody came alongside her, then led the way down into the darkness.

As they descended the cave began to curve, bending in a circular fashion to the west. At the bottom of the tunnel she could see a vague glow, like the distant light of a raging fire. The dark walls began to brighten as they walked on, reflecting the glow of the tunnel before them. The scent of the air changed, too; rather than growing more dank, as Rhapsody had expected, it began to freshen and take on a salty tang. She recognized it after a moment as the smell of the sea.

As the light became blindingly bright, Elynsynos stopped. 'You go on ahead, Pretty,' she said, nudging Rhapsody forward with her brow. Rhapsody complied, walking slowly toward the glow, squinting to avoid the pain her eyes had initially felt. She put one hand out in front of her, hoping to both shield her face and avoid walking into something unseen.

After a moment her eyes adjusted, and she saw she was in a vast cavern, almost half the size of the grotto that held Elysian's lake. The blinding glow was the reflection of the radiance of six huge chandeliers, each large enough to light the ballroom of a palace, each illuminated by a thousand candleless flames. The illumination was mirrored by more sparkling items than Rhapsody could even imagine, let alone count, piles of gems in every color of the rainbow and mountains of shimmering coins in gold, copper, silver, platinum, and rysin, a rare green-blue metal mined in the High Reaches of Serendair by the Nain of the old world.

The chandeliers were fashioned from the ship's wheels from hundreds of vessels, the coins piled high in captain's chests and hammocked in massive sails strung from ropes that were moored to the walls of the cave with rigging hardware. Wrecked prows and decks of ships were lovingly displayed throughout the cavern, as were anchors, masts, and several salt-encrusted figureheads, one of which bore a startling resemblance to Rhapsody.

In the center of the great cave was a lagoon of salt water, complete with waves that rolled gently to the muddy edges. Rhapsody walked down to the water's edge and bent to touch the sand. When she looked at her fingers she saw that it was laced with traces of gold.

She looked into the lagoon at the rocks that held more treasures: a golden statue of a mermaid with eyes fashioned from emeralds and a tail that was made from individually carved scales of polished jade, intricately woven caps of merrow pearls, a tall bronze trident with a broken point. A secluded spot in the sand held scores of globes, the orb-shaped maps Llauron had shown her, charts and nautical renderings, as well as sea instruments – compasses, spyglasses and sextants, pulleys and tillers, and chests full of ships' logs. It was a veritable maritime museum.

'Do you like my hoard?' The harmonious voice echoed in the vast cave, causing the water in the lagoon the ripple out of pattern. Rhapsody turned to face the dragon, whose prismatic eyes were glowing with unmasked excitement.

'Yes,' Rhapsody answered, her voice filled with awe. 'It's incredible. It's – well, it's – ' words failed her completely. 'It's the most beautiful hoard I've ever seen.'

Elynsynos laughed in delight. The sound was like nothing Rhapsody had ever heard before, higher and thinner than the dragon's gargantuan size would have suggested, with a bell-like quality that rang in Rhapsody's bones. 'Good, I'm glad you like it,' she said. 'Now, come over here. There is something I want to give you.'

Rhapsody blinked in astonishment. Everything she had ever heard about dragons had reiterated that they were avaricious, coveting their treasure above anything else. She had heard tell in the old world the legend of a dragon that had laid waste to five towns and several villages, all to recover a plain tin cup that had been inadvertently taken from its hoard. And now the matriarch of wyrms and wyrmkin of this land, Elynsynos herself, was offering her a gift from her hoard. She was unsure how to react, but she followed the giant serpent over piles of winches, bells, oars, and oar locks.

On the other side was a large net secured by a harpoon thrust deep into the rock wall. Rhapsody shuddered at the thought of the strength needed to bury prongs that far into solid rock. Elynsynos rustled with an extended claw in the bulge of the net and drew forth a waxwood lute, beautifully polished, pristine as the day it was finished by the harper. She wrapped her serpentine tail around it, lifted it out of the net and held it out to Rhapsody.

The Singer took the lute with wonder, and turned it over in her hands. It was in perfect condition, despite unknown years of exposure to the salt air and water. 'Would you like to hear it?' she asked the dragon.

The iridescent eyes twinkled. 'Of course. Why else would I have given it to you, if not to play?'

Rhapsody sat down on an overturned dinghy and tuned the lute, quivering with excitement.

'What would you like to hear?'

'Do you know any songs of the sea?' asked the dragon.

'A few.'

'And are they from your home, the old world?'

Rhapsody felt her heart skip a beat. She had not revealed anything to Elynsynos about her origins, as far as she could remember. The dragon smiled, revealing swordlike teeth.

'You are surprised I know where you come from, Pretty?'

'Not really,' Rhapsody admitted. There was little she could imagine that was beyond the dragon's power.

'Why are you afraid to talk about it?'

'I don't know, actually. The other people in this land, they seem very curious about where I come from, but they are very reticent about their own backgrounds. It seems that being Cymrian means to be sworn to secrecy, like it is something to be ashamed of.'

The dragon nodded knowingly. 'The man who brought you here, he wanted to know if you are Cymrian, yes?'

'Yes.'

The dragon laughed. 'You may as well tell him, Pretty. He already knows. It is obvious.'

Rhapsody felt heat rise in her cheeks. 'It is?'

'I am afraid so, Pretty. You have fire, and time, and music in you. Innate lore is a sure sign of a Cymrian – no other human type has it.' She cocked her head as Rhapsody looked down. 'Why does that make you sad?'

'I don't know. I think it's because the Cymrians here seem to be incapable of being honest, especially with themselves.'

'That is Anwyn's fault, too,' said Elynsynos, an ugly note coming into her voice. 'She is to blame for that. She is the one who reached back into the Past and gave it power. She is the one.' The electric charge returned to the air.

'Gave what power?'

'The evil one; the F'dor.'

The sound of her own heartbeat suddenly filled Rhapsody's ears. 'What do you mean, Elynsynos? There was a F'dor spirit here, in this land? Are you certain?'

Elynsynos's eyes gleamed with hatred. 'Yes. It was a demon from the old world, weak and helpless when it came, but it grew in power rapidly.'

The dragon's nostrils flared threateningly. 'Anwyn knew; she knows everything that happens in the Past. She could have destroyed it, but instead she opened my lands to it, thinking it might be of use to her one day. And it was. She is bad, Pretty. She allowed it to live, even when she knew what it was capable of, like the one that took him away from me. He never came back. I never saw him again.' The air in the room grew even more full of static, and outside the cave Rhapsody could hear the thunder roll overhead. The dragon's innate bond with the elements was beginning to assert itself.

'Merithyn?' she asked gently.

At the name the buzzing stopped, and the dragon blinked back tears again.

'Yes.'

'I'm sorry, Elynsynos. I'm so sorry.'

Rhapsody reached out and stroked the immense forearm, running her hand gently over the millions of tiny scales. The skin of the beast was cool and vaporous, like mist; Rhapsody had a momentary sensation akin to putting her hand into a raging waterfall. There was a solidity to the dragon's body that seemed at the same time ephemeral, as if her mass was not flesh but generated by the force of her own will. Rhapsody withdrew her hand quickly, fearing the undertow.

'The sea took him,' the dragon said sadly. 'He does not sleep within the Earth. If he did, I would sing to him. How can he rest if for all eternity he is doomed to hear the endless crashing of the waves? He will never know peace.' An immense tear rolled down the scales of her face and splashed the cave floor, making the golden sand glisten.

'He was a sailor,' Rhapsody said before caution could intervene. 'Sailors find peace in the sea, just as Lirin find it on the wind beneath the stars. We commit our bodies to the wind through fire, not to the Earth, just as sailors commit them to the sea. The key to finding peace is not where your body rests, but where your heart remains. My grandfather was a sailor, Elynsynos, and he told me this. Merithyn's love is here, with you.' She looked around at the multitude of nautical treasures that filled the brimming cave. 'I'm sure he is right at home.'

Elynsynos sniffed, then nodded.

'Where is my sea song?' she demanded.

Her tone sent chills up Rhapsody's spine. Hurriedly she tuned the lute strings and began to pick out a simple sea chantey, humming softly. The dragon sighed, its warm breath a rush of hot wind billowing through Rhapsody's hair, making her close her eyes for fear they might burn. The lute strings grew hot, and she quickly concentrated on her lore, drawing the fire into her fingertips to spare the strings from igniting and burning the lute.

Elynsynos rested her head on the ground and closed her eyes, breathing in the music as Rhapsody played and sang. She sang all the sad sea chanteys she knew, ignoring the splashing of enormous tears that soaked her clothes and made her boots wet, understanding the need for a good cry to wash away the recurrent pain of a great loss, and wishing it were an option for herself. The lyrics to most of the songs were in Old Cymrian, a few in Ancient Lirin; Elynsynos either understood both languages or was not particularly concerned about the words.

How many hours she sang Rhapsody did not know, but finally she ran out of chanteys and other sea-related songs. She put down the lute and leaned forward, resting her elbows on her knees.

'Elynsynos, will you sing for me?'

One enormous eye opened slowly. 'Why do you want me to, Pretty?'

'I would love to learn what dragon music sounds like. It would be the most unique song I have ever heard.'

A smile came over the serpent's face. 'You might not even recognize it as music, Pretty.'

'Please. Sing for me.'

The dragon closed her eye again. A moment later, Rhapsody could hear the water of the lagoon begin to lap in a different rhythm, an odd, clicking cadence that sounded like the beating of a three-chambered heart. The wind began to whistle in through the mouth of the cave, blowing across the opening in varying intensities, producing different tones. The ground beneath the boat she sat on rumbled pleasantly, the tremors rattling the coins in the chests and making the hardware clink and bang into itself. *An elemental song*, Rhapsody thought in fascination.

From the throat of the dragon came a rasping sound, a high, thin noise that set Rhapsody's teeth on edge. It was like the whistling of a snoring bed partner, accompanied by deep grunts and hisses in irregular time. The song went on for an indeterminate interlude, leaving Rhapsody breathless when it was over. When she regained her composure she applauded politely.

'Liked it, did you, Pretty? I am glad.'

'Did you like the Cymrian songs, Elynsynos?'

'I did. You know, you should make them your hoard.'

Rhapsody smiled at the thought. 'Well, in a way they are. The songs and my instruments; I have quite a few of them at home. The music and my garden, I guess that's my hoard. And my clothes; at least one of my friends would say so.'

The great serpent shook her head, stirring a cloud of sand that rose from the ground and blinded Rhapsody temporarily. 'Not the music, Pretty. The Cymrians.'

'Pardon me?'

'You should make the Cymrians your hoard, like Anwyn did,' Elynsynos said. 'Only you would not bring harm to them like she did. They would listen to you, Pretty. You could bring them together again.'

'Your grandson is after the same thing,' Rhapsody said tentatively. 'Llauron seeks to reunite them as well.'

Elynsynos snorted, sending a puff of steam over Rhapsody and the lagoon she sat beside. 'No one will listen to Llauron. He sided with Anwyn in the war; they will not forgive him for that. No, Pretty, they will listen to you. You sing so nicely, and your eyes are so green. You should make them your hoard.'

Rhapsody smiled to herself. For all her ancient wisdom, Elynsynos clearly did not understand the concept of social class and lines of succession. 'What about your other grandson?'

'Which one?'

Rhapsody's eyes opened in surprise. 'You have more than one?'

'Anwyn and Gwylliam had three sons before the Grievous Blow, the act of violence between them that began the war,' said the dragon. 'Anwyn chose the time to bear each of them. Firstborn races, like dragons, have control over their procreation. She chose well, for the most part. The eldest, Edwyn Griffyth, is my favorite, but I have not seen him since he was a young man. He went off to sea, disgusted by his parents and their war.'

'Who is the other one? The manuscripts did not mention him.'

'Anborn was the youngest. He sided with his father, until he too could stand it no more. Eventually even Llauron could not take Anwyn's bloodthirstiness and went to sea. But Anborn stayed, trying to right the wrongs he had committed against the followers of his mother.'

Rhapsody nodded. 'I didn't realize Anborn was the son of Anwyn and Gwylliam, but I suppose it makes sense.' She thought back to the scowling general in black mail interlaced with silver rings, his azure blue eyes gleaming angrily from atop his black charger. 'My friends and I met him in the woods on the way to visit Lord Stephen Navarne, and his name was mentioned in a book we found in the House of Remembrance.'

'Your friends – there are three of you together?'

'Yes, why?'

The dragon smiled. 'It makes sense, too.' She did not elaborate further. 'Why did you go to the House of Remembrance?'

Rhapsody yawned; she hadn't realized how exhausted she was. 'I'd love to tell you, Elynsynos, but I'm afraid I can't keep my eyes open much longer.'

'Come over here by me,' said the dragon. 'I will rock you to sleep, Pretty, and will keep the bad dreams away.' Rhapsody pushed herself off the rowboat and came inside the arms of the reclining beast without fear. She sat down and leaned back against the dragon, feeling the smoothness of her copper scales and the heat of her breath. That there was anything strange about the situation did not occur to her at all.

Elynsynos extended a nail on her claw and with infinite tenderness pushed back a loose strand of hair from Rhapsody's face. She hummed her strange music and moved the crook of her arm back and forth in a rocking motion, lifting Rhapsody off the ground as she did.

'I dreamt you saved me, Elynsynos; you lifted me up in your arms when I was in danger,' she said drowsily.

Elynsynos smiled as sleep took the small Lirin woman she was holding. She leaned her head down close to Rhapsody's ear, knowing that the Singer would not hear her anyway.

'No, Pretty, that was not me in your dream.'

8

He couldn't breathe, couldn't keep his eyes open in the searing heat. Caustic smoke had filled the cavern all the way to the ceiling, squeezing the life from his lungs. Grunthor waved his arms wildly to clear the burning ash from the air in front of him, but the flailing movements only made it harder to draw breath.

Around him in the fetid air sparks were igniting and ripping into flame. The giant covered his eyes and tried to cough the burning cinders from his lungs, but only succeeded in drawing the acid further into his chest. He struggled to his feet, holding his breath, then staggered blindly forward, groping desperately for the tunnel that he knew opened somewhere before him in the smoky haze.

But the cavern was collapsing all around him, chunks of rock and debris falling from above, the tunnel walls closing in. Grunthor's lungs swelled in agony and he inhaled the filthy air, drowning.

He stumbled over soft mounds that clogged the street, shuddering as he felt the crunch of bone and heard the muted gasps below his feet. Bodies careened off him from all sides, pushing, crushing in a great rush toward the air. Grunthor had not seen them come forth from the Loritorium's silent buildings; he had still been asleep, gathering his strength when the world collapsed in a rolling cloud of stinging fumes. He was only vaguely aware they were there, a great throng of people hurrying forward in panic, blocking the exit, struggling for breath, as he was, in the acrid air.

The burning black fog swirled before his eyes, and one of the people grabbed him by the upper arms, shouting something unintelligible. The sergeant gasped, mustered the last of his strength, and flung the man into the caving wall. Then he stumbled forward again, trying to keep from inhaling. His sight was growing dimmer.

It took a moment for the world to stop spinning. Achmed clutched his head and rose shakily, still reeling from the impact. Grunthor's reaction had caught him by surprise; he could tell by the wild glaze in the giant's amber eyes that the sergeant was in a delusional state and panicking, but he had hardly expected to be hurled across the street into a lamppost.

'Grunthor!' he shouted again, but the great Bolg sergeant didn't hear him. Grunthor clawed at the air, lurching through the empty streets of the Loritorium, locked in a life-and-death battle with unseen demons. He was fighting ferociously, but it seemed to Achmed that Grunthor was losing the fight.

Achmed steadied himself against the half-wall, his fingers brushing the oily substance in the channel that scored the top of the wall. Absently he noted a strong odor, similar to the one emitted by pitch when it burned. Then he ran down the street toward the central garden after Grunthor.

The giant was on his hands and knees now, gasping for breath. Achmed approached him carefully, calling his name, but Grunthor didn't seem to hear. He swung his arms wildly to the side as if trying to clear an invisible passageway, panting with exertion. He scrambled over a section of the circle of benches that surrounded the reflecting pond of the fountain, veering off toward the southwest, his olive skin flushing to a frightening shade of purple.

Then, just before Achmed caught up to him, Grunthor's face went blank, then relaxed. His eyes cleared and grew wide, and slowly he turned toward the south as if hearing his name being called. Achmed watched as the giant rose to a stand and walked forward through the small garden, following a call that only he could hear.

When he came to the foot of one of the altar-shaped displays, Grunthor sank to his knees, then leant over the altar, resting his head there.

Through the pandemonium Grunthor heard it ring like a bell on a windless night. The chaos and smoke died away in an instant, leaving only the clear, sweet tone, a sound that rang through his heart and reverberated there. It was the song of the Earth, that low, melodic hum that had played in his blood since he had first heard it, deep within the belly of the world. And it was singing to him alone.

Grunthor felt the nightmarish vision of smothering death sheet off him like water. He rose, the fire in his lungs instantly abating, and followed the music that permeated him.

It was coming from a single source, decidedly louder than the ever-present melody that always was at the edge of his consciousness. His skin flushed with warmth and tingled as it had so long ago, back when they first emerged from the Fire at the heart of the world. It was back; the unconditional, loving acceptance he had felt then. He never knew how much he had missed the feeling until it returned.

His sight cleared as he came nearer to it. He could see the source singularly, as if all the rest of the world had melted away into oblivion. There at the far side of the Loritorium's central square was a piece of earth shaped like an altar, a block of Living Stone. Grunthor had never seen Living Stone before, but had once heard Lord Stephen make reference to it in the Cymrian museum while discussing the five basilicas the Cymrians had built and dedicated to the elements.

This is the only non-Orlandan basilica, the church of Lord All-God, King of the Earth, or Terreanfor. The basilica is carved into the face of the Night Mountain, making it a place where no light touches, even in the middle of the day. There is a hint of the old pagan days in Sorboldian religion, even though they worship the All-God and are a See of our religion. They believe that parts of the earth, the ground itself, that is, are still alive from when the world was made, and the Night Mountain is one of these places of Living Stone. The turning of the Earth itself resanctifies the ground within the basilica. It is a deeply magical place.

A deeply magical place. Grunthor came to a stop before the altar of Living Stone, choking back the pain and wonder that were clutching his throat. The great block of earth was radiating a vibration that soothed the last vestiges of his panic, whispering wordless consolation. It erased the pain that had been pulsing in his chest, easing his breathing. Somehow, without hearing any words, Grunthor knew the living altar was speaking his name.

He knelt down before it, as reverently as he ever had, and put his head down, listening to the story it told. After a moment he looked back up at Achmed. His eyes were clear with understanding, and sorrow.

'Something happened near here. Something awful. You game to go deeper, find out what it was?' Achmed nodded. 'Are you sure, sir?'

The Firbolg king's brow furrowed. 'Yes; why do you ask?'

'Because the Earth says it was your death, sir. That you don't know it yet, but you will.'

Deep within the Earth, the Grandmother woke again to the sound of the child trembling. Her ancient eyes, well accustomed to the lack of light in the Colony's caverns and tunnels, scanned the darkness furtively. Then she swung her brittle legs off the earthen slab that served as her bed and rose slowly, the grace of her movements belying her great age.

The child's eyes were still closed, but the eyelids fluttered with fear from whatever nightmare lurked behind them. Tenderly the Grandmother brushed her forehead and took a breath. From her highest throat the familiar clicking sound issued forth, a fricative buzz that sometimes helped to calm the child. In response the child began to mutter incoherently. The Grandmother closed her own eyes, and wrapped her Seeking vibration, her *kirai*, around the child. The deepest of her four throat openings formed the humming question.

'ZZZhhh, zzzzhhh, little one; what troubles you so? Speak, that I may aid you.'

But the child continued to mutter, her brow contorted in fear. The Grandmother watched in measured silence. This time would be no different than any time before; the prophecy would not be fulfilled. The child would not speak the words of wisdom that the Grandmother had been waiting for centuries uncounted to hear. She caressed the smooth gray forehead again, feeling the cold skin relax beneath her long, sensitive fingers.

'Sleep, child. Rest.'

After a while the child sighed brokenly, and settled back into deeper, dreamless sleep. The Grandmother continued her tuneless hum until she was certain that the worst of it was past, then lay back down again, staring into the darkness of the cavern high above her.

Grunthor recapped the waterskin and handed it back to Achmed, then leaned back against the stone altar and exhaled deeply, driving the last of the tension from his lungs. The Firbolg king's eyes watched him intently.

'Are you past it now?'

'Yeah.' Grunthor rose and shook the grit from his greatcloak. 'Sorry about that, guv.'

Achmed smiled slightly. 'Well? Care to enlighten me? What did you see?'

Grunthor shook his massive head. 'Chaos. Swarms of people chokin' to death in tunnels filled with burnin' smoke. Like I was there. Smelt like a smithy does.'

'The forges, perhaps?'

'Maybe.' The sergeant ran a taloned hand through his shaggy hair. 'Deeper than that, though. A place we never been. I don't think it was part of the Cymrian lands.'

'Do you think you can find it?'

Grunthor nodded absently. He was thinking about Rhapsody, and all the times he had held her as she thrashed about in her sleep, battling dream-demons as he just had. He had never understood the ferocity with which she fought until now.

Somewhere in the back of his mind he recalled the words they had exchanged upon parting.

You know I'd take the worst of them dreams for you if I could, Your Ladyship.

I know, I know you would. And believe me, if it was within my power, I'd give you the worst of them.

Perhaps she had. Perhaps that joking comment had evoked her Naming ability. Perhaps that ability, tied to the truth, which had changed Achmed's name and broken him free of the demon's hold, had inadvertently done the opposite for him – had opened the door to whatever it was that gave her visions in her sleep, and sometimes even when she was awake. Maybe he had carried the burden of one of those nightmares for her. It made him miss her all the more.

'It'll take a good deal more tunneling,' he said at last. 'But distance-wise, it ain't too far. When you're ready, sir, we can have at it.'

A perfunctory canvass of the streets of the Loritorium yielded a detailed inventory of the defenses and traps that had been erected and built into the complex. Grunthor shook his head in amazement.

'Seems like overkill to have so many for such a small place,' he said, a note of disdain in his voice. 'One good explodin' side-to-side or a ceiling cutoff would have done it. Plus the idiot didn't account for an escape route, by all appearances.'

'Gwylliam may have been losing his grip on reality by the time the Bolg began to infiltrate Canrif,' Achmed said, examining an enormous semicircular cistern that was carved into the western wall. He ran his fingertips over the wide channel that led up to a stone block in the center of the cistern wall, then smelled them, recoiling slightly at the harsh odor. It was the same as that of the thick residue in the channels that scored the half-walls with lampposts.

'This must be the reservoir of lampfuel,' he said to the sergeant. 'The manuscript describes how one of Gwylliam's chief masons discovered a huge natural well of an oily substance that burned like pitch, only brighter. They incorporated it into the lamppost system to provide light for the scholars to read by.'

''How did it work?'

Achmed studied the stone block for a moment, then looked around the Loritorium. 'The reservoir is up behind this cistern, not as far down as we are now. Gwylliam devised a flow system to allow the cistern to collect the lampfuel until it was full, then distribute it into the channels that score the half-walls. The fuel ran up the hollow tubes in the lampposts and lit the wicks, burning continuously. The weights inside this main channel balance the outflow through this stone plug, so that if the cistern begins to overfill faster than the lamps are consuming the fuel, it closes automatically, opening again when the fuel level in the channels subsides. The balance of the system is fairly important; the lampfuel is highly flammable, and only a little was needed to light the streets.'

Achmed wiped his hands on his cloak and followed the main channel into the center of the small city. He stepped carefully into the dry reflecting pool, avoiding the gleaming silver puddle, and gingerly touched the wellspring of the plugged fountain, quickly withdrawing his hand.

'This wasn't a fountain of water, it was a firewell like that ever-burning flame in the Fire basilica in Bethany,' he said. 'Smaller, perhaps, but it has the same source. It vents directly from the inferno at the center of the Earth. One of the great pieces of elemental lore that this place was designed to study. This was what Gwylliam used as the firesource that sparked the street-lamp system and kept it alight, as well as for heat.'

'Blimey,' said Grunthor. 'What made it go out?'

'It didn't, I suspect. Looks like it was dammed, intentionally or otherwise. A piece of rubble from the ceiling is lodged in the vent. The heat from the wellspring is still there. Give me a hand, and we can unseal it.'

'Perhaps we should wait for Her Ladyship,' Grunthor suggested. 'First off, she's apt to be mighty put out that we didn't wait for her like we said we would. Second, she seems to be immune to fire and the like; she can probably unplug it without burning her face off. I'm not so sure that's true of you, sir, with all due respect.'

'According to Jo, it might be an improvement if I did,' Achmed said wryly.

'I wouldn't worry about that, sir. Those pigs you've been fornicatin' don't seem to mind.'

Achmed chuckled. 'By the way, you did release her, didn't you?'

'Yep.'

'Good. Well, I think I've seen enough until Rhapsody gets here. Do you still want to search out whatever it was that gave you the vision?'

Grunthor regarded him seriously. 'That's really more your call than mine, sir. I told you what I heard.'

Achmed nodded. 'Well, if I died and don't know it yet, I'd like to find out what happened. Where do we begin?'

Grunthor pointed toward the south. 'That way.'

The two Bolg gathered their gear and went to the southeastern wall of the Loritorium. Grunthor took a last look at the beautiful altar of Living Stone; walking away from it would be immensely painful. He swallowed, took a deep breath, then leaned into the stone wall as he had before, opening a tunnel before him as he faded away into the earth. Achmed waited until the initial rubble had fallen, then followed him.

They were too far away to notice the glimmering silver shapes, manlike bodies that rose from the pools in the Loritorium's silent streets like mist, hanging in the air for a moment, then disappearing again.

9

The air in the underground caverns was warmer than the air of the world above. The change in heat was the first thing Achmed noticed when Grunthor broke through to the hidden complex of tunnels that lay deeper in the earth to the south of the Loritorium. It was a warmer, staler air with an age-old hint of lingering smoke, heavy and dry with no scent of must or mold, absent of any humidity, humming with static.

The second thing he noticed was the ancient woman standing in the tunnel before them.

Grunthor stopped in his tracks, jerking backwards in surprise. Until this moment the Earth had been singing to him, had drawn his attention to each crack, each unstable area, cautioning him of danger, alerting him to formations that were rare or unique. There had been no warning that another living creature was waiting for them on the other side of the rock wall.

And yet, there she stood, taller than Achmed, slighter than Grunthor, wrapped in a robe of brown cloth, her head covered, nothing showing but her face and thin, long-fingered hands. That glimpse was enough to tell Achmed what he needed to know.

100

The skin of her face and hands was translucent, wrinkled with age and scored with a network of fine blue veins, like iridescent marble. Though impossible to discern completely due to the hood of the robe, the woman's head appeared to taper from a great width at the top of the skull down to a slender jawline, with large, black eyes making up most of her face. Those eyes were heavily lidded and without apparent scleras; no white at all could be seen, rather they resembled two wide ovals of darkness, broken only by a large, silvery pupil. They glittered with unspoken interest and a keen intelligence.

Despite her obvious age, the woman's body was unbowed, tall and straight as the trunk of a heveralt tree. The wide shoulders, long thighs and shins, and gangly arms ending in strong, sinewy hands were unmistakable hallmarks, despite this being only the second time Achmed had ever seen one of her race. The woman's eyes twinkled in the light of their torch, though her thin mouth remained set in the same nonchalant expression as had been there the moment the ground crumbled before her and the two of them stepped into her realm.

She was Dhracian. Full-blooded.

Achmed's sensitive skin tingled again in the dry static of the air. Instantly he realized that he was wrapped in the woman's Seeking vibration, the electric hum that Dhracians emitted through the cavities in their throats and sinuses. It was a tool their race used to discern the heartbeats and other life rhythms of whomever they sought to find or assess. He had used it himself, mostly when hunting his prey in the old world.

The woman seemed amused, though her expression remained unaltered. She also seemed satisfied; she folded her hands patiently before her and waited. When neither Grunthor nor Achmed moved, she spoke.

'I am the Grandmother. You are late in coming. Where is the other one?'

Both Firbolg involuntarily shook their heads as the vibration of her voice scratched their eardrums. The woman was speaking in two different voices, each coming from one of her four throats, neither of which contained actual words in any language either of them knew. Despite that, both of them understood exactly what she was saying.

The address that Achmed heard was a fricative buzz that formed a bell-clear image in his mind of the meaning of her words. In the manner she addressed him, 'Grandmother' meant *matriarch*. He was not certain how he knew it, but there was no doubt of it.

Grunthor, on the other hand, had been greeted in a voice that was deeper, a more ringing tone that mimicked the speech pattern of the Bolg. The explicit image the Grandmother conjured in his mind was that of a maternal caregiver a generation removed from a child. The men looked at each other, then back at the Dhracian woman. There was no mistaking that the other person she referred to was Rhapsody.

'She's not here,' Achmed answered, his own words feeling odd in his

101

mouth. The elderly woman's eyes twinkled again, and his face flushed with embarrassment. He swallowed his anger at the stupidity of his answer. 'Obviously she's not here. She's traveling overland. She will be home soon, with any luck.'

'All three of you must come one day soon,' the Grandmother responded, again in her separate, clicking tones. 'It is necessary. It was foretold. Come.'

The elderly Dhracian woman turned smoothly in the rocky tunnel, and walked quickly away. Grunthor and Achmed looked at each other, then hastened to follow her.

Jo muttered to herself all the way from the cavern entrance to the Blasted Heath above the gates to the Cauldron.

Her life as an orphan on the streets of Navarne's capital had given Jo a number of skills, including the abilities to remain motionless for a long time while hiding in an alley shadow, to react with speed and agility in dangerous situations, and to belch and break wind silently.

It had also given her a vast and colorful vocabulary of curse words, improved upon immensely by her exposure to Grunthor and Rhapsody who, despite her mother-hen attitude, could make the Bolg blush with the vulgarity of the oaths she uttered when inspired – Rhapsody had spent her own time on the streets. Jo repeated many of those oaths now in the course of her grumbling.

It was fortunate that she had saved some of the choicest ones for last. As she rounded a corner of the mountain pass that led down to the Heath something grazed her head, catching her off-balance.

Jo ducked, miscalculated the muddy terrain, stumbled, and slid forward on her stomach, planting her face squarely into the excrement that had been hurled at her head. She lay, prone, trying to recapture the wind that had been knocked out of her. When she did, that wind had a repulsive stench that reached down into her blood and brought it to a boil.

As the initial shock began to abate, she could hear the tittering laughter of the Bolg children hiding behind the rocks. The Bolg as a race were not given to easy laughter, and the sound of it, harsh and shrill, was irritating to Jo's ears under normal circumstances. Since something even more foul was now irritating her eyes and nose, she was even less inclined to appreciate it.

Jo raised herself out of the mud and swiveled to one side. A plethora of small dark faces, hairy and grinning repulsively, had sprouted from behind the rock slabs ringing the Heath. She recognized a number of Rhapsody's adopted grandbrats among them.

A flood of red darkened Jo's vision as fury roared through her. She let loose a howl of rage that reverberated up the rockwalls. The grins disappeared, followed a moment later by the heads.

'You misbegotten little *bastards!* Get back here! I'll use your heads for target practice! I'll strain your clotted blood through my teeth! I'll flay you alive and salt you like hams!' She scrambled to a stand, sliding in the mud that caked her clothes and hair, then took off at breakneck speed after the scurrying children.

As she crested the rise of the rocks where they had been hiding she could see them disappearing in all directions, the older ones swifter and all but out of sight.

'I'll suck your lungs out through your nostrils!' Jo panted, struggling to keep the slower ones in view. 'Peel – your eyes – like plums and swallow them!' She drew her bronze-backed dirk, the thin, deadly dagger Grunthor had given her on the day he and the others had freed her from the House of Remembrance; it caught the sun, and the attention of the Firbolg children. The expressions on their faces dissolved from impish glee to panic.

Jo let loose a war cry and doubled her speed. She was bearing down on two of the slower ones now. One stopped and spun about, looking frightened, then leapt over a rockledge to escape. His scream trailed away as he fell, then was cut abruptly short.

Jo froze in horror.

'Oh no,' she whispered. 'No.' She took a few slow, numb steps, then ran to the rockledge and peered over.

The Firbolg child was lying in a crumpled heap on a ledge that jutted from the cliff side quite a distance below. Even from above Jo recognized him as Vling, Rhapsody's third youngest Firbolg grandchild. Her face tingled, then grew hot as nausea and remorse swept through her.

'Gods,' she choked. 'Vling? Can you hear me?'

From down the cliff a muffled whimper rose.

Jo sheathed her dagger. She glanced around for a handhold, and found a long, dead root sprouting from the rocks of the cliff face. She tugged on it to test its strength, then quickly lowered herself down the embankment to where the broken child lay.

'Vling?'

There was no answer.

Jo was growing sick. 'Vling!' she shouted, rocks crumbling beneath her as she slid down the cliff face to the ledge.

The child looked up as she bent beside him, an expression of undisguised terror on his dirty face, and tried to crawl away.

'Hold still,' Jo said as gently as she could. 'I'm sorry I frightened you.' The child, who didn't speak Orlandan as she did, shook his head violently and tried to inch away again, then collapsed against the ground with a moan.

Struggling to force back her dislike, Jo reached out and cautiously patted the child's head. His eyes widened in shock, then narrowed suspiciously.

'All right, all right, you have every reason to doubt my intentions,' Jo muttered darkly. 'I'll admit I've considered tossing you into the cavern on several occasions, but I didn't, now, did I? It's my fault you fell, and I'm sorry, and I'm here to help you.' The glint in his eye did not recede. 'Look, Vling, Rhapsody is going to kill me if I break one of her grandbrats.'

The child's face melted. 'Rhapz-dee?'

Jo exhaled loudly. 'She's not here.'

'Rhapz-dee?'

'I said Grandma's not here, but she wouldn't want you to stay out here, injured, and become food for the hawks.'

Vling sat up slightly. 'Rhapz-dee?' he repeated hopefully.

'Yeah, that's right, Rhapsody,' Jo said. 'Come with me, and I'll take you to her.' She put out her hand to the child, who recoiled slightly, then allowed her to help him stand. His arm was hanging at an odd angle, she noted. The sight of it made her feel dizzy, and her stomach surged into her mouth.

A look of pain shot across Vling's face as he stood, replaced a moment later by the stoic, slightly sullen countenance of the Bolg race. Jo knew immediately what was crossing his mind. A show of weakness was a disgrace among the Bolg, who were still trying to absorb the concept that the injured could be healed. For millennia uncounted it had been common practice to leave the injured to die, no matter how valuable they might be, as a matter of honor. Lesser forms of the attitude still persisted in the Teeth, despite the changes instituted by Achmed at Rhapsody's insistence. The Bolg child was going to lose face with his peers if she carried him in, or even if he was perceived to have been helped.

Jo grasped the vine again and hauled herself and the child back over the ledge, then sat down behind a large rock to think. Vling seemed to be holding on to consciousness, but she could tell he was in tremendous pain.

A thought finally occurred. Jo reached into her pack and pulled out a length of rope. She gave one end to the puzzled child, then tied the other end loosely around her own wrists.

'All right,' she said in her best approximation of Bolgish, through clenched teeth. 'Let's go. Take me to Grunthor's barracks.'

The child blinked, then understanding spread across his face. He looked up at her and smiled wanly, then gave the rope a playful tug. He led her back to the Cauldron, swaggering importantly, clutching his arm and grinning as she howled mock threats the entire way, knowing what prestige he would be accorded when the other Bolg children saw what he had captured.

10

Her dreamless sleep in the arms of the dragon was the best in Rhapsody's memory. She slumbered for hours, uninterrupted by nightmares or the need to sit watch, and awoke refreshed and happy.

The face of the dragon sleeping next to her made her heart skip a few beats upon wakening, but her gaze was immediately drawn to her own chest. A small blanket of shining copper scales was draped across her midsection, glimmering in the half-light of the cave. She picked it up carefully. It was a mail shirt, light as air and made of thousands of intricately connected dragon scales. It gleamed in her hands.

'It is yours, Pretty,' said Elynsynos, her eyes still closed. 'I made it for you last night, while you slept. Try it on.'

Rhapsody stood and untied her cloak, laying it on the ground. She slid the shimmering armor over her head and pulled it down like a vest. It fit perfectly. She had heard legends of the detail of dragon sense; now she could see the reputation was warranted. Her hair caught the light reflected by the scales and sparkled with a red-gold sheen.

'Thank you,' she said, touched by the thoughtfulness, and something more. If she had feared that the dragon would not let her go when she first agreed to stay, she no longer did. The gift of armor proved that Elynsynos expected her to go back into the world again. She leaned over and kissed the enormous cheek. 'It's beautiful. I will think of you whenever I'm wearing it.'

'Wear it often, then,' said Elynsynos, opening her eyes. 'It will help keep you safe, Pretty.'

'I will. You asked me a question I was too tired to answer last night; what was it?'

'Why you went to the House of Remembrance.'

'Oh, yes.' Rhapsody stretched her arms above her head, enjoying the whisper of the dragonscale armor, then sat back down on the overturned rowboat. 'We went to the House of Remembrance at Lord Stephen's suggestion, because it was the oldest standing structure that the Cymrians built. We found a number of children being held hostage, and equipment to drain them of their blood. Tangled a bit with the forces of a man who wielded dark fire as a weapon against us.' Her face went sallow in the demi-light of the dragon's cave. 'It was the first time I ever killed anyone.'

Elynsynos snorted and cuffed Rhapsody playfully with her tail, knocking her off the rowboat and onto her rump on the golden sand.

'And you call yourself a Singer?' she said humorously. 'That was the worst telling of a tale I have heard in seven centuries. Try again, and take your time. Details, Pretty, details. Without them a story is not worth hearing.'

Rhapsody brushed the sand from her clothes and climbed shakily back onto the rowboat. When she had caught her breath she told Elynsynos the story, in excruciating detail, from Llauron's suggestion that they go to learn more about the Cymrians at Haguefort, to the aftermath of returning the stolen children of Navarne and adopting Jo. It took a long time to relate, because even with the level of detail she provided in the retelling, Elynsynos still interrupted her for clarification of the smallest of points.

After it was finally over, the dragon seemed satisfied. At last she stretched herself and raised up to her full height.

'What did the man who attacked you at the House look like?'

'Truthfully, I don't know,' Rhapsody said. She was staring at the plate of hard rolls and raspberries that had appeared when the dragon sat up. 'I didn't really see anything but a flash of him running by, nor did Grunthor. The only one who engaged him was Achmed, and even he didn't get a good look at his face. He wore a shielded helmet.'

'Eat.'

'Thank you.' Rhapsody picked up a roll and broke it in two. 'Are you having some?'

'No. I ate three weeks ago.'

'And you're not hungry yet?'

'Six stags take a long time to digest.'

'Oh.' Rhapsody began to eat.

'It must have been the Rakshas that you met.'

She looked up at the dragon's face; Elynsynos was watching her inquisitively. 'Can you tell me about the Rakshas?' The dragon nodded slightly. 'Who is he?'

'The Rakshas is an it, really. It is the plaything of the F'dor.'

A chill went up Rhapsody's back. 'The demon you told me of last night? The one Anwyn gave power to?'

'Yes. The F'dor created the Rakshas in the House of Remembrance twenty years ago. A shame, really; it was such a beautiful memorial to the brave Cymrians, in those days before Anwyn's war. And then he poisoned it, took it over. The sapling of Sagia was the first thing to suffer desecration. It was a branch-child of the great Oak of Deep Roots, the holy tree of the Lirin of Serendair that the Cymrians brought with them from the old land and planted in the House's courtyard. I could feel the tree screaming, even this far away.'

'I tended to it while I was there,' Rhapsody said, wiping the crumbs from her lips with her pocket handkerchief. 'I left my harp playing in it, renewing the song of its healing. It should have bloomed this spring, but I wasn't there to see it.'

'It did.' The dragon chuckled. 'Along with the leaves, there were white blossoms, like starflowers. A nice touch, Pretty.'

'What do you mean?'

The dragon laughed again. 'The sapling is an oak tree. In your land did you ever hear of an oak tree with blossoms?'

Rhapsody's throat went dry. 'No.'

'Of course, every oak flowers a bit in the fall to produce acorns, but the flowers are generally too tiny to see with eyes like yours. These were fluffy and white and covered the tree like snow. In your song you told the tree to bloom?' Rhapsody nodded. 'Well, I am impressed. It is an honor to have a Namer of such power visit my lair. How often does a beast meet someone who can successfully command an oak tree to blossom? I am sure the

106

Rakshas was livid, after all it had done to despoil the tree – or at least its master was.'

'Please tell me more about this Rakshas. You said the demon created it – but it looked and acted just like a man.'

'A Rakshas looks like whatever soul is powering it. It is built of blood, the blood of the demon, and sometimes other creatures, usually innocents and feral animals of some sort. Its body is formed of an element, like ice or earth; I think the one made in the House of Remembrance was made of earth frozen with ice. The blood animates it, gives it power.'

'You said something about a soul?'

'A Rakshas made just of blood is short-lived and mindless. But if the demon is in possession of a soul, whether it is human or otherwise, it can place it within the construct and the Rakshas will take the form of the soul's owner, who of course is dead. It has some of the knowledge that person had. It can do the things they did. It is twisted and evil; you must beware of him, Pretty.'

Rhapsody shuddered. 'And that person – that thing – that we fought, are you certain that was the Rakshas, the one made by the F'dor?'

Elynsynos nodded. 'It must have been. And hear me: it is very close to here now, nearby. When you leave, be careful.'

Cold acid began to bubble in Rhapsody's stomach. She put down the rest of the hard roll. 'Don't worry, Elynsynos. I have the sword.'

'What sword, Pretty?'

'Daystar Clarion. I'm sure you know what it is.'

The dragon looked puzzled. 'You have it at home?'

Rhapsody shook her head. 'No, I'm carrying it now. Shall I show you?'

The dragon nodded, and Rhapsody drew the sword forth from its scabbard. The leaping flames glittered off the reflective scales, sending millions of rainbows dancing around the cavern in the darkness. The flames in the ships' wheel chandeliers roared in greeting when it came forth.

Elynsynos's eyes opened wide, sending undulating waves of enchantment coursing through Rhapsody. She tried to look away but stood, transfixed, as the giant serpent bent her head to examine the sword momentarily. Then she ran a claw over the scabbard at Rhapsody's side.

'Of course,' she said, her massive face relaxing a moment later. 'Black ivory. No wonder I could not sense it.'

'I don't know what you mean,' Rhapsody stammered, struggling to break free of her trance.

'Black ivory is the most effective shield known to beast,' said Elynsynos. 'It is a misnomer, not really ivory at all, but a form of rock akin to Living Stone. It can be fashioned into boxes or scabbards, or other containers, and the object kept within it becomes undetectable, even to the sense of a dragon. That is good, Pretty. No one will know that you have it unless you draw it. Where did you find it?'

'It was hidden within the Earth. I found it on our way through from the old land.'

'You came through the Earth, not on a ship?'

'Yes.' Rhapsody's face flushed at the memory. 'We left long before the Cymrians did. We only arrived recently.'

Elynsynos laughed. Rhapsody waited for her to explain, but she didn't. Instead the dragon looked at her intently.

'Have you been to see Oelendra?'

The name on Serendair was legendary for a celestial occurrence. 'The fallen star?'

Elynsynos looked confused. 'No, she is like you, Lirin. She used to carry the sword.'

Rhapsody's face brightened, remembering the name from Llauron's tale. 'Is she still alive?'

The dragon seemed to think for a moment. 'Yes. She lives in Tyrian, the Lirin forest to the south. If you go to her, she might agree to train you in its use. She does that, I believe.'

'How would I find her?'

'Go to Tyrian and ask to see her. If she wants to see you, she will find you.'

Rhapsody nodded. 'Is she nice?'

Elynsynos smiled. 'I met her but once. She was kind to me. She came with the one who held the position of Invoker that Llauron now holds to tell me of what befell Merithyn, to give me his gifts and a piece of his ship. Then I knew he had tried to return, but he died. He was so fragile; I miss him.' Great tears formed in the spellbinding eyes once more. 'I gave the man a gift. It was a white oak staff with a golden leaf on top.'

'Llauron carries it now.'

The dragon nodded. 'I would have given Oelendra a gift, too, but she would not take one. But you will keep the shirt, Pretty, yes?'

Rhapsody smiled at the beast. She was such a contradiction, powerful and vulnerable, wise and childlike. 'Yes, of course. I will keep it next to my heart, where you are.'

'Does this mean you will remember me, Pretty?'

'Of course. I will never forget you, Elynsynos.'

The dragon smiled brilliantly, displaying rows of swordlike teeth. 'Then perhaps because of you I shall achieve a little immortality after all. Thank you, Pretty.' She chuckled as Rhapsody's brows drew together in uncertainty. 'You do not understand what I mean, do you?'

'No, I'm afraid I don't.'

Elynsynos settled into the floor of the cave, her iridescent skin catching the fleeting light of the chandeliers and flashing in the dark.

'Dragons live a very long time, but not forever. There is no time within the Earth, the element from which we come, so our bodies do not grow old and die. In this you and I have something in common: Time has stopped for you as well, Pretty.' Tears glinted in Rhapsody's eyes, mirroring Elynsynos's own, but she said nothing. 'This makes you sad. Why?'

'How I wish that were true,' Rhapsody said, her voice clogged with emotion. 'Time went on without me, and took everything I loved with it. Time is my enemy.'

The dragon eyed her pragmatically. 'I think not, Pretty,' she said, a hint of humor in her voice. 'I know Time well, and she rarely chooses sides. She will smile on those who embrace her, however. Time may have gone on around you, but it has no power over you anymore – your body, at least. Unfortunately, Time always has power over the heart.

'You come from Serendair, the island where the first race, the Ancient Seren, originated. That was the first of the five birthplaces of Time. You have come here, to the last of those birthplaces, where dragons, the youngest race, originated, crossing the Prime Meridian in the process. You have tied the beginning of Time to its end, as the Cymrians did, and more: in the completing of that arc you traveled within the Earth, a place Time has no dominion. In doing so you have defeated Time, broken its cycle. It will never scar your body again. This prospect does not make you happy?'

'No,' said Rhapsody bitterly. 'It doesn't.'

The dragon smiled in the dark. 'You are wise, Pretty. Longevity that borders on immortality is as much a curse as it is a blessing. Like you, time has stopped for me. There is a substantial difference between us, however. Unlike me, you are immortal.'

'I don't understand.'

'You have a soul,' the dragon said patiently. 'It sustains the life within you, because the soul cannot die. As long and endless as your life might seem, you will go on after it is finally over, because of your soul. It will remain even after you decide to give up your body and go on to the light, to the Afterlife. That will not happen for me.'

Rhapsody swallowed hard to choke down the knot in her throat. 'Everyone has a soul, Elynsynos. The Lirin believe that all living things are part of one universal soul. Some call it the Life-Giver or the One-God, others just call it Life, but we each have a piece of it. It binds us to one another.'

'And that is true for the Lirin,' Elynsynos said. 'It is not true of dragons. You are a special kind of Lirin, are you not? Liringlas?'

'My mother was.'

'What does that mean in your tongue?'

A faint gust of wind rose from the cave floor, heavy with sand, and settled on Rhapsody's cheeks, drying the unshed tears in her eyes. She smiled involuntarily at Elynsynos's gesture of comfort. 'It means *Skysinger*. Liringlas sing their devotional prayers to the rising and setting sun, and mark the appearance of the stars in the sky at dusk.'

'And Lirin in general? What do men call them?'

'We are often known as Children of the Sky.'

'Exactly.' The great beast shifted importantly in the sand of the cave floor. 'You are a Singer, and part of the lore Singers learn is about the passage of the soul, yes?'

'Yes,' said Rhapsody. 'Sometimes, during the dirges we sing, a Singer can actually see the soul leave a body on its way to the light. But I did not learn much else, and I know there is much more to the lore of the soul.'

'Well, then,' said the dragon, 'I will tell you a bit more of the lore of the soul, Pretty, and the story of the Earth-born. Perhaps you know parts of it already.

'In the Long-Ago, the Before-Time, when the world was being born, the one you called the Life-Giver painted all of what exists with the Five Gifts, that which we know as the elements of Ether, Fire, Water, Air and Earth. You know this lore, yes?'

'Yes,' Rhapsody said.

'Each of these Gifts, these elements, gave birth to a race of primordial beings known collectively as the Firstborn. From the stars, the Ether, came the Ancient Seren, like Merithyn.' Elynsynos cleared her throat, a titanic rumble that rattled the rowboat on which Rhapsody sat. 'From the sea the Mythlin were born, and the Wind gave birth to the race known as the Kith, from whom your own race is descended.' Rhapsody nodded in agreement. 'The Earth-Mother brought forth my race, the Wyrms, dragons, which of course are the masterpiece of the Creator, which is why he made us last.' Elynsynos chuckled as she caught the glimmer of Rhapsody's hidden smile.

'Second-born among the primordial races was that of the F'dor, the children of Fire. But from the very beginning, the F'dor longed for nothing more than the destruction of the Earth. I suppose that is to be expected; fire consumes whatever feeds it, for without that fuel it burns out into nothingness. But, as also can be expected, the other Firstborn races could not allow this to go on unchecked, as it would mean that the Creator's Gifts would all vanish from the eye of Time, leaving nothing but Void again. So the other races, the Seren, the Kith, the Mythlin, and of course the dragons, formed an uneasy alliance to force those demonic spirits into the center of the Earth where they could be contained.

'Needless to say, we dragons were not particularly pleased with this plan from the beginning. It was abhorrent to us that the Earth, our Mother, was given the task of imprisoning those monstrous, evil entities within Her heart, but we were also aware that the escape of the F'dor would mean the Earth's destruction.

'Our contribution to the effort to contain the F'dor was the building of the vault that became their prison. Dragons carved it from our most sacred possession, Living Stone, the pure element of Earth, the one substance we knew was powerful enough to contain them. This was a tremendous sacrifice, Pretty. It is one of the reasons that dragons are bad-tempered and territorial; we feel we have more invested in the lands we consider our own, since we have had to sacrifice the sanctity of those lands to protect them.'

'I believe that characterization in the mythos is exaggerated,' Rhapsody said, smiling. 'I haven't found dragons to be particularly bad-tempered unless you skimp on the details of a story.'

A look of profound fondness came into the dragon's prismatic eyes, replaced a moment later by a more solemn aspect. 'The primordial races in the alliance that had bodies like your own, and Kith, Seren, and Mythlin, became known as the Three.'

Rhapsody sat up quickly, almost falling off the rowboat in the process. 'The Three?'

'Yes.'

'Llauron told us a prophecy about the Three, how three known as the Child of Blood, Child of Earth, and Child of the Sky would come, and be the only means by which the rift between the Cymrians could be healed and peace returned.'

Elynsynos laughed. 'Your time perspective is a bit off, Pretty. At the time of which I speak there were only five races in existence, the Firstborn. Their children, the Elder races, were not even in existence yet. The Cymrians were by and large Third Age races, children of the Elder races. This name, the Three, is from very long ago, millions of years. You cannot comprehend this yet, because you are so young, but one day you will. You may even live to see a history of this scope yourself. After a few thousand years, you will begin to understand.' She laughed as Rhapsody shuddered.

'The Three all had bodies that resembled, at least in some way, the modern human form,' Elynsynos continued, 'while dragon form was serpentine and the F'dor had no bodily form at all. The reason for this is that that the Creator showed his image to the Three at the time of their origination, and the forms they assumed were inspired by that image. Dragons were shown the Creator's image as well, but chose to ignore it; you have heard how much we hate being told what to do. As you can also imagine, F'dor were never given the opportunity to see it. The Creator knew that the bastard children of Fire were innately evil, and refused to share this knowledge with them. This may be why the F'dor are without physical form.

'This leads me to the lore of the soul. You say you traveled within the Earth on your way from Serendair to here?'

'Yes,' Rhapsody said.

'How did it feel to you? Were you, Lirin as you are, comfortable there, within the Earth, separated from the sky?'

Rhapsody closed her eyes, struggling to keep the memory that continually lurked at the edges of her consciousness at bay. 'It was like a living death.'

Elynsynos nodded. 'The sky is the connection to the soul of the universe, to the Creator, and those that would seek to be part of the collective soul have to be in contact with it. Without it, they have no connection to their fellows in life, no immortality after death. Your race is descended of the wind and the stars; they were born with that understanding. That is why you can hear the singing of the universe, why you add your own voice to it: you are part of that collective soul. Those who do not become part of the sky, part of an eternal Afterlife – for them, after death, there is only the Void, the great Nothingness.

'Because they chose to live away from the sky, dragons, F'dor and even Mythlin have no souls. The Mythlin chose to reside within the seas, staying apart from their fellow races, just as dragons remain within the Earth. The sea children who eventually came from the Mythlin, mermaids, merrows, the sea nymphs and their like, live for millennia, but when they die their souls do not ascend to the stars; they turn into foam on the waves of the sea and disappear, their only immortality in the memories of those who knew them.

'And so it will be with me. When finally I tire of living, when the pain of it has gotten too much to bear, I will lie down to rest with no will to rise again; that will be my ending. Then my body will decay here, within my lair, my blood seeping into the earth and one day forming the veins of copper that men will mine and form into coins and bracelets.

'Do you like copper, Pretty? It is really nothing more than the spent blood of dragons of my kind, just as the vein of gold that formed your locket once ran in the veins of a golden dragon. Emeralds, rubies, sapphires – nothing more than the clotted life's blood of ancient dragons of various sub-races, various colors. It is what we leave behind in the hope that Time will maintain our memory, but it never does. Instead, it serves only to adorn the breasts of women and the empty heads of kings.

'But if you remember me, Pretty, really remember *me*, not the legends, not the history, then in a way I will go on, at least a little. I will achieve a little of the immortality, the eternity, that I did not gain because I am without a soul, because I stayed within the Earth and did not touch the sky.'

The words of the great beast were spoken wistfully, with only a trace of melancholy, but to Rhapsody's enchanted heart they were the saddest she had ever heard. Grief welled up within her, consuming her, and without thinking she leapt from the rowboat and threw her arms around Elynsynos's foreleg, weeping.

'No,' she choked, strangled by the strength of the pain in her heart. 'No, Elynsynos, you are wrong. You shared a soul with Merithyn; I'm sure a piece of it is with him now. You had children; surely that is a form of immortality. And you *have* touched the sky; you are touching a child of it now. You have touched my heart so deeply that the bond will always remain. I'll be your soul if you need me to be.'

Tenderly the dragon caressed the Skysinger's golden hair with one of her foreclaws. 'Careful, Pretty; you do not want to rename yourself. There is a power in you that might make it real, and then you would be enslaved to me. But I am glad to know that I do have a soul, and that it is so Pretty.'

The dragon patted Rhapsody again, and the Singer sat back down on the boat. 'You are right about my children,' she continued, 'though they seem so distant, so alien that I hardly think of them as my own, especially Anwyn.

'The races without souls sometimes have a great desire to have progeny of some sort, because it grants them a form of immortality. That is why the F'dor made the Rakshas. It wanted progeny, but of course the Rakshas is a bastard child, because the F'dor would have had to break open its own life essence to make a child totally its own, and that would have weakened itself more than it was willing to allow. Is that not the way with every parent? One trades a piece of one's soul to achieve a little immortality?'

'I suppose,' said Rhapsody, brushing a strand of hair off her face. 'I never really thought of it that way before.'

'There are many reasons, selfish and unselfish, that children are brought into the world. The F'dor wanted the Rakshas to do its bidding in the world of men. It is a toy, a tool to be used to accomplish its ultimate goal.'

'What is that goal, Elynsynos? Is it looking for power? To rule the world?'

Elynsynos chuckled. 'You are thinking like a human, Pretty. To understand the motives of the F'dor you must think like a F'dor, as much as that is even possible, for they are forces of chaos and their intentions and actions cannot be readily predicted. F'dor use men as tools to achieve their ends as well. They do not seek to rise to power and rule over the masses or oppress their enemies; they are very single-minded. All they contemplate is ruin and death, and the friction of conflict that gives them power and pleasure. Their ultimate goal will destroy even themselves, as they seek to consume the Earth. They will then exist only in the Underworld, and in nightmares. As will we all.'

II

The words of the dragon echoed through the dark cave, leaving a thudding silence when the reverberation ceased. The flames that illuminated the chandeliers flickered across the Singer's face, suddenly ghostly pale in the darkness.

Elynsynos lowered her head slowly until she was eye to eye with Rhapsody. There was a look of sympathetic understanding in her eyes, though the expression on her enormous face was solemn.

'What is it, Pretty?' she said softly, her voice as quiet as the hum of cricket's wings. 'What are you remembering?'

Rhapsody closed her eyes, wrestling with the memory of the most frightening nightmare she had seen during her sojourn within the Earth. Achmed had woken her from her restless sleep, had taken her to a vast tunnel at the bottom of which he could hear an immense beating heart, pulsing in the slow serpentine rhythm of hibernation.

Something terrible rests in there, something more powerful and more horrifying than you can imagine, something I dare not even name. What sleeps within that tunnel, deep in the belly of the Earth, must not awake. Not ever.

He had been afraid to speak, to give voice to the words of the ancient story; it was the first time she remembered him not being insolent or arrogant. It was the first time she saw fear in his eyes.

In the Before-Time, when the Earth and seas were being born, an egg was stolen from the progenitor of the race of dragons, the Primal Wyrm. That egg was secreted here, within the Earth, by the race of demonic beings born of elemental fire. The infant wyrm which came from that egg has lived here, deep in the frozen wastes of the Earth's interior, growing, until its coils have wound around the very heart of the world. It is an innate part of the Earth itself; its body is a large part of the world's mass. It sleeps now, but soon that demon wishes to summon it, and will visit it upon the land. It has the power to consume the Earth; that was the intent of the thieves who put it here. It awaits the demon's call, which I know for certain is intended to come soon. I know this, because he planned to use me to help bring this about.

What if it didn't hear the call? she had asked. *If we could obscure the call, keep the beast from hearing it properly, or feeling it, perhaps it would just stay asleep and not answer. At least for a little while.*

They had taken steps to prolong its slumber, had placed a musical web in the tunnel, spinning endless discordant melodies, aimed at interfering with the call of that demon. Achmed had warned her that the solution was only a temporary one.

Even then, Rhapsody, you will only be buying time. You will never have the power to destroy it completely, nor I, nor any living soul.

'It sleeps still,' said Elynsynos, shattering her thoughts and causing her heart to pound. The dragon had read her mind. The great beast chuckled at the look of panic that crossed Rhapsody's face. 'No, Pretty, I cannot discern your thoughts, except when you are thinking about the Sleeping Child.'

Rhapsody blinked. 'I wasn't,' she said. 'I was thinking about – '

'Do not put words around what you were remembering; I know what you saw within the Earth. You were thinking about something just now that only dragons and F'dor know about, something infinite and ancient that is a holy abomination in the lore of my kind. You saw it by accident. You are now one of a very few living beings that even knows it exists.

'The entity that was in your thoughts a moment ago is our antithesis of your Life-Giver. It was the First Child of our race, kidnapped as an egg and raised by beings that were our opposite – where we cherish the Earth and all its riches, the F'dor seek to consume it for the fulfillment of their own ridiculous lust. That child is no longer a wyrm; the F'dor have poisoned it, possessed it, much as they would a human host. It is part of the Earth now, a vast part, and will one day rise and claim that Earth as its own. If that is our destiny, then so be it. But it is a sacred mystery, one that no dragon gives voice to, except in the song of prayer. We pray that the

First Child will remain asleep – that is what dragonsong is for. A lullabye to the Sleeping Child.'

'The Sleeping Child,' Rhapsody murmured. 'Those words had a different meaning in the lore of Serendair. In our legends the Sleeping Child was Melita, a star that fell from the sky. It fell into the sea near the Island, taking much of what was once land with it into the sea forever. But the sea did not quench it. Instead it lay beneath the waves, roiling in unspent fire, until finally it rose – ' Her voice began to waver, and she stopped. When she could control herself again, she continued. 'It rose and took all of the Island back to the depths with it, this time in a hail of volcanic fire.'

'Perhaps that name, however it is used, foretells the death of our respective races,' suggested Elynsynos. 'Merithyn used to sing me a song from your homeland that spoke of the Sleeping Child. Would you like me to tell you the words?'

'Yes, please.'

The great beast sat up straighter and cleared her enormous throat with a mighty cough. The sound rattled the chandeliers above them and sent backward waves of frenetic ripples across the lagoon, pounding in the same furious rhythm as Rhapsody's heart. When the dragon spoke, her voice was no longer the harmonically diverse tone that she had originally addressed Rhapsody with, but a deep, melodic baritone, a sonorous voice the carried with it the sound of magic, the ring of ages past. Merithyn's voice.

> *The Sleeping Child, the youngest born*
> *Lives on in dreams, though Death has come*
> *To write her name within his tome*
> *And no one yet has thought to mourn.*
>
> *The middle child, who sleeping lies,*
> *'Twixt watersky and shifting sands*
> *Sits silent, holding patient hands*
> *Until the day she can arise.*
>
> *The eldest child rests deep within*
> *The ever-silent vault of earth,*
> *Unborn as yet, but with its birth*
> *The end of Time Itself begins.*

The words echoed off the cavernous walls and hung in the stale air, reverberating in the silence. Rhapsody said nothing, fearing if she uttered a sound her own heart would shatter. Finally the dragon spoke.

'When my daughters were born, their eyes were closed, like kittens,' Elynsynos said. Her multitoned voice had returned. 'They seemed asleep, and I thought for a moment that they were the three children in the prophecy, but of course that could not be right. I knew what the eldest born was – as any dragon would. Merithyn had referred to the Sleeping Child off the coast of his – your – homeland. That would be the middle child, I presume.'

'So there is another?' Rhapsody asked nervously. 'Another Sleeping Child? The youngest-born?'

'Apparently,' said Elynsynos, smiling. The sight of the massive maw wreathed in a grin, swordlike teeth glittering in the pale light, was both endearing and gruesome. 'It would also appear that each of these sleeping children might become a tool of the F'dor, something to help bring about the end of the world, to allow it to be consumed in one way or another.'

'I had prayed that the ascension of the middle one, the Sleeping Child that took the Island, was the end of all that,' Rhapsody said. 'We thought the F'dor that planned to summon – ' her words choked off as a warning look came violently over the dragon's enormous face. 'We thought the F'dor Achmed had known of in the old world was dead. Its last remaining servant, one of the thousand eyes it had called the Shing, told us that before it dissipated. It said the F'dor was dead, man and demon spirit. And that meant what – what we feared it might do would never come to pass.'

The massive serpent stretched, causing a hailstorm of lights to flicker off her millions of copper scales. 'The demon he knew may well have been destroyed as you thought. That does not matter – any F'dor would know the secret of the Wyrm, would know how to summon it if it becomes powerful enough.'

'And the other you spoke of, Elynsynos? Was that a different demon? Not the one Achmed knew of?'

'I do not know. There may have been another that escaped when the star beneath the waves erupted. It is hard to say, Pretty. There are not many of them left over from the dawn of Time, but they come without warning, and hide within the host, biding their time, gaining strength as the host does. When they become powerful enough, they take on a another host with more potential, usually one that is younger than the body they currently reside in. A F'dor can only take possession of someone weaker than itself or similarly strong; it cannot subsume someone of greater power.'

Rhapsody nodded. 'Do you know who it is, Elynsynos?'

'No, Pretty. It has changed hosts often over the years. I can sense it when it is near, but it has remained far away, probably knowing that. It could be anyone.

'If there is but one thing you remember about what I have told you, let it be this: they are consummate liars, and that will work against you, as a Namer, since you are sworn to the truth. Their greatest power is in using their victim's advantages against him; in our case, they were able to play upon the dragons' naturally destructive nature and turn it from something benign into a weapon to achieve their own wanton ends. It will do the same to you, only what it will target will be your truthfulness. Beware,

Pretty. They are like a guest in your lair that you cannot see has stolen from your hoard until it is too late.'

'Llauron told me a prophecy Manwyn once related about an uninvited guest,' Rhapsody said. 'Could that have been about the F'dor?'

The air around the dragon hummed, signaling her intense interest. 'I do not know this prophecy.'

Rhapsody closed her eyes, trying to recall the night in the forest Llauron had related it to her. Achmed and Grunthor had been there as well. She rummaged in her pack and pulled out a small journal where she recorded some of the lore she had learned in this new world. 'Here it is,' she said.

> *Among the last to leave, among the first to come,*
> *Seeking a new host, uninvited, in a new place.*
> *The power gained being the first,*
> *Was lost in being the last.*
> *Hosts shall nurture it, unknowing,*
> *Like the guest wreathed in smiles*
> *While secretly poisoning the larder*
> *Jealously guarded of its own power*
> *Ne'er has, nor ever shall its host bear or sire children,*
> *Yet ever it seeks to procreate.*

Elynsynos sighed. 'Manwyn always was the strange one,' she murmured. 'I do not know why she does not just say what she means. Yes, Pretty, it sounds like the F'dor. There is a great deal of power and risk to a demon like that in undertaking to acquire progeny. Should it do so through the body of its human host it weakens itself, breaks its own life essence open and gives some of it up to the child. F'dor are far too greedy and power-hungry to give up any of their own power, which is why they have to resort to other means of procreation.'

'Like creating the Rakshas?'

'Yes, My Pretty Soul. In a way the F'dor is really no different than the ancient dragons where propagation outside their species in concerned. When we realized the mistake of refusing to take a form like the Creator's we tried to rectify it. It is ironic, really; those few humans whose blood is mixed with that of dragons, rather than trying to become more human, generally seek to give up their humanity and attain dragon form, which is in a way tantamount to sacrificing their souls.

'Since dragons could not interbreed with the races of the Three, they tried to carve a humanlike race out of what few fragments of Living Stone remained after the vault was made. Rare and beautiful creatures were the result. Those creatures were called Children of the Earth, and had a humanoid form, or at least as close to one as the dragons could fashion.

'They were in some ways a brilliant creation, in other ways an abomination, but they were able to interbreed with the Three. Unlike the Rakshas, the Children of Earth had souls, because unlike the F'dor, the dragons were willing to commit some of their life essence to bring them into being. Their progeny, the Elder races they produced, are the Earth-born, those who seek to live within Her bosom, but whose souls touch the sky.'

Rhapsody was writing furiously in her journal. 'And what form do those races take?'

'The offspring of the Children of Earth and the Seren were a race known as Gwadd, a small, slender people deeply tied to the Earth's innate magic. A blending of earth and stars.'

Rhapsody stopped writing and looked up sadly. 'I remember the Gwadd from the old world,' she said wistfully.

'They are my favorite of all dragon grandchildren,' Elynsynos said. 'I am also particularly fond of the Nain. The Nain were the issue of the Children of Earth and the Mythlin.

'They are natural sculptors, miners, and molders of stone because from one parent they know the lore of the Earth, from the other the lore of the sea. To them it is as if granite is liquid, and yields willingly to their hand.'

Rhapsody nodded and returned to making notes. 'And the Kith? Did the race of air produce any Earth-born children?'

'Yes,' Elynsynos said. 'That pairing spawned a race known as Fir-bolga, literally, wind of the earth.'

The Singer's mouth dropped open. 'Fir-bolga? Firbolg? The Bolg are descended of dragons?'

'Well, in a way. They are more a sort of adopted grandchildren, since the Children of Earth were sculpted from Living Stone by dragons, not tied directly to their blood. The Kith were a harsh race, and so the Bolg are as well, but they love the earth genuinely, and I am very fond of them, despite their crude ways. Of all the Earth-born they have the most in common with their wyrm grandparents.'

Rhapsody laughed. 'I guess I really could be the soul of a dragon,' she said. 'I've adopted a dozen Firbolg grandchildren myself.' Her face grew serious. 'To that end, Elynsynos, I need to ask you something.'

'What, Pretty?'

'You don't intend to punish the Bolg in any way for having the claw dagger in their possession, do you?'

'Of course not. Just because I am a dragon does not mean I am totally wanton or specious in my revenge.' One enormous eye closed, and the dragon regarded her severely with the one that remained open. 'Have you been reading that tripe, *The Rampage of the Wyrm*?'

Rhapsody's face grew red in the light of the ships' wheel chandeliers. 'Yes.'

'It is nonsense. I should have eaten the scribe who penned it alive. When Merithyn died I thought about torching the continent, but surely you must be able to tell that I did not.'

'Yes, I thought not.'

'Believe me, if I were to rampage, the continent would be nothing but one very large, very black bed of coal, and it would be smoldering to this day.'

Rhapsody shuddered. 'I believe you. And I'm very glad to hear you don't hold the Bolg responsible.' The faces of her friends and her grandchildren rose up in her mind. 'And, as much as I would love to stay here forever with you, I really need to be returning to them.'

'You are going now?'

Rhapsody sighed. 'I should. I wish I could stay longer.'

'Will you come back, Pretty?'

'Yes, most definitely,' Rhapsody answered. Then she thought of Merithyn. 'If I am alive, Elynsynos. The only thing that will keep me from visiting you is death.'

The dragon began walking with Rhapsody back toward the tunnel. 'You must not die, Pretty. If you do, my heart will break. I have lost my only love. I do not wish to lose my only friend.' She stopped before one of the ships' figureheads, paint peeling and encrusted with salt. 'This is from the prow of Merithyn's ship.'

Rhapsody looked at the wooden statue. It was of a golden-haired woman, naked from the waist up, arms outstretched, reaching out to nowhere. Her water-faded eyes were green as the sea.

'She looks like you,' said Elynsynos.

Rhapsody looked doubtfully at the figurehead's ample bosom, then down at her own bustline. 'Not even on the best day of my life, but thanks for the thought.'

12

The darkness in the underground series of tunnels was so complete that it was difficult to see the Grandmother as she led them even deeper into the earth. Occasionally Grunthor could make out a whisper of her robe or the crackle of the ground beneath her bare feet, but by and large her passage through the tunnel was silent and all but invisible in the dwindling light of their torch.

The failing torchlight illuminated little of the tunnel walls, but what they could see caused Achmed and Grunthor to wish they were traveling more slowly with an opportunity to examine them. Unlike the newly hewn earthen walls of Grunthor's burrowing passages, these corridors had been mined centuries before and bore the hallmarks of deliberate architectural planning, though very different from that of the Cymrians. They were smooth and even, carved with the vestiges of the ancient reliefs that had once adorned them, all marred with a heavy layer of dank soot and the smears of fire ash, the byproduct of forges where iron was smelted.

However long it had been since they were despoiled, the odor still remained, now a permanent part of the stone passageways and the air they held within them.

After a short distance the tunnel opened before them into an immense cavern. The basalt ceiling was almost as tall as that of the Loritorium, hewn from the Earth itself and polished. Over the opening to a chamber deeper within the cavern was an immense arch on which words were inscribed. The letters, each at least as tall as a man, were in no alphabet that either of the Firbolg men recognized. The walls of the cavern were thick with ancient smoke and stained with the black streaks of soot from the fires of a forge or smithy. From this large central cavern tunnels ran in all directions.

The Grandmother stopped before the chamber and pointed a long bony finger at the massive inscription in the arch above it. 'Let that which sleeps within the Earth rest undisturbed; its awakening heralds eternal night,' she translated. Again her speech came forth wordlessly in two different voices. Grunthor and Achmed shuddered inwardly with the memory of their walk along the Root that ran the length of the Axis Mundi. They had seen something that slept deep within the bowels of the Earth for themselves. Neither disagreed with the words of the inscription.

The Grandmother folded her hands again and eyed them seriously. 'This place was known in its time as the Colony,' she said in her hissing, clicking language without words. 'Before the end it was a city-state of 112,938 Dhracians. Extinguish your torch. I will show you the reason my ancestors built the Colony in this place.'

Achmed tossed the remains of the torch to the ground and stamped out its light. A plume of smoke rose in the cavern, to dissipate a moment later. The Grandmother turned and walked away into the chamber beyond the words of warning. The men followed her through the archway into the deepening darkness.

It took Achmed's sensitive eyes a round moment to adjust to the darkness within the chamber, thick and palpable as liquid night. Just as they did the Grandmother struck something against the wall, sparking a tiny burst of light. Achmed saw that it was a spore like the ones they had used in their travels along the Root, a fungus that gave off light when friction was applied to it. The small light threw his focus off again, and it took another moment to adapt once more.

The elderly Dhracian woman climbed up a set of steps to an earthen slab and reached high above her head, then moved away as the light from the spore began to expand. Achmed and Grunthor could see after a minute that she had set it into a small lantern, a globe of muted light that hung from the ceiling of the chamber. With the aid of its glow they were able finally to see the room's dimensions.

It was three-sided, with a passageway secured by massive iron doors that led back to the cavern from which they had come. The polished walls tapered up to a curved triangular point from which the globe was suspended on a long, tarnished chain. The walls of the chamber were utterly without ornamentation.

Beneath the globe was a large obsidian catafalque, a platform on which a coffin might rest. In the shadows cast by the globe it did in fact appear that a body was laid out on the catafalque as if it was lying in state. Achmed and Grunthor drew nearer.

The sleeper was like none they had ever seen before. While her body was as tall as that of a full-grown human, her face was that of a child, her skin cold and polished gray, as if she were sculpted from stone. She would have, in fact, appeared to be a statue but for the measured tides of her breath.

Below the surface of filmy skin her flesh was darker, in muted hues of brown and green, purple and dark red, twisted together like thin strands of colored clay. Her features were at once coarse and smooth, as if her face had been carved with blunt tools, then polished carefully over a lifetime. Beneath her indelicate forehead were eyebrows and lashes that appeared formed from blades of dry grass, matching her long, grainy hair. In the dim light the tresses resembled wheat or bleached highgrass cut to even lengths and bound in delicate sheaves. At her scalp the roots of her hair grew green like the grass of early spring.

'She is a Child of Earth, formed of its own Living Stone,' the Grandmother said softly, the delicate rhythms of her buzzing language more present on their skin than in their ears. Gently she ran a thin hand over a rough lock of the child's hair. 'In day and night, through all the passing seasons, she sleeps. She has been here since before my birth. I am sworn to guard her until after Death comes for me.' She looked up, her black oval eyes gleaming. 'So must you be.'

The elderly woman rested her aged fingers on the child's forehead, then climbed the steps next to the catafalque and extinguished the light. 'Come,' she said, and left the chamber. The two Bolg stared at the stonelike face of the Earth Child as it receded into the darkness again, then followed the Grandmother.

When Rhapsody came out of the cave, the earth seemed disproportionately greener, the sky more intensely blue than when she had left. *How many days have passed?* she wondered. *Two? Five?* She had no idea.

She looked around her to try to get her bearings, plotting a course southeast. That route would take her to the forest edge of Tyrian, the kingdom of the Lirin, outside the borders of Roland, and, with any luck, to Oelendra.

Rhapsody made her way off the slippery rocks and down to the edge of the lake when something touched her arm.

'Rhapsody?'

She jumped in fright and instantly drew her dagger; her assailant was too close for the sword. Ashe held up his hands and took a step back.

'Sorry.'

Rhapsody exhaled furiously. 'Will you *please* stop doing that? You're going to give me a fatal fit.'

'I apologize, I really do,' he said, folding his hands passively. 'I've been waiting here since you went in to make sure you came out again.'

'I told you I'd be fine.' Her breathing was almost back to normal when she heard Elynsynos's voice in her memory.

And hear me: it is very close to here now, nearby. When you leave, be careful.

Beads of cold sweat appeared on her brow. *The dragon couldn't have meant Ashe*, she thought. When she stopped to contemplate it, the prospect seemed impossible. He had been alone with her for weeks now. If he had meant to do her harm he would have had ample opportunity.

Unless he had reason to follow her.

'Rhapsody? Are you all right?'

She looked up into the hood, seeing nothing in the darkness. Then the memory of his face came back to her, the hunted, uncertain look in his eyes, and her reservations vanished.

'I'm fine,' she said, smiling up at him. 'By any chance, do you know the way to Oelendra's?'

'I know how to get to Tyrian.'

'Can you draw me a map? I'm heading there next.'

'Really? Why?'

Rhapsody's mouth opened, then snapped shut again. 'I'd like to see her – Elynsynos thinks I should. Maybe I can find some answers there, among the Lirin.'

Ashe nodded. 'Could be. Well, as luck would have it, Tyrian is on the way to where I need to go next also. Shall I escort you there?'

'I'd hate to impose on you again,' she said uncertainly, remembering the conversation around one of their many campfires. She knew he must be anxious to return home to his lover who had been waiting for him all this time.

'As I just said, I'm on my way there anyway. It would be no imposition, and it would make me feel better knowing you're in Oelendra's capable hands. What do you say?'

'I say "thank you,"' she replied, checking her gear. 'Well, then, shall we go?'

Ashe nodded and turned to the south, stepping easily over the slippery rocks of the reflecting pool that glowed with mist from the dragon's cave. Rhapsody followed him around the shore of the lake, back to the sleepy glen, until the cave entrance was almost out of sight. Then she stopped and looked at it one last time.

'Goodbye, my friend. I love you,' she whispered.

The wind in the trees picked up slightly, caressing her face and the loose strands of her hair.

13

Rhapsody was like a child with a secret. She glowed for days following her visit with the dragon, though she was hard pressed to explain why. Ashe had the impression she would have been forthcoming if she had been able, but that she was having trouble articulating what she had seen and felt in the cave.

As a result, the tone of their walk was vastly more cheerful than it had been recently, despite all the rain and mud they were now braving. She seemed to have forgiven him for his poor judgment at the Tar'afel, and alternately joked with him outrageously or walked in a comfortable silence that was brimming with excitement just below the surface. It was an heightened state that fascinated his dragon nature, causing it to become even more obsessed with her, as the human side was doing as well.

Occasionally, when they would stop for a meal or when sitting around their fire at night he would find her looking at him thoughtfully, as though she were trying to place the features she had glimpsed inside the darkness of his hood from memory. When she became aware that he was noticing this she would smile at him. Even though the smile she gave him was the same one he had seen her use naturally on other friends or acquaintances, he felt somehow that there was a special element to it that made it his alone, that was reserved for him. The effect it had on him made him glad of his near-invisibility.

After three days of traveling, through even more rain and mud, they came to a clearing. In the distance Rhapsody could hear the sound of falling water, but for some reason the direction was not easy to determine. She was convinced after a few minutes that they had been traveling in circles, and became sure of it the third time they passed the same filbert bush. She stopped in the middle of the forest path.

'Are we lost?'

'No.'

'Then why are you leading me in circles?'

Ashe sighed, and Rhapsody thought she heard a smile in his voice. 'I forgot for a moment that you are Lirin. Anyone else would not have been able to tell.'

'Well?' There was a hint of annoyance in her voice.

He was silent for a moment. 'I'm sorry. I will explain when we get to our shelter.'

'Shelter?'

'Yes, there is a place here I thought we might camp for the night, a place we can both have a bath and at least one of us can actually sleep in a bed tonight. Both, if you're willing.' The teasing tone was back.

'But it's a place you don't want me to be able to find again.'

Ashe sighed again. 'Yes.'

Rhapsody sighed as well. 'Would it help if I closed my eyes?'

He laughed. 'That's not necessary. Come, I'll show you where it is.'

The noise of the water grew louder as they entered a grove of ash and flowering crabapple trees, the latter just beginning to bloom. Rhapsody was enchanted. She held aside a heavy branch and walked into the grove, turning slowly around as her eyes took in the delicate pink and white blossoms and the pale green of the new spring bark. The afternoon sun broke through the forest canopy, streaking the glen with shafts of light so heavy that she put out her hands, trying to catch it. The forest air was sweet, rich with the scent of recent rain.

'What a beautiful place,' she murmured. 'I'm not surprised you'd want to keep it to yourself.'

Ashe smiled; she could hear it in his voice. 'I don't,' he said. 'You're here, aren't you?'

'I'm not sure,' Rhapsody answered, still looking around. 'I might be dreaming.'

'I don't think so,' said Ashe. 'I've witnessed your dreams, and I doubt they look anything like this.' Rhapsody winced. He was right, of course, but the reminder of how disturbing her night terrors were to other people flushed her with embarrassment. She resolved to try and sleep as far away from him as she could that night.

They went deeper into the glen, and the birdsong became louder, competing with the splashing noise of the water she had heard. Finally in the distance she caught a glimpse of a waterfall. It staggered down a hidden hillside in four different drops. The stream that made it ran in front of a deep gorge; it was gaining power as the rains that fed it swelled with the advent of spring.

'Let me see your boots,' Ashe directed. Rhapsody bent her knee and held up the sole of one. He nodded, seeming satisfied. 'You'll have to take my hand on this one, Rhapsody. The gorge is steep and the shale around the waterfall is extremely slippery. You don't have a rough enough sole to maintain any purchase here. If you give me your hand I promise not to pick you up if I can avoid it.'

His tone was light, but Rhapsody knew his intent was serious; he was keeping his promise.

'What do you know about the roughness or smoothness of my soul?' she joked. 'Are you the All-God now, too?'

Ashe laughed. She gave him her hand, noticing that he glanced at her wrist, as he always did whenever their hands were joined.

He led her into the water. 'I've been accused of being many things, but that was never one of them.' They forded the stream, slipping only once. Rhapsody was glad to have his weight supporting her when she looked down over the second drop to the gorge below. He navigated them across the waterway and over to the other bank, where scrub and leafy vegetation flanked the rockwall of the hill. He held a large branch aside for her and stood back, letting her pass.

Rhapsody found herself in a hidden part of the glen, a place more dark than light. It took a moment for her eyes to adjust and when they did, she realized that there was a small hut there. It was made of stone and the roof seemed to be made of turf. The flora of the forest grew in and around it, making it difficult to see. It was free from any adornment, and had but one window and door. It was situated on the side of a large pool formed by backflow from the waterfall.

'Is this where we're staying?'

'Yes. Is that all right?'

'I think it's wonderful,' Rhapsody said, smiling up at him. 'I never would have known it was here.'

'That's the whole point,' Ashe said agreeably, taking her hand again and leading her over to the hut. 'This is the only place in the world I can shed my cloak and be as a normal person, or at least the only place on land. I don't wear it when I'm at sea, either.'

Rhapsody puzzled about his statement. If the mist from his cloak hid his vibrational signature so that he could not be detected, then it must be the water that occluded him from the sight of whatever power that could find him. She recalled Achmed mentioning something similar in his vibrational makeup when they had first traveled to Elysian. Things began to clarify in her mind; it was no wonder Achmed was uncomfortable around Ashe. Unlike the other people in the world, Ashe would not register on Achmed's vibrational senses. The churning of the waterfall must have the same effect, along with being hidden against the gorge. Then a thought occurred to her.

'No, it's not the only place,' she said excitedly. 'You would be safe to take off your cloak in my house, too.'

Ashe shuddered visibly. 'In the Cauldron? No, thank you.'

Rhapsody shoved him playfully. 'My house is not in the Cauldron,' she said. 'And it is even harder to find than this place, I'll wager.'

'Really.' Ashe's tone was noncommittal. He opened the door and held it for a moment, to allow the breeze from the forest to clear the air of the hut. Rhapsody looked inside.

It was a small room, with a single rumpled bed and a tiny fireplace. It had one doorless closet, separated from the room by a ragged curtain, which seemed empty of its contents, largely because they were scattered messily on the floor. Dishes were left on every horizontal surface, as well as socks and undergarments, one set of which hung from the coatrack, unwashed. Rhapsody's eyes looked around at the disarray, astonished at the slovenly place.

'Gods. This is your room?' she asked in disbelief. 'How do you fit in here?'

'Easily, for your information,' said Ashe defensively, but with a chuckle in his voice. 'It's just the right size for one person, and perhaps a nonjudgmental guest. All others can sleep outside, thank you.'

Rhapsody pushed him aside and went in. There was no decoration to the place; it was completely without ornament, unless the filth counted. In addition to the bed there was a small table and an old, dilapidated chair with hideous upholstery, now worn to the nap. The smell of the dirty laundry was unpleasant.

'Well? What do you think?'

'I think what this place needs is a woman's oversight – or a maid.'

Ashe laughed. 'You are welcome to provide either service if you'd like.'

'I've worked as a maid. There's no shame in it.'

'Certainly not,' he said. 'I don't think there would be shame in anything you'd do.' Rhapsody colored but said nothing. *Shows how little you know,* she thought to herself.

'On second thought, perhaps a flood would be more warranted.'

'I can arrange that, too.' He touched the hilt of the water sword. 'Well, are you going to stay? It'll cost you.'

Rhapsody turned to face him. 'Oh? What's the price?'

'An answer.'

'What's the question?'

'There are two.'

'Go ahead.' Rhapsody folded her arms.

'Are you Cymrian, and if so, what generation? You said you don't lie, so I know whatever you say will be accurate.'

Rhapsody lowered her head, considering. 'All right, I have the answer to your question. Your first one, that is: the answer is no, I'm not going to stay.' She walked toward the door where he was still standing. Ashe put his hands out in front of him.

'Wait. I was just joking.'

'No, you weren't. Stand aside.'

'I apologize,' he said as he stepped out of her way. He knew better than to try and block her exit. He watched as she walked to the pool and sat down beside it, pulling her pack from her shoulders.

'No need to. I'll be perfectly happy here.' She took out her bedroll and began unrolling it.

He bent down beside her. 'But I won't be. Rhapsody, you are the first person I have ever shown this place. I brought you all the way here so that we might both get some real rest before you head off to Tyrian. I'm tired of sleeping outside; I do it all the time, and I want one night's rest in my bed. I know the place may not seem like much, but it's the only place I have. Please come inside. I'm sorry about the mess and the stupidity. You don't have to answer any questions, and I'll stop bothering you about whether or not you're Cymrian; I promise. Besides, part of our arrangement is that one watches while the other sleeps, and I can't very well do that if I'm inside while you're out here. It would be a dereliction of my duty as your guide. So please, come back in.'

Rhapsody looked up at the cloaked figure beside her. His voice had a desperation to it that she didn't understand, and she felt sorry for him, this exhausted wanderer who was constantly on the move, hiding from the eyes of his stalkers. She felt ashamed for her lack of gratitude, after all he had done for her, putting his life and his relationship in abeyance to escort her here. She heard again the melodious, sensible voice of the dragon.

The man outside, he wanted to know if you are Cymrian, yes?

Yes.

You may as well tell him, Pretty. He already knows. It is obvious.

She stood up and brushed the dirt off her garments, then picked up her gear. 'I'll make a bargain with you, Ashe,' she said, slinging her pack over her shoulder again. 'I will tell you the answers to your questions.'

'No, I had no right – '

'Let me finish. I will answer either question you put to me, or both, as long as you answer the same question about yourself first. Do we have a bargain?'

He thought for a moment. 'Yes.'

'All right, then, let's go inside.'

Sorry about the mess.'

'Don't be,' said Rhapsody. 'First off, it's your room, you're entitled to keep it in any manner you choose. Second, this is neat as a pin compared to Jo's.'

Ashe laughed. 'She must live in a trash heap.'

'Yes, she does, but she lived much of her life on a real one before I met her, so I try not to bother her about it, no matter how much I dislike untidiness. I'm afraid fanatical housekeeping is part of my upbringing.'

He nodded. Rhapsody went to the chair and picked up the dirty woolen socks lying there; she folded them and sat down, depositing them in her lap.

'Here, let me take those,' said Ashe hastily. 'You don't need to hold them.' He dropped them into an empty basket in the closet.

'Aren't you going to take off the cloak?' Rhapsody asked. 'You must be dying to get out of it.'

Ashe pulled back the hood, leaving the cloak in place, and sat down on the bed. She took in a breath when she saw his face again; it was strange seeing it again. From across the small room she could not see the strange pupils in his eyes, but the metallic sheen to his hair was as startling as it had been when he first revealed himself to her. He seemed to notice her staring at him, and looked uncomfortable.

'So,' he began uneasily, 'are you Cymrian?'

'You first.'

'Yes.'

'Well,' she said, 'you already know, but yes, I am.'

'Achmed and Grunthor, too?'

'I can't speak for them without their permission,' she said regretfully. 'You'll have to draw your own conclusions.'

Ashe nodded. 'What generation?' When she looked at him askance, he smiled. 'On my father's side, third. On my mother's, it's so far removed that it's hardly worth mentioning.'

'Explain this to me again,' Rhapsody said. 'First Generation Cymrians were born in the old world; their children, born here, are Second Generation?'

'Yes.'

'What if someone was Seren, lived in Serendair, but didn't sail with the Fleets?'

Ashe, who was watching her face intently, blinked, and his face went suddenly blank. 'And survived the cataclysm?'

'Obviously, or there wouldn't be a reason to discuss it, would there?'

Ashe nodded. 'No, there wouldn't. Of course, how stupid of me. This happened to a great many people, in fact, if my historical studies are accurate. Not everyone who evacuated Serendair wanted to go with Gwylliam; a lot of them thought he was insane, or that the journey would be too much for them, particularly the races that were not inclined to sea travel. They left prior to the sailing of the Three Fleets, and went to other places, land masses closer to the Island.'

Rhapsody rose and pulled the cloak from her shoulders. 'So, would they be considered Cymrians?'

The searing blue eyes trained even more intensely on her, the vertical slits expanding in the darkness of the room, soaking in her answers as if they were sunlight.

'Yes,' he said thoughtfully. 'Even though they didn't greet the indigenous population with Gwylliam's aphorism, I think a native Seren who left Serendair prior to the cataclysm would still qualify as a Cymrian. The members of the Second Fleet never did, either; they landed in Manosse or Gaematria, and didn't set foot on this continent until many generations later, when the first Cymrian Council was called. And they are Cymrians; they felt the call of the Council horn deep in their souls when it was winded, were compelled to answer, to come to the Moot. Yes; I think anyone who once lived in Serendair and left would be a First Generation Cymrian.'

Rhapsody turned away from him and hung her cloak on the peg near the door so he would not see how hard she swallowed. 'I guess that makes me a First Generation Cymrian, then,' she said, smoothing out the mantle's folds, brushing the dirt from them. Then she turned and looked back at Ashe. She studied his face, but no gleam of victory came into his eyes, just the fragment of a smile.

'How did you survive? Where did you go? It must have been somewhere you could get to by rowboat or ferry, since you said you never sailed on any other kind of ship. How did you come to be here, half a world away?'

'That's more than two questions,' said Rhapsody hastily. The memory of her endless sojourn through the bowels of the Earth reared its head; she shook her own to banish the sensation of crawling along the Axis Mundi, still hovering close to the surface of her consciousness. It was a struggle not to think about it, and when she did, she felt despair she could not easily overcome. 'Besides, I thought we agreed we would try to avoid talking about the Past as much as possible.'

'I'm sorry,' Ashe said quickly. 'You're right, of course. Thank you for telling me what you have.'

Rhapsody eyed him uneasily. 'You're welcome. So now that you've extracted this information from me, what are you going to do?'

Ashe stood up. 'Bathe.'

Rhapsody stared at him again. 'That's it? You've been nagging me the entire length of this trip to know this answer, and you're going to bathe?'

'Yes,' Ashe answered with a laugh. 'In case you haven't noticed, while you have taken advantage of every sheltered spot in the river and each secluded pond to swim yourself clean, I have had to make do with the mist from the cloak; hardly fair, and certainly not conducive to us sharing a small room tonight. So if you will excuse me, I'll be going now.' Rhapsody watched in amazement as he picked up a scrap of woven cloth from the floor that may have, in less ratty days, been a towel, and walked out the door, whistling.

Ashe had just finished lacing his trousers when the door of the cottage opened and a hailstorm of dirt and debris flew out. Rhapsody had apparently found a large branch to use as a broom and was sweeping his room with a furor that rivaled a windstorm. She emerged for a moment; their eyes met, and she gasped. She was staring at his chest.

Commencing at his navel and extending to his left shoulder was a hideous wound, black and twisted, festering red in the light of the glen. The enormous gash seemed to be an old one, but one that had never healed; it was raw and open, with burned flesh blistered beneath charred skin. Blue veins spread radially across his chest, forming a starlike shape above his heart. The sight of it was enough to bring tears to Rhapsody's eyes.

Customarily I'd cut your heart out, although it's fairly obvious someone already has.

Ashe turned quickly away and pulled his shirt over his head. When he turned back she was gone. He ran his hands through his now-clean hair and waited for her to reappear, but she didn't. Finally he decided to break the awkward silence.

'Rhapsody?'

She reappeared at the door. 'Yes?'

He pointed at the backflow pool of the waterfall. 'I've dammed a spot in the pool to make a little lagoon, if you want to use it.'

Her face brightened. 'Perfect! Thank you. I'll be right out.' She vanished into the hut, emerging a moment later with a full basket of clothes. He stared in dismay; they were his.

'What are you doing?'

'Laundry.' She went to the small pool that he had made for her to bathe in and dropped the clothes, garment by garment, into it, followed by a bar of hard soap. A pair of soiled pants, a shirt with an immense grease stain and several sets of dirty undergarments fell into the water, to his intense embarrassment. He strode around the shore and reached for the basket.

'Here, give that to me. I'll do it.'

Rhapsody's eyes twinkled. 'Nonsense! You offered me the position of maid, and I accepted, for today at least. It's my way of paying for your services as my guide. Laundry comes with the territory. In fact, if you want to strip out of those, I'll wash them, too.' She pointed to the clothes he was currently wearing and picked up a stick.

'No, thank you.'

'You may as well take advantage of the service while you can. Once our account is squared, you'll be washing your own clothes and sweeping out your own hovel – er, house.' The water in the lagoon began to bubble, steam emerging in the cool air of early spring. She had used her fire lore to boil the laundry and now stirred it along with the soap, creating a lather in the lagoon that washed out among the rocks, avoiding the waterfall itself.

When the clothes were done Rhapsody pulled them from the water, suddenly cool enough to touch, and hung them on the rope line she had strung in between the trees of the glade. Ashe went to each garment and touched it, removing the excess water instantly.

'Are you going to bathe?' he asked.

Rhapsody looked up through the canopy of trees at the patches of sky. The clouds were thickening and beginning to grow gray. 'I don't think so. It looks like rain.'

Ashe looked at the sky as well. 'You're right. Let's get inside.'

They snatched the laundry, hurried into the hut and shut the door just as the raindrops began to pelt the roof. Ashe stopped in amazement. His room was tidy and scrubbed, cleaner than it had ever been. The bed was made, the floor swept, and a pot of tea had been set to steep on the table, which had been washed and polished.

'How did you do all this in such a short time?'

'Experience.'

'I see. Well, this wasn't necessary. Thank you.'

Rhapsody smiled at him from the doorway. 'It's part of my job as maid. We provide some of the services you would get without cost if you were married.' Her words choked off almost as soon as they had left her lips. She was still not sure that he wasn't.

Ashe laughed. 'If that's the case, there are some others I would far rather have.' His eyes twinkled merrily.

'Sorry,' said Rhapsody, taking the laundry he held and dropping it on the bed. 'This is just a temporary arrangement until my debt to you is paid off. Basic housekeeping. Other services cost extra, and there are some things you just can't afford.'

Ashe turned away, smiling. 'There are some things worth begging, borrowing, or stealing for, too.'

She laid the laundry across the bed and began to fold it. 'Yes, but I hardly think that's one of them.'

Ashe picked up a cambric shirt from the bed and took it to the closet where he hung it on a peg. 'I doubt you even know which one I'm talking about, Rhapsody.'

Rhapsody picked up her pack from the floor and opened it. She began rearranging items in preparation for repacking her clean handkerchiefs and the clothes she had washed with Ashe's laundry. 'I can guess,' she said dryly.

'You might be wrong,' said Ashe humorously. 'Why don't you hazard a guess. What wifely service might I like you to provide?'

She removed a series of pouches from the bottom of the satchel. 'I don't want to guess. Why don't you tell me, and I'll try not to belt you if I'm not offended.'

Ashe picked up his leather gloves and pulled them back on. He sat down in the threadbare chair and put his feet up, enjoying the prospect of making mischief with her. 'All right.' He looked her up and down as she continued to ignore him, sorting through her supplies. *Child rearing*, he thought.

'There's a town that's part of the southern Nonaligned region called Gallo. Men use their wives as shields when they enter into battle. The women walk before them to absorb the arrow shots.' He waited for the eruption, but she said nothing. He tried again. 'In addition, when they are trading horses, if one needs to somehow make up the difference in the value of a – ' He stopped when he saw her looking down at her hand in amazement. 'What's the matter?'

'Look at this,' she said, her voice filled with wonder. Ashe stood up and came over to where she stood. She was holding the dragon's claw dagger she had returned to Elynsynos. 'I gave this back to her.'

'Obviously she wants you to have it.'

'I suppose. I wonder how she got it in here without my noticing.'

Ashe smiled at her. 'Never underestimate the determination of a dragon when it comes to something it loves, Rhapsody. It will always find a way to get what it wants.' He put his folded laundry in the closet and went out into the rain.

14

The tea's ready. Want some?'

'Yes, thank you,' Rhapsody answered. She looked around the interior of the room again as Ashe laid a fire with the wet branches he had found behind the hut. She went to the hearth to light it, moving the little screen out of the way.

'It's here on the table,' Ashe said.

'Thanks.' Rhapsody looked at the wood that a moment before had been green and wet; it was now dried as though seasoned for a year or more, every drop of water having been removed from it. She touched the kindling and spoke the word for ignition, then the one for sustenance, and sparks leapt up, catching the edges of the wood. She smiled and looked up at Ashe, who was kicking the towel he had dropped on the floor under the bed.

'Are you tied to water yourself, or just through the sword?' She rose, picked up the mug he had set out for her, and went to the old chair, settling down in it.

He looked startled, then relaxed a bit. He took off his battered scabbard and laid the sword across his knees, running his hand over the tattered leather. 'It's hard to say, really. I've had Kirsdarke for so long now that I can't remember that element not being a part of me. I've always felt the sea in my blood, even as a child. My family were seafarers by and large, and so it comes naturally, I guess.' Rhapsody waited for him to go on, but instead he went to the hearth and picked up the fire iron. She shifted in the chair; it was so old and the fabric so threadbare that it was difficult for her to sit upright.

'So what do you want from me now?' she asked.

Ashe bent to stir the embers of the fire, and as he did she felt a thrill run up her back, as though his ministrations to the flames were being applied to her body. She felt a moment's panic, then realized almost immediately that it was a function of her communion with the fire rather than anything he was doing intentionally. She concentrated on separating herself from it as he replaced the screen and turned to face her.

'What do you mean?'

'Well,' Rhapsody answered, sipping her tea, 'you have been after me for weeks to yield the information I just gave you about my Cymrian lineage. It has seemed very important to you, so now that you've broken me down and you have your answer, I'd like to know what you plan to do with the knowledge. What do you want from us? From me?'

'Nothing you aren't prepared to give.'

Rhapsody sighed. 'You know, I don't make a very good Cymrian, and I certainly don't much like being one. You people can't answer a question directly to save your lives.'

Ashe smiled in spite of himself. 'You're right. I'm sorry. I know it's annoying, but it comes from centuries of breeding, from paranoia and distrust cast in the forge of a terrible war, Rhapsody. They're all like that, I'm afraid, and I am among the worst.'

'I can tell. I mean, how many people walk around by choice in a cloak of mist, hiding from the eyes of the world?'

Blue eyes of startling intensity met her own. 'Who said it was by choice?' She was unable to break his gaze or to say anything for a moment. 'I'm sorry,' she said when she could finally speak again. 'I had a sense when you first showed me your face that it wasn't.'

'Why?'

Rhapsody considered her answer. Until the moment he had lifted his hood and let her look at him, she had assumed he was malformed in some way, the victim of an accident or a battle injury, or perhaps of a difficult birth. She had felt an affinity for him because of it; she sometimes felt that way herself, knew the desire to shield her countenance from the stares and gawking looks that often came her way in the street.

She had examined her face at great length in the glass, trying to determine what was so unusual about it, coming finally to the conclusion that her Liringlas blood had produced a visage in her that the people of this land were not used to seeing, or found to be alien. Even though she didn't consider herself ugly, the stares sometimes made her feel that way.

But Ashe was not ugly. On the contrary, there was a beauty to his face, a handsomeness that could be seen even through the scraggly beard and unkempt hair. He had an aristocratic look to him, despite his simple clothes and the muscularity of his body; he was obviously a man who had wandered far, as evidenced by the long, strong sinew in his legs. His shoulders were broad and his waist narrow, like a man who had labored on a farm or chopped wood, and his hands had seen hard work and hard times. And Rhapsody knew, from the moment she beheld him, that the misty screen was a necessity, not a measure of vanity. She knew he was hunted, sought by predators with extensive reach and power. Seeing the terrible black wound on his chest only served to confirm that belief. And in her heart she hurt for him, even though she did not really know him.

The sound of pounding rain could be heard on the turf roof, and air of the room became damp. 'You never answered my question,' she said finally. 'What do you want from me now, if anything?'

He went to the bed and sat down, giving her a studied look. 'It would certainly be nice to have you as an ally. Your friends as well, but you especially.'

'Why me in particular?'

He smiled slightly. 'You seem a good person to be with in a fight.'

Rhapsody laughed. 'Well, thank you, but you are a poor judge of fighters. If you have to go up against something hostile, you want Grunthor if you can get him. Or, better yet, Achmed.'

'Why Achmed?'

'Achmed is – well, Achmed is – talented.' She decided she had said too much already. 'Before I can be your ally, I have to know what you're fighting. Can you tell me?'

'No.' His word was abrupt, sweeping the smiles from both of their faces. 'Sorry.'

'Well, that does make it a little difficult to agree to be your ally.'

'I know.' He sighed heavily.

'Do you trust anyone enough to tell them?'

'No.'

'What an awful way to live.' She ran her finger around the rim of the mug of tea, all but empty now. 'Don't you think there are some things worth the risk, the gamble?' Her voice was gentle.

'I'm not a gambling man, I'm afraid. Not anymore.'

A stillness descended, thick and palpable. Rhapsody cast a glance at the fire, snapping and hissing within the grate, then looked back at Ashe, the strange vertical pupils of his eyes accentuated by its light. There was a look in those eyes she could not identify, but it filled her with a sadness that squeezed her heart.

'Do you at least leave the door open to the possibility?' she asked.

'I don't know what you mean.'

Rhapsody stared into her teacup, then took another sip. 'My past is a corridor of doors I left open, never meaning to close them. I never closed a door if I didn't have to, in the hope that things would be right again one day if I only left the chance open. Maybe you aren't ready to gamble now, to trust anyone with your secrets, but perhaps one day you will be. Is that possible?'

Ashe looked into the fire. After a long moment he spoke.

'I don't think so. I believe that door is not only closed, but locked and bolted. And sealed shut.'

Silence thudded between them. Rhapsody set her teacup down.

'Then I guess we had best stand by our bargain and try to avoid talking about the Past,' she said gently.

'Agreed.'

'Perhaps it's better if I tell you in broad terms what I'm willing to fight to support, and then, if your agenda fits into that, you will know that I'm your ally, even if you can't state your cause.'

His face brightened a little, and the vertical pupils twinkled. 'That would work.'

'Right. First, if you are planning to assault the Bolg or wrest the mountain from Achmed, we will be fighting each other.'

'No. Not at all.'

'Well, I thought not, but one never knows. Anyone planning to harm a child in any way is my enemy; likewise any innocent person or Lirin holy tree or forest. I would like to see peace take a lasting hold. I am generally on the side of the defender, not the aggressor, unless I have a good reason not to be. I will castrate any rapist or child molester I catch in the attempt.

'Other than that, I may build myself a goat hut in the forest one day, if the Lirin will accept me, and live there in peace, not harming anyone, puttering with my plants and working on my music. Someday I'd like to build or help build a healing place and use my music to treat illness or injury, and teach others to do so. As I've told you before, I doubt I will survive these dangerous times, so I don't hold out much hope for the longer goals. I expect to go down doing something I believe will make the world better in one way or another. So, am I your ally?'

Ashe was smiling. 'It sounds like it.'

Rhapsody looked seriously at him. 'And would you tell me if I was not?'

'Probably not.'

She sighed. 'I didn't think so.' Thunder rumbled in the distance. 'So is that all that you want?'

Many emotions passed over Ashe's face, but when he spoke his words were simple. 'I would like have you as my friend.'

'I'd like that as well,' she answered, putting her feet up on the end of his bed. 'And, as long as you really are what you seem, I think I am.'

'And are you really what you seem?'

She laughed. 'Totally. I don't know what I seem to be, but anything I am is out in the open. I'm afraid I've never learned to hide my faults, and I'm very unsophisticated. You know I try never to lie if I am not forced to.'

He looked interested. 'How can one be forced to lie?'

Rhapsody thought back to Michael, the Wind of Death, and the cruel gleam in his eyes as he laid his terms out to her.

You will want me, too, and tell me so. You will not only meet my needs, you will engage in their succor willingly, with relish. You will make love to me with your words, as well as all your other attributes. Now, can you do that? Can you promise me a reciprocal situation?

She closed her eyes and tried to block out the memory of the child's screams of fright.

All right, Michael, I'll say whatever you want. Let her go.

Rhapsody crossed her arms over her waist. She thought about the victorious smile on Michael's face; either she would be truthfully telling him what he wanted to hear, or she would have to lie, a fate far worse. Either way, he won.

'Take my word for it; one can be,' she said finally. Her eyes met Ashe's, and she caught her breath. He had the same crystalline blue irises as Michael had had.

'Is something wrong?'

She shook her head, and as she did, the thoughts cleared out of her mind. Michael may have had the same blue eyes, but they were certainly not slit vertically. Perhaps whatever odd nature caused his strange ocular formation was part of why Ashe was hunted.

'No,' she said. 'Nothing is wrong.' She drained the rest of her tea and put the cup down on the table next to her chair. 'I just hope you never find yourself in the position of being forced to lie. It's one of the worst things in the world. Anyway, I guess the things you want are possible. I will try to be your friend, and your ally. I can't speak for Grunthor or Achmed, but if I put in a good word for you, as long as they don't object to whatever action you are undertaking, they will probably be willing to ally themselves with you as well.' She watched Ashe's face wrinkle in something that appeared to be disgust. 'What?'

'Sorry,' Ashe said, looking contrite. 'Sometimes it amazes me that you have anything to do with those two, especially Achmed.'

'Why?'

'He's a repulsive person, that's why.'

Rhapsody bristled. 'You don't even know him. How can you say that?'

'I have been the recipient of his hospitality twice now, and I can't say that I enjoyed it much either time.'

'I'm very sorry,' Rhapsody said sincerely. 'He can be a bit abrasive. Why did you stay?'

Ashe went back to the fire and gave it another stir. It seemed unwilling to participate fully in warming the room. 'You and Jo were pleasant enough to be around. And when you mentioned Elynsynos, I knew I could help you find her. I'm one of the few living foresters who has ever approached her lair.'

She sat up at his mention of the word *forester*. 'You're an official forester?' He nodded. 'Were you trained at Llauron's?'

'Yes.'

'I've been there! What a lovely man he is. Did you have much direct instruction from him?'

Ashe replaced the screen. 'Some. Generally Llauron doesn't do too much of the forester training himself, he leaves that to Gavin, with occasional help from Lark.'

'Yes, I met them, too. Lark taught me a good deal about herbalism. I'm sorry; I got us off the topic. Achmed is really not that bad. He is rough around the edges, and he has an interesting perspective on the world, but he is a good person to know. He and I actually have a great deal in common.'

Ashe shuddered. 'Short of being Cymrians of the First Generation, I can't think of anything.'

'I didn't say Achmed was a First Generation Cymrian – you're inferring that. For one thing, both our appearances seem to rile the sensibilities of the people of this land.'

Ashe stared at her in amazement. 'What?'

'Yes, in case you haven't noticed, we both tend to walk about in hooded cloaks because when we don't, we get stared at or worse.'

He shook his head in amazement. She had no idea why she was getting the reactions she was. Even though he was aware of this before, the realization never ceased to bewilder him. 'Achmed is an ugly person.'

She was beginning to grow angry. 'How judgmental you are! It's foolish to assume a person's appearance is the same as his personality.'

'I was referring to his personality.'

'As I said, you don't know him.'

He leaned back on the wall next to the fireplace. 'You never did answer my question about you and he.'

'What question?'

'About whether you would mate with Achmed – I mean marry him.' The words caused a large knot in his throat that Rhapsody could almost see.

'Maybe,' she said. 'We certainly haven't discussed it. He might be horrified at the thought. As I told you, I don't expect to marry anyone, but if I were to live that long, he's probably my best prospect.'

Ashe looked sick. 'Why?'

Rhapsody drew her knees up to her chest. 'Well, let's see; he knows more about me than anyone else in the world, he understands my strengths and weaknesses, and he doesn't seem to be put off by my appearance.'

'Rhapsody, no one is put off by your appearance.'

She ignored the comment. 'And I don't think he would expect the things from marriage that others might.'

'Such as?'

'Love, for instance. Achmed is aware of the fact that I am without a heart, and it doesn't seem to bother him. I think he would be satisfied with what I am limited by, and what I would be able to share. This is speaking theoretically, of course. As I told you, we have never talked about it.'

'I don't know, Rhapsody, but it seems a shame to me that you would limit yourself at all in your expectations of that relationship you claim to hold in high esteem.'

She was growing annoyed again. 'What difference does it make? I mean, why are you the custodian of my marital prospects?'

Ashe turned away. It was far more difficult to talk to her without the anonymity afforded by the mist cloak's hood. 'I'm not.'

'I find it strange that you really seem upset by the prospect of my loveless marriage.'

He turned and looked at her directly. 'I'm surprised you're not. You say you have a great respect for the institution.'

Rhapsody considered his words. 'Fair enough. I guess that applies in my mind only to those who have the capability to enter into a loving one.'

'And you are not one of them?'

'No.'

'Why not?'

She sighed and stared at the fire, now beginning to catch. 'I am forsworn, prohibited from it.'

Ashe sat down on the bed across from her. 'Why? Are you a member of a celibate religious order?'

Rhapsody choked, then laughed. 'Hardly.'

'Then why?'

Rhapsody looked down at her hands. 'Back in the old land, I traded my ability to ever love that way for something I wanted to protect.'

'Which was?'

'A child,' Rhapsody answered. She looked up and mild surprise was on her face; she had a hard time believing she was answering his questions so easily, as he was the first person she had ever told about it.

Ashe looked down, not meeting her eyes. 'You had a child?'

'Not of my own, but I wanted to protect her anyway.' Ashe nodded.

Rhapsody thought she sensed relief, but he said nothing. 'Anyway, I vowed I would never love anyone else, and I have kept my word.'

'Anyone other than the child?'

'No, I guess I'm not explaining this correctly. I gave my word to a man that I would never love another until the world ended.'

'And who was this man that you loved? What happened to him?'

Rhapsody grimaced. 'I never said I loved him. He was a pig.'

'You're losing me; why did you vow to love a pig?'

She sighed. 'All right; let's go over it again, since it seems to be important to you. The most reprehensible, evil, cruel bastard I have ever known had possession of an innocent child that he would have raped repeatedly and butchered if I didn't intervene. I vowed, in return for her safety, never to love anyone else, and I haven't. I never said I loved him.'

'Not until the end of the world, right?'

'Right.'

'That's a hefty oath to give to someone like that.'

'Well, I guess it depends on what the likelihood was that I would find love I wanted anyway.'

'And you didn't expect to?'

'No. It really was not a big sacrifice.'

A warm smile crossed Ashe's face, and he rose from the bed and came to Rhapsody, crouching down before her. 'I have wonderful news for you.'

'What's that?'

'If you should ever decide that you do want to love someone again, you can, free and clear, without breaking your oath.'

'How do you calculate that?'

'Because you vowed not to love again until the end of the world?'

'Yes.'

'Well, guess what, Rhapsody? Your world did end; it's been gone more than a thousand years. You're free of him, and any promises to him.'

Tears welled up in Rhapsody's eyes for more reasons than she could count. Ashe reached out and took her hands comfortingly, anticipating her allowing the tears to fall. But, as required, she choked them back, struggling with intense effort against giving herself over to her sorrow and the relief that his words had stirred inside her. Ashe stared at the contortions of her face in its battle against the tears, and he reached up to touch the corner of her eye, only to be pushed away.

'Don't,' she whispered. She looked away. 'I'll be all right in a moment.'

'You don't have to be,' Ashe said gently. 'It's all right, Rhapsody; you can let it down now. You're safe here. Have a good cry. You look like you need one desperately.'

'I can't,' she said quietly. 'I'm not allowed to.'

'Allowed by whom?'

'Achmed. He forbade it.'

Ashe laughed unpleasantly. 'You're joking.' She shook her head. 'You're not joking? What a lovely person he is. Look, Rhapsody, crying is not a sign of weakness.'

'I know,' she said, blinking to drive the moisture from her eyes. 'It's annoying.'

'Annoying to Achmed? Tempest take him, he's not here. If you need to cry, cry. It will not annoy me in the least.'

Rhapsody smiled. 'Thank you, but I don't need to. I'm fine.'

Ashe shook his head. 'No, you're not. I'm a minor expert on salt water, be it sea water or tears; an effect of the sword, you know. I can assure you that the body and the soul both need the cleansing that comes with tears. The blood is far cleaner and healthier afterward. I would think Achmed would know that if anyone would.' Rhapsody's eyes narrowed slightly at the comment, and Ashe hurried on. 'If you have been withholding the natural action of weeping all these centuries, given the amount of grief you have undoubtedly experienced in that time, you are not just doing yourself a disservice, you are doing yourself harm. Please, Rhapsody, I can hold you if it would help.'

Her eyes went to the monstrous wound beneath his shirt, and she flinched at the memory of the pain she had inadvertently caused him with the embrace she had given him in the forest. 'No, thank you. I appreciate the offer, however.'

'Or I could leave for a while, take a walk, if you like.'

'No, thank you,' she repeated, firmly this time. 'I really am fine, and you don't need to be soaked to the skin. What you could do for me is to pass me the lute Elynsynos gave me. Would you like to hear it?'

Ashe rose and went to the closet where she had stored her gear. 'I would love to. Are you sure you – '

'Yes,' Rhapsody said, taking the instrument when he held it out to her. 'What would you like to hear?'

He sighed, and decided to let the matter drop. 'Do you know any songs of the sea from the old world?'

'A few,' she said, smiling, thinking of Elynsynos. 'Some of my family were seafarers, too. A minarello really is a better instrument for that, but I'll do the best I can.' She tuned the lute and began to play. The strings were ancient, but the dragon's magic had held them in perfect condition, and the wood had mellowed since its carving into a sweet, rich sound that resonated in the room.

Ashe stretched out on the bed, listening to her play, enraptured. She had no idea of the depth of his feelings, even without the protection his face no longer had from his hood. He let the music creep into his head and wind its way through his heart, soothing the constantly throbbing pain a bit, erasing the headache that had been brewing since the discussion of Achmed. Her voice was so beautiful, airy and ethereal, like the singing of the wind, and it made him drowsy. He would have given the remainder of his soul at that moment if she would only stay for a few more days, singing to him alone, opening the heart she said she didn't have.

After a few sea chanteys she stopped singing and let the music continue through the lute alone, a haunting melody that made him feel immensely sad. He felt on the verge of tears himself when a discordant note rang out, jarring him out of his reverie. Rhapsody blinked, then played the passage correctly, continuing on until the next wrong note. Then she stopped altogether.

Ashe sat up and looked across the room at her. She was asleep in the chair, her fingers still on the lute strings. He thought about carrying her to the bed, but the scene at the Tar'afel rose quickly up in his mind, and he discarded the thought immediately. Instead he got up and slid the lute out of her hands, setting it on the table, and then covered her with one of the blankets. She sighed in her sleep and turned over on her side in the chair.

Ashe looked at the black velvet ribbon. He longed to unbind her hair, but decided that would be intrusive as well. So he put another log on the fire, now burning quietly and steadily, then went back to the chair where Rhapsody slept. He stared down at her for a long while, enjoying the picture of her, asleep in the firelight. After almost an hour he felt exhaustion overtake him. He gave her a soft kiss on the head and slipped in between the covers of the bed, knowing it would not be long before she woke in the night, sobbing in her sleep.

When she did, he went to her in the dark and whispered words of comfort until she grew quiet again. The pounding storm had given way to a steady, insistent rain. Reluctantly he returned to bed and left her to her unsettling dreams.

15

The rain continued, unabated, for most of the following day. By the time it began to let up the sun had gone down again, leaving the darkness silent except for the dripping of water from the leaves onto the pool and hut. The relentlessness of the downpour had left Rhapsody strangely tired, so they stayed one more night in the hut to allow the ground the opportunity to dry out somewhat.

They had passed the day in pleasant enough conversation, mostly in regard to plants and trees, wars that Ashe had fought in, tales of the subdual of the Firbolg, and things he had heard from companions about training with Oelendra. A formidable warrior and a legendary hero, she had a reputation as a stern and humorless teacher, an occasionally brutal taskmaster, but was regarded as the best in sword instruction, he had said. He himself had not trained with her, had only met her once and they had not spoken.

Rhapsody was beginning to feel a creeping sadness that she could not fully place taking root in her soul. She felt it each time Ashe smiled at her, or passed in front of her, so she knew it had something to do with him, but why her heart tugged at her she did not know.

That she had grown somewhat fond of him was no secret, either to her, or, she assumed, to him; they were at a comfortable place. He reminded her a great deal of her brother Robin, the second oldest, of whom she had also been very fond but with whom she was not particularly close. She did not understand Robin, nor did she understand Ashe. Perhaps one day she would, but the comparison to Robin made the sadness deepen. She had run away from home just as they were finally getting to know one another, much the way she and Ashe were parting now. She never saw Robin again. She wondered if it would be that way with Ashe as well.

He had been kind to her, for the most part, and had done a great deal for her, extending himself more than any other had in this new land. Unfortunately, she knew there was something beneath the surface of his generosity, something calculating that pressed for personal information but refused to share any, that sought her trust but did not offer his own. He was using her in some way, she knew. She just hoped that it would not be fatal, or worse.

They stayed in the hut that night, waiting for the rain to clear and the night wind to dry the ground. He had insisted that she take the bed, and, upon finding resistance futile, she thanked him and slipped into it, tired suddenly from the lack of the exercise she was accustomed to and the prospect of what was to come.

Her dreams were haunted by images of demons and destruction, of a blind Seer with no irises in her eyes that reflected the image of her own face. She felt a chilling cold, a cold that reached down into her blood and drank it, like the root of a poisonous willow, stripping her of her heat and her music, leaving her without a voice with which to even cry out for help. She woke gasping in Ashe's arms and clung to him, holding on as if he were the only person in the world who could hear her now that her music was gone.

He stretched out beside her on the bed, staying on top of the covers, and held her until she stopped trembling. It took more than an hour, but eventually she quieted and slept dreamlessly. When he was sure she was truly asleep he wistfully removed her arm from his waist; she had placed it there to avoid the wound, he knew. With great difficulty he stood up and looked down at her, curled around the hay pillow like a dragonling around its treasure; perhaps her visit to Elynsynos had left some residual effect. He stood over her a long while, at last returning to his chair, wondering if anything in his life had been as difficult as leaving her in that bed alone.

The passageway down which the Grandmother led them opened up into a vast vertically cylindrical cavern almost the size of Canrif City that stretched out of sight above and below them. Circular ledges ran around the interior perimeter of the cavern, forming stone rings the size of wide streets. The rings encircled the inside of the cavern at various heights above and below the ledge on which they stood, punctuated with hundreds of dark openings that appeared to be tunnels like the one they had come down. There was something about the cavern's size and shape that vaguely reminded Achmed of the tunnels that sheathed the Root of Sagia that ran along the Axis Mundi, the centerline of the Earth. It reached up into the darkness, a mute memorial to the civilization that had once pulsed through its tunnels.

A crumbling stone bridge stretched out before them across the enormous open space of the cavern. In the center of the great cylindrical space stood a giant rock formation that resembled a pedestal; its flat surface was roughly the size of the Great Hall in Ylorc. The drop on either side of the bridge caused Grunthor to shudder involuntarily. From the depths of the colossal cave a dank wind rose, stale and heavy with the odor of wet earth and desolation.

The Grandmother said nothing, but stepped out onto the bridge and crossed, never looking down into the giant circular ravine that it spanned. The dead wind rippled her dark robe, causing it to snap ominously. The two Firbolg followed her across the ravine toward the great flat formation in the center of the vertical tunnel.

As they came closer to the central rock formation they could see something suspended above it from an immensely long strand of what appeared to be spider-silk, anchored to the ceiling above out of sight. The object at the thread's terminus swung slowly back and forth across the rock plateau in a measured gait, like the slow rippling of lake tides or a sleeper's heartbeat. It glinted in the dark.

Once they stepped onto the flat surface the wind from the belly of the cavern increased; the sound of it was as heavy as the dust that hung thickly on its currents. Involuntarily Achmed drew his veils about his face; there was something within the gusts and eddies of that lifeless wind that whispered of death. The Grandmother pointed to the floor on which they stood.

Carved into the canter of the stone floor was a circle of runes in the same language that formed the words over the arch of the Earth Child's chamber. Within the circle was a large faded inlay, once beautifully rendered in exquisite detail, now stained with soot and marred by time. The symbols on the floor depicted the four winds, the hours of the day, and the seasons. Achmed closed his eyes, remembering his upbringing in a monastery in the foothills of the High Reaches of Serendair. Those symbols had been carved into the floor there as well.

He looked up to the long thread and its slowly moving weight and recognized the device as a pendulum clock; the swinging weight was silently marking the moments, the hours, the seasons of a long-dead realm, each pass of the pendulum counting another fragment of endlessly passing time. 'This is where the Thrall ritual was taught, where training took place, where dedications were consecrated,' the Grandmother said. The multiple voices had reduced to one, the thin hiss with which she had been addressing Achmed. Apparently she determined it was not necessary to impart the information to Grunthor. 'In the old days, this was a place of much traffic, great noise and distraction, of myriad vibrations to sort through. It made for a good environment in which to teach the discerning of the right heartbeat, the exclusion of the world's other sounds in the hunt for the F'dor.' Achmed nodded.

The Grandmother dark eyes ran over the giant Sergeant-Major. When she spoke again her voice was duotoned as it had been before. 'Once these mountains housed our great cities, our council chambers. The tunnels were the veins of the Colony through which its lifeblood flowed. We were that lifeblood, the *Zhereditck*; the Brethren. This place was our Colony's heart.'

'How did the fire start?' Achmed asked.

'There was no fire.'

The two Bolg stared at the Grandmother, then looked at each other. Grunthor's vision had been frighteningly clear, and the hallmarks of smoke and soot lingered still, the odor of smelting fumes still hanging, rancid, in the air around them.

The Grandmother's face remained unchanged, but her eyes glittered as if in amusement. 'There was no fire,' she repeated, looking pointedly at Achmed. 'You are Dhracian, but you are not *Zhereditck*, not Brethren. You were never part of a Colony.'

'No.' Bile rose in Achmed's throat. The Past was entombed in his memory; he had no desire to exhume it. He steeled himself for more probing about his history, but the Grandmother merely nodded.

'None of the Brethren would have used fire, even in the smallest of ways. Fire is the element of our enemy. There was sufficient heat in the pools from the wellspring.' The spoken vibrations against their skin caused an image in the minds of the two men of sulfurous ponds and hot springs bubbling in muted hues of green and lavender, of pockets of steam rising from streams that ran off from the ground beneath the Loritorium on the other side of the wall of rock. It was the same source as the darklight, the underground glow that illuminated the cavernous passageways with an mute ambient radiance. It had been the same in the tunnel along the Root.

The Grandmother pointed to the ground. 'Sit,' she said in her fricative, hissing tones. 'I will relate the tale of the death of this place.' As the two men complied, she stared at Achmed, then looked off into the darkness again. 'It is only right that you should hear it in its entirety, since in a way it is the tale of your own death as well.'

16

In the night, Oelendra woke from a dream of deep darkness. She stood as she had twenty years before with Llauron, the son of Anwyn, at the feet of her sister, Manwyn, the prophetess of the Future. She trembled in her bed as the words of the madwoman came back to her.

Beware, swordbearer! You may well destroy the one you seek, but if you go this night the risk is great. If you fail you will not die, but, as a piece of your heart and soul was ripped from you spiritually in the old land with the loss of your life's love, the same will happen again, but physically this time. And that piece it takes from you will haunt your days until you pray for death, for he will use it as his plaything, twisting it to his will, using it to accomplish his foul deeds, even producing children for him.

Oelendra bolted upright in her bed. The fur blankets were wet with sweat and tears; she was shaking violently. Slowly she crawled out of bed and made for the fire. It was dying quietly on the hearth, with but a few infinitesimal embers remaining, clinging to the gray ash. Oelendra blew on the embers; they gleamed red-orange for a moment, then settled back into the impotence of the overly weary. *There is nothing left*, they seemed to say. *Admit it; there is a limit to even the most raging fires eventually. This is what it looks like.* Oelendra did not need the reminder. She had seen the same thing each morning in the looking glass.

She had not had the dream in years, a decade even. Why now? The sword had returned; she had felt it when it came forth from the earth, only to feel its fire drift farther and farther away until it was gone. But now she could sense it once more, at sunset and with the rising sun; it was very near. Oelendra looked into the dark fireplace and sighed as the last spark burned out. She rested her head against the mantel and closed her eyes.

I'd like to alter our route to Tyrian a bit.'

Ashe craned his neck forward hear her voice better. She was dressing in the small closet, her words muffled by the ever-present timpani of the rain water dropping from the forest leaves.

'Oh?'

The curtain pulled back, and Rhapsody came into the room, lacing her boot leggings. 'I'd like to go by way of the Filidic settlement at Gwynwood. Since you trained at the Circle, I assume you can find it again – yes?'

The wind around them died down suddenly, leaving a pulsing silence. Ashe was silent for a moment as well. 'I believe so,' he said finally. 'My training was a very long time ago.'

Rhapsody blinked in surprise at what sounded like uncertainty in his voice. He had led her all the way from Canrif through Bethe Corbair, Yarim, and Canderre, into the northern part of the forest of Gwynwood itself to the lair of the dragon without a map or a misstep of any kind. He traveled the virgin woods and endless fields that reached to the horizon in all directions as if he were some vagabond lord and they were his own lands. It seemed strange that he was unsure of the way to enormous Filidic settlement at the foot of the Great White Tree, which in her estimation was somewhere nearby.

'Well, if you can't find it, I'm sure I can,' she said, shifting her pack to the other shoulder. 'I imagine if I were to concentrate I could hear the song of the Tree from here. In fact, I think we are very near the outer ring of huts now. Are we in Navarne now, or actually in Gwynwood?'

There was a long moment before he spoke. 'Gwynwood.'

Rhapsody pulled the other bootlace taut. 'I thought so. I believe I've been through this part of the forest with Gavin.'

'I can find the Circle,' Ashe said; there was a slightly terse tone to his voice. 'Why do you want to go there?'

'I need to send a message back to Ylorc, to let them know my plans have changed. I can't go off for several months of training and not at least let them know I'm safe and where I am. Llauron has messenger birds. He would send a missive to Achmed if I asked, I believe. But if this is a problem for you, I certainly understand. As I've already said, I don't want to impose.'

Ashe shook his head. 'I'll take you to the Circle; I don't wish to broach it, however. I will wait for you in the forest to the south while you send your message, and then escort you the rest of the way to Tyrian.'

Rhapsody smiled. 'Thank you,' she said. 'I'm grateful.'

Ashe turned over in the chair and sighed. He stared at the tiny window for a moment, then closed his eyes.

'If you are, you can show it by letting me go back to sleep. It's not dawn yet.'

The next morning the sun was back and the forest floor had dried sufficiently. They set out, closing the door on the little hut regretfully, and slipping in front of the waterfall once more.

They walked in near silence. Ashe's hood was up again, and it seemed to swallow his thoughts as well as his countenance. Rhapsody's own thoughts were roaming far and wide, scattering themselves before her like leaves in a high wind.

She closed her eyes and listened for the song of the Tree; she heard it almost immediately, deep and resonant, humming in the earth and the air around her. It was a slow song, full of dormant power, with much the same timbre as a yawn and stretch after a long sleep; a song of awakening.

A thrill shot through her, resonating in her skin. There was a sense of rebirth all around her, and she felt part of it, here in this place of spring. She was smiling for the joy of it when a thought occurred to her. She stopped and turned quickly to Ashe.

'You took your forester training here? From Gavin?'

'Yes.'

Rhapsody looked off through the trees to the south. 'There's a waymarker blazed in a small-leafed linden tree to the south of the Circle lands, about halfway to Tref-Y-Gartweg,' she said. 'Do you think you can find it from that limited description?'

'Yes,' Ashe said again. She thought she heard a slight smile in his voice.

Having seen his face, and found it to be pleasing, picturing him smiling was more pleasant than it had been before when it was left to the supposition of her imagination.

'Well, then, why don't we plan to meet there tonight? It's about three foot-trod leagues from here, so I should be able to make it if they don't delay me.'

'I'll wait for you.'

'Only until tonight. If I don't come, go on without me. I don't want to be responsible for keeping you from your love one more moment than necessary. I'm sure there are foresters heading south to Tyrian into whose company Llauron can put me.'

Ashe shook his head. 'Don't do that,' he said; the warmth had left his voice. 'The fewer people who know where you are going, the better, Rhapsody. I wouldn't even share that information with Llauron if you don't absolutely have to.'

Rhapsody sighed. 'You know, you and Achmed have a lot more in common than I ever realized,' she said, pulling up her hood. 'All right. I'll be discreet. Goodbye, Ashe. If I don't see you this evening, thank you again for your aid.'

'You're welcome. I will walk you as far as the hostels before we part. And you will see me this evening.'

She smiled. 'I'm certain I will – as much of you as you're usually willing to let me see.'

The wind picked up, almost swallowing his soft reply.

'I've allowed you to see far more than most. Let's hope neither of us lives to regret it.'

Outside the ring of forest huts that formed the widest circle of the Filidic settlement was a hostel, a series of small wayfarers' cottages with a main lodge between them. Rhapsody recognized the group of buildings as one of the pilgrim hostels. It was to one of these hostels that Llauron's Tanist, Khaddyr, had brought her when she first came to the Circle.

Ashe had circumvented a number of similar hostels before pointing her in the direction of one somewhat smaller building.

'Why this one?' she asked. 'Why not one of the dozen or so we passed earlier?'

'I think you might find Gavin here,' Ashe replied.

Rhapsody laughed. 'It's easier to find a specific grain of flax in a ten-stone sack than to find Gavin anywhere you are looking for him,' she said. 'He could be anywhere on this side of the continent.'

Ashe shrugged. 'Well, then he has just as much chance of being here as anywhere else,' he said nonchalantly. 'Do you need to see him specifically?'

'No. Anyone who can get me to the Tree Palace without being stopped will do.'

'Then you are in the right place. Just ask one of the foresters; I'm sure they'll be more than happy to oblige you. But Rhapsody – only one. And keep your hood up. I'll see you tonight.'

Rhapsody watched him walk away into the trees and disappear from her view. She turned back to the budding forest before her.

A few acolytes dressed in the cowlless robes of the Filidic order were walking through the hostel's grounds, chatting with each other. Rhapsody waited until they had faded off into the woods, then walked up to the door of the main building and prepared to knock.

Before her knuckles touched the door it opened. Standing there, looking surprised, was a brown-skinned man with a full, dark beard, attired in the green and brown garb of the foresters regiment, the woodsmen who served as guides to the pilgrims on their journeys to pay respect to the Circle and to the Great White Tree. Rhapsody froze so as not to rap him in the face.

'Gavin! I'm sorry.'

'Rhapsody?' Gavin stared at her, then smiled. 'What are you doing here?'

'I need to ask a favor of Llauron,' Rhapsody said. 'Do you think you might be able to get me in to see him?'

'I imagine I can,' he said, stepping out of the cottage and pulling the cord handle to shut the door behind him. 'I'm on the way to the Tree Palace now, in fact. Llauron holds a meeting of the chiefs after each new moon. You're welcome to accompany me, if you'd like.'

'Thank you,' she said, following him off the doorstep and through the glade. 'I'd like that.' She hurried to keep pace with his swift passage through the greenwood, and made note to compliment Ashe – who was about the same height as Gavin – the next time they met up on how nicely he had managed to rein in his stride to keep her from having to chase him as they walked.

17

At midday they came to the wide forest meadow that encircled the Great White Tree. Rhapsody had been following its song since the outer forest edge; what had begun as a deep humming in her soul was now a vibrant melody, slow and varying only slightly from note to note, but filled with enchanting beauty and unmistakable power.

How like Sagia's song it is, she thought, remembering the melody of the Tree on the other side of the world through which she, Grunthor, and Achmed had escaped. Only there was a youth to it, a vibrancy that Sagia didn't have. Sagia's song, on the other hand, contained a mellow wisdom, a depth of tone missing in this one. Perhaps that was because Sagia had grown in the place where the first element, ether, was born, and the Great

White Tree stood where the last one, earth, had appeared. Age and Youth, tied together by history and the Axis Mundi.

When finally they could see the Tree, Rhapsody stopped inadvertently, awed by the wonder of the sight. The Great White Tree was easily fifty feet across at the base, and the first major limb was more than a hundred feet from the ground, leading up to more branches that formed an expansive canopy blooming with new leaves, green-white with fresh life. The midday sun shone on its bark, giving it an almost ethereal glow, and casting patches of golden light in between its enormous branches, forming hazy shafts of illumination that rained down on the ground below, filled with dreamy magic.

Around its base, set back a hundred yards from where its great roots pierced the earth, had been planted a ring of trees, one of each species in the known world, some of them the last surviving example of its kind, Llauron had said.

On the other side of the meadow stood a great copse of ancient trees, vastly tall and broad, though no match for the Great White Tree in height or breadth. Built throughout and around this grove of trees was a large, beautiful house, simple yet breathtaking in design simultaneously. The sight of it brought a welcome warmth to Rhapsody's soul.

Llauron's tree palace was set at many odd angles, with sections placed high in the trees or on stilts with windows that faced the Tree. Intricate woodwork dressed the exterior, in particular the large section with a tower that reached high above the forest canopy. With the arrival of spring, the house had taken on a glow similar to the bark of the Great White Tree; it stood, gleaming quietly, in the cool shade of the tree grove around it.

A great stone wall, lined with blooming gardens that had been sleeping when last she was here, led up to a section on the side of the smaller wing, where a heavy wooden door, ancient and marred with what appeared to be salt spray, was guarded by soldiers on either side.

In the upper corner of the door was a hex sign, a circle formed by a spiral. In the door's center was the image of some sort of mythical beast, a dragon, or a griffin perhaps, that had at one time been rendered in gold leaf, but had been eroded by the passage of time and the elements. And more – Llauron had said this door had once been the entryway to an inn in Serendair, a place significant in the history of the war that was brewing when she and the others had left the Island. Seeing the door always served as a reminder of her homeland, and how lost in time she was.

'It's good to see this place again,' she said to Gavin as they passed the wide flower beds, blooming with a riot of color. The bloom on the gardens of the Filids was far ahead of the rest of the flora of the western continent. 'I've missed it.'

Gavin smiled and nodded to the guards at the door, who saluted him. 'You can live here, you know. You can stay in my cabin if you dislike the luxury of Llauron's home; I'm never there anyway.' He opened the door.

Rhapsody followed him into the entryway of the wooden palace.

Sunlight streamed through the glass panes in the vaulted ceiling, revealing the forest canopy above the towering roofline. The scent of cedar and fresh pine boughs filled the air of the oddly angled house, mixed with the spicy aroma of herbs and flowers. Rhapsody breathed it in gratefully, finding the odors soothing.

In the center hallway stood a small group of men and women in farm clothes and simple robes, talking quietly until Gavin closed the door behind him. Rhapsody recognized Khaddyr, Llauron's Tanist and chief healer, first. Khaddyr was the man the Circle elders had chosen to be the Invoker's successor one day, but now he passed his days instructing the acolytes in medicine and caring for the injured and the dying in the hospices of the Filid settlement. Despite an occasionally gruff manner, Khaddyr was a devoted healer and spent untold hours compassionately tending the patients in his care.

Talking with him was Lark, the quiet Lirin herbalist with whom Rhapsody had also studied. Lark was shy and withdrawn, and tended only to speak when asked a question or when discussing the subject with which she was most familiar.

Further down the hall stood Brother Aldo, also very shy, the healer of forest animals and chief of the physicians who assisted the local townspeople with their livestock. He was conversing with Ilyana, the chief of agriculture and the manager of Llauron's greenhouses. They stared as she pulled down her hood, as did the other Filidic chief priests.

Khaddyr finally shook his head and broke into a smile.

'Rhapsody! What a surprise! How nice to see you, my dear.'

'Thank you, Your Grace; it's nice to see you as well.' She bowed politely to the others. 'Is Llauron about?'

'Indeed he is,' came a cultured voice to her right. Llauron stood in the doorway of his offices, attired in his usual robe of simple gray, carrying a sheaf of papers.

The Invoker's face was pleasant and wrinkled, with a good many lines around his eyes, his hair silver and white with heavy brows and a matching mustache, neatly trimmed. His build was tall and somewhat slight, though he appeared in good health. His skin had the weathered look of someone who spent most of his time outdoors. 'And he is most pleased to see you, but I had no idea you were coming. Excuse me for a moment, will you, Your Graces?'

The others nodded, and Llauron handed the papers he was holding to Gavin. He gently took hold of Rhapsody's arm and led her into his study.

Once the door was closed the Invoker kissed her on the cheek and went to the fireplace where a steaming kettle hung.

'Tea, my dear?'

'No; thank you very much, though, Llauron. I'm sorry if I disturbed you, dropping in unannounced.'

'Not at all; it's a delightful surprise. Make yourself comfortable. I need to tend to this meeting of the chief priests, but I will let Gwen and Vera

149

know you are here. They can roust you up some lunch and set to preparing your room. How long can you stay, my dear?'

'I'm afraid I can't,' Rhapsody said uncomfortably. 'I'm en route somewhere, and I have to be on my way shortly.'

'I see.' The cool blue-gray eyes of the Invoker narrowed slightly, though his face remained in a pleasant expression.

'I was hoping to impose on you, and ask a favor.'

'By all means. What can I do for you?'

Rhapsody took off her gloves; her hands were sweating suddenly. 'I need to send a message home to Achmed, and I don't want to wait for the guarded caravan. I was hoping you might allow me to make use of one of your messenger birds.'

Llauron nodded thoughtfully. 'Certainly. So that's why I haven't heard from you in such a long time; you've been traveling.' Rhapsody steeled herself for the inevitable questions, but Llauron seemed to sense her unwillingness and didn't ask them. 'Well, by all means we can send a message home for you. Why don't you have a seat and rest your legs, my dear. I will have Vera bring you some lunch, and set to reprovisioning you. Do you need any herbs, any medicines?'

'No, no, thank you,' she replied, following his outstretched finger to the horsehair sofa where she sat down.

'Well, perhaps we can find you some special stores for you to take home with you anyway. I'm sure the Bolg can make use of them. Now, my dear, I want you to watch this.' He went to a door hidden among the molding and bookshelves of the far wall of his study and swung it open; Rhapsody had seen it before, and knew it led into his private office.

'Do you remember Mahb, the young ash tree in my medicine garden in the back?'

'Yes.'

'There is a hidden entrance behind him which you can enter, opening it much the same as you would open this one. The next time you come, please feel free to make use of that entrance. It will lead you into my private office, and that way if your travels are of a sensitive nature, as I sense they are this time, no one else need know of your arrival.'

'Thank you,' she said gratefully as Llauron closed the door again.

The Invoker smiled warmly. 'Think nothing of it. Now, let me attend to this meeting while you refresh yourself, and I will help you send your message when I return.'

Rhapsody had barely finished the meal Vera had brought to her in the study when Llauron came back, closing the door behind him. A small satchel was slung over his shoulder. In his hand he held a small blue-gray winterbird, a hardy flier of the type that he often used to send messages to her in Ylorc.

'Hello again,' he said, stroking the animal's tufted head. 'Have you had enough to eat?'

'More than enough, thank you, Your Grace,' she said, wiping her mouth quickly with the linen napkin from the tray.

'Here is Swynton; he's one of my best long-distance messengers; I think you've seen him before. There's a quill, an inkwell and some vellum on the desk there if you would be so kind as to write your note; he's getting a bit flustered. I woke him rather rudely and pulled him from the rookery, and I don't think he's of a mind to forgive me yet.'

'I'm sorry.' Rhapsody hastened to the desk, jotted a brief note, blotted the ink dry and rolled it into a tiny scroll. Llauron smiled, reached into his pocket and removed a small metal leg container, which he offered her. She slid the message inside and the Invoker attached it, then nodded to the concealed door in the wall.

'Let's go out through the hidden entrance to be sure you can find it again,' he said. 'Next time you come, I hope you'll have more time to stay and chat. I've missed you terribly.'

Rhapsody opened the door in the wall. 'I'd like that very much,' she said. She followed Llauron's lead to the hidden entrance, which led through a dark earthen tunnel to the quiet alcove behind the invoker's kitchen. They waited until there was no one in sight, then stepped out into the brightness of late afternoon.

'Do you think you will be able to find it again?' Llauron asked as he let the bird go.

'I believe so.'

'Good, good.' Llauron shielded his eyes as the winterbird banked into the wind, then disappeared over the towering canopy of the Great White Tree. 'There he goes. Have no fear, my dear. Your friends shall receive your message safely.'

Rhapsody smiled at the elderly man. He had not pried into her quest at all, nor asked her the content of her message. She looked into his face and read fatherly concern in his expression.

'Many thanks again, Llauron,' she said, taking his hand. 'I am sorry for my rudeness in dropping in like this and hurrying on my way.'

'Well, sometimes it can't be helped, no matter how much we'd all love to visit with you, my dear. Gwen has your provisions ready.' He pulled the satchel from his shoulder and handed it to her. 'If you'll allow me a blessing, I'll ask the One-God for his protection for your journey until you are safely back in Ylorc with your friends.'

'Thank you.' She bowed her head respectfully, and Llauron rested his hand on it, speaking a few words in Old Cymrian, the language of her childhood that was now considered an ancient cant, and used for religious purposes only.

When his invocation was finished, the old man patted her cheek gently, then lifted her chin up and studied her face.

'Be careful, my dear; I would not wish to see any harm come to you. If you need anything while in my lands, please tell whomever you meet that you are under my protection, and any aid they give you will be considered a favor to me.'

'Again, thank you, Llauron. Now, I must be off. Please thank Gwen and Vera for me.' Rhapsody reached up and put her arms around the elderly gentleman's neck, giving him a quick embrace. 'Please take care of yourself as well.'

The Invoker returned the embrace, and when he released her his eyes were shining with a fond light.

'For you, my dear, anything in the wide world. Travel well, and give my best to your friends back in Ylorc.'

When she arrived at the waymarker that night, Ashe was waiting for her.
'I see you found it.'
He chuckled. 'Yes. Were you able to send your message?'
'Yes, thank you. Ashe?'
He had turned toward the south, preparing to leave. 'Yes?'
'Thank you for not making me run to keep up.'
'You're more than welcome, Rhapsody. As I told you back in the Teeth, if you should run I doubt *I* would be able to keep up.'

Their journey south through the wakening forest was uneventful, marked by thickets of blossoming trees and endless stretches of new green leaves. Rhapsody was beginning to wonder when the world would seem like more than just the endless forest through which they traveled.

The burgeoning spring had reached down into her blood, causing her to drink in the air deeply, making her eyes shine. Rhapsody walked amid the awakening forest with a sense of awe, wondering what Elynsynos was feeling through her bond with the blossoming earth, and hoping the season was bringing the dragon comfort.

After several days she sensed that they were approaching the Lirin lands. Finally, late one afternoon, she turned to him and touched his arm.
'Ashe?'
'Yes?'
'We're in Tyrian now, aren't we?'
'Yes, I believe so.'
'In fact, I think we've been in Tyrian for several hours.'
'You may be right.'
'Well,' Rhapsody said, coming to a gradual stop, 'then this is where I should go on alone.'

Ashe said nothing, but loosed his pack and laid his walking staff on the ground.

Rhapsody dropped her gear as well, then looked up into the dark hood, hoping for a glimpse of blue eyes. She saw none.

' "Thank you" ' really isn't adequate to express my gratitude for all you've done for me,' she said, hoping she was looking up at the correct angle. 'But thank you, anyway.'

'I'd be happy to wait for you and escort you back to Ylorc,' said Ashe.

Rhapsody laughed. 'Again, thank you, but I think I've imposed on your time long enough. I assume you have a life to get back to. If not, for goodness sake, go find one.' There was no response. 'Besides, I'm hoping Oelendra will take me on as a student, and if she does, I expect to be here quite a while. And I *can* take care of myself. Really.'

'I know.'

'But if the Lord Roland invites me to his wedding, you can escort me there,' she said, still laughing. 'Our garments already match.' She held up the edge of her cloak.

A sudden cold breeze cut through the glade where they were standing, blowing the loose strands of Rhapsody's hair across her face and accentuating the thudding silence. She patted Ashe on the arm. 'Well, goodbye,' she said. 'I'd give you a kiss on the cheek, but of course I don't know where it is.'

Ashe rested a gloved finger on her lips, as if to silence her. 'If you'll allow me to guide you one last time, I'll lead your lips to where they should be.'

Rhapsody grinned, closed her eyes and tilted her chin. His hand gently realigned the angle of her face, and then, when his finger returned to her lips, she followed it upward and inside the wide hood. His hand moved away, and instead of the hardscrabble wire of his beard, her lips met the warmth of his, and clung to them for a moment. She was not really surprised.

She gave him one more swift kiss, and then bent to retrieve her gear. 'Well, goodbye,' she repeated as she stood to leave. 'Travel safely, and please be careful.'

'You as well.'

Rhapsody's face grew serious. 'And Ashe?'

'Yes?'

'Please think about what I said. About the beard.'

From beneath the hood she thought she heard a chuckle.

Rhapsody pulled up her own hood, turned and walked away. When she had gone ten or so paces she turned around. 'I hope I see you again one day.'

She could almost hear a smile in the voice that came from inside the misty cloak. 'If I were a gambling man I would wager on it.'

Rhapsody gave him a studied look. 'Yes, but we both know that you're not a gambling man.'

She smiled at him once more, then turned and was gone.

Ashe watched her go for as long as he could. He could hear her voice for some time after that, singing the whispered song of the forest trees, whistling the wordless tune of the wind across the highgrass, humming with the vibration of the earth in this place where she hoped to find answers, and that he hoped she would one day rule. Becoming one with Tyrian; learning its song, its secrets.

She was half a league gone before he had breathed out the scent of her completely and could no longer physically recall the way the fragrance of her hair reminded him of morning. It was two leagues more before he ceased to feel the warmth of the fire radiating from her. The spicy-sweet taste of her mouth and the detached softness of her kiss would remain on his lips for many weeks afterward. He knew that the image of her as she said goodbye, and the way she had looked in the shadows of the firelight, would be with him all his life.

He had not touched her, except with gloved hand and the brush of a friendly kiss. His fingers still stung, and the painful sensation spread through the rest of his body, awakening him with a sickening severity to the reality of his solitude. The agony, almost dormant, resurged violently. The dragon resented the loss of her intrinsic magic; the man missed much more.

And with the return of his loneliness and pain came the memory of what was coming, and the part he would play in it. The realization that she, too, would know pain this horrific was more than his disfigured heart could stand.

Ashe dropped to his knees and curled up until his forehead struck the ground. Holding his head in his hands he wept, breathing in the acrid dust of the forest path, soaking the ground with dragon tears, leaving thereafter a patch of obsidian flecked with stains that sparkled gold in the flickering sunlight.

18

For a long time the only sound in the great heart of what had once been the Colony was the soft whir of the ancient clock's pendulum as it swung slowly through the darkness. The elderly Dhracian drew her robe closer about herself and turned, silently surveying the empty ruin. When finally she spoke, her wordless voice echoed up the hollow cavern, then was swallowed by the thick, dank wind.

'On the day of the Colony's destruction, this place was as alive as it is dead now.' Her eyes scanned the dark passageways, as if reliving the memory of them in use. 'Death came in the night.' She closed her eyes. Achmed saw the translucent skin of her face stretch as the muscles contracted beneath it, armoring her face against the memory. The fragile veins that scored her skin grew darker with the increased flow of blood from her heart, and quickened pulse that Achmed could feel in his own skin.

'F'dor,' the Grandmother whispered, her eyes still closed. Achmed felt his blood begin to pound against his eardrums, thudding thickly in his head. Beside him he could hear Grunthor's stout heartbeat quicken as well, the pressure of the blood passing within the sergeant's veins increase. The ancient woman opened her eyes and stared directly into Achmed's own.

'Even the word angers you,' she said. The Firbolg king nodded slightly. 'Your blood sings with hatred, as does mine, because of an ancient promise made by our ancestors, the Kith. They were the sons of the wind, one of the first five races of this world.' As she spoke Achmed could feel ambient vibrations in the air of the ancient ruin begin to hum softly. The dank wind from the depths of the cave freshened a bit, as if participating in the story she was telling.

'In the days of the Before-Time four of those ancient races undertook to imprison the F'dor within the depths of the world,' the Grandmother continued. 'Each race chose a task in the undertaking. The youngest of the races, those known as *Wyrmril*, dragons, built the vault in which the F'dor would be imprisoned for all time. Out of Living Stone they built it.' The black eyes glittered ominously. 'Just as they had built the Children of the Earth.' Achmed glanced at Grunthor, but the giant Bolg said nothing. He was listening intently to the second of the Matriarch's voices, speaking to him in a deeper vibration.

'The other two races, the Mythlin and Seren, set the trap and imprisoned the F'dor spirits within the cage of Living Stone, deep within the Earth. It was an organic vault, a living prison, because the stone from which it was fashioned was alive as well. Its dual nature gave it the power to contain spirits which could pass, as F'dor can, between this world and the spirit-realm of Underworld.

'The Kith chose the task of guarding the imprisoned F'dor, acting as jailers to them. They took on this task because they had the gift of *kirai*, the ability to read, or taste, or feel, or change the currents of the air to derive knowledge from it. Their sensitivity to vibration made them able to see the F'dor, to contain them, when they had no corporeal form. They could, with the vibrations they emit, spin a web of carefully constructed noise to hold the demon-spirits in a thrall should they ever escape the cage.

'Taking on the task was a great sacrifice, because it required the sons of the wind to live forever within the domain of the Earth, away from the sky and the spirits of the air. Those guardians, that sect of the race of Kith that would act as sentinels, the keepers of the F'dor, were what evolved into the elder race known as Dhracians.'

The Grandmother's eyes narrowed; Achmed knew immediately by the change in the hum on the surface of his skin that she was assessing him with her Seeking vibration, trying to ascertain how much of the information was new to him. He dropped his own defensive *kirai* and allowed her to be aware that much of it was. He had known that the F'dor had been imprisoned by the other four races, but the means that had been used had been unknown to him until the Grandmother's tale.

She stared at him a moment longer, then her face relaxed into the same nonchalant visage she generally maintained.

'All remained as it was planned until a star fell from the sky and hit the Earth. It ruptured the vault of Living Stone, the prison of the F'dor. Before the surviving guardian Dhracians could mend the vault, some of the demon-spirits escaped. That was the beginning of the Primal Hunt, the blood-quest that all Dhracians are part of, their fealty sworn before birth, lingering even after death. It is our reason for existence, to hunt down those F'dor that escaped and destroy them. You have known this, haven't you?'

'Yes,' Achmed answered steadily. There was a change in the Grand-mother's tone that made his skin itch.

'Those Dhracians that joined the Hunt, that left their watch at the vault within the Earth and came back up into the air again to search for the F'dor, banded together in colonies, living underground but venturing up into the wind to search. Great crusades were undertaken to find and extinguish the F'dor, to locate their human hosts, hold them in thrall, and destroy both the man and the spirit. You have known this as well?'

'Yes.'

'But you are not one of the Brethren. You are *Dhisrik*, one of the Uncounted, those Dhracians not tied to a Colony. You are also Untaught; you have never mastered the Thrall ritual.'

'I've seen it performed.' The bile was back in Achmed's throat. He struggled to keep the memories that her words were calling forth in abeyance.

'You cannot remain Untaught,' the Grandmother said, her eyes still scanning the silent cavern above her. 'I will train you in the Thrall. Without it you will be unable to fulfill what was foretold.'

Achmed cleared his throat, swallowing the acid that had collected there. 'Perhaps you'd care to enlighten me as to what that was.'

The Grandmother looked down to the circle of words that enclosed the pendulum clock's symbols. 'You must be both hunter and guardian. It is foretold.'

'Bugger foretold,' Achmed growled. 'What does it mean? How can I do both at once? I know what I am to hunt, more or less. What am I supposed to guard? The vault?'

The Grandmother shook her head, still examining the runes on the floor. 'No, but it, like the vault, is of Living Stone.'

'The child.' The words came from Grunthor.

The Grandmother inclined her head. 'Yes. All that you see here, and everything else that once was the Colony, was built in this place to protect her. F'dor seek her, and her kind, crave to find them above anything else on the Earth.'

'Why?' Achmed asked.

'Because the Children of the Earth were made of animated Living Stone, like the prison vault of the F'dor. Their bones, specifically those from the rib cage, could serve as a key to unlock the vault.'

The wind from the depths of the cavern gusted through; until it did,

Achmed had not noticed how deep the silence had become. The taste of ashes was in his mouth. In distant memory he remembered being given such a key.

It was wrapped in the tendril of a vine that seemed made of glass itself, spiked with obsidian thorns. The vine had grown from the floor of the Spire, the unholy temple of the demon that had been his master in the old land.

Take it.

Achmed closed his eyes, trying to barricade his mind against the memory, but it was too strong, the horror too profound. He had plucked the key from the vine. The obsidian tendril shattered like the stem of a fragile wineglass in his hand.

He had held the key up before his half-Bolg eyes, the night eyes of a people who had risen up from the caves, and examined it closely. It appeared to made from a dark bone, its shaft curving like a rib might. It had glimmered in the darkness.

You will take this key to the base of the failed land bridge to the northern islands, his master had said. *The foundation of this bridge contains a gateway unlike any even you have ever passed through. The fabric of the Earth is worn thin there; you may experience some discomfort. If you have passed through correctly, you will find yourself in a vast desert. You will know the direction to go, and an old friend of mine will come to meet you. Once there, you will agree to the time and date when you shall serve as his guide through the gateway to this side. My only concern is that it be as soon as possible. Return to me, and I shall prepare you as his guide.*

Achmed had done as the demon demanded. That experience was the singular reason he and Grunthor had sought to escape the Island. Neither of them had any compunction about death, they did not shrink in the presence of evil, but what he had encountered in the wasteland beyond the horizon defied any horrific description of which his mind might be capable. In the face of the destruction that would ensue, the devastation they knew would come over the world, they decided instead, for the first time in either of their lives to run, to abandon all they had, to risk an eternity of something worse than death. Anything else would have been unthinkable.

The demon's last words to him rang in his ears now. Achmed could, all these centuries later, still recall the stench of human flesh in fire that clung to the demon's breath.

I want this done quickly. It will make whatever trivial catalogue of death you think yourself responsible for a mere jot, an afterthought of inconsequence. I am the true master, and you will be my thrall until you follow me willingly, or are swept away in my victory.

He had used the key instead to open the trunk of Sagia, the Oak of Deep Roots, remembering the description of a different, beloved master. Father Halphasion had used the same words when telling him about the Tree that had been their means of escape.

157

Sagia is rooted in the Lirin woods at the far crescent of the Pool of the Heart's Desire. The Lirin believe her roots stretch throughout the Earth, tying her to the trees that grow in each of the places where Time began. If ever you should walk there, my son, be reverent; it is a place of great holiness. You will sense the fragility of the universe in the vibrations that issue forth from that place, for the fabric of the Earth itself is worn thin there.

Once they had entered the Tree, and crawled along its root, and passed through the fire at the core of the Earth, the key had lost its glimmering power; it had been unable to open the other side. Now it rested, wrapped in a velvet pouch, inside a locked reliquary in the floor of his chamber in Ylorc, all but forgotten.

He shook his head to fend off the fuzz of the vibration on his skin; the Grandmother was observing him closely. A moment later she seemed satisfied; she sat smoothly down beside them, with a grace that belied her great age, and folded her hands to her lips.

'What's wrong with her?' Grunthor demanded. 'Why is she always asleep?'

For the first time the old woman looked sad. 'At the dawn of the Age of Man she was grievously injured in a bloody battle between the *Zhereditck* of a Colony in Marincaer, a province on the continent west of the wide central sea, and those polluted demon-hosts who sought to harvest her bones to free their imprisoned fellows from the vault. She is one of the last of her kind still living, perhaps even the last. There was no recourse; the stakes of the battle for her life could not have been higher, so it raged with the furor of the boiling seas. In the end the Brethren prevailed, and brought her here, irretrievably broken, to hide her for all time, deep within the impenetrable mountains.

'For centuries these mountains *were* impenetrable. The child remained here, healed from the greatest of her pain but unable to be revived, safe within the Colony that was built around her. While the Brethren lived mainly within the earth, in those days patrols still went Above, still gathered food and maintained a watch for enemies. No one came to disturb the vibrations of the wind within the peaks. Those were safe days, good days, it was said.

'Then one day the men came. The winds brought the news of them long before they were in sight. The Brethren knew they were not an invasion force by their number and the condition they were in; ragged, tattered men and women, old and young, with children in tow, many races melded in one long caravan fleeing north across the desert lands. They were struggling to survive and remain together, and it was clear that they sought refuge within the arms of the mountains as well.'

'The Cymrians,' Achmed said. 'Gwylliam and the Third Fleet.' Grunthor cleared his throat in agreement.

'We never knew what they called themselves,' said the Grandmother. 'Once their intentions were determined the Brethren went into hiding, went In, retreated within the earth and concealed all trace of the Colony's whereabouts. We are a people of silent passage, and the Colony was able to remain undetected even as the enormous population of men settled here and began burrowing within the earth themselves. They were builders of a great order; the mountains rang with the sound of their forges and the earth trembled as they formed it to fit their will.

'Through it all, the Colony seemed to remain undiscovered. There was never any contact between the Builders, as they were known to us, and the Brethren. Even when they opened a new passage just on the other side of the mountain wall, the place from which you entered the Colony, there was no sign that they knew we were here. The *Zhereditck* had built listening places within the perimeter of the Colony to maintain a surveillance, but there was never any indication that the men were aware that they shared the mountains with us.

'Before the Last Night, there seemed to be rumblings within their realm, but no one believed it in any way was directed at the Colony. The Listeners caught vibrations of strife which had become more heated over the passing of years, but it seemed part of that realm's culture. The Brethren are a simple race of simple needs, and a singular life goal. It seemed the Builders had grander aspirations, grander needs – and greater hostility. It had been that way for centuries.

'In those days I was an *amelystik*, a tender of the Sleeping Child. Tending to her was a responsibility afforded to a future matriarch of the Colony. There were several of us, each one a candidate that would be chosen eventually by destiny to be the new Grandmother upon the Old One's passing. On the Last Night, by Fate I was the one to whom the task of tending had fallen.

'I had noticed before I lay down to sleep beside her that she was restless. It was the first time I had ever seen her so, though now it is an almost constant state. My own dreams were troubling; I awoke from one of them to the taste of ash and terror in my mouth and throat. Hot smoke and caustic fumes were filling the tunnels. There was panic throughout the Colony, the *Zhereditck* choking and gasping in the poisonous air.

'Because Fate is kind even in her cruelty, I did not have to witness much of it. The last act of one of the Brethren was slamming shut the great iron doors of the Earthchild's chamber; I can still recall his face as he closed me in with her. I could see the great mass of flailing, struggling Dhracians behind him as the portal closed, separating the Earthchild and me from the burning smoke and the rest of the Colony. Even as our eyes met, my savior and I both knew what he had done was the only thing that could have been done. It was the first priority, the reason for our Colony's existence: the protection of the Sleeping Child.' The hum of the Grandmother's two voices diminished a little.

'Despite being cut off from the sight of the Colony's destruction, I lived it nonetheless, because Dhracians who live in a colony are of one mind, much like bees in a hive, or ants in a hill. I felt each agony, endured each struggle for breath, watched through thousands of dimming eyes the sight of our race's life being snuffed out. It is an image that haunts me with each waking breath. Only in sleep do I find respite from it, even now, all these centuries later.

'I waited a very long time, until the doors cooled, until the noise abated. Even on the other side of the doors the choking and muffled screams, the pounding of the ground was audible. I waited for another of the *amelystik* to come to relieve me, but no one ever did. I was a young woman myself, a girl really, and so decided there was wisdom in waiting until I could no longer feel the vibrations of death and smoke in my skin; that was a very long time. I watched the child for signs that her terror had abated; that took even longer.

'When finally the noise died away, when I could no longer feel the heat through the door or smell the soot in the air, when finally the Earthchild had fallen back into undisturbed slumber, I opened the doors. It was as I expected; the haze of lingering smoke hanging in the air of the silent tunnels, the bodies of the Brethren choking the passageways.

'I waited for the victors to break through the walls, to take the Colony now that all the *Zhereditck* were dead. No one ever came. There was no invading army, no plunderers. To this day I do not know if it was a horrific accident or a deliberate act of genocide. It is important to know this if it can be determined, because if it was intentional, if the F'dor were responsible, then they know the child's whereabouts, and they will be back for her.

'I have waited since that moment, almost four centuries ago now, but there has been no sign. Fate seems to have handed the Brethren a horrific tragedy from which were no survivors save for the Earthchild, whose life is eternal death; to protect that life an entire civilization died. And me, chosen by Fate to be Matriarch, who would never bear child; mother, guide, guardian to none of my own kind. And now you, a mere ghost.'

Achmed closed his eyes, remembering the odor of candle wax in the monastery, and the soft, dry words of Father Halphasion. *Child of Blood*, the Dhracian sage had said, *Brother to all men, akin to none*.

'You have finally arrived, although you are late in coming. There is time still; I have remained, waiting for you.'

'Perhaps you should tell us whatever prophecy you were given,' Achmed said quietly.

The memory that had clouded the Grandmother's eyes vanished, and her gaze became clear and hard.

'The words are not for you alone.'

'You said I was expected to be both hunter and guardian. I can't do either of those things if you won't tell me the prophecy.'

'No,' the Grandmother said again. The tone of the word was flat and burned against his skin. 'There must be three. It is foretold.

'One thing you must come to understand about this land, as the *Zhereditck* learned when they came here: this is the last of the places where Time was born. Speaking the words of prophecies forces their fulfillment

160

more quickly here. It must be done sparingly. Sometimes it can only be done once. Otherwise they may be fulfilled in a way they were not intended.' Achmed nodded reluctantly. 'Bring the other with you when you come back. Time grows short.'

The Grandmother rose smoothly and beckoned them to rise as well. 'Destruction is far simpler than creation, than sustenance, than deliverance; it takes but one to destroy a world. But the deliverance of that world is not a task for one alone. A world whose fate rests in the hands of one is a world far too simple to be worth saving.'

The sun was beginning to set as Grunthor finished moving the boulders in place that would conceal the entrance to the Loritorium. Achmed shielded his eyes and looked to the west to watch the coming of night. The red light of the vanishing sun was washing the leeward faces of the Teeth with wide rivers of crimson and scarlet, making the mountains seem as if they were on fire. His brain, honed from what he had just experienced, felt much the same.

The sergeant clapped his hands together, brushing the remaining dirt from his tattered goatskin gloves.

'That about does it, sir. Ready to head back?'

Achmed scanned the path from Grivven post to the high peaks, trying to locate the entrance to the Cauldron in the distance. A moment later he found it, obscured by a swarm of tiny human figures forming a disorderly mass by the gate. He rolled his eyes.

'*Hrekin*,' he swore. 'The second wave of ambassadors are here from the outlying lands, as well as some of those returning from Roland with answers from their lords. They made better time than I thought they would in the muddy terrain.'

Grunthor loosed a long sigh. 'Can't be helped, I guess, sir,' he said, pulling off the sweat-soaked gloves and stuffing them in his pack. 'Kingly duties, so to speak. May as well get it over with.'

Achmed watched a moment longer. There was a dark mist clinging to one area of the group, an afternoon shadow, most likely, and nothing more. Nevertheless his mind was clouded with the images of desolation and death from which he had just come.

'When did Rhapsody say she would be returning?' he asked, still shading his eyes as the glory of the bloody sunset began to dim to a soft pink, the threat of a pallid gray looming with the onset of dusk.

'She didn't,' Grunthor answered. 'If all worked out the way her message said, she should be in training about now. Might take a while.'

Achmed scowled. 'Let's get back,' he said, shouldering his pack. 'I have a missive I need to send to Tyrian with the next mail caravan.'

19

The border watchers of Tyrian had been following her for more than an hour when Rhapsody finally decided to call a halt to the game. She had been aware of their notice, several miles after she and Ashe had parted. They had come down silently from the trees, unseen, to observe her as she walked, whistling, through their forest. She had expected them to show themselves fairly early on, but instead they moved silently behind her, covering the ground with no more disturbance than the wind. If she hadn't been in tune with the song of the forest she would never have known they were there.

Finally she stopped in the middle of the forest path. 'If you're concerned about my presence here, come out and greet me,' she said, looking at the four different spots she knew they were standing, hidden. 'My intentions are peaceful.'

After a moment one of the guards came out, a tall, broad-shouldered Lirin woman with eyes the same color as her fawn-brown hair. Those eyes were large and almond-shaped, her body lithe and long of line, with skin that bore the marks of the sun and the elements in its hue; she was a perfect specimen of her race. She had been standing in the spot where Rhapsody's gaze had come to rest.

'I am Cedelia,' she said in Orlandan, the common tongue of Roland. 'Are you looking for something in particular?'

'Yes, actually,' Rhapsody answered, smiling. 'I have come to see Oelendra.'

The woman's face betrayed no reaction. 'You be in the wrong part of Tyrian for that.'

'Well, can I get there from here?'

'Eventually,' answered Cedelia. She moved slightly, and Rhapsody saw she was returning an arrow to her quiver. Rhapsody had not seen the bow until just then. 'You be more than a week's journey away. 'Twill be easiest if you head west through Tyrian City. Who are you?'

The Singer bowed slightly. 'My name is Rhapsody,' she answered respectfully. 'If it would be preferable to you, we can speak in the Lirin tongue.'

'Whichever language you are more comfortable with is fine.' The Lirin woman's face betrayed none of the hostility that Rhapsody had seen humans occasionally exhibit toward those of mixed blood. She leaned to the east slightly and emitted a series of birdlike whistles. Rhapsody heard a faint rustling in the trees and nothing more. 'I will escort you as far as Tyrian City.'

'Thank you,' Rhapsody said. 'It will be good to have a guide.' Cedelia gestured to a barely visible trail off the forest path, and Rhapsody followed her into the greenwood, amid the sounds of birdsong and the wind in the trees of Tyrian.

They walked in virtual silence for the entire journey. Rhapsody tried several times to make conversation, and though Cedelia answered her pleasantly, she never sought to continue the dialogue. Eventually Rhapsody recalled that her mother tended to only speak when there was a need to say something significant, too, so she lapsed into a state of quiet contentment, satisfied to observe the beauty of spring as it came to the forest.

The leaves were in full bud now, lacy foliage appearing with the eagerness of a toddler's smile, green and silver, fresh from the long sleep of winter. Rhapsody felt her heart opening as she passed through the woods, following her silent chaperone. There was something renewing about being here, in the land of her mother's people, though the Lirin of the wood were not Liringlas, as her mother had been. It was an honesty, a simplicity about the life they led; each village they passed seemed fruitful and peaceful, the people they encountered were pleasant and seemed to treat each other well. There was joy here, or something close to it. Tyrian felt like paradise. Rhapsody felt her inner fire grow steadily day by day.

Cedelia sat the watch each night. Rhapsody had offered to share it with her, but she had politely declined, citing no need for sleep. Rhapsody's own need for sleep was less than that of her Bolg friends, and far less than Jo's, but even she required a few hours' rest, where Cedelia did not. So each night she climbed awkwardly into her bedroll, feeling the eyes of her guardian escort on her. She hoped she would be more welcome at Oelendra's.

On the fourth day it rained, heavy, pelting rain that stung as it fell. Even Cedelia felt the need to take shelter from the storm, and led Rhapsody into a cottage that she would not have seen had it not been pointed out to her. Inside it was sparsely furnished with a few cots and tables, and stores of dried food. Cedelia pried open a chest and offered Rhapsody some salted venison strips. She accepted so as not to appear rude. Finally she decided to attempt conversation once more.

'What is this place?'

Cedelia looked up over her food. 'One of the houses of the border watchers.'

'It's cleverly hidden. I wouldn't have seen it.'

"Tis the point; you're not supposed to.'

Rhapsody wilted under the cool tone. 'Have I done something to offend you, Cedelia?'

'I know not. Have you?' The fawn-colored eyes narrowed slightly; otherwise her expression didn't change. She took another bite of meat.

'I don't understand,' Rhapsody said, color rushing to her cheeks. 'Please explain what you mean, Cedelia. We've been traveling together for four days and I still have no idea what's bothering you.'

Cedelia put down her food. 'You were seen with a man in a hooded gray cloak five days ago at the Outer Forest lip.'

Rhapsody looked puzzled. 'Yes.'

'Who was that?'

Her heart began to pound. 'Why?'

'Because a man in a hooded gray cloak led a raid on a Lirin village on the eastern edge of the Outer Forest lip that same night. The settlement was burned to the ground.'

Rhapsody leapt to her feet. '*What?*'

Like lightning a bow was pointed at her heart, the arrow nocked. 'Sit down.' Rhapsody obeyed. 'Fourteen men, six women, and three children perished in that raid.'

Rhapsody began to tremble. 'Gods.'

'Hardly; try again.' Venom dripped from Cedelia's voice. 'Who was that man?'

'His name is Ashe.' Her voice was barely above a whisper.

'Ashe? Ashe what?'

Rhapsody looked out the window at the greenwood. 'I don't know.'

'Do you always kiss people you don't know?'

She looked back at Cedelia. 'No.'

Cedelia nocked a second arrow on the string next to the first one. 'Why are you really here?'

Rhapsody's glance hardened. 'I told you the truth. I'm looking for Oelendra.' Cedelia continued to stare at her. 'What are you going to do now?'

'I told you the truth as well. I am escorting you as far as Tyrian City. What happens after that will be up to Rial to decide.'

When they left the house of the border watchers Cedelia returned the arrows to her quiver and slung her bow across her back.

'You are being covered from all angles. 'Twould be decidedly unwise for you to try anything untoward.'

Rhapsody sighed. Her vision of paradise had dimmed considerably with the knowledge that they had been followed all along, that the Lirin thought she might be responsible for the heinous attack on the village. She could not allow herself to even think about Ashe.

In the first joyful hours of her walk when she was alone, communing with the forest through her music, she had learned much about the place. The forest of Tyrian was more than a hundred miles wide east to west; it was closer to two hundred going north to south. On its western edge it bordered the sea, running north to the Roland seaside province of Avonderre and south to the lands of the Lirinwer, the plains Lirin.

The wonderful impression she had of the attitude and plight of the Lirin who lived in Tyrian appeared to be borne out by what she had learned from the wood itself. It seemed macabre that she was now a virtual prisoner of unseen jailers, on her way to judgment by someone named Rial. Elynsynos had certainly not mentioned him, nor had Ashe. At the thought of Ashe Rhapsody went cold again.

'This way,' said Cedelia politely. Rhapsody shouldered her pack and followed her down the muddy trail, rainwater dripping off the new leaves like tears.

Two more days of silent travel through thick vegetation brought them in sight of the city. Rhapsody had seen the guard towers long before she realized what they were; a wall of ancient heveralt trees, a cousin species to the Great White Tree, had been set on a hill-like rise and reinforced with a wide stone and wood barricade at their bases, from which ladders ascended into the platforms that connected their upper canopies.

The wall stretched north for as far as she could see, giving her the impression that the size of Tyrian City as akin to that of Easton. Before the wall lay a wide and steeply sided ditch, slick moss coating the bottom. Hundreds of Lirin guards, men and women, traversed the connected aerial platforms through the trees as effortlessly as walking on the earth. The sight filled Rhapsody with wonder and sadness. The possibility that she would ever be welcome in this marvelous place was becoming more remote by the moment.

Half a mile or so outside the clearing that surrounded the city, Cedelia took a turn off course and led her into another hidden structure similar to the border watcher's house. It was larger and better appointed inside, with no sleeping bunks but several long tables and many chairs. The windows each contained a mounted crossbow stand and windowbox-like vessels that held hundreds of bolts. A weapons rack with impressive contents took up the rest of the wall that the door was in. Cedelia drew forth her bow and nocked an arrow, holding the weapon ready but not pointing it at her. 'Take a seat,' she said.

Rhapsody laid down her own bow and removed her pack, dropping it onto the table. She pulled out a roughhewn pine chair and sat down, sighing heavily.

They waited that way, Rhapsody and her guard, for more than an hour. Just when she was about to ask for water the door opened and a tall, silver-haired man came into the longhouse. He wore the same forest-colored clothing as Cedelia, with a dark red cape and a polished wood buckle on his belt. His face was lined with age but tanned and healthy, and his eyes smiled as he looked at her. He turned to her guard and nodded politely.

'Thank you, Cedelia.' Cedelia slung her bow and returned her arrow to the quiver on her back. She took her leave silently and quickly, closing the door behind her.

The man crossed the room and came to a halt in front of her. 'How do you do?' he said, extending a hand to her and assisting her in her effort to rise. 'I am Rial. I hope Cedelia has treated you well.'

'Yes, thank you. My name is Rhapsody.'

Rial looked her over intently but in a way she did not feel invaded by. Then he released her hand and pulled out a chair next to the one she had been sitting in. Rhapsody sank into her seat again, her back aching at the hardness of the wood. 'You have a beautiful voice,' Rial said as he sat down.

Rhapsody looked at him in surprise. 'Excuse me?'

'I heard you singing a week or so ago, at least I assume that was you.'

'You have been following us?'

'Nay,' said Rial with a smile. 'I've been here in Tyrian City. There are some things that transcend distance in Tyrian. Music of the kind you were making is one of them.'

Rhapsody flushed with embarrassment. 'Does that mean everyone heard me, or just you?'

His smile grew warmer. 'I'm afraid 'twas everyone. 'Tis nothing to be embarrassed about. It may have been the forest's way of telling its people something they need to know. Tyrian is more than a wood, 'tis a living entity; it has a soul. Your music delighted the soul of Tyrian in a way it never has been before. Tyrian decided to share it with its people.'

Rhapsody ran a hand awkwardly over her hair. 'Well, I'll try to keep that in mind before I open my mouth again.'

'I hope you won't,' said Rial. ''Twould be a shame if you became self-conscious about something that might be useful to the people of your blood. You are Liringlas, are you not?'

'My mother was.'

'Aye, I thought as much. Well, 'tis an honor to meet you then, Rhapsody. I have only seen Liringlas visitors once before, when some of Cymrian descent came from Manosse to pay homage to the Great White Tree and stopped to pay a visit to Queen Terrell.'

'Queen Terrell is the ruler here, then?'

'She was,' said Rial, his dark eyes shining. 'She has been dead three hundred years now. Her son's reign has come and gone as well; he died quite young, leaving no heir.

'At the moment the Lirin have no sovereign. I serve as Lord Protector. There are three others who serve as liaisons to each of the other Lirin factions that were subject to the queen as well, the Lirinwer of the plains to the southeast, the sea-Lirin to the southwest, and the Manossian contingent. The Manossians have their own government, but see themselves ultimately as subjects of Tyrian, or at least they did when there was a ruler. Now we are a fragmented people, almost as divided as Roland. 'Tis a shame, really.'

Rhapsody didn't know what to say. She had expected to be interrogated for the murderous act of pillage that Cedelia quizzed her about, and instead she was receiving a lesson in Tyrian politics from the Lord Protector himself. Her forehead came to rest in her hand, her elbow on the table.

Rial rose and went to the door. He whistled a strange trill, and a moment later a guard came with a skin of water. Rial thanked him and brought it to her.

'Here; I can see you are overwhelmed. Why don't you have a drink and rest for a moment?'

Rhapsody accepted the skin, smiling. 'Thank you. You're right; I am overwhelmed. I'm horribly sorry to hear about the raid on the Lirin village, but I didn't have anything to do with it, I really didn't.'

166

Rial nodded. 'I didn't think that you did. These border incursions have been going on for years, Rhapsody; your arrival in Tyrian had unfortunate timing. What can you tell me about your companion?'

Rhapsody thought for a moment. She was still unsure, after all these months in this new land, whom she should trust. Ashe had asked her to be his ally, and yet if she had inadvertently led him into Tyrian and he was guilty of the raid, she was responsible as well. She owed it to the people of her blood to help them find the aggressor.

On the other hand, if for some reason Rial and the Lirin were involved in something corrupt, something to do with the demon Elynsynos spoke of, she might be responsible for delivering an innocent man into evil hands. Lord Stephen had said that his wife had died in a brutal raid at Lirin hands. Achmed's policy of total isolation, trusting none but themselves, was looking better all the time.

'Not much that's accurate, I'm afraid. He calls himself Ashe. He guided me here from Ylorc – er, Canrif. He has done nothing to harm me, or anyone else in my time with him. He always walks hooded and cloaked. I have no plans to see him again.'

Rial nodded again. 'And why is it that you have come to Tyrian now?'

'I am looking for Oelendra.'

'Would you mind if I asked the reason?'

Rhapsody looked at him directly. 'No, I don't mind. I'm hoping she will train me in the sword.'

Rial leaned back and looked thoughtful. 'And how did you come to hear about Oelendra? She does not commonly train those outside of Tyrian anymore.'

Rhapsody thought of Elynsynos and smiled to herself. 'Someone thought she would be the best person to train me in the sword I carry.'

'You have a unique kind of sword?'

'Yes.'

'Interesting. I am a bit of an aficionado of the sword myself. May I see it?'

Rhapsody considered the wisdom of fulfilling his request, then decided to grant it. She prepared herself in case she had to fight her way out of the longhouse. Rial looked like a formidable adversary, and she would probably have to unleash all of her fire lore to get by him.

'Very well,' she said, and drew Daystar Clarion.

The sword came forth with a blinding flash that filled the cabin with stark white light, then settled into the flames that licked up the glowing blade. Rial's eyes opened wide in shock and he rose slowly to his feet, unable to take his eyes off the weapon.

'Daystar Clarion,' he said. His voice was filled with awe.

'Yes.'

After a long moment he tore his eyes away from the sword and stared at her. 'You are the Iliachenva'ar.'

167

'I believe so, if that's what this sword's bearer is called,' Rhapsody said, trying not to sound flippant.

Rial lapsed into amazed silence again. Finally he spoke.

'I will take you to Oelendra now.'

20

Rhapsody's new guide was a man named Clovis, whose hair and eye color were so close to that of Cedelia that they could have been twins. He had a readier smile, however, and Rhapsody felt slightly more at ease with him as she was led from the longhouse and onto a southerly path. Rial touched her arm as she prepared to go.

'Rhapsody, I hope you know that you are welcome here in Tyrian. The forest itself has made that abundantly clear, and I hope I have as well.'

'Thank you,' she answered, smiling up at the Lord Protector. 'Now let's see if Oelendra agrees with you.'

'She will, no doubt. Oelendra has her eccentricities and her temper, but she is a wise woman. She wants more than anything to see the world safe and at peace; remember that.'

Rhapsody tried to keep her smile from fading as Rial bent over her hand and turned to leave. She remembered Ashe's comments about his friends finding Oelendra to be a harsh, humorless taskmaster, but decided that whatever lack of humor she possessed, it could not be as bad as Achmed's. She watched as Rial faded into the trees, then followed Clovis down the forest path.

After an hour's walk they came to the edge of a large clearing. It was a vast garden, almost a park, with sparsely spaced ornamental trees, tall grasses, and wildflowers giving it a feel that was more akin to a wild land than a formal garden. But here and there were touches that showed the work of Lirin hands. A well-manicured path, a bed of flowers whose colors were too perfectly suited to be the haphazard choice of nature, the lack of any underbrush all pointed to guidance and intervention rather than random growth.

Off the neatly trimmed path, not far into the garden, stood a group of children, all with wooden swords, laughing at a joke by the sole adult crouched in their midst. Rhapsody turned to Clovis, who had stopped. He gestured toward the children.

They were gathered around an older woman with long silver-blond hair touched with streaks of gray and white. She wore no armor and bore no weapon, and was dressed in a simple white shirt and brushed leather trousers that looked as if they had seen much wear. The woman spoke in soft tones to the children, patiently adjusting one child's hold on his toy sword. Then she stopped as if she had heard something.

The woman stood, saying something in a low voice to the children before she began to approach Rhapsody. Rhapsody caught her breath as the woman crossed the garden, struck by the sight of her. She had shoulders almost as broad as Achmed or Ashe did, and coloring that made Rhapsody's hands grow clammy; the silver-blond hair, the rosy-gold skin, the long, thin limbs: She was Liringlas, one of the People of the Fields, a Skysinger, the same kindred as Rhapsody's own mother, a breed of Lirin that Rhapsody had seen no other traces of since long before she left the Island.

'Mhivra evet liathua tyderae. Itahn veriata.'

Rhapsody felt her heart miss a beat. Spoken in Ancient Lirin, the words were from another time: *In you two rivers meet. How appropriate.* The accent, the dialect, were exactly as Rhapsody's own mother would have spoken, and the metaphor of joining rivers was one from Serendair used to describe those Lirin of mixed blood.

'Welcome,' the woman said as she came close, smiling. Rhapsody found herself unable to move or answer, as a tangle of old emotions rose up in her heart. She opened her mouth to speak but no sound came forth. Her eyes met the eyes of the woman and found the memory of a time long forgotten in them. A look of wonder spread slowly over her face, following the path of a tear that fell, unnoticed. 'I am Oelendra.' The woman placed her hand on Rhapsody's shoulder in a gesture of tenderness. 'I am most happy to see you.'

She finally found her voice. 'Rhapsody. I am Rhapsody,' she said. 'Oelendra, like the fallen star.' An infinitesimal musical sound danced in the air as she spoke the word, whirling like an invisible funnel cloud until it shattered lightly, unseen, on the wind. 'They didn't tell me you were Liringlas.' She smiled, oblivious to her own tears.

'And they didn't tell me you were the Canwr that we heard filling the forest with music, but that makes sense. You must have traveled very far, and I can see you are weary. Come with me and I will get you something to drink and a place to rest yourself.'

Rhapsody considered the woman's statement. She had not rested for more than two hours at a time since she had entered the woods of Tyrian; by her best recollection that had been eight days ago. The call of the woods and the deepening magic all around her had lulled her, as if in a dream, and she had not felt the need for rest until now. Now it was as if she could finally let down a burden she had been carrying for a long time, in a place where it would be safe. Exhaustion roared through her, unchecked.

'I am a little tired,' she admitted.

'Thank you, Clovis.' Rhapsody's guide nodded, and walked back up the path, disappearing, as Rial had, into the woods. Oelendra took Rhapsody's arm. 'Come along; you're exhausted, no doubt.' She led Rhapsody across the meadow and through an arbor of flowering trees, until they came to

169

the edge of a field near the hollow of a hill. There a small turf-roofed house stood, close to the steepest part of the hillside. It had white plastered walls which revealed the wooden framework of the building, glass windows with heavy shutters, and a stone chimney which presently produced little smoke. Oelendra led her inside through the sunken front door.

'Please, sit down, make yourself at home.' She crossed over to a rather large fireplace, where a small pot hung over the low embers. 'Sit anywhere.'

Once inside, Rhapsody saw that much of the house was also sunken, built at a level below the ground, which made it far larger on the inside than it appeared on the outside. They had entered through a small foyer into a much larger room which seemed to make up almost half of the house.

Like Oelendra herself, the furniture was not what Rhapsody would have expected. The house was starkly decorated, with little in the way of comfort or ornamentation. Two hard-backed chairs were positioned before the large stone hearth which served as the inside wall of the room. A sofa was placed nearby, and in the corner was a simple willow rocking chair. At the other end of the room was a solidly built dark pine table, with two long benches and two thick chairs. Aside from this, a series of large pillows, none of which appeared to match, seemed to serve as the rest of the furniture. The weapons rack near the door held a battered steel sword, without ornamentation, and a strange curved bow made of white wood.

Rhapsody sank gratefully into the willow rocking chair and sighed in relief. Her feet burned from all the walking she had done. She looked about the room as her host busied herself at the hearth. The room had a high ceiling open to roof, along the edge of which ran a balcony. The large fireplace had several iron doors that seemed to be ovens for baking, and a central hearth in which a small set of logs presently burned in low embers.

The walls inside the house were like those of the exterior, whitewashed with wooden framework exposed. A ladder led up to a loft, which overlooked the large room. The floors were bare except for a single rug woven in a complex geometric design. Rhapsody smiled. Without knowing why, here at last she felt at ease and at home. Oelendra turned around and walked over to her.

'Here, this may warm your heart a little,' she said as she handed Rhapsody a large ceramic mug. It was hot to the touch, but Rhapsody welcomed the warmth in the cool spring air. The mug was filled with a golden-red liquid from which the rich smell of spice wafted forth. Rhapsody took a sip, and her mouth was at once filled with the sweet taste of a gentle mead and oranges mixed with a medley of hibiscus, rosehips, cloves, and cinnamon blended with other subtler spices. The flavor brought back a wealth of memories she had all but forgotten.

'*Dol mwl*,' she said softly, closing her eyes and smiling sadly. 'My mother used to give this to us after we came in from playing on a cold day.'

'Aye, I thought perhaps you knew it,' Oelendra replied, 'though I would hazard that your mother used honey rather than mead. Mine did.'

'I haven't had this since I was a child.'

'Humans just don't appreciate it. Even the Gwenen and Lirin of the wood couldn't make it. They always used sickly sweet mead rather than the mellow, lighter variety. The only good *dol mwl* I could get outside of the longhouses was at the Crossroads Inn in the old land, and that was a long time ago. Now I'm afraid it has faded from our culture, swallowed by the sea along with countless other treasures. Alas, I am the only one who seems to enjoy it, or at least I was until you came.'

'They don't know what they're missing,' Rhapsody said. She opened her eyes and looked at the woman in front of her. Oelendra sat on the arm of one of the chairs with an air of ease that made Rhapsody relax. Her gray eyes gleamed as she waited comfortably through the silence that might have seemed awkward in other company.

She's beautiful, Rhapsody thought, but the warrior's build was far from the traditional feminine figure. Her shoulders were broad and well muscled, her skin, though rosy, was not the skin of youth, but carried the fine lines of age and years in the wilderness. Each movement showed a gentleness of spirit and an easy confidence that held no trace of arrogance. In her silver eyes Rhapsody thought she saw a nostalgic sadness. She tried to imagine how many generations those eyes had watched be born and die.

'You must have a million questions,' Oelendra said, bringing Rhapsody back from her musings. 'Let's start answering some. I am Oelendra Andaris, the last Iliachenva'ar before you. I've been expecting you.'

'You have? How did you know I was coming?'

''Twas more a matter of hoping than knowing, Rhapsody. I've been waiting for two decades for the sword to return. Sooner or later I knew it would come back, and that meant the Iliachenva'ar would come with it. I have to say, that she is a woman, Cymrian, and most especially Liringlas does my heart good.'

'How did you know I was from the old world?'

Oelendra smiled. ''Tis written all over you, dear, but besides that, I have not seen another Liringlas since I landed here myself. There were some that sailed with the Second Fleet that landed in Manosse, I've been told, but other than that, 'tis you and me. We're all that is left of what was once a vast and noble line, some of the greatest warriors and scholars the world has ever seen.'

Rhapsody looked uncomfortable. 'You are, Oelendra, but please don't ascribe those things to me. I'm a peasant, and my mother was a farm wife.'

'Nobility has nothing whatsoever to do with social class or family lineage, Rhapsody, it has to do with the heart. Tell me why you're here.'

'I came to learn the sword, if you will teach me,' Rhapsody said, taking another sip of *dol mwl*. 'I don't really deserve to be carrying such a weapon unless I can use it well.'

'The first characteristic: a desire to be worthy of the weapon,' said

Oelendra, more to herself than to Rhapsody. Her gray eyes began to shine with a distant light. 'And what do you intend to do with this new knowledge, should I agree to impart it to you?'

'I'm not sure, exactly; I know that sounds inane, but I believe Daystar Clarion came to me for a purpose. Perhaps I can help mend the rift between the Cymrians, or the Lirin, and help put a stop to these terrible border incursions.'

'An aspiration to serve a higher cause,' murmured Oelendra. 'And what if you die in the attempt?'

'I expect to, actually,' Rhapsody said, smiling slightly. 'I have a sense my time is limited, despite everything I've heard about Cymrian immortality. I hope to go down doing something worthwhile that will leave this place a little better than it was when I arrived here.'

'The acknowledgment that there are things greater than one's self, and a willingness to give one's life for them,' said Oelendra softly. Her voice grew stronger as she put one last question to Rhapsody. 'And what if you decide to use this power against the Lirin?'

'You have my permission to dispatch me immediately, and without argument. I would never betray my own people.'

'A loyalty and devotion to cause and kin,' said Oelendra. Her eyes cleared and she smiled finally. 'Nay, Rhapsody, I'm afraid you're wrong. You are no peasant, you are definitely Liringlas in your soul, whatever your father may have been. And you were born to be the Iliachenva'ar. I will be honored to train you.'

'Perhaps you had best tell me what it means to be the Iliachenva'ar,' Rhapsody said awkwardly. 'I don't want to promise to be something I don't even understand.'

'Fair enough,' said Oelendra, settling back with her mug in the chair. '*Iliachen*; how would you translate that?'

'Light into darkness, or from darkness.'

'And of course you are familiar with the suffix "*var*"?'

'Bringer, bearer.'

'Aye. So, obviously, the word means "bringer of light into a dark place."'

'Or from one.'

'Exactly.' Oelendra looked pleased. 'In the old world, Daystar Clarion had two other names, *Ilia*, meaning Light, and Firestar. I'm sure you've noticed why that second appellation came about. So do you now understand the role of the Iliachenva'ar?'

'I'm to be a lamplighter?'

Oelendra laughed; it was the merry, bell-like sound that her mother's voice had made in happy times, and Rhapsody felt her throat constrict suddenly. 'Well, the sword would certainly make that job easier. You are suited to this role perfectly, Rhapsody. The Iliachenva'ar seeks to bring light into places and situations that are tainted and despoiled by evil.'

Rhapsody shifted uncomfortably in her chair. 'I'm not so sure, Oelendra. I don't know if I would recognize evil if I saw it. You see, my judgment is not always the best. People who are generally considered monstrous or subhuman are some of the people I love the most, while I seem to be distrustful of those in regal positions and of honorable reputation. I'm not good at discerning who I should trust and when I should keep my mouth shut. I could be very dangerous in a position like that. In fact, perhaps I should just give the sword back to you.'

'Oh? To do what with?'

Blood rushed to her cheeks. 'I – I don't really know; I mean, you were the Iliachenva'ar before.'

'And you think I should be again?'

'I guess that's for you to decide, Oelendra. I didn't mean to be presumptuous.'

The Lirin warrior smiled. 'You're not being presumptuous, Rhapsody, you're misinformed. That's easily correctable; you just need information.'

Rhapsody sighed. 'Of all the things I have been searching for since I've been in this land, Oelendra, I find that information, honest information, is the hardest commodity to come by. People are unwilling to part with it as if it were the family silver. That and trust.'

'You're more discerning than you think, Rhapsody. Let me tell you three things. First, I understand completely how you feel, and will accommodate you in any way I can as far as information goes. Ask me anything you want, and I will tell you everything I know about it without hesitation.'

Rhapsody's breath came out in a whistle. 'Thank you. I'm not sure if I can handle that or not.'

'You can. Second, what you see as the inability to tell the difference between what everyone else sees as good and evil is uncommon wisdom. Not everything that is good is beautiful, and not everything that is beautiful is good. Generally that rule is imparted in childhood to keep pretty girls from becoming vain, and make those less blessed feel better. The truth of it goes far deeper; what is good and valuable is not always visible to the eye. That goes for evil as well.'

'Are there specific duties to being Iliachenva'ar, other than just brightening a room and scaring off unspecified evil?'

Oelendra laughed again. 'Well, traditionally the Iliachenva'ar acts as a consecrated champion; that is, an escort or guardian to pilgrims, clergy, and other holy men and women. The sect does not matter. You are to protect anyone who needs you in the pursuit of the worship of God, or what someone thinks of as God.'

Rhapsody nodded. 'And the third thing you wanted to tell me?'

Oelendra's face lost its smile. 'Daystar Clarion chooses who it wishes to carry it, not the other way around. It has chosen you, Rhapsody. I can't be the Iliachenva'ar, even if I wanted to, which I do not.'

'Why did you stop being the Iliachenva'ar, if you don't mind my asking?'

The older woman stood up slowly and went to the hearth; she bent as stirred the embers beneath the pot of *dol mwl*. From a barrel beside the fireplace she ladled water into a dented kettle and hung it beside the *dol mwl*. Rhapsody could see the muscles in her brawny back tighten as she stood back up and turned to face her. A sharp look was in her eyes.

'I've never told anyone the story before, Rhapsody. I suppose I do owe it to you, however.'

'You owe me nothing, Oelendra,' Rhapsody blurted, her face flaming red. 'I'm very sorry to have pried into something that was none of my business.'

'No one else has ever asked, largely because they think I'm insane.' Oelendra came back to her chair and sat down heavily. 'I had been railing at them for centuries, trying to tell them what was living in their midst, what had followed them from the Island, but they refused to listen.'

'The Cymrians?'

'The Cymrians, at first, then the Lirin.' Oelendra disappeared into the kitchen and came back with a pair of knives and a black cast-iron pot filled with potatoes and onions. She put it on the pine table and went to the bins by the door, rummaging and coming up with dried meat, carrots, and barley, which she deposited next to the pot. Rhapsody rose and came to the table. She pulled out a chair next to the one Oelendra had sat down in and picked up one of the knives. With a practiced hand she set about peeling the potatoes while Oelendra sliced onions savagely, an outward manifestation of the look in her eyes. When she spoke, however, her voice was calm.

'You see, Rhapsody, when the Cymrians left Serendair, I was the protector of the First Fleet, the people who were sent initially to settle and build up the place Merithyn had found. He reported that the land he had discovered was uninhabited, except, of course, for Elynsynos, the dragon.

'Gwylliam, the last of the Seren kings, the Visionary, kept the army back until the third and final sailing, since they wouldn't be needed in an uninhabited place. He had no desire to make the dragon feel threatened, or to appear that we intended to fight or invade its land. We had been invited, and so we had come in peace, the architects, the masons, the carpenters, the physicians, the scholars, the healers, the farmers. Our passage was difficult, we lost Merithyn and many others along the way, but the land welcomed us and, once we found our home, the plight of the First Fleet was easy, certainly compared to those who came later.' Oelendra tossed the onions into the pot with the potatoes Rhapsody had peeled and chopped, then began to strip the meat.

''Twas more than a year before they landed, the Third Fleet, almost fifty more before we met up again. That was a day of great celebration; it wasn't until later that the hard feelings emerged. And in all the revelry and jubilation of being reunited with our countrymen, I felt suddenly uneasy. Deep within me I could feel it, the smell of the same kind of demon that had been responsible for the Great War, that had almost destroyed the island centuries before. You have heard of F'dor?'

'Yes, a bit, but please tell me about them anyway.'

'The F'dor were one of the Firstborn races, like dragons; one of the first five to walk the earth. They were naturally tied to fire, dark fire, and innately evil, a deeply twisted, spiritlike people who sought only destruction and chaos, the masters of manipulation, spending eternity trying to figure out ways to get around the limits of their own power. They are gifted liars, able to take pieces of the truth and mix them in with half-truths and outright lies, and be convincing with the whole. Because they are noncorporeal they can bind themselves to the souls of men and women, becoming an intrinsic part of their host.

'Sometimes the binding is slight and temporary; the victim performs some act he is not aware of and is never bothered again. Sometimes they bind to a soul, owning it for the Future, payable upon the death of the victim.

'And then, by far the worst kind, there is the taking of a true host, the individual who it becomes. It is more than possession, it is a complete insinuation of the demon into the victim. It lives in that body, growing stronger as the host does, taking on other forms as it grows more powerful or when the host dies. And it is, to most, including myself, indiscernible. I had suffered greatly at the hands of these creatures, Rhapsody, as did many that I loved. And as soon as we met up with the Third Fleet I knew that one had come with them. It had bound itself to someone on the last ship out. Gwylliam had failed in his guardianship. 'Twas his task to keep the evil from following us. But no one believed me.'

Rhapsody shuddered. 'That must have been terrible. What did you do?'

'When the Lord and Lady were chosen to rule over the reunited Cymrian people, I warned both Gwylliam and Anwyn of what I felt. They dismissed it, and nothing particularly bad had happened, so my warnings were laughed off as paranoia.

'What they didn't understand was just because something like that is out of sight, doesn't mean it's gone. More than likely 'tis hiding in the dark, festering, growing stronger. But Anwyn and Gwylliam seemed to feel their wisdom was borne out. The F'dor never surfaced; they ruled in relative peace for three centuries, until it all fell apart one night in Canrif, the place now called Ylorc. Whether the demon played some part in that, or if 'twas just their own folly, will never be known. The war came, and it went on for centuries, Rhapsody, more than seven hundred years. All along I had been training champions, sending them forth to find the demon. None of them ever returned.' Oelendra threw the meat into the pot and began to clean the barley.

'And that by itself wasn't enough to convince them?'

'During the war, the loss was insignificant; soldiers disappeared all the time. And after the end of the war, in the relative peace that followed, 'twas eventually assumed that I was somehow responsible for the loss of the champions myself. The Cymrians, and then the Lirin, began to believe I was insane, chasing this demon that didn't exist. Even I began to wonder myself if somehow I had just misread the signs, had just been so lost in the pain of the Past that I had imagined it all. Slowly, the Cymrian families stopped sending their sons to me to learn the sword, fearing I would bring about their deaths with my wild goose chase. I sought the F'dor endlessly myself until I finally decided they were right.'

Rhapsody went to her pack and pulled out one of the pouches of spice. She threw a handful of dried herbs and some wild horseradish into the pot. 'What made you realize they weren't?'

'Finding Gwydion.'

At the name, Rhapsody looked up. 'Gwydion of Manosse?'

'Aye. You know of him?'

'I've heard his name once,' Rhapsody admitted. 'That barely even qualifies as knowing of him. It was in the keep of Lord Stephen Navarne, in a place Lord Stephen keeps a few remembrances of him.'

'I hardly knew him either. I had only seen him once, at his naming ceremony when he was an infant. I did know Stephen, however; he studied with me. Stephen and Gwydion were childhood friends, but were raised in different provinces until they met up again when Stephen came to Gwydion's father for further training.'

Rhapsody retrieved the dented kettle of boiling water and began pouring it into the cast-iron pot. Oelendra stared at her hands, unshielded from the red-hot iron. Rhapsody felt her glance and looked up at her, smiling.

'So who was Gwydion's father?'

'Llauron, the Invoker of the Filids, in Gwynwood.' Oelendra moved rapidly out of the way to avoid being burned by the steaming water as Rhapsody dropped the kettle on the table. Rhapsody quickly mopped up the water with one of the towels hanging beside the drysink.

'I'm terribly sorry. Are you all right?'

'Aye, are you?'

'I'm fine. Did you say that Gwydion of Manosse was Llauron's son?'

'His only son, only child, only heir. Llauron's Lirin wife, Cynron, died giving birth to him.'

'How sad.' Rhapsody absorbed Oelendra's words slowly. She felt grief for her gentle mentor; it was no wonder that he buried himself in his work. The trappings of Cymrian royalty obviously couldn't replace what he had lost, so he kept to himself, to his studies, tending to his garden and his followers, and eschewing the riches and titles of his lineage. It also explained his close friendship with Lord Stephen, his son's best friend. 'What do you mean, you found Gwydion?'

Oelendra's eyes took on a distant look. 'Twenty years ago I came upon Gwydion, broken and bloodied, hovering near death, outside the forest of Gwynwood, in Navarne, not far from the House of Remembrance. He had gone after the demon; he is the only one I know of who ever did and

176

escaped. But in spite of getting away he was grievously wounded, his entire chest cavity torn asunder, a piece of his soul ripped open. I knew he was dying the moment I saw him, and I knew what had killed him.'

Rhapsody hung the pot over the fire and watched the flames crackle as she came near them. 'The F'dor?'

'It was obvious. His soul was hemorrhaging; he was surrounded with a bloody light that pulsed in a way I will never forget. The soul is thought of as an ethereal thing, something with no physical form, but the F'dor had succeeded in slashing it open. 'Twas a hideous sight.'

'I can't even imagine. What did you do?'

'I panicked, but not from fear for Gwydion. I had seen enough death in my time to be unaffected by it. What frightened me, Rhapsody, was knowing how powerful the F'dor had become. Gwydion was a formidable opponent. He had grown up wandering the wilds of Manosse, he had sailed to distant and dangerous lands with the Sea Mages and was a veteran of more than one war. But more than that, the powers and Rites of Command he had received through his lineage were unparalleled.

'From Gwylliam, his grandfather, he had been given the bonds to the land that only those of ancient royal blood inherit, the lineage of kings. From Anwyn, his grandmother, he had the blood of Elynsynos the dragon and Merithyn, who was Seren, another of the five Firstborn races, races sprung from the elements which make up the fabric of the universe.

'And on his mother's side of the family he had the lineage of MacQuieth. He was the Kirsdarkenvar and the Chief of the House of Newland, the most senior of the Manossian houses. And despite all that, the crown prince of the Cymrian dynasty was reduced to a quivering pile of bleeding meat. If it could destroy Gwydion of Manosse, its power had grown beyond what I could hope to defeat alone. That was twenty years ago, Rhapsody; I shudder to think what it can do now.' She looked up at her new pupil and her brows furrowed.

Rhapsody was trembling.

'Gwydion was the Kirsdarkenvar?'

'Aye; he carried the elemental sword of water, Kirsdarke, handed down to him through the generations. Through the rights of blood and rite of passage, he had wielded that sword with as much power as anyone ever had. And if he, using a blade that was forged specifically to kill evil beings just such as this, could be slain, I knew the time had passed when any but the Three could destroy it. Rhapsody? What's wrong?'

She was staring out the window into the fading twilight that had crept up on them while they were conversing.

Are you tied to water yourself, or just through the sword?

It's hard to say, really. I've had Kirsdarke for so long now that I can't remember that element not being a part of me.

Rhapsody thought back to the hidden glen, the unexpected sight of Ashe after his bath, naked from the waist up, the grisly wound festering in the filtered red light. Unexpectedly her memories shifted to another hidden glen.

It must have been the Rakshas that you met. The F'dor created the Rakshas in the House of Remembrance twenty years ago. A Rakshas looks like whatever soul is powering it. It is built of blood, the blood of the demon, and sometimes other creatures, usually innocents and feral animals of some sort. A Rakshas made just of blood is temporary and mindless. But if the demon is in possession of a soul, whether it is human or otherwise, it can place it within the construct and it will take the form of the soul's owner, who of course is dead. It has some of the knowledge that person had. It can do the things they did. It is twisted and evil; you must beware of him, Pretty. And hear me: it is very close to here now, nearby. When you leave, be careful.

Cedelia had stared at her.

Have I done something to offend you, Cedelia?

You were seen with a man in a hooded gray cloak five days ago at the Outer Forest lip. A man in a hooded gray cloak led a raid on a Lirin village on the eastern edge of the Outer Forest lip that same night. The settlement was burned to the ground. Fourteen men, six women, and three children perished in that raid.

She remembered the look in Achmed's eyes as she read to him from the contract they had found in the House of Remembrance.

The parties involved are Cifiona and someone called the Rakshas, and through him his master; that's strange – his master is not referred to by name. Among those services shall be counted the commitment of the blood sacrifice of thirty-three persons of innocent heart and untouched body of Human descent, and an equal number of Lirin or half-Lirin origins.

'Rhapsody?' Oelendra's strong hands closed around her upper arms.

Rhapsody turned around. 'Yes?'

'What are you thinking?'

Rhapsody looked back out the window and swallowed; the night was coming.

'We can talk more after supper, Oelendra. We have to hurry now, or we'll miss devotions.'

'Devotions?'

She looked at the ancient Lirin warrior in surprise. Surely she must have been familiar with the songs of the rising stars and the setting sun; Oelendra was full Liringlas, a Skysinger. But she was staring at Rhapsody in what seemed to be confusion. Perhaps she knew them by another name.

'Here, Oelendra, come with me. We can do them together. It has been so long since I've had someone to sing with who knew the songs.' She took Oelendra by the hand and together they left the cabin, hurrying toward the nearest clearing in the advancing twilight.

21

The twilight was already darkening to the deepest of blues when the two women came into the clearing. The daystar had set, and one by one the others were beginning to come forth, glimmering in momentary uncertainty before claiming their places in the night sky, shining through the wisps of cloud that passed before the rising moon.

Rhapsody cleared her throat and her mind. She was rushed, having allowed the afternoon to slip away unnoticed, and so took a few moments to place herself in a calm and reverent frame of mind. The horrifying things Oelendra had related to her were forgotten for now, lest they interfere with the age-old ceremony she practiced as the last vestige of communion with her mother. As the last ray of sun disappeared over the edge of the horizon she began the first note of the farewell vespers, the evensong that bade the sun Godspeed in its journey through the darkness and reaffirmed the promise to greet it in the morning with joy.

She sang softly, waiting for Oelendra to join in, but the Lirin champion stood silently, listening to her. Her voice increased in power as the night deepened and the stars grew brighter; she could feel their light in her eyes. There was something right about singing in Tyrian, a sense of freedom and ease. The song was not held by the normal bonds of wind and the pull of the earth, but floated free and easily to the sky above. The Lirin of this land might not have been Liringlas, singers to the sky, but they were still its children.

The greeting to the stars did not take long; each verse was short and succinct, and within a few moments Rhapsody was finished. She did not complete any of the more complex lauds, as she was unsure of the reason Oelendra was not joining her and did not wish to exacerbate the situation if she was in some way displeasing the older woman. She took a deep breath of the sweet evening air and turned to Oelendra. Her smile faded when she saw the look on her face.

'Oelendra? What's the matter?'

The Lirin Champion was staring at the sky with the eyes of the lost. There was a sadness to her expression that moved Rhapsody to pity for a moment. Then Oelendra looked back at her, and her face relaxed into the same look of gentle wisdom Rhapsody had been drawn to when they first met.

'Nothing, dear. I was just thinking. Why don't you go back in the house? I'll be there momentarily.'

Rhapsody nodded and obeyed. She retraced their steps through the glade and back to Oelendra's dwelling, opening the door and leaving it ajar behind her.

Oelendra waited beneath the canopy of night, staring at the stars. Rhapsody's song had awakened a memory in her, the memory of a ritual practiced faithfully, each morning and evening, every day of her life before she had left her homeland and come here. A ritual she had forgotten until this moment.

Her own devotions had not been only the standard Liringlas vespers that Rhapsody had sung, but the Dirge of the Fallen Star as well, the star for which she had been named. How long had it been since that song was sung? Did anyone now living still remember her extinguished star, or had her unintentional neglect erased the memory of it forever?

She felt her cramped heart expand with the returned memories, the songs that had brought her consolation in her hours of grief and guidance when she was lost were now hers once again. She had not even realized they were gone. And this girl had given them back to her; the first dark place into which Rhapsody was bringing light was Oelendra's own heart. And the place that the light had originated was dark as well in the depths of the silent sea. Light to and from darkness. The Iliachenva'ar.

The brisk wind of the spring night caught the edges of Oelendra's cloak, but it was not the breeze that stung the warrior's eyes. She wiped the tears from her cheeks as she stopped at the edge of the clearing to observe her own house. *How could I have forgotten?* she wondered. *It must have been when the sword went silent, the moment it and Serendair were parted forever.*

The darkness now closed in around her. The pool of light from within her home was like an island of warmth in the black sea of night. Inside the house she could see Rhapsody moving about. She stirred the stew on the fire, then turned to arrange a vaseful of spring flowers on the table that she must have gathered in the dark.

Oelendra smiled. *This one has potential. Real potential,* the ancient warrior thought as she watched the young Singer. *She has a noble heart and a selfless devotion to others. She knows that there are things greater than herself, and she wishes to serve them. She just might succeed where they – where we have failed.* Inside the house the girl readied two bowls at the table, then looked momentarily out the window before returning to tend to the stew again. *How long has it been since someone has set me a place for supper?* Oelendra wondered as the girl moved out of sight.

This one was different, and that would be harder. She knew her scarred heart must invest itself one more time, would risk the pain again, to believe in this girl, to help her and love her and pray in tears that she would survive the ordeal for which she was destined.

Rhapsody handed the dried plates to Oelendra to put away, then took a seat before the fire. 'Will you finish telling me about Gwydion, please?'

Oelendra closed the cabinet and smiled. She came over to the willow rocking chair and sat down in it, one leg bent beneath her. 'We did leave the story incomplete, didn't we?

'Despite being mortally wounded, Gwydion was still alive when I found him. There was nothing I could do to save him, or even to ease his pain, so I carried his broken body deep into the Great Forest, past the Veil of

Hoen, and into the keeping of the Lord and Lady Rowan. They worked to heal him; for days they struggled to keep him alive.

'In the end, when nothing was working, and Gwydion was in mortal agony, I took a piece of a star from sword's hilt and gave that to the Lady Rowan. You see, Daystar Clarion had piece of Seren, the name-star of our homeland, set into the hilt that I had put there. 'Twas my bond with the sword, a pure fragment of elemental ether, and I knew that nothing else in my possession but the sword itself was as powerful as that piece. I offered it to them in the hope they could use it as a last effort to save him, and they did, but he was too far gone. Perhaps it is just as well, because living with that kind of elemental power might have been worse than death for Gwydion.'

'Why?'

'Because Gwydion was the great-grandson of Elynsynos, and as such was wyrmkin; in other words, he was a man with dragon's blood mixed with the human blood in his veins. That kind of intense power source might have brought the dormant dragon nature into full-blown status. I doubt he would have wanted to live as a dragon, since he had the soul of a man. 'Tis probably a blessing to us all that he did not survive; if the F'dor had been able to bind him, to command the dragon, I shudder to imagine how it would have used that power to control the elements themselves. Anyway, giving up the piece of the star for him was a desperate gesture, and one that did not work, but I don't regret trying.'

'I'm sure your kindness and generosity were appreciated in his last moments, Oelendra.'

'I doubt he was aware of anything but his own agony, Rhapsody. 'Twas the worst I had ever seen a human being endure, and I have seen some very terrible suffering.'

Rhapsody was thinking of Llauron. 'I wonder if Gwydion is buried under the white ash tree in the Invoker's garden, the one Llauron calls Mahb.'

'Perhaps. 'Tis the word for son.'

'Did you bring back the body?'

Oelendra shook her head. 'No; the Lord Rowan told me 'twas time to return to the land of the living. The Lady was still blessing the body when I came back through the Veil. I couldn't even tell Llauron what his son said or did, if anything, in his last moments, because I wasn't there.'

Rhapsody was perplexed. 'Land of the living?'

A faraway smile came over Oelendra's face. 'The court of the Rowans is a mystical place, Rhapsody, on the other side of the Veil of Joy. In order to enter one must be near death, or in a situation that is truly life-or-death. Time does not pass there as it does here; one can be gone for years within their realm to find himself but a moment older when he returns.'

'And who are the Rowans? Healers?'

Oelendra's smile dimmed into sadness. 'Of the greatest magnitude, though the healing they give is oftimes hard to accept. The Lady is the Keeper of Dreams, the Guardian of Sleep, Yl Breudiwyr. The Lord is the

Hand of Mortality, the Peaceful Death, Yl Angaulor. That's why I know Gwydion is dead without having seen his last moment; the Lord himself told me 'twas time. And I left, for then I was not needed or welcome any longer. When I next see the Lord and Lady, I shall pass forever into their realm, and walk no more upon this earth. When I saw you, I knew that time was not far off.'

A cold wave of nausea ran through Rhapsody. 'Are you saying that my coming will be the cause of your death?'

'Nay, but I have lived past my time, waiting for a guardian to come and replace me. Now that I have someone to pass my stewardship on to, I will eventually be able to find the peace that I have longed for. I will at long last be reunited with those I love. Immortality in this world is not the only kind, you know, Rhapsody.'

The look in Oelendra's eyes went straight to Rhapsody's heart. She had longed for the same things herself.

'And it was then that you gave up the sword?'

Oelendra smiled and took a sip of *dol mwl*. ''Twas then that the sword gave up me. I turned back to it after removing the piece of the star, and it had vanished into the earth where I had left it, leaving nothing but its light behind for a moment, and then even that was gone. 'Twas almost as if it had died when Gwydion did, buried there beyond the Veil of Hoen. It seemed an appropriate place. I knew it would return eventually, and now it has.' Rhapsody nodded. Now she understood how it had come to be within the Earth.

They passed the remainder of the evening in pleasant conversation. Rhapsody played a few of the old world tunes on her lute from Elynsynos, singing some in Ancient Lirin. Oelendra listened raptly, but did not join in. She told the Singer of times long gone, of the final days of glory after the war and before the cataclysm when Serendair had peace for the last time, of friends and comrades and the stuff of enduring memory.

At last the weariness from her long journey overtook Rhapsody, and she fell asleep by the fire. Some time later she was awakened by a gentle hand on her shoulder.

'Come, dear, let me show you to where you will stay.'

Rhapsody rose, rubbing her head hazily. 'I need to get a message back home to Ylorc soon, if that is at all possible,' she said.

'Aye,' Oelendra agreed. 'I will take you into Tyrian City in the morning. The mail caravan stops there on a weekly basis. I'm sure your friends will be glad to know you arrived here safely. Now come; you're exhausted.'

Half in a dream, Rhapsody followed the older woman past the large hearth and down a hallway. Oelendra led her into a small room at the far end of the house with an ironworked window. A large four-poster bed stood against one wall, and a heavy wardrobe against the other. The bed was covered with a variety of bedspreads and furs, enough to last a frozen winter.

'This is your room, for as long as you want to keep it,' Oelendra said.

'Make yourself at ease, and get some sleep. Tomorrow if you'd like I will show you about the city. For now, however, sleep as late as you can. I suspect you need it.'

'Thank you.' Rhapsody was barely able to keep her eyes open. 'I should probably warn you, I have nightmares. If you should hear me in the night, I apologize in advance.'

'I shouldn't doubt it, after all you've been through. I had them, too. They eventually go away. You will sleep without them one night, and then they become fewer and farther between until they stop haunting you. Sleep well.' Oelendra touched Rhapsody's shoulder as she left. Rhapsody undressed and crawled immediately into bed.

Her dreams were not of the old land, or the demon, but of a handsome face, smiling uncertainly. She could see it, looking down at her in the light of the forest glade again, bidding her farewell on the doorstep of the dragon.

It is twisted and evil; you must beware of him, Pretty. It is very close to here now, nearby. When you leave, be careful.

The face in her dreams smiled uncertainly again. Then the sun shone through the leaves of the forest and he began to melt, great icy tears running from his eyes, until he dissolved completely into a pool of steaming water that still reflected his image.

What have you to drink?'

'Port. Or a young brandy.'

'Anything stronger?'

'Hmmm. Not a good day, I take it?'

'I guess you haven't been paying much attention to the status of my life recently.'

'Not true, which is why I have this wonderful Canderian whiskey on hand.'

'That'll do nicely.'

'I confess I'm a bit surprised to see you. Why are you here?'

'I think it's the warmth of the welcome. Hard to resist.'

'Now don't get testy. You know I'm always delighted when you come.'

'Of course. Did I interrupt something critical? Plotting the destruction of anyone interesting?'

'I'll ignore that. Here's your drink. What do you want?'

Ashe took a sip and let the burning liquid sting his mouth for a moment before swallowing. The whiskey scorched his throat. 'I want you to reconsider your plans for Rhapsody.'

'Really? And why is that?'

He took another, larger swallow and sat down at the ornate wooden desk. 'If she's who we think she is, it is unwise to abuse her good will.'

'If she's who we think she is, she will understand. It's as much her destiny as it is ours.'

'You know, I think you have a serious misunderstanding about destiny. Other people don't always embrace it, or, in fact, interpret it, as you would have them. Particularly when it involves bringing harm, or pain, or tragedy upon themselves.'

'You would not, by any chance, be speaking personally, now, would you?'

Ashe was silent for a moment. 'No. Of course not.'

'I thought not. And when, might I ask, did you become so concerned about my protégé's welfare?'

'You are not the only one who thinks of her as his protégé, you know. She is studying with Oelendra as we speak.'

'Good, good. That will help. Now, don't avoid the question. Where did all this worry about Rhapsody come from? Has she proven not to be up to the task?'

'Hardly. In fact, if anything, she may be more powerful than we originally thought.'

'Then why are you concerned?'

Ashe spun the last of his drink in the glass, then downed it. The alcohol was having no numbing effect whatsoever. 'I would hate to have all this come to naught because you have misjudged your influence with one of the Three.'

He looked up to see eyes of blue granite staring back at him, an almost reptilian gleam blazing from them. *So out of place in the kindly old face*, he thought.

'Now, let me be perfectly clear. I need Rhapsody to play the part I've cast her in. Neither of the other two can. But that part is minor. When it comes to currying favor, the only one within whose good graces I need to remain is Achmed. He alone is irreplaceable.'

Ashe smiled, then rose and ambled to the liquor chest. 'You don't understand that power structure at all,' he said, filling his glass to just below the rim. 'Achmed is devoted to Rhapsody. It is her loyalty to you that might influence him, not any of his own. He couldn't care less about you and your plans. And if you harm her in any way, he will come after you.'

It was Llauron's turn to smile. 'You know, your lack of thoroughness disappoints me. I'm afraid you are mistaken. Achmed has other reasons to do as I plan. Reasons that are much older, and much stronger, than any love or friendship his hideous heart might have for her. You obviously don't know them as well as I had hoped you would come to in all this time you've spent with them. A waste.'

Ashe fell silent, staring into the lapping flames of the fire in the dark study. *Except for the mist*, thought Llauron, *he could be one of the shadows in the room*. His voice grew gentle as he laid his hand on his son's shoulder.

'Does she know?'

'Know what?'

'That you love her.'

'No.'

'Good. It's better for all concerned.'

An ugly choked laugh came from the misty shadow. 'Really? I await with eagerness your explanation of that belief. How is it better for anyone but you?'

The old man sighed and went back to his chair. 'There was a time when you believed without question that I knew what was best for everyone, mostly because what benefits me also benefits you, and ultimately, the rest of the land.'

'I suppose twenty years of wandering the world alone in physical and spiritual agony tends to dim even the most ardent hero-worship.'

The voice from the chair was cold and hollow. 'It's temporary. And it will be over soon. This matter is insignificant. When your dominion comes to rest over this land, your pain will end. And, of course, you can have any woman you want then.'

'There is only one woman I will ever want.'

'Forgive me if I remind you that I have heard this from you before.' He did not flinch as Ashe hurled the whiskey glass into the fire, causing the flames to bellow out of their stone boundaries and roar with smoke and shards of glass. 'Besides, there is no reason you can't have Rhapsody then, if you still want her. She will undoubtedly have tired of being the Bolg's courtesan by that time. If you really want a used whore, I'm sure she will jump at the chance.'

Ashe turned. Silhouetted against the inferno, Llauron could see the fury of blue eyes within the dark hood, and could almost see the dragon within them coil. 'Don't ever say anything like that again,' he said, his voice deathly calm. 'You have already pushed the limits of my loyalty farther than you think. This is not a subject on which you want to tread heavily.'

Llauron smiled into his own glass. 'You forget, we differ in our opinions of the value of court trollops, Gwydion. Some of the best women in my life were whores in my court. I certainly meant no insult to Rhapsody.'

Ashe was silent for a moment. 'You know, Father, there may be nothing you don't know about power and strategy and fashioning destiny,' he said finally. 'But you know nothing about trust and the human heart.'

'You think not?'

'Without question. You promise me Rhapsody as if you had some control over her feelings. She will probably hate me when this is done, and she will have every right to. There are some things you cannot manipulate, and some things you cannot repair once they are betrayed. You can't expect someone to stand by you when you've used them as a pawn to accomplish your own ends to their detriment.'

Llauron looked away. 'Why not?' he said to the floor. 'It has always worked with you.'

Ashe's voice was hardly above a whisper. 'I will not be a party to this.'

The reply was as sympathetic and warm as the bristling fire. 'Too late, my boy; you already have been.'

The biting wind that rustled the papers on Llauron's desk was the only sign that Ashe had gone.

22

'Good morning,' Oelendra greeted Rhapsody as she emerged from her room, blinking the sleep from her eyes. She set a mug of tea at the place at the table where Rhapsody had sat the night before. 'I hope you slept well.'

'Very well, thank you,' Rhapsody responded, yawning. She was wrapped in the red silk robe embroidered with an ornate image of a dragon that had been left at the foot of her bed. It was far too large for her, and would no doubt have been too large for her host as well. She took her seat and sipped the tea as Oelendra returned to her kitchen. The warrior was already dressed, and had likely been up for hours. She returned with a plate of fruit and a pastry-like bread in the shape of a waxing moon.

'First a little breakfast, then a chance to stretch; we can take a walk up to the city. After we get back I would like to see how you handle yourself with a sword.' Oelendra gave Rhapsody a plate and joined her at the table. They ate in comfortable silence, while Rhapsody stared out the window at the garden, drinking in the songs of the birds. The feeling of magic she had experienced during her first lovely hours alone in Tyrian was returning.

When they had finished breakfast, Oelendra showed Rhapsody around Tyrian City. It was laid out along a series of hills, the tallest and steepest of which was called Tomingorllo and served as the court of the king. It was the wall near this north-central hill which Rhapsody had passed that first day. As they came through the gates now they walked down an underground hallway and out into a great bowl in the center of the rise that formed the Garden of Tomingorllo. The sides of the bowl were wall-like, much like the outer slopes of the hill, so that ascending or descending them directly would be nearly impossible.

The only ways into the Garden were through the underground halls they had just come through or a well-hidden path by which Oelendra led her out of the Garden. The actual seat of the king was in the fortress castle in a vast courtyard at the highest point of Tomingorllo, and could be reached only through the great halls that lay beneath the massive hill's surface. The fortress was visible from any clearing in the city. Rhapsody watched it in delight as they passed along the pine-laden slopes of the Garden, before descending into the rest of the city. It was a great round building with many pillars and a dome of silvery marble that seemed to glisten in the morning light.

The rest of the city was more akin to the Lirin cities of home, and more like what she had seen in the villages Cedelia and she had passed. Most of the buildings were of simple design, with high roofs and short walls, built along avenues created by the forest itself. Here and there, in the largest of the trees, were high platforms or structures, some smaller ones in the mighty oaks, other, larger buildings built between several trees. Between them ran rope bridges that connected a second series of avenues high above the woodland paths. Goats, sheep, and pigs ran through parts of the city, but for the most part, the animals who wandered the streets were forest creatures that lived harmoniously among the Lirin.

The defenses of the city were less obvious. There were blind and hidden guard posts, designed to catch invading forces unaware and trap them in a deadly crossfire. There were sudden ditches which would have broken any organized charge.

There were more conventional, human-style defenses as well. Each of the six outer hills was crested with a walled defense, and between these was a series of palisaded ramparts and ditches, each one taller or deeper than the one before. At the bottom of each ditch was set a series of sharpened sticks that made falling deadly. These ditches were crossed by bridges, which could be easily collapsed from inside the ramparts. Rhapsody wondered what Achmed or Grunthor would have made of these defenses, and took note of them for possible use in Ylorc.

It was the life of the city, however, that really interested Rhapsody. Tyrian was a bustling place, brimming with activity and foot traffic. The Lirin, though reserved with outsiders, were warm and friendly within the city walls, and Rhapsody found herself laughing merrily with people to whom she had been introduced just moments before. She was greeted with affection and cordiality wherever Oelendra took her.

They ate the noonday meal in an outdoor café, dining on spiced venison, olives, and delicious nuts that Rhapsody found hard to stop eating. Crowds of children ran through the streets laughing, stopping to stare for a moment as they passed by her table, occasionally reaching out to touch her or to drop a flower in her lap before they broke into a run again.

The people of Tyrian, with their large, almond-shaped eyes and whimsical appearances, gladdened Rhapsody's heart in ways she didn't fully understand. *This must be what Elynsynos meant about the Cymrians*, she thought, finding herself smiling continuously as she watched them. *I can see now how someone can come to think of a people as treasure.* She grinned at two little girls who stood before their table.

'If you're finished, I'll show you the castle,' Oelendra said, digging in her pocket. She held out her open palms to the children and nodded. Both girls grabbed for the contents as Oelendra's hands closed, rapid as the recoil of a snake. They examined their results, both of them squealing with delight and each popping a red kiran berry into her mouth, the trophy of defeating the speed of the Lirin champion. Rhapsody laughed and applauded the victors.

'Yes; that was delicious.' She rose and folded her napkin, waving to the children as they ran off, giggling. 'Lead on, Oelendra. I will follow you anywhere.'

This is the Court and Throne of Tomingorllo,' Oelendra said as she swung open one of a pair of heavy oak doors. Beyond the doors was an enormous marble rotunda with an overarching dome held up by pillars that stood ten feet from the wall. The dome had a large hole in the middle of it, leaving the center of the room open to the cloudless sky.

On the other side of the room was a large throne carved of black walnut, far less ornate than Rhapsody had expected. It was instead austere, with pillar-like arms and a low, even back. Two great stone fireplaces, wider than the whole of Oelendra's house, stood dark and cold at each of the other directional points in the circle.

Running along the walls of the round room was a wooden bench that circled the room unbroken, except for the gaps for the doors and the throne. In the center of the room itself was a small glass case on an ornate silver stand that did not seem to match the austerity of the rest of the room. A balcony encircled the room above, looking down on the center display case. The only other decorations in the room were the four star-shaped grills that were part of the floor. The air in the room was clean and cold.

'This is where the king would sit, if there was one, and where the first alliance of the New World was made, and broken. Come over here.' Oelendra walked toward the odd display in the center of the room. Rhapsody joined her and looked within the glass case.

'The Crown of the Lirin Kingdom,' Oelendra said.

'How beautiful.' Rhapsody stared down at the diadem that lay in the case before her. It was made of countless tiny star-shaped diamonds. Eight similarly-shaped larger stones formed the center ring of the crown. They glimmered in the sunlight that shone down from the opening overhead into the throne room. Rhapsody had never seen their like before.

'The fragments that make up this crown were once the Purity Diamond, a stone the size of a man's fist that shone with the light of the stars. We brought it from the old world and gave it as a sign of friendship to the Lirin tribe Gorllewinolo, the first indigenous people we met here, aside from the Seers. They were the ancestors of the people who live in Tyrian now, and together with some of the Lirin of our Island, they founded this city, the main hill of which bears, in part, their name.'

'Tomingorllo: tower of the Gorllewin, the people of the west,' Rhapsody said to herself.

'Aye. Over the years the name changed, but the city and the people remained the same.'

'But what happened to the diamond? You said that these pieces were once a single diamond. Did they break it?'

'Nay, they did not. Anwyn did.'

'I don't understand. Why would she do such a thing?'

'No one understood. The Lirin of this land were our friends and allies. They had stood by us when all others had failed, and they supported Anwyn throughout the war, even when her own people deserted her. The alliance between the Lirin and Anwyn was older and deeper even than that of Anwyn and the Cymrians, who had chosen her centuries before as their Lady. The Purity Diamond was a symbol of that alliance to the Lirin. At the time her actions made no sense. It was not until years later that I began to suspect the reason. I should have guessed right away, I suppose.' Oelendra ran a finger absently through the fine layer of dust that had built up on the case.

'It happened just before her scheduled meeting with Gwylliam, the one which he did not live to attend. She came into the throne room and to this place, where the diamond was on display. Raising her hands, she called starfire down from the sky and spoke words of deep power that shattered the stone into thousands of pieces, driving the light it contained out of it forever. Then, without a word, she left.

'It was because of that act that the Lirin, and indeed many of even her staunchest supporters, refused to recognize her claim to the sole leadership of the Cymrians after Gwylliam's death. She had destroyed the gift that the First Fleet of Cymrians had given to the Lirin of this place, the very symbol of the peace and unity with the land they believed their way of life represented.

'To the Lirin, 'twas the breaking of the treaty, the greatest betrayal, but to her own people 'twas just the final one. She returned to the Tree to find that, not only had the Lirin turned their backs on her, but her own people denied her as well. So she left, having accomplished what she had set out to do, destroy Gwylliam, but at the cost of the prize she sought. In the end she simply sat alone to let her hatred fester, until at last none visited her but her son and a handful of pilgrims who sought answers to questions about the Past.

'When Llauron came years later in an attempt to repair the damage, offering himself in a marriage of alliance to the Lirin queen, she showed him this crown, made of the shards of what had been a gift of peace. Can you repair this?' Queen Terrell asked him. Llauron acknowledged that he could not. Then what makes you think you can repair the alliance so easily?'

'Llauron explained his desire to right the wrongs his parents had inflicted on the Cymrians and the Lirin, and the wish to see them united as they had never been before. Queen Terrell declined both his offer and his marriage proposal, but told him that when and if he, or anyone, could restore the stone to life, could make it shine with the light of the stars as it once had, that the Lirin would recognize that person as Chieftain of the Cymrians and Lord of both peoples. Until such a time, the Lirin would remain separate, following their own monarch.

'Llauron accepted this, and, as the Invoker, blessed the crown and the queen who made it before returning to Gwynwood. Since that time the crown has remained in this place, waiting for the coming of the Lord or Lady Cymrian to right the wrong that was done here.'

'Why do you think Anwyn destroyed it?' Rhapsody asked, walking around the case to see the crown from all its sides.

''Twas the price she paid to be rid of her husband.'

She looked up. 'What do you mean?'

189

The look on Oelendra's face grew harder. 'She struck a deal with the demon. It was actually the first confirmation I had as to what kind of evil had followed us, because F'dor are afraid of diamonds; they fear them, it seems, or are injured and weakened by them. I have never discovered exactly why, but I believe 'tis because diamonds hold the light of the stars, as Daystar Clarion does, an element that precedes the existence of fire, and, as an older element, is more powerful. This was a diamond immense enough to capture and destroy the essence of even the greatest of the demon spirits.

'I knew that evil, and I hated it. It had been responsible for most of the trouble on our Island, had destroyed all I loved, killed my grandfather, killed my husband. I knew it lurked somewhere, that it was hiding among us, clinging to the souls of innocents, staying always out of sight, always in the background, waiting for its power to rise and its time to be perfect.

'I had only suspected its presence by smell that first day when the First and Third waves reunited – F'dor have a ghastly smell in their true form, and you can sometimes catch a whiff of it when they are insinuated into a host – but I had no confirmation until the day the diamond was destroyed.

'But Anwyn knew. Anwyn had always known. She was the Seer of the Past. She knew it escaped the moment after it stepped on that ship; she knew which soul it clung to as soon as it took up residence. It could not hide from her, and had she told me who it was, we would have been done with that evil many generations ago. But she was wyrmkin, a dragon's-child, and hoarded that information as she hoarded everything, certain that one day it would turn to her benefit. And surely one day it did, but, as with all things touched by F'dor, that benefit was twisted.

'After seven hundred years of war with Gwylliam, she turned to the only power she knew could defeat him, the one power in the world ancient enough to know secrets that were beyond even her gift to recall. She turned to the demon, and it offered a bargain: the F'dor would grant her heart's desire, 'twould kill her husband, who was immortal, who to all other threats was invulnerable, and in return she would destroy the Purity Diamond, the one thing the demon feared even more than Daystar Clarion.

'She was a fool. She thought because she was of the mixed blood of two of the ancient races, Seren and dragon, that she could bargain with the F'dor and her knowledge of the Past would protect her. What she failed to understand was that the demon was not just descended from an elder race, but was itself from the Before Time, and knew things she could never dream of.

'She agreed to its terms, and who knows what else, and destroyed the gift that was surely one of our greatest weapons against the F'dor. In return, it killed Gwylliam, the last of the Seren kings, and so won the battle it had lost on the Island, in the old world. Then it destroyed the remains of the Cymrian alliance, disposing of the leaders of two of the houses, and breaking their tie with the Lirin, and the different Lirin factions' ties with each other. The F'dor destroyed the Cymrians as a unified people, and Anwyn had opened the door for it. Gwylliam may have started the war, but Anwyn lost it for us all.

'I spent the next few years hunting it. Anwyn refused to help me find it, because I had stayed out of the war, being unwilling to support either side in the destruction of the other. I also counseled the Lirin to stay out of it, but they turned a deaf ear and followed Anwyn, much to their eventual regret. I sought it everywhere, but the demon was far too clever to be found. It had gone to ground, biding its time, waiting until conditions were ripe to emerge again. Well, with war brewing, and border incursions on all sides, and racial hatred flourishing, that time can't be far off.'

Even though she stood in a shaft of warm spring sunlight from the hole in the center of the dome, Rhapsody shivered. It was becoming horrifyingly clear what Oelendra expected of her. Since the destruction of the diamond, the only obvious weapon powerful enough to kill the F'dor was the sword she carried. It was no wonder Oelendra was willing to train her in its use.

Very good,' Oelendra said, sheathing her sword.

Rhapsody collapsed onto the ground, her breath harsh and labored. 'You must be joking,' she said between gasps for air. 'I've never been so humiliated in my life.' She had not expected to hold her own with the Lirin champion, but she had hoped to spare herself outright embarrassment. Oelendra laughed and held out her hand, which Rhapsody stared at for a few seconds before taking.

'Oh, come now, you were wonderful.' The older woman pulled the tired Singer from the ground, showing little sign of exertion herself. Rhapsody, by contrast, felt utterly exhausted. Her arm was numb and her fingers ached with the sting of the shocks that had resounded through her steel blade. She had not used Daystar Clarion in their first sparring, since Oelendra had wanted to see how well she fought without any special advantages.

'If I had been that wonderful in combat, my severed head would be decorating somebody's flagpole.'

'Don't be so hard on yourself. You held your own, you didn't fall for any of my invitations to get in over your head, and you didn't let your guard down even though you were tired enough to drop. Most of all, you know how to move on the ground and are very good on the parries and dodges. That's the hardest part, you know.'

'No, I didn't.'

'Absolutely. You've had some good training.'

'Thanks – I'll make sure to tell Grunthor.'

'He's your Bolg friend you were telling me of on the way back from the city?'

'Yes, he was my first trainer in the sword.'

'Well, that makes some sense. As I said, you've got a good start, but now we're going to train you to fight like our people do.'

'Do you think that the Lirin way of fighting is better than that of the Firbolg?' Rhapsody asked between breaths.

'Aye, at least for Lirin. The Bolg are big, strong, and clumsy, the Lirin are small, fast, and weak. Not every person of either race falls into those categories, but enough of them do that their fighting styles tend to reflect it. You rely too much on your strength, not enough on agility and cunning and, no offense, you just don't have the body mass to fight like a brute.'

'No offense taken,' Rhapsody said, picking up the weapon. 'Where do we start?'

'We start by having a drink of water.' Oelendra took a sip from a wineskin and passed it to her. 'The first lesson is to listen to your own body. There are times you have to ignore it, and you've already shown me you know how to push yourself well beyond the point of normal endurance.'

'Well, I've had to do a lot of that.' Rhapsody took a deep drink.

'It shows,' Oelendra said. Rhapsody looked for signs of ridicule or sarcasm in the warrior's expression, but all she saw was honest admiration. 'Now 'tis time to learn to listen to your body, to learn the rhythm that you move to, then learn to read that rhythm in others and match your movements to theirs. You are already a Singer, Rhapsody; now we will make you a Dancer.' Oelendra drew her sword again, and they returned to the lesson.

They spent hours that day going through a basic series of attacks, defenses, and the motions to get between them, until, at the end of the day, Rhapsody could perform the ritual without effort. When the sun was sinking low and the clouds were touched with pink, she ran through the paces with Daystar Clarion, and the moves seemed much more fluid than they had before.

As she swung the sword through the brisk open air the flames of the blade seemed to pick up the soft pastels and touches of crimson that appeared in the sky, the silver hilt glistening gold in the deepening hues of the sun. Rhapsody felt moved by the dance, and as her arm swept through the last of the strikes, a slow slash from above, she felt a comforting sense of balance and strength. She took a deep breath on finishing the routine, and let it out slowly before turning to her teacher for her comments. Oelendra stood with arms crossed, a slight smile on her face.

''Tis a good start,' she said, 'Now, come with me.'

She began to walk out of the clearing and down a forest path. Rhapsody followed, sheathing her sword. The air became more chilly with the promise of night as they passed beneath a series of trees whose ancient boughs stretched above their heads like the arches of a basilica. The bright leaves filtered the light of the setting sun into a peaceful shade of green, broken by the occasional glitter of gold. They walked quickly, and Oelendra did not speak. At last they broke free of the forest, and came to a small bald hill, the sky around them rapidly turning a deep shade of orange, the clouds trimmed in scarlet.

''Twas your mother that taught you the evening song?' Oelendra asked as she made her way up the hill.

The question and the memory it evoked caught Rhapsody off guard. 'Yes, in my childhood, that and the morning aubade and all the other lauds and songs of the Liringlas. My father used to joke that she had a song for every occasion.'

'She probably did,' Oelendra said seriously. ''Twas the way of our people. Would you mind if I joined you in the evening song tonight?'

'No, of course not,' said Rhapsody, a little surprised. 'As I told you last night, it will be wonderful to sing with someone who remembers the songs.'

'I remembered them last night for the first time,' Oelendra said, stopping at the rounded top of the hill, where the reddening sun was touching the western forest with the colors of fire and blood. 'I had lost them when I came to this place. 'Twas you that brought them back to me, Rhapsody. You are probably the only person in the world who might be able to understand what not having them, and then getting them back, has meant to me.' Rhapsody blinked, then smiled, and the ancient warrior turned away, scanning the horizon. ''Tis time. You should draw Daystar Clarion, and hold it through the song. 'Tis, after all, bound to the stars as well as to fire, and through exposure to the stars that its power grows.'

Rhapsody did as she was told, noting that the fires of the sword now matched the color of the sky. She closed her eyes and felt the sword's presence, became aware of its increasing power. The sensation tingled through her hands and into her being, as if Daystar Clarion was awakening, and as it did was awakening a piece of herself as well.

Then she heard Oelendra's voice begin the evening song. It was a voice that had been weathered by age and sorrow, but there was a sympathy to it that moved Rhapsody. It was like the voice of a grandmother singing to a well-loved child, or a widow singing the lament of the husband who had fallen in battle. It was a strange and sad voice, to which Rhapsody softly joined her own.

As they sang, the sun slipped beneath the western hills, the outer reaches of the sky turning from blue to orange to crimson to indigo. Above the western horizon a twinkling light became visible. The sun set, the evenstar appeared fully, and the flames of Daystar Clarion changed from hues that mimicked the sun to a silvery white.

As if in answer, Oelendra began to sing a new song, one with which Rhapsody was intimately familiar. It was a song to the star called Seren, the star that the Lirin of the old world believed had watched over their home, the Island that was no more. Rhapsody tried to join her, but quickly choked; Seren was the star she had been born beneath, the one Ashe had heard her call *Aria*. She could hear again, as clearly as if the memory were

193

the Present, her mother's voice singing the laud, teaching her the song of her guiding star. Her eyes swam with forbidden tears, and Rhapsody's face became hot with the effort to hold them back.

Unwelcome images from the Past, the memories she had fought to keep in abeyance, flooded her mind; pictures of the last time she had seen Barney and Dee at the Hat and Feathers, Pilam the baker and the other townspeople in her daily life from the old times. She thought of the children she had played for at the fountain in the town square, Analise and Carli and Ali and Meridion, who used to ask her for the same tune over and over.

The roaring flood of memories came more quickly now, thoughts of childhood friends dead a thousand years; images of her brothers, her father, her mother. As the picture of her mother's face formed, unbidden, in her mind, she looked up and saw Oelendra singing to the sky, her lined face silvery in the light of the stars.

The serendipity was too much for her. The tune was quickly abandoned; she lost her struggle as tears flowed freely down her face, and her body began to shake. Achmed's mandate to her drowned in the sorrow she had held behind the dam that his harsh words had created in her soul their first night on the Root, a barrier that had withstood the loss of everyone she loved, the world she had known, the life she had been taken away from that night. Rhapsody bent over and clutched her waist, trying to invoke the fail-safe that had always been able to drive the tears back before, but the attempt was useless. She sank to the ground and dissolved into wracking sobs.

Darkness swallowed the hillside as she felt the touch of a hand on her shoulder. Words were spoken in a kind tone near her ear, but she didn't hear them. She looked up into Oelendra's face, and the warrior spoke the words again.

'I know.'

Tears from an even deeper well of sorrow came forth. Oelendra took Rhapsody into her arms and drew the young Singer's head to her strong shoulder as she wept. The younger woman choked out words that were meaningless to anyone but herself. Oelendra slowly rocked her back and forth, gently stroking the shining hair that gleamed in the starlight.

'Let it come, darling, let it all come. This – this is where we begin.'

They sat thus all through the night, Rhapsody cradled in Oelendra's arms. At times she would grow silent, only to return to crying so hard that she thought she would die. All the while Oelendra spoke words of comfort that were not meant to stop the mourning, but to ease and encourage its passing, as one might hope to ease the pain of childbirth.

The morning found them still on the hillside. Rhapsody awoke to the soft singing of her mentor, who was greeting the rising of the daystar and the sun with the ancient song of their people. Her head cloudy from tears, Rhapsody joined in, her voice breaking sporadically. Her hand shook as she pulled the sword from its black ivory scabbard and held it beneath the heavenly bodies rising in the sky, its rippling flames reflecting soft tones of blue and rose and gold as the sun crested the horizon.

When the sun stood clear in the sky and the evenstar was no longer visible through the morning light, Oelendra rose from the ground and helped Rhapsody to stand. They returned to Oelendra's house and Rhapsody settled into the pillows on the floor with the cup of tea her mentor put gently into her hands. Over breakfast they reminisced about the old world, speaking fondly of people and things that they missed and knew they would not see again. There was healing laughter, a few tears, and much plain talk. Finally, when Rhapsody was feeling better, Oelendra gave her a discerning look.

'You have not really mourned your loss until now, have you?'

Rhapsody drained her mug of tea. 'No.'

Oelendra nodded. 'Do you mind if I ask why?'

'I was forbidden to.'

'By whom?'

She smiled. 'The leader of the expedition here. My sovereign, I guess. Someone I hated at the time, but have come to trust implicitly. One of my dearest friends.'

'Why did he forbid you to cry?'

Rhapsody thought for a moment. 'I'm not entirely certain; I think it offends his ears. He's rather sensitive to vibrations, that might be part of it. But he was very clear about it. I was not to cry ever again.'

'An unwise order, if I have ever heard one. Rhapsody, the rules I am teaching you as your mentor in the use of Daystar Clarion are essential to your survival, but there is more to life than just surviving. This one is offered as your friend and one who has lost what you have, and so understands what it has cost you. If the first rule is listen to your body, the second is listen to your heart.

'You have a remarkable ability to keep going when both parts of you are desperately in need of rest and renewal. Take the time to attend to yourself better, not just your body, but your soul as well. The cost of not doing so is too great to endure. Grieve if you need to. Carrying that much pain will defeat you eventually as surely as going into battle overwrought physically. Look after yourself. If you don't, you will never be able to look after anyone else.'

Rhapsody smiled. 'I will. Thank you, Oelendra, thank you for all you've done. Now, if you're ready, I think I'd like to get back to work.' She rinsed her mug in the water barrel and went to the sword rack, belting her sword as her mentor smiled.

195

23

Steel clashed against steel as the two Liringlas women sparred in the courtyard of Oelendra's garden. Blow after blow Rhapsody landed, and blow after blow Oelendra parried with little effort. Now and again the Lirin warrior would lash out with the flat of her blade, smacking Rhapsody in the calf, thigh, or occasionally on her side, but most of the blows to the vital areas the Singer managed to block or dodge.

In her mind she could hear Grunthor bellowing at her.

STRIKE! Get your pretty head out of your arse and pay attention, or I'll rip it off and stick it on my poleaxe!

Rhapsody grasped Daystar Clarion with both hands and pressed forward. She mustered all her strength and brought the sword down hard on the warrior.

Oelendra held up her sword with her left hand and parried the blow with ease. Then she punched out with her right fist, landing a jab on Rhapsody's chin. The world vanished as white pain flashed before her eyes.

She stumbled and fell to the ground three feet back, hardly able to believe she could have received a harder blow from Grunthor. Rhapsody blinked the spots away from her eyes as she lay sprawled on the ground, uncertain where, or even who, she was for a moment. A time-weathered face appeared above her.

'You are not a Bolg, Rhapsody,' Oelendra said as she stood over her student. 'If you try to fight like one, you will be killed. I've told you before your physical strength is not your strongest point, you shouldn't rely on it so much. If you have need of strength, you can draw on it from the sword, but you shouldn't rely on it alone. You won't live long as the Iliachenva'ar if you let the sword wield you. Now, are you all right?'

'Yes,' Rhapsody said as her bloodied lip began to swell. 'Just a little dizzy.'

'Very well, we'll rest a moment before we give it another try.'

'No, I'm all right.' Rhapsody gingerly touched her bruised chin as she came to her feet. She assumed a ready position, and the two returned to sparring. This time Rhapsody's movements were more carefully considered, and at the end of the match Oelendra nodded in approval.

Finally the rhythm became intrinsic, and Rhapsody began to land more blows, driving her instructor back and occasionally unbalancing her. She breathed deeply and concentrated on the music she could feel in her body, and how it matched with the vibrational blur that was her opponent and friend. With her eyes nearly closed, she waited for the moment when Oelendra's hand swung up, sword poised, then slashed her across the side, following her stroke with a blazingly fast blow to her teacher's wrist. She opened her eyes in alarm when she heard Oelendra's sword clatter on the cobblestones of the courtyard.

Oelendra was uninjured and smiling broadly; it was the most delight Rhapsody had ever seen on her mentor's face. The warrior extended her hand. Rhapsody took it and received a congratulatory handshake.

'Good work. Now we'll stop fooling around and get serious.'

Rhapsody looked at her in dismay. 'That wasn't serious?'

The smile faded from Oelendra's face. 'I'm afraid not, dear. With what you have to face, what you just accomplished was enough to keep you alive long enough to see it kill you.'

'Wonderful.'

'Well, 'tis an improvement. Before, you wouldn't have even known what hit you.'

Rhapsody grimaced. 'And you think seeing it is an improvement, given that choice? No wonder they think you're insane, Oelendra.'

The warrior wrapped an arm around the Singer and led her home, laughing.

Their days soon settled into a quiet routine. Each morning, after devotions, Rhapsody meditated, clearing her mind of thoughts, trying to feel the rhythm of her own body and the world around her. This exercise complete, Oelendra would have her run through her sword routines, practicing her movements slowly and carefully until they seemed second nature to her. This would be followed by a sparring session, in which the two would enter mock combat, with Oelendra stopping to point out faults or where improvements could be made.

They would spend the afternoons wandering the woods or the city, talking of the history of the new world or telling stories of personal events, getting to know each other well. Rhapsody felt Oelendra to be a kindred soul, someone who understood where she had come from often better then she did herself. Though she kept some of the details of her exploits with Achmed and Grunthor, and all of her knowledge of Ashe, to herself, she found herself confiding her fears and dreams to the Lirin champion, trusting her as she had not anyone else for as long as she could remember. Oelendra was a perfect listener; she answered questions forthrightly and shared parts of her own heart and past as well. These times were as strengthening to the growth of Rhapsody's soul as the physical exercises were to her body and ability as a sword bearer.

The evenings were filled with mental exercises, aimed at enhancing Rhapsody's bond with the sword, as well as her own natural talents.

'As a Singer, you already know the world is made up of vibrations, waves of color, of light, of sound,' Oelendra said as they entered her chambers one evening not long after Rhapsody had arrived. 'The world is full of constant motion which most people never see, and 'tis through such motion, such vibrations, that you are able to affect the world through music. This will be true of the use of Daystar Clarion as well. If you concentrate, focus on the patterns you can already see as a Namer, you can discover weaknesses in armor, areas of injury or vulnerability. When

197

you have had more experience with this kind of concentration in combat, I will ask some of the Lirin soldiers to spar with you, especially those who have technique that is not perfect. Then you can practice finding your opponent's weaknesses in combat.'

Rhapsody looked perplexed. 'Isn't this what we're doing now?'

Oelendra smiled. 'Do you do it blindfolded?'

'Oh.'

'At first I will have them go easy on you.'

'There's really no point to that,' said Rhapsody, smiling. 'My Bolg friends never do, and I tend to doubt my enemies will either, so you may as well let them at me without holding back. If I survive, I'll be better for it.'

Oelendra returned her smile. Rhapsody's matter-of-fact nature and simple honesty reminded the warrior of herself when she was younger. The young Singer was different in her outlook on life than she had been, however. Probably because she had grown up among humans, she lacked the natural reserve of the Lirin, and instead plunged into life with an eagerness that touched Oelendra's heart in its recklessness.

It was an intense desire to celebrate the joy she saw around her, an insistence on believing there was good in situations where Oelendra herself saw none. Age and experience had taught her this was a life philosophy that guaranteed hurt, but it was scintillating to be around, exciting to be part of. She hoped Rhapsody's need to burn brightly would more reflect her tie to the stars and their enduring, steady light, than the momentary glory of the fire to which she was also tied, which roared with passion and died quickly as the fuel that sustained it was consumed.

The lack of caution that was evident in almost every move Rhapsody made did not apply to the commitment of her heart, however. That she guarded with diligent wariness. Oelendra had noticed that she was willing to smile at the young Lirin men who handed her flowers in the street when they were out on their walks, or who left small gifts on Oelendra's doorstep for her, but was unwilling to fulfill their requests for meetings in the glen or walks in the moonlight.

Whenever a man got his courage up to ask her to her face, she would either arrange for him to join the two of them for a meal, knowing how intimidating dining with the Lirin champion could be, or beg off, citing her need to train. Oelendra respected her privacy about it but wondered all the same. She was wise enough to know that she could train Rhapsody's body but not her spirit. *Ryle hira*, she thought. Life is what it is, the old Liringlas expression. All she could do was give her tools and pray for the best.

One night they sat before Oelendra's hearth, quietly drinking mugs of *dol mwl* before the roaring fire. Oelendra stared past the flames, her mind wandering down old roads. Rhapsody's own thoughts were closer to home, and to the world she had awoken into.

'Oelendra?'

'Hmm?'

'How can we find the F'dor? If you've been unsuccessful all this time, does that mean it might be unable to be found at all? That we will have to wait until it strikes, and react defensively?'

Oelendra put down her mug and regarded the Singer thoughtfully. 'I wish I knew,' she said at last. 'Certainly that would be unfortunate, as it gives all the advantages to the F'dor.

'I've spent centuries pondering ways to find it. I had hoped that the Cymrians would be reunited by now; Llauron has been working on that goal for centuries. There is a good deal of power in that population, and those that remember the Seren War would be eager to focus their talents on destroying the F'dor, if they can be convinced that it exists. 'Twould need to be a new, wiser group of leaders then we had in Anwyn and Gwylliam to do it, however.

'Without the reunited Cymrians, I suspect the crown of the Lirin might be useful in locating the demon if there were a monarch to wear it. Sadly, the greatest power the Purity Diamond would have had – the capability of trapping and holding the demon within it, is gone forever. This, no doubt, is why it sought to have the diamond destroyed.

'When I was Iliachenva'ar in the old land, I was sometimes able to see hidden evil things through the flames of Daystar Clarion. Your bond with fire may permit you to see such things through the sword in ways I am no longer able, especially since the F'dor are bound to fire. The Three may come, though I have given up hope of that. The only other thing I can think of is that we may come across a Dhracian somewhere in the world; Dhracians are the only race that can find F'dor by natural ability.'

Rhapsody opened her mouth to ask about the Three, but Oelendra's final comment caused it to close rapidly. She thought back to where she had first heard of the race. It was in the darkness of the Root, on the first night she had come to think of Achmed as something other than an obstacle.

What, did you think you're the only half-breed in the world?

Of course not.

Grunthor is half-Bengard.

And you?

I'm half-Dhracian. So you see, we're all mongrels.

'What can you tell me about Dhracians, Oelendra?'

Oelendra rose and threw another log on the fire. 'Dhracians were one of the Elder races, older indeed than all but the Firstborn, and they were the ancient enemies of the F'dor. They had a racial hatred of the demonic spirits that ran immensely deep, and they set forth on an ancient crusade to rid the world of them.

'The Dhracians, though humanlike, were also in many ways insectlike, and lived in deep caverns within the earth; some may still. They were said to be very quick, very agile, and they could see the world in shades of vibrations, as you have learned to. I am not certain, but I believe this is how they could sense the F'dor. They had a natural ability to turn the tables on them, to bind them, in a way.

199

'A Dhracian, by the strange pattern of its own natural rhythms, can hold a F'dor in thrall, make it impossible for it to escape from the host while the ritual is in force. In theory, a Dhracian could help sniff the demon out, and hold it in its human body while someone else killed it. Then both parts, the human and the demon, would be destroyed. I always hoped to happen across a Dhracian in my travels, but of course I never did.'

Rhapsody thought back to the moment of Achmed's accidental renaming on the streets of Easton. 'Did you know the Brother?'

'The Brother?' Oelendra gave her an odd look. 'Now there's a name I haven't heard in a very long time. Nay, I did not know him. What makes you ask about him?'

Rhapsody hesitated for a moment. 'I heard the name once and wondered what it meant.'

'The Brother was the greatest assassin the old world had ever known, if the tales were true. Half-Dhracian, he was said to be the first of that race to be born on Serendair, and so was granted a bond to that land that increased his natural vibrational sensitivity. The Dhracians were all innately vibrationally sensitive, but in part due to his physiology, and in part to his status as the Eldest, his talent was greater than any other. What is more, he was bound to blood, much as you are to fire. Together, these skills made him a deadly foe.

''Twas said he could hear the heartbeat of an intended victim anywhere in the land and lock his own to it; I think that was part of the reason for his name. Once that happened, there was no place on the Island that his intended victim could run to escape him. And his skill was not only that of a seeker, but also of a slayer. He knew more ways to kill than anyone, but 'twas his speed and accuracy that proved the most dangerous. He could slay most opponents before they had the capacity to draw their swords, and that was only if one were lucky enough to have seen him coming. For the Brother did not need to see his victim; with his uncanny vibrational awareness, all he needed was to get within range of his weapon and fire – and the cwellan, his weapon of choice, had an astonishing range.'

'About a quarter-mile,' Rhapsody said absently.

'I wouldn't know,' Oelendra replied. Rhapsody looked quickly at the woman, who was gazing at her purposefully.

'I'm sorry; please go on.'

The Lirin champion gave her a long look, then continued. 'He had always served as an independent, neutral to all causes and serving no one lord, but rather whoever interested him and paid for his talents at the moment.

'Then, that seemed to change. We never knew for certain, but it seemed that during the early days of the Seren War he began to serve the enemies of the Seren king. He performed services that did not include just standard assassinations, but also other tasks, and several of our leaders and allies met their ends through the deadly disks of the cwellan.

'It seemed quite odd to us, for, as I told you, Dhracians are the ancient enemy of the F'dor. It was strange enough for the Brother to have chosen sides in a political argument, but for him to have served the F'dor, or even their allies, seemed to be against the natural order of things. And then one day he vanished, never to be seen again. 'Twas one of those mysteries to which we never found the answer.'

Rhapsody nodded, but remained quiet. She turned slightly away from the fire, hoping Oelendra wouldn't pressure her for answers. She did not. The older woman just watched her for a while before returning to silently staring at the flames.

Ashe's face haunted her dreams that night, as it had for weeks. Oelendra had come the first night when she had woken, crying out in her nightmare, to find Rhapsody sitting up in bed, shivering beneath the heavy furs, her eyes staring wildly.

'Are you all right, dear?'

After a moment Rhapsody nodded. 'I'm very sorry, Oelendra; I'm afraid I do this a lot. Perhaps it's best if I sleep in the garden.' She began to rise from the bed.

'Don't be foolish,' said the older woman, sitting down on the edge of her bed. She reached out and gently stroked the Singer's hair. 'You can't help it if you're prescient. 'Tis actually a useful skill, if it doesn't ruin your health due to sleep deprivation.'

'Or that of your friends,' Rhapsody said. 'You've known other people who are prescient?'

'Many of the First Generationers were. I think it contributed to their eventual insanity.'

Rhapsody sighed. 'Well, I can easily see how it could.'

'Don't let it discourage you, Rhapsody, and don't underestimate the importance of the power. It can be a bellwether, a forewarning or a clue when there is no other. What's a little sleep lost if it saves your life, or ends the threat of war?'

Her words came back to Rhapsody now as she woke again, clammy from the sweat of fear. In her dream Ashe sought her endlessly, hunting her wherever she went. Each time she found safety he would be there momentarily, following her ceaselessly. Finally he had caught her; she had been unable to wrest herself free as he spun her forcefully around, took her head in his hands and jerked it skyward. He took her sword hand in his own and raised Daystar Clarion to the heavens, pointing it at a distant star.

'Hiven vet.' *Say it.* 'Ewin vet.' *Name it.*

She had whispered the name of the star, though upon wakening she had forgotten what it was. With a furious roar, starfire descended from the sky and struck a figure some distance away; its body arched in agony and burst into flames. As she watched it burn, the figure turned slowly.

It was Llauron.

She woke once again, alone in the dark, trembling.

★

201

Rhapsody, you're not concentrating.' Oelendra's voice was patient, but had a touch of scolding in it. ''Tis easy enough for you to call upon the fire aspects of the sword, and that's good. You have a natural affinity for those powers that I did not have, it helps you link to it, but you need be able to utilize all of its attributes if you are to fight the enemy that is waiting for you. Fire is not enough to destroy the F'dor – 'tis their own element. You need to make that link with the ethereal aspects of Daystar Clarion. You need to reach out to the stars. If you do not know the *seren*, you will die when you face the F'dor. Now try it again, and this time concentrate.'

'I know, I'm sorry.' Rhapsody tried to clear her thoughts and focus on her breathing. She held the sword before her, closed her eyes and reached out with her mind. In a moment she saw the world like a grid, lines roughly forming the silhouettes of rocks and trees. Oelendra appeared as a glowing human form. She hummed her naming note, *ela*, and the sword seemed to change its vibration to match the tune.

At once the clarity of her vision increased, and even through the brightness of the sun the stars suddenly seemed to come out. The landscape of the garden appeared on the imaginary grid, everything plotted in proportion and place except for the river that flowed through the field. She noted that she could not see through it. It caused a disturbance in her vision, and she began to wonder if that was how Ashe would appear. At the thought her concentration broke and her inner vision of the world vanished. Rhapsody sighed heavily and lowered her sword.

'I'm sorry. My mind just keeps wandering.'

Oelendra sat on a garden bench and pointed to the seat next to her. 'Do you want to tell me about it?'

Rhapsody stood quietly for a moment, then came over and sat beside her. 'How do you know for certain whether to trust someone?'

'You don't,' Oelendra replied, 'not really. You have to take people as individuals, listen to what they say and judge that against what you know. You have to give others the benefit of the doubt, but hold a piece of your trust in reserve until they prove themselves one way or the other. You are blessed with extraordinary wisdom, Rhapsody. Look into his or her heart and see what you find there.'

'What if there isn't time to wait until they prove themselves? What if you don't know anything about the person? What if you can't see into his heart? What if you can't even see his face?'

Oelendra sighed, her eyes clouding with memory. 'That's a hard place to be, Rhapsody. I was really only in it once. When I first became the Iliachenva'ar, I met a man who seemed to be willing to help me, but those were troubled times, more so perhaps than even today, and I was a hunted woman. Then he came my way out of nowhere and offered his assistance. I didn't know whether I could trust him or not. F'dor are masters of deceit; in those days there were more of them, and my enemies had countless servants. 'Twas quite a dilemma; if I made the wrong choice it meant that I could be killed and that Daystar Clarion would fall into the hands of our enemies. That was a blow my allies might not have survived. Finally, I just had to trust my heart. 'Tis all we really have in the end, anyway.'

Rhapsody looked crestfallen. 'That's not good news. My heart has not proven reliable.'

Oelendra smiled. 'We all make mistakes. I think perhaps you should give your heart a second chance. I know you well enough to trust what you would discern.'

'You shouldn't gamble your life on anything I would decide.'

Oelendra her reached out and touched the young Singer's face. 'In a way I already have. And I am confident the wager was a winner.' Rhapsody smiled and looked down.

'What ended up happening with this man?'

'I married him,' Oelendra said with a broad smile. 'His name was Pendaris, and in our short time together we loved a lifetime's worth.'

'What happened?' Rhapsody asked gently.

'He died in the Seren War; he didn't live to see the exodus of the Cymrians,' Oelendra answered. Her smile grew nostalgic. 'Not long after we were married we were captured by F'dor and those that served them. They tortured him to death.'

Rhapsody touched her hand. 'I'm sorry, Oelendra.'

''Twas a terrible war, Rhapsody, one you should be grateful that you missed. But in the end, at least he and I were able to share the time together that we did. The truth is, if I hadn't trusted him when I did, I probably would have survived, but I never would have had the happiest moments of my life. That is something to always remember when you face a choice – the cost of what might have been.'

Shrike was slightly late, and it irritated him. In addition to disliking being tardy for any meeting, he knew that his master would hardly appreciate being kept waiting. Given who that was, it made for some discomfort.

As he rode into sight of the meeting place, he saw, as he knew he would, that he was being awaited. In the center of the road stood his master's steed, as beautiful a piece of horseflesh as Shrike had ever seen, with its rider atop it, glaring at him. Shrike sighed. The day had started out with a drenching thunderstorm. It seemed about to get worse.

'Where the blazes have you been? It's almost dark.'

'Sorry, m'lord,' said Shrike breezily, trying to diffuse his master's anger. 'I wanted to be assured that I was not followed.'

'Well, how went your visit?' The beautiful stallion turned about in the road.

Shrike's own horse stepped in place nervously. 'It was as you suspected. The Firbolg warlord is the one you saw last year, and his Bolg general was there as well. The blond girl you mentioned didn't live up to the description in my opinion, however.'

'What do you mean?'

Shrike looked uncomfortable. Generally he was not afraid of his leader's wrath, and ordinarily their discourse was easy. Today, however, the subject of the takeover of Canrif was making him testier than usual. The light in his azure eyes was fierce, and his tone of voice was harsh. Shrike could guess the reason.

'Well, this girl was in her teen years, and she was somewhat plain of face and sallow of skin. Unremarkable. Given your experience and proclivities, I would hardly think you would have seen her as comely. In addition, she was unformidable.'

'It must be another, then,' said his master, drawing the reins up tighter. 'There was no mistaking either of those characteristics in the woman I saw.' The silver rings interlaced in his black chain mail flashed.

'There is another, then, most likely,' Shrike agreed.

'And what of Canrif?'

'It is surprisingly intact, though unrestored, which, of course, is *not* surprising. What is interesting is that the Bolg are manufacturing goods of impressive quality, and have even managed to produce a preliminary pressing from the ancient vineyards.'

His master nodded. 'And their forces?'

'Substantial and well trained. I would credit the giant Bolg commander for that. He didn't say much, but his hallmark is clear in the reaction of the various Bolg guards.'

'Have they found the vaults? The library?'

'Undoubtedly.'

Anborn scowled. 'Damnation. All right, Shrike, let's get out of the rain. There's a tavern not far from here, decent food, reasonable wenches. We have some planning to do.' Shrike nodded and spurred his horse, trying to catch up with Anborn as he galloped up the road into the coming darkness.

24

Oelendra smiled to herself as her pupil landed a solid blow to Urist's midsection, spinning gracefully to parry the strike Syntianta had aimed at her back. She watched as Rhapsody whirled to face her first opponent again; pulling her killing strike before the sword actually touched the Lirin soldier's throat. 'Gained!' they said in unison, then they both laughed. Rhapsody had no time to savor the moment; Syntianta was on her now, swinging two-handed, a skill she was renowned for. In addition, Rhapsody was blindfolded. She was doing amazingly well regardless.

Oelendra decided she was doing too well. Quietly she approached the sparring match, picking up a quarterstaff from the ground. She waited until both Urist and Syntianta had Rhapsody fully engaged, then crept up on her from the side and slapped at her knees with the staff, attempting to trip her up.

The flurry of moves that resulted was almost impossible to follow with the eye. Rhapsody spun gracefully and knocked Urist to the ground, jumping over the staff and rolling out of the way in time to unbalance Syntianta, who stumbled into Urist. Then, with a ringing sweep, she slapped the quarterstaff out of Oelendra's hands with Daystar Clarion, sending it spinning into the trees.

Oelendra laughed aloud and embraced her student, pulling the blindfold from her eyes. 'That's enough for today; let us celebrate. Congratulations, Rhapsody; you now dance almost as beautifully as you sing.'

That night Rhapsody decided to trust Oelendra with one of her greatest secrets. Unlike the others she had already imparted to her, this one affected her friends. She remembered Achmed's caution to her, and decided to follow Oelendra's advice and trust her heart. It told her she was safe.

She tiptoed down the upstairs hallway to Oelendra's bedroom. A light was still burning; Rhapsody knew that many nights Oelendra did not sleep at all. Being full-blooded Lirin she had no need to, as she was refreshed and rejuvenated by the subconscious meditation that resulted from the vibrations that her physiology drew from the forest. She tapped softly.

'Come in, dear.'

Rhapsody opened the door. Oelendra was sitting up in bed, unbinding her long thin braid. The sight of her caused tears to well up in Rhapsody's eyes. Her mother had taken down her own hair each night when they were alone, and she had brushed it and Rhapsody's before the fire. Oelendra represented her mother in so many ways that it never failed to cause her the pain of memory when something reminded her of this. Oelendra knew instantly that it had happened. She patted the bed next to her.

'Sit down.' Oelendra began brushing her hair.

Rhapsody complied. 'Oelendra, tell me of the Three, and the prophecies about them.'

Oelendra smiled. ''Twere rantings, Rhapsody. Manwyn was trying to spare her sister from being cast out by the Cymrian Council. It didn't work. The Council banished Anwyn in spite of her sister's promises that saviors would come to undo the wrongs she had committed. After four hundred years, I think 'tis time we give up the fantasy and make different plans.'

Rhapsody nodded. 'Do you remember exactly what she said?'

'Aye; I helped write them down. Why?'

The Singer smiled. 'Well, you know me, always searching for lore.'

Oelendra looked at her seriously, then began to recite the words in the language of the Cymrians.

The Three shall come, leaving early, arriving late,
The lifestages of all men:

Each man, formed in blood and born in it,
Walks the Earth and sustained by it,
Reaching to the sky, and sheltered beneath it,
He ascends there only in his ending, becoming part of the stars.
Blood gives new beginning, Earth gives sustenance, the Sky gives dreams in
*   life – eternity in death.*
Thus shall the Three be, one to the other.

Rhapsody nodded. 'And there has never been a further explanation?'

'Not really,' Oelendra answered. 'The sages studied Manwyn's words, trying to discern their meaning, and finally decided 'twas an allegory that meant anyone could kill the F'dor, since she spoke of the lifestages of all men. I didn't believe that at the time, but I have decided since that 'twas more or less useless information. Why are you so interested tonight? Did you have a dream?'

'No,' Rhapsody answered. 'And there was no other explanation?'

'Well, actually, Anborn, Gwylliam's son, asked Manwyn before the Council how the Three would repair the rift.'

'Do you remember what she said?'

Oelendra nodded and thought a moment.

As each life begins, Blood is joined, but is spilled as well; it divides too easily
*   to heal the rift.*
The Earth is shared by all, but it too is divided, generation into generation.
Only the Sky encompasses all, and the sky cannot be divided; thus shall it
be the means by which peace and unity will come.
If you seek to mend the rift, General, guard the Sky, lest it fall.

Rhapsody laughed. 'Well, that was helpful.'

Oelendra put her hairbrush down on the bedside table. 'Now do you see why I don't put any stock in the babbling of a madwoman?'

'Yes, but perhaps you should.'

Oelendra looked sharply at her. 'Say what you mean, Rhapsody.'

The Singer regarded her seriously. 'You know I didn't sail with you, Oelendra, yet you know I am also a First Generation Cymrian. You have assumed that instead of sailing with the Cymrians I went to a country nearer to Serendair, as so many Liringlas did, but I did not. I actually have only been in this world for a very short time. I have told you about Grunthor, my Bolg friend who taught me the sword. I should probably tell you that he is Cymrian as well. We came with a third friend.' Her voice grew softer as Oelendra's eyes widened. 'He is Dhracian.'

Oelendra took her hand, clutching it. 'You're one of the Three?'

Rhapsody shrugged. 'I think so. I mean, I don't know, really, but Grunthor is tied to the Earth, and Achmed to blood. And since I am Liringlas, I would guess that could make me a child of the sky.'

'Leaving early, arriving late,' Oelendra murmured to herself. 'None but the sky encompasses all, thus shall it be the only means by which peace will come and unity will result.' Her eyes began to shine. '"Tis you, Rhapsody; I knew it from the moment I saw you. Even if you weren't one of the Three, I believe in my heart that you are the one to do this; the true Iliachenva'ar. The sword has borne out Manwyn's prediction.' Her hands trembled slightly from excitement.

'Now, Oelendra, don't get carried away,' Rhapsody warned. 'I know nothing of the Three, and if it is foretold, nobody foretold me. I just thought you should know that I didn't come alone.'

'And you will never be alone again, Rhapsody. Whatever it takes to prepare you for this fight, whatever your destiny may be, I am here for you.'

25

Rhapsody had awakened early, the sonnet from her dreams still nattering in her head. She had bathed, and dressed, but it still wouldn't leave, driving her to distraction.

She listened at the door to see if her predawn putterings had disturbed Oelendra, but there was no sound from the hall. Rhapsody eyed the lute in the corner with annoyance, then gave in with a sigh, knowing that once the composing session began she would have to see it through or be unable to think of anything else.

She made herself a cup of tea. As she sipped the steaming liquid she remembered Ashe's insulting comments and wondered what the problem was. It didn't taste that bad to her.

She settled into the comfortable chair across from the fireplace, tuned the lute, and began to play. At first the song was cold, uncooperative, but after a few minutes the notes began to flow with more regularity and the melody started to take shape. Rhapsody played softly so as not to disturb her host. Soon the room began to hum with creative energy, adding to the light and warmth within it.

The fire sang on the hearth, crackling in rhythm to the notes from her lute, hissing in time. Rhapsody was lost in the music when the door opened.

'Are you ready?' Oelendra asked, entering the room. She was dressed in her customary leather armor, worn from years of workouts, and carried her high-collared cape.

Rhapsody looked up from her lute to the iron-grated window. Morning was still at least an hour away.

'It's dark outside, Oelendra,' she answered, her fingers continuing to work on the strings.

'Aye, but you're awake, or at least you do a good impression of it.'

Rhapsody smiled at her. 'I am almost finished with this sonnet,' she said, her eyes returning to her instrument. 'It will be completed before the sun comes up. As soon as I'm done I'm at your disposal.'

'Funny,' Oelendra said quietly, 'I was of the notion that you were at my disposal regardless.'

It was an odd comment, and Rhapsody looked up. Oelendra was studying her intently. When her eyes met Rhapsody's, she smiled. Rhapsody smiled back, feeling as if she was missing something.

'My focus should be better today,' she said, returning to the sonnet. 'Once this song is out of my head, I should be able to concentrate again.'

'Really?' Oelendra's voice was kind.

'Yes,' Rhapsody said, tuning a string that had slipped flat. 'This lute is a harsh taskmaster. It nagged at me all night while I slept; that's why I got up so early. It keeps drawing my attention back to the song, demanding I finish it. I don't think it will let me rest or focus until it's done.'

'What an annoying instrument. Well, if that's all – ' Oelendra reached out and yanked the lute from Rhapsody's hands. As Rhapsody opened her mouth in protest Oelendra smashed the instrument into the wall, then threw it across the room into the fireplace, where it splintered into crackling fragments and the whine of burning gut strings. Rhapsody's eyes stung in astonishment as she watched the wood begin to kindle.

'Well, then,' Oelendra said lightly, 'now that 'tis not a problem anymore, are you ready to start?'

It took a moment for Rhapsody to regain her voice. 'I cannot believe you just did that.'

'I'm waiting.'

'What in the name of the One-God is the matter with you?' Rhapsody shouted. She gestured at the fireplace. 'That instrument was priceless! It was a gift from Elynsynos, filled with lore and history. And now it's – '

''Tis going to keep the room warm.'

'You think this is *funny*?'

'Nay, Rhapsody, I do not.' All pleasantries had been stripped from Oelendra's manner, replaced by a cold, angry determination. 'I don't think this is funny, and I don't think this is a game, though you seem to. This is about as deadly serious as it gets, and you'd better begin acting like you understand this. You are now the Iliachenva'ar. You are one of the Three – you have a job to do.'

'That doesn't excuse what you did! I do have other responsibilities, Oelendra, besides this. I'm a Namer, too. I have to practice my profession, or I'll lose it.' Rhapsody swallowed rapidly, trying to contain the anger that was burning behind her eyes.

Oelendra began to pace the room restlessly. 'Perhaps, but, rare as they may be, there are other Namers in this world. There is but one Iliachenva'ar. You have a tremendous responsibility to live up to. The rest of your interests do not matter.'

Rhapsody felt her fists begin to coil in fury. 'Pardon? Are you now dictating what I am? I don't remember volunteering for this assignment.'

'Nay, you were conscripted,' said the Lirin champion, a harsh edge in her voice. 'Now get up.'

'Oelendra, what is the matter with you?'

A washbasin and pitcher shattered against the floor, sending shards of crockery flying, as the Lirin champion slammed the washstand into the wall. 'I can't kill the damned thing; that's what's the matter with me!' Oelendra snarled. 'If I could, it would have been ashes on the wind ten centuries ago. But I failed; I made mistakes, and the price has been great. You can't let it escape, Rhapsody. Your destiny is foretold, and you can shrug at it all you like, but you will kill the F'dor, or die trying. You have no choice. My responsibility is to give you a chance to be successful at it, and you are wasting my time.'

Rhapsody closed her mouth; it had been open since Oelendra's tirade began. She tried to formulate the words to calm her mentor down, but realized immediately that she couldn't. There was more than rage in Oelendra's eyes, there was something even deeper that Rhapsody couldn't fathom. She remembered the warnings about Oelendra's fury and her reputation as a harsh taskmaster. All she could do was try to stay out of her way.

'Listen to me, Rhapsody. I have sent eighty-four fully trained warriors after this beast, and not one of them, *not one*, has returned. You have more raw talent, more potential, than any of them to defeat it, but you lack the discipline and the will. Your heart wants to save the world, but your body is lazy. You don't understand the depth of the evil lurking out there, waiting to destroy you.

'And if you can't find a shudder over your own death and damnation, think of the people you love. Think of your friends, of your sister, of the children you look after. Do you have any idea what's in store for them if you fail, as I did? Nay, you do not, because if you did you would be out there right now praying to get hold of this thing and drive your blade through it again and again and *again* – to taste its death on your hands and relish the joy of retribution for all the heinous things it has done over the millennia of its life!'

Rhapsody looked away; she could not bear to watch Oelendra rant. Deep within her a sense of calm descended, the feeling of peace that signaled imminent danger to her. But it was not Oelendra who threatened her, it was the panic that rose in her throat as she contemplated the task ahead of her.

'Do you know what befell your family, your friends, at this thing's hands? Do you know happened to Easton, Rhapsody?'

'No,' Rhapsody whispered.

Oelendra's eyes cleared; it was as if the Singer's tone had brought her around. 'Be grateful; 'twasn't pretty,' she said in a calmer voice. 'You have the chance to end it, Rhapsody, end the suffering for all time. You have a natural tie to the stars and to fire, and the aid of a Dhracian. You're one of the Three. It knows you're here, you realize. It has been waiting for you as long as I have. But if you're not ready it will catch you unaware, and what it will do to you and those you love will make death seem like a blessing. And then I may as well have handed the sword to it myself long ago.'

Rhapsody took a deep breath, and willed herself to be calm. There was a desperation under Oelendra's obstreperous tone that touched her; deep within herself she felt it resonate, and she could identify the song. It was the sound of unspeakable pain, pain as she herself had felt upon coming to this land. Clearly the ancient warrior was not as much at peace with the Past as she had seemed at first. Moreover, as impossible as it seemed, there was a cold fear in Oelendra, a fear whose depth knew no bottom.

'Oelendra, we have to resolve this,' she said, struggling to keep her voice steady. 'I don't want there to be anger between us. Please, will you sit down and talk to me for a moment? After that I will gladly go with you to the field, and you can work me through sunset and beyond if you wish. But it will be unproductive unless we settle this.'

Reluctantly the older warrior took a seat at the table. Rhapsody pulled back the chair opposite her, and sat down.

'Oelendra, I can't be the Illachenva'ar that you were.'

'Don't be ridiculous, Rhapsody. I wasn't born with the sword in my hand. I had to learn it too, just like you. It takes commitment. And focus. And dedication. You can't be a reluctant warrior.'

'I can only be a reluctant warrior,' Rhapsody answered. 'I have no other choice. That's not what I meant, however. I know I can learn the sword. I have a far better teacher than you did – the best, in fact. But each of us has different gifts. You are blessed with strength that I don't have, and a mind like a fine instrument.' She looked to the burning ashes of the lute in the fireplace. 'Well, maybe that wasn't a good analogy.'

Oelendra smiled in spite of herself, her anger diminishing somewhat. 'I get the gist.'

'And I have skills that you don't have. I am a different person; if I try to be you I will fail. It seems to me in a fight against a foe of this strength that every skill can and must be brought to bear. So I have to become the best swordsman I can be, and I no doubt will, because I have your wisdom and experience to guide me, not to mention your boot on my hindquarters. But I don't think it makes sense to ignore the other weapons at my disposal, either. You keep telling me to maximize my strengths in combat; "rely on your speed and skill, don't fight like a Bolg" – isn't that right?'

'Is there a point?'

Rhapsody exhaled. 'Maybe. I hope so. There are many kinds of weapons, and all of them are powerful in their way and time. The point is, music for me can be my most powerful weapon, even more powerful than the sword. It is not a pastime or recreation; it's my best skill, Oelendra, my *best*. That doesn't diminish in any way my commitment to the sword.'

Oelendra stared at her for a long moment, then she looked down and let her breath out slowly. 'You're right. I really had no right to take my pain out on you today. I'm sorry about the lute.' Something in her voice sounded wrong; there was an undertone that made Rhapsody frown.

'Oelendra, look at me.' When there was no response, Rhapsody pressed her again. 'Please.'

After a moment the older woman raised her head, and her eyes met Rhapsody's. There were tears in them that startled her.

'Oelendra? What's wrong? Please tell me.'

'Today.' It was a whisper.

'What about today?'

Oelendra looked into the fire. 'The anniversary.'

'Today is your wedding anniversary? Oh, Oelendra.'

The warrior smiled sadly. 'Nay, Rhapsody, not the anniversary of our wedding. 'Tis the anniversary of his death.'

Rhapsody's face melted in sorrow. 'Oh, gods. I'm so sorry.' She bolted from the table and ran to her mentor, wrapping her arms from behind around her broad shoulders. She held her for a long moment, as Oelendra's hand came to rest on her own. Then she released her, and went to the sword rack.

'All right, Oelendra,' she said, belting her sword. 'I'm ready now.'

In the darkness of her dream Rhapsody could see a pinprick of light. It shone across the room from her, lighting the corner, and she sat up to watch as it grew in brilliance. She squinted in the dark. She could see the light source twinkle; it was a tiny star on top of a thin strand of spider-silk, hovering in the air.

As she stared at the infinitesimal star, she became aware of other lights in the darkness, pools of illumination composed of hundreds of dimmer points, glowing softly around her. In the dark they looked like brooches in a jeweler's case, sparkling gems against the black velvet of night. Then she looked down, and Rhapsody could see she was no longer in her room in Oelendra's house, but was sitting on a thin wisp of a cloud in the sky, hovering above the land wrapped in night.

From her lofty perch she watched as the sun rose, clear and golden, at the edge of the eastern horizon. The sunlight touched the land, and as it did she could see that the tiny star was the minaret in Sepulvarta, the towering Spire in the pictures Lord Stephen had showed her. The solar light glinted brightly off the Spire, and then touched the rest of the land, illuminating all of Roland at her feet. The jeweled pins were revealed as cities, which ceased to glow as the sun came up.

In the back of her mind, Rhapsody felt the urge to sing her morning aubade, but her voice would not sound. She shook her head, and as she did, she watched a shadow cross the land, a deep shadow that was moving toward Sepulvarta. She felt horror rise in her heart as the shadow fell across the Spire, and then consumed the basilica, plunging it into darkness.

In the darkness stood an old man. Rhapsody was now no more than a few feet away from him as he stood praying at an altar of a vast basilica, his face white as death. Black fire burned around him, and as he chanted, blood began to pour from his mouth and nose, staining the white vestments he wore a brilliant crimson. She watched, still unable to speak, as the dark fire consumed him.

A moment later the image cleared, and five men came into the basilica. They ran to the pool of blood where the old man's body had been and stood over it, praying. Two of the men, a callow youth and a decrepit elderly man with hollow eyes, stared helplessly at the pool of blood on the floor. Two of the other men drew swords, and instantly began sparring across the pool. The last, an older man with a kindly face, began sorting papers and making tea for everyone, cleaning up the mess. He turned to Rhapsody and smiled, his hand extended, offering her a cup of tea as well. She shook her head, and he went about his business.

Rhapsody heard a sound at the window of the basilica, and went to look out. Traffic was the same as every other day, townspeople walking about, merchants selling their wares, all amidst a great river of blood that ran through the streets, drenching them to the knees. The people seemed oblivious to it, even as it rose above their heads, drowning them. She could hear the baker making change for the washerwoman at his window as his mouth filled with blood.

She heard a tremendous crack and looked skyward. The star on the top of the Spire dangled from the tower for a moment, then fell into the red sea that had been Sepulvarta, exactly as the star of her earlier dreams had. As it hit the street a great light slashed across the sky, blinding her. When she could see again she was sitting in the Great White Tree, the diadem of Tyrian on her brow, surrounded by Lirin who sang gently with her as the tree descended slowly beneath the waves of the ocean of blood.

There was more to the dream, but Rhapsody was jarred awake by her own screams. Oelendra was sitting on the bed across from her, holding her arms at the elbows.

'Rhapsody? Are you all right?'

Rhapsody could only stare at her and shake. She blinked hard, trying to recall the image clearly. It had obviously been a vision of some kind, a warning she was afraid to ignore. Oelendra sensed her struggle and disappeared, leaving her to find her way to clarity again.

''Tis warm enough?'

Rhapsody took a sip of the *dol mwl* and nodded. 'It's fine. Thank you for bringing it. I'm sorry to have awakened you.'

Oelendra watched in silence as her pupil drank deeply, willing her heart to stop racing. She had grown accustomed to Rhapsody's nightmares, and was only rarely aware of them now; this was the first time she had awakened to the sound of screaming. Having heard the content of the dream, she was not surprised at the Singer's reaction.

When Rhapsody finished she set down her mug. 'I have to go to Sepulvarta in the morning.'

Oelendra nodded. 'The man in the white robes fits the description of the Patriarch, certainly, although no one outside of his inner circle ever sees him, so I don't know what he actually looks like. I don't know who any of the others are, if they are not just symbols.'

'I recognized the young man who came in with the five as the Blesser of Canderre-Yarim,' said Rhapsody. 'I met him once when negotiating a peace treaty between Roland and Ylorc, and he seemed a decent fellow. I imagine the death of the Patriarch would cause the consternation he showed in the dream.'

'Perhaps the others are the four remaining benisons,' suggested Oelendra.

'Perhaps,' said Rhapsody. 'I'm sorry to have to leave so abruptly. I wish we could have more time together.'

"Tis time,' said Oelendra simply. 'You know all you need to, Rhapsody; I was wrong to say you weren't ready. You are. You are strong, and skilled in the ways of the sword now, and have a wise and giving heart. Nothing remains but for you to follow your destiny. I will help you in any way I can. Remember that you are welcome here at any time, for as long as you want to stay. And if you do decide you have it within you to try to unite the Lirin as well as the Cymrians, come to me and I will support you in that as well.'

Rhapsody smiled at her, but there was grave sadness in her eyes. 'I think it will be harder for me to say goodbye to you than to anyone I have met so far, Oelendra. In the short time I've been here I have felt at home for the first time since I left Serendair. It will be a little like losing my family all over again.'

'Then don't say it,' Oelendra answered, rising and walking toward the door. 'As long as someone is thinking of you here, you will have never really left. And, I can assure you, someone always will be. Try to rest. Morning will be here soon.'

'The High Holy Day in the religion of the Patriarch is the first day of summer,' said Oelendra, handing Rhapsody a saddlebag. The Singer nodded as she positioned the pack across the back of the chestnut mare Oelendra had given her. It was a strong animal, and gentle; Rhapsody could see innate intelligence in her eyes. 'If you ride overland and avoid the roads you can make it just in time.'

Rhapsody was not so sure. 'Sepulvarta is two weeks from here, you said. If I don't follow the roads I'll get lost. I've never been there before.'

Oelendra smiled. 'The Spire is an enormous beacon lighted by a piece of a star. If you concentrate, you should be able to feel it in your soul, even without Daystar Clarion. With the sword to guide you to it, you will never be lost. No Lirin soul is ever lost under the stars at night, anyway.'

'My grandfather used to say the same thing about sailors,' said Rhapsody, smiling. Her smile dimmed as she heard her mother's voice again.

If you watch the sky and can find your guiding star, you will never be lost, never.

'I have one last lesson for you, one you mustn't forget,' said Oelendra, her eyes glistening. 'I would have told you this one day, but I didn't know our time together would end so quickly.

'In the old land, there was a brotherhood of warriors called the Kinsmen. They were masters of the craft of fighting, and dedicated to the wind and the star you were born beneath. They were accepted into the brotherhood for two things: incredible skill forged over a lifetime of soldiering, and a selfless act of service to others, protecting an innocent at threat of one's own life.

'Someday you may attain this honor, Rhapsody; you are excellent Kinsman material. You will know if you have by the sound of the wind in your ear, whispering to your heart. I have never met one in this new land; I don't know if the brotherhood still exists. But if it does, a Kinsman will always answer your cry for help on the wind if you are one yourself. Listen well, and I will teach it to you.' In a quavering voice Oelendra began to sing. The words were in Old Cymrian.

By the Star, I will wait, I will watch, I will call and will be heard.

'Don't forget to call if you have to,' said Oelendra. 'I don't know if I will hear you, but if I do you can be certain I will come to you.'

Tears stung Rhapsody's eyes. 'I know you will. Don't worry, Oelendra, I'll be fine.'

'Of course you will.'

Rhapsody patted the mare. 'Well, I had best be off. Thank you for everything.'

'Nay, Rhapsody, thank *you* for everything,' the Lirin warrior replied. 'You've brought far more here than you leave with. Travel well, and be safe.'

Rhapsody leaned down and kissed the ancient cheek. 'I'll tell you all about it when I return one day.'

''Twill be a marvelous tale, to be sure,' said Oelendra, blinking back tears. 'Now, go. You have a long day's ride ahead of you.' She gave the horse a gentle slap on the flank and waved as Rhapsody rode off, the latest in a long line of pupils to carry her prayers forward with them. Somehow it was different this time, she knew. She didn't dare to hope anymore; she had seen too many young champions take their leave, never to return. But this time, her heart was riding off with this one. If she never returned, it wouldn't, either.

26

The ride to Sepulvarta proved to be invigorating. Summer was preceding her by a day like an elusive quarry as she rode northeast, following its trail of new grass and reborn needles on the evergreen trees that lined the forest. Each day the air grew warmer, the leaves fuller, the meadow grass higher, and Rhapsody felt the fire in her soul growing stronger in the flourishing heat. The blossoms and pale leaves of spring had given way to rich green foliage that shaded the ground, ground that grew drier and firmer in the advent of the season of the sun.

The rush of the wind, the pounding of the horse's hooves, the speed of her desperate journey loosed a wildness in Rhapsody that had been held in check for too long. She had pulled the ribbon from her hair the first day she left the forest and entered the wide plains of Roland; her tresses streamed behind her as she and her mount flew over the ground. She turned her face to the sun and drank in its warmth, letting the burning rays of midday shine down on her countenance, turning her rosy skin a golden pink. By the time she had crossed the fields of Bethany and Navarne she felt healthier and stronger than she ever remembered being.

It took eleven days of furious travel to reach the outskirts of the city of Sepulvarta. The star-topped spire had been in view for three days before that. Rhapsody had first seen it at night, glowing dimly in the distance. It looked exactly as it had in her vision, and the sight of it caused her dreams that night to be especially intense. The nightmare that had made her undertake this journey had returned to her almost every night, a nagging reminder of her need to press on with all possible speed.

The road to the city was teeming with people, pilgrims on their way to the holy shrines, clergy traveling to and from assignments, as well as the typical humanity that wandered the thoroughfares from province to province, looking for commerce or other interaction, some honorable, some nefarious. It was fairly easy to blend in with the crowd and wend her way past the gates of the city proper, winding up eventually at the rectory of Lianta'ar, the Great Basilica of Sepulvarta, high on the hill at the outskirts of the city. It was a beautiful marble building attached to the basilica itself, its engraved brass doors guarded by soldiers in bright uniforms. Rhapsody tied her horse to the hitching area, tended to the mare's needs with water and oats, and approached the guards directly.

She had not gotten within ten feet of them when their spears crossed, one in front of the other.

'What do you want?'

Rhapsody stood up as straight as she could. 'I need to see His Grace.'

'Days of Pleas are in the winter; you're too late.'

She felt the fear she had carried since the first nightmare had come dissolve into irritation. 'I have to see him anyway. Please.'

'No one sees the Patriarch, even on Days of Pleas. Go away.'

Impatience was threatening to take over. Rhapsody kept her voice as calm as she could. 'Please tell His Grace that the Iliachenva'ar has come to stand as his champion. Please.' The guards said nothing. 'All right,' she said, attempting to control her rage, 'until you take my message to the Patriarch you will be unable to deliver any other.' She spoke the name of silence.

The guards looked at each other, then began to laugh. Pity crossed Rhapsody's face as they found themselves utterly without sound, and their faces contorted in confusion and fear. The younger of the two men clutched at his unresponsive throat, while the more experienced guard leveled his spear at her.

'Now, now, don't get testy,' she said, looking unimpressed. 'If you really want to set to it here in the street, I'd be glad to oblige, but I'm afraid my weapon is far better than yours; it really would be unfair. Now, please, gentlemen, I've been traveling for a long time and I really have no more patience left. Either take my message to the Patriarch, or get ready to defend yourselves.' She gave them her warmest smile to take the threat out of her words.

The younger of the two guards blinked, and his face went slack. He looked at the other guard, then back at Rhapsody, before turning and entering the rectory. The other guard kept his spear leveled at her. She, in turn, sat down on the stone steps of the manse to wait.

The view of the city from the steps of the rectory was majestic, sweeping from one edge of the hill to the other. Many of the buildings of Sepulvarta were constructed of white stone or marble, and the resulting effect was a city that glinted in sunlight, appearing somehow otherworldly, like a disappointing vision of the afterlife. Some of the ethereal light was doubtless imparted by the enormous pinnacle in the center of the city. The Spire was so tall that it looked down on the top of the basilica, despite the church being set on the hilltop hundreds of feet above the city itself. When the sun caught a facet of the star a broad slash of light flashed through the air, making the rooftops gleam in momentary glory.

The guard returned just as Rhapsody had decided to stand and stretch her legs.

'Please come with me.'

She followed him up the stone steps and through the heavy brass doors.

The bright sun of the city disappeared the moment Rhapsody entered the rectory. There were few windows, and the marble walls blotted out the light completely, leaving a dark and dismal feel to the interior of the beautiful building. Heavy tapestries hung on the walls and ornate brass candlesticks held large wax cylinders that provided the only light. The pungent scent of incense did little to mask the sharp odor of mildew and stale air.

She was led down several long hallways, past sallow-faced men in clerical black who stared at her as she walked by. Finally the guard stopped before a large carved door of black walnut and opened it slowly for her. He gestured with his hand, and Rhapsody went into the room.

It was approximately the same size as the meeting room behind the Great Hall in the Cauldron, with a large gilt star embossed on the floor. Other than that it was without ornament, and unfurnished except for a heavy black walnut chair sitting atop a rise of marble stairs, similar to a throne but without the grandeur customarily associated with one. In the chair sat a tall, thin man in richly embroidered robes of golden silk patterned with a silver star. He regarded her sternly as she stopped before him; he was no one she had ever seen before, not even in her dreams. She waited for him to speak.

He continued to watch her for a long moment, then his brow darkened. 'Well? What did you want to see me about?'

Rhapsody let her breath out slowly. 'Nothing.'

The stern face molded into an expression of anger. 'Nothing? Then why were you so insistent? Don't toy with me, young woman.'

'I believe you are the one who is toying with me,' answered Rhapsody as politely as she could, though a hint of her anger did creep into her tone. 'I need to see the real Patriarch. Misrepresentation of this nature hardly becomes him, or you.'

The anger vanished from his face in the flood of bewilderment that followed her statement. 'Who are you?'

'As I told the guards, I'm the Iliachenva'ar. It's all right if you don't understand what that means; I'm not here to see you. But the Patriarch does understand, or will, if you haven't seen fit to tell him I'm here yet. Now, with all due respect, sir, please take me to see him. There isn't much time.'

The man stared at her for a moment, then rose. 'His Grace is in preparation for the High Holy Day celebration. No one can see him.'

'Why don't you let him make that decision?' Rhapsody asked, folding her arms. 'Really, I think you will find he wants to see me.'

He considered her words. 'I will ask him.'

'Thank you. I am grateful.'

The man nodded and came down the stairs. He paused as he came past her, looking her up and down, and then left the room. Rhapsody sighed and glanced up at the ceiling. It was constructed of marble as well; the unrelenting solidity made her feel entombed. She itched to get back outside into the air again.

After what seemed like an eternity the door opened once more, and the man she had spoken with returned, attired in simple clerical black this time. He gestured for her to follow him, and she did, down more endless corridors until she was so deep within the building that she had totally lost her bearings.

Finally they entered a long hall of simple cells, many with open doors, that looked like a hospice. As they walked past she could see that each room contained a single bed, or occasionally two, with reclining figures beneath white linen sheets, sometimes moaning in pain or muttering in dementia. The man stopped before a closed door near the end of the hallway, knocked, and opened it. He gestured for her to enter.

Rhapsody came into the room, vaguely aware of the door closing behind her. In the bed rested an elderly man, frail of body, with a fringe of snow-white hair and bright blue eyes that twinkled merrily in the prison of his fragile physical form. He was dressed in the same white linen bedsmock as the other patients she had seen on the hall, and Rhapsody recognized him instantly as the cleric in her dreams. A look of awe came over his face as she came to him, and he held a shaking hand out to her.

'Oelendra?' His voice was a thin croak. 'You have come?'

Rhapsody took his hand gently and sat down on the stool beside the bed so he would not have to crane his neck to see her. 'No, Your Grace,' she said softly. 'My name is Rhapsody. I am the Iliachenva'ar now. Oelendra trained me. In fact, I just came from training with her.'

The elderly priest nodded. 'Of course, you are far too young to be her. I should have realized it when you came in. But when they told me a Liringlas woman who said she was the Iliachenva'ar had come – '

'I'm honored by the error, Your Grace,' Rhapsody said, smiling. 'I hope to be worthy of the comparison one day.'

The Patriarch's face broke into a wide smile. 'My, you are lovely, child.' His voice dropped to an impish whisper. 'Do you think it would be a sin for me just to lie here and look at you for a moment?'

Rhapsody laughed. 'Well, you would know better than I, Your Grace, but I doubt it.'

He sighed. 'The All-God is kind, sending me such consolation in my last days.'

Rhapsody's brow furrowed. 'Your last days? Have you had a vision, Your Grace?'

The Patriarch nodded slightly. 'Yes, child. This celebration of the High Holy Day will be my last; within the year I will go to be with the All-God.' He saw the consternation in her eyes. 'Don't pity me, child, I'm not afraid; in fact, I am eager to go, when the time comes. What matters now is to complete the High Holy Day ceremony tomorrow night. Once that is done the year is assured.'

'I don't understand. What does that mean?'

'You are not of the faith, then?'

'No, Your Grace, I'm not. I'm sorry.'

The blue eyes twinkled. 'Don't apologize, child; the All-God calls each person to his or her own discernment. If you believe differently, perhaps you are here to teach me something as I prepare to go to meet Him.'

Rhapsody looked uncomfortable. 'I hardly think I could teach you anything about matters of faith, Your Grace.'

'Don't be so certain, child. Faith is a curious thing, and it is not always greatest in those who are the most schooled in it. But we will return to this thought, yes? Let me tell you about the High Holy Day.

'Each year, on the eve of the first day of the season consecrated to the sun, I perform a sacred ritual, alone in the basilica. Throughout the year other celebrations take place, but none of them are as important, because the High Holy Day ceremony recommits the faithful to the All-God, and the Patriarch to His service. The sacred words are part of a holy bond with the Creator, the fulfillment of a promise that each year the Patriarch, on behalf of all the faithful, dedicates the collective soul of the people to the All-God. In return, we are granted His divine safekeeping for another year.' Rhapsody nodded in understanding; the ritual he described was a form of Naming.

'Thus, since an entire year of the All-God's protection is assured by this holy ritual, there is nothing that can be allowed to delay or interrupt it,' the frail old man continued. 'The populace of Sepulvarta retires for the night early and remains indoors to ensure there are no distractions to me. In fact, they are encouraged to pray for me at this time, so that I may be diligent in my duties, though I'm sure most of them are sleeping, rather than sitting vigil.' The old man stopped and took several rasping breaths from the exertion of his discourse.

Rhapsody poured a cup of water from the pitcher on the bedside table and handed it to him. 'Are you in pain, Your Grace?' She steadied the trembling glass for him.

The Patriarch drank deeply, then nodded to indicate he was finished. Rhapsody set the glass back down. 'Only a little, child. Growing old is a painful process, but the pain helps us to focus on leaving our bodies behind and strengthening our spirits for the journey. There are so many others here who suffer so much more. I wish my strength were not failing me so. I would tend to them as I usually do, but if I do, I fear I will not be able to complete my service tomorrow night.'

'I will tend to them for you, Your Grace,' Rhapsody said, patting his hand.

'You're a healer, then?'

'A little,' she answered, rising and removing her cloak and pack. She draped her cloak over back of a chair on the other side of the room, and began to rummage through the satchel. 'I also sing a bit. Would you like to hear a song?'

The pale face lit up. 'Nothing would please me more. I should have known you were a musician with a name like that.'

'I'm afraid the only instrument I have with me is my lark's flute,' said Rhapsody regretfully. 'My lute met with an unfortunate accident recently, and I left my traveling harp in the House of Remembrance to guard the tree there.'

'Harp? You play the harp? Oh, how I would dearly love to hear that. There is no more beautiful sound in all the world than a harp played well.'

'I didn't say I played well,' Rhapsody said, smiling. 'But I do play enthusiastically. Perhaps someday I'll return and bring my new harp, if you'd like.'

'We'll see,' said the Patriarch noncommittally. Rhapsody knew that his eyes were already looking into the next world. She put the tiny flute to her lips and began to play an ethereal melody, light and breezy, the song of the wind in the trees of Tyrian.

The Patriarch's face relaxed, and the muscles of his forehead went slack as the pain he carried eased with the sound of the instrument. Working with the Bolg as she had, Rhapsody had become accustomed to watching the face for signs of relief, and could tell when the music had alleviated suffering to a degree that would last for a while. When she saw that stage occur in the Patriarch, she brought the song to an end.

The old man sighed deeply. 'Truly the All-God sent you to ease my passage, child. If only I could keep you here with me for the rest of my days.'

'There is a song of passage the Lirin sing when a soul prepares to travel to the light,' Rhapsody said. She saw the Patriarch's eyes spark with interest. 'It is said to loose the bonds of the Earth that keep the soul in the body so that it doesn't have to struggle through them. That way the soul feels nothing but joy in its journey.'

'How I wish I was Lirin,' said the Patriarch. 'That sounds wonderful.'

'You don't have to be Lirin to have it sung for you, Your Grace. Surely there must be many Lirin in your fold.'

'Yes, perhaps one could be found who knows it when the time comes,' he said. 'Your song has relieved my pain, child. You have a rare gift.' A knock sounded on the door. After a pause it opened, and the man who had impersonated the Patriarch came in, carrying a set of pristine white robes on a hanging rope.

'Are these satisfactory for tomorrow night, Your Grace, or shall I have the sexton unpack the Sorboldian linen set?'

'No, Gregory, those will be fine,' the Patriarch replied. The man bowed and disappeared through the door again. He turned back to Rhapsody. Her face was as white as the robes. 'Child, what's the matter?'

'Those are the robes for your ceremony tomorrow?'

'Yes; on the High Holy Day the ceremonial vestments are of the purest white. It is the only celebration for which I wear white; all others are of some color, generally silver or gold. Why do you ask?'

Rhapsody took his hand; hers was trembling more than his. 'I have to tell you why I came, Your Grace,' she said. Slowly and carefully she related the details of her vision, trying to describe the people she saw as accurately as possible. The elderly priest seemed alarmed initially, but as she continued he became thoughtful, nodding at intervals and listening attentively. Finally when she finished he took a deep breath, then let it out slowly.

'How very distressing. Not only the possibility that the High Holy Day ceremony might be compromised by my death, but the behavior of my benisons as well. I think your vision accurately portrays what will happen after my demise, Rhapsody. I had hoped they would rise above it, but I fear I was too optimistic.'

'What do you mean, Your Grace?'

'Well, the first two men you saw, the young man and the old one, are the Blessers of Canderre-Yarim and the Nonaligned States, respectively, Ian Steward and Colin Abernathy. Ian is wise for his years, but green, inexperienced. His appointment to the benisonric had more to do with the fact that his brother is Tristan Steward, the Lord Regent of Roland and Prince of Bethany than his own worthiness, though in time I believe Ian will make a fine benison. Colin is older than I, and in almost as poor health. Neither is suited to carry on in my stead, and in fact will undoubtedly panic when faced with the situation.

'The gentleman you saw making tea is most likely Lanacan Orlando, the Blesser of Bethe Corbair. His actions in your dream bespeak his personality perfectly. He is an unassuming chap, always looking to facilitate things and fix uncomfortable situations. Lanacan is my chief healer and minister; it is him I send to bless the troops or to comfort the dying. He's not much of a leader, but he is a wonderful priest.

'And the other two, well, therein lies the difficulty. Those are the Blessers of Avonderre-Navarne and Sorbold, bitter rivals and both in contention for the Patriarchy when I die.

'Philabet Griswold, the Blesser of Avonderre-Navarne, is internationally influential due to Avonderre's proximity to the shipping lanes and the wealth of the provinces in his See. Nielash Mousa, the Blesser of Sorbold, is the religious leader of an entire country, not just an Orlandan province, and is not from the traditional Cymrian lineage, which more and more is falling out of favor in Roland. They hate each other, I'm afraid, and though I've tried to ameliorate their differences in the Past, I fear the power struggle that will ensue after I'm gone. I'm not sure any of them are worthy of being the Patriarch, especially if the year is not assured.' He bit his lip; Rhapsody could see that his trembling had increased.

'Tell me what I can do to help you,' Rhapsody said, squeezing his hand. 'Whatever it is, you can depend on me.'

The Patriarch looked at her sharply, as though assessing her soul. Rhapsody held his gaze, letting his fading eyes wander over her face unrestricted. Finally he looked at their joined hands.

'I believe I can at that,' he said, more to himself than to her. He removed a ring from his finger; she had barely noticed it before. It was a clear, smooth stone set in a simple platinum setting. He opened her hand gently and put it into her outstretched palm.

Rhapsody examined it more closely. Inside the stone, as though internally inscribed, were two symbols on opposite sides of the oval gemstone. They looked like a plus and a minus. She looked inquisitively at the Patriarch.

He touched the stone and spoke the word for containment in Old Cymrian; Rhapsody's eyes opened wide. He was using the ability of

Naming again. 'There,' he said, a small smile of satisfaction coming over his face. His eyes met hers again. 'Child, you now have the office of the Patriarchy in your hand. As long as it is present tomorrow night in the basilica, I will still officially be the Patriarch for purposes of performing the ritual. After that, it doesn't matter if there is an official Patriarch, as I will have no more celebrations to offer. I know I will be gone within the year in any case. Keep it safe for me, will you? It contains the wisdom of my office, and the deep powers of healing that go with it.'

'How can your office be in the ring? Isn't it inherent in you, Your Grace?'

The Patriarch smiled. 'Actually, child, crowns of kings and rings or staves of holy men are often repositories for the wisdom of their offices; otherwise, that wisdom would die when the person holding the office does. That is why a crown, or a ring, is passed from king to king, Patriarch to Patriarch; it contains the wisdom of many kings, of many Patriarchs, not just the current wearer. That is also why a king is coronated with a crown, a Patriarch invested with a ring. It is not just a symbol; it holds the actual office, and its powers, safe. The collective wisdom gives each king, each Patriarch, the additional wisdom he needs to rule or to lead, rather than just having to rely on his own.' His hand trembled as he squeezed hers. 'I know you will protect it.'

'I'm honored by your trust, Your Grace,' Rhapsody said haltingly. 'But wouldn't it be better left with one of your order?'

'No, I don't think so,' said the Patriarch with a smile. 'My wisdom, informed by the ring, says you are the one to entrust it to; you will know the right thing to do with it. It is an ancient relic from the Lost Island, brought by the Cymrians when they came. It holds many secrets that I have never been able to gain access to; perhaps you will, or the one you to whom you give it. If a peaceful and righteous solution to the ascendancy of this office is reached after I die, you will come to Sepulvarta to help invest the new Patriarch, won't you?'

'Yes.'

'I thought you would agree. That's good, since they can't really do it without the ring.' He laughed conspiratorially.

'Let me stand with you tomorrow night, Your Grace,' Rhapsody said seriously. 'If the vision I saw foretold your death at the hands of an assassin, rather than at the All-God's choosing, I should be there as your champion to defend you. The ritual can be completed, and the year assured. Then your days will be easy and peaceful until the All-God calls you.'

'I was hoping you would say that,' he whispered gleefully. 'A named champion is the only escort the Patriarch can have present during the ritual. I think you'll find it rather dull, but it still will be good to have you there.'

'Are you sure, Your Grace? I can wait outside the basilica and guard the entrance, if you wish. Since I am not of the religion, I wouldn't want to – '

'Do you believe in a God?'

'Yes, most definitely.'

'Then it isn't a concern.' The old man shifted in his bed. 'My child, will you tell me something?'

'Certainly.'

'What is it you do believe, if you don't adhere to our religion? Are you a follower of Llauron?'

'No,' Rhapsody said, 'although I have studied a bit with him. His interpretation is a little closer to what I believe than yours, if you'll forgive me for saying so, but it's not exactly the same as mine, either.'

The Patriarch's eyes brightened in interest. 'Please tell me what you do believe.'

Rhapsody thought for a moment. 'I'm not sure I can articulate it exactly. The Lirin use the name One-God,' just as you do All-God,' but the concept is the same. I believe God is the combination of all things, that each thing, and each person, is a part of God, not just something God created, but an actual part of God. I think the reason people convene to worship is that there are more parts of God present, and God's presence is more easily felt and celebrated.'

'That is similar to one of the tenets of our faith. Our religion believes that all people belong to the All-God, and their prayers combine to reach him.'

'So why, if your God is the God of all, are you the only one allowed to pray to him?'

The Patriarch blinked. 'I am merely the channel of their prayers. Anyone can pray.'

'Yes, but they pray to you. Prayer, to me, which usually takes the form of song, is my way of communing directly with God. I need that to feel close to him.'

'Don't you believe the All-God would want to have as many of his faithful's prayers combined, so that the glory and honor we give Him is that much greater?'

'I don't know. I suppose if I were a God of many people, I would want each of them to be as close to me as possible. Otherwise, what's the point? I don't think he created us to give him glory, I think he made us because he loves us. I don't think he expects to have that love returned through a channel. Essentially, I see God as Life. It's an easy concept to ascribe to, but a hard one to live.'

'Why?'

She thought for a moment. 'Liringlas have an expression – *Ryle hira*: Life is what it is. I used to think that was inane, a useless truism. Then I lived a little more, and came to understand the wisdom of those words. The Lirin see God as all of life, too; that each individual, each thing in the universe is but an infinitesimal part of God. So life, whatever it hands you, is to be revered, because it is as it should be, even if you don't understand it at the time. I guess that comes from them living so long, and watching so much come and pass away in their time. Probably the reason it is hard for me to understand is that I'm only half-Lirin, so I don't have the natural long-term view.

'So I try to accept that all things are part of God, even the ones I don't understand. In the meantime, while accepting life as it is, I think my part as a piece of it is to try to make it better in any way I am able, even though I recognize that my contribution is very minor, since I am such a small part of the whole. I'm afraid I am stubborn and impatient, and I want things my own way. I don't make a very good Lirin, when it comes right down to it. I may look like my mother, but I guess I'm really more my father's child.'

'You have gained wisdom from both of them,' said the Patriarch fondly. 'If I had a daughter, I would want her to be just as stubborn and impatient, and wonderful, as you.' His face grew slightly paler.

'Why don't you lie down, Your Grace?' Rhapsody said, taking his arm and helping him recline. 'I have tired you too much. You rest, and I'll go tend to the others. I have some medicines with me, and I can sing or play for them if they'd like. When you wake you can tell me more about what I need to do tomorrow night.'

The old man nodded. Rhapsody rose and went to the door. He called to her as she opened it.

'You'll be back?'

'I will.'

'And tomorrow?'

'I'll stand by you, Your Grace,' she said. 'It will be my honor to do so.'

27

The Great Basilica in Sepulvarta was the centerpiece of the city, with towering walls of polished marble and an overarching dome that was taller than any in the known world. It had seating for the thousands of souls that sought solace within its walls, though on this, the holiest of nights, it was completely empty.

Rhapsody had been shown around the basilica that afternoon, and had delighted in the beauty of its architecture. The myriad colors and patterns of the mosaics that graced the floor and ceiling, along with the exquisite giltwork on the frescoed walls and the windows fashioned in colored glass all contributed to its grandeur, but it was the sheer height and breadth of it that took her breath away. Even in Easton, the largest city on the Island of Serendair, there was nothing to even remotely compare to this; the basilica there held perhaps three hundred and was singular in that it had contained some pews for the richest of the faithful to sit during services.

The reason for this contrast, aside from a vast difference in the wealth of the respective lands, was that Serendair had been for centuries polytheistic, with many temples catering to the faithful of several different deities. At the time she left the Island it was only a recent event that the king and country had adopted a monotheistic approach, and the turnover was still resisted in many sectors. The use of the epithet 'gods,' a word that was a simple oath to monotheists like Rhapsody's family, had caused citizens to come to blows in the street. As the population embraced a single God, however, more and more of the old temples stood empty.

It was the same here on this night, but for a different reason. As the cleric had explained to her, the High Holy Day celebration was performed alone, witnessed only by the Patriarch, in keeping with the direct-channel practice of the religion. At the stroke of midnight the elderly priest would begin his rites at the altar, chanting and offering sacrifice for the protection of the faithful for another year. This act of renewal interested Rhapsody, as it was strikingly similar to the Filidic rituals of the seasons. Perhaps the two religions were not as antithetical as their members believed them to be.

For this night, the Patriarch had performed a simple ceremony naming Rhapsody his champion. The technical name he gave her was the Ordained Avenger, and she struggled to keep from laughing during the sober rite by which this name was bestowed on her. Then she became solemn, realizing that the word Avenger implied that she might fail in her guardianship, and be required to exact revenge on behalf of the Patriarch's faithful. The prospect was too portentous to be contemplated; she preferred to concentrate on her successful stewardship to see the Patriarch through the night.

So she stood in the darkness of the basilica, Daystar Clarion at the ready in its scabbard, her eyes scanning the vast empty church for signs of movement. She was positioned in the lector's circle, a gilded design painted on the marble floor in the shape of the star that crowned the pinnacle of the city, at the edge of the huge set of marble stairs that led up from the front of the basilica to the altar. The altar itself was a plain stone table edged in platinum that stood in the very center of the basilica on the cylindrical rise that was the sanctuary. Positioned thus, all the faithful could see the altar, and as a result she had a good vantage point for her guard duty.

The only light in the dark basilica was cast from the reflection of the star atop the enormous tower she had seen. Though the spire itself was on the other side of the city, its light source illuminated the basilica, shining down through the openings in the great dome above the altar. It cast the place in an eerie glow, turning the face of the Patriarch white as he set about preparing the altar for his ritual. Then he walked slowly, with a shaking gait, over to where she stood at the top of the sanctuary stairs.

'I'm ready, my dear.'

Rhapsody nodded. 'Very well, Your Grace, commence your ritual. If anything should happen, try to keep going. I'll be standing watch.' She smiled at the frail old man, who seemed both lost and strikingly noble in the voluminous robes of his order. She drew her sword, and he blessed her. Then he returned slowly to the altar and stared into the solitary beam of light descending from the dome.

When he began to chant, Rhapsody closed her eyes and concentrated on the notes of his sacred melody. They were in the pattern of a song of protection; this made sense to her, since the rite itself was a request for a year of protection for his faithful. She pointed Daystar Clarion at the Patriarch, holding it steady until she could catch one of the repetitive notes. Then, with a careful hand, she drew the musical tone in a circle around the altar, hovering over the cleric.

Like a floating ring of light in the air, the protection circle whirled around the altar and the Patriarch. It made the cone of light from the dome above shine more intensely and look as if it were almost solid around him. His voice seemed to grow a little stronger as the circle picked up on the tones in his chant and held them in a spinning ring. She sheathed her sword and stood respectfully, honored by the knowledge that few other than she had ever witnessed the ritual.

As Rhapsody watched she felt a prickle of heat behind her, and the small hairs on the back of her neck stood on end. She turned around slowly to see two figures enter through the locked doors and begin to walk toward the central basilica. One figure stopped at the arch that led into the nave. She could see little detail except that it wore a great black cloak and a horned helmet of the same color. Around its neck in the distance she could make out a vaguely round symbol that seemed to be set in the center with a stone, the color of which she could not determine.

The second figure also wore a black cape, but it was thrown back to reveal armor of shining silver. It strode down the long aisle with an air of cocky confidence beneath which lurked a sinister, purposeful menace. Rhapsody heard the chant of the Patriarch grind to a halt, and the old man backed away from the altar, his eyes wide in fear. She crossed and stood as much in front of him as she could, hoping he would stay behind the altar that was between them, but instead he tottered forward and stood behind her.

When the walking figure got to the center of the church it threw its hood back and Rhapsody gasped. Outshining the silver armor was red-gold hair, bright as burnished copper, though in the dark it did not gleam metallically as it had in the sunlight of the hidden glen behind the waterfall. The handsome, hairless face she had last seen beneath a scrub of beard smiled broadly, and her heart cramped in the memory of the admonition she had given him to shave. Even at this distance she could see his blue eyes gleaming clearly at her. He came to a stop at the edge of the first row of pews and grinned at her.

'Hello, dear. It's been a long time; I've missed you.' His words echoed in the open air of the vast basilica.

Rhapsody stared at him in disbelief. A single word formed silently on her lips.

226

'Ashe.'

'Oh, you do remember me, then? I'm flattered.'

Her voice was low and steady. 'Leave now, and no harm will come to you.'

An ugly laugh escaped him. 'How very generous. I'm afraid I can't do that, but I can extend the same offer to you.' Slowly he dropped his cloak to the polished floor of the basilica and took a step toward her.

Rhapsody felt the bony hand of the Patriarch touch her shoulder. 'Leave now, my child. I can't ask you to make this sacrifice.'

Rhapsody's eyes never left the handsome face that smiled at her as it had in her dreams since she first beheld it in the forest. She reminded herself that, whatever kindness he may have seemed to show her in the Past, he was now her adversary. Her stomach turned in sickening betrayal. She addressed the Patriarch without looking back. 'You didn't ask. I came unbidden, remember?'

Her opponent moved nearer. 'Listen to His Grace, darling. This is not your fight. Go back home to the Firbolg lands; go pleasure the Lord of the Monsters. That's something I could never understand; such a beautiful woman, such a horrible fate.'

'Stay inside the circle, Your Grace,' said Rhapsody, gently shrugging the trembling hand from her shoulder, watching her opponent's approach. 'Go about your ritual and don't worry. Focus on your celebration.'

The crystalline blue eyes lost their insolent twinkle. 'I tire of this game,' he said, his voice growing nasty. 'The more you make me play it, the more I shall play with you after I kill him. I have waited a long time to have you, dear.'

Rhapsody's face hardened with anger. 'Come, then,' she said, her eyes narrowing, her voice calm and deadly. 'I'll try to ensure the experience is memorable for you.' Her hand came to rest on the hilt of Daystar Clarion.

'Promise?' he asked suggestively, moving slowly to the side, his hands open and at the ready. 'I can hardly wait.' He drew a sword, one she had not seen before. It was black tempered steel slashed with a white band, and the air around him hissed as he raised it before him.

Rhapsody felt her sword in its scabbard and changed her grip ever so slightly, as Achmed had taught her, focusing her awareness on herself first. She was as strong as she had ever been, and as well prepared, and standing on sacred ground. She could feel with a sense that had run in her since the old days, in that seemingly other life, the protection of the basilica. It was the sense that this ground would not hurt her, even if she fell. Rhapsody closed her eyes and concentrated as Oelendra had taught her.

At the edges of her awareness, moving closer now, were the three others. The familiar sound of the Patriarch was channeling through the ring. The being farthest away appeared as an unfamiliar burning at the edge of her vision. Her immediate adversary, the one she had called Ashe, closed quickly, directly in front of her. Rhapsody searched it for blood close to the surface, any sign of weakness or injury. She found none, but saw that it did have the same vibrational signature in its blood as the figure in the back of the basilica. Strangely, it did not register on the vibrational grid in her mind as a man, but as a thing, a ghost or a machine about to attack her. It seemed no more alive than its sword, which meant that she did not know if she could kill it.

A Rakshas looks like whatever soul is powering it.

Elynsynos's words echoed in her memory. Rhapsody opened her eyes and glanced at the figure in the back, grateful that she was on blessed ground, on this, the holiest night of the year, for surely the host of the F'dor itself must have been behind the shield of the horned helmet. She wished she could make out any detail, any clue of its identity, but instead her focus was drawn back to the foe approaching her now.

She moved slowly down the iridescent marble steps that led up to the altar, extending the arc of the musical cylinder that hovered above and about the Patriarch as she came to a stop on the bottom stair. From the altar behind her the faltering voice of the ancient cleric began to chant the solemn words that would mark his final High Holy Day ceremony.

At the back of the hall the figure with the horned helmet gestured impatiently. The warrior, now uncloaked, whom she had trusted, had traveled with, that she had fought beside, slept beside, charged across the aisle at her with murder in his eyes.

Peace descended on Rhapsody in the seconds before their impact. It was the calculated calm that she had always been blessed with in dangerous situations, tempered by her training and honed by the sword itself, as if time had slowed dramatically, and all angles, all functions, every plane and arc was clear to her, ready to put her in position. Her face was set with a look of deadly serenity; she took a deep breath and increased her concentration on the vibration of the musical circle and the man approaching her, who was reduced now to mathematical calculations and vectors. She no longer saw him as someone she knew; he was merely the enemy, and every fiber of her being, and the sword's, was poised for its destruction.

'You will not get by me,' she said, speaking with a Namer's authority.

Rhapsody saw his face in the half-moment before he struck, contorted with rage and smoldering with hatred. The eyes she had dreamt about were spewing fire, the pupils tiny pinpricks in blazing blue light, the vertical slits gone. She judged his strength and his body mass to be twice her own; she believed she held the advantage in speed and technique, though his weapon was unknown to her. His fury was greater; whether this would work to his advantage or hers, she had no idea.

She had seen him in combat before, but never like this. He moved with the speed and agility of a wolf, and the horrific snarl that issued forth from him was more feral than human. In only a moment he had closed the distance between them in the wide aisle and, circling his sword with his wrist, he was upon her.

She stood deliberately rooted in place as he crossed, leaving only enough time to draw Daystar Clarion before he would be on her, timing the flash the sword would produce as it appeared from its dark sheath to coincide with the passing of the apex of the musical circle above her. As his blade swung at her throat, aiming to decapitate her, she heard the sound Oelendra had spoken of, the whisper of the wind denoting that, live or die, she had attained the status of Kinsman by her act of guardianship.

Without a sound, with the speed born of experience, she drew Daystar Clarion, holding it with all her strength in a path to intersect and parry his blow. The sword came forth, blazing with a ferocious light, its brilliance magnified and dispersed throughout the basilica by the humming circle above her.

A ringing sound of metal in motion like a silver trumpet call rent the air. The sword clanged against the black weapon with the timbre of a great forge, its reverberation picked up and echoed by the bells of the basilica, causing a wave of sound that rocked the Spire and swept down over the land, shaking the very Pinnacle itself.

Rhapsody used his own strength and size against him to direct his strike to the floor. She dragged her blade across his side, and where it bit through his armor it flashed, searing him. She spun quickly back to her place between him and the steps leading up to the Patriarch, half expecting him to be down. Instead, he was there still, barely favoring his wounded side, almost on top of her. She had to block again, but this time aimed her counter at his eyes. Even as she felt the sword cut him once more he was pushing her, grasping at her with his sword hand while he raised the other arm to shield his face.

Rhapsody dodged, slipping from beneath his grasp. She wrenched herself around, trying to find an opening, but he was too close. With a sharp move she gripped Daystar Clarion with both hands and hacked his thumb from the hilt of the black sword. The weapon clattered to the ground, followed by the bleeding digit, as she elbowed him down the stairs. She took two steps up to give herself another view of the situation.

'You – will not – get – by me,' she repeated, catching her breath.

Rhapsody felt the anger of both adversaries deepen and intensify. Looking at their vibrational signatures, she could see them pulsate into a dark red flame, burning black with fury. The rage of the masked figure in the rear of the basilica seemed to be with the now very public nature of their confrontation; it glanced around the back of the basilica, hearing the sounds of response begin to issue forth from the land. Warning bells and shouts could be heard from the town below, growing in intensity through the formerly silent night.

The wrath of her opponent, however, was not directed solely at her. She could see an irate bewilderment in his eyes, as though he had somehow misjudged her abilities. The possibility of this seemed remote to her; certainly Ashe had been around her enough, and with her in enough combat, to accurately assess her skills. And he was aware of her training with Oelendra as well. Whatever his confusion, it was momentary. His face darkened with hate and he leapt at her, soaring through the air with an unnatural lupine grace and knocking her to the ground, pinning her beneath him.

Obviously he had determined himself outweaponed, so he set about pressing his physical advantage of size and strength. With his uninjured hand he grabbed her forehead and slammed her head backward into the marble stair. Rhapsody's return sword blow glanced off him, but the heel of her free hand made contact with his nose, striking upward and drawing blood. What came out was more like lye than blood; it stung her eyes and burned her skin. It hissed as it contacted her flesh, sending stinging waves of pain through her entire body.

He remained locked onto her as they grappled, rolling off the stairs. She landed on her back and tried to rise. A gloved hand closed around her throat and gripped with crushing strength, smashing her to the floor again. Rhapsody felt the world darken for a second as her air was cut off. With his lower torso holding hers to the ground, he rose above her, pressing her even harder to the basilica floor. He was panting; blood filled one eye and poured from his nose, his face twisted in malignant fury.

Rhapsody's arms sprawled out to her sides, and pain coursed through her. She was overwhelmed with the nauseating stench that filled the air like a poisonous cloud around them; it seemed to issue forth from his blood. She didn't struggle in his grasp, but slowly, imperceptibly slid her arms up above her head until they were directly over it, her abdomen and chest vulnerable to him but shielded by the mail shirt of drangonscales. His grip on her throat grew stronger; he now clutched her neck with both hands, having risen to almost a sitting position, his legs astride her, his genitals out of reach of her knees.

'What a shame,' he panted, bouncing hard on her abdomen. 'It had been my intention for a long time to have you in this very position, but I think we both would have enjoyed my original plans a little more.' His words were labored, and his breathing shallow. 'Well, no matter. I think I will take your body with me and have you anyway. It probably will be more enjoyable than if you were alive; at least you won't be talking. And all this time I had been so looking forward to sodomizing you; just the screams alone would have been music to my ears. Oh well.'

Rhapsody concentrated on his helmet. As her consciousness ebbed and returned she thought she had a fix on the seam in his mail at the neck. With infinite patience she rotated the hilt of the sword in the palm of her sword hand and brought both hands together, resting her free one on the pommel. She summoned her strength, and the strength of the sword, and when she felt they were in harmony she exhaled all her breath and went limp in his grasp, letting the sword fall out of her hands to the basilica floor.

He gave her neck another crushing squeeze, then relaxed his grip, his hands moving to his bleeding face. He raised up on one knee, reaching for her sword.

As he did Rhapsody called in her mind to the sword. Daystar Clarion leapt back into her hands and she bolted forward, driving the blade point-first into the slit in his cuirass. She hit the mark with such accuracy that the force carried him backward, Daystar Clarion lodged in the mail at his throat.

An ugly, choking gasp came out of his mouth, and his eyes opened wide in surprise and pain. Rhapsody saw that the pupil of his bloodless eye was now dilated and round. She pulled the sword from his neck with a strong backward motion, then slashed him across the knees, causing him to fall backwards. He scrambled on his elbows, trying to grasp his sword, but she swept it out of his reach with Daystar Clarion, sending it spinning into the aisle behind them.

'I am sorry to disappoint you,' she said, following his retreat. 'If it's sodomy you're longing for, I'd be happy to oblige. Roll a little to one side.' She waved the sword at him threateningly, then sensed its harmonic vibrations suddenly jolt. She felt shame; in her fury she was taunting him while he was compromised. It was unseemly behavior for a Kinsman, and the Iliachenva'ar.

'Hold still, and I will end it quickly,' she said in a kinder tone. She raised the sword, pointing it at his throat.

Suddenly from the back of the room she heard a roar. She barely had time to roll clear of the wall of flame that leapt between her and her bleeding enemy. Out of the floor an inferno of black fire had risen, smoking with the same hideous stench that burned in his blood. The wall of heat and flame climbed as high as the top of the altar, surrounding her on all sides. Rhapsody was powerless to break through. This was not natural fire; it hissed and snarled with an evil intent that was tangible, and on the other side of the burning wall Rhapsody could see hasty movement.

She summoned her lore around her like a cloak and was preparing to broach the fire when it vanished. The two assassins were gone. The Patriarch, still chanting in a wavering whisper, was almost at the conclusion of his rite.

Rhapsody remained standing respectfully, breathing shallowly, still drawn, until the cleric finished. As he descended from the altar and came down the steps to her, she sat down, rubbing her fingers over her bruised throat. Her head throbbed as her body slowly began to recognize the pain it had bought as a result of the fight.

The Patriarch's voice shook with alarm. 'Child! My child! Are you all right?' He was quaking so violently Rhapsody feared he would pitch down the altar steps.

'Yes, Your Grace, I'm fine,' she said, struggling to her feet and holding out both hands to the frail old man. She steadied him; his eyes were wide with concern, but seemed without fear.

'Let me see your throat,' he said, pulling the collar of her jerkin aside and examining the swelling purple marks. 'You look terrible.'

Rhapsody winced as his fingers brushed her neck. 'Yes, but he looks worse, and that's what counts.'

The Patriarch cast a glance around the basilica. 'Where did he go?'

She was leaning over now, breathing slowly, trying to control the mounting pain. 'I don't know. He turned tail and ran, with help from his ugly friend.'

'Friend?'

'Yes, there was another one, wearing a horned helmet. I'm fairly sure he was the one that called the fire.'

'Fire? I can't believe I missed all this. I heard the roar, but by the time the rites were over, the only thing left here was you. Protecting me has cost you dearly. It might have cost your life.'

Rhapsody was touched by the anxiety on his face. She gave him a comforting smile. 'That you weren't distracted is as it should be, Your Grace; it means we both were attending to our duties. You were able to successfully complete the ritual?'

'Oh, yes. The High Holy Day celebration is complete. The year is safe, and, with the All-God's help, this time next year another will be in my place. I can go peacefully now. Thank you, my dear, thank you. If not for you, I – ' He was staring at the floor, his mouth opening and closing silently, no words coming forth.

Rhapsody patted his hand. 'It was my honor to stand as your champion, Your Grace.' The doors of the basilica opened, and cacophony swept in, as guards, soldiers, acolytes and townspeople rushed to check on the Patriarch. As the mob swarmed into the basilica, Rhapsody sheathed her sword and knelt down before the cleric.

'I'll guard the office in the ring for you, Your Grace, until there is another in your place. Pray for me, that I may do so wisely.'

'I have no doubt that you will,' said the old man, smiling down at her. He rested his hand on her head, asking a blessing in Old Cymrian, the sacred language of his religion. Rhapsody hid her smile, remembering the last times she had heard the tongue used in the old land. What were now mystical holy words were once the vernacular of cursing guards and the advertisements of prostitutes, they had been screeched by bickering fishwives and slurred by drunkards. Yet pronounced now, solemnly and with awe, they were as meaningful to her as any Lirin song. Finally, his last blessing was a simple statement that she had heard attributed to the Ancient Seren as a child.

'Above all else, may you know joy.'

'Thank you,' she said, smiling. She rose, with some difficulty, bowed, and prepared to take her leave. As she turned to go, the Patriarch touched her shoulder.

'My child?'

'Yes, Your Grace?'

'When the times comes, would you, perhaps, consider – ' His voice trailed off into awkward silence.

'I'll be there if I can, Your Grace,' she said softly. 'And I'll bring my harp.'

28

Madeleine Canderre, Lord Cedric Canderre's daughter, was the sort of woman genteel people often described as 'handsome.' Her face was pleasant enough, its features correctly balanced into the perfect aristocratic aspect that only centuries of exclusive breeding could produce. The skin of that face was dewy and fashionably pale, the eyes a famous shade of hazel. The hue was an allowable variant on the traditional azure blue or aquamarine of the Cymrian royal and noble lines.

While the color of those eyes was attractive, the shape of them, and the expression they usually held, was not particularly so. Small and closely set, Madeleine's eyes routinely seemed to be conveying displeasure. Perhaps this was because, as a rule, she was routinely displeased.

That displeasure was more than slightly evident this morning, even as she sat in her carriage, preparing to return to her father's lands. Tristan Steward sighed. He had come down to bid her goodbye an hour before, and still she was here, methodically listing all the problems that needed to be worked out before that auspicious moment a few months hence when she would join herself, inexorably, to every aspect of his life for Time Immemorial. The idea was causing him to grow more nauseated by the moment.

'I still don't understand why you won't go to Sepulvarta and see the Patriarch yourself,' Madeleine whined, rifling through the many pages of her list of notes. 'Surely he will make an exception and marry *us*; after all, you *are* the only Prince of the highest House in all of Roland. What could possibly be more important, Tristan?'

'I believe the man is dying, dearest,' Tristan answered as patiently as he could. *Would that the same could be said* – he thought bitterly.

'Nonsense. Word all over is that he just survived an assassination attempt in the basilica on the High Holy Day. If he's hale enough to live through his own murder attempt, he can stand in front of the altar, perform the Unification ritual and bless the most important marriage in the land.'

Tristan swallowed angrily. He, of course, was familiar with the news, but from different sources, and for different reasons. The Patriarch's rescuer had been a slight, slender woman, according to the gossip among the prostitutes who serviced his guards, or so Prudence had said. A woman with the face of an angelic spirit, with the warmth of a raging fire in her green eyes. He had no doubt there could only be one.

'I'll consider it, Madeleine,' he said curtly, snapping the carriage door shut. He leaned in through the open window and gave her a peck on the cheek. 'Leave your list with the chamberlain, and I'm sure he'll see to your other concerns. Now, travel well. We don't want to keep your father waiting; you know how he worries.'

Tristan turned his back, too late to miss the shock that flooded his fiancée's face, and gestured to the quartermaster, who whistled to the coachman. The carriage lurched forward, Madeleine's startled expression visible only a moment longer before the coach jolted away out of view.

'I thought you were never going to come.'

'Prophetic words, no doubt. Once I'm married I can assure you that I never will again, at least in the manner I do with you.'

Prudence tossed a pillow at the Prince, smacking him squarely in the chest. 'It's not too late,' she said, smiling. 'Madeleine's finger is still ringless, as is her neck. Wring one and not the other.'

'Don't tempt me.'

The gentle smile faded from Prudence's face. 'Stop whining, Tristan. If you can't stomach the thought of spending the rest of your life with that – woman, grow a spine and break the engagement. You're the bloody Lord Roland. Nobody's forcing you to marry her.'

Tristan sat heavily on the edge of his massive bed, and began pulling off his boots.

'It's not that simple, Pru,' he said. 'The marital pool from which I can draw is very limited. Lydia of Yarim had promise, but she also had the very bad taste to fall in love with my cousin Stephen Navarne and marry him; lost her life in the process.'

A painful shock ran up his spine to his neck as Prudence's foot connected with his back.

'An ugly thing to say, Tristan, and beneath you, even when you've spent a month with Poisonous Madeleine and are toxic as a result. Lydia was killed in an unexplained incursion, as so many others have been over the years. It could happen to anyone; it does all the time, in fact. To imply that Stephen was in any way at fault – '

'All I'm saying is that it is ridiculous for a duchess to be traveling with so small a contingent, in pursuit of a pair of baby shoes for Lady Melisande. I didn't say Stephen was at fault. I just think he could have taken better care of his family, of the woman he loved.'

'Hmm. Well, what about that Diviness in the Hintervold – what was her name? Hjorda?'

Tristan dropped the other boot to the floor and began to unlace his trousers. 'Not Cymrian.'

'So? I thought all you needed in your fiancée's background was royalty, nobility, or even landed gentry. The Diviner is royalty in the Hintervold. What difference does it make if his daughter is Cymrian or not? That might actually work to your advantage, given what most of the population thinks about you Cymrians, no offense.'

Tristan rose and slid his trousers off, then turned to face her. She was propped against the gauzy white pillows, beneath the drapes of royal blue velvet that hung about his bed. Her strawberry ringlets cascaded over the shoulders he noticed had grown bonier with time, as age stretched her skin and reapportioned her flesh from the silhouette of a young girl into the shape of an older woman. It was a sight that never failed to make his throat tighten with many emotions, none of them pleasant. He looked out the window.

'Madeleine is the daughter of the duke of Canderre and the cousin of the duke of Bethe Corbair,' he said, staring at the fields beyond the courtyard, ripe and green in the heat of summer. 'Stephen Navarne and I are cousins. Once we are wed, I will have family ties to every province in Roland except Avonderre.'

'So? Why is that important? You're the Lord Regent now without it.'

'I want to be prepared, in case there is a call to reunite the provinces of Roland under a Lord Cymrian again. There are those who feel it might be a way to end the violence that is plaguing the realm from the coast to the Bolglands, and in Tyrian and Sorbold as well. There might be a call.'

Prudence rolled her eyes and sighed. 'There might be a call to have the sky painted yellow, too, Tristan, but I wouldn't saddle myself with a woman who is the stuff of nightmares in anticipation of it if I were you.'

The Lord Roland smiled in spite of himself, and pulled his long tunic off, dropping it to the floor on top of the pile of rumpled clothing. 'Madeleine's not that bad, Pru.'

'She's as cold as a war-hag's tit, and twice as ugly. And you know it. Open your eyes, Tristan. See clearly what you are enrolling in, and for what purpose. Whoever you marry will become Cymrian just by virtue of being your wife, may the All-God help her. It's not as though the line is pure, anyway. Marry someone who will make you happy, or at least who won't make your life a misery. If you are so lucky as to become Lord Cymrian, or king, or whatever, no one will care who she was, just who she is now.'

The clarity of her words loosened the muscles in Tristan's forehead, which had been clenched from the moment he had heard of Madeleine's arrival. There was wisdom in Prudence's words, as there always was.

He tore off his knee-length undergarments and grabbed the coverlet, tossing it and the satin counterpane aside, then swept Prudence up in his arms. The warmth of her skin felt comforting against his chest. He had missed her this last month.

'I think I should behead Evans and make you my chief counselor and ambassador,' he said, his hands sliding down her back and clutching her buttocks. 'You're infinitely wiser. And far more beautiful.'

Prudence shuddered comically. 'I should certainly hope so. Evans is seventy if he's a day.'

'Indeed. And he doesn't have exquisite golden hair.' The Lord Roland ran his hand down her locks, tangling his fingers in her ringlets.

Prudence broke free from his embrace and sat back, pulling the covers up over her breasts.

'Neither do I, Tristan.'

'Of course you do,' he stammered, lightheaded, his stomach suddenly turning cold. 'Red blond, I meant. It's sort of gold.'

'Spare me,' she said, looking out the window. 'You're thinking of her again.'

'I was not – '

'Stop. Don't you dare lie to me, Tristan. I will not be played for a fool. I know who you're thinking of, and it isn't me.' Prudence smoothed the sheet over her legs. 'And I don't mind, by the way. I just want you to be honest about it.'

Tristan sighed. He stared at Prudence for a long moment, his expression flickering between guilt for the hurt he knew he had caused her, and amazement that she was always so willing to forgive him any transgression. In his life there would never again be anyone who accepted him so unconditionally, fully cognizant of his faults, loving him nonetheless.

When he saw a hint of a smile creep back into her eyes he pulled down the covers, carefully this time, and slid into the bed beside her. Gently he drew her into his arms, bringing her head to rest on his shoulder.

'I really don't deserve you, you know,' he said, something approximating humility in his voice.

'Yes, I know,' she said, her face buried in his chest. It was smooth and broadly muscled, humming with the youth and vitality that Tristan's Cymrian heritage had bequeathed him, along with an extended life expectancy that Prudence herself would not enjoy.

'There is something I want you to do for me.'

Prudence sighed and lay back on the pillow. 'What?'

The Lord Roland lay back as well, staring at the ceiling. This was so much easier at night, after lovemaking, the time they usually discussed his obsession with Rhapsody. Then the darkness cloaked the room, held in by the bed curtains, keeping any decent feelings of shame at bay, allowing him the candor he would have had with his confessor, had he been able to talk to one.

But where the royal rank had its privileges, it also had its curses. The only clergyman of suitable station to hear his crimes and channel his prayers for absolution to the Patriarch, other than the Patriarch himself, was his bother, Ian Steward, the Blesser of Canderre-Yarim. It was becoming more and more likely that Ian would be performing the Unification Blessing of the marriage ritual, Madeleine's wishes notwithstanding. As a result he was left with no other confidant to hear his adulterous thoughts than the servant woman in his bed, his childhood friend, his first lover. The only person in the world he was certain he loved.

He covered his eyes with his forearm, affording himself some dimness in the absence of the night.

'I want you to go to Canrif – er, Ylorc, as the Firbolg call it.' He could hear Prudence exhale beside him, but she said nothing. 'I want you to deliver the Firbolg king's wedding invitation – and, uh, the one for his emissary.'

'Emissary? Come now, Tristan, surely you can do better than that.'

'All right! *Rhapsody*. Are you happy now? I want you to take the invitation personally to Rhapsody. Gauge her reaction. If she seems open to it, try and get her to come back with you to Bethany, or to at least come soon, so that I can see her once, alone, before I throw my future away, before I wed the Beast of Canderre.'

'For what purpose, Tristan?' Prudence's voice was soft, without a hint of accusation. 'What do you hope to gain?'

He sighed again. 'I don't know. I only know that if I don't I will live in agony for the rest of my life, wondering what she might have said. Wondering if there had been a chance that I never took, that I never even knew about.'

Prudence sat up in the tangle of sheets and pulled his arm away from his eyes.

'A chance for what? Do you love her, Tristan?' Her dark brown eyes searched his face, interested but otherwise expressionless.

He looked away. 'I don't know. I don't think so. It's more – more – '

'Desire?'

'Something like that. An overwhelming, inexplicable need. Like she is a bonfire in the depths of winter. It's like I'm wandering, shirtless, in the snow, and have been since I first beheld her. You've been right about my attraction to her all along, Prudence. I lost my head and committed a full brigade of my own soldiers to a grisly death rather than let her walk away from me. And, if you can believe this, she doesn't even know it; at least that's what the Firbolg king said.

'You knew better, of course, Pru, but I couldn't let myself believe you. Poor Rosentharn had orders to bring her back with the army when the Firbolg were crushed.' He blinked rapidly at the memory of the Firbolg warlord, sitting on the edge of this very bed, playing with the crown of Roland like a child's toy, calmly dispensing the news of the slaughter of Tristan's army.

Don't worry; the cloaked monster had said in a sandy voice that whispered of death. *She has no idea that she was the one who inspired the massacre. Of course, I do. Why do you think I sent her to you? You are a man of free will. If you had genuinely desired peace, you would have greeted my offer, and my emissary, with open arms, no doubt. Any man, especially one who is betrothed, with less-than-honorable intentions toward a woman, would be untrustworthy as a neighbor as well. It's just as well that you threw two thousand lives away trying to win her attention now. You learned your lesson early. The cost would have been far greater later on.*

The man-shadow had risen silently from the chair as the Firbolg king prepared to make his exit.

I'll leave you now to get ready for the vigil you will no doubt want to hold for your men. The Lord Roland saw no more of the monster's departure than he had of his arrival.

It had taken Tristan Steward almost twelve hours before he was able to speak again, another six before his speech was even vaguely coherent. A caustic, burning sensation had ripped through his gullet, swamping his mouth, with acid he could still taste now, these many months later. The death of his army had left him terrified and aghast.

But not aghast enough, apparently, to shake loose the image of the woman which still clutched his mind. Tristan lay back against the pillows and let out a painful sigh.

'I don't know what it is, this hold she has over me, this craving that makes me stupid, incapable of sensible thought,' he admitted. He closed his eyes, blocking out the image of his tertiary infantry and horsed crossbowmen, and the poor unfortunates that had been unassigned to other duties that morning, their bodies never found, rumored to have become a grisly feast for their monstrous vanquishers. 'It's more than carnal, but I don't know that it's love, either. I think part of what's driving me is the need to find out just exactly what it is.'

Prudence watched his face a moment longer, then nodded.

'All right, Tristan. I'll go. That bonfire must be spreading; now I have an inexplicable need as well. My curiosity won't be satisfied until I see this creature for myself.'

He grasped her face and pulled her to him, kissing her gratefully.

'Thank you, Pru.'

'As always, anything for you, m'lord.' Prudence twisted free from his hands and rose, walking to the dressing table where she had left her clothes, ignoring the look of blank shock on his face.

'Where are you going?' he stammered.

Prudence slid her dress over her shoulders, then turned to face him.

'To make preparations for my trip to see the object of your erection. Where else?'

'That can wait. Come back to bed.' He opened his arms to her.

'No.' Prudence drew on her undergarments, then turned to the looking glass, running her fingers through her tangled curls.

'I mean it, Prudence, please come back. I want you.'

The servant woman smiled. 'Well, had it occurred to you that perhaps the feeling is not mutual, m'lord? And if you're mortally offended by my rejection, perhaps you should consider beheading me and taking Evans to bed.'

She left the room, Tristan's astonished face vanishing from view as she closed the door soundly.

Rhapsody slept beneath lacy shadows cast by the moon through the leaves of a brindled alder, the tallest of the trees in the thicket where she had sought shelter for the night. The wind rustled through the thicket from time to time, and the chestnut mare snorted occasionally, but otherwise there was silence at the western edge of the Krevensfield Plain.

A sweetness was carried on the wind that cleansed her dreams, making them more intense in the summer heat. Rhapsody turned on her side and inhaled the scent of the clover beneath her head, breathing in the fragrance of the green earth. It was a scent she remembered from childhood, when on nights like these she and members of her family sometimes fell asleep in the pasture under the star-sprinkled sky.

She sighed in her sleep, wishing that the memory would turn to dreams of her mother, but Rhapsody had not been able to conjure up her image since before Ashe came to the mountain. Her mother had come to her then, one last time it seemed, and showed her a vision of her birthstar, her Aria, the star called Seren.

She relived that dream again now, though without her mother's soothing voice narrating it as she once had. Rhapsody sat up in her sleep and stared through the slender trees to the Plain beyond them. In the darkness of the field she could see a table, or an altar of some kind, on which the body of a man rested. The figure was wreathed in darkness; she could discern nothing but his outline.

Above her in her dream Seren winked in the night sky, shining large as it once had on the other side of the world. A tiny piece of the star broke off and fell onto the body on the altar, causing it to shine incandescently. The intense brightness gleamed for a moment, then resolved into a dim glow.

That is where the piece of your star went, child, for good or ill, her mother had said in the dream. *If you can find your guiding star, you will never be lost. Never.*

Other voices filled her head. She could hear Oelendra speaking, the sadness permeating her words.

In the end, when nothing was working, and Gwydion was in mortal agony, I took a piece of a star from the sword's hilt and gave that to the Lady Rowan. I offered it to them in the hope they could use it as a last effort to save him, and they did, but he was too far gone. 'Twas a desperate gesture, and one that did not work, but I don't regret trying.

'Oelendra, is that what I'm seeing?' she murmured in her sleep. 'Was it the attempt to save Gwydion's life?'

That is where the piece of your star went, child, for good or ill.

Above the image of the body hands appeared, disembodied hands she had seen in a vision while in the House of Remembrance. They folded together, as if in prayer, then opened as if in blessing. Blood poured from between them into the lifeless form, staining it red as it filled.

Words, absent of any voice, spoke in her ear next to the ground.

Child of my blood.

The multitoned voice of the dragon spoke in the other ear, the ear turned toward the wind.

A Rakshas looks like whatever soul is powering it. It is built of blood, the blood of the demon, and sometimes other creatures, usually feral animals of some sort. Its body is formed of an element, like ice or earth; the one made in the House of Remembrance was made of earth frozen with ice. The blood animates it, gives it power. If the demon is in possession of a soul it can place it within the construct and the Rakshas will take the form of the soul's owner, who of course is dead. It has some of the knowledge that person had. It can do the things they did. It is twisted and evil; you must beware of him, Pretty.

With a shudder Rhapsody woke and sat upright. She was still in the thicket, the mare beside her, alone and unnoticed except for the touch of the night wind. She shivered and ran her hands up and down her arms, trying to warm herself.

'What are you, Ashe?' she asked aloud. 'What are you really?'

The only answer was the warm breath of the wind. She could not make out what it was trying to tell her.

Seventy leagues to the west, the wind blew warm through the open gates in the ancient stone walls of the House of Remembrance, rustling the leaves of the tree that stood in the center of its courtyard. A figure, garbed in a heavy gray cloak with the hood pulled close about the face, stood at its base, gazing thoughtfully up into its branches.

At eye level, planted resolutely in a crotch above the first hollow of the trunk, was a small musical instrument that resembled a harp. It was playing a roundelay quite unlike any he had ever heard before, a simple melody that filled the entire courtyard, humming through the age-old stones. The man reached up to touch the instrument, the cloak falling away from a hand whose newly formed thumb bore only the slightest sign of red, healing skin. The fingers of the hand hovered for a moment over the strings, then withdrew quickly.

It would do no good to try to remove the instrument, the Rakshas decided. It had become an intrinsic part of the tree itself, playing its namesong, the repeating melody sustained by the life within it. The will of the sapling was now tied to the same source as its mother, Sagia, had been, its vestigial roots sunk deep within the Earth, wound inextricably around the Axis Mundi. The song of the harp had broken his master's hold on the young tree, had healed it from its desecration. There was no doubt in his mind about who had put it there.

Slowly he lowered his hood, letting the wind whip through the shining curls of red-gold hair, while he pondered what to do next. The one who was his master, his father, had been very specific about the need to monitor the Three and keep them contained, not to try to destroy any of them yet, at least up until the confrontation in Sepulvarta. That debacle had proven how badly they had misjudged the situation, thinking that each of the Three was occupied at the time of the assassination attempt. Its failure had been a serious setback, even more serious than the rout that had occurred here, at the House of Remembrance.

The Rakshas turned away from the tree and slowly paced the courtyard, trying to focus his limited powers of reason. Something nagged at the back of his mind, perhaps something from before his rebirth, something he had experienced when he was Gwydion. He couldn't put a context around the thought, so he returned to the place where that rebirth had occurred.

At the western edge of the garden stood a long, flat table fashioned of marble, the altar on which he had first come to awareness. He closed his eyes again, recalling the first words he had heard as his father prayed above him.

Child of my blood.

The pulse of light, the pain of rebirth.

Now shall the prophecy be broken. From this child will come forth my children.

The Rakshas closed his crystalline blue eyes, as he had then, against the intensity of the light in his memory. When he opened those eyes again, they were gleaming with that same light, but now the light was that of inspiration.

Quickly he crouched down in a feral stance, like the wolf whose blood had been added to his father's own to form him, and scratched at the earth beneath the altar. He dug for some time until he finally came upon it, a root from the tree that still bore the pocked scars of its original pollution. The tree's savior had not found all the tap roots – she had probably not even looked beneath the altar when she had done whatever anointing she had undertaken to heal the tree. The Rakshas threw back his head and laughed aloud.

There was one left, one root still desecrated.

It was enough.

He glanced around quickly and scowled for a moment. Stephen Navarne's men had stripped down the slaughtering equipment, the vats that had been carefully erected to collect the blood of the children he had stolen. That blood had fed the tree then, had twisted it to his master's whim. There was no longer any here to be found – the place had been scoured clean of it.

His master had committed a good deal of his life's essence to bring him into being, he mused. It had been a blood sacrifice on the demon's part as well, and more; it was a substantial commitment of precious power that could wink out if it was not jealously guarded. By nature F'dor were only smoke, ephemeral spirits that clung desperately to a human body. The more power, the more *will* they expended, the more tenuous that hold became. With his limited abilities to reason, the Rakshas felt honored at the life offering his master had made to give him existence.

The Child of Earth that the legends of ancient demons said slept beneath the mountains of the Teeth was one of the two tools most critical to his master's plan. The sapling's root had been the F'dor's way in – fed by the blood of innocents, connected to the power of the Axis Mundi, the centerline of the Earth itself, pulsing with ancient magic of incalculable strength. That root system ranged throughout the world, even into the flesh of the unassailable mountains. And it could be manipulated, or so his master believed. Surely reestablishing control over this holy tree's root was worth the commitment of more of his, and his master's life essence.

He tried to concentrate, tried to force his circumscribed intelligence to calculate the right answer. The repetitive music of the small harp jangled his thoughts, making focus impossible. He eyed the instrument angrily, then, as dawn crosses a valley, a smile spread slowly over his face, lighting each of the features it touched until it came at last to his eyes.

He had his answer.

With an arrogant flip of the wrist, a dagger was in his hand, a hand that no longer bore any sign that it contained a new thumb. Quickly he slashed his forearm twice, drawing deep, bright bands of red across the skin, and then turned his arm over to allow them to drip onto the exposed root. There was no real pain; such a trifling injury could not compete with the agony that constituted his waking life.

As the blood splashed the ground smoke began to rise. Scarlet and black against the night sky, it twisted into a tendril, then a spiraling column, catching the wind.

The ground began to smolder, then to burn. The Rakshas closed his eyes, listening to the deep voices begin to whisper, then to chant darkly, ominously, speaking in obscene countersigns, murmuring in pain.

The agony surged, roaring through him like hot lightning; he felt his head crackle with the intensity of it. The odor of burning flesh in fire crept into his nostrils, and he clenched his fists, knowing that the spilling blood was taking some of his master's power with it into the earth.

Bloody light filled the darkness, dancing frenetically to the chanting voices of F'dor spirits imprisoned in their deep vault within the Earth. The Rakshas struggled to stand upright in the waves of power pouring from his pulsing heart like blood from the artery he had opened. *I am merely the vessel*, he thought, pleased, as the ground beneath his trembling feet turned crimson. *But I am a capable vessel*. He lost the battle with gravity and stumbled forward from his crouch, kneeling in his own burning blood.

When the root and the soil around it was soaked into red mud the Rakshas exhaled in exhaustion, then held the skin-flaps around his wounds together for a moment, sealing them shut again. He carefully reburied the root, whispering the words of encouragement he had routinely spoken over it when he was still Master of this house.

'Merlus,' he whispered. *Grow.* 'Sumat.' *Feed.* 'Fynchalt dearth kynvelt.' *Seek the Earth child.*

He stood slowly and watched in delight as the root swelled, engorged with tainted blood, then withered, dark and vinelike, before it slithered back into the ground and disappeared. He pulled up his hood, casting one last look around the old Cymrian outpost, and went to meet up with the one who was waiting for him.

29

'Grunthor, stop hovering, I'm fine. Jo, make him stop.'

Jo gave the giant a playful smack across the back of the head. 'She says she's fine. Leave her alone.'

'I heard her,' said the Bolg indignantly, 'and I can also see her neck, thank you, little miss. You look like the loser in a game of Badger-in-the-Bag, Duchess. You got your charmin' little arse booted, didn't you?'

'I beg your pardon,' said Rhapsody with a tone of mock offense. 'I'll have you know he did not draw one drop of blood on me, *not one.*'

'Not above the surface of the skin, anyway,' said Achmed with a smirk. 'What do you think bruises are?'

'Aye, well, you should have seen him when it was over,' said Rhapsody, pushing the giant hand away from her throat again. 'Will you leave me alone?'

'If the Patriarch is such an almighty healer, why didn't the old bastard fix your neck, miss? I like his mettle; if you'd come and stood by me, saved my hairy arse, I would at least given you something for the pain.'

Rhapsody smiled at her friend, genuinely touched by his concern for her. 'I didn't give him a chance, Grunthor. I just wanted to get home as soon as I could. Besides, the bruises are much better. Ten days' ride without incident does wonders for minor wounds.'

'Still say I don't like it. We're a team, you and me. From now on I don't want none of this galavantin' off by yourself. Got it?'

'We'll see. I don't intend to go anywhere anytime soon, but I do have something I need to discuss with you all.'

Achmed nodded; she had briefed him thoroughly before the other two had arrived, telling him all about what she had learned in her travels, and giving him her take on the situation in Roland, on the incursions and the future reunion of the Cymrian states. He caught Grunthor up quickly while Jo opened some of the gifts Rhapsody had brought back with her. Finally, when they returned to the massive table, Rhapsody took a deep breath and crossed her arms.

'I've decided I want to help Ashe,' she said. Jo smiled, Grunthor and Achmed looked at each other.

'Help him what?'

'Help him get his soul back. Kill the demon that took it in the first place. Help him heal. Help him become Lord Cymrian, eventually, and help unite the Cymrian people.'

'Stop,' said Achmed. 'Why?'

'I've had ten days to think about it, to sort things out. After being around him, and around the land, I think it's the right thing to do.'

'Are you knobbing him?'

'You're a pig,' Rhapsody retorted, holding her hands over Jo's ears.

'Too late; I heard him already,' said Jo. 'Well, are you?'

'No,' said Rhapsody indignantly. 'What's the matter with you three? I've helped you all at one time or another, and I'm not knobbing any of you.'

'Well, it's not for want of tryin' on my part, I can assure you.'

'You be quiet. The Rakshas is going to be after us sooner or later, I expect, after the House of Remembrance and our confrontation in the basilica. And I can't believe you don't have the desire to hunt down and kill the F'dor, Achmed. I thought that was intrinsic to your race.' The Firbolg king said nothing. 'As for uniting the Cymrians, I think it makes some sense for us to take a role in the healing of the people who came from the same place we did.'

'Well, that leaves me out,' said Jo, rising from the table. 'I came from Navarne, and as far as I'm concerned they can all die of the pox there. I'm going to bed. Do whatever you want, Rhaps; you know you can count on my help.'

'Thanks, Jo.' Rhapsody blew her a kiss as she left the room. Jo had little stomach for long political arguments.

Jo turned out to be astute in her decision to leave, Rhapsody decided some hours later. They had argued and debated endlessly, getting nowhere. Even more than Achmed was suspicious of Ashe, he did not trust Llauron. Grunthor could not get past the idea of the Rakshas and Ashe being two separate entities.

'So you say this thing ain't him, it just looks like him, right?'

'Right.'

'And have you ever seen them together?'

'No,' she admitted. 'I think if the Rakshas had found Ashe, he would be dead, or, even worse, his soul would be the F'dor's entirely. Powerful as Ashe is, in a confrontation with the Rakshas he would be fighting against his own soul. He is damned either way, win or lose. That's the main reason he hides behind the mist cloak, I think.'

'Ashe told you this?' Grunthor asked suspiciously.

'No,' Rhapsody admitted reluctantly. 'I've pieced it together from my own observations, and what Elynsynos and Oelendra told me. And my visions.'

'If you haven't seen them together, then how do you know it ain't him just actin' different?'

'I don't know it for sure,' Rhapsody admitted again. 'But I have seen them both, and watched them fight, and they seem very different.'

'No. Not good enough. I think they're one and the same. Maybe Ashe don't even know it, but perhaps the Rakshas is nothing more than his own evil side.'

'Let's go over this again,' Rhapsody said, trying to maintain her patience. 'There are two possibilities. The first is that Ashe and the Rakshas are one and the same; that Gwydion died, for all intents and purposes, and the F'dor was able to reanimate him somehow, and use him as its servant.'

'That would be my guess, miss.'

'And if that's true, I just traveled safely across the better part of the continent with him, during which time he never once made a move to harm me.' Her voice caught in her throat as she remembered the scuffle where he drew his sword on her. 'Well, maybe once, but he didn't actually harm me.'

Grunthor's amber eyes narrowed. 'What does that mean?'

'Nothing. It was a misunderstanding. And obviously he did what he said he would do – he took me to where I asked to be taken, and then he left. If he was this twisted, evil minion of the F'dor, why didn't he just kill me when he had the opportunity, and thwart the prophecy?'

'Maybe he was following you to get an idea of your mission,' the giant suggested. 'Might be spyin' for the F'dor.'

Rhapsody swallowed her frustration. 'The second possibility, the one I believe to be correct, is that there are two beings, Ashe and the Rakshas. Ashe is Gwydion, and, despite what Oelendra and Stephen think, he's alive; he survived the F'dor's attack. He is wandering the world alone, in pain, trying to remain hidden so that it doesn't find him and take the rest of his soul. The Rakshas is a separate entity, a construct built around the piece that the F'dor took. It's made from ice, earth, and the blood of the F'dor, and probably some sort of feral animal. That's what the dragon said.'

'But she didn't say Ashe and the Rakshas weren't the same, now did she, miss?'

'No.'

'Then I think we can't take the chance that they are.'

'Well, what would you have me do, then?' Rhapsody asked in exasperation.

'I say we kill him. And if we're wrong, and another one shows up, we kill him too.'

Rhapsody paled; she knew the Bolg giant wasn't joking. 'You can't go around killing people if you're not sure whether you're right.'

'And why not? Always worked for us before. Seriously, miss, this is too big to take chances with, if you're not sure.'

'That's ridiculous, Grunthor.'

'No, it's not,' said Achmed. He had been quiet for the better part of the evening, taking in the arguments and sorting through them while Rhapsody and Grunthor had at each other. His silence had made Rhapsody occasionally forget he was even there. 'What's ridiculous is your insatiable need to reestablish the world you lost.

'Your family is gone, Rhapsody; we're it now, Grunthor and Jo and I. Your town is gone as well; you live here, among the Bolg. The king your family honored is dead two thousand years; the leaders here could not hold a candle to him and his reign. He certainly never led an entire generation to its death over a domestic squabble. Those who came from Serendair to this place were shoddy examples of our culture. They don't deserve another chance to get it right. And as for Ashe, why do you want to duplicate your old relationship with a twisted madman all over again? Do you really miss the Wind of Death that much?'

Rhapsody's mouth dropped open. 'How can you say that?' she sputtered. 'Ashe has never hurt me, or tried to compromise me in any way. He's *hunted*, Achmed – I would think you of all people could sympathize with that. A piece of his soul is the source that powers the Rakshas. It's in the hands of what appears to be a F'dor of great power, which means damnation in both life and death. The wound where the demon ripped that piece of his soul from his chest has never healed; he is in unspeakable pain. Despite all that, he has never even asked for anything from me except that we consider being his allies. How can you even think to compare him to Michael? Michael was a bastard of the lowest order, and a liar.'

'And that is precisely the problem I have with all the Cymrians, Ashe included. They are all liars, too. At least in the old world you knew who sided with evil gods because they professed what they stood for. Here, in this new and twisted place, even the allegedly *good* ones are calculating users. The ancient evils could never wreak the level of havoc that the "good" Lord and Lady Cymrian did. And you want to hand yourself over on a silver platter to the potentially biggest liar of all.'

Rhapsody had had enough. 'Well, if I do, it is my choice to do so. I will take the risk, and live or die of my own volition.'

'Wrong.' Achmed rose slowly, anger evident in the tight, methodical movements of his body. 'We may all suffer that fate, because you aren't just compromising yourself, you are throwing all of our neutrality into the pot, and if you overbet your hand, we all lose.'

Rhapsody looked at him. His eyes were burning with intensity, his shoulders knotted with a rage she had not seen in a long time.

'Why are you so angry? Just because I want to help someone else doesn't mean my loyalty to you is any less.'

'That has nothing to do with it.'

'I disagree.' She stood up and came to his side of the table where he stood, struggling to contain his wrath, and sat on the tabletop in front of him. 'I think it does. And I might remind you that, in the course of helping you accomplish what you wanted in these lands, I have done a number of things that I was not sure about, or in fact was repulsed by. But I did them anyway, because you asked me to, and because you said it was right. I believed in you. Why shouldn't I believe in him as well?'

'Because he has told you none of this. He has played mystery games with you, seeking information but giving none in return. He doesn't trust you. For all you know, he might be the F'dor himself.'

'I don't think so.'

'Well, that's reassuring. You are the worst judge of character in the world. Your intuition is suspect here as well.'

Angry tears sprang into Rhapsody's eyes. 'How can you say that? I love you and I love Grunthor. How many non-Bolg do you think would be able to see past your obnoxious behavior to the good in you?'

'None. And that's because they would be reading us more correctly than you do. You have been misinterpreting my intentions since the moment we met.'

'What do you mean?' Rhapsody's stomach knotted suddenly.

Achmed put his hands on the table on either side of her, and leaned forward until he was inches from her face, forcing her to stare into his mismatched eyes. 'Do you remember the first thing I ever said to you?'

Rhapsody swallowed. 'Yes. You said, "Come with us if you want to live." '

'And you understood me to mean that I would save you if you came with me?'

'Yes. And you did.'

'Wrong *again*,' Achmed spat. 'Perhaps I should have worded it for you differently. Make no mistake, Rhapsody, no matter what has grown between us since then, no matter what I have come to feel for you over time, at that moment what I should have said to you was "Come with us or I will kill you." Do you understand now? You are too willing to believe that people are as good as you want them to be. On the whole, they're not. Not me, not Grunthor, and certainly not Ashe. His soul is in the hands of an old-world demon – do you know what that means?'

'No.'

'Well, I do. You forget, I've been there.' He slammed both fists down on either side of her, making her jump. 'Unlike you, I *do* understand what Ashe is going through. I know what it is like to have a piece of yourself in demonic hands. You will do anything, betray anyone, to keep from allowing the rest to be taken. I don't fault him for that, Rhapsody; if it were me instead of him you were talking about, you shouldn't trust me, either.

'I've told you before, F'dor can possess their victims in different ways. Ashe doesn't have to be its actual host in order to be enslaved to it. Sometimes a F'dor plants a single suggestion in some unwitting person's mind, just long enough to perform some act it wants accomplished. Sometimes it owns the victim, can see through him, or command him at will, but stops short of binding its spirit to that person's body. That means anyone and everyone we meet in this place is suspect. Why can't you understand this?

'It's bad enough that you keep adopting orphans that may or may not have ever encountered the beast. The Firbolg and even Stephen's children are most likely harmless, but we found Jo in the House of Remembrance, remember? She was the prisoner of the Rakshas. Who knows whether or not she has been bound to the F'dor?'

Rhapsody was trembling. '*I* know,' she said. 'She's not. You forget, Achmed, she was there to be sacrificed for her blood, along with all those other children. Why would the F'dor or the Rakshas waste their time, energy and *life force* possessing someone they expected to destroy?'

The furor in the mismatched eyes did not cool at all. 'That is the *only* reason I allowed you to bring her along. It was a serious lapse in judgment on my part.'

'How can you say that?' Rhapsody demanded. 'I thought you liked her.'

'I *do* like her, most of the time. And the fact that you keep bringing up such an inane point shows me that you do not even *begin* to understand the severity of what we're dealing with. Love and friendship mean nothing here, *nothing*. It is worse than life and death when you are dealing with the F'dor.

'I know you love Jo, and Grunthor does, too. That notwithstanding, I am continually regretting that I didn't kill her the first time she did something stupid to compromise us. She has done so repeatedly, in both your presence and your absence. I am beginning to believe it is a pattern, Rhapsody, that there is a reason for it we can't see, and that she can't help. If that turns out to be the case, the consequences for us, and for the Bolg, will make the destruction of Serendair pale by comparison. And those consequences are eternal – they will not end with death.'

'For gods' sake, Achmed! She's a teenager! Didn't you ever do anything foolish or misguided when you were a teenager?'

'No. And that's not the point. The F'dor or its minion can *be* a teenager, or a child, or the handsome young imbecile who passed you on the street and dropped a flower in your path. It can be anyone, Rhapsody, *anyone*.'

'But it can't be *everyone*, Achmed. Eventually we will have to choose sides, to intervene. We just can't hide, stay locked away in Ylorc for the rest of eternity. If any of the mythos is right, and we are destined to some hideous form of longevity bordering on immortality, sooner or later there's going to be a confrontation with us. Besides, if you really believe that someone you care about might be tainted by the F'dor, don't you think you have an obligation to try and spare that person from damnation? To reclaim whatever part of them is in its hands?'

Achmed turned away and ran an angry hand through his hair. 'You're not talking about Jo now, are you? You're back to Ashe again. I hadn't realized he had been elevated to the level of "someone we care about." '

'We can help him,' she whispered. 'We can find and kill the F'dor. We're the only ones who can. Remember the prophecy Llauron told us of? Haven't you figured it out yet? We're the Three. You're the Child of Blood; that's obvious. Grunthor is the Child of Earth; you know that as well. And I am Lirin; that's what they call us – Children of the Sky. It's us, Achmed. Our coming was foretold in this place.'

He whirled and glared at her. 'So we should merrily follow the prophecies because some insane Cymrian seer said so? You want to blithely go out and rid the world of this evil that these people brought on themselves by bringing them back into power? Where's the guarantee? How do you know you won't end up its next victim?'

'Where's the guarantee that won't happen anyway? Don't you think it knows about us by now? It came on a Cymrian ship. Probably its original host, and many of its subsequent ones, were Cymrian. It attended the

Councils; it knows the prophecies. And aside from the purely random chance that we will come up against it anyway, there is a good possibility that it will seek to destroy us *just because some insane Cymrian seer said so.* Forget about Ashe, forget about Llauron. We have to kill the damned thing anyway, for ourselves.'

'She's right, sir.' Grunthor spoke up from the corner he had retreated to during the heat of their argument, causing both of them to start. 'If it's out there, and we're the only ones who can kill it, I say we do so and be done with it. I don't want to spend the rest of my life lookin' over my shoulder again.'

Achmed watched his sergeant for a moment, then nodded. 'All right,' he acquiesced, still glaring at Rhapsody. 'I suppose there is wisdom in us getting to it first, at least. So what's your plan?'

'I'll call Ashe to Elysian, alone, and give him the ring. Once he's healed, we can go after the Rakshas and kill it.'

'Why not just call him here?'

Rhapsody thought about the distance Ashe always maintained. 'Because Ashe will never agree to it. He will only come to a place he knows he can be safe. Elysian's waterfall is perfect to shield his vibrational signature from anyone who might be able to find it.'

'No. That wouldn't be safe for *you*,' Achmed muttered. 'There's no speaking tube down to Elysian. You wouldn't be able to call for help if you needed it.'

'No, but the gazebo is there. It's a natural amplifier. Believe me, Achmed, if I send you a signal you will hear it.'

'No doubt,' he said sourly, his eyes boring a hole through hers. 'Is that before or after he has coerced all of our secrets out of you?'

'I would never give Ashe any help that I thought would make him a threat to you, Achmed,' she said, returning his stare with a mild expression. 'My loyalty is, first and foremost, to my family.' She smiled at Grunthor, and breathed a little easier when she saw him hide a slight grin. 'That's part of the reason I've helped you subdue the Bolglands. Not that you couldn't do it on your own, but with any luck the Bolg will turn out to be more within your vision of the nation you want them to be. The united Cymrians will pose no threat to them, particularly if I'm right about Ashe. We'll be allies. He will feel that he owes us. And if I'm wrong, I will kill him myself. I promise.'

'We'll see.'

'But our help has to be freely given, otherwise it's not worth as much.'

'You know, Rhapsody, sometimes I wish you wouldn't treat strategy like a sale in the market. It is acceptable to not always get the most that something is worth from time to time.'

She leaned forward and kissed his cheek. 'You'll let me help him, then?'

'You are a grown woman, Rhapsody. I don't have to let you do anything.'

'But you'll help.'

249

A strange smile came over his face. 'Yes. But not for him. Only for you. Now, before you invite that useless idiot into my lands, I would appreciate your help in taking care of something else first. Crack open whatever nice vintage you brought home with you, and Grunthor and I will tell you about the Loritorium.'

30

Hours later, the bottle of Canderian brandy Rhapsody had bought for Achmed was empty.

'Did you happen to gain any insight into the mystery of who the host of the F'dor might be while you were gone?' The Firbolg king tossed the empty decanter into the fire.

'A little. I think I figured out what happened to Gwylliam based on what Oelendra told me. Do you remember that other body we found with his in the library, the one we thought was a guard?' The two Bolg nodded. 'That was probably the host of the F'dor, the one that actually killed him. The host would have been far less formidable than Gwylliam himself, which is why the king was able to kill the guard before he succumbed to death himself. Remember how you suspected at the time there was a second guard?' Achmed and Grunthor nodded simultaneously again. 'Well, undoubtedly there was. He or she was the innocent witness. And when the F'dor's host died at Gwylliam's hand, the demon-spirit took possession of the second guard and left the vault.'

Achmed nodded. 'Makes sense.'

'I wish I could have found out who it is now,' Rhapsody said regretfully. 'Oelendra actually has seen F'dor in a human host before, and has been looking more than a thousand years for this one with no luck. But I did find a few clues.'

'Such as?'

'Well, I'm fairly certain the second assassin in the basilica that night was the F'dor. I got the same vibrational reading from it that I did from the Rakshas. I assume that was a factor of them having the same blood.'

Achmed nodded. 'Sounds right. Did you see any distinguishing marks?'

'I didn't see his face, he was wearing a helmet. But I had seen the helmet itself, or one like it, before. It had horns on it. Do you remember when I rode out to meet the Lord Roland to sign the peace treaty?'

'Yes.'

'There was a benison there, the Blesser of Canderre-Yarim. He wore a horned helmet, and a sun symbol like the F'dor in the old world wore, although I couldn't see the stone in the amulet up close.'

'That's the uniform of the officers and nobility in Yarim. The ambassador wore the same type of thing when their delegation visited.'

'Hmmm. I haven't been to Yarim yet, but it's got a reputation as a decadent place. That's where Manwyn the Oracle, the Seer of the Future, lives.'

'Tell me about the benison,' said Achmed.

'He's Tristan Steward's younger brother, the newest of the five Orlandan benisons, and the weakest. I doubt he has much of a chance at the Patriarchy, given his ties to Bethany and his lack of experience.'

'Perhaps killing the old goat was the only way he could assure the title. If that ring contains the office, maybe Ian Steward's plan was to take it from the Patriarch when he was vulnerable in the midst of his religious rite.'

'Maybe,' said Rhapsody uncertainly. 'You know, it's hard for me to imagine that a clergyman of that visibility could be the demon's host. They spend so much of their time in the basilicas, on holy ground, that it seems impossible for them to be both demon and benison. The power of those sacred places would certainly thwart a demon, even an old-world one. The F'dor, if that's what it was, couldn't enter the basilica at Sepulvarta. It had to stop in the nave. The best it could do was throw a fiery shield to let the Rakshas escape.'

'Then maybe it's one of the Orlandan nobles that the benisons share power with,' Achmed said, resting his hand on his chin. 'If there was a tug of war between the clergy and the state, who would have been on the other end of the rope from the Patriarch?'

'That would be our old friend, the Lord Roland, Tristan Steward.'

'Ah, yes,' said Achmed, smiling. 'Well, we can hope it's him.'

'Why?'

'I hardly need to remind you what a dolt he is.'

'True.'

'But that could also be an act. F'dor are particularly good at deception. They can be as convincing as a Namer speaking truly, but their medium is the combination of lies, half-lies and a judiciously rare usage of the absolute truth.'

Rhapsody shuddered. 'No wonder it felt at home among the Cymrians.'

'What makes you think it's got to be someone powerful?' asked Grunthor finally. 'Why wouldn't it just stay out of sight?'

'It could be someone who is not in the public eye, but is still very powerful,' agreed Rhapsody. 'The way the thing works is to bind itself to someone who is as powerful as it is or less; it can't possess a soul of greater strength than its own. It uses that lifetime to grow in capacity, then takes over a newer, younger life of equal vitality. Given that it almost destroyed Ashe without breathing hard, I would say it's a fair guess that it is almost at the apex of its power. Whatever else you think of Ashe, Achmed, you have to admit he's someone to be reckoned with.'

'Yes, he is.' Achmed leaned against the wall. 'I still think it's Llauron.'

'Llauron is Ashe's father.'

'So? If it's the demon, it wouldn't care who was standing in the way, even his son.'

'That's not the point. Because Llauron has a son, it *can't* be him, remember? It shall bind to no body that has borne or sired children, nor can it ever do so, lest its power be further dispersed."

Achmed sighed. 'You are assuming that what you think you know is true. Perhaps Ashe is a bastard; I'd lay a wager on that one. Believe me, Rhapsody, the depths of deception possible are beyond your comprehension. It's probably better if you don't even try to understand it.'

Rhapsody rose and gathered her things. 'You're probably right,' she said, kissing Achmed on the cheek. 'I think it's better for me to just decide how things are going to work out, and then they will. In a day or two I'll go with you to the Loritorium, and to the Colony, to see if I can help with the Sleeping Child. Then I'll let you know what comes to pass with Ashe. Now, if we're finished, I think I'll look in on the hospice. Is there anyone in pain who needs to be sung to?'

Achmed rolled his eyes. 'As far as I'm concerned, there never is anyone who needs that,' he muttered.

Grunthor looked at him seriously. 'I'd have to take exception to that, sir,' he said. Rhapsody had once sung him back from the brink of death.

'That's different,' the king scowled. 'No one's dying currently. She's talking about easing the pain of Bolg with minor injuries. It's a waste of time, and it makes them feel awkward.'

Rhapsody chuckled as she gathered the debris. 'You know, Grunthor, you could help with the healing as well. You like to sing.'

The Sergeant's expression was both amused and doubtful. 'I believe you've heard the content of my songs, miss,' he said, scratching his head. 'Generally they tend to be more on the threatnin' side. And I don't think anyone's ever gonna mistake me for a Singer. I certainly got no trainin' in it.'

'Content makes no difference at all,' Rhapsody said seriously. 'It can be any kind of song. What matters is their belief in you. The Bolg have given you their allegiance. You're their version of The Last Word, to Be Obeyed at All Costs.' In a way, *they've* named *you*. It doesn't matter what you sing, just that you expect them to get well. And they will. I've always maintained the Achmed will do the same for me one day.' The Firbolg king rolled his eyes.

The giant rose. 'All right, then, Your Ladyship, I'll go with you,' he said. 'I can treat the troops to a few choruses of "Leave No Limb Unbroken."''

The ambassador blinked nervously. The voice that spoke was light and pleasant, in marked contrast to the look in the red-rimmed eyes.

'Well, that was an unpleasant surprise; I do loathe surprises. But I'm sure there is a very reasonable explanation. Perhaps you'd like to enlighten me, Gittleson. Now, if I remember correctly, in the report of your ambassadorial call to the court of Ylorc you said that each of the Three was there when you visited, is that not so?'

'Yes, Your Grace.'

'And when I quizzed you on what constituted the Three, you told me that it was the Firbolg king, his giant guard, and a young blond woman, am I right? That's what you saw in Canrif?'

'Yes, Your Grace,' Gittleson repeated apprehensively. 'That was my report.'

'Well, that is the correct answer. It seems you did in fact meet the Three. And yet when we arrived in Sepulvarta, one of them was there waiting for us in the basilica. Now, Gittleson, how could that be?'

'I don't know, Your Grace.'

'Did she fly there, do you suppose? Hmmm?' The red tinge at the edge of his eyes darkened to the color of blood.

'I – I – I can't explain that, Your Grace. I'm sorry.'

'And you positioned your escort so that they were watching the mountain pass, and the road out of Ylorc, as I instructed?'

'Yes, Your Grace. She did not leave the Firbolg realm alone or with the mail caravan. I don't understand how she could have gotten to Sepulvarta before you. It seems – quite – impossible.' His words ground to an impotent halt under the withering stare from the icy blue eyes.

'And yet, Gittleson, she was there, wasn't she, my son?'

A third voice spoke, a pleasant baritone, warm as honey. 'Yes, indeed.'

'Your Grace, I – ' A hand raised, and Gittleson fell silent, his protest choked off in mid-word.

'Do you have any idea what this setback has cost us?' The voice had lost its cultured edge, and now had grown icy, a cold, threatening whisper.

'She – she seemed as if she could pose no threat to anyone, Your Grace,' the ambassador stammered. Two sets of Cymrian-blue eyes stared at him, then looked to one another in silence. After what seemed like forever, the holy man spoke.

'You are an even bigger fool than I imagined, Gittleson,' he said, the aristocratic tone returning to his voice. 'A blind man couldn't miss the immense innate power in that woman. How could you possibly misjudge her so badly?'

'Perhaps he hasn't,' said the Rakshas thoughtfully. 'I would think that even Gittleson could not have been this wrong about her. In fact, I tend to think he would have stood, slack-jawed and glassy-eyed, abusing himself if he had gotten within sight of her.' Gittleson swallowed the insult, grateful for the possible salvation that lay behind it. 'Besides, if you had thought to ask me, I could have told you that she was in Tyrian not all that long ago.'

The reddened eyes narrowed. 'Go on.'

'How old was the woman you saw?' the Rakshas asked the ambassador.

'Quite young,' Gittleson said hesitantly. 'A girl, really. Perhaps fifteen or sixteen.'

The elder man sat forward. 'Describe her further.'

'Thin, with pale blond hair. Sallow skin. Unremarkable in all ways, except for a quick touch with a dagger – she was playing mumblety-peg with one.'

Across from him the two faces contorted, one in a scowl, the other in a smirk. After a moment the holy man sat back in his desk chair.

'And if I were to tell you, Gittleson, that the woman in the basilica was painfully beautiful with a soul of elemental fire – '

'She isn't the one I saw in Ylorc, Your Grace.'

'Now, you see, Gittleson, you are already ahead of me. You have reached the same conclusion I was about to put forward.' The holy man poured himself a snifter of brandy.

'The Three rescued a girl from the House of Remembrance that fits your description,' said the Rakshas. 'That's probably who you saw.' He turned to his master. 'Perhaps I should pay her a visit. We spent some time together; I think she was somewhat enamored of me, actually.'

'Has she seen your face?'

'Not fully. She might have caught a glimpse. I would be happy to look into it, Father, if you'd like. She's undoubtedly our best chance to get back into the mountain.'

'Do that, but be careful. The Firbolg king is wily, and he may sense you far better than you think. Oh, and while you're at it, I think it's time to move our plan into its next phase. Take care of that while you're there as well.'

31

The snowcaps of the high crags in the Teeth caught the late morning sun and turned the color of fire against the clear sky. Prudence pulled the coach's window curtain further aside to take in the view, closing her eyes for a moment and letting the warmth of the wind ripple across her face. Then she rose slightly from the cushioned seat and leaned out of the window.

For the fourth time that morning the coachman and the guard were showing the traveling papers under Tristan's seal to yet another set of Firbolg soldiers who had stopped them. Prudence's gaze returned to the mountains. This land was so strangely beautiful and threatening, dusky, multicolored peaks scratching the sky at the horizon like the fangs of a great beast that lay in the near distance. Having never before left the wide plains of Bethany, she was mesmerized by the dark magic she felt in this place, Ylorc, the mountainous land of monsters.

She felt eyes upon her, and turned inadvertently to meet the gaze of one of those monsters. Like the other Firbolg soldiers she had seen since they had crossed the border at Bethe Corbair, his face was dark and hirsute, his build wiry, but not particularly grotesque. The man was studying her with an expression that was direct but not insolent. Embarrassment crept into

Prudence's cheeks as she realized his expression must mirror the one she wore herself.

They're monsters, humanoid beasts that eat rats and each other, Tristan had said. *And any human they can catch as well, by the way.* And yet now, seeing them up close, it seemed an exaggeration worthy of a child's tale. The Bolg had appeared each time as if from thin air, stopping the carriage silently, crossbow-like weapons trained on the horses. Once satisfied with the intent of the mission they motioned wordlessly for the coach to continue on its way, then disappeared again. Prudence couldn't help but wonder if the Bolg were only humoring them.

The carriage shuddered and began to roll again. Prudence settled back against the cushioned seat, the place where she and Tristan had made secretive love on numerous occasions. After a moment the tiny slat door in the wall across from her slid open, and the upper part of the guard's face appeared.

'Not too much longer, miss. We're within an hour of the main outpost, the place where the mail caravans enter.'

Prudence nodded, and the small door slid shut again. She glanced out the window one last time and saw the Firbolg scout still staring at her as the carriage rolled away. There was a look in his eyes that worried her.

After a time the road beneath the carriage wheels seemed to smooth out somewhat, offering her a less bumpy ride. Prudence pulled the curtain aside, then reached forward quickly and banged on the little slat door.

'Stop, please.'

The carriage rolled to a slow halt, and Prudence opened the outside door, rising as she did. The coachman was still descending from his perch and was not quick enough to offer her his assistance in alighting from the step. She gathered her skirts and jumped down to the road, then crossed to the wide meadow beyond.

Before her stretched a great bowl-like amphitheater, cut into the earth by time and nature, though it seemed to have been enhanced by the work of men. Now forgotten by all but history, the structure seemed to have at one time been a gathering place for an enormous number of people. A twisting rock formation in the dead center of the far slanted wall looked for all the world like a speaker's podium. The amphitheater was vast in size and breadth, surrounded by rocky ledges and rimmed internally in gradated rings that leveled out onto a wide, flat floor, all overgrown with highgrass and brushy scrub. Prudence recognized it from the descriptions Tristan had read her once from a Cymrian history text.

'The Moot,' she murmured to herself. It was the place that Tristan's strange, all-but-immortal ancestors had once convened their meetings, intending to keep peace within the Cymrian realm. The failed intention had been a good one, at least.

'Excuse me, miss?' the coachman asked.

Prudence turned to him. 'Gwylliam's Moot,' she repeated, excitement creeping into her voice. The natural wonder was bigger than the Fire basilica and Tristan's palace together.

The coachman and the guard exchanged a smirk, then the coachman opened the door again.

'Yes, miss, whatever you say. Please, now, make haste and come back inside. We need to be at the post in no more than an hour so we can leave before dark, or we won't meet up with the second-week caravan three days hence.'

Prudence took the man's outstretched hand and climbed back into the carriage, a look of displeasure darkening her features. She had seen that smirk several times since she had left Bethany, and knew its genesis. The coachman and the guard thought of her as Tristan's peasant whore, and it amused them to be driving her about alone in splendor generally reserved for royalty, or at least nobility. She heard the coachman chuckle as he closed the door behind her.

With a jolt the carriage lurched forward again. Prudence cast one last look back at the ancient marvel, lying forgotten in the endless rich green of the foothills. Then she took out her looking glass and began to polish her face, preparing to do yet one more ridiculous favor for the man she loved.

'First Woman?'

The midwives and Rhapsody looked up simultaneously. The guard took an involuntary step back at the expressions on the faces of the Bolg women at his interruption.

'Yes?'

'Messenger here for you. Woman. From Bethany.'

'Really?' Rhapsody handed one of the midwives an herb they had been examining together. 'What does she want?'

'Talk with you.'

'Hmm. Where is she?'

'Grivven post.'

'Very well. Thank you, Jurt. Please tell her I'll be down directly.' Rhapsody gathered the remaining herbs and medicines and passed them to each of the thirteen midwives, some of the most powerful Bolg in all of Ylorc. 'Are we finished, then?' she asked. The broad-shouldered women nodded and Rhapsody rose. 'Thank you for coming. I'll check in with you at week's end to see how those tonics are working. Please excuse me.'

Prudence waited in the shadow of the bay geldings, feeling safer next to the enormous horses than inside the guard quarters where she had been offered shelter. She swallowed hard. While she was waiting she had been steeling herself for the meeting, and she had been waiting for quite some time, but was still unprepared for the sight of what was approaching.

A giant Firbolg dressed in battle armor walked beside a much smaller figure, cloaked from head to mid-shin in a gray hooded cape, despite the blistering heat of summer. From behind the giant's back a plethora of blade hilts protruded, making him appear to have a mane of thorns.

The smaller figure remained hooded until it had reached her, then took down its mantle. The face that emerged from the hood was the most singularly beautiful Prudence had ever seen, crowned with shining golden hair pulled loosely back in a black ribbon. The woman was attired in a simple shirt of white linen and soft brown trousers, and it was all Prudence could do to keep from bursting into tears at the sight of her.

Suddenly Tristan's words made sense. Looking into this woman's face was much like staring into a crackling fire, hypnotic and compelling on a level she could feel in her soul.

'Hello,' said the golden-haired woman, smiling and extending a small hand. 'My name is Rhapsody. Did you ask to see me?'

'Ye – yes,' stammered Prudence. She looked down at the woman's open palm, then recovered her wits and shook hands. The woman's hand was deliciously warm, and Prudence had to struggle to pull her own away. To cover the awkward jerking motion, she dug quickly within the pouch Tristan had given her and produced two vellum sheets folded neatly and sealed with gold. 'His Highness, Lord Tristan Steward, Prince of Bethany, asked that I deliver these invitations to you personally.'

Rhapsody's brow furrowed, and Prudence felt her heart sink suddenly. 'Invitations?'

'Yes,' Prudence said, her words falling over each other. 'To his wedding, on the eve of the first day of Spring, this year to come.'

'There are two of them?'

'Yes. One for His – er, Majesty, the King of Ylorc, and one for you.'

The woman's emerald eyes opened in astonishment. 'For me?'

Hot blood rushed to Prudence's cheeks. 'Yes.' She watched nervously as Rhapsody turned the folded card over in her hand and stared down at it. 'You seem surprised.'

The giant beside her let out a roaring laugh, causing Prudence to go pale in fright. 'Well, well, Duchess, listen to that. The Prince wants you at 'is weddin'. Isn't that lovely?'

Rhapsody handed one of the invitations back. 'There must be a mistake. Why would the Lord Roland send me an invitation?'

Prudence ran her hand over her throat, and felt herself trembling. 'Duchess? I do beg your pardon, I hadn't realized. I hope you will forgive me any offense in addressing you improperly, m'lady.'

'No, no,' Rhapsody said hastily. 'He's just joking.'

The giant's amber eyes twinkled merrily. 'What are you talkin' about? The Duchess of Elysian she is, miss. The highest born Lady in Ylorc.' Prudence nodded, the expression in her eyes changing.

'I don't think you understand how little that means,' Rhapsody said, casting an annoyed glance at Grunthor. 'To your Lord I am still a peasant. My role to his court has been that of messenger for the king of Ylorc. And while our last meeting was civil, on the whole our intercourse has been somewhat strained. So for all those reasons I am astonished that he would send me an invitation to such an auspicious event. I'm sure this was merely an error.'

'You've been having intercourse with him?' Grunthor gasped in mock horror. 'You said he was a dolt!' Rhapsody elbowed him as subtly as she could, then looked back at Prudence, who now was trembling visibly. The look of irritation on her face melted into one of concern. She reached out and touched the servant woman's arm.

'Are you unwell?' she asked.

Prudence looked up into the golden woman's face and felt herself warmed by the worry she saw there. 'No, I'm fine,' she said, awkwardly patting Rhapsody's hand.

'Here, let's get out of the sun,' Rhapsody said, pulling Prudence's thin hand into the crook of her arm. 'I've been a terrible host thus far – I haven't even asked your name.'

'Prudence.'

'Well, please forgive my discourtesy, Prudence. Allow me to welcome you to Ylorc properly. Would you and your escort like something to – '

Suddenly the world shifted. Rhapsody's ears filled with the pounding of her own blood, and her eyes clouded over. Grunthor's hand shot out quickly as she pitched forward onto her face and grabbed her before she hit the ground. He turned her quickly over in his arms to see her face contorted in fear, and something more.

'You all right, Duchess?' he asked anxiously, patting her smooth cheek with an enormous hand.

Rhapsody blinked rapidly, trying to stave off the sensation that the sky was closing in on her. She looked up past Grunthor into the Orlandan messenger's face. Prudence was a pretty woman with pale skin and strawberry-blond curls, Rhapsody noted absently. Something approaching panic was glittering in her dark-brown eyes.

Then, as Rhapsody watched Prudence's face, it began to rip away, as if being torn by the claws of a brutal wind, leaving gouges of exposed bone and muscle. Her eyes vanished from the sockets, leaving dark holes filled with dried blood. Rhapsody gasped.

'M'lady?' Prudence voice was shaking.

Rhapsody blinked again. Prudence's face was as it had been.

'I'm – I'm very sorry,' she said. Grunthor gently pulled her to a stand, and she brushed the dirt from her clothes. She gave the frightened messenger a weak smile. 'Perhaps the sun is getting to me as well. Inside Grivven post there is a place we can sit and cool down. Would you come inside with us?'

Prudence glanced over at the guard post, where six Firbolg guards were watching her with interest. One of them smiled at her, a grisly expression that approximated a leer. She shuddered.

'I – I really must be getting back,' she stammered. 'The mail caravan is three days ahead of us, and we should make haste to meet up with them.'

Rhapsody's expression grew serious. 'You did not come with the guarded caravan?'

Prudence swallowed. Tristan had been quite specific about the need for discretion and secrecy in her mission.

'No,' she said.

'Do you mean to tell me that the Lord Roland sent a civilian woman into Ylorc without the protection of the weekly armed caravan?'

'I have a guard, and the driver is an Orlandan soldier as well,' Prudence answered. *Ironic*, she thought. She and Tristan had had this same discussion. It was bitterly amusing to be defending the position now that she had objected to then.

Rhapsody's expression grew thoughtful for a moment, then resolved suddenly. She put out her hand to Prudence. 'Please come inside with me,' she said. 'I promise you will be safe.'

The words had such a clear tone of truth to them the Prudence could feel their veracity in her soul. Almost involuntarily she took the woman's hand, and allowed Rhapsody to lead her into the post.

Grivven post was a guard tower hollowed out of the mountainside that eventually culminated in one of Ylorc's tallest peaks. Inside the rocky structure the walls were honed smooth and straight, with floors of polished stone. Above them stretched a many-tiered tower taller than Avonderre's lighthouse, built into a low crag with inner rings of wood on three sides facing the west, north and south. These platforms were connected by ladders so tall she could not see their tops, cemented to the walls. Prudence looked around in amazement as she followed the giant Firbolg and the small woman through the outpost's barricades scored with rows of hidden windows and lined with hundreds of mounted crossbows.

They passed offices and barracks and several large meeting halls, Prudence's wonder growing by the moment. She had lived her entire life in Tristan's keep, and knew the ramparts of his stronghold were only a fraction of the size of this. And this was just an outpost, not part of the main mountain fortress. She made note to tell Tristan how seriously he was outmatched.

Finally Rhapsody stopped before a heavy door, lacquered and bound in black iron. She swung the door open and gestured inside.

'Please come in,' she said.

Prudence obeyed, her eyes taking in the weapons racks that flanked the door. Inside the room was a long, heavy table of roughhewn pine surrounded by crude chairs. Rhapsody lingered in the hall long enough to exchange some words with the Firbolg giant, then came into the room as well. She gestured to the table.

'Please, Prudence, make yourself comfortable.'

Prudence complied as Rhapsody removed her long gray cloak and hung it on a peg near the door. She sat down in a chair facing Prudence.

'I'm sorry I didn't have the opportunity to properly introduce Grunthor,' she said. 'He's gone to arrange some refreshments for us.'

Prudence nodded. 'Now, then, while we're alone, why don't you tell me why you really came here?'

Prudence looked away. 'I don't know what you mean.'

'Forgive me, but I believe you do. Although the Lord Roland and I have had a few unpleasant exchanges, and despite the fact that he has made several serious errors in judgment, I can hardly believe he would be so foolish as a matter of routine to send a special messenger who is obviously not a soldier to deliver a wedding invitation, particularly when there is a weekly caravan that makes these sorts of deliveries, escorted by two score and ten armed guards. Why are you really here, Prudence?'

The tone in Rhapsody's voice was gentle and filled with understanding. Prudence looked back into the woman's eyes, and found a look of consummate sympathy there. She was beginning to understand what Tristan meant about being unable to break away from the thought of her. There was something compelling about this woman, whether in the music of her words or just in the warmth that exuded from her. Either way, Prudence found herself struggling to keep from being drawn in to it.

'The Lord Roland regrets his past transgressions with you,' she said haltingly. 'He is, frankly, embarrassed by the way he has treated you.'

'He has no need to be.'

'Nonetheless, he wishes to make amends. To that end he asked me to invite you to Bethany for a visit, so that he might apologize in person, and further demonstrate his good intentions toward the kingdom of Ylorc. He also would like to show you the city, and promises a tour with all appropriate protocol and guard.'

Rhapsody hid a smile. The first time she had been to Bethany she had accidentally caused a riot in the street and had almost been seized by both Tristan's soldiers and the town guard.

'That's very kind, but I'm still not certain I understand. Why didn't he send this invitation to me in writing, or at least have you travel with the caravan? These are unsafe times, not just in Ylorc, but everywhere.'

'I know.' Prudence sighed heavily. 'I'm just doing my lord's bidding, m'lady.'

The golden-haired woman considered for a moment, then nodded. 'Please, just call me Rhapsody. I'm afraid I've just returned from a rather lengthy sojourn, and I need to spend some time tending to my duties here in Ylorc. So as much as I might like to accept your Lord's invitation, I'm afraid I can't. I'm sorry.'

Prudence's throat went dry, envisioning Tristan's disappointment. 'I'm sorry to hear that. I hope you won't be declining the wedding invitation as well.'

Rhapsody sat back in her chair. 'I'm not sure what to say about that. It still seems very strange to me that the High Regent of Roland would want a commoner at his nuptials.'

'I assure you, he was most sincere.'

'Hmm. Well, do you need an answer at this moment?'

'No, not at all,' said Prudence in relief. 'You can respond when the King of Ylorc does.'

The door opened. Grunthor came into the room, followed by a Bolg soldier bearing a tray with a pitcher, glasses, honey muffins, and fruit. The man quickly deposited the food on the table and left the room, closing the door behind him.

Rhapsody smiled at Grunthor, then turned back to Prudence and gasped again. Tristan's messenger lay slumped crazily in her chair, her empty eye sockets staring hollowly at the ceiling. Her face was mangled, her nose gone; in the moment Rhapsody had looked away she appeared to have been savaged by wild dogs or other predatory animals.

Rhapsody closed her eyes against the vision, but the picture wouldn't leave. Instead, the darkness framed the image of Prudence's broken corpse, sprawled on a green hillside. She was recognizable only by the remains of her tattered hair, red-gold strands matted with black blood, blowing about in the wind.

Steeling herself, Rhapsody took a deep breath, trying to calm her racing heart and willing the vision to come forward. The picture expanded in her mind, pulling farther and farther away from her until Rhapsody recognized the place where the mutilated body lay.

It was Gwylliam's Moot.

A huge, strong hand closed gently on her shoulder, and the vision vanished. Rhapsody opened her eyes. Prudence was staring at her again, the same look of fear on her face from before, now intensified.

'Prudence.' Her voice came out as only a whisper. 'Prudence, you must stay here tonight. Please. I fear for your safety if you were to leave now.'

Prudence already feared for her safety if she didn't. 'Thank you, really,' she said, 'but there's no need for concern. I am well guarded, and will be meeting up with the second-week caravan less than halfway back.'

Rhapsody choked back the tears that had come suddenly into her eyes. 'That would make for at least three days when you would be traveling alone. The next caravan, the third-week caravan, will be coming by in that time, three days hence. When they arrive you can join up with them, and return with them to Bethany, which is the first stop after Bethe Corbair. You can remain here in the meantime, safe, as our guest. Please, Prudence; a small carriage, unguarded, is vulnerable, and these are dangerous times.'

The desperation in Rhapsody's voice frightened Prudence even more, and she rose from the table, trembling visibly. 'No. I'm sorry, but I must return to Bethany at once. I have delivered the message I was sent to bring you; now, if you'll excuse me, the guards are waiting for me.' She blinked, struggling to fight off the compelling effect the woman's tears were having on her. Tristan was exactly right; it was as if she was lost in a world of endless snow, and Rhapsody the only source of warmth. Deep in her heart she wondered if there was not something demonic about her.

She pushed the chair away quickly, then bolted to the door, opened it and ran from the room.

Grunthor watched the reverberating door for a moment, then turned his gaze to Rhapsody, who was still sitting at the table, staring at the wall ahead of her.

'You all right, now, miss?'

She remained lost in thought for a moment. When she looked up, there was a resolute gleam in her eye.

'Grunthor, will you do something important for me?'

'Anything, darlin'. You know that by now.'

'Follow her, please. Now. Take as many troops as you would need to defend against something powerful, and follow that carriage until it is safely past the Moot and over the border into Roland. Make sure it is out of Ylorc and onto the Krevensfield Plain, well on its way to the second-week caravan and far from our lands before you turn back. Will you? Will you do this for me?'

Grunthor regarded her seriously. 'Of course, Duchess. We'll take the field tunnels, and she won't even know we're there.'

Rhapsody nodded. The Cymrian breastworks was a labyrinth of disguised ditches, gullies, and tunnels mined into the fields at the base of the Teeth centuries before by Nain artisans loyal to Gwylliam. Grunthor had discovered them, ancient and abandoned, scoring the steppes in crumbling disuse. Achmed had made it a priority to recommission them, and now the Bolg traversed the wide fields before the mountains, silent and unseen. Prudence was already frightened enough. It would hardly improve the situation for her to discover that she was being followed by the giant sergeant and a sizable fragment of the Bolg army.

Grunthor gave Rhapsody a kiss on the cheek and left the room. She waited alone for a few moments longer, then went and climbed the high tower of Grivven post, staring out into the dusky light of the setting sun, watching as her giant friend and his regiment set off across the field after the distant coach, disappearing into the ground before her eyes.

32

Achmed checked the bindings on his gear, then looked out of the tunnel again.

'Grunthor's coming,' he reported.

Rhapsody nodded. She gave Daystar Clarion one last cleansing wipe and sheathed it in the new scabbard lined with Black Ivory that the Bolg artisans had forged for her in her absence. A song drifted up over the rockledge, the ringing bass voice echoing off the tunnel walls.

In love and in war
(Two things I adore)
They tell me that all things are fair,
So don't be surprised
As I pluck out your eyes
While I bugger your fat derriere.

Your children and wife
will be put to the knife
When we've sated our carnal desire,
Though long after you're cold
They may live to grow old
Because we don't easily tire.

Rhapsody laughed. 'Utterly charming,' she said to Achmed. 'Is this a new one?'

The Firbolg king shrugged. 'In all the years I've known him, he's never been at a loss for a marching song,' he said. 'I'm sure there are thousands more I've not heard yet.' A moment later the Sergeant emerged from the hidden crevasse and entered the tunnel.

'Is she gone, Grunthor? Did she make it out of the Bolglands safely?'

'Yeah,' the giant replied, sponging the sweat off his brow. 'We followed her as far as the breastworks allowed, into the province of Bethe Corbair and onto the Krevensfield Plain before we turned back. She's a good ways into Roland, miss, and many leagues past the Moot.'

Rhapsody sighed in relief. 'Thank you,' she said earnestly. 'I can't tell you how grisly the vision was that accompanied her. Well, at least now she's safe and on her way back to Tristan Steward, that imbecile. I can't believe he sent her out here, unguarded like that.'

'Obviously she's expendable, or whatever he wanted was too important to wait for the mail caravan,' Achmed said, pulling up his hood.

Rhapsody smiled slightly. 'It's the latter, though I can't understand why. It's a shame. She clearly loves him.'

Grunthor blinked. 'I don't remember hearing that part.'

'She didn't say it, but it's obvious.'

Achmed stood up and shook his cloak out, an air of irritation wrapped around him. 'Well, maybe he'll make it all worth her while when she gets back, then,' he grumbled. 'Can we go now? I could scarcely give a damn as to whether or not Tristan Steward's knobbing a servant girl.'

Rhapsody rose as well. 'Yes. Show me the Loritorium. I've been thinking about it since I left for Elynsynos's lair.'

The Firbolg king specifically positioned himself at the entrance to the underground vault so he could watch Rhapsody's face as she entered the Loritorium for the first time. Despite being prepared for her reaction, he felt a chill run through him as the wonder of the sight spread slowly across her countenance, lighting it with a glow that rivaled the sun in the world above.

'Gods,' she murmured, turning slowly beneath the high marbled ceiling, staring into the firmament of the cavern. 'What a beautiful place. And what a shame that no one ever saw it finished. It would have been an unrivaled work of art.'

'I'm glad you like it,' he said impatiently, annoyed by the reaction he had experienced yet again in watching her. Rhapsody's extraordinary beauty was a source of power he had made glad use of when it served his purposes. He was not happy to be reminded that he was occasionally vulnerable to it himself as well. 'Now can you please help us determine what this silver hrekin is.' He pointed to a pool of the glimmering liquid. It shone up from the cracks between the marble slabs, the puddle noticeably smaller than it had been when he first found it.

Rhapsody bent over the gleaming liquid and extended a hand toward it. She felt a strong vibration dance across her outstretched fingertips, causing them to tingle, then burn. She closed her eyes and hummed her naming note, trying to discern the origin of the vibration.

Her mind suddenly filled with a jumble of images, some thrilling, some of them ghastly. The swirl of pictures caught her off balance and involuntarily she stepped back.

'What is it?' Achmed asked as he gripped her arm, helping her regain her equilibrium.

'It's memory,' Rhapsody said, rubbing her eyes. 'Pure, liquid memory.' She looked around the square at the altars placed at each of the directional points, then walked to each of them, trembling with excitement. She pointed at the case designed to hold one of the August Relics that had been shaped somewhat like a stone birdbath.

'Listen,' she said, trying to remain calm. 'Can you hear the song?'

'Stay back, miss,' Grunthor warned. 'It's trapped.'

'I know,' Rhapsody said. 'It's telling me that, too.'

'What is?' Achmed demanded.

Rhapsody's face glowed even brighter. 'In that basin is a single drop of water – can you see it?' The Bolg squinted, then nodded. 'It's one of the Ocean's Tears, a rare and priceless piece of living water, the element in its purest form.' She whirled and pointed to another of the cases, a long, flat altar carved from beautiful marble in muted shades of vermilion and green, brown and purple.

'And that is a slab of Living Stone,' she continued, 'still alive from when the Earth was born.'

'The Earthchild is formed from the same substance,' Achmed reminded her.

'It looks as if the case for wind is empty,' Rhapsody said. She pointed to the hole in the vaulted ceiling overhead. 'I would guess that Gwylliam intended that to be the place where he would house the piece of a star, the *seren* – ether – that he brought with him from the Island. The manuscripts you showed me seemed to indicate it.

'That explains how these pools of memory were formed. Action causes vibration, and vibration remains behind, dissipating only when it blends with other vibration or is swallowed by the wind or the sea, the two greatest repositories of vibration. This place was sealed, airtight, and filled with pure and powerful forms of elemental lore, like the altar of Living Stone and the Ocean's Tears. All that magic blended with the vibrations of what transpired here and made the memory solid.' She bent beside the little gleaming pool. 'I suspect it has begun to dissipate since you opened the tunnel and let in some of the air from the world above. Still, centuries of trapped vibrations have left a strong signature in this place.'

Achmed nodded. 'And can you discern from that liquid memory whether or not the firewell was plugged intentionally, or by accident?'

Rhapsody walked over to the blocked fountain in the heart of the Loritorium and walked around it slowly. The heat from the vent grew suddenly more intense, as if the fire beneath it was responding to her presence. She closed her eyes and reached her hand out to the plugged pipe, then let her fingers come to rest on it. As her mind cleared, she began to hum a note of discerning.

Grunthor and Achmed watched in amazement as silver mist from the pool around the fountainhead rose into the air like heavy rain, forming an indistinct image of a human figure. The figure was hazy, its actions not clear, but it seemed to be looking over its shoulder. It turned and approached the fountain, then dissipated into the air.

Rhapsody opened her eyes, and in the torchlight the men could see them gleaming in emerald intensity.

'The answer to your question is yes, it was deliberate,' she said quietly. 'The fountainhead was plugged, as were the other wells that vented the smoke from Gwylliam's forges. All that caustic vapor was directed into the Colony.' A moment later she lapsed into a thoughtful silence. Achmed waited for her to come around again, anxious for more details and the chance to question her further. After a few minutes he saw her eyes clear.

'Now I remember,' she said softly, almost to herself. She turned to the two Bolg. 'The man who plugged the fountainhead did so on purpose, and a long time ago. I had seen him once before, though I didn't recognize him at first.'

'But you eventually remembered who he was?' Achmed asked.

'Well, in a way. When we first came here, when we were exploring the royal bedchambers of Canrif, I had a vision of Gwylliam sitting morosely on the edge of his bed, a corpse with a broken neck lying beside him.' Achmed nodded. 'The man who plugged the vent was that corpse.'

'Can you describe him?'

Rhapsody shrugged. 'Unremarkable in appearance, blond hair with traces of gray in it, and blue-green eyes. Other than that I don't recognize him from any surviving manuscripts or frescos we have found. But it doesn't matter. If that was the F'dor's host, and somehow I suspect that it was, it has taken on another host by now, since that man is dead.'

Achmed exhaled slowly. 'So the F'dor knew about the existence of the Colony.'

'So it appears.'

'It must know the Earthchild is here, then. That means it will be back.'

'Is that residue in the channels cleared?'

Achmed twisted the oily rags into a knot and tossed them into a heap at the edge of the Loritorium's square. He ran a finger through the gutter below the nearest streetlamp.

'Yes, at least near enough to keep from igniting when you open the wellhead.' Rhapsody looked at him askance, and he bristled, then turned to Grunthor for confirmation. 'What do you think, Sergeant?'

The giant Bolg was otherwise occupied. He was standing before the altar of Living Stone, gazing down at it as if listening to distant music. Finally he shook his head as if shaking off sleep, and turned to see the quizzical expressions on both of his friends' faces.

'Hmmm? Oh, sorry, sir. It's clear enough, I suspect.'

'What about the vents, Grunthor?' Rhapsody asked. 'Can you tell if there will be any adverse affect on the Colony if this is unsealed?'

Grunthor closed his eyes and stretched out a massive hand; he brought it gently down on the altar, trembling slightly, as if touching a lover's face for the first time. The thrill of the contact almost unbalanced him. It shot through his fingertips and up his arm, setting his shoulder afire with heat and life.

Within his mind he could see the veins of the earth around him, the ravines and cracks in stone and clay layer, the strata of rock above them, surrounding them. He let his mind follow the vent of the firewell through its ancient outlets and intakes, noting their unobstructed passageways. The sensation was a bit akin to following a dear friend through the hallways of a beloved ancestral estate, each nook and special alcove lovingly proffered for viewing. With great difficulty he tore his mind away before he became utterly lost to the journey.

'No, miss, it's all clear,' he said. 'What few passageways remain within the vent system have long since been emptied. Besides, the Grandmother's dug out a few ventilation tunnels of her own since then.'

Rhapsody nodded, satisfied. Carefully she slid her small hands into the fountainhead's pipe on either side of the rock that was wedged there. Basalt, Grunthor had said it was. And he had known the true name of the rock; the Earth had spoken it to him. She called on her abilities as a Namer and carefully spoke the word, singing the song of the basalt.

The rock, wedged for centuries, began to hum in the presence of its name. Rhapsody took a breath, then changed the song. *Magma*, she sang, *just cooled, still molten*. Her fingers slid further into the hot stone, now molding around them like clay. She gave the blockage a strong pull, freeing it from the fountainhead, and then heaved it to the ground before it could solidify on her hands.

With a roar, a small jet of fire from the Earth's core leapt up through the wellhead, splashing liquid heat and light to the Loritorium's ceiling. The flame that issued forth from the firewell was blindingly bright, the illumination so intense that the three cried out in pain to a one as it shot forth from the fountainhead. Rhapsody fell back, shielding her eyes.

In the new light the Loritorium took on an entirely different aspect. The polished marble gleamed with a new radiance, making the streets shine. The half-finished frescoes on the walls were revealed in all their exquisite detail, the intricate carvings in the stone benches made obvious for the first time. The crystal domes of the streetlamps twinkled like stars in the fire's reflection. In but a single moment the new, pure light was banishing the darkness of the place's ignominious history. The firejet settled into a bubbling flame, burning quietly within the confines of its receptacle.

Once her eyes adjusted, Rhapsody looked at the fire fountain with satisfaction, then around to the system of lamps and channels connected to the great repository of lampfuel. 'This place will be magnificent when you finish it,' she told Achmed excitedly. 'It will be perfect for scholarship and study, just as Gwylliam intended it to be.'

'Assuming we live that long,' Achmed said impatiently. 'Now that the silver sludge has confirmed that the F'dor once knew about this place we have to expect that an attack will be coming. It's just a matter of time.'

'If that was the case, why didn't it happen before now, before the Bolg were organized?' Rhapsody asked.

'That's what we're bringing you down to the Colony to determine,' he said, gesturing toward the opening. 'The Grandmother won't tell us the prophecy unless we're all there. I'm hoping there might be some answers in whatever the Dhracian sage foretold.'

Rhapsody picked up her gear and slung it over her shoulder. 'I see,' she said teasingly. 'Whatever that may be, we're going to do it because some *Dhracian* seer said so.' She smothered a laugh at the scowl that twisted the Firbolg king's face, then followed the two of them through the tunnel Grunthor had burrowed into the buried Colony.

Grunthor could see the annoyance building in the lines of Rhapsody's brow, even by the light of his torch. She and Achmed had been arguing without stopping since they had left the Loritorium and begun their descent into the tunnel that led to the Colony.

'It makes even more sense that the F'dor is Llauron,' Achmed was saying, ignoring the thunderclouds building in her eyes. 'He lived here, in Canrif, before the war. He very well might have had access to the Loritorium in those days. He undoubtedly plans to reform the Cymrian state – you even acknowledged that he sought your help in reuniting them – and make Ashe their Lord.'

'That makes no sense whatsoever,' Rhapsody growled. 'If Llauron was the F'dor, and he wanted to make Ashe the Lord, why would he rip his chest open, and almost kill him?'

'Enough!' Grunthor snarled. 'She can feel you both arguin', and it's upsetting her.'

The other two stared at him, astonished. Rhapsody recovered her voice first.

'Who, Grunthor?'

'The Sleepin' Child, naturally. Be still now, miss. She knows you're coming.'

The Singer looked up into the solemn face of her giant friend. 'All right, Grunthor. Perhaps on our way to the Colony you can explain to me just how you know that.'

33

The Grandmother was waiting for them in the darkness at the tunnel's end.

Her eyes ran over Rhapsody with interest, the silvery pupils expanded into thin oblong mirrors.

'Well met, Skychild,' she said.

Achmed and Grunthor looked at each other; in addition to the two voices which she had used to communicate with them, a third was now sounding, dry and sandy like Achmed's own. This one, however, used words.

'You are late in coming.' The Grandmother's words were full of accusation.

'I'm sorry,' Rhapsody stammered, taken aback at the brusque tone; she had not been expecting to hear spoken words, either. 'I've been away.' She stared at the woman before her, all concerns of her own rudeness drowning in the amazement she felt.

In the Grandmother's strange features she could see some decided similarities to Achmed; now, finally, she was able to assign to his Dhracian heritage what could not previously be seen in standard Bolg traits. They had guarded his Dhracian heritage as one of their closest secrets; she had never spoken the word to anyone save for Oelendra, not even Jo. The rare magic she could see before her explained far better than words could why it had been so important to keep the secret.

The woman was thin as a rapier, with skin that was more exposed vein than dermal covering. While in Achmed this trait had a nightmarish effect on most people, in the Grandmother it was a thing of beauty, like an ink etching or intricate body painting; at least it seemed so to Rhapsody. She reminded herself that she had never seen the woman in the light. Here in the dark, the woman was breathtaking.

Looking into the Grandmother's eyes was much like staring into a mirror in a dark room. Black as ink but reflective, they stared back at her now, their silvery pupils drinking in the limited light. Then the woman looked at the two Bolg, and the loss of her gaze all but ripped Rhapsody's breath away. The Grandmother's stare was almost as hypnotic as that of Elynsynos.

In the sharpness of her features, the dryness of the air around her, Rhapsody was suddenly put in mind of animal races that were born of the wind, as the Dhracians were – crickets, with their brisk, scratching sound; raptors, with their gracefully quick movements; owls, with their unblinking gaze, best suited to the night.

The Grandmother nodded curtly, then turned and began to walk away. 'Come.'

The Three followed the Colony's lone survivor down the dark tunnel and into the chamber of the Sleeping Child.

The large iron doors to the chamber were closed. The Grandmother paused before them, then turned to Rhapsody.

'You are a skysinger.' There was no question in her words.

'Yes.'

The Grandmother nodded. 'First you will meet the Earthchild,' she said, nodding to the heavily banded doors. 'Then I will take you to the canticle circle. You will find the prophecy there in its entirety. But first you must tend to the child.'

'How am I to tend to her?'

The Grandmother took one of the enormous door handles in her thin hand. 'The wind of the stars to sing the mother's-song most known to her soul," she recited. 'That is the piece of the prophecy I believe applies to you. You must be her *amelystik* now. I will soon be too aged to do it.'

Rhapsody rubbed her eyes with her thumb and forefinger. 'I don't understand; you are going too quickly,' she said.

The black scleras of the Dhracian woman's eyes expanded explosively. 'No; you are going too slowly,' she snarled in a voice full of sandy spit. 'You are late, all of you. You should have been here long ago, when I was still strong, before Time broke me. But that did not occur.

'Nonetheless I have waited, waited alone these many years, these centuries, watching as the pendulum clock counted each hour, each day, each passing year. I have waited for you to come and relieve my watch; now you are here.

'But even now, it is not as simple as the mere passing of guardianship from my hand to yours. The child has begun to dream, is tormented by nightmares. I cannot hear them; I do not know what bedevils her mind. Only you can free that knowledge, Skychild. Only you can sing her back to a peaceful slumber. It was written in the wind. It is so.'

The last words were spoken in a voice that trembled. Rhapsody's chest tightened; she knew the fear in those words, recognized the vulnerability

269

behind them. The Grandmother was more than the stalwart, solitary guardian of an invaluable tool that the F'dor prized; she loved the Earthchild as her own. It was the same sound that had been in Oelendra's voice when the lute met its destruction. The same fear that had been in the Lirin champion's eyes when she bade her goodbye.

'I understand,' she said. 'Take me to her.'

The iron doors opened with a metallic sigh, and the three companions followed the woman into the dark chamber. The Grandmother struck a spore against the cave wall, bringing forth a spark, then set about lighting the lamp over the catafalque.

Once the chamber was no longer completely dark, Rhapsody and the men drew nearer. The child rested, as she had when they first discovered the Colony, on her great stone altar, beneath a blanket of woven spider-silk as soft as eiderdown. Her smooth gray skin was still as cold-looking as stone, but there was a decided difference in her appearance since the men had seen her last. The roots and the length of her hair were green as summer grass, withering down to the dry brushy scrub ends that had once made up the entirety of her tresses. Summer was high, and the child of the Earth felt it; she was reflecting it in the only way she could here in her dark cave, away from the season of the sun.

Rhapsody rubbed her hands up and down her arms, trying to fend off a sudden chill. Slowly she walked around the Child of Earth's catafalque, her eyes absorbing the sight in the darkness pooling around the muted light from the lantern above. The wonder on her face made Grunthor's heart twist.

Elynsynos's words echoed in her heart.

Since dragons could not interbreed with the races of the Three, they tried to carve a human-like race out of what few fragments of Living Stone remained after the vault was made. Rare and beautiful creatures were the result. Those creatures were called Children of Earth, and had a humanoid form, or at least as close to one as the dragons could fashion. They were in some ways a brilliant creation, in other ways an abomination.

'She's beautiful,' Rhapsody said softly.

The Grandmother nodded. 'She thinks well of you, too.' She pulled the cover over the child again. 'She is calmed by your vibration, by the music in the air around you.' Her eyes narrowed slightly, and she stared at the Singer. 'She wonders why you hold back tears.'

Rhapsody blinked self-consciously, trying to drive the water from the edges of her eyes, and cast a wry glance at Achmed. 'Crying is forbidden in the Bolg king's presence.'

'Why do you mourn?'

'I mourn for her,' the Singer answered. 'Who would not? To be condemned as she is to a living death; to never wake? For so rare and beautiful a child to never have a life? Who would not mourn for her?'

'I would not,' said the Grandmother shortly. 'You are incorrect that she is without a life. This is her life, her destiny; this is what it is, what it will always be. It is to be endured, to be appreciated, just as a life of solitary guardianship is to be endured and appreciated. Just as your life is, no doubt, sometimes to be endured, sometimes appreciated. That it is not recognizable as life to you does not make it so to her. Life, what ever it is, is what it is.'

'*Ryle hira*,' Rhapsody whispered. The wisdom in the Lirin adage settled on her softly, like the falling of snow, until it rested solidly on her shoulders. Finally she was coming to understand fully the meaning of the words she had been taught so long ago.

The Child of Earth's lips moved silently, as if echoing the Lirin refrain. The Grandmother quickly bent down, leaning over the child as if trying to catch the soundless words. She waited, but no more was forthcoming. She sighed silently.

'Does she speak?' Grunthor asked.

'Not as yet,' the Grandmother answered softly, running her hands along the grassy hair that faded from summer's green to winter's blanched gold. 'The last prophecy of the greatest Dhracian sage said that she one day would, but in all this time she never has.

'From the oldest days it has been recorded that wisdom resides in the Earth and stars. All else, the churning seas, the evanescent fire, the fleeting wind, all these are too ephemeral, too transitory to hold on to the lessons taught by Time. But the stars see all, though they don't reveal what they know. The Earth alone holds the secrets passed down through the ages, and the Earth sings; it imparts this knowledge constantly, in the changing of the seasons, the destruction and rebirth of wildfire. There is much to learn in the repositories of the Earth.

'That was one of the saving graces of going In. Though it meant that we would never see the sky again, never read the vibrations of the wind, the Earth that was a prison to us as much as it was to the F'dor was also our teacher. The *Zhereditck* studied the Earth's lessons, learned its secrets. And the wind, in bidding us farewell, gave us one last message: that ultimate wisdom would come from the lips of the Earth Child.

'I have been waiting all my life to hear what she has to impart, waiting for those words of wisdom. Through the centuries she has said nothing intelligible, has given not a single answer, not one clue. But though she has formed no words, I know her heart.' The long fingers that tenderly caressed the smooth cheek trembled a little.

Lines of worry puckered the old woman's forehead as the child began to whisper more rapidly, her eyelids twitching.

'Now her heart knows fear,' the Grandmother said. 'I just cannot put a name to it.'

'Can you do anything for her, Duchess?' Grunthor asked anxiously.

Rhapsody closed her eyes and considered the question. *The mother's song most known to her soul*, the prophecy had apparently said. She tried to summon the image of her mother in her mind, a picture that had one been

271

clear as the summer sky, and now was almost impossible to call forth. It had been so ever since the last time she had heard her mother's voice in her memory.

Fire is strong, her mother had said in the final dream Rhapsody had had of her. *But starfire was born first; it is the more powerful element. Use the fire of the stars to cleanse yourself, and the world, of the hatred that took us. Then I will rest in peace until you see me again.*

She could still remember the words, but not her mother's voice. It was a loss she felt keenly.

Rhapsody moved closer to the catafalque, bending nearer to the child's ear. Gently she rested her hand on the grassy hair, brushing away the stray strands that had fallen into her eyes as she tossed restlessly. The Grandmother made no move to stop her, but rather removed her own hand and slid it silently back into the folds of her robe.

'My mother had a song for everything,' she said quietly. 'She was Liringlas, and every event had a song ascribed to it. I heard them all so often; it was like breathing the air. I don't know which one is the mother's song that the prophecy refers to.' Almost as soon as the words were out of her mouth a thought occurred to her. 'Wait,' she said, 'perhaps I do at that.'

'It is tradition among the Lirin that when a woman discovers she is with child, she chooses a song to sing to the growing life within her. It is the first gift she gives to the baby, its own song; perhaps that's what meant by mother's-song.' She sings it through the course of each day, through mundane events, in quiet moments when she is alone, before each morning aubade, after each evening vesper. It's the song the child comes to know her by, the baby's first lullabye, unique to each child. Lirin live outside beneath the stars, and it is important that the infants remain as silent as possible in dangerous situations. The song is so familiar that it comforts them innately. Perhaps this is what the prophecy meant.'

'Perhaps,' said Achmed. 'Do you remember yours?'

Rhapsody swallowed the disdainful retort that rose to her lips, remembering that Achmed had never had a family and could therefore not understand. 'Yes,' she said. 'And it's a wind-song, so perhaps it's the one the prophecy refers to.' She sat down on the slab of stone next to the catafalque that served as the Grandmother's bed and drew one knee under her, all the while leaving her hand on the child's forehead. Closing her eyes, she sang the song from a lifetime ago.

> Sleep, my child, my little one, sleep
> Down in the glade where the river runs deep
> The wind whistles through and it carries away
> All of your troubles and cares of the day.
>
> Rest, my dear, my lovely one, rest,
> Where the white killdeer has built her fair nest,

Your pillow sweet clover, your blanket the grass
The moon shines on you as the wind whistles past.

Dream, my own, my pretty one, dream,
In tune with the song of the swift meadow stream,
Take wing with the wind as it lifts you above,
Tethered to Earth by the bonds of my love.

When she finished, Rhapsody opened her eyes and looked at the Earth child. She had grown silent during the song, but as soon as it ended she began to twitch again, building quickly into thrashing movements; it seemed as if she was even more agitated then she had been before. Rhapsody looked on in dismay. Grunthor's huge hand closed gently on her shoulder.

'Oh, don't feel bad, Duchess,' he said. 'It wasn't that bad-soundin'.'

The Grandmother was growing agitated as well; Achmed could tell by the electricity in her vibration. 'Isn't there something else?' he asked Rhapsody, who was making soothing sounds, trying to hush the child's panic.

'My mother sang me hundreds of songs,' she answered, running her hand over the child's flailing arm. 'I have no idea which one the prophecy refers to.'

'Perhaps you're interpreting it wrong, then,' Achmed said. 'Maybe it's not *your* mother the prediction means; maybe it's *hers*.'

A note of clarity rang through Rhapsody's head. 'Yes, yes, you're probably right,' she said nervously. 'But how can I sing her own mother's-song? I don't even know who her mother was.'

'She had no mother,' said the Dhracian matriarch firmly. 'She was formed, as you see her, out of Living Stone.'

'Perhaps the dragon that made her, then?' Rhapsody suggested.

'No,' said Grunthor quietly. 'It's the Earth. The Earth is her mother.'

The three others stared at him in silence. 'Of course,' Rhapsody murmured after a moment. 'Of course.'

'And you know that song as well, Duchess. Heard it over and over again, you did; sang with it all the time we was travelin' inside the Earth. Can you sing it now?'

The Singer shuddered. It took a great deal of effort to force herself to think back to those days on the Root, the living nightmare they had endured to escape Serendair. Rhapsody closed her eyes again and concentrated on trying to hear the hum, remembering the first time she had actually listened to it, the great, slow vibration that modulated ever so lightly in the endless cavern towering above them.

It was a song deep as the sea, thrumming in her skin, rumbling through her heart, though soft as the falling of snow, almost inaudible. It was more a feeling than a sound, rich and full of wisdom, magical and unique in all the world. The melody moved slowly, changed tones infinitesimally, unhurried by the need to keep pace with anything. It was the voice of the Earth, singing from its soul. And in the background, deep and abiding, was the ever-present beating of the heart of the world, a cadence that had steadied her in her moments of despair, that reassured her in the dark of the Earth's belly. She heard it again now in her ear, as she had each time she had slept with her head against the ground.

Then the realization came. More often than not she had slept not with her head on the earth, but on Grunthor's chest. The two sensations were very similar; the giant's chest was broad and strong, solid as basalt, the beating of his heart matching the rhythm of the Earth's song exactly. It rang through him, comforting her in her nightmares. *You know I'd take the worst of them dreams for you if I could, Your Ladyship*, he had said. Rhapsody reached out and touched the Sergeant.

'Grunthor,' she said, 'will you help me do this? Like you did with the wounded soldiers?'

A slight grin broke through the consternation on his face. 'Of course, miss,' he said. 'You want a few choruses of that old Bolg mother-song, Maw's Claws'?'

'No,' she said. 'I just need you for percussion. Bend down so I can reach your heart.'

Grunthor complied amid the soft squeaking of armor, the rustle of his greatcloak. Gently Rhapsody ran her hand over his chest until she could feel his heartbeat, the slow, steady pounding she had come to know over what seemed like a lifetime. It was still the same, attuned to the rhythm of the Earth.

Rhapsody closed her eyes and cleared her mind of everything but that sound. It rang in her head, vibrating in her sinuses and through the roots of her hair, making her skull tingle. She took a deep breath and drank it in further, feeling it run down her spine and into her muscle, out to the very edges of her skin. When it had reached her fingertips she extended her free hand and touched the Earth child's chest, slipping it inside the folds of the child's garment until it came to rest on her heart as well. The rhythms matched exactly, though there was a tremolo to the child's pulse that worried Rhapsody. She bent closer to the child's ear, pressed her lips together, and began to hum.

She knew the exact pitch when she found it, because instantly her mind was filled with the musical images from that mystical, horrific time, the deep basso of miners singing as they carved their way through the depths of the world, the slow, melodic rumbling of the magma beneath the surface, peppered with the occasional staccato hiss or pop, the sweet, steady tune of the Axis Mundi that bisected the Earth, and the Root that had wound around it. It was an ancient symphony of earthsounds, wordless and almost just beyond hearing, but filled with power and awe.

She sang the earthsong as best as she could, keeping time with Grunthor's steady heartbeat, only changing the tone subtly, as slowly as it would within the Earth. In the near distance she heard Achmed exhale softly, and realized it was a signal; they must be seeing some effect, some transformation from the song.

Beneath her fingers the trembling vibration within the child's heart vanished, replaced by smooth, steady tides of respiration. Rhapsody recognized the state; the Earth Child was finally sleeping dreamlessly, deeply and soundly. She felt the same state of calm come over herself, as if she, too, was sleeping deeply and soundly. So deeply, so soundly, in fact, that the hideous gasps that issued forth from Grunthor and the Grandmother did not disturb her at all.

It was the thudding sound of their bodies hitting the sandy floor that did.

34

Achmed was already on the floor, checking the Grandmother, when Rhapsody opened her eyes.

The child was still sleeping, beads of crystalline sweat dotting her forehead like dew, as though she had just broken a fever. She was breathing easily, not moving.

Once she was certain that the child was safe for the moment, Rhapsody ran to where Grunthor was lying sprawled on the floor. She helped him to sit up, examining him worriedly as he clutched his head.

'Somethin's comin',' he muttered. His eyes were glassy, his breathing shallow.

'What, Grunthor? What's coming?'

The giant continued to mutter, becoming more disoriented by the moment. 'It's comin'; it had stopped but now it's on the way again. Somethin' – somethin's comin'.' Rhapsody could feel his gargantuan heart racing, pounding ferociously, and it frightened her.

'Grunthor, come back,' she whispered. She spoke his true name, a strange collection of whistling snarls and glottal stops, followed by the appellations she had given him so long ago when they passed through the Fire at the Earth's core: *Child of sand and open sky; son of the caves and lands of darkness*, she sang softly. *Bengard, Firbolg. The Sergeant-Major. My trainer, my protector. The Lord of Deadly Weapons. The Ultimate Authority, to Be Obeyed at All Costs.*

Grunthor's eyes cleared, and focused on her again. 'That's all right, darlin',' he said woozily, awkwardly pushing her hand away. 'I'll be fine in a minute. Help the Grandmother.'

'She's all right,' Achmed said from the other side of the catafalque. A moment later he rose, assisting the elderly woman to a stand. 'What happened?'

The Grandmother seemed steady, though her hand remained at her throat. 'Green death,' she murmured in all three of her voices. 'Unclean death.'

'What does that mean, Grandmother?' Rhapsody asked gently.

'I know not. It is repeated over and over in her dreams; I could hear the words suddenly. Now I cannot make the voice grow still.' The elderly woman's hand trembled; Achmed took it carefully between his own. 'It was as if your song broke them free from her mind, gave them to me.' The Grandmother's strange eyes glittered nervously in the dark. 'For that I thank you, Skychild. At least I now know some of what plagues her, though I understand it not. Green death; unclean death.'

'She's also dreamin' about somethin' comin',' Grunthor added. 'He took the handkerchief Rhapsody held out to him and mopped his sweating brow.'

'Any idea what?' Achmed asked. The giant shook his head.

'I'm so sorry,' Rhapsody said to them both. 'I fear I may be responsible for your visions. I was thinking about how you said you would take the worst of my nightmares on yourself, Grunthor. Perhaps I've inadvertently condemned you both to do that for her as well.'

'If you did, it was because we were both willing to accept them,' said the Grandmother. She leaned down and kissed the Sleeping Child, brushing the last of the moisture from her forehead. 'She sleeps peacefully again, at least for now.' With a final caress, the Grandmother rose to her full height again.

'Come.'

Rhapsody bent down and kissed the Sleeping Child's forehead as well. 'Your mother the Earth has so many beautiful clothes,' she whispered in the stone-gray ear. 'I'll try and write a song for you so that you can see them, too.'

The letters on the arch above the Chamber of the Sleeping Child gleamed as the torchlight passed over them. Time had begun to fill the carvings in soot and the crumbling detritus of the centuries.

'What does this inscription say?' Rhapsody asked.

The Grandmother slipped her hands inside the sleeves of her robe. 'Let that which sleeps within the Earth rest undisturbed; its awakening heralds eternal night,"' she answered.

Rhapsody turned to Achmed. 'What do you think that refers to?'

His mismatched eyes darkened angrily in the dim light of the passageway. 'I think you've seen it once yourself.'

She nodded. 'Yes. I think you're right, but only partly.'

'Explain.'

'It seems to me that there is an entity known as the Sleeping Child in more than one mythos,' she said. 'There was the star that slept beneath the waves off the coast of Serendair, a story from Seren lore. I think we know how correct the prediction was of the consequences of its awakening. There was the – ' She flinched under the intensity of the look Achmed shot at her – 'the one we saw on our journey here, the one the dragons refer to as the Sleeping Child. Those consequences would be even greater should it happen to waken.'

'And now there is this one, the one that rests here in the cavern. It seems to me that the prophecies of the Dhracians, if that is what this inscription is' – she pointed at the archway above the child's chamber – 'are warning of the same cataclysmic possibilities should this child wake.' Rhapsody stared back into the Sleeping Child's chamber, now wreathed in darkness.

'Freeing her from her nightmares might be the way to keep her asleep,' Achmed said.

The Grandmother turned and stepped into the shadow of the hallway leading to the vast cylindrical cavern. Her word echoed in the hollow corridor.

'Come.'

The enormous pendulum swung through the hollow cavern, crossing the circle on the central stone slab with each pass. Rhapsody could see the weight at the end of the spider-silk strand glitter in the darkness.

'What weights the pendulum?' she asked, her voice heavy in the sand of the dead wind.

'It is a diamond from Lorthlagh, the Lands Beyond the Rim, the birthplace of our race,' the Grandmother answered. Her heavy cloak flapped stolidly in the musty air of the cavern. 'It is a prison; within it is held captive a demon-spirit from the battle that wounded the Sleeping Child. Diamonds of great purity and substantial size, properly used, can house a captive spirit, though not as well as Living Stone can. And only a special kind of diamond, found only at places where pieces of stars have fallen to Earth, leaving ethereal crystals behind. These crystals come from a time before the Earth was formed, before fire came into being – they predate all elements save for ether. Their power is greater than that of the F'dor.'

As if in sullen response, the pendulum's weight flashed angrily. A slash of red light bounced around the cavern's walls, then vanished.

'The Purity Diamond Oelendra told you about must have been such a crystal,' Achmed said. 'Sounds like it was big enough to imprison even the strongest of demon-spirits.'

'Small wonder the F'dor wanted it smashed,' Grunthor said.

'Why would you suspend such a valuable and potentially dangerous object like that over an endless chasm?' Rhapsody asked, staring down into the circular abyss that surrounded the flat central formation. 'Isn't there a greater risk that the diamond will be lost if the strand breaks?'

The Grandmother's vibration grew more intense, causing their skin to itch.

'What you are witnessing is the power of the winds at work,' she said. 'This is why the training in Thrall ritual was done here; all four of the winds from Above are knotted here, around that rocky pedestal. They are anchored in this place; they hold the pendulum steady, in time with the turning of the Earth. The diamond is safer there than anywhere else in these mountains.' She turned to Achmed. 'When you are undergoing training, the winds will be your teachers.' She pointed to the crumbling bridge that spanned the dark chasm.

'Follow me to the canticle circle, and I will show you what has been written about you. It is your destiny. Deny it, and it would be better to hurl yourselves into the abyss now.' The matriarch ignored the glance that passed between the Three as she stepped out onto the bridge, braving the billowing wind.

'Why do they call this the canticle circle?'

Rhapsody stepped carefully around the pattern on the floor, making sure to stay out of the pedulum's path. She recognized the symbols for the four winds, but none of the other inscriptions, despite being told that they were in part an ancient clock.

The Grandmother gazed up into the silence of the endless cavern, as if staring into the Past. She let the Singer's question hang heavily on the dusty air as her black eyes scanned the ancient hallways, now nothing more than empty holes in the hollow shell of what had once been the great civilization's heart. At last she spoke.

'Lirin are the descendants of the Kith and the Seren, the children of the wind and stars. Dhracians are begotten only of the wind; the *Zhereditck* are direct descendants of the Kith, different only in that we were the clan chosen for our diligence and endurance to forsake the world Above and live within the Earth, guarding the vault of the F'dor for all time. It was only when that prison was broken open that we came Above again, joining in the Great Hunt to find and destroy those demons that escaped. But our roots were in the wind, not the Earth.'

The elderly woman finally broke her eyes away from the towering edifice above her and focused instead on the ancient stone bridge that connected the place where they stood to the rest of the Colony.

'Our race heard the vibrations in the music of the wind, just as yours does. We are even more sensitive to those messages than you are, Skychild. It was the greatest sacrifice we made, separating ourselves from the wind by going in. Some, born later, like me, have never even known it, have never felt it on our skin, free from the bonds of the Earth that surrounds us. That break cost us dearly; it denied us the Present, the ability to ascertain what was going on in the world, in the life all around and above us. We lived in darkness, and in the absence of knowledge, except for one.

'Just as one of our Colony was raised from birth to be the Matriarch, one was also raised to be the Zephyr, our Prophet. Candidates for the Zephyr were generally chosen for the sensitivity of their skin-webs and their abilities to taste the wind, to absorb its vibrations, to read its hidden wisdom. For while the wind is a fleeting repository of knowledge, it is a wide one, and much can be learned by listening to it. You have heard the wind speak, Skychild? You have heard it sing?'

'Yes,' Rhapsody said. 'And the Earth, and the sea. I have heard the song of fire as well, Grandmother, and, though earlier you said the stars do not reveal what they know, I can assure you that they sing as well; they impart their wisdom to those who observe their passage through the sky. That was the belief of my mother's people, the reason the Liringlas sing their devotions to the sunrise and star-rise.'

'And all those vibrations, no matter what lore they come from, are carried on the wind,' the Grandmother said. 'The Zephyr could hear them, even below the ground, here, within the canticle circle. High above, there is a hollow structure that resembles one of the mountain's peaks, through which the wind reaches down into the Earth, here. It dances about this flat central stone outcropping, forming a corridor of air that brings with it random vibrations from the above. The wind sings; its holy song was the canticle of the Brethren. The Zephyr heard the song, and brought the news it carried to the rest of the Colony. This was the way the *Zhereditck* were able to still keep in touch with the world Above, even though they were no longer part of it.

'From these vibrational signatures the Zephyr not only drew knowledge of what was happening Above, he or she also could sometimes tell what was to come. These prophecies were extremely rare; I only know of one, in fact. You stand within it now.'

The three looked at the words which encircled the design that had been inlaid in the stone floor. Achmed bent down and touched the letters, lost in thought.

'The wind that brought this prophecy was a hot one, a strong one, from the other side of the world,' the Grandmother continued. 'It carried death on it, and hope. That was many centuries ago, and but a short time before the Builders came.'

Achmed caught Rhapsody's eye, and saw the same thought mirrored there as had formed in his own mind. He winced at the memory of his Master's last minion, the one remaining Shing that had followed him from Serendair. The lone survivor of Tsoltan's Thousand Eyes, it had spoken very softly before it vanished.

Where are the other eyes? Rhapsody had demanded. *The rest of the Thousand? Gone*, the dying Shing had said, *long dissipated on the wind in the heat of the Sleeping Child. I alone remained, having crossed the wide ocean in search of him.*

In the heat of the Sleeping Child. The wind that told of the destruction of their Island home.

The wind that foretold their coming.

'What was the prophecy?' Grunthor asked.

'Can you read it?' the Grandmother asked Achmed. 'Any of it?' He shook his head. 'Then we will need to instruct you in the language as well as the Thrall ritual.' She bent and touched the letters as well.

Within a Circle of Four will stand a Circle of Three
Children of the Wind all, and yet none
The hunter, the sustainer, the healer,
Brought together by fear, held together by love,
To find that which hides from the Wind.

Hear, oh guardian, and look upon your destiny:
The one who hunts also will stand guard
The one who sustains also will abandon,
The one who heals also will kill
To find that which hides from the Wind.

Listen, oh Last One, to the wind:
The wind of the past to beckon her home
The wind of the earth to carry her to safety
The wind of the stars to sing the mother's-song most known to her soul
To hide the Child from the Wind.

From the lips of the Sleeping Child will come the words of ultimate
    wisdom,
Beware the Sleepwalker
For blood will be the means
To find that which hides from the Wind.

'Blood will be the means,' Rhapsody murmured. 'I don't like the way that sounds. Does it foretell the certainty of war, then?'

'Not necessarily,' Achmed said, 'though I would guess it will be unavoidable.'

'Wonderful.'

'What do you expect, Rhapsody? You know the history. The only thing F'dor crave is conflict, destruction, chaos. Where better to find that than in war?'

'If we had some of the F'dor's blood, could you track it, Achmed? As you did in the old world? The F'dor's blood is old; you should still be able to match your heartbeat to it.'

The Bolg-king's eyes grew steely. 'If I had some of its blood, I wouldn't need to track it,' he growled. 'Having its blood presumes we know who the host is, since we would have *gotten* it from the host.'

'Can we get it from the Rakshas?' Rhapsody asked. 'It was made from the demon's blood.'

'Commingled with several others, a wolf, and them kids, if I'm not mistaken,' Grunthor said, forestalling another impatient remark from Achmed. 'It would have to be pure, miss, to find the right one.'

Achmed looked above him again, at the empty, hollow cavern that had once been the heart of the Colony, the center of a great civilization.

'Mark my words, Rhapsody: by the time we discover who the demon's

host is, there will have been more blood than you could imagine
commingled, soaking into the earth. And if we don't discover it soon, it
will be enough to fill the sea.'

Prudence was dreaming fitfully in darkness. After traveling for many hours
over the rough terrain of the Krevensfield Plain, the roadway had finally
smoothed out again, and she had fallen into a light slumber, her neck
resting against the pillowed back of the carriage seat. The support it
offered her was probably the only thing that spared her from injury when
the carriage hit something large in the road and shuddered, rocking wildly
from side to side. Just as the carriage righted itself, it happened again,
thudding, careening, and then rolling to a slow stop.

She sat up in terror, her heart pounding audibly. The moon was new,
having vanished the night before, and no light filtered through the heavy
curtain at the coach's window. Prudence listened for the small slat to pull
back, but heard only silence.

After what seemed like an eternity had passed, the carriage door
opened.

'Are you all right in there, miss?'

'Yes,' she called back, her voice much louder than she had intended it to
be. 'What happened?'

'We hit something in the road. Let me help you out of there.'

Prudence rose unsteadily and took the guard's hand. She stepped out of
the carriage and into profound darkness, black as pitch and hanging heavy
in the humid air of summer. She squeezed the man's hand, trying to stop
her own from trembling.

'What is it?'

'I'll go look,' he said, and gently loosed her hand.

In response she gripped his tighter. 'No,' she choked. She could not
even see him, so dark was the night, and he was standing right beside her.
She was afraid if he let go she would be lost to the starless black void all
around her. 'No, please.'

'As you wish, miss, but I really should have a look.'

Prudence tried to breathe deeply and failed. 'All right,' she said at last,
'I'll go with you.'

The man gave her hand a comforting squeeze, then turned her toward
the back of the coach. Slowly they picked their way through the stones in
the road, Prudence keeping her free hand on the carriage for balance,
pausing for a moment at the wheel. Dark rain had pooled beneath the
wooden cogs where the wheels met the earth, muddying the ground at
Prudence's feet. She walked through the mire and around the back of the
carriage, her sleep-fuzzy mind trying to remember if the rain had begun
before or after she had dozed off. When her eyes focused, she choked.

Lying in the road behind the carriage was a tattered pile of clothes that
had once been the body of a man. Not far behind him in the road was a
similar broken bundle.

Stifling a scream, Prudence clutched the guard's hand in a viselike grip. She looked down at her shoes, thick with the mud of the road. The scream tore loose from her throat as she realized the muck she had stepped in was earth thickened with blood, running in a small river from the wheel to the body behind the coach. She lurched forward, then backed up into the guard, unable to tear her eyes away from the grisly sight.

'Sweet All-God,' she whispered. 'Who is that? Where did he come from?'

The man behind her released her hand and brought his own hands to rest on her upper arms, giving her another comforting squeeze.

'I believe that's your driver, and he came from the coachman's perch.'

The words echoed through Prudence's ears, making no sense. Distantly she was aware of a coldness in her limbs as the blood rushed away from her extremities, filling and coursing through her racing heart. She looked at the second body, farther up the road, the silvery symbol of Tristan's elite regiment barely visible within the crumpled fabric of its cape.

It was her guard.

Time slowed, and with it Prudence's breath. A resolute sense of calm fought with her abject fear and won; she stood stock-still in the hands of the man who she had mistaken for the soldier Tristan had sent to ensure her safety. After a moment he chuckled softly, then lowered warm lips to her ear.

'If it makes you feel any better, they were dead before they hit the ground, and certainly before the wheels went over them. They felt nothing.'

Panic coursed through Prudence again, and she bolted forward, only to be held firm as the man's grip tightened. Slowly he turned her around to face him. She found herself staring up into the darkness of a hooded cloak, gray or black, almost invisible against the backdrop of night.

The man said nothing. Within his hood Prudence thought she saw the twinkle of blue eyes gazing down at her with an almost sorrowful expression, but realized it was merely the reflection of her own terrified tears.

'Please,' she whispered, 'Please.'

The man released her right shoulder, then gently ran his fingers through her hair.

'Now, don't cry, Strawberry,' he said. His tone was almost wistful. 'It would be a shame to mar such a pretty face with tears.'

Prudence felt blackness close in at the edges of her consciousness. *Strawberry*. It rang hollowly in her memory, a name from the distant past.

'Please,' she whispered again. 'I'll give you whatever you want, please.'

'Yes, yes, you will,' he said soothingly. His hand ran down her hair one last time, and then moved to her cheek, caressing it with his fingers. 'More than you know, Strawberry. You will be the beginning of everything. You'll give me Tristan. And Tristan will give me everything I want, one way or another.'

Her stomach writhed in agony. 'Who are you?' she stammered. 'I – I am only his servant. I'm nothing to him. Let me go. Please. *Please.*'

The hand was back in her hair again, gently unwinding the curls. Prudence could tell by the strength of his grip that she was no match for him. For a moment, the hooded man said nothing. When finally he spoke, his words were tempered with sadness.

'There is so little time left; you really shouldn't sully it by denying something as real as his love for you, Prudence. It has been very clear, ever since childhood. Even if he is a selfish snob who would never compromise his chance at the throne to marry you.'

'*Who are you?*'

The gentle tone vanished, replaced by something darker. 'I'm crushed you don't remember me, Strawberry. I certainly remember you. And while I've changed a good deal, I daresay so have you.'

Crystalline realization cleared her vision as the memory of the childhood nickname finally returned, only to be obscured again. 'It can't be,' she choked. 'You're dead. You've – you've been dead. Years. Tristan mourned you for years. It can't be.'

The man laughed aloud, a barking laugh, then released her hair and pulled down the hood of his cloak; laughing again as she made a strangling sound.

'Well, you're not entirely wrong,' he said humorously. 'I'm not really alive, at any rate.'

The coppery hair gleamed in the dark. He looked the same as he had all those years ago, laughing and roughhousing with Tristan and his cousin, Stephen Navarne. Stephen's best friend. The Invoker's son – what was his name? *Strawberry*, he had called her then. Pulling her curls, admiring their mutual redheadedness. Oblivious to the class difference between them in a way that Tristan never was. *Pleasant fellow*, she had told Tristan, *but seems sad, melancholy when no one is watching*. Finally, after what seemed like a lifetime, his name came to her lips.

'Gwydion. Gwydion, please, come back with me to Bethany. Tristan will give you – '

'Don't,' he said pleasantly. 'Don't waste your breath, Prudence. I have other plans for you.'

His eyes gleamed in the dark, glittering with naked excitement in an otherwise passive face. Distantly Prudence was aware of the tears pouring down her cheeks, but she fought to keep her voice calm.

'All right,' she said, trying to keep her shaking voice from betraying her utter panic. 'All right, then. But not like this, Gwydion. Give me a moment to collect myself, and I promise you I will make it worth your while. I am quite experienced in pleasuring a man. But please, not here. I swear to you – '

'Don't be ridiculous,' he said, amusement in his voice. 'With all due deference to your charms, that was never my intention. I'm really not myself these days, Prudence. I only take a woman in that manner if she serves a different purpose than I intend for you. It's really not my call, anyway; I have no free will, I only follow orders.'

Prudence could no longer summon control over any of her limbs. Numbness was taking her over.

'What are you going to do with me?'

The cloaked man laughed again, then drew her into a warm embrace, and bent his lips to her ear again.

'Why, Prudence, I'm going to eat you, of course; what else is a strawberry for? Then I'll carry your carcass back to Ylorc and toss it in the Moot. And if you don't cause me any trouble, for the sake of our old friendship, I'll try to make sure that you're dead before I begin.'

35

Lord Stephen Navarne nodded to the captain of his guard, then stepped out of the carriage. The coachman shut the door behind him, bowing deferentially to Philabet Griswold, the Blesser of Avonderre-Navarne, as he did. The benison's face molded automatically into the beneficent smile he bestowed on the faithful, then withered back to the grim expression he had worn the moment before as the soldier turned away. The two leaders exchanged a glance, then made their way up the palace steps that led to Tristan Steward's offices.

His cousin's missive had been terse and direct, and Stephen reflected on the words as he climbed the stairs. *The Nonaggression pact with the Bolg has been broached in a grievous violation resulting in the gruesome and totally unwarranted execution of three Bethanian subjects, two of them soldiers in the royal guard*, it read. *I therefore declare the peace agreement to be void.* Simple words that foretold the death of the continent.

When he reached the great elevated courtyard at the top of the stairs Stephen turned for a moment. From this vantage point, the tallest in Bethany except for the towers and balconies of the palace, he could see much of the city proper. Within the white stone rings of the great circular basilica of Fire next to the palace he could make out a number of clergymen, huddling together in apparent fear of the clamorous muster that was taking place within Bethany's walls.

He had seen signs of it on his way in from Navarne with the benison, and had been greatly disturbed at Tristan's ability to raise such a large army in such a short time. The air in the lower courtyard crackled with the electricity of conflict amid shouted orders and the clashing of the smithy's anvils. Soldiers streamed through the streets. He could see no townspeople.

'Sweet All-God,' he murmured, watching the ferocity with which the Lord Roland was making ready for war.

'*Rinê mirtinex*,' intoned the benison in agreement, the holy response in Old Cymrian. 'Let's get in there before he's half-way across the continent.'

'Tarry a moment, Your Grace,' Lord Stephen said, shielding his eyes from the morning sun. In the streets that bordered the Fire basilica a morass of soldiers was surrounding what appeared to be the coach of a high-ranking clergyman. The guards accompanying the carriage were taking exception to the scrutiny, and ugly sounds were beginning to make their way into the air.

The armor of the retinue accompanying the coach was not that of guards from any Orlandan province, but the scarlet and brown uniform of Sorboldian soldiers. The sun glinted off the many small hinged plates of their mail, woven in intricate meshwork to keep out the heat of their arid, mountainous home. The Sorbolds were used to a harsher clime, and a harsher mentality; they were grievously outnumbered in their dispute, whatever it was, and did not seem bothered by that fact at all.

'It must be Mousa,' said Griswold disdainfully. Nielash Mousa was the Blesser of Sorbold, and his chief rival. It had long been assumed that one of the two men would be the Creator's choice to replace the Patriarch upon his demise. Stephen said nothing, but moved closer to the edge of the stairs. His own contingent of guards was logjammed in the crowded streets, near the brewing conflict.

His eyes moved quickly to the streets near the city gate where his coach had entered. Llauron and his contingent had been following them, and would be entangled in the imbroglio themselves in a moment. He felt his stomach twist into an even tighter knot than had been there since Tristan's urgent summons had arrived.

As if reading his mind, the benison touched his arm. 'The Invoker and his retinue were right behind us,' Griswold said. 'There will be a far worse incident if some harm befalls them even before they reach Tristan's hold. Between Mousa and Llauron, war is about to break out on every border Roland has.' Stephen nodded in dismay.

A flash of scarlet caught his eye, and Stephen looked down to the steps of the Fire basilica. Standing there on the tallest rise was a man in the gleaming red robes of the benisonship of Bethany, wearing a great horned helmet. The man stood silent, the amulet around his neck reflecting the sun which it had been designed to resemble. Ian Steward, the Blesser of the See of Canderre-Yarim, Tristan's younger brother.

As Lord Stephen and Griswold watched, the youngest of the Patriarch's benisons raised his hands to command the attention of the throng swirling below his feet, but the soldiers paid him no heed. In a abrupt violent scuffle the door of the Sorboldian carriage was torn open. The Sorbold guards began slashing with their weapons as the tide of Orlandan guards surged forward toward the carriage. Ian Steward's shouts for calm were swallowed in the chaos that erupted.

Suddenly, with an infernal roar, the fire from the wellspring in the center of the basilica thundered out of its brazier, sending flames of pure heat and light soaring into the sky above the temple. Ablaze with the intense colors that burned in the inferno at the center of the Earth, from which the firewell sprang, the flames reached to the clouds above, showering the area around the basilica with ash.

The commotion screeched into silence. The soldiers in the streets, both Orlandan and Sorbold, froze where they stood, staring at the conflagration in the sky. The flames billowed over the clouds and then receded in a heartbeat, leaving nothing in their wake but silence.

Stephen was aware of the trembling of Griswold's hand, still resting on his forearm. 'Sweet Creator, what was that?' the benison asked in a shaking voice. 'I had no idea Ian Steward could command the element of fire.' The symbol around his own neck, fashioned to evoke a drop of water, clinked against its chain.

Lord Stephen cast a glance at the benison on the temple steps below, who was standing as rigid as Griswold. For a moment he seemed as shocked by the sudden eruption as the soldiers had been. Then he gathered his robes and walked purposefully down the steps of the basilica into the sea of humanity.

The crowd parted immediately before him, forming a wide river in the human sea. The scarlet-robed cleric strode to the carriage in the center of the fray and gestured at a Sorbold soldier to open the door. The man leaned in at the window, then obeyed. The bension reached in and drew back, assisting another man clothed in clerical robes fashioned in rich shades of vermilion and green, brown and purple. Philabet Griswold's face twisted into a scowl.

'Mousa. I knew it.'

'Tristan undoubtedly summoned him as well,' Stephen said, watching a second man alight from the carriage. From this distance it was impossible to recognize his face, but he could tell by his manner of dress that it was not the Prince of Sorbold himself; he had apparently sent an emissary. 'I think it's wise that Sorbold is represented in these discussions. Perhaps their presence will have a tempering effect on Tristan.'

Griswold nodded curtly, then turned and made his way across the courtyard to the heavily guarded doors leading to the Lord Roland's offices. Stephen watched a moment longer to be certain the two Sorboldian dignitaries and Ian Steward made it safely to the lower courtyard, then turned and followed Griswold.

As soon as the palace gates closed behind the Blesser of Canderre-Yarim, the street erupted again into the frenetic preparations for war.

'M'lords, Your Graces: His Grace, Llauron, the Invoker of the Filids, has arrived.'

The chamberlain stepped away from the door and bowed politely. Lord Stephen, standing at the sideboard by the window, looked up and smiled wanly at his old friend. Llauron stood in the entryway, attired in his simple gray robe cinched with a rope belt, his blue-gray eyes twinkling in an otherwise solemn face. Despite his modest vestments, in marked contrast to the rich robes of state worn by the benisons of the Patriarch, he cut a royal figure among all the nobility and high clergy clustered in the room around him.

For a moment the conversation in the room died away. Then Tristan gestured impatiently at the Invoker, waving him into the room. Llauron smiled and nodded to the chamberlain to close the door behind him.

Stephen refilled the brandy snifter he had drained the moment before and poured a second glass, then crossed the thickly carpeted room and handed the second snifter to Llauron.

'Well met, Your Grace,' he said.

'Thank you, my son,' Llauron answered, still smiling. He took the glass Stephen proffered, saluted the duke of Navarne, and took a sip. He chuckled and leaned closer to Stephen. 'Canderian brandy. I see that Tristan does not limit himself to the fruits of his own province out of a selfless loyalty to his merchants and vintners. Bethany boasts its own credible brandy, though of course it cannot compete with that of Canderre.'

'Tristan has never done anything selfless in his life,' Stephen answered, casting a glance at the group of dukes and benisons engaged in heated discussion around the Regent. 'And he is about to prove my words ringingly true yet again.'

Tristan's hands were in the air, gesturing toward the immense table in the center of his library. 'If you will all be seated, we can begin,' he said. His voice was thick and strained, matching the exhaustion on his face and the obvious pain in his eyes. Stephen had yet to make it to his side for a private word, but could see that Tristan was more than deeply troubled by whatever had transpired that now brought them together. It was not a good sign.

As the assembled nobility and clergy took seats around the table Tristan dismissed the servants, then signaled for silence.

'The time for tolerance is long past,' he intoned gravely. 'As I believe each of you know from the missive I sent you, the Bolg have broken the peace accord and murdered three of my citizens, two of them soldiers. The pact is forfeit. It is time to end this insanity once and for all. The muster of my troops will be complete in three days' time, at which point I will be calling for the marshaling of all of Roland's forces. Our purpose today is to determine a time and meeting place for the assemblage of that joint army.'

The dukes and benisons immediately broke into a soft cacophony of mutterings and exclamations, but were brought to silence again by Tristan's upraised hand.

'I have asked Anborn to serve as Lord Marshal for the Orlandan forces in this campaign,' he said. He turned to Llauron. 'I hope this invitation to your brother is not displeasing to you, Your Grace.'

Llauron looked amused. 'Whether it is or not, my son, it appears to have been displeasing to Anborn.'

Tristan and the others cast a glance about the table. Anborn was not there.

'Where is he?' Tristan demanded.

'With Anborn, who's to say?' said Griswold. 'Are you certain he planned to attend, my son?'

'I'm certain he received my missive. If he was unable to attend I expect he would have had the courtesy to reply thus.'

Llauron chuckled. 'Actually, my son, not to reply was uncharacteristically courteous for Anborn. I shudder to think what he would have said if he had.'

'Probably something rudely similar to what I have to say,' said Quentin Baldassarre, the duke of Bethe Corbair. 'Tristan, are you out of your mind? Go to war with the Bolg?'

A wave of agreement broke over the gathering, as voices were raised in simultaneous assent. Martin Ivenstrand, the duke of the coastal province of Avonderre, could be heard above the others, the fury in his tone apparent.

'My citizens have been dying in these unexplained border incursions for the last two decades,' he said angrily, 'as have many innocent victims in the other provinces and Tyrian. We have heard nothing from you in all this time, even when you, yourself, Tristan, were suffering casualties. So why now do the deaths of three Bethanian citizens suddenly constitute a need for war?'

'I cannot believe you would even consider taking on the Bolg, especially over something like this,' agreed Ihrman Karsrick, the duke of Yarim. 'If Anwyn could not defeat Gwylliam, in the land she ruled for three centuries, what in the name of the gods makes you think *you* could wrest the mountain from the Bolg? You'd be slaughtered in a heartbeat, just like your forces were during Spring Cleaning. And ours as well, if we were foolish enough to stand with you. Where is this madness coming from?'

The look of utter shock on the Lord Roland's face caused the group to dissolve into silence. After a moment, Lanacan Orlando, the gentle Blesser of Bethe Corbair, cleared his throat nervously.

'My son, what makes you think the Bolg are responsible for your loss?'

'Indeed,' Baldassarre chimed in, 'to my knowledge they have stayed within their own lands, within the mountains. We have not even seen them in Bethe Corbair, which borders Ylorc. How did they make it all the way to Bethany?'

Tristan slammed his fist down on the heavy table, causing the crystal goblets to shudder and clink threateningly. 'The victims weren't in Bethany,' he snarled. 'They were within the borders of Ylorc. The third-week mail caravan found them, torn limb from limb and partially *eaten*, for gods' sake, strewn across what used to be Gwylliam's Great Moot.' His face went pale. Stephen Navarne began to rise, but Tristan glared at him and he sat back down.

'The Bolg attacked the mail caravan?' asked Cedric Canderre, the duke of the province that bore his family's name, and Tristan's future father-in-law. 'I can't imagine that. It was King Achmed's suggestion to implement the weekly caravans in the first place.'

'I did not say that the Bolg attacked the caravan. They – the victims were not with the caravan.'

'Why were your citizens, your soldiers, in the Bolglands without the mail caravan?' asked Ivenstrand. 'That seems foolhardy. It is difficult for me to work up tears at the loss of reckless idiots, Tristan. Whoever ordered them there should face military justice. Perhaps you should start by disciplining whichever of your commanders is responsible, and let the rest of us go home and tend to our own troubles.'

'Did any of you hear what I just said?' Tristan demanded, his voice raw and shaking. 'Partially eaten. Torn to shreds. All but unrecognizable. Doesn't the sheer savagery of this abomination merit better than this dismissive attitude?'

'I'm sorry to hear about it, certainly,' said Ivenstrand, 'but it hardly compares to the children who were kidnapped from my province and Stephen's, slaughtered like swine and drained of their blood, and in the House of Remembrance of all places, gods help us. There have been repulsive acts of violence throughout this land for quite some time, Tristan. As the central authority it has been *your* responsibility to determine the source of this violence, and thus far we have seen no solution to it, have been presented with no explanation for it. And now that it has touched you, for some reason, suddenly you expect us to commit our forces en masse to a suicide mission. It's insane.'

The bells of the tower began to chime the noon hour, and the room became still. When the twelfth knell rang and died away, Nielash Mousa spoke.

'I have something to add,' he said in his soft, dry voice.

Tristan Steward broke his stare away from his fellow regents and fixed it onto the benison from the neighboring nation of Sorbold.

'Yes, Your Grace?'

The benison nodded at the emissary who had accompanied him to Roland. The man produced a folded piece of parchment and handed it to him. The benison opened the folds and read over the paper quickly, then looked up to the assemblage again.

'His Highness, the Crown Prince of Sorbold, has received word from King Achmed of Ylorc by way of avian messenger. The king denies any incursion or assault by the Bolg against any Orlandan citizen.' As the men began to murmur among themselves, Mousa produced another, smaller piece of parchment, sealed with the crest wax of Ylorc, then folded his hands, waiting for the silence he was granted a moment later. 'In addition, the Prince asks that I deliver to you, Lord Regent, a message that was included in King Achmed's missive and addressed to you.' Mousa extended his hand with the note.

Tristan Steward leapt to his feet and snatched the parchment, broke the seal, and scanned the message. The other regents and holy men watched as the blood drained from his face, and he sat slowly back down. He stared at the message for some time, wrapped in the silence afforded him by the other men. Finally he looked up once more.

'Will no one stand with me in this matter?' he asked, his voice cracking.

'Not I,' said Martin Ivenstrand firmly.

'Nor I,' added Cedric Canderre. 'I'm sorry, Tristan.'

'Cowards,' Tristan sneered. 'It is simple enough for you to stay out of it, isn't it? Your lands are far from the Teeth, and your subjects need not fear the cannibals, at least not yet, anyway. But what say you, Quentin? Ihrman? Your provinces border Ylorc. Will you not fight to spare Bethe Corbair and Yarim?'

'Not for this,' said Quentin Baldassarre stiffly. 'For all I know, your soldiers were attacked by wolves. You have given us no evidence to the contrary.'

'In my judgment, it would be a disaster that we would be bringing upon ourselves, especially in light of Achmed's denial,' said Ihrman Karsrick. 'If what the Firbolg king says is true, and you attack the mountain, *you* would be the aggressor who broke the accord. And then ten percent of Roland is forfeit, assuming the Bolg would even let you sue for peace again. I want nothing to do with this. It's madness.'

Desperation and dark rage contorted the Lord Roland's face, and he turned to his cousin, Stephen Navarne.

'Stephen, stand with me. Help me make them understand.'

Stephen sighed and looked away, catching the sympathetic eye of the Invoker. When he turned back to Tristan the expression in his green-blue eyes was direct.

'How can I make them understand when I can't even comprehend your perspective myself? You have my loyalty and my life, Tristan, but not the lives of our innocent subjects. I cannot stand with you in this.'

A thick silence descended again. Slowly the Lord Regent rose from the table and walked brokenly to the tall library windows that looked out over his fair city. He leaned on the glass, lost in thought.

After a few moments, the dukes and benisons began to talk softly again among themselves. Philabet Griswold turned to Ian Steward.

'That was a very impressive display this morning, Your Grace. Would that I could command the sea as readily as you brought forth fire from the earth.' Ian Steward said nothing; he was watching his brother intently, a worried expression on his young face.

Stephen Navarne looked over at Llauron, whose face was impassive. Though the basilicas of the Patrician religion were dedicated to the five elements, in truth that lore was more or less lost in the faith as it was now practiced. Instead, the worship and manipulation of the lore of the elements was more akin to the practice of the Filids, who worshipped nature. It was his belief that the sudden roar of the fire was more likely the work of the Invoker than the Blesser of Canderre-Yarim, but Llauron betrayed no sign that he was even listening.

As the others dissolved into various discussions of different matters, Stephen rose and walked to the window where Tristan still stood, staring blankly over the city. He waited patiently for the Lord Roland to speak. Finally Tristan sighed.

'I wish I had been more available to you some years back, Stephen, when Lydia died,' he said. 'I'm sorry.' His eyes remained locked on whatever old pathways of remembrance he was walking down.

'Who was it, Tristan? It wasn't – it wasn't Prudence, was it?'

Tristan only nodded and left the room, his absence scarcely noted by the chattering holy men and the other regents.

Trying to absorb the shock of Tristan's answer, Stephen's eye caught the crumpled parchment note the Lord Roland had left behind when he departed from the library. Stephen picked it up slowly and read the few words written on it in a spidery script.

I thought you had learned your lesson early. I see I was wrong. I told you the cost would be greater later on. And you paid the price both times for nothing – she still doesn't know.

'I know your pain is very great, my son.'

Tristan looked up. He had not heard the door open. As he turned he caught a glimpse of his own face in the looking glass, a face that had never before borne the ravages of time quite so clearly. He was haggard, from the deepening lines around his mouth to the crevice that had been carved somehow into his forehead between his eyebrows. There was no hiding the redness in his eyes, born of grief and the lack of sleep that grief had caused.

The eyes that looked sympathetically into his own glimmered red for a moment as well, as if in empathy.

'Yes, Your Grace,' the Lord Roland murmured.

A hand came to rest gently on his head.

'The others, they do not understand,' the sonorous voice intoned without a hint of condescension. 'They only see what is immediately before them. It is very difficult to be the one who alone comprehends the severity of the situation to come, who sees the danger when it is still down the road yet. The eyes of a visionary weep often over time, it is said.' The hand moved to Tristan's shoulder, giving it a comforting squeeze.

The Lord Roland exhaled brokenly and lowered his head to his fists, clutched on the table before him. The hand on his shoulder passed over his back, and then was removed, disappearing within the sleeve of the robe above it.

'This land is divided against itself, my son. After the Great War, your Cymrian forebears chose to allow Roland to remain divided thus, under these disparate houses, because they feared the chaos and death that Anwyn and Gwylliam's union had wrought in its undoing. It was folly to believe that it could remain this way without even greater chaos following. Look at me.'

The last words had a ring of irritation to them, an undertone of threat, and Tristan raised his head to see kindly blue eyes staring intently back at him. For a moment he thought perhaps there was something else within them, something dark, something *red*, but then the holy man smiled, and Tristan felt warmth course through him for the first time that day, a day which had begun with such promise and had ended in such a debacle. It was a feeling of acceptance, of approval; of *respect*.

'You are the eldest, Tristan, the heir apparent of the Cymrian line.'

Tristan blinked painfully. 'Your Grace – '

'Hear me out, m'lord.' The holy man bowed slightly as he uttered the last word, and deep within his soul Tristan felt the sickening gnaw of the morning's humiliation miraculously abate. Something in the tone of the word had reached into that hidden vault of royalty within him, a place long denied in the attempt to maintain a friendly consensus with his cousin and the other Orlandan heads of state. It was the first pleasant sensation he had felt since Prudence had left his arms and ridden away to her grisly death. Involuntarily he smiled slightly, and was smiled at warmly in return. Tristan nodded for him to continue.

'The lines of succession may seem unclear to to you, because no one in those days after the War was willing to assume the throne. Indeed, if they had tried, the non-Cymrian population would have unseated them anyway, such was the hatred for all the descendants of the Seren, not just the line of Gwylliam.

'As you can see, now that war looms again, this fragmented system has yielded no real leadership. An obvious act of aggression has taken place, but the others are unwilling to band together to support you, even the dukes of Beth Corbair and Yarim, whose own lands border the Firbolg realm.

'What will happen, then, when the violence escalates? When the Firbolg swarm down from the Teeth and begin swallowing the lands of Roland? Will you and your fellow regents just sit back and watch while your subjects are devoured, literally, by those subhuman monsters?'

'Of – of course not,' the Lord Roland stammered.

'Really?' The warm voice grew instantly icy. 'How do you propose to prevent it? You couldn't convince them to join together before the slaughter begins. Once the mayhem starts, how do you expect to field an army that will be able to fend off the wave of death that will come with those cannibalistic demons? By the time the Firbolg reach the boundaries of your central lands, Tristan, it will be far too late to stop them. They will possess all of Bethe Corbair and Yarim, Sorbold too, perhaps. They will eat you alive, or drive you into the sea.'

An inkwell and several bound books fell violently to the floor, swept off the table by the force of the Lord Roland's reaction. *'No.'*

The warmth returned to the holy man's eyes as black ink pooled like dark blood from the shards of the inkwell, staining the floor.

'Ah, a hint of viscera. You see, I was right. You may be the one after all.'

Despite the warmth in the eyes locked on to his, and the heat lingering in the room from the angry dissension that had taken place there, Tristan felt suddenly cold.

'The one for what?'

The screech of the legs of the chair as it was pulled back ripped through Tristan's ears as the man sat down across from him.

'The one to return peace and security to Roland. The one to have the courage to put an end to the chaos that is the royal structure of this land and assume the throne. If you had dominion over all of Roland, not just Bethany, you would control all of the armies you sought in vain to bring together today. Your fellows, the dukes, can say no to the Lord Regent. They could not refuse the king. Your lineage is as worthy as any of the others, Tristan, more so than most.'

'I am not the one in need of convincing, Your Grace,' said Tristan bitterly. 'In case this morning's fiasco didn't prove it, let me assure you that my fellow regents do not see the clarity of the succession scenario that you do.'

The holy man smiled, then rose from the table slowly. 'Leave that to me, m'lord,' he said, the words soft, their sound pleasant against Tristan's ears. 'Your time will come. Just be certain that you are ready when it does.' He walked slowly to the door and opened it, then looked back over his shoulder on last time.

'And m'lord?'

'Yes?'

'You will think about what I said, hmmm?'

The Lord Roland had nodded agreement. True to his word, when the dukes and religious leaders had finally left Bethany, he pondered the suggestion, endlessly, in fact. He thought of little else with each waking breath, almost as if he had no other choice, turning the sage words over and over in his mind, like an insistent melody. All other thought, other reason, was drowned in the noise of it.

The suggestion had wound around his soul like a cinnebara vine, a ropelike plant he had once studied that made an excellent trap, hanging loose and harmless until the victim sought to pull away. Then it clung with a strangling insistence until the animal caught within it stopped struggling. The sensation of pondering the suggestion was eerily similar.

It was only at night that he found respite from the words, in an older, deeper obsession – his insatiable hunger for the woman he had sacrificed everything for, including the only love his life had ever known. Even now, after all that had happened, he still dreamt of Rhapsody.

In his sleep she called to him, wrapped in a fiery warmth. He dreamt of making love to her, fiercely, passionately, looking into her face as the thunder rolled up inside of him to see an older, more familiar face beneath his, lined with age, the golden tresses replaced by strawberry curls.

Curls matted with black blood.

From these dreams he would wake in a cold sweat, shaking violently, willing her to leave his thoughts, wishing he could somehow exorcise this beautiful demon who still haunted his dreams.

The Lord Roland did not know that his obsession with her, deep and intrinsic as it had become to his soul, was the one thing saving him from being given over completely to the command of another, much darker demon.

36

The cold stone steps leading up to Elysian's gazebo gleamed in the diffuse sunlight. It had taken a vast amount of effort to clean the centuries of grime and lichen off the marble columns, as well as the charred black soot, but it had been worth it, Rhapsody decided. The small pavilion glistened like a holy shrine in the quiet green of the underground cavern.

She had spent the morning puttering in her gardens, stalling. Jo and Grunthor had come to visit, Jo because Rhapsody missed her and had been longing to see her, Grunthor because Jo was utterly incapable of finding the underground realm of Elysian. She was even unable to locate Kraldurge, the area above the grotto that the Firbolg thought was haunted, or the guardian rocks that hid it, no matter how many times she visited. It had become a joke among the four of them.

They ate their noonday meal in the garden, the rich blossoms of Rhapsody's many plantings filling the air with a heavy, sweet scent, the blooming colors a symphony to the eye. Jo said very little, but spent most of her time staring at the shady gardens and the cavern above her, amazed more by the alien nature of the place than the sheer beauty of it. The stalactite formations, the glistening waterfall, and the iridescent colors of the cave held both her eye and imagination. Grunthor caught Rhapsody up on all the gossip and they exchanged bawdy jokes, Jo laughing along.

It was a good and pleasant meal, and Rhapsody was sorry to see it end. But finally Grunthor stood up, wiped his tusked mouth politely on his napkin, and patted Jo on the head.

'Come on, little miss, time we was gettin' back. The meal was scrumptious, Duchess.' Rhapsody gave him a hug, and then Jo. They walked down to the banks of the lake, still chattering away.

While Grunthor made ready the boat, Rhapsody pulled Jo aside. 'Well? Have you thought about coming here to live with me?'

'A little,' said Jo uncomfortably. 'Don't get me wrong, Rhaps, I miss you like crazy, but I'm not sure I could live down here.'

Rhapsody nodded. 'I understand.'

'I can't even find the place, you know. That could be a problem.'

'I know. It's all right, Jo. I'll try to come and see you more often in the Cauldron, unless Achmed gave my room away.'

'Not yet, but he keeps threatening to sell your clothes.' Jo smirked as Rhapsody laughed. 'Give me a little while to get used to the idea,' Jo said. 'Can I have the room with the turret?'

'Anything you want,' Rhapsody answered, hugging her again. She could see Grunthor was ready. 'Take however long you need; we have all the time in the world.'

Jo smiled and gave her a kiss. Then she ran to where Grunthor was waiting, and got in, waving as they rowed across the lake. Finally, when the boat was out of sight, Rhapsody stopped waving and sighed. She had just run out of excuses.

The evening had come, and she could hear the birds singing in her tiny trees, planted recently. They had found their way underground, and occasionally she would see one in the garden or hopping on the grass. The sunlight was leaving the sky in the world above, so the darkness had already come below the ground in Elysian. Only the warmth of the evening air told her the night was still at least a few moments away.

Rhapsody took a deep breath and steeled her resolve. What she was about to do put many of the things she loved at risk – Elysian and its status as a safe haven among them. Far more important, her friends and their safety might be compromised if she was wrong, though what she had told Achmed about his strength and position she still believed to be true.

She walked through the gardens and around the benches, up the walkway to the gazebo. Rhapsody climbed the steps slowly, turning in a circle once she was inside to survey the glory of the cavern around her. She closed her eyes and listened to the music of the waterfall high above splashing into the lake below. Then she stood still, breathing shallowly, and concentrated on the face she had seen in the forest glen, the face that had smiled uncertainly. The face with the dragon eyes.

In a high, clear voice she sang his name, the tone sweet and warm. It was a long name, and it took a moment to get it all out, but once she had finished, it rang like a bell in the grotto. The natural podium that was the gazebo amplified her song and held it hovering above the lake, spinning in circles faster and faster. She sang it again, and again, then attached to it a clear directional thread, a note for him to follow. The lingering note would lead him to this hidden place, this place where, if he came, he would find healing.

When she was finished the song continued to hover for a moment, then rose and expanded through the cavern, permeating the walls and echoing for miles around. Then it dissipated, but she could hear it in the distance, ringing through the night on its way to the one she hoped would hear it.

★

Ashe woke from his dream of Rhapsody to the sound of her voice calling his name. He shook his head and settled back under the tree beneath which he had been sleeping.

He dreamt of her almost every night. In this dream she was dancing with the wind through the highgrass of the heath, her arms spread wide, like she was flying. Then the wind took her; it blew her over the edge of the chasm and into the canyon below. He cried out her name, but his scream was swallowed up by the gale. He ran to the edge of the heath and looked down, but he could not see her.

Then he heard her voice calling him, and he turned to see her standing once more on the heath, attired in a dark dress and her signature black ribbon, the ever-present locket around her slender neck, holding out her hand to him. He reached for her in the darkness, and awoke to find himself alone, as he always did.

At first he had cursed the dreams. Waking itself was a painful enough process, the agony that was centered in his chest, radiating outward, returned full force once sleep was gone. But to have to endure the loss of her at the end of each night was depressing beyond belief.

Eventually, though, he took to looking forward to his nightly visits with her in his mind. In the realm of the Lady Rowan, Yl Breudiwyr, the keeper of dreams, the guardian of sleep, Rhapsody was his own on most nights. She knew of his feelings and returned them with joy, she slept in his arms, she made love to him without fear. Occasionally a nightmare would creep in and she would be cold, distant, or he would be unable to reach her. Once he dreamt that he had sought her endlessly to discover her in the bedchamber of the Firbolg king and had been unable to convince her to leave. From that dream he woke in a cold sweat and with a headache that lingered for hours.

Worst of all were the nights when no visions of her came to him in his sleep. Once he had not dreamt of her for three nights in a row, and he grew so despondent that when his mission was over he made a foray back to his small room behind the waterfall.

When he opened the door he could still smell the fresh, sweet scent of her; it lingered on the bedsheets and in the clothes she had washed and folded for him. Ashe stretched out on the bed, remembering their last night together, Rhapsody curled around the pillow like a dragonling. He grew wistful as he thought of how he had comforted her in her endless quest for a peaceful night's sleep. That night he had dreamt of her again, singing to Lirin children, large with child herself.

He heard her voice a second time, calling him not by the name she knew, but by his real given name in all its complications.

Gwydion ap Llauron ap Gwylliam tuatha d'Anwynan o Manosse, come to me. His name had been the bane of his existence his entire life, as a child because of its ridiculous length and the associations with it, now because it might lead the demon to him. He had never considered it beautiful until he heard it on the wind, spoken by the voice that sang in his dreams.

Ashe was still unsure as to whether or not he was dreaming, but the voice kept calling, softly but insistently, moving farther away, leading him to somewhere he did not know. *It could be a trick of the demon,* he thought. Similar entrapments had been tried before. But unlike those snares, the voice did not coax or wheedle him, it merely called to him surely, with a gentle firmness.

Gwydion, come to me.

Where would she have gotten his name? In the eyes and mind of the world, in history itself he was dead, gone a score of years. Only his father knew he was alive; great care was taken when he visited to always enter through the secret door in the back of Llauron's compound. His family and friends believed him dead as well. For all intents and purposes his life had effectively come to an end that night twenty years before. There was no one else who knew, no one except possibly the F'dor. The more he thought about it, the more certain he became that what was calling him was demonic.

Gwydion.

Ashe stood up and shook off his slumber. The agony surged back, as it always did, but somehow his head was clearer than it usually was. He thought of his father, and the reconnaissance Llauron expected shortly; he thought of the latest border incursion, and how he would again find no explanation anyway. He closed his mind and sensed the voice; it sounded for all the world like Rhapsody. He knew her voice; he had memorized it with each word, each tune, each aubade, each vesper. He had to follow it, whatever the risk.

Rhapsody was sewing by the fire in the darkness that came with early afternoon when she felt a strange stirring within her. Ashe had come to Elysian, though she was uncertain how she knew. She was sitting in her bedroom and so leapt up and ran to the room with the turreted window, sitting on the window seat as her eyes scanned the dark water for the boat that was bringing him to her. It had been five days since her song went out; she was surprised he had come so quickly. He must have been very nearby when the song reached him.

Then her stomach knotted with the realization that she had no idea that this was, in fact, Ashe. She had hoped to ensure it by the way she had called, but, having seen the demonic powers of the Rakshas put to use, she was unwilling to assume anything. She went downstairs to wait.

On her way past the looking glass she checked herself to be sure she did not appear vulnerable, and winced at what she saw. She was dressed in a pleated white linen blouse, the pintucks lined in azure blue, the same color as the wool skirt she wore. Her hair ribbon matched her skirt; all in she looked like a schoolgirl. It couldn't be helped, she decided. There was no time to change.

Rhapsody paced back and forth in front of the parlor fire, trying to calm her nerves. She went over all the things in her mind that she, Achmed and Grunthor had fought about.

They are all liars, too. At least in the old world you knew who sided with evil gods because they professed what they stood for. Here, in this new and twisted place, even the allegedly good ones are calculating users. The ancient evils could never wreak the level of havoc that the 'good' Lord and Lady Cymrian did. And you want to hand yourself over on a silver platter to the potentially biggest liar of all.

Well, if I do, it is my choice to do so. I will take the risk, and live or die by my own volition.

Wrong. We may all suffer that fate, because you aren't just compromising yourself, you are throwing all of our neutrality into the pot, and if you overbet your hand, we all lose.

She fought the panic that was rising within her. *Please let me be doing the right thing,* she whispered. *Please don't let me be wrong.* She owed Ashe nothing, no allegiance, no friendship, not like she owed Jo and the two Bolg.

I say we kill him. And if we're wrong, and another one shows up, we kill him too.

You can't go around killing people if you're not sure whether you're right.

And why not? Always worked for us before. Seriously, miss, this is too big to take chances with, if you're not sure.

There was a knock on the front door of the house at Elysian.

37

From the moment he had entered the Bolglands, Ashe had felt a sense of awe. His amazement grew as he followed the voice, through the dark mountains and over the heath, into the depths of the Hidden Realm. He had stopped only long enough to hide from the sentries, then followed his beacon once more.

When he came into the meadow at Kraldurge the voice became clearer and stronger. He looked around at the rockwalls towering above him, knowing he never would have found this place, even with his dragon sense. And because of that, a feeling of safety was beginning to come to rest on him.

You would be safe in my house, too.

In the Cauldron? No, thank you.

My house is not in the Cauldron. And it is even harder to find than this place, I'll wager.

As he descended into the cavern, his wonder began to grow beyond all bounds. The place was magical, with its crystalline lake, the splashing waterfall, and the gleaming stalactites and stalagmites that sprang from the earth within the grotto.

But what dazzled him the most was the song of the cave. It was joyful, unlike the feeling of the Bolglands; it rang through the air, touching the edges of his senses with a harmonious, peaceful tone. That could only be Rhapsody, he thought. If this was a place that had been here before the Bolg, had been inhabited at one time by Gwylliam and Anwyn, it would have been polluted by hate, the tangible, twisted anger that had laid waste to the old Cymrian lands, leaving them barren and lifeless. That it felt warm and easy was a sure sign she was here.

When the little house came into view, he knew she was. He could feel her within the structure, moving from room to room, carrying her heat with her. The lights of the cottage twinkled merrily in the dark of early afternoon, smoke curling up the stone chimney. With his dragon sense he noted and recorded every detail of the place, from the shimmering gazebo with the golden birdcage, where the song of his name still echoed, to the sweeping gardens bursting with the heady bloom of early summer. The beauty of it was almost enough to ease the pain he carried by itself.

He steeled his nerve. He had resolved to tell her of his feelings, to end the game of Cymrian silence. This, if anywhere, was the place to do it, and now was the right time if there was one.

Rhapsody opened the door. He was standing there, his cloak draped over his arm, smiling uncertainly at her as he had that first time in the forest when he revealed his face. Her eyes went immediately to his pupils; they were slit vertically, as before. Then she gasped. The scruffy beard was gone, the face clean-shaven, as it had been in Sepulvarta. His smile faded immediately.

'Is something wrong?'

Rhapsody stared for a moment longer, then shook her head. 'No, sorry. No, nothing's wrong. Please come in. I didn't mean to be rude.'

Ashe came into the parlor and looked around. His eyes drank in the cozy sight, and he felt a longing that he could not have named as he looked about the room.

It had been lovingly furnished with a colorful rug of woven wool and a pair of matching chairs before the fireplace on one side of the room, a small sofa across from them. Vases of flowers were everywhere, and throughout the room simple but beautiful objects decorated the walls and tabletops. Musical instruments were closeted in a cabinet made of cherry wood and lined in cork. The scent of spicy herbs and fresh soap was in the air, along with a trace of vanilla. Ashe sighed as he breathed it in.

'Nice place.'

'Thank you.' Rhapsody reached automatically for his cloak; she realized her error just as he put it into her hands, dropping it inadvertently. She could not believe he had given it to her. It felt cool in her hands, radiating a fine mist, but otherwise it was not apparently different than any other garment. After she hung it on one of the pegs near the stairs, she turned and faced him.

'What happened to your beard?'

Ashe looked at the fire and smiled. 'Someone whose opinion I respect seems to feel I look better without it.'

'Oh.' She fell awkwardly silent, not knowing what to say next.

Ashe turned and looked at her. 'Well? You called?'

'Oh,' she said again. 'Yes. I hope I didn't drag you away from anything important.'

'What did you want?'

She leaned on the banister. 'Two things, really. The first is upstairs in my bedroom. Do you mind coming up?'

Ashe swallowed hard, trying to beat back the arousal that had flared within him the moment she had opened the door. 'No,' he said, his voice somewhat terse with the effort.

Rhapsody smiled at him, and he felt the surge that he always did upon receiving her beaming glance. He followed her up the stairs after hanging his swordbelt next to hers on a rack near the door.

Her bedroom was beautiful too, tastefully decorated and filled with things she loved. The open door of the cedar closet revealed a carefully organized wardrobe of tastefully colored dresses, none of which he had ever seen her in. A large dressing screen stood in one corner of the room, painted in the same sunset colors as the pitcher and basin on the washstand, brass andirons gleaming in front of the fireplace. Rhapsody went to the heavily carved mantel and picked up two small paintings that were displayed on it. She handed them to Ashe, who had joined her in front of the fire.

One painting was an oil of two human children, a boy entering adolescence, and a girl several years younger. They were both handsome, of obvious noble blood, the girl blond and fair, the boy darker. By contrast, the other picture was crowded with grinning faces, sketched in charcoal. The faces were coarse and hairy; in a moment Ashe recognized these children as Firbolg. He looked up at Rhapsody quizzically.

'These are my grandchildren,' she said, her emerald eyes searching his face.

Ashe still did not comprehend. 'Oh. Yes. You did mention them. I remember now.'

'I thought you might like to see these especially,' she said, pointing to the oil painting. Her voice was gentle. 'These are Lord Stephen's children.'

As she expected, tears welled in Ashe's eyes, and he sat down numbly on the sofa before the fire. She assumed he had never seen them, and may not have known of them at all; apparently Llauron had not bothered to keep his son abreast of the significant events in the life of his best friend. Rhapsody's heart ached for him. She leaned over the back of the sofa, one hand coming to rest on his shoulder as she pointed with the other.

'The little one, Melisande, was born on the first day of spring; she's a genuine sunbeam. Her brother is more solemn, more introspective, but when he smiles he can light a room. His birthday is the last day of autumn.' She paused, trying to avoid overwhelming him. 'His name is Gwydion.'

Ashe looked up at her, his eyes suddenly full of an emotion Rhapsody did not recognize. He stared at her for a long moment, then looked back at the picture.

'Would you like to get a sense of what they're like?' she asked. Ashe nodded distantly. She rested her other hand on his shoulder as well and began to sing the song she had written for them when she first met them, a song that described them perfectly. Melisande's tune was a sprightly melody, airy and unpredictable, Gwydion's a haunting song of deep and mellow tones, repeated in a more complicated pattern with each refrain. When she was finished she looked over the back of the sofa to find Ashe in tears. In great distress she ran around the loveseat and knelt down in front of him.

'Ashe, I'm so very sorry. I never meant to upset you.'

Ashe looked up at her hand and smiled awkwardly. 'Don't apologize; you didn't. Thank you.'

'I suppose that leads into what I want to say to you,' Rhapsody went on as he wiped his eyes with the back of his hand. 'Obviously, I know who you are.' Ashe nodded warily. 'I mean, I know exactly who you are.'

'And who is that?'

'Please don't play games with me, Ashe,' she said, mildly annoyed. 'Obviously I understand the connection between you and Lord Stephen. I knew your name enough to call you. I assume you know that means I knew it in all its implications.'

Ashe sighed. 'I guess it does at that.'

'Does it bother you?'

He shook his head. 'Not really. In a way, it's a relief.'

'Well, before the night is gone I hope to provide more of that relief.'

'How so?'

'You'll see in a moment. First, I have something important to tell you.'

Ashe nodded, and met her gaze with his own. 'I'm listening.'

Rhapsody nodded as well. 'Right. I've decided something, and, since it affects you, I thought you deserved to know about it.'

'Yes?'

She took a deep breath. 'I've had enough of the Cymrian mystery. I have decided to trust you, and frankly, I don't really care if I'm right or not. I hate being uncertain of my feelings, and refuse to be from here out. So, I have decided to be your friend, whether you ever are mine or not. As such, I will care about you, and will protect you with my life. I will fight the minions of the Underworld to keep you safe, just as I would for Achmed, or Grunthor, or Jo. And if you are leading me on, if you have nefarious plans for me, please don't tell me. I would prefer it if you would kill me now, rather than betray me later, but either way, I'm taking a stand. You don't need to reciprocate, you just need to cooperate. Please extend your ring finger.'

'Excuse me?'

She coughed in embarrassment. 'I guess that was a little brash. I would appreciate it if you would put on this ring.' She held up the signet the Patriarch had given her, the ring that contained his holy office and all the wisdom and powers of healing associated with it.

Ashe's eyes opened wide in astonishment. 'Where on Earth did you get that?'

'Sepulvarta. I stood with the Patriarch and fought the Rakshas when he attacked – yes, I'm afraid that was me.' The news of the battle had spread like wildfire throughout Roland; she was sure it had caught up with him at some point. 'No one knows it, but His Grace gave me his office that night. He asked me to keep it safe, to guard it with my life. Since I have issued the same pledge to you, and since I know it will heal you, I give it to you now. Put it on.' Ashe just stared at her.

'Oh, by the way,' Rhapsody continued, 'I know all about the Rakshas, too. I will kill it for you, and get whatever piece of your soul it has back. Then you can go about the business of becoming Lord Cymrian. I will help you in any way I can to unite the realm.'

Ashe stood up suddenly and walked to the fireplace. He rested his hands on the mantel and took several deep breaths. Rhapsody watched in silence as he assimilated everything she had told him. Finally he turned to her.

'I don't know what to say.'

'Why do you have to say anything? All I asked you to do was put on the ring.'

'I don't think you understand what you are giving me.'

Her brows drew together in annoyance. 'You must really believe I'm stupid, Ashe.'

'I – I don't think that at all. On the contrary, I – '

'I didn't find the ring in the attic in a box of old undergarments, or on a table in the market, I got it from the Patriarch himself on the night of his High Holy Day ritual, a ritual I witnessed. What makes you think he would have given such a critical thing to me, the most precious thing he had, if I didn't understand its significance?'

'Then perhaps you don't understand about my father, that he – '

' – is the head of the opposing theology, and that one day you will likely be as well? Yes, I understand that, too. Are you aware that there was only one religion when the Cymrian arrived from Serendair, a combination of the practices of Gwynwood and Sepulvarta, and that it was the Cymrian split after the war that forced the schism? If you are planning to heal the rift in the governance of the Cymrian people, why not heal the religious rift as well? I've witnessed holy rites in both churches, and they are much closer to each other than you may believe. Who needs a Patriarch *and* an Invoker? Why can't you be both? Or why can't the Lord Cymrian be the unifying head of both sects, and leave the ecclesiastical rule to the leaders

302

of each faction? Recognize the right for people to have different belief systems, but still be united as one monotheistic people.'

She stopped; Ashe was staring at her in disbelief.

'What?' she asked.

'You're amazing.'

'Why?'

Ashe shook his head, smiling. 'And scary. Amazing and scary.'

'Now I don't understand.'

He held onto the mantel and put his head down again, the light from the fire gleaming off his metallic hair. He remained that way for a few moments, gathering his thoughts, breathing deeply; Rhapsody wondered if he was ill. Finally he stood up and turned to her.

'How did you find out all of this?'

'It wasn't simple,' she said, crossing her arms. 'You were no help, certainly. So, let me see if I do understand now, Ashe; or shall I call you Gwydion ap Llauron ap Gwylliam and so on?'

'No, thank you, Ashe will do.'

'You are the son of Llauron, the only grandchild of Gwylliam and Anwyn, and the Kirsdarkenvar, which you get from your mother's side. You are also a Manossian noble, and chief of the house of Newland, not to mention the Heir Presumptive to the title of Lord Cymrian, should the Cymrians be reunited.'

Sweat began to form on his brow. 'You're sure of this?'

Annoyance crept into the sympathy of her expression. 'Don't interrupt me – I've had to find all this out without any assistance from you, so you just stand there and listen and wait your turn. Sure? No. When I'm sure of something, I'll say so. But I have more than a passing suspicion that I'm right, so please don't chime in again unless you're correcting my facts. Understood?'

'Yes,' he said, lowering his eyes and smiling.

'Twenty or so years ago, in an attempt to kill an old-world demon that came to this land by stowing away on Gwylliam's ship, you had a piece of your soul torn out, leaving you in constant agony and giving that demon the power to find you. You went into hiding, letting everyone who knew you think you were dead, walking around in a shroud of mist, trying to find the new demonic host and to stop the petty wars it was causing. You've been rather unsuccessful at both, if you'll pardon my saying so.

'In the meantime, the demon that took the piece of your soul built a machine of sorts around it, something that looks like you, and is powered by your soul, but is generated from the F'dor's own blood. It is responsible for much of the terror that has been bringing the land to the brink of out-and-out war, and should anyone ever encounter it and live, they would blame you for those acts, assuming they believed you were alive.

'It's not likely that they would, however. Not even the demon knows you are still alive, I would guess. Nonetheless, the Rakshas has been seeking you all this time on behalf of its master, trying to get your body and the rest of your soul, probably for the purpose of making you the F'dor's new host. It is searching for you still, which is why you walk in a cloak that hides your whereabouts. How am I doing so far?'

Ashe nodded numbly.

'Oh, and I also know how you were mostly healed by the Lord and Lady Rowan. And that you're a dragon, at least partially. That's how you knew in which of several hundred hostels I would find Gavin.'

'What are you going to do with this information?'

Her eyes twinkled. 'Well, first, I'm going to hope that you don't kill me now.'

'I think you're safe for the moment.'

'Oh, good. Next, I plan to help you. I believe I've outlined how already, but you still haven't put on the ring.'

'I know.'

'Are you afraid to?'

'A little.'

'Why?'

Ashe sighed. 'Rhapsody, this is not what I expected to hear from you.'

She smiled, and a look of interest came into her eyes. 'Really? Just what did you expect to hear?'

'I have no idea, actually. I guess I thought you might need help, or wanted to let me know you were back.'

'I see. Look, Ashe, you have been one of the few people since I've been here to actually assist me in finding the things I needed to; you've helped me, and I would really like to return the favor. I've been pretty isolated since I've been in this land; until now, I've spent my time chiefly with Achmed and Grunthor. Except for Jo, you're about the only friend I have.

'I know you're used to being on your own, and have been unable to trust anyone except Llauron, but please, let me help you. I think you need a friend as much as I do; more, probably.' Ashe smiled. Rhapsody sat down on the sofa and patted the seat next to her. 'Please; I know you don't want to trust me, but you have to, you really do. Sooner or later the demon will catch you off guard. You need someone to watch your back. Besides, no woman should have to beseech a man this much to put on a ring; it's demeaning.'

Ashe laughed. He came to the couch and sat down beside her, taking her hand. 'I wish I knew what to say to you.'

'As I told you before, there's really no need to say anything. Please, Ashe, just put it on. It's the first step in making you whole again. Once you are healed and out of agony; then I'll work on killing the Rakshas for you. Here.' She held out the ring once more.

Ashe took the ring in his palm, and slowly closed his fingers around it. Just holding it eased his pain; he could feel intense power radiating from it. He looked back at the woman on the sofa beside him; her eyes were sparkling with anticipation. His wounded soul cried out a warning, that this was an illusion, it was too good to be as it seemed. *A trap*, whispered the dragon. *She's from the demon, she will have us. Forbear.* At the same time, that element of his nature was fascinated by the power of the ring. More than anything, his human soul wanted to believe her. He swallowed hard, and put on the ring.

At first he felt no change. Then, after a moment, he felt a sensation of goosedown falling gently on his head, like snowflakes. He looked up but could see nothing. Then he felt something heavier, like a warm cloak, descend on his shoulders, and as if from the floor a strength rose through him, increasing the volume of his blood and the power of his heart. His lung capacity grew, and his dragon sense could feel the knitting and repair of thousands of vessels and the muscles within his chest cavity, the growth of new bone and new skin, until each wounded piece was made perfect again. And at that moment power roared through his newly perfect body, surging through his blood and to his mind, and his thoughts expanded, as well as his capacity to understand, as the wisdom of the ring permeated him.

He looked back at Rhapsody, who was watching his transformation in awe, and knew innately that she was not a demonic minion, but was totally without pretense; she was exactly as she seemed. Tears came into his eyes at the thought, and a great shuddering gasp escaped him.

The look of intense amazement on her face shifted rapidly into concern. 'Are you all right?'

He nodded, smiling slightly, and released her hand. He could sense the blood return to her fingers, and felt guilty in the knowledge of how tightly he must have squeezed it. His fingers trembled as he unlaced the top of his cambric shirt and opened it. The ugly gash that had sundered his chest was gone, replaced by a thin pink scar and new, healing skin. He looked back at Rhapsody. Tears welled in her beautiful eyes, and she broke into a smile that made his heart leap.

'How do you feel?'

The pain was gone; he felt dizzy and hollow, but marvelous.

'Better,' he said, mentally kicking himself for the inadequacy of his answer.

'Good. I'm glad it worked.'

Ashe, for yet another time that afternoon, was unable to express adequately the vast extent of what he felt: relief, joy, anticipation, validation of his hopes. How could he explain what this meant to him, to be freed of decades of anguish and suffering, to be offered hope for the first time in as long as he could remember? He opened his mouth, but nothing came out, and in the back of his mind, the dragon cursed his inadequacy.

Rhapsody, on the other hand, seemed satisfied. 'Well, now that that's over, will you do me a favor?'

He took a deep breath. 'Anything. Anything at all.'

She patted his hand. 'Would you do me the honor of bestowing on me your first pain-free embrace? I've felt terrible about what I did to you in the forest.'

Rather than risk making a fool of himself, Ashe didn't speak, but just opened his arms, and she came to him. He pulled her close, almost not daring to allow himself to sense her for fear the dragon would consume his self-control. Like a child entering the cold water of a swimming hole, putting one toe, one foot in at a time, he gradually allowed his senses to appreciate her. The scent of her hair was still like morning, as fresh as a meadow after a summer rain. The crisp fabric of her blouse held in the warmth of her upper body, a heat that made his hands shake.

But before he could fall deeply into her she released him and stood up. 'How about some tea?' she asked. Smiling. 'I know you hate the way I make it, but you can steep it yourself. I'll get the pot. Why don't you rest here? I'll be right back.'

She left the room, Ashe's heart following her out the door.

38

After she returned with the tea, she sat down next to him on the floor and handed him a cup. He took a sip, then decided to plunge ahead.

'May I ask you something?'

'Certainly.'

'Why did you do this?'

'Do what?'

He held up his hand with the ring. 'This. And everything you must have done to get it.'

Rhapsody looked confused. 'I told you all that a moment ago; there is nothing I wouldn't do for a friend. I told you what I would do, what being your friend meant, didn't I?'

'Yes.'

'Well, there you have it.'

'Are there any other reasons?'

'Other reasons for what?'

'Other reasons for giving me this incredible gift; for helping me like this.'

Rhapsody was surprised. 'Other reasons? Other than the ones I've just given you?'

'Yes, if there are any.'

She considered, looking down into her lap, and rested her hands on her knees. 'Well,' she said after a moment, 'I suppose there are two other reasons, but they aren't as important as the first.'

'Tell me,' Ashe said, looking down at her. He was very uncomfortable with their seating arrangements; she was sitting at his feet in the traditional position that a servant assumed in a human royal court.

'Well, I'm not sure I can really explain this, but ever since I met Lord Stephen and saw the shrine he has to you in his museum, I believed you weren't dead, and I felt a sort of inexplicable need to help you.'

'Shrine?'

'That might be a bad word for it, but Lord Stephen has a little area in the museum in his keep with a plaque dedicated to you and some artifacts that were yours. I asked him who this Gwydion was, and he told me a little of your story. It was somehow clear to me that he, I mean you, not only might still be alive, but, in fact, were. I can't explain it past that.

'As you know, I've had dreams and visions of the Future for a long time, and sometimes they are frighteningly accurate, so I tend to trust my instinct. That instinct said you were alive, and so I guess I became a little obsessed with finding you and helping you. I obviously didn't know that you were Gwydion when we first met, but as it has become more and more apparent, I have done what I can to help you.'

'And I can't begin to express my gratitude,' he said, looking at her with an unfamiliar expression in his eyes. Rhapsody felt the color rise in her face, even though she was not sure why. His eyes were so strange; the vertical pupils were unnoticeable from a distance, but it was evident there was something different about them. Perhaps that accounted for the odd look.

'What else? You said there were two things.'

Rhapsody looked uneasy. 'It might make you a little uncomfortable to hear it,' she said, her face continuing to redden, her eyes clear and green as the forest canopy, shining up at him.

Ashe couldn't bear to hope. 'What?'

She looked down at her hands again. 'If things go the way we expect, you will eventually be the Lord Cymrian. Since I am Cymrian, you will be my sovereign lord, and I will be your subject, so I owe it to you as my liege to help you in any way I can.'

The expression on Ashe's face when she looked back up caused her to move away a little. It was a combination of sick disappointment and horror.

'I'm sorry if I've reminded you of anything painful,' she said, wishing she had kept silent.

It took him a moment to formulate a response. He fought to keep his voice calm and gentle. The last thing wanted was to frighten her with the intensity of his feelings.

'Rhapsody, I don't want you to be my subject.'

She looked at him with a surprised expression, one that was even a little hurt.

'Really?'

'Yes.'

She took a deep breath and dropped her eyes again, looking like she was coming to understand what he said.

'Well, all right then,' she said slowly, 'if that's the way you feel, I'll stay away from Roland. I can live here, I suppose. These are Achmed's lands; they won't be under Cymrian domain. Or I can probably go live in Tyrian; Oelendra said I was always – '

She stopped as he moved like quicksilver to the floor beside her, seized her face and kissed her.

His lips were warm and insistent, his kiss intense, if not intimate. Her eyes opened wide with shock, her lashes fluttering against his face. Rhapsody froze in his grasp; when he released her, unwillingly, she stared at him in utter amazement, then dropped her gaze when she saw the look of desperation on his face. She rose and crossed the room, running a hand self-consciously over her hair.

After a moment she spoke. 'You know, it's amazing the lengths people go to just to get me to stop talking. Achmed once threatened to have me stuffed and roasted on a spit and fed to Grunthor if I – '

'Don't dodge this, Rhapsody,' Ashe said quietly. 'It's not like you.'

'I'm not dodging,' she said, nervously twisting her hands. 'I'm just trying to decide which action, his or yours, was the more extreme measure. I mean, he had chosen the marinade.'

'Frightening. He was probably serious,' said Ashe, annoyed at the turn in the conversation.

'I know he was serious,' Rhapsody replied, looking away. 'What I don't know is if you are.'

'Completely.'

'Why?' she said, incredulously. 'What in blazes was that about?'

Ashe watched her face, a look of disbelief replacing the shock that had been there a moment before. 'I guess I just couldn't hide it anymore, Rhapsody. I can't bear you talking to me like I'm your lord, or your brother, or a stranger who cares nothing for you, or even just your friend. I may only be those things to you, but it's not because I want it that way.'

'What is it you do want?'

Ashe sighed and looked up at the ceiling for a moment, then returned his gaze to her. 'I want to be your lover, Rhapsody.'

The confusion dissolved, and, to his surprise, her face relaxed and she began to smile.

'Well, now I understand,' she said kindly. 'You've been in terrible pain for so long, Ashe; and you're feeling better. It's natural that the things like that would come back as – '

'Don't be stupid,' he said, a bitter ugliness in his voice that stopped her in mid-sentence. 'You insult both of us. This is not a recent physical need to satisfy because the pain I've carried is gone. I have wanted this all along. Gods. You don't understand me at all.'

'No argument here,' she replied, her anger rising. 'Now, why might that be? Let's see – first you refuse to tell me anything about what you want, or what you think, or even who you are. Then, when you finally did tell me what you wanted from me, I believe the roles you outlined were "friend" and "ally." Oh, yes, and "maid." Please correct me if I'm wrong – did you mention this other one and I just didn't hear you? How stupid of me not to make the connection between these things and "lover." '

'Perhaps I should have figured it out when you thought I was a courtesan, and then had the very bad taste to tell me so? Or maybe I should have realized it when you were telling me to stay away from you, that you didn't trust me, to leave you alone? I don't know how I could have missed it with intimacies like that on a daily basis, Ashe. That kind of sweet talk usually makes me want to find the nearest horizontal surface and lie right down.'

Unable to contain her fury anymore, she turned away from him and put her clenched fists to her burning forehead. 'I can't believe it. You're right, Ashe, I am stupid. All this time I thought you had learned to like me, at least a little, as a person, not as just another potential conquest. I felt comfortable with you because I thought you didn't just want what they all want, that you were finally learning to trust me. It proves what a fool I am, I guess. I should have known it was too much to expect from anyone but Achmed.' The fireplace roared along with her, leaping flames filling the hearth, splashing angry light around the room and onto the pictures on the mantel. The eyes of the grandchildren seemed to glitter in silent accusation.

Ashe stood in that silence for a moment, examining the interwoven patterns in the carpet on the floor. Then he went to her and stood at her back, watching the flames twist and dance in confused fury.

Finally he let out a deep, painful sigh. 'No, Rhapsody, you aren't the one who's been the fool; I think I have that honor. Please, don't start doubting your own senses. Surely you must know you were right about my learning to trust you.'

Rhapsody stared at the fire. 'Actually, Ashe, I think it would be safe to say that I know nothing about you, nothing at all.'

'Please say you don't mean that.'

She turned and faced him, her face filled with regret. 'I'm sorry; that would be lying. And you know that's something I try never to do.'

Ashe took her by the shoulders carefully, looking directly into her eyes. 'How could you possibly doubt that I trust you, Rhapsody? Look at me. Can you see me?' She nodded slightly. 'Well, that makes you the first person in almost twenty years. Even my own father hasn't seen my face in all that time. Yet here I am, uncloaked before you, unarmed and open in your domain. And this isn't the first time you've seen me. Doesn't that tell you something?'

Rhapsody gave him a gentle smile to ease the desperation she could see on his face. 'I suppose so. I guess I'm just not sure what.'

'I know you don't understand the significance of some of these seemingly simple things, but that's because you have no idea what it has been like for me to wake up every morning, year after year, wishing more each day that I was dead, and knowing I couldn't even take my own life because it wouldn't help.'

He slid his hands down her arms until they held her own, and he spoke even more seriously.

'Out there somewhere is an abomination that looks just like me, with part of my soul powering it, giving it abilities to inflict unspeakable acts. And for all this time it has been committing atrocities untold to innocents I can't protect, because it is totally chaotic and random in its violence, even though it obviously is enacting a plan of cruelty that even my twisted mind can't fathom. It has been my first thought, every moment, each time something bad happens anywhere. It haunts me with each heartbeat, with each breath.

'How, then, can a soul as pure and innocent as yours be able to comprehend this?' A choked laugh escaped Rhapsody but her ironic smile faded when she met his eyes; their gaze was steady and sure, and he spoke as though he was certain of what he was saying.

'Don't laugh, Rhapsody; you *are* an innocent, even if you have been through the mill yourself. You believe in people who have no right to that belief; you love people who really don't deserve it. More than anything you want to find something or someone to trust in, because it is your nature to do so. It doesn't matter what your experiences have been, or what you've done – it hasn't touched you. It's like you are a virgin, a real one, in body and soul.'

Rhapsody laughed again. 'You have no idea how funny that statement is,' she said. 'If that's what you're looking for, you are definitely in the wrong place.'

'I'm not looking for anything – that's the point,' Ashe replied seriously. 'I have been hiding, Rhapsody, for two decades, trying to avoid all contact with the world, and doing a credible job of it. And then out of nowhere, one day there you were, like an unavoidable beacon, and everywhere I went, no matter how much I struggled to put you out of my mind, no matter how far I went to stay away, you were there, in the stars, in the water, in my dreams, in the air around me. I have tried to exorcise you from my blood, Rhapsody, but it's no use. I can't make you go away.

'And probably the paranoia, the pushing away, the attempts to offend you into hating me and leaving me alone, were not only my way of trying to break free of the hold you have on me, but they were experiments of a sort; testing to see if you were really what you seemed.

'You have to remember, the way this demon enacts its evil is to bind itself to innocents, and then to work through them. For all I knew, you could be the F'dor yourself. I had no idea if you were seeking me for the same purposes that its countless other minions have been since that night twenty years ago, looking to destroy what is left of my soul, or worse, to use it in a more despicable manner than it is being used now.

'And what a wonderful way to finally catch me off guard – throw an innocent heart my way, wrapped in an exquisitely beautiful package, flavored with powers of an old world that disappeared beneath the waves before my father was even conceived – what better bait for a dragon? I was especially suspicious when I realized you are a virgin – what is the probability of that?'

'Not great,' Rhapsody said humorously. 'It's really only a technicality.'

'It doesn't matter,' Ashe went on. 'Can't you see what I am saying? You are the ultimate in everything I, man or dragon, could ever desire – you are far too good to be true. So of course I was suspicious of you. I have to be paranoid – it's what has kept me alive these twenty years.

'And there you were, offering me comfort, seeking to help me, taking me into your heart; it wasn't possible that it was real. So I waited for you to reveal your other nature, to turn on me. I waited and waited. But it never came about, of course. If anything, you left yourself far more vulnerable to me than I could ever have been to you.

'And then, slowly, my heart began to wish that it *was* real. It has been hoping that from the moment I first saw you, but the more sensible parts of me have beaten it back. And finally, I couldn't stand it anymore. So, like you said that you have just decided to trust me and live, or die, with the consequences, I had decided the same thing – that I just had to tell you and pray that I wasn't delivering the rest of my soul into the F'dor's hands.

'And truthfully, Rhapsody, if I am, I don't even care. I would have come to you even if you hadn't called. I was still trying to figure out how to tell you, and I suppose I have botched it now, but I couldn't lie about it anymore. Not to a woman who won't even lie to save her own life. How could I ever hope to be worthy of you if I did?'

The irony of his words overcame her, and, against her better intentions, she broke into laughter. 'I'm sorry, Ashe, please forgive me,' she said, struggling to contain her mirth. 'That's just too funny.'

Ashe was thunderstruck. 'Why?'

Rhapsody took his hands. 'You are the future Lord Cymrian, the convergence of the royal lines of all three Cymrian waves. I am a peasant, and more common than most. And *you* hope to be worthy of *me*? Don't you see the humor here?'

'No,' said Ashe shortly. 'I don't. I'm actually surprised at you, Rhapsody. Of all people I would think you would understand that a person's family lineage doesn't dictate her worth.'

'Not her worth as a person; of course not,' Rhapsody said, growing serious under his terse tone. 'But when one is talking about lovers, well, people like you don't generally take people like me into that role except by fiat or for recreation, and I don't expect that you would ever try either of those things with me. I believe we settled that some time ago on the banks of the Tar'afel.'

Ashe turned toward the mantel; she could see he was gathering his thoughts. Absently he picked up the painting of the Firbolg children and looked at it carefully.

'Now I see the basis of our confusion,' he said at last, more to the painting than to her. 'You don't understand what I meant when I said I wanted to be your lover.'

Against her will, Rhapsody laughed again. 'I think I actually have a far better understanding than your dragon sense has led you to believe. There are many things you don't know about me, Ashe.'

'And one very significant thing you don't know about me, Rhapsody.'

'Only one?'

'Only one that matters.'

'And that would be – ?'

Ashe looked up from the painting, fixing her with a direct stare from the crystalline blue eyes. 'I love you.'

Rhapsody sighed silently.

'Don't,' Ashe said, a warning note in his voice. 'Don't dismiss this, Rhapsody; I know what you're thinking.'

'Really?'

'Well, I believe so; you be the judge. You are thinking I'm throwing around sacred words like countless other fools have at you, either because your beauty has deluded me into believing it, or because I am trying to get you into bed.'

'Actually – '

'Don't you dare lump me in with those imbeciles who took one look at your face and professed their love for you while drooling on their shoes. I am not one of them, Rhapsody. I fell in love with you even before I beheld you; I could feel your magic *leagues* away. What do you think I was doing in Bethe Corbair in the first place?'

'Shopping?'

'No, dear.'

'I really have no idea; I'm sorry if I'm being thick.'

'I was looking for you, Rhapsody; looking to find whatever it was that was calling to my heart on the Krevensfield Plain two leagues away. I came to find you and when I did, I knew I was lost to you. Did you think I came to Ylorc just for the pleasure of having Achmed insult me repeatedly?'

'Well, that certainly is a rare treat. And besides, the view from the Teeth is lovely in the spring.' The humor was beginning to return to Rhapsody's eyes, and it washed over Ashe like warm water.

'Yes, it certainly is,' he said, remembering the sight of her running through the mountain fields, dancing with the wind across the heath. 'Well, am I right?' He smiled at her to test her new mood, and was delighted to see her smile back at him.

'About what?'

'About what you were thinking?'

Rhapsody chuckled. 'Well, not really,' she said, taking the picture of her grandchildren from his hand and looking at it herself. 'But thanks for making the attempt.'

'What, then?'

'Well,' she said, turning her back to the fire and letting it warm her shoulders, 'I was thinking about one of our conversations on the road.'

Ashe leaned an elbow against the mantel. It was spotlessly polished and completely free from dust. 'Really? Which one?'

'Do you recall when I said to you that in my experience foresters and other wanderers sought different things from women?'

'Yes,' he answered, his face warming with the memory. 'You said most men were looking for release, while wanderers sought contact.'

'Yes, that's the one.'

'Why are you recalling it?'

Rhapsody sighed. 'I can't help but wonder what the point is for you in starting something with someone who clearly is only a temporary diversion in your life, especially when there is so much risk involved.'

'I have no idea what you are talking about.'

She turned and stared at him. 'No? Perhaps I can remind you of a few situations you seem to have forgotten. First, as I mentioned before, we are of totally different social classes; about as far apart as one can get, actually. So obviously your interest in me can only last so long before you choose someone else who is suitable as a life partner, someone royal, or at least noble, as she will have to take on the role of Lady Cymrian.'

'You really don't understand the way the succession works, Rhapsody.'

'Are you telling me that you are not in line for the Lordship?'

Ashe's face grew solemn. 'No, but – '

'And is there not an expectation that the Lord will take a suitable wife, who then becomes the Lady?'

'Yes, but – '

'Well, there you have it, Ashe,' she said simply. 'Our timetable to find and kill the F'dor, and reunite the Cymrians, is within the year. I am not sure how long after that is considered suitable for you to remain unmarried, but I can assure you, as I believe I have mentioned before, that I make it a point not to consort with married men, ever, no exceptions. So anything we might undertake together would have a very brief life; I'm not sure I understand why it would be worth your time and effort, given what you've said to me about longevity.'

Ashe removed his elbow from the mantel and crossed his arms. Her logic, from her perspective, was perfect; there was no point in arguing with it, at least not now. 'So you don't think love is worth anything if it lasts only a short time?'

Rhapsody looked up at him, and her eyes were filled with memory. She thought back to her talk with Oelendra about her husband: *in our short time together we loved a lifetime's worth.* 'No,' she said softly, out of respect for the thought, 'I definitely wouldn't say that.'

'What, then?' Ashe could feel his desperation rising again. 'What do I have to do to convince you to give me a chance?'

'A chance at what?'

Ashe felt like shaking her. 'A chance to act on my feelings for you, Rhapsody. A chance to cherish you, and spend time with you; a chance to be as honest with you as you have been with me, to trust you with my heart, even if – ' He stopped, unable to finish.

'Even if what?' Her voice was gentle, and when Ashe looked up he saw the same mildness in her eyes.

'Even if you don't want to keep it.' The pain in his face and his voice went straight to her heart, and she felt it tug in a way that was not altogether unknown to her. She stared at the floor, afraid that if she continued to look in his eyes she would begin to weep. For a few moments they stayed there, Ashe watching Rhapsody, Rhapsody watching the fireshadows flicker on the rug. Finally she looked up.

'So you would be willing to become lovers, knowing that it was only for a short while?'

'Yes. I would be grateful for any moment with you, any time at all, no matter how brief. I know it would be worth whatever it cost me.'

'And that would be enough?'

'If it had to be. When you want something this badly, anything you can get is enough.'

She nodded after a moment, as if finding her way out of a lost thought. 'And what of yourself would you hold in reserve during this temporary arrangement?'

'Nothing. I don't believe I would be able to hold back anything from you, Rhapsody – I don't really want to, either. We tend not to discuss the Past because it is painful, but I will, if you want to.' She shook her head. 'There are things that we both know we can't share with each other, because they are other people's secrets. But I would have none of my own from you.' His heart rose a little when he saw the expression in her eyes change, and he hurried ahead.

'I know the prospect of being loved by a dragon is a scary one, especially if you know anything about the nature of the beast – we do tend to be possessive on a rather grand scale. But it is the human part of me that loves you most, and it would never stand in the way of your happiness if the time comes when you want to leave.'

Rhapsody shook her head in amazement. 'I think you have it a little off,' she said, laughing. 'I'm not the one with all the royal commitments.'

Ashe just smiled. 'You'll think about it, then?'

Rhapsody handed him back the painting and turned again to face the fireplace. She was silent for a long time, lost in thought; Ashe was used to her quiet moments, and he waited patiently. He knew her mind was racing a million leagues with each passing second, and when she came out the other side of the thought she would be that distance away, so he resolved to remember to put the question to her again. At last she spoke, though her question seemed directed to the fire.

'Do you believe in the concept of soulmates? You know, two people sharing halves of the same soul?'

'Yes.'

'And did you ever meet yours?'

Ashe was silent himself for a moment.

'Yes,' he said finally.

Rhapsody glanced up, and for the first time in a while her eyes seemed clear and focused on him. 'Really? If you don't mind my asking, what happened to her?'

'She died,' he answered, his face twisting in pain.

Rhapsody flushed with mortification and sadness at the sorrow her question had caused. 'Ashe, I'm so very sorry.'

'Not only that,' he said, unable to keep the words inside, 'she died believing I betrayed her, because I didn't say goodbye.'

Rhapsody looked away. For at least the second time that afternoon she wanted to take him in her arms and comfort him. But then she thought back to the first time she had, on the forest road to Tyrian, and remembered the pain her embrace had caused him. She didn't want to repeat the mistake, she told herself, then silently owned up to the truth: she was afraid of what might happen within her own heart if she did.

Ashe looked up to find her averting her eyes. 'What about you?' he asked. 'Do you believe in soulmates?'

'No,' she said softly. 'I mean, yes, I guess there are for some people, but I don't believe I have one.'

'No? Why not?'

Rhapsody sighed, wishing she could change the subject gracefully and knowing she couldn't. 'Well, I thought so once, and I was consummately wrong.'

'What happened?'

'Oh, nothing out of the ordinary. I fell in love with someone who didn't love me back. Standard fare.'

Ashe laughed aloud and shook his head.

Rhapsody was annoyed. 'What? Is that so hard to believe?'

'Actually – yes.'

She was flabbergasted. 'Why?'

Ashe put the painting of the Firbolg children back in its place on the mantel and walked to the sofa in front of the fireplace. He leaned back against the arm of the sofa, arms crossed, studying her, watching the firelight play off her features, responding to her mood. The flames were burning quietly, with the occasional crackle and hiss.

'Rhapsody, in case you hadn't noticed, men profess their undying love for you from little more than a glance. Even when you walk about cloaked and hooded, ox carts run into each other, men stumble into walls, and women stand with their mouths agape. The mere sound of your voice causes those who have been happily wed for thirty years to cry for the sorrow of never having known you. And your smile – your smile warms the coldest of hearts, even those that have wandered alone and wounded for decades.

'Yet I suppose I could understand a man not loving you for these things, for they are only physical. But as beautiful as your bodily form is, it's only a shadow of the soul that wears it. How someone could come to know the person that you are and fail to lose his heart to you is, frankly, beyond me. Gods know I lost mine immediately. Whether you understand it or not, Rhapsody, I do love you, and not just for your appearance, but for the myriad and contradictory things that you are.'

'What does that mean? How am I contradictory?'

'Almost everything about you is a contradiction, and I love each one. I love that you are a Singer, but that most of the songs you know are in a tongue no one understands. I love that you are the Iliachenva'ar, but hate to have to use your sword, whether it's for the pain or the mess that it causes. I love that you are a virgin, and yet you seem to know the charms and enchantments of a prostitute.' Rhapsody blushed, and Ashe had to avert his eyes quickly to stifle his laugh when he saw the look of shock cross her face.

'You want the rest of the litany? All right, here it is, good and bad. I love that you make what is perhaps the worst pot of tea I have ever been asked to endure. I love that you still tear up at sad songs you have sung a thousand times. I love that your best friends are a giant half-Bolg and the most obnoxious creature I have ever laid eyes on, they are rude to you beyond measure, and yet you love them like brothers. I love that you think of food as a musical instrument – '

'You said that was manipulative,' Rhapsody interjected.

'Don't interrupt. I love that you have a better right cross than I have, and, even though you're half my size, you're not afraid to use it on me. I love that you sing the Ballad of Jakar'sid and always get the words of the refrain wrong. I love the way you look after Jo as if she were a little girl when she clearly lost her innocence years ago. And I especially love that you speak your mind to me, even when I don't want to hear it.

'I love that you can't conceive of jealousy in anyone else because there is none in you; that you think that all women have the same effect on men that you do – that you don't even realize you are beautiful at all. I love that your beauty – the thing so highly prized and sought after by almost everyone else – is the bane of your existence.

'I love that you have survived the cataclysm of your whole world, and have lived among monsters, and still always attribute honorable intentions to people. I love that you have the mind of a scholar, the will of a warrior, and the heart of a little girl who only wishes to be loved in spite of all that she is. I love all these things – I love you, and I cannot see how anyone could come to know you, truly know you, and not also love you, not for what you appear, but for who you are. Whoever this man was that didn't was the world's most consummate imbecile.

'But perhaps that's the answer. Perhaps no one else truly does understand you. I know you, Rhapsody, I really know you. I know what it is like to lose those you love, to have to leave them behind and to know that they continued on with their lives until the end of their days, never knowing what became of you. I know the sorrow that brings, though no doubt I do not know that pain to the depths you do.'

Rhapsody, whose face had been growing rosier at each word, paled and turned to face the fire, her back to Ashe, her shoulders straight. The dragon within him sensed the tears brimming, but the dam inside him had already ruptured, and he could not stop the words from pouring out.

'I also know what is worse is that you feel you cannot even fill the holes it left in your life with new friends, new loves, for fear of showing your face. That, I think, is the worst pain of all.

'You are a woman who longs to be taken at face value, but the nature of your beauty forces you to hide yourself behind a cloak, unable to show yourself for fear of the consequences that will ensue. And then there's the fear of whether or not you can trust that the love so abundantly expressed is genuine, or motivated by something else – something as innocent as blind infatuation with your physical attributes, or as sinister as wanting to possess or destroy your soul.

'I know that fear. I know, perhaps better than anyone, what it is like to live behind the mask, remaining unseen, unknown, even though your heart cries out for recognition. It is hideously lonely, in ways no one could ever expect. It makes you want to turn your back on it all and go live in a goat hut, but you can't. Your destiny won't let you, and I know what that feels like, too. I know what it is like to live in that pain, Rhapsody. I know what it is to need that kind of healing. And I would give my very life to spare you from one more moment of it.' His voice broke, and he fell silent.

The fire had died down to softly burning embers while he was speaking; now a few flames licked up, catching new life from parts of the wood revealed as the spent logs crumbled. Rhapsody turned to face him again.

Ashe's dragon senses had told him that she was crying, but the actual sight of her in tears caught him off guard. Her face had never been more beautiful, and his heart, now whole and freed from its former pain, twisted into tiny knots at the sight of it.

She smiled through her tears, and came and stood before him, looking down at him for perhaps the first time. Her fingers carefully touched the coppery hair, brushing the strands gently off his forehead, a look of wonder and discovery on her face. As on that day in the forest where she first saw him without his disguise, her eyes sparkled as they took in his features. Then she bent down and rested her forehead on his.

'So,' she said, closing her eyes, 'you came here hoping to heal me, too?'

'Not really,' Ashe answered. 'I came because you called. I came intending to tell you the truth about how I feel.' His face grew florid in the firelight. 'If the whole truth be told, if you want to know my deepest desires, I came hoping to make love to you.'

Rhapsody smiled again. 'You just did,' she said softly.

She kissed him gently, and then stepped back and opened her eyes. The look of hope and love and fear on his face broke her heart in that instant.

He reached out his hands to her, and she came into his arms and kissed him again.

Ashe began to feel the control he had over his senses give way. The warmth, the sweetness of her mouth was intoxicating him; he was growing dizzy with joy. He pulled her even closer and pressed her lithe body to his, and the burning in his fingers from when he had first let his dragon nature sense her cooled and disappeared as he touched her. Headiest of all was the sensation of being whole again, being without pretense, knowing that she was aware of his feelings and responding to them without fear. And as he gave himself over to the ecstasy of holding her, the dragon arose and reached out to sense more fully the woman in his arms.

I want to touch this.

But as its awareness began to envelop her, Rhapsody pulled away. She pushed out of his grasp and turned from him, her hands covering her face. Ashe could acutely feel each muscle in her body begin to tremble and hot tears fall onto her hands; tension knotted her shoulders and her heart began to race. She was crumbling before his eyes.

'I can't. I can't. I can't. Oh, I'm sorry, I'm sorry, I can't. I can't do this. I can't. It isn't right; it isn't fair. I can't.'

'Fair to whom?' Ashe asked.

Within him he felt the fabric of the universe tremble. The power that the dragon held over the forces of nature began to rise. Though no outward sign betrayed the inner battle that was waging in his soul, Ashe stood at the brink, fighting his own nature and the longing that both parts of it shared. He held as physically still as he could, praying that Rhapsody would not look at him while the dragon was dominant, for the guile it would use to enchant her would be evident in his eyes. And though every part of his senses was primed for what the dragon wanted, it was finally the man who prevailed. The human soul longed for her far more than the dragon could ever covet her, and the human understood that her love had to be given, not taken, so the wyrm was forced back into submission, and the man was left, human and alone.

'Fair to you,' she answered, her voice thick with tears. 'You really deserve someone better, someone who has the capacity to love you back. Someone with a heart. I'm sorry. I'm so sorry.'

Ashe stood up, walking until he stood behind her.

'Please turn around,' he said.

Her body went rigid, but she did not pull away. Slowly she obeyed, looking up at him through strands of shining hair that had fallen out of place, her eyes dark, her chin trembling slightly. He held up his hand.

'May I touch you?' he asked softly.

Rhapsody's eyes cleared. He was remembering his promise. She nodded slightly.

He reached out, and, gently caressing her cheek, he traced the trail of a tear. Her eyes closed at his touch, and her head tilted slightly toward his hand. His fingers traced on, down the line of her neck, to her collar and the neckline of her blouse, which he traced down to the hollow of her bosom before stopping. Lightly he rested his hand upon her chest, just above the heart, and felt it pounding.

Rhapsody drew in a sharp, broken breath, and stood trembling beneath his hand. She wanted this; some part of her wanted this, and deep within her being the part of her bound to fire rose at his touch and flowed into the void places of Ashe's soul where the fire had been taken. Slowly she opened her eyes and looked at him.

They stood just so for a moment, neither one moving or breathing. Ashe felt the racing of her heart beneath his palm and saw the bewildered look on her face as the swarm of conflicting emotions fought within her.

'It feels like you have a heart to me,' Ashe said at last. He watched her, breath held, trembling, vulnerable but not defenseless, and he wanted her. As Ashe, as Gwydion, as man and dragon, he wanted her. Not to vanquish or possess, but to cherish. He wanted her, and he waited in fear of her answer. 'You do have a heart, Rhapsody. Why don't you trust what it tells you?'

Her answer was a whisper. 'It lies.'

'You never lie. No part of you could either.'

'Then it has terrible judgment. I believed it before, and it couldn't have been more wrong.'

'Give it another chance. I thought you believed in taking risks.'

He had to bend nearer to hear her soft reply. 'It's fragile. I wouldn't survive it being wrong again.'

Ashe removed his hand from her chest and caressed her face again. 'You seem to have appointed yourself the guardian of my heart, Rhapsody. Why don't you make me the protector of yours? I promise I will keep it safe.'

The conflict around and within her was making Rhapsody's head spin. She struggled to hold on to what she believed was reality as her eyes searched his for assurances. They seemed so alien, and yet more human than she had ever seen them, and the depth of feeling she could see in them amazed her. *How could I have been so wrong about him?* she thought, remembering their sibling-like bickering during their travels, the distance at which he held her when she tried to learn more about him, their platonic level of comfort. *I didn't know him at all.*

He was as much a contradiction as he had said she was – handsome and alien-looking, hunter and hunted, dragon and mortal, Lirin and man, pushing her away from him while all the time wishing her closer. And she herself had known things about him even before they had met; known that he was still among the living when the rest of the world had given him up for dead. Why?

As her mind turned the questions over and over, deep within her she felt a part of her awaken that had stood closed and neglected for many years. At first she was aware of it as a trickle, like finally noticing the sound of a stream that had been flowing slowly in the distance all along. Then it came with more force than she had known the whole world could muster. She was drowning in longing, and hurt, and desire – and something else, something strange and wonderful and long forgotten. Rhapsody was lost in a flood of emotion too fast for her thoughts to keep pace, and all the lyrical beauty of her abilities as a Singer, a Namer, deserted her. She was left with the heartfelt, unpoetic entreaty of a vulnerable woman.

'Please be what you seem. Please, please don't hurt me.'

Tears stung Ashe's eyes. 'I am. And I never will.'

And then she was in his arms again, mingling her tears with his, holding on to him as though their lives depended on it.

The element within her that was fire found its way into the dark places of his being that had felt no warmth since the night his soul was torn open, until at last it touched his wounded heart. The flames filled in the empty parts of his soul and he felt it heal, if only for a while.

And then her lips were on his, freely given, and as their kiss deepened into heady darkness the dragon again came forth from where he had held it to sense the wonder that was this woman.

I want to touch this.

Yes.

His awareness expanded and Ashe could feel the moment when her tears stopped and her breathing eased as her defenses came down. His hands glided over her body and the dragon could feel each place that his touch pleased her. Minutiae became magnified, and he reveled in the tiniest detail of information the dragon could sense. He surrendered to it.

A trickle of sweat made its way down her back; her muscles rippled and flowed as she moved within his arms. Her blouse caught slightly in his embrace and was pulled tight; he felt its fabric weaken, thread by thread, at the seam. There was a small crack in a floorboard in the next room that widened ever so slightly as their weight shifted in this one.

Rhapsody's eyes kindled from dark green to a brilliant emerald. She drew in a deep breath; on the hearth the fire leapt and crackled, sending embers up the chimney where they lodged in the bricks and smoldered quietly.

Currents and eddies of power flowed through this place and circled around them and the lore they held – music, fire, time, dragonlore – drawn into their passion and passed out again as a whirlpool of essence exhaled like a breath. Flowing faster, more wildly, but with no direction, it swirled through the air, across the land, and over the waters which echoed with its passing. The grotto became alive with that power, alive as it had not been for centuries uncounted, since the war that had begun here.

Within the lake a fish leapt, causing a splash that sounded softly through the cavern, echoing off the rockwalls and drowning in the sound of the waterfall, which tumbled down into the pool with a musical flow that poured over its brink, creating the mist that refracted the light of the moon to form a barely visible rainbow, and sent forth the myriad vibrations that helped to hide this place from the prying eyes that hunted and searched for them both. The churning water caused the waves that lapped against the shore of the small island covered in gardens upon which the house stood with its smoke rising through the air, up the chimney from the fire fed by the rising passion of Rhapsody.

Rhapsody, from whose body fire and heat flowed into Ashe's own and beyond. Rhapsody, whose soft voice was musical even in the breaths she took as they kissed, and whose back still held the healing bruises from her fight with the Rakshas. Whose blood flowed faster with the pounding of her heart and the movement of his hands over her body. Rhapsody, the woman he had loved from the moment he became aware of her.

Ashe unbound the ribbon in her hair and, with eyes closed, sensed every strand as it fell across her shoulders to her waist. He pulled away, cradling her face in his hands, and looked at her. The light sparkled in her eyes as she searched his face, the fire bringing life to her hair. She breathed deeply and caught her breath; her mouth was open slightly, but she said nothing.

He kissed her again, and his hands innately went to the places he knew she desired to be touched. She responded in kind, her own hands gliding smoothly over his shoulders. They rested for a moment on the muscles of his chest, and he felt them burn. Then they moved under his shirt and gently touched his skin, and the scar which until that night had been so painful for so long.

Ashe caressed her face, and slowly slid his fingers into the shining waterfall of hair, drawing them down through the glistening locks that were even silkier than he imagined, sending tremors through his entire body and making the arousal he felt even more unbearable. Then his hands slipped beneath her blouse, under the lacy camisole, and his fingers played lightly upon her breasts, reveling in their firm softness. He felt her shiver, and his lips sought the hollow of her throat, drinking in the scent of her hair, her skin. Rhapsody ran her hands through the coppery hair, amazed that something that looked metallic could feel so soft. Her fingers entwined around the shiny curls, holding tight as he began to kiss down the line of her neck.

Ashe's hands encircled her waist, his fingers caressing the small of her back as he gently loosed the laces of her skirt. When the last tie was unbound he spanned her waist again and lifted her free from the garment as it crumpled to the floor. She smiled down at him as her hands went to the laces of his broadcloth shirt; he waited for her to finish untying them before rising to kiss her mouth once more.

They moved in a wordless dance, drawing each other free from their outer clothing. The sight of his bare chest brought tears to Rhapsody's eyes again; the blackened flesh and gnarled scar gone, in its place new, healing skin, no different than that on her own leg. She turned away, overcome, and he wrapped her in his arms and held her fast against his chest, both of them celebrating his freedom from pain.

She reached up behind her neck and unfastened the clasp of her locket, holding it tightly in her palm for a moment before dropping it to the table near the sofa. Ashe's lips caressed the nape of her neck; then he turned her gently around and looked into her eyes to find, for the first time, his own euphoria reflected back at him.

They embraced once more, slowly moving to the floor as each removed the few remnants of clothing that remained. He leaned over her, pulling away from their embrace for a moment, and let his eyes see for the first time the form his dragon senses knew so well. She was luminous, perfect; her skin glowed with a radiance the like of which he never could have imagined.

'You are beautiful,' he said, awe making his voice husky. 'So beautiful.'

Rhapsody smiled at him. 'I'm glad you think so,' she said, and brushed his face gently with her hand. Ashe closed his eyes, and took her hand in his. He kissed it, then the crook of her arm, and then he was lost to her. As the fire blazed behind them they made love upon the floor of Elysian.

In time he gathered her in his arms and moved to the bed, where their lovemaking continued until the night had passed into the new day, and the flames had diminished down to sleepy coals that glowed on the hearth like firegems, spilling warmth from the room into the fog that swirled around the silent lake.

In the night Ashe woke and felt the top of her head near his lips in the darkness as she lay on his chest, sleeping softly. The dragon had wrapped itself around her dreams, guarding her from her nightmares, and so she was silent, breathing easily. He brushed the crown of her hair with a kiss and pulled her even nearer, burying his face in her neck. He took in a deep breath, inhaling her scent and the warmth and sweetness of her skin.

In her sleep Rhapsody felt warm tears in the hollow of her shoulder and the heat of Ashe's breath. She sensed him shiver, and sleepily she turned on her side and slid her arms around his neck, drawing his head against the bare skin of her shoulder and breast, shielding him like a child from whatever demon dreams were causing him to wake.

But Ashe was not sad; his were tears of gratitude that this time the dream he had been holding in his arms was real, and was still there when he awoke. His lips stroked her shoulder, then lowered to her breast, and with the warmth of his mouth he caressed the fragile skin, feeling its sleepy softness stir at his touch and respond to him.

Ashe deepened his kiss, gliding his fingertips up her side. He was filled with longing to give her pleasure, to see her as happy as she had made him. She stretched with drowsiness and as she did his hand traced down the slender abdomen, over her flat stomach and came to rest on an exquisite leg, trembling as he touched her.

In her sleep she sighed, a soft, musical sound that stirred him even more. He waited for her to wake, but her eyes remained closed and her arms drowsily entwined around his neck again as her fingers absently caressed the hair at the back of his head. She was well and truly asleep.

Ashe was lost in the dilemma of what to do next. His desire for her grew more intense by the moment, but the dragon could tell she was tired, weary from being emotionally overwrought and worn out from the cataclysmic lovemaking that had begun on the floor in front of the fire as the sun was setting and had gone on long past midnight. She had satisfied him in ways he had not even dreamed of, and she was irresistible; the more of her he got, the more he wanted. Whatever stores of energy she had were spent, and now she was sleeping deeply, her body trying to gain it back.

He imagined making love to her again now, taking her in ways that would return to her some of the joy she had given him, but he looked into her face and decided not to. Exhaustion was taking her, too, like an overly insistent lover, and her sleep was undisturbed by the dreams that frightened her and made her wake, trembling, in the night. It was the first time he had seen her slumber in complete peace. So he swallowed hard and let his need pass, difficult though it was, and cradled her in his arms, guarding her dreams and her rest. He could wait.

In the gray haze that preceded dawn in the underground grotto Ashe rose slowly from the bed, careful not to waken Rhapsody. His feet recoiled at the chill of the floor as he moved to the fireplace where the dragon had sensed the sign. He knew what it was, and exactly how much of it there was, yet he went all the same, just to see it with his own almost-human eyes. On the floor were three drops of blood, Rhapsody's blood, blood he had let in passion.

He had known she was untouched, of course; the dragon had sensed that from the start, but three drops – as with Emily, it was three. An omen, no doubt, but of what he did not know. That this was his grandmother's house did not escape him, nor was her office as Seer of the Past insignificant. Three drops of blood, just like Emily. A sign of things to come, or a completion of things past?

Ashe turned back toward the bed and looked at Rhapsody, still softly sleeping. Her face was free of regret or fear; her dreams were happy, or at least seemed to be. His smile was melancholy as he left the room and went down the stairs to the front hall where his cloak hung on a peg. He reached inside it, feeling the cool moisture of the mist, and from it drew out a small silver button he had kept there for years. Then, leaving the cloak where it hung, he walked out of the house, down to the waters' edge.

He stood there, letting the waters of Anwyn's cottage speak to the waters of his soul, as he held the silver button and contemplated the omen in blood. He closed his eyes, drew in a deep breath, and, tightening his hold for a moment, leaned back and threw the silver button out into the waters of the grotto.

'Good-bye, Emily,' he whispered, then stood silently for a moment, tears touching the corners of his eyes.

Rhapsody woke to the knowledge that Ashe was no longer in bed, but to the equal certainty that he was still nearby. She could feel his presence as surely as she had heard his breath as he lay beneath her while they slept. And though she was confused by everything that had transpired, she was assuredly happy he was there.

She drew a blanket about her as she stood and moved to the window where she knew she would see him. In the distance she could make out his form, naked and wrapped in the mist of the lake, staring out into the distance, watching what she did not know. She felt her skin tingle and knew the dragon sensed her movement as surely as she had felt his presence a moment before. The thought comforted her.

At the sight of him she felt a tug at her heart, a melancholy that at first she did not recognize, though she had felt it before. It had been with her a long time, and she realized she had felt it on each occasion that she had thought about Ashe over the past few months. It was not until now that she recognized it for what it was, because it had been so long since she had felt anything like it.

What a strange man you are, Ashe, she thought. At times as unassailable as a rampant dragon, now he looked as lost as a kitten. Whatever he was, for good or ill, he had her heart, the heart she hadn't realized was still there. There was no turning back now.

Down by the water's edge he shivered and rubbed his hands on his arms as though chilled. Rhapsody hurried to him, bounding down the stairs, throwing wide the door to the cottage, and running to the beach before slowing her steps as she came up behind him. She took the blanket from herself and draped it around him, leaving her arms with it.

Ashe turned and smiled down at her, then drew her under the blanket with him. He kissed the top of her head, trying to decide which was shining more brightly – her hair or her face.

'Sleep well?'

'Very, thank you,' she replied. 'I've discovered something, and I thought you should know.'

'Yes?'

'I love you, too. And I'm sure of it.'

His reply was a deep, sustained sigh; wordless, but it spoke volumes.

Rhapsody laid her head on his chest, and there on the shores of the lake they held each other until the early light of dawn had given way to the brighter sun of midmorning. The green light that filtered through the bushes that grew above the firmament made the grotto seem as though it lay in some deep forest.

Against all likelihood, a small silver button washed up on the shore of the island, unnoticed.

39

'Clear your mind. Relax your skin-web. Concentrate on the rhythm of your own heart.'

Achmed closed his eyes in the heavy wind of the vast, echoing chamber. He stood within the canticle circle, feeling the dust that hung heavy in the dead air settle on his bare skin.

'Exhale. With the breath expel your *kirai*.'

Achmed complied; he had done this before each hunt in the old world. It was a technique he had known from birth, honed by Father Halphasion's instruction, a step in the process that removed the routine rhythms of his body – the beating heart, the tides of breath, the movement of air within his sinuses, the infinitesimal whisper of growing skin – and made it blank, clear, pristine, waiting to be inscribed with the life rhythms of whomever he sought.

Despite his nakedness, his body did not feel the chill of the great chasm that tunneled around and above him. His skin-web, the complex mesh of veins and nerves that scored the surface of his face and neck, hummed placidly at the ready, cleared of the flow of blood for the moment.

The great pendulum of the clock swung slowly through the darkness. From behind his eyelids Achmed could feel it pass, could hear the whir of the spider-silk chain as it went by. In the weight at the end of the pendulum the captive essence of the long-trapped F'dor spirit from the battle of Marincaer burned within its diamond prison. Achmed could sense its smoldering rage, could hear its anger approaching in a crescendo as the pendulum swung toward him, diminishing to a whisper as it swung away again like a spark from a campfire flaring out into the dark night. It gave him cold satisfaction.

'Let your identity die.' The scratchy hiss of the Grandmother's voice crackled in the empty cavern. Achmed obeyed and felt suddenly cold; no vibrational signature radiated from him at all. He was as gray as the rockwalls of the cavern. He had done this before as well.

'When you have subdued yourself, reach out and catch the essence of that which you seek. Command it stop.'

Slowly Achmed exhaled, loosing his *kirai* again. His skin-web hummed, this time forming a net of vibrations that rose from his body like mist off the sea, tethered to the sinus cavities above his eyes. He breathed again, his throat joining the vibration, pushing the invisible pulsing net higher into the heavy air.

As the pendulum passed once again, he concentrated blindly on the furious heat flashing inside the facets of the diamond weight. He held up his right hand. *Zhvet*, he thought. *Halt*. The net of vibrations expanded around the heat, then contracted suddenly, catching the evil essence in the invisible snare.

Like a fish on a line the demonic spirit snapped and twisted against his will, screaming in fury at its bondage. The pendulum froze in place, hovering in the air above the chasm. Achmed raised his left hand.

'Within your mind, call to each of the four winds,' the Grandmother instructed softly. 'Chant each name, then anchor it to one of your fingers.'

Bien, Achmed thought. The north wind, the strongest. He opened his first throat and hummed the name; the sound echoed through his chest and the first chamber of his heart. He held up his index finger; the sensitive skin of its tip tingled as a draft of air wrapped around it.

Jahne, he whispered in his mind. The south wind, the most enduring. With his second throat he called to the next wind, committing the second heart chamber. Around his tallest finger he could sense the anchoring of another thread of air. When both vibrations were clear and strong he went on, opening the other two throats, the other two heart chambers. *Leuk.* The west wind, the wind of justice. *Thas.* The east wind. The wind of morning; the wind of death. Like strands of spidersilk, the currents hung on his fingertips, waiting.

The Grandmother noted with satisfaction that the wind-symbols at the edges of the canticle circle had begun to glow. Four notes held in a monotone. He was ready. Now to the true test.

'Cast the second net,' she ordered. Achmed's hand contracted, and with a graceful swing of his arm he tossed the ball of wind that had formed in his palm out into the darkness of the cavern. Behind his eyelids he could feel the four winds knot together, anchored to his palm, then wrap fiercely around the struggling demon-spirit.

'Tie it,' the Grandmother said. 'Cut it.' This had been the most difficult part of the ritual for Achmed to master; being half-caste, his physiology did not contain the anatomical structure that allowed full-blooded Dhracians to easily sever the ties of the first net, leaving the strength of the winds alone to maintain the cage he had formed. He and the Grandmother had worked for many hours to find another way for him to perform this last critical step of the Thrall ritual.

He concentrated now on the back of his first throat. He took in a breath and forced the air up over his palate. A harsh fifth note sliced through the monotone of the other four: Achmed felt the threads attached to his fingers go slack. Quickly he clicked his tongue, tying off the ends of the wind-cage, and allowing his first net to dissipate. Then he clenched his thumb to snap the wind-thread taut against the flailing spirit.

The struggle ceased immediately as the diamond weight flinched, then went rigid. The demonic spirit was caught in the grip at the confluence of the four winds under the command of a Dhracian, the Winds' son. Slowly Achmed twisted his palm, wrapping the tether around it like a kite string. Once secure he gave the tether a strong pull, feeling the unwilling spirit coming closer with each revolution of his hand. He opened his eyes.

Hanging in the air, an arm's span away from him, was the spider-silk chain of the mammoth pendulum. Its weight, the walnut-sized diamond with the demon housed inside it, hovered before his eyes. Achmed looked at the Grandmother. She was nodding.

'You are no longer Untrained,' she said. 'You are ready.'

'Now that you are adept in the Thrall ritual, we must prepare you for the hunt.'

Achmed stood silently as the Grandmother pulled the covers over the Earthchild and gently released her hand. He had been standing vigil for hours it seemed, watching wordlessly as the Matriarch tried to console the child's terrors. She had pitched fitfully from side to side on her catafalque, gasping in fright, ignoring all the Grandmother's ministrations, refusing to be soothed.

'ZZZhhh, zzzzhhh, little one; what troubles you so? Speak, that I may aid you.'

The child had shaken her head violently, moaning intermittently. ' "Green death," ' the Grandmother muttered. ' "Unclean death." What does she mean? Speak, child. *Please.*' But the only response had been the hiccoughing sobs, the violent thrashing about. Achmed's teeth set in anger.

It was bad enough that Rhapsody had thrown in her lot with the son of Llauron; the Invoker was still his best guess to be the F'dor's host. Even worse, she had not returned to the Cauldron in almost a week, though she had sent word through the amplification of the gazebo that she was safe. Now, watching the convulsing child, feeling the Grandmother's despair in his skin, it was all he could do to keep from striding down to her accursed duchy, killing Ashe where he stood and hauling her back to the Colony by her hair. *She should be here*, he thought bitterly. *If she could witness this and still go to him –*

Sour bile flooded his mouth. He dismissed the thought from his mind, unwilling to follow it to the conclusion that haunted his dreams.

Finally the child settled into a less agitated sleep. The Matriarch of the dead Colony brushed her stone-gray forehead with one last gentle caress, then extinguished the light, crushing the spore beneath her heel. She nodded to the doorway of the chamber, and Achmed followed her out into the corridor.

'Her fear is growing stronger,' the Grandmother said.

'Does she have any idea why?'

'If she does, she cannot form an image around it that I can understand. All her mind whispers is "green death, unclean death." '

Achmed exhaled. He had no patience for riddles; this, too, was Rhapsody's bailiwick. *She should be here*, his mind repeated furiously.

'What do you wish me to do?' he asked, casting a glance at the soot-stained relief on the wall across from him. It was a geometric pattern that had once had been a map of some sort in the days before the Colony's destruction, as were many of the images that decorated the walls.

The black ovals of darkness that were the Grandmother's eyes regarded him seriously.

'Pray,' she said.

★

327

In a lush glen on the Krevensfield Plain, Nolo winced in the heat of the afternoon. In all the memory of his ten summers he could not recall a more frustrating day. The minnows had been too swift, the haze of the sun too blinding, and he was too hot, too hungry to remain in the fields any longer. He dragged his line out of the water, squinting in the light that reflected off the pond.

'Hie, Fenn,' he called as he looped the string around his palm, but the little dog was otherwise engaged, stalking grasshoppers, no doubt.

Nolo rose and shook the pond scum off the fishing line, then crammed the string into his pocket. The sack that once held his breakfast had been empty since sunrise, but he checked it again anyway, on the happenstance that a crust of bread or a crumb of cheese had made its way into the seam to hide. Upon examination the sack proved to be as empty as his stomach.

'Fenn!' he shouted again. His eyes scanned the meadow beyond the trees of the glen. He could see movement in the highgrass, could hear rustling. *Stupid mongrel*, he thought to himself. Nolo crammed the sack into his pocket with the string.

His bare feet stung in the hot grass of the field once he stepped outside the glen's shade; it seemed to him that the ground beneath them trembled ever so slightly. Nolo glanced around again. There was no one in sight, but suddenly he felt the cold grip of fear, though he had no idea why.

'Fenn, where are you?' he howled, his voice cracking. In answer he heard airy panting a stone's throw away, and a moment later Fenn's little yipping bark pierced the humid air. Nolo exhaled in relief and trotted over the brushy scrub to his dog. Upon cresting a small swale, he could see what had held the pup's attention.

The carcass of a rabbit was impaled on a low-lying bramble, a thick, black vine with long, spiked thorns that looked sharper than those of a blackberry bush. Nolo's eyes opened wide with interest. The dog must have spooked the coney badly; it had obviously leapt backward with a tremendous force, judging by the point of the thorn that protruded from its chest. Otherwise it would almost appear to have been stabbed forcibly from behind with a murderous intent, but of course that was impossible, Nolo knew. A small puddle of fresh blood pooled around it, a dollop of which adorned Fenn's nose. The dog's eyes glittered excitedly, anxiously.

Nolo thought about freeing the carcass from the bramble and taking it home to his mam for supper, but decided rapidly against it. Something about the day wasn't right, something that diluted the leisure of his respite from chores and lessons, a waste of the freedom of the Fore-midsummer holiday.

'C'mon, Fenn,' he urged, and gestured to the dog. Nolo turned and ran, the pup at his heels, all the way back to the settlement, to the small thatched house where the candles would soon be lit in the solitary window.

As soon as the boy was out of sight, the bramble flexed slightly. The pool of blood began to recede, disappearing into the skin of the thorn with a greedy eagerness until there was nothing left but dry ground. Then, with but a whisper of sound, the bramble sank into the earth and vanished.

40

The gardens of Elysian were a marvel to behold, even by Ashe's Filidic standards. Prior to the beginning of his nightmarish ordeal twenty years before he had overseen his father's conservatories, as well as his own, vast country estates with formal gardens and massive greenhouses devoted exclusively to the holy and ceremonial plants of the religion. His knowledge of horticulture was deep, though limited in scope, and he had overseen hundreds of nature priests toiling in the fields and monastic farms as well. He had seen many strange planting techniques in his life, but nothing prepared him for Rhapsody's unique gardening style.

She was up each morning before the sun, tidying Elysian, baking muffins and bread, filling the air with heavenly aromas. As she worked she sang softly, so as not to wake him, but the dragon knew she was gone the instant she left the bed, and began a long, unconscious process of vaguely sensing to be sure she was still within his reach. The lovely melodies would lull him back into semi-sleep until finally, when she had finished her work in the house and gone outside, he would wake, rise grumpily, and set about making himself human again.

Most days she left whatever she was baking in the oven and went out to tend the gardens, knowing he would sense the moment that the pastries were perfectly done and be there to remove them from the heat. It served as an effective and gentle wake-up call, and Ashe enjoyed the simple domesticity of sharing the cooking chores with her. He would lumber, still in the hazy throes of dragon-sleep, down the stairs, pull whatever she had made from the hearth, and then set to preparing the morning's repast, arranging it on a tray.

Finally he would emerge with the tray and carry it out to the garden to share breakfast with her. Inevitably he would find her on her knees in the dirt, her hair tied in a shining knot, often in a frumpy kerchief. She would be caressing the leaves of tiny plants, singing merrily, or humming to herself as she worked with the shovel.

She had a song for each flower, and a method by which she soaked and tended each seed, producing thriving gardens almost overnight. By the time she had called him to Elysian the place was ablaze in summer colors and soft, shady hues, the scent of spice and a rich herbal tang hanging in the air. Now it was a virtual paradise, delighting the eye and nose with the perfect balance of greenery to brighter hues. She had a gardener's eye and a farmer's touch, and both had brought to Elysian a healthy, jubilant air that it had certainly not seen before her.

One morning he had awakened to a particularly beautiful song, a tune that put him in mind of the seasons without hearing the words. Later, when he had caught the lyrics wafting over the garden wind, he had smiled at them.

> White light
> Draw back the night
> And wake to the call of spring,
> *Come and see, come and see,*
> What the warm winds bring
> The butterfly's wing
> The meadowbirds sing
> A new year in its birth
> Welcomes the Child of the Earth
>
> Cool green
> In forests unseen
> The summer sun's high in the sky
> *Come and dance, come and dance,*
> On the verdant ground
> In merry round
> Where joy is found
> The season of mirth
> Laughs with the Child of the Earth
>
> Red gold
> The leaves grow old
> And fall on the breath of the wind
> *Stay and dream, stay and dream*
> At summer's flight
> In colors bright
> Autumn's fight
> To hold fast for all she is worth
> Comforts the Child of the Earth
>
> White light
> Yon comes the night
> Snow drapes the frozen world,
> *Watch and wait, watch and wait*
> Prepare for sleep
> In ice castles deep
> A promise to keep
> A year whose days left are dearth
> Remembers the Child of the Earth

On that day he had commented to her about the song. *Lovely,* he had said as kissed her. *Much too lovely to be about Grunthor. Needs more guts and phlegm, maybe some lice.* Rhapsody had smiled, but her eyes darkened slightly in the way that indicated she was not telling him something. *There are things that we both know we can't share with each other because they are other people's secrets,* he had said to her on their first night as lovers. He had changed the subject.

She had planted a small orchard at the edge of the subterranean meadow, the only spot where the fruit trees would receive enough light. Sometimes he would find her among the baby trees, speaking to them softly and caring for them as tenderly as she would a child. Inevitably when he would come upon her like that she would break into an embarrassed grin and run to him, taking his arm and walking with him to the gazebo or the stone benches in the middle of the perennial herb garden where they usually had breakfast.

This morning had been no exception. He had woken in a surly mood with the realization of her absence hanging in his mind, but had become reasonable after breaking his fast. Then he rolled up his sleeves and proceeded to dig in the dirt with her, helping her separate the roots of plants she was dividing and moving to the bank that led down to the lake in front of the turret.

They worked in the half-sun of the grotto for hours. Rhapsody sang joyfully; she had ceased to be self-conscious with him some time before when he had begun singing along, seeking to learn her songs of growing. He had taught her a few more from this land that he knew from his days in Gwynwood, which she learned enthusiastically. Today she was exceptionally happy; when he questioned her as to the reason, she smiled and kissed him.

'Look in the lake,' she said.

He wandered down to the bank and gazed down into the water, but saw nothing unusual. He shrugged, and she smiled again.

'Must be muddy this morning,' she said, kneeling down once more and turning back to the pile of leaves and loam that she was working into the soil. 'Usually it reflects better than that.'

Ashe felt warmth spill over him. He went up behind her and bent down, hugging her from behind.

'I love you.'

She kept digging. 'You do?'

He nuzzled her neck. 'Yes. Can't you tell?'

'Not at the moment.'

Ashe blinked. 'Why?' He felt his chest tighten.

She did not favor him with a glance. 'Because no man who really loved me would be standing on my newly planted spritewort.' She gave his foot a playful push out of her flower bed.

'Oh. Sorry about that, old girl.' He gave the shining knot of hair beneath the ugly kerchief a playful tug, and patted her hindquarters affectionately.

'Keep your hands off my muffins, sir.' She looked up at him in mock annoyance.

'Your what?'

'Well, you're the one who called them that,' she laughed, brushing the strands of hair that had fallen down back under the kerchief and turning back to her digging.

He crouched down next to her. 'What are you talking about?' His fingers gently caressed the stray strands.

She tried to hide her smile as she kept working. 'Whoever taught you Ancient Lirin had a poor understanding of idiomatic usage. *Kwelster evet re marya* – you have the most beautiful muffins.'

Ashe's face colored in embarrassment and humor. 'You're joking. That's what I said?'

She nodded. 'Why do you think I make them for breakfast most every morning? I've never had a man think my baked goods were visually pleasing before.'

Ashe erupted into laughter, and pulled her to him, scattering moss and leaves as he did. He kissed her, interrupting her own laughter and smearing the dirt from her brow across his face. 'I guess I have to work on my idioms, then, eh?'

'No, not necessarily; I thought it was delightful.'

'Oh, good. So, now, what do I say if I want to see your crumpets?'

She wrapped her arms around his neck. 'I suggest "please," although myriad other things come to mind.'

'In that case, please.'

She smacked him gently on the back of the head with her trowel. 'Gods, you are insatiable.'

'That's your fault, you know.' His dragonesque eyes twinkled, and her emerald ones did the same. They both knew that when it came to romantic fulfillment, she seemed almost as unquenchable as he was. She tried to return to her gardening.

'What makes you say that?'

Ashe removed the tool from her hand and pulled her lovingly into his lap. 'You've become my treasure, Rhapsody. You must know that the thing a dragon obsesses about most, can never have enough of, is its treasure.' He smiled down at her, but in the back of his mind he was unsure if his light tone of voice was undercutting the sincerity of his words. He sensed that she was still a little uneasy in the knowledge of his other nature, and he hoped she wasn't put off by the truth of his statement. Aside from the prospect of being taken by the demon again, there was nothing that worried him more than the prospect of what would happen later, when and if she turned away from him, as he knew she expected to one day. He knew the rampage he would undertake then would leave a scorching trail of devastation in his wake.

Rhapsody took his face in her hands and kissed him. 'Then maybe I'm part dragon, too.'

'Why?'

'Well, I must be equally obsessed with you to allow you to continually divert me from my work in the garden, which hithertofore was my second-favorite thing in the world.'

'The first being music?'

'Of course.'

'But you've been working in the garden all morning. Surely you must be getting tired by now.'

Rhapsody stood and stretched, then shook off the remaining dirt and grass. 'Actually, I am.' She gave him her hand and helped him up, then wrapped her arms around his waist. 'And hot, too; I feel like a human flame, in fact.'

'I can vouch for that.'

'There you go again, you randy thing,' she chided as he pulled the kerchief off her head and began to unwind the knot in her hair. 'Can't you think of anything else?'

'Excuse me,' Ashe scolded in mock offense. 'I wasn't being lascivious; I was referring to your fire lore.'

'Oh,' Rhapsody smiled. 'Well, as a human flame, then, I feel the need to be enveloped by water.' She hugged him tighter.

'I thought you'd never ask,' he murmured, kissing her neck.

'Ask what? I'm going to take a bath.' She wriggled out of his arms and ran back to the house with him close behind.

Ashe had stayed in another part of the cottage while Rhapsody filled the tub with cold, clear water from the pump. When it was finally full she sank her hands beneath the surface and concentrated on the heat in her soul. The water began to grow warm, as did the room a moment later. She tossed a handful of spiced rose petals into the tub.

She looked around. It had taken quite some time to get enough water for the bath, and she had expected Ashe to come in by now, but still he had remained elsewhere. Finally she walked to the door and looked out; he was nowhere to be seen.

'Ashe?'

'Yes?' His voice came from downstairs.

'Where are you?'

'In the parlor.'

'What are you doing?'

'Reading.'

'Oh.' Rhapsody tried to keep the disappointment out of her voice. 'You're welcome to join me in the tub.'

'No, thank you.'

She tugged on the tie of her white robe. 'Are you sure?'

There was no answer for a moment. 'Maybe I'll be up in a while.'

Rhapsody sighed. 'All right.' She went back into the bathroom, chagrin beginning to spread through her. She hadn't meant to offend him; usually he enjoyed being teased about their fervent attraction for each other. Perhaps she had taken the joke too far. She hoped she hadn't hurt his feelings.

The temperature of the tub water was perfect. She shook off her dripping hand and listened for footfalls, but they did not seem to be forthcoming. Rhapsody sighed one more time and resigned herself to having to wash her own back. She was standing before the glass, brushing the plant fragments out of her hair, when the door opened and Ashe came in, dressed in his robe, a bound book in his hand.

Rhapsody's eyes sparkled with excitement, but her expression remained neutral. 'I thought you were otherwise engaged with your book.'

'I am, but I thought you could use some company while you bathed.'

'I see.'

'From over here across the room, of course. I don't want you to think I'm looking for an invitation or anything.'

'No, of course not.'

Ashe looked hurt. 'I assure you, my intentions are purely honorable.'

'Right.'

'No, they are; really. I only came in here to read.'

Rhapsody looked at him with amusement in her eyes. 'This is hardly the place to read,' she said, watching as the warm, soggy air laden with scented moisture lazily swirled around her. 'Parchment tends to fall apart in steam.'

He came closer, ambling through the hot mist, hands folded politely before him. The vapors curled around his ankles like a playful kitten. The brightness of his smile matched the white robe.

'Tell you what: let's make a bargain. If you let me stay, I promise you I will not touch you unless you ask me to. I won't bother you at all. In fact, I'll sit all the way over here by the door. Fair enough?'

'You won't be able to see much over there.'

'I've told you already, I didn't come in here to play the voyeur, I – '

'I know, you came to read,' Rhapsody said, smiling. 'Well, enjoy yourself.'

'Oh, count on it,' said Ashe, returning her grin.

Rhapsody went back to the tub, watching the vapors hover over the steaming water. Clouds of roiling mist were rising around her, and water droplets settled on her lashes, making her eyelids feel heavy. Apparently the same thing was happening to Ashe; he had sat down on the marble floor next to the door, leaning up against it, and closed his eyes. She gave him one last chance.

'You know, you're welcome to join me if you want.'

He held up his hand, eyes still closed.

'All right,' she said. 'Suit yourself.' She drew a slender leg up over the rim of the tub and tested the water with her toe; it was hot, but she knew it would be comfortable, and so she walked a few feet over to the towel hook, slid the nubby robe off her shoulders and let it drop to the ground. She cast a glance back over her shoulder, but Ashe was still resting against the door, eyes closed, almost as if asleep.

Rhapsody reached into one of the glass apothecary jars on the table below the towel rack and extracted more dried rose petals mixed with sweet-smelling spices; the soothing aromas of cinnamon, rosemary, and vanilla melded with the perfume of lime flowers and joined the clouds of mist wafting through the air, filling the bathroom with a heavenly aroma. She bent to pick up her robe, hung it on the hook, and then turned toward the tub.

Ashe still looked as if he was sleeping, but the smile on his face broadened as she turned around.

'Ah HA! You're peeking!' Rhapsody declared, laughing.

'Who in this world could resist?' Ashe said, eyes still closed. 'Besides, I didn't say I wouldn't peek. I just said I wouldn't touch.'

'Frankly, I prefer the latter to the former, but have it your way.' Rhapsody walked unselfconsciously to the tub and tossed the spicy mixture in. The potpourri hissed as the heat released more of the aromatic oils, and the water swirled with a shimmery film. She took hold of the long fall of her hair and twisted it up on top of her head, securing it with her standard black ribbon. Then she stepped slowly into the tub, enjoying the warmth of the waves. The water closed around her as she sat down and stretched out, luxuriating in its torridity, and slipped beneath its surface up to her neck. Her body relaxed and her mind began to follow.

She slid back up to a sitting position again, her shoulders breaking the watery surface, and laid her head back against the pillow on the edge of the tub. The gentle waves swirled and surged around her, caressing her skin and lapping lightly at her breasts. She smiled, enjoying the tickling sensation as the heat of the water, then the coolness of the air, alternated against her upper body as the undulations came and went. Her nipples, normally pale pink as the inside of a seashell, warmed in the water and the sensation, and darkened to a deep rose.

Rhapsody sighed as the water continued to kiss her, and the porcelain skin rippled in tiny goosebumps. She settled a little further into the tub and slid her feet up the edge, her knees cresting the surface. Then she felt a vibration, much like a current within the depths of the water, swirling between her knees and gently separating them. Her body began to tingle as the current swirled lower, stroking her hips and back and then settling between her legs, whirling and rushing. She felt the water lightly surge around her thighs, growing in its intensity, darting in and around her most sensitive spots. Her body was beginning to tremble, and she felt heat, internal this time, rushing to the places it was caressing.

The waves became more insistent, whirling and throbbing into areas of her that were growing more excited at each motion. It was as if the water was becoming solid and was seeking out places to pleasure her. Rhapsody felt a flush course through her body as the water created a need within her that was beginning to beg to be met.

'Ashe,' she said; the word caught in her throat and came out husky. 'Ashe, what are you doing?'

'Reading.'

She struggled to open her eyes and saw him, still leaning against the door, eyes still closed.

'Please,' she said as the water began to pulse in and out of her, 'Please stop it.' Her breath was growing shallow as she fought the growing excitement.

'Stop what?' He smiled, but did not open his eyes.

'This is turning into a sexual experience here,' Rhapsody said, trying but failing to maintain her composure. 'Now knock it off. Please.'

'You have something against sexual experiences?' he asked playfully, still not favoring her with a glance.

'Yes, if they're not with you.'

Finally Ashe sat up, opened his eyes and looked at her seriously. 'My love, that is me,' he said sincerely. 'I can feel you every bit as much as you can feel me, maybe even more so.'

'But that's the point,' she said as the solid water began to throb, making her desperate. 'It's not you, it's water, whether you can sense through it or not. You are the only thing I want touching me like this. Please, Ashe. Please don't do this.'

There was a desperation in her voice and on her face that he suddenly recognized; it was the same as the day at the Tar'afel River when she pleaded with him not to carry her across. He jumped to his feet and came to the edge of the tub; the vibrations in the water immediately ceased.

'I'm sorry, Rhapsody,' he said, watching her anxiety fade and calm return to her face. 'I certainly didn't mean to upset you.'

Rhapsody sat forward, drawing her knees up in front of her. 'I know,' she said; she reached out a wet hand and rested it on his cheek. 'I know, and it's not your fault; it's mine.'

Ashe wanted to take her in his arms, but he remembered his promise to wait for her invitation to be touched, and he held back. 'How can this be your fault? All you did was try and bathe. I'm sorry for being an idiot.'

Rhapsody looked into his eyes, and the confusion she saw there went to her heart. She drew his head forward and kissed him tenderly.

'No, *I'm* sorry, Ashe,' she said softly. 'You didn't do anything wrong. It's just that in the Past I've been used in unspeakable ways by men to vent their sexual excitement, and it was the worst part of my life. And the element of it I don't think I'll ever get over was being put on display and – ' Her eyes dropped as her voice broke for a moment.

'I was happy to think that I would never have to experience anything sexual again when I came here – that I could live a chaste existence and be so much better off. And then you came along, and brought it back into my life, for literally the first time in a positive way. I never would have believed that could happen. You made love to me for the first time, really. And making love with you is such an incredible thing, a beautiful thing, that I've tried very hard not to let anything in my past touch it; I don't want them associated at all. And through sheer force of will I've prevented myself from becoming inhibited in most ways – I'm sure you've noticed.'

For the first time, Ashe smiled, and Rhapsody caressed his face with fingers that were beginning to wrinkle from the warm water. 'There are just a few things that still remind me of those days. The truth is I don't mind anything you want to do with me as long as you are holding me in your arms, or at least on the same side of the room as me. It's probably screamingly ironic that someone like me turns out to be so old-fashioned sexually, but I can't help it. Every charm, every fantasy, anything I can do to please you is yours, but only because it's one of my ways of expressing that I love you. And it's my choice to give myself to you. I'm no one's toy any longer.'

He looked into the emerald eyes and it was as if he could see straight into her soul. The honesty of her heart and her words made him tremble.

'Rhapsody, if making love reminds you of something you dislike – '

'Don't say that,' she said quickly. 'That's not what I meant at all. I do want to make love with you, very much; so much so that when you said you were going to read instead I thought – well, never mind what I thought. It's just I want you to hold me, you yourself, not some disembodied force. There's a sort of communion that doesn't happen when one partner is on the other side of the room. Besides, it gives me a chance to reciprocate.' Her words made his face flush, and he gripped the sides of the tub, straining to keep his promise.

Rhapsody laughed as she watched his knuckles turn white. 'I do admire your forbearance,' she said, and leaned forward. She gave him a warm, wet kiss and as she did she unbound the tie of his bathrobe. 'Consider this your invitation,' she said, her eyes sparkling with mischief, and she moved back to the far end of the tub to allow him room.

Ashe dropped his robe and stepped into the tub. He knelt down and took hold of the edges of the tub and, holding his own body suspended over her, he leaned forward and gently kissed her.

She returned his kiss warmly, running her hands up his arms, feeling their strength. Her fingers traced the lines in his back, stroking the corded muscles as they held him hovering above her. As her tongue flickered into his mouth she wrapped her arms around him and pulled to draw him nearer. She rose out of the tub as unexpectedly he held his grip; he chuckled at the look of surprise that flashed across her face as her upper body and back were suddenly exposed to the colder air of the room.

'Show-off,' she scolded in mock annoyance. 'Very well, have it your way. Stay out here and freeze when it's lovely and warm in the water.'

'I'm just enjoying the pleasant effect the brisk air is having on you,' he said with a wicked smile, glancing at her chest. He laughed as her body grew suddenly rosier under his gaze, following the reddening glow up her abdomen as it crept into her face.

'Why, Rhapsody; you're blushing!'

'Don't tell anyone; you'll ruin my hard-bitten reputation,' she answered, laughing with him. She gave him another impatient pull.

Ashe's lips brushed her cheek, moving up the line of her face until they were just above her ear.

'Your secret is safe with me,' he whispered. Then his hands released their hold.

Rhapsody let loose a little cry as together they started to fall, but the water caught them as if it were a cushion, and her yelp turned into a laugh. Then Ashe felt the temperature of the water begin to rise until he was surrounded in a blissful heat. A silky leg brushed the back of his thigh and wound itself sensuously around his own, causing his skin to prickle into the same gooseflesh he was admiring on her a moment before.

Despite the warmth of the bath Ashe began to shiver and as he did, swirling waves swelled from the tub floor beneath Rhapsody and spun around her until they broke over her shoulders and toes, the few remaining areas of her outside the water. Ashe's hands followed the rhythm of the waves and flowed over her body, gliding upward from her back until they encircled her waist. Her own hands matched his movements, running up his back and over the broad shoulders to his strong neck, where they parted and came together again, cradling his face.

Ashe looked deep into her eyes, wordlessly communicating the depth of the love he felt for her that was rising now into a passion almost beyond his control. Then his own eyes closed and his lips sought hers, crushing them with an intensity that made her tremble beneath him.

Their kiss grew deeper as his hands followed the tremors down her body, enjoying the smoothness of her skin, his palms and fingertips taking in the sensation of the pleasure his touch was giving her and making him tremble in response. One of his hands slid around her back and drew her to him in a strong embrace as the other continued its downward path, tracing the contour of her breast, her side and waist, down the line of her hip and her upper leg, turning artlessly inward. The water surged forward, from her toes, past her knee and met his hand as it moved to the sensitive areas of her inner thigh and upward.

Their lips parted and Rhapsody began to gasp at his touch and the simultaneous pulsing of the water, her back arching as her hands grasped his shoulders again. Ashe's mouth moved to the hollow of her throat, caressing with fondness the area he had first come to desire when they met, tracing up the long slender neck until his lips touched her ear. In ancient languages he whispered his deepest feelings to her as his hands sought her pleasure, blending carnal delight with the expression of a passionate love the depth of which he could not measure. His own excitement grew as he watched her face transform into radiant happiness at the combination of his efforts to please her.

'I love you,' he whispered.

She echoed his words between broken breaths that grew shallower as his hands intensified their motions, his touch gently increasing in perfect rhythm with her desires. His lips returned to the hollow of her throat and then moved lower, lovingly caressing her breasts as they crested the water, warm with longing and arousal. Tiny whirlpools were left behind, tickling where his lips had been moments before as Ashe descended, brushing her slender abdomen with appreciative kisses.

His head disappeared beneath the waves that Rhapsody's trembling body was causing in the tub, tracing a careful line as he moved to the top of her thigh, then lower still. The soft musical sounds she was making became airy whimpers, and the water began gradually to warm, becoming almost too hot to bear. She gripped the edges of the tub, eyes closed, waiting for him to come up for air, but he did not stop his efforts until she cried out in delight, shivering beneath his hands that had closed around her waist again.

Warm, peaceful sensations began to take over her body as she languidly ran a hand over his hair, his head resting on her abdomen. Her eyes remained closed as he sat up slowly in the tub and positioned himself above her again, the warmth of his grin perceptible even without being seen.

At last his lips pressed gently against hers in a final loving kiss, and she opened her eyes. An inquisitive smile was on his face; his eyes, with their strange vertical slits, sparkled warmly in a way she was beginning to treasure. She returned his smile as she ran a lazy hand over his hair again. It was barely damp. He slipped his hand behind her and eased next to her in the wide tub, pulling her into his arms. She snuggled against his chest and sighed, feeling totally happy.

'Now, was that more of what you had in mind?' he asked playfully.

In response, Rhapsody caught him off guard, pulling him over on top of her, aware that his needs were still unmet.

'Actually, no,' she said, mischief making her eyes darken and flash like an emerald catching the light. 'But if you'd like, I'd be happy to show you what I meant.'

Rhapsody parted her legs, and as she wrapped them about her lover, Ashe let loose a deep sigh of pleasure. As always he was amazed at the depths of desire she stirred in him, and at the intensity of longing her touch brought forth. He closed his eyes and began to shiver uncontrollably as she drew him within her; when her warmth closed around him he clung to her, pleading with her softly not to let him fall too fast into the blissful oblivion that threatened to overtake him.

Her answers were tender, reassuring; she comforted him even as she pushed his excitement forward to new heights, assuring him of her love. Then she set about manifesting it physically, and Ashe felt her fire filling him, starting from where they were joined and flowing into the furthest reaches of his soul.

They rolled briefly beneath the surface of the water, Ashe turning in ways she found implausible, so that when they surfaced she lay astride and above him. The ribbon in her hair had been swept away, and as she broke the surface it fell like a golden waterfall around her shoulders. The sight of her reminded him of the legends he had heard long ago when sailing with the Sea Mages, of merrows and mermaids, and of sea nymphs, whose songs could enchant a man into losing his heart forever. He thought for a moment that perhaps this was what she was.

Ashe watched her face in awe, the feelings she was experiencing showing openly, changing like a kaleidoscope as the pleasure grew, transforming her beautiful countenance into something indescribable. She was lost in the joy of a man who loved her, and that man was able to see, clearly and without question, what it meant to her. And his thankfulness for that meaning was immeasurable.

With each caress, each motion, each touch of a wave, Rhapsody felt them moving together toward a dual ecstasy, one that would wildly satisfy their physical desires while, in a deeper, more profound way, comfort their wounded souls with the healing salve of trusting love that neither had believed in for many years. The heady, daredevil feeling of risk she felt in their earliest moments of exploration had given way as each barrier disappeared, and the sickening reminders of how far she had gone past the point of no return were fading away. Even the knowledge of the temporary nature of their relationship, the danger of what was coming, the lack of future in it all no longer dampened the happiness they were discovering, layer by layer, together.

And in that moment, as he made love to her with his body, and his soul, and his words, and even the water around them, Rhapsody lost forever her fear of that part of his nature that was alien to her, the strange dragonesque part, and the power it held over the elements. It was just another piece of him to be cherished, along with the rest. The dragon in him was no different than the music in her; it was something powerful that made him special. And as she sought to please the man she loved, she wanted to make that part of him happy as well.

She took his hands in her own and guided them through her hair, knowing how that excited the dragon, and as she drew them over her body she let him envelop her, wrapping herself up in him. Ashe began to tremble violently; she knew she was reaching both parts of his nature, and the knowledge mixed with the sweet excitement that his efforts were causing in her, pushing their lovemaking toward a culmination that threatened to consume them both.

Rhapsody closed her eyes as the waters of the tub surged around them, caressing her back. She could feel a tingling warmth that started in her fingers and toes begin to move inward, building in intensity; she knew when it reached her center there would be an explosion. She clung to Ashe, who was in the midst of his own battle for dominion over the moment; he was losing. She opened her eyes and studied his face. It was enthralled but pensive, in the struggle to maintain control.

'You're holding back,' she scolded gently between breaths. 'Let go.'

His eyes closed in response, and he shook his head slightly.

Rhapsody was at the edge of a realm she had no desire to enter alone.

She slowed the delicious rocking slightly, and Ashe's hands gripped her waist tighter. 'Please,' she whispered. 'I'm not going without you. Let go.'

He did. The waves began to churn with vibrancy like a raging river, rapids tumbling over themselves as the rhythm of their movements increased. The water roared white with the force of their passion, sloshing over the edges of the tub and flooding the floor. The currents in the tub, responding to his rapture, crashed over Rhapsody like waves against the rocks on a shoreline. Even the air of Elysian took on an electric hum, and in the distance she was vaguely aware that the musical sounds of the waterfall had been replaced by a raging torrent. The fire on the hearth in the next room leapt and roared in response.

She had no idea how long the pleasure actually lasted, but it seemed almost long enough to erase a lifetime of sorrow. Finally fire and water melded in ecstatic release, and they cried out together as the waves broke over them, submerging them in froth.

After a moment Rhapsody broke the surface again, and put her head down on Ashe's chest as it rose from the water. She gasped for breath, and caressed his shoulder as he held her tightly in his arms. The waters, still hot but now calm, had drenched the floor, and through her weary delight Rhapsody was glad for the marble tiles.

They lay in the tub for a long time without speaking until the water finally grew tepid. Ashe kissed her forehead and looked down at her, his heart in his eyes.

'You all right? Didn't breathe in any water, did you?'

A long sigh escaped her, and she turned to look at him, smiling. Her eyes shone up at him like starlight reflected on the water. Ashe felt his throat tighten.

'Amariel,' he said softly to her, in the language of her childhood. 'Merei Aria. Evet hira, Rhapsody.' *Star of the Sea; I have found my guiding star. It is you, Rhapsody.* Her eyes twinkled; his idiomatic usage was perfect.

'What a romantic thing to say.'

He smiled at her. 'I guess you've made me a romantic. What a feat.'

Rhapsody laughed and leaned up to kiss him. 'A romantic dragon. Isn't that a contradiction in terms?'

'Yes.' His face began to shine. 'Do you love me anyway?'

She looked seriously at him and spoke, using her ability as a Namer for declaring the truth. 'Always.'

He drew her closer, kissing the top of her head. 'Aria,' he whispered again. And from that moment on Aria became his special name for her, the name he used in the most intimate moments and as an expression of a love that no other language or image could approximate.

Grunthor waited impatiently in the afternoon sun at the edge of Kraldurge's guardian rocks, listening to the howl of the wind as it whined through the fanglike formations. He had come in answer to Rhapsody's call, and was growing more frantic by the moment, wondering where she was. The message she had sent him on the wind had contained no hint of fear or panic, just a simple request, amplified out through the gazebo, to meet her in the meadow above Elysian.

At last he could see her coming out of the shadows, wrapped in her familiar cloak, despite the sweltering summer heat.

'About time you checked in, Duchess,' Grunthor groused as she approached. 'If one more day had passed, I would have been down there with my entire elite regiment.' He swept her into his arms and held her tightly, feeling the panic and annoyance drain out of him like water through gravel. 'You all right?'

'I'm fine, Grunthor,' Rhapsody answered, laughing as he put her down again. 'In fact, I'm better than fine.'

Grunthor eyed her suspiciously. 'And why is that, exactly?' he demanded, noting her glowing countenance and gleaming hair, unbound from its ever-present black ribbon. Before she could answer, he held up a massive hand. 'Ah. Never mind. Please don't say it, miss.'

The light in her face diminished a little. 'Why?'

'Just don't, please,' said the sergeant simply. He sighed deeply. What she intended to say was as clear as glass to him. What he feared would happen had come to pass. A dragon had taken her as its treasure, just not the one he had believed would.

He thought about how Achmed would react, and shuddered. Grunthor looked away from her face, now wreathed in a puzzled frown, and off into the sunlit crags of the Teeth, their rocky trails green in the fervent bloom of high summer. 'You're not in any trouble then, or need any help, do you?' he asked finally.

'No, of course not,' Rhapsody said falteringly: 'I would have called for you right away had that been the case.' She tried to swallow the knot in her throat that his reaction had formed. She reached up and touched his broad face, turning it gently back toward her. When the amber eyes met hers there was great sadness in them, but his face was set in his standard mask of nonchalance.

'I thought you wanted me to be happy, Grunthor,' she said softly.

Grunthor looked down at her thoughtfully. 'I do, miss. More than anythin'.'

'Then can't you be happy for me?'

The giant turned away again and stared off into the tallest crags. Once they had seemed insurmountable; now the Bolg scaled them regularly, maintaining the ancient ventilation systems, rebuilding the Cymrian observatory. Everything that had once seemed so distant now seemed within easy reach. The irony tasted bitter in his mouth.

'I'll do my level best, miss,' he said at last. 'Now, if that was all, I need to be on my way. I'm off on a scouting mission to the deep Realms. If you need me, I'll be back in a fortnight or so.'

'Wait,' Rhapsody said, fumbling inside her cloak. 'There is something you can do for me, if you're willing.' She drew forth a folded piece of parchment, carefully sealed, and handed it to him. 'This is for Jo. I wanted to explain – what has come to pass, and give her a chance to adjust to the situation.' She wiped a bead of sweat from her brow. 'Jo has – a fondness for Ashe, and I want to be sensitive to her feelings,' she added awkwardly. 'Will you make sure she gets it, please, Grunthor? Before you go, if possible? I want to give her as much time as possible.' The giant Sergeant nodded, tucking the letter inside his doublet. 'And let Achmed know as well?'

Grunthor nodded again, stone-faced. It was clear by the lightness of her tone, and her consideration of the task as an afterthought, that she had no idea of the difficulty of what she was asking. For the first time since he had known the Firbolg king, he would have to struggle to find words. 'When are you comin' round again?'

'I thought I'd wait for a few weeks, give Jo a little time,' she said. 'I'll try and coordinate my return with yours. Then I want to sit down with you and Achmed and talk about going after the Rakshas.'

Grunthor ran a finger under the neck of his jerkin. 'All right, miss. Now, I need to be off.' He patted her head clumsily with his enormous hand, then pulled her close in an unwieldy embrace.

'Are you all right, Grunthor? You look tired, haggard.'

'Not been sleepin' too well at that,' the giant answered. 'Nightmares; somethin' comin' out of the darkness. Can't put a face on it yet. Now I got an idea what you've been sufferin' all this time, miss.' He sighed deeply, and gave her a final squeeze. 'You be careful, eh? And let our misty friend know if he's not a gentleman, he'll be answerin' to me.'

Rhapsody smiled within the depths of his armor. 'I'll do that,' she said, then pulled back and kissed the giant's hidelike cheek. 'Give my love to the others, and to my grandchildren.'

Grunthor squeezed her shoulder, then turned and left the windy meadow, now blooming in bright colors of heartsease, flowers Rhapsody had planted there at winter's end. Blossoms of condolence, often given to mourners or planted on graves and battlefields, they did little to gladden either of the hearts that had stood for a moment within their glorious panorama.

The ring of the Patriarchy came into its power on the night of Summer's midpoint. It was a night of great significance in both of their traditions, so Rhapsody and Ashe were glad to be able to observe it together. They had camped out on the heath, Ashe waiting to perform the rites of the religion his father led, Rhapsody observing the ceremonies that the Lirin held sacred. Afterward they lay in a patch of sweet woodruff and watched the night sky, her head on his shoulder, wordlessly. A shower of shooting stars passed overhead, and a moment later Rhapsody could feel the muscles in Ashe's chest stiffen beneath her. She sat up and looked down at him.

'What's the matter?'

He was staring at his hand, a strange look coming over his face. 'Fascinating,' he murmured.

'What?'

'Well, I was just thinking about a Gwadd chemist, First Generation, an apothecary by the name of Quigley, reputed to know the secret to every medicinal tonic and potion ever mixed, primarily because he invented most of them. I know his history, and the story of his trip with the First Fleet – Gwadd are not generally seafarers and the voyage was terrifying to him. In spite of that, he developed an herbal remedy for seasickness from dried seaweed in the course of the journey. I was thinking what a marvelous person that would be for you to meet.' Rhapsody nodded. 'Then I realized I have no idea how I know any of this.'

'How very strange.'

'Yes, but not as strange as the thoughts I was having about the Mountain Knives. They are a band of stout, strong men, Nain, I suppose, who are so gifted with their blades that they can eviscerate an entire army before the soldiers even know it. One legion of their victims kept traveling for a mile before they felt apart, literally. They are pig-headed and merry, and when they are victorious they celebrate with a war dance and ear-splitting, hooting cries, even if they are still in imminent danger. Also First Generation; also a thought I had never had until a moment ago.'

'And you think it has something to do with the ring?' Her comment became moot a moment later when the white stone in the center began to gleam, and a broad smile crept over Ashe's face.

'I know it does. Rhapsody, this is marvelous. I suddenly have knowledge of all the living First Generationers, where they are, what they are like, even whether they are loyal to the Cymrian cause or not. There are some marvelous people still alive, Singers, healers, nobles and peasants, priests and pirates, and I know of them all. I wonder if the Patriarch had this knowledge, too.'

'I doubt it,' she said. 'He told me it was a ring of wisdom, and it gave him the knowledge to perform the duties of his office well. I imagine it is telling you these things because the office you will hold is that of Lord Cymrian, and it is giving you information you might need in that capacity. It must believe you're the best candidate.'

'How disappointing.'

'Stop that; you're insulting my liege lord.' She bent and kissed him. Then a thought occurred to her. 'What about leadership? Does it give you any inkling as to who would be a good set of counselors, or who would make a good Viceroy?' He nodded.

'It's as though, for those reasons only, I can judge any of their worthiness, not as people, but as leaders.' Rhapsody drew her knees to her chest and grew quiet. Ashe noticed. 'What, Aria? What's wrong?'

'Nothing's wrong,' she answered, looking at the ground. 'What about potential candidates for the Lady Cymrian? Any First Generationers alive that qualify?'

Ashe looked at her seriously, and turned his attention to her question. 'Well, as a matter of fact, there are several.'

Rhapsody looked up at him and smiled slightly. 'Well, that's good, anyway. It gives you a group to choose from, so you should have no trouble picking someone you'll be happy with.'

'Not really,' Ashe answered. 'There is only one obvious choice, someone of a nobility that would be unquestioned among the Cymrians. She's also someone of great wisdom and accomplishment; both the Cymrians and I would be lucky to have her as our Lady.'

'Well, that sounds promising,' Rhapsody said, smiling. 'I'm glad to know you will be happy in your choice of wife.'

'First of all, the Lady Cymrian doesn't have to be my wife. And even if it makes sense to do it that way, just because I choose her, and ask her, doesn't mean she'll have me, Rhapsody. Cymrians are strange like that. She may be reluctant; in fact, I know she is. If she had wanted to, she could have taken the title on her own. She's had the power at her disposal to do so for some time.'

Rhapsody leaned over and kissed him. 'I have no doubt that she will accept you, Ashe. You said she was someone of great wisdom. Anyone who would turn you down would have to be a fool.'

'I hope you're right.' He felt her grow colder beside him, as if her internal fire was burning down a little, and he drew her back into his arms to warm her. 'Are you all right?'

'I'm fine,' she said shortly. 'But I'm cold; who would have believed it on Midsummer's Night? Can we go in now?'

'Of course,' Ashe said. He stood as she did and offered her his hand. 'There's a fireplace waiting for us back in Elysian that holds a special place in my heart. Since this is a night of reflection and remembrance, why don't we go relive the first memory we made there?'

She nodded and took his hand, and together they made their way back underground to Elysian in the dark.

41

There was a coldness to the stone within the corridors of the Cauldron that the torches, spaced in wall sconces every ten feet, could not dispel. It was an old chill, one that had been in the granite since before the Firbolg had taken the mountain, one that suited the history made here. It was a negative place, and dreary. Footsteps echoed for a fragment of a second and then were swallowed up by the inert stone. It was somewhat like walking inside a coffin.

Ashe could not remember the last time he had been in such a bad mood. For close to three weeks he had lived in unfettered bliss, alone and undisturbed with Rhapsody in the paradise she had made in Elysian just by being there. He had never known such simple joys – cooking inventive meals for each other, swimming by filtered moonlight in the crystalline lake, watching her sew or mend weapons in the firelight, helping her hang laundry, singing with her, brushing her hair, making love, making memories – and he deeply resented being snapped back to the reality that deprived him of even a moment alone with her. His clear understanding of the long-term need of this visit to the Cauldron did nothing to assuage this annoyance.

By mutual unspoken agreement they had not discussed the Past – both of them knew it was painful ground for the other and risked breaking the spell of their magical hideaway. For the same reason they had not discussed the Future, either. But they had agreed to this being the day that their request would be put before Achmed, and so here he was, with a headache throbbing behind his eyes, striding down the dingy corridors of the Firbolg seat of power, to the council room behind the Great Hall where Rhapsody's odious companions would meet them.

Rhapsody, walking beside him, sensed his frame of mind and gave his hand a supportive squeeze. She was dressed for work again in her traveling outfit – the plain white linen shirt, the soft brown pants tucked into high, sturdy bootleggings tied with rawhide – and, of course, the infernal cloak. He had found good reasons to get her to undress twice already that morning, but still the black ribbon had made its way back into her hair, neatly binding the shining waterfall into a demure fall. The exquisite colorful clothes had been returned to the cedar closet in favor of the disguise she wore to hide herself from the world.

This was the way he had first seen her, and he had lost his heart to her utterly, despite her being camouflaged by the plain costume. But now, having seen her true self revealed, he could barely stand to see her forced back into hiding. The jubilance she exhibited in being allowed to walk around in Elysian, free of obscurement, hair flowing without restrictions, in any garment of her choosing made his heart glad in many ways, and he hurt for her to see that freedom taken away.

But she seemed to be taking it all in stride, smiling at him, clasping his hand, hurrying him along to a meeting with the last people in the world he wanted to see.

The council room behind the Great Hall held a large, roughhewn wooden table made smooth by centuries of use. On the walls hung a few ancient tapestries, smelling of rot and darkened beyond recognition by smoke and time. There was a firepit taking up most of the far wall, ablaze with a foul-smelling inferno that cast the only light in the room; despite the lack of ambient illumination, the lanterns would not be lit until nightfall.

As they entered the room, Grunthor hopped up from his massive chair, clicked his heels and made a gracious bow in Rhapsody's direction. She ran to him and embraced him while Ashe stood in amazement that something that big could move so gracefully. Then his eyes scanned the rest of the room.

Achmed remained seated, one foot propped on the table, reading from a sheaf of bound yellowed vellum. He did not look up as they came in.

Rhapsody walked behind the Firbolg king and bent down to kiss the top of his cloaked head. Then she glanced around the room, a look of displeasure taking hold. Her nose wrinkled up and she shook her head in disgust.

'Gods, Achmed, what are you burning? Never mind – I don't want to know.' She set her pack on the table and rifled through it, pulling out an amber glass bottle of sweet flag boiled in vanilla-anise oil and a chamois pouch folded into several different compartments. From one of the middle folds she extracted some dried spices mixed with flakes of cedarwood and, squinting to avoid the rancid smoke, tossed them on the fire, followed by a hefty splash from the bottle. Instantly the putrid smell dispersed and was replaced by a fresh, sweet odor that dissipated into neutrality within a moment.

'Oh, how lovely,' said Grunthor. 'Now we can all smell like a field of daisies. I'm sure the troops will love it. Thank you, my dear.'

Rhapsody's expression was growing more pained as she turned in a circle, surveying the room with distaste.

'You didn't do *anything* to redecorate, did you? What happened to the silk tapestries I had sent from Bethe Corbair?'

'We used them to make the floor of the stable quieter,' said Achmed, still reading. 'The horses thank you.'

'Oh, and I buried one of my favorite lieutenants in one,' added Grunthor helpfully. 'His widow was genuinely touched.'

Ashe struggled to contain his amusement. Whatever problems Rhapsody's friends posed, it could not be denied that the relationship between the three of them certainly made for good entertainment. Still, his head ached and he couldn't wait to get back to Elysian with her, alone. He coughed politely.

'Oh, hallo, Ashe,' said Grunthor. 'You're here too?'

'It apparently couldn't be helped,' Achmed said to Grunthor. 'If you're ill, Ashe, I can get you a leech.'

'That won't be necessary, thank you,' said Ashe.

'Well, there's the little miss,' said Grunthor in a jolly tone as Jo came into the council room. 'Gives us a kiss, darlin'.'

Jo complied, then she and Rhapsody hurried to each other and embraced warmly.

'What's been going on?' Jo asked as Rhapsody put an arm around her waist and walked to the table. 'Where have you been?'

Rhapsody looked puzzled. 'What do you mean? Didn't you get my letter?'

'Letter?'

For the first time Achmed looked up, in the direction of Grunthor.

'Uhhhhrrrumph.' Grunthor cleared his throat awkwardly, his bruise-colored skin flushing suddenly.

Rhapsody turned to Grunthor with an incredulous look. 'Uhhhhrrrumph? What do you mean, uhhhhrrrumph? You didn't give her my letter?'

'Let's just say I've been keepin' it next to my heart,' the giant Firbolg replied sheepishly as he removed the folded parchment from his breast pocket.

'I'm so sorry, Jo,' Rhapsody said, looking daggers at Grunthor. 'No wonder you're confused.'

She glanced at Ashe, and her look spoke volumes. They had worked on the letter together endlessly, trying to explain their new relationship in a way that Jo could accept, in language simple enough for her to read, endeavoring not to hurt her feelings. The intervening weeks had been carefully timed to allow her adequate opportunity to adjust. All their good intentions had obviously just gone to smash.

Jo took the letter and began to read it. Her brows furrowed together after a moment, and Rhapsody tried to intervene.

'Here, Jo, why don't you give that to me? There's really no need for a letter now that I'm here; we can just go and talk. Gentlemen, we'll be back in a – '

Jo held up her hand suddenly and Rhapsody fell silent. The girl's sallow countenance grew florid and she looked around the room wildly. Realization, then humiliation, crawled over her face as she absorbed the first blow, then the understanding that her friends had all known about it and had been worried about her reaction. The second embarrassment seemed much greater.

Rhapsody could see that she was mortified, and tried to put her arm around her again. With a violence that almost knocked her down, Jo broke free and ran from the council room in tears.

The four stared at each other in helpless silence. Then Rhapsody spoke, a stricken look on her face.

'I have to go after her.'

'No, let me,' said Ashe gently. 'It's my fault for not talking to her sooner; besides, you three will probably be better off meeting without me anyway.'

'You're a wise man,' said Grunthor.

'Let's not get carried away,' said Achmed.

Ashe kissed Rhapsody's hand, and she touched his shoulder in a final thought. 'Don't pursue her too excessively,' she said, looking up into his hood. 'She might not want to be found, and she may need her privacy right now. And please – don't use your dragon senses or anything that might upset Achmed. He's sensitive to that sort of thing.'

'As you wish,' he answered, and was gone.

Grunthor took one look at Rhapsody's scowl as she turned from the door. 'It's probably best if you talk for both of us, sir,' he said nervously. 'I'd agree to about anythin' she wants just to get that look off her face.'

42

Highgrass and heather bent low in supplication before the twisting wind that seared the steppes and moaned through the canyons of the Teeth. It laid low the brushy scrub that clung to the desolate bluff, desperately trying but failing to infuse the jagged land with life. The late afternoon sun was baptizing the rocky crags of Ylorc in a blood-red light, casting inverted mountains of shadow onto the valley ridges and moraines.

Jo was oblivious to the anguished dance of the landscape, immune to the buffeting of the wind, as she made her way, stumbling, crawling, to the open plain at the top of the world. When she reached the apex of the ravine she stopped to catch her breath, resting her perspiring head on raw hands that held fast to the rocky outcroppings of the cliff. Then she pulled herself up over the precipice and staggered forward until she reached the first place on the heath where the ground felt solid. Still panting, she put her hands on her hips and turned in a circle, surveying the wasteland behind her and the beginning of the moor that led to the deeper, hidden realm of the Firbolg.

Night was beginning to set in; at the eastern horizon she saw a star appear and vanish behind the gauze of clouds riding the wind across the blackening sky. With the coming of the night came a wintry wind, strange in the waning days of summer, but not unknown in the Teeth. The endless expanse of mountains loomed large around and below her, circling her world in a dismal embrace. Jo turned toward the setting sun and willed it hurry. In darkness the only things visible would be the sky and the flat land; its clawlike underbelly of crags and fissures would disappear like a forgotten nightmare. Perhaps if she stayed here long enough she could disappear with it.

'Why are you out here?'

Jo whirled around to see the twilight advancing on the cloaked figure behind her. The wind flapped at his mantle and hood, revealing momentary glimpses of the familiar coppery hair and sea-blue eyes, as well as a look of sympathy and concern.

A guttural sound of frustrated fury tore loose from Jo. 'Gods, not you! Damn! Get out of here, Ashe! Leave me alone!'

He had to sprint to catch up with her, and grabbed her arm as she made a blind dash back in the direction of the cliff. 'Wait! Please wait. Whatever I did to upset you, I'm sorry. Please don't run off. Talk to me. Please.'

Jo wrenched her arm loose from his grip and glared at him. 'Can't you just leave me alone? I don't want to talk to you. Go away!'

Even beneath the hood Jo could see the hurt look cross his face. He took a step back and dropped his arms to his sides, adopting a posture that would not threaten her. 'All right. I'm sorry. I'll go if you want me to. But for goodness sake, don't run over the edge for nothing. I was trying to help, not cause you to plummet to your death.'

Jo waited in sullen silence for him to leave, but instead he stood and watched her.

'Well? I'm waiting. Go away.'

The wind shrieked across the heath and around them. Jo had to struggle to keep upright. His reply was nearly lost in its howl.

'I'm sorry. I can't leave you alone out here. It isn't safe.'

Rage contorted her face again. 'I don't need your help. I can take care of myself.'

'I know that. But you don't have to. Friends watch each other's backs, don't they? We are still friends, aren't we?'

Jo turned back toward the setting sun. It was slipping over the outermost rim of the Teeth, casting its final rays in momentary brilliance before disappearing. To Jo it looked like the end of the world.

'If you were my friend, Ashe, you would leave me alone and not try to force me back where I don't want to be.'

He walked around her until he was facing her again. 'I would never force you to do anything, and I did not say you had to go anywhere.' He watched her anger cool a few degrees as she looked at him quizzically. 'I just don't want to you to be alone. I'll stay here with you. As long as you need me to. All night, if necessary.'

Jo felt her ire evaporate, and the old annoying longing flooded back. She struggled to keep it at bay, but it was all she could do to keep her feelings from showing on her face. 'What about Rhapsody?'

'What about Rhapsody?' he repeated.

'Well, won't she be wondering where you are?'

'Why would she?'

'Oh, I don't know; that's the funny thing about lovers. They have a tendency to expect you to be with them.'

Beneath the hood she could see him smile. 'Don't worry about Rhapsody. She'll be fine. She would want me here with you.'

Rhapsody came back to the large table around which her companions sat and took a chair.

'I thought we agreed you would leave your pets behind when you came to visit,' said Achmed, still not looking up from his reading.

Rhapsody ignored the slight. 'Do you already know why I'm here? Can we skip the formalities and go straight to the answer?'

Amusement crossed the Firbolg king's face, and he stared up at the ceiling. 'Let's see, why are you here? The fine wine, the excellent service, the ambiance – '

Rhapsody sighed. 'All right. Since you're going to make this difficult, let's start over. I've come to ask, as you damn well know, for your help in killing the Rakshas.'

Achmed put down his papers. 'For all you damn well know, it could have just left the room.'

'No,' said Rhapsody. 'It's a separate entity; it just looks like Ashe. Please, Achmed, don't torture me.'

Grunthor's face lit up. 'There you go; I knew she liked me best. Oh, can I do it, please, sir? I can be back in a jiffy with my thumb screws.'

Rhapsody glared at him. 'You shut up. I'm still not speaking to you.' The jocular look on the monstrous face turned into one of embarrassment.

Achmed's smile was wry. 'Funny about that. Refusing to talk is what torture is designed to change. If you're not speaking, I guess we really aren't torturing you.'

'No, you're doing a mighty fine job of it. Please, will you help me? I don't want Ashe to hunt it. If it finds him, the F'dor will know where he is, and try to take the rest of his soul. The demon has no hold on us; we can probably kill the Rakshas easily of we work together. This has been on our list to do since the House of Remembrance, anyway. I just want to make it a priority. Please. Help me kill the Rakshas.'

Achmed leaned back in his chair and sighed. 'All right, let's review. Do you know for certain where it is, or who it is, or what it is?'

'Where it is, no. But I brought back some dried blood from the wounds it took in our combat. The Rakshas was made from the F'dor's blood, and it's from the old world. I thought you might be able to use the blood to track it.' Achmed didn't respond. 'Who it is, you know this already. What you really mean is who it's not – it's not Ashe, Achmed. I'm sure of it.'

'How can you be so sure?' Grunthor asked.

'Do you want the list, or will you just take my word for it?'

Achmed and Grunthor glanced at each other. 'Give us the list.'

'Well, let's see. Ashe has the eyes of a dragon. They are very different from the Rakshas's – his pupils are slit vertically, while the Rakshas's are round, the same as ours.'

'Why would that be? I thought they were identical.'

Rhapsody struggled to keep calm beneath the jeering tone in Achmed's voice. 'The piece of Ashe's soul was ripped from him when the dragon within his blood was still dormant. When the Lord and Lady Rowan put the piece of a star in his chest, that pure, unbridled elemental power brought the dragon nature out, making it more dominant. I suspect his eyes were normal, like Llauron's, before he was wounded.'

'He told you this?'

'No,' Rhapsody admitted. 'We don't talk about the Past.'

'No? You talk about the Future, then?'

'Not really. That's a painful subject, too; we don't have one together.'

'Well, that's a relief.'

'I don't think so,' Grunthor interjected merrily. 'If they're not talking much, what do you think they're doin'?' Rhapsody's brow blackened with anger, and he hurried to deflect the coming assault. 'Is that the whole list? What else is different about them?'

'Well, when I fought the Rakshas I cut off one of its thumbs. Ashe has both his thumbs – '

'He's all thumbs. He probably had an extra. That proves nothing.'

Rhapsody had had enough. 'Look, this is stupid. If you don't want to help me, I'll go after it myself.' She pushed back the heavy chair and rose to leave.

'I would have to object to that, Your Ladyship,' said Grunthor gently. 'No disrespect intended, but I think he might just boot your charmin' little arse if you're alone.'

'Never mind.' She stepped around the chair and pushed it up to the table.

'Show me its blood.'

Rhapsody regarded Achmed for a moment, trying to gauge his intent. Finally she reached into her pack and pulled forth the clothes she had worn in Sepulvarta when she and the Rakshas fought in the basilica. They were soaked in a considerable amount of blood, though much of it had been obliterated by burned patches where it had ignited on contact.

Grunthor sat forward, looking impressed. 'Is that all from him?' She nodded. 'Well, then, I stand corrected; actually, I sit corrected. You must have been payin' attention to the sword lessons, darlin'.'

Achmed turned the garments over in his hands, concentrating on the stains. Rhapsody could feel a strange vibration emit from him, one she did not remember feeling before. There was a scratchiness to it, not unlike the sound a cricket made in the dark. Finally he looked up at her again.

'Do you have any of Ashe's blood?'

'No.'

'I could get some,' Grunthor offered helpfully.

'No. That's two, Grunthor. One more and you're out of the will.'

Achmed looked at Rhapsody for a few moments. Finally he spoke.

'If I help you kill the Rakshas, can I expect your help in addressing whatever needs to be done in the Colony?'

She eyed him seriously. 'You can expect it even if you don't.'

'You may be required to fight.'

'I know.'

The Firbolg king nodded. 'We'll make plans for the first day of winter, then.'

Rhapsody's face began to glow. 'You'll do it, then? You'll help Ashe? Help me kill the Rakshas?'

'Yes. No. And yes,' Achmed stated flatly. 'I told you before, my help is only for you. I'm also willing to do this because it needs to be done. Now get the map.'

The only sound on the heath for the longest time was the unrelenting whine of the wind. Jo sat in staunch silence, casting the occasional sidelong glance at her uninvited chaperone, who sat patiently at a respectful distance, watching her. The awkwardness and embarrassment she felt was making it impossible to maintain her anger, and finally she worked up the courage to address him civilly.

'Look,' she said, trying to sound like an adult, 'why don't you just go back to the meeting? I promise to go inside in a few minutes.'

His answer was nearly lost in the wail across the billowing highgrass. 'Nope.'

Jo sprang to her feet. 'Damn you, Ashe, I'm not a child! I have been taking care of myself my whole life; poor, stupid Jo doesn't need you to protect her from the dark! You're probably missing something important. Just go.'

She watched him rise and begin to walk toward her, and her knees turned to water. As much as she wanted to hate him, at that moment all she could feel was the same wondrous, sickening cramp in her stomach that she had felt the first time she'd seen him in Bethe Corbair. She wanted to run from him, too, but she stood frozen to the spot as he stopped in front of her.

His voice was gentle as he reached out and brushed the whipping strands of hair out of her eyes. 'What could possibly be more important than making sure you're safe?'

'How about convincing Achmed to help Rhapsody kill the Rakshas?'

Jo couldn't see the his reaction, but the tone of his answer was solemn. 'Achmed will do whatever he thinks is in his best interest, regardless of anything I might say. Besides, being with you is more important to me.'

Her question slipped out before she could stop it. 'Why?'

He came a little closer, and his fingers moved from the flying strands of hair to caress her cheek. They stood, looking at each other, and Jo thought she could see the blue eyes twinkle inside the dark hood, like stars in the now-black sky above. There was a warmth in his voice that made her skin tingle.

'Do you really need to ask me that, Jo?'

The swirling wind spun all around her, and the blood rushed from Jo's head, leaving her dizzy. The revulsion she felt at the craving that had descended on her body quickly succumbed to the craving itself, and she dropped her eyes in the useless hope that they would not betray her. She could feel the blood pounding in places she wished it wouldn't.

'Let's go back,' she said.

'Not yet; tarry a moment,' he replied, and his hand moved from her cheek to her chin. He lifted her face, and with the other hand took hold of his hood.

Jo's voice was a panicked whisper. 'I want to go in now.'

'So do I,' he said, and pulled back the hood. Even in the dark, the features that had originally stolen her heart – hair the color of burnished copper, eyes as blue as the center of the sky – had the same effect on her now. They were set in a face more handsome than even her insistent dreams had imagined. Jo felt her stomach melt, and the flesh between her legs began to burn with unwelcome desire. She watched, half in giddiness, half in horror, as he untied the mantle of his cloak and threw it on the ground. It was lined with brindled fur, and with the toe of his boot he spread it out until it covered the patchy grass next to them.

Jo began to shake. 'Ashe, what are you doing?'

His second hand joined the first at her cheek, and he cradled her face as his eyes, even more beautiful in the dark than she had remembered, roamed over her. 'Nothing that you don't want,' he said, smiling down at her, his voice as warm as a crackling fire. 'I told you I would never force you to do anything, didn't I, Jo?'

'Yes,' she whispered weakly.

'And I meant every word, Jo. I would never compromise you in any way.' His lips lightly brushed her mouth, his tongue teasing the rim of her lips. 'You do believe me, don't you, Jo?'

Her reply was barely audible. 'Yes.'

'I thought so. I'm glad you trust me,' he said, and then his lips took hers deeply, passionately – almost harshly.

The heat of his kiss made Jo tremble violently. A rush of ardor surged up from the depths of her soul, from painful places that had been stunted by the life she had led, seeking solace, seeking acceptance. Her body grew clammy as the biting wind chilled the places soaked with sweat, and she wrapped her arms around his neck, returning his kiss, beseeching his body for warmth. He pulled her closer, and the crush of her body to his made Jo suddenly, painfully aware of the intensity of his arousal, and the disproportionate amount of strength between them.

Now she was frightened. But more than that, she was jolted by the sudden thought of Rhapsody. With a sickening thud the reality of what was happening hit her, and she squirmed away, breaking free from his embrace.

'Gods, what are we *doing*?' she moaned. 'Ashe, please, let's go back now.' She wheeled around and started back toward the path to the Cauldron.

His hands closed on her shoulders from behind, gently but decisively. He held her stationary as his lips brushed her ear and cheek. His voice was warm and toneless above the howling wind.

'I'm sorry if I've displeased you, Jo,' he murmured, gently nuzzling her neck beneath the straw-colored hair. 'That was the last thing I wanted.' He turned her carefully around and looked down at her again.

There was a decided look of sympathy in his eyes – *perhaps that's what makes them look so much more human,* she thought. The brightness of his smile made her heart quiver again, and guilt fought with desire within her once more.

'You didn't,' she answered, haltingly. 'I just don't want to hurt Rhapsody.'

'Ah, yes, Rhapsody,' he said. 'She's lucky to have you for a friend, you know; being so concerned about her feelings. But who guards your feelings, Jo? Who appreciates you for all that is special about you?'

Jo hung her head. 'Don't make fun of me, Ashe.'

He knelt down on one knee before her and looked up at her face from below. 'I'm not – I swear I'm not. Why would you think that?'

'Because you know as well as I do that there is nothing special about me,' she replied fiercely, choking back tears.

'That's not true.'

'Really? How would you know? I hate to tell you this, but some of us don't throw power around like it was bread crumbs or carry swords of solid water; we don't smile and have flowers bloom at our feet. Some of us were born in a back alley and will die on a trash heap somewhere, and no one will notice.'

Tears were flowing freely now. He took her hand and kissed it. Her wet face stung as the frigid wind blasted through again, and he drew her down to the ground where he knelt and cradled her head against his chest.

'Jo, Jo, what's the matter with you? You are full of hidden treasures – you just have to be willing to let someone mine them.' Jo lifted her face, and he kissed her again. Desire won its battle and guilt was abandoned as she responded with all the want and hurt and need that had flooded her soul.

In the distance a wolf howled, a long, high, sustained lament that blended discordantly with the moaning of the wind. A pale moon rose, casting eerie white shadows over the swirling landscape. Jo felt the sensation of falling as he laid her down on the fur of his cloak. She opened her eyes and saw gleaming blue light reflecting back at her; she saw an eagerness in those eyes that unnerved her. But she was too far gone to care.

And then his hands were ripping at her vest and roughly pulling open her shirt. She heard an intake of breath and an exhale of admiration.

'You see, Jo – hidden treasures. Waiting for plunder.' She gasped as his mouth went to her breasts; its liquid warmth whirled around her nipples, drawing them into aching points as his hands moved to the laces of her pants. The force with which he tore them open exposed her suddenly to the cold wind, and, grabbing hold of his head, she clung to him and shivered as she welcomed the heat of his fingers between her legs.

His coarse exploration left her pulsing with unmet need as his hands set about unbinding his own trousers. She moaned aloud in frustration, surprising them both. He laughed, an unpleasant, barking laugh, and his mouth went to her abdomen and moved lower, his tongue tracing the line leading to where his fingers had been.

He pleasured her, almost brutally, for a moment as he pushed aside her clothing that remained in the way, then his mouth moved up her body again as he positioned himself over her. Jo opened her eyes as she felt his head rise above hers and looked into his face; the naked excitement in his expression had a tinge of cruelty in it that frightened her.

Jo began to panic as the wind whipped over their bodies again and she felt the sting of icy raindrops beginning to fall. She trembled, partly from longing, but more from fear, and began to cry out for him to stop. In response his lips moved from her breasts to her mouth, and his tongue delved into all the spaces there, swallowing her pleas and breathing heat back into her. Then she felt a far more intense heat, and pain, as he drove into her, erasing her virginity and making her one with him in frenetic motion. She clutched his back, her fingers turning white, and gave herself over to the ferocious waves of carnal indulgence mixed with agony as he came further and further inside her.

His lips left hers and he began to keen, a harsh, animal sound punctuating the rhythm of his movements, driving her insistently against the ground and the rocks beneath his cloak. Jo cried out as well, screaming his name over and over, praying for it to end and at the same time dreading that it would.

Through it all the wind of the mountaintop roared around them and over them, muting their guttural cries and carrying them, like the voices of seagulls, down into the valley and canyons below. And the Firbolg who heard them took to whatever shelter they could find, fearing the coming of demons.

And then, when Jo was beginning to think about praying for death, it was over in a rolling fireball of climatic fury. He lay above her, motionless, and she held fast to him until she could move on her own again. And as she lay there she felt a creeping sensation, starting from their point of physical connection, wending its way through her body and soul, wrapping tightly around her inner core like a vine growing up her spine and spreading tendrils throughout the whole of her. The feeling reached all the way into her skull and grew out through the bone like a shaft of hair, then it dissipated.

She began to shiver. As she did the wind died down to a barely perceptible breeze, and he raised his head and looked into her face. Any of the ugliness she had seen in passion was gone. He smiled at her, then kissed her gently.

'Are you all right?'

She nodded, unable to speak.

'Good.' He disengaged himself, rose slowly and began to lace up his trousers. 'You see, Jo, you are more than special; you are unique in the wide world. Now get dressed.'

As if in a dream Jo gathered the fragments of her shirt and fastened her torn trousers as best she could. She put on her vest with hands that trembled and watched as he shook the dirt from his cloak, drawing the mantle around his shoulders. Then he reached out and pulled her into his arms for a final embrace, carefully running a hand down the fall of her hair.

He walked her to the edge of the Cauldron, gave her a swift kiss on the head, and then sauntered off into the shadows of the Teeth. The darkness swallowed him up, and he was gone.

It wasn't until she was alone, aching in body and soul, back in her chambers in Ylorc that Jo realized she had no idea what his final words to her meant.

Merry laughter was coming from the council room behind the Great Hall as Ashe returned to the Cauldron; the scent of roast boar and spiced apples hung in the air. The lamps had been lit, and the pungent aroma of the food and sweet smell of the wood fire were tainted by the caustic odor of burning fat. Lantern light made the room shine like a beacon in the dreary hallways of the Cauldron.

Upon his entrance Rhapsody leapt from her seat and ran to him in welcome. She had changed from her traveling clothes into a long fitted gown of pale green silk, so he knew she had been celebrating. As he bent to kiss her his glance caught Achmed's gaze; there was a studied amusement in the surly eyes. He slid one arm around her waist and accepted the tankard proffered by Grunthor with the other hand.

'Good news, I take it?'

Achmed said nothing.

'Depends on how you look at it,' said Grunthor.

'Where's Jo?' asked Rhapsody.

Ashe looked around at the unlikely trio before returning his attention to Rhapsody. 'I couldn't find her,' he said.

He watched as the lovely face fell in disappointment, then clouded over in worry. 'Maybe I should go look for her,' she said, turning to Achmed.

'Leave her be, Your Ladyship,' said Grunthor, refilling his glass. 'If she'd wanted to be found, he would of found her. Perhaps she just needs a bit of time to get used to, well, things, you know?'

'Don't we all,' said Achmed.

Rhapsody was staring down into her glass, lost in thought. Ashe ran his hand gently down the fall of her hair, and she looked up at him and smiled. 'I guess you're right,' she said at last, then took Ashe's hand and led him to his seat at the table.

She pushed the crockery and silverware aside and showed him the large parchment field map they had been working on in his absence. 'Achmed and Grunthor have agreed to help us,' she said, smiling warmly at the two Firbolg. 'We're targeting the first day of winter.'

'That's wonderful. Thank you. Thank you both.'

'Please,' said Grunthor, 'Don't mention it.'

'Please,' added Achmed, 'Don't remind me.'

They laid their plans late into the night, amidst drinking, dining and joking banter. Outside the mountain the wind shrieked and raged, and the dark sky cried icy tears for no one in particular.

43

'Rhapsody, starlight shines through water all the time. It will be fine.'

Rhapsody looked at Ashe doubtfully. She was holding the sword near the surface of Elysian's lake, watching the flickering light sparkle on the surface of the water and cast bright shadows into the depths below.

'What if I extinguish it? Oelendra will hunt me down and kill me herself.'

Ashe laughed and kissed the top of her head. 'All right, if it's going to cause you so much worry, perhaps it's better if we don't do this.'

Rhapsody peered into the water. Not far off shore below the surface she could glimpse shimmering stalagmites rising from the floor of the lake, glowing as the radiance from Daystar Clarion touched them. They gleamed in soft hues of green and blue; she was sure they were the beginning of an underwater field of the spiked formations, probably left over from before the cavern filled with water. The picture had haunted her dreams at night, and as a result she had been stalking the shores of the lake all morning, trying to find a way to explore the depths in the darkness of the underground grotto.

It was Ashe who suggested she take her sword swimming with them. He had broken into merry laughter at her horrified reaction as she imagined the ancient weapon of champions sizzling as it touched the water, then being snuffed out forever. He had tried to explain to her about the tempering process of swords, about the unquenchable light that had been ingrained in the weapon, but he could see she still was uncertain. He drew her into his arms.

'Aria, you won't kill the sword, I promise. But if you are still concerned, let's do something else. There are any number of interesting places to explore down here.'

Rhapsody smiled. She loved the time they had spent discovering the hidden treasures of Elysian. They had crawled through underground caves full of beautiful purple crystal formations, the light of Daystar Clarion illuminating the walls into feverish iridescence; it made the two of them seem trapped within a faceted gemstone.

Together they traced the hidden source of the stream that formed the waterfall and followed it to where it swelled through the rock. They had stepped into the stream and ridden it over the edge, plummeting into the lake below. And they had found a small underground meadow with rock walls surrounding it, rising a thousand feet or more to the open sky above, like a subterranean version of the one inside the guardian walls of Kraldurge. It was the perfect place to picnic in the sunlight, and to watch the stars at night. And to make love.

'No,' she said decisively. 'I want to see this place, and if you're sure it won't hurt the sword, I'll trust you.' She stuck the tip into the water. Below the surface its light changed from the licking flames that normally leapt up the blade to a radiant glow, but Ashe was right; it didn't go out.

Rhapsody began to glow herself with excitement. 'Come on,' she said eagerly, 'get undressed.'

They shed their outer clothes and stepped into the water, frigidly cold until Rhapsody entered it. Then, as she willed her fire lore to put forth warmth, the water temperature rose in the area immediately around them, heating the lake like the summer sun would have if it could reach it directly.

'Here,' said Ashe, 'let's trade swords. Kirsdarke will let you breathe beneath the surface, being a water sword. I can breathe without it. If you don't mind, that is.' He knew the natural reluctance to relinquish a sword like the one each of them carried, but he had not felt it himself just now.

Obviously Rhapsody didn't either, as she happily handed him Daystar Clarion and took the blue-scrolled weapon he held out to her. The blade altered the moment she took it; the glimmering ripples that danced along its surface ran rapidly from the hilt down the blade and disappeared as if they had drained out of the sword. The faint light that had gleamed from the scrollwork vanished as well, and the entire sword suddenly became more solid. The weapon she now held was beautiful, the silver blade inlaid in elaborate patterns of turquoise, but it no longer appeared as it had in Ashe's hand, where it looked as if it were composed only of water hanging suspended in the air.

'I killed it,' she whispered nervously.

'Oh, no!' Ashe gasped in mock alarm, then laughed at the size to which her eyes had opened. 'I'm just teasing you, Aria – it's fine. That's what it looks like in any hand other than that of the Kirsdarkenvar.'

Rhapsody ran her fingers over the now-solid blade. 'Are you sure I haven't damaged it?'

'Yes; it's fine. See, your sword doesn't respond to me the way it does to you, either.'

He was right. Daystar Clarion now resembled a regular sword, gleaming intensely with the starlight that it had been imbued with, but no flames licked up the blade. Rhapsody's brow furrowed.

'How very strange,' she murmured. 'Both Achmed and Grunthor have held it, and the fire didn't go out like that.'

Ashe's eyes were touched with melancholy. 'The piece of my soul that the F'dor ripped from me was the part tied to fire, Rhapsody. It left my soul void of that element, until you came into my life.' He smiled and put his arm around her, drawing her near. 'The sword senses that, and doesn't respond to me because of it. The only fire in my heart is also in my arms.'

Rhapsody kissed him. 'Not for long.'

Ashe winced involuntarily. She was referring to her plan to hunt down the Rakshas and destroy it, retrieving the piece of his soul in the process. It was a thought that turned his stomach, so he drove it out of his mind, concentrating instead on his golden-haired lover and the world they were about to explore together.

'If you're ready, let's go. Just remember, whatever you do, don't swim back to the surface too quickly, you'll injure yourself seriously.'

'Understood.' She kissed him again and gingerly lowered Kirsdarke into the lake. Beneath the surface of the water the blade disappeared, leaving nothing visible in her hand but the hilt. Ashe smiled in contentment at the trust between them the exchange had demonstrated. Then he ducked beneath the surface. Rhapsody could see the light of Daystar Clarion still gleaming in his hand under the water.

She took a deep breath and centered herself before following. As soon as she was beneath the surface she was aware of a paradox – within the vast silence there was an almost deafening noise. The water was filled with subtle sounds, almost drowned out by a great rushing clamor that resembled a strong wind, but was clearly aquatic. It was alien to her ears, and very beautiful. She closed her eyes for a moment and traced the origin of the sound. It came from the base of the great waterfall that spilled from the rock outcroppings into the lake below.

Rhapsody floated upright in the water for a moment, eyes still closed, absorbing the sound of the underwater world, when she heard a strange baritone note, like the sound of a bell wrapped in linen. She opened her eyes onto a world of strange light and beauty, one in which certain colors seemed to have been taken away, leaving everything within it a diminished hue from what it would look like above the surface.

The noise she had heard was Ashe's laughter, and when she turned to him she was amazed by his appearance. He floated free in the water, hovering slightly above her, illuminated by the crystal light of Daystar Clarion. His red-gold hair floated freely about him, moving slowly and metallically, reflecting the radiance of the sword. His skin was pale, as was her own, and his broad smile gleamed his teeth resembling pearls. His eyes seemed the strangest of all, for here within his element, they shone like sapphires, blending in with the waves around him. Suspended in the water as in if in flight, holding the glowing blade of the stars in his hand, Ashe looked more like an angelic apparition than a man. Rhapsody's heart swelled with the intense sensation that occurred each time she felt her love for him grow, and she caught her breath.

At once she was filled with a sense of panic, fearing she had breathed in water. She felt a mad desire to rush to the surface, to break back into the world of air, but fought it and willed the fear away, taking another breath. Calm returned as she found she could breathe easily in the water, and her panic was replaced by a giddiness at the wonder of the new world she saw about her. Ashe's smile had vanished when he saw her struggle momentarily, and he was beside her instantly; she nodded to reassure him. Then he gestured toward the depths.

Together they swam to the middle of the lake, following the beacon of light the sword cast before them. About twenty feet off shore the stalagmite formations Rhapsody had thought she'd seen began to rise from the slanted floor of the lake, glimmering brilliantly in the reflected radiance. They were crystalline and smooth, unlike their jagged, toothlike counterparts above the surface, and gleamed in soft hues of pink, green and blue, with violet appearing more frequently as they swam deeper.

The stalagmites at the edge of the field ranged from tiny stakes up to Rhapsody's knee to the largest ones that came up to her shoulder. In the depths they were vastly taller, some towering higher than the cottage would have been had it resided on the bottom. As the light from Daystar Clarion touched these formations they took on a magical quality, a soft, glittering beauty that was further enhanced by the encroaching darkness at the edge of the light. They gleamed for a moment as the sword hovered overhead, then slipped back into the inky black of the deep.

Ashe had been right again; with Kirsdarke Rhapsody could breath easily beneath the surface. She kicked to dive even farther down, following his lead. In this part of the lake the formations took on a lacier appearance, rather than the solid heft of the stalagmites at the field's edge. The multicolored rocks became thin and wispy, with fragile extensions reaching out like ghostly arms in the darkness. In places the frail-looking structures bent from the weight of the water above them, resembling domes and arches. It made the stalagmite field look like a city formed from frosting and spun sugar, a resplendent realm for the dark fish that swam between the rocks, skittering away when the light touched them.

As they passed over a large structure of intertwined green and azure rock threads, a glint of silver caught Rhapsody's eye. She signaled to Ashe, who nodded and dove to retrieve it from the floor of the lake. She followed him down into the enormous underwater basilica, born of dripping water and time, and looked around her in wonder. The upper expanses reached into the lake above her at a height that seemed similar to that of a real basilica, taking her artificial breath away. The sheer size of it astounded her, the thought of this hidden realm, this underwater land lying beneath the surface high above, as well as the thousand feet of dome above that, secreted within the hidden meadow of Kraldurge. It seemed a shame that such exquisite beauty existed, unseen and unappreciated.

Her contemplation was interrupted by a strong arm wrapping around her back. She turned to see Ashe hovering beside her, his floating hair gleaming in the circle of light. He looked up at the towering formations above them and smiled, nodding as she grinned in response. He leaned near and kissed her, holding the sword as far from their sides as possible. Then he gestured toward the surface.

Reluctantly Rhapsody nodded as well, and swam behind him as they slowly ascended to the air, following the slant of the water as it grew more shallow. They had not gone anywhere near the deepest part of the lake; she could only imagine what treasures were hiding down there in the constant night.

As they retrieved their clothes from the shore, Rhapsody looked at Ashe and smiled. 'What did you find down there?' she asked, pointing to the metal object in his hand. He held it out for her inspection. Rhapsody gasped, then burst into laughter. It was the trowel she had been digging with in the meadow when she and Achmed had first discovered Elysian, though it was almost unrecognizable with the coating of pearlescent rockthreads that had attached themselves to it.

'You've seen this before?'

'Yes,' Rhapsody said, shaking the sand from her clothes. 'It's the reason we found this place. I was planting seeds of heartsease in the meadow above to drive away some of the mournful sadness that hung in the air there, and the ground just swallowed the trowel. I could almost swear I heard it belch. It must have fallen into the lake through one of the holes in the firmament that let in the light.'

'That's one for the museum,' Ashe commented. He looked at her as she wrapped herself in one of the drying cloths they had left on the lakeshore. Her wet hair was gleaming in the dim light that filtered from above, making her look like a sea nymph smiling at him. He took her in his arms.

'Shall I read more to you from those maps we were looking at earlier?'

Rhapsody sighed. 'No, I think we had best get supper started. I was hoping to go back to the Cauldron tonight and spend the evening with Jo. I have a gift I've been waiting to give her for a while. She seems sad lately, and I haven't seen her alone in a very long time. Would that be all right?'

No. Stay. Mine, whispered the dragon urgently. *My treasure. Don't share.* 'That's fine,' he said, squelching the insistent inner voice. 'I'll walk you there. Are you planning to stay all night?'

'I'll see how she feels,' Rhapsody answered, toweling off her hair. 'If things go well, then yes. Maybe she and I can get back to where we left off before – '

'Before I came into the picture and spoiled things.'

She glared at him. 'Don't finish my sentences unless you know what I am going to say. And that, by the way, wasn't it. Before things changed. Jo is a big girl. I told her what you said to me on the road about the difference in your ages and your life expectancies before I called you back here. She seemed to be fine about it. If anything, it's me who had spoiled things by being selfish and not paying more attention to her. I've just found it so hard to leave Elysian, and you, to go back to the Cauldron.' She shuddered involuntarily.

'I don't think being happy qualifies as being selfish all the time, Rhapsody. You've had some terrible things happen to you in your life. Maybe it's about time things got better for you.'

She grinned and reached up to kiss him. 'Funny; I think I gave the same speech to you a few days ago.'

'Well, I'm not above stealing words if they convey the right message.' He kissed her again, and tried to contain the longing in his eyes as she turned to go into the house. 'I'll be there in a minute,' he called to her.

Rhapsody turned back and smiled at him. 'I'll be waiting upstairs. It's summer; I suppose supper can be delayed for a little while.' She doffed her drying cloth teasingly, then walked into the house, leaving the door open for him.

Ashe sighed, feeling the warmth that always crept through him when she smiled. He took a deep breath, trying to recall the pain he had carried for so many years, and was unable to. She had cast it out, and filled his soul with a sweetness that was almost tangible. If only it could stay this way.

At the outskirts of his senses the dragon noticed something silver, glinting in the hazy afternoon light. Ashe walked to the edge of the water and looked down. There on the beach amid the rocks and sand was the tiny silver button he had thrown into the lake the morning he had finally let Emily go. He bent to pick it up.

It was still shiny, unmarred by its ordeal, glimmering up at him in his hand. For the first time seeing it brought no tears to his eyes, and no pain to his heart. Emily was a happy memory now, something with which he had come to terms. He could keep her in the back of his heart, tucked away in his memory. He was happy, as he knew she would have wanted him to be.

44

Rhapsody crept down the cold gray hall, watching furtively for any Bolg that might have wandered into the inner sanctum. It had been a while since she had spent the night in the Cauldron, and she was unsure as to the timing of the changing of the watch, the excuse the Bolg sentries had used in the Past to steal a peek into Achmed's private rooms.

She was dressed in a long blue nightshirt, covered with a hooded robe, and was carrying an enormous basket of sweetmeats from the bazaar in Sepulvarta, a peace offering to Jo, who had seemed distant and testy of late. With any luck, Jo would be alone and open to the idea of a late night chat. Rhapsody shifted the huge hamper to one arm, bracing it against her shoulder, and knocked.

After a few moments the door opened slowly, and Jo looked out from behind it. Rhapsody swallowed at the sight of her – she was thinner, with a dullness in her expression and her skin; her straw-colored hair was darker and without its usual shine. She stared past Rhapsody.

'Yes?'

'Jo, are you all right?' Rhapsody asked, concern knotting her stomach and rising into her throat. 'You don't look like you feel well.'

'I'm fine,' she said tersely; then she looked down at Rhapsody. 'What do you want?'

'Ah – well, I thought you might, I thought we could have kind of a girls' night again,' Rhapsody said awkwardly. 'I've missed you, Jo; I've missed our talks and spending time together. If you're not up to it, though, I understand.' Her voice trailed off self-consciously.

Jo stared at her for a moment, then her gaze relaxed. 'Sure,' she said, opening the door wider. 'Come in.'

Rhapsody handed her the basket. 'This is for you. I know how you love bonbons. There was a wonderful confectioner in Sepulvarta who had all kinds of sweets and dried fruits – ' She stopped in shock. Jo's formerly messy quarters, once full of carefully scattered possessions to provide hiding places for her most prized valuables, were neat as Rhapsody's own. And the hundreds of small candles Rhapsody had given her were nowhere in sight. In their place was a single lantern, casting a dim light and filling the room with a noxious smell.

Jo took the basket to her bed and sat down, cross-legged, and began sifting through its contents. Rhapsody pulled the jug of spiced mead from the basket and filled the two small cups she had tucked into her robe pockets, leaving one for Jo on her bedside table and taking one with her to the pile of pillows across the room. She settled into them and took a sip, hoping the warm liquid would ease the conversation that for the first time seemed so labored. It had always been a comfort-bringer with Oelendra.

'So, what's been going on up here?'

'Nothing.' Jo unpacked the basket systematically, cursorily examining its contents, setting her preferences aside. Rhapsody took another drink, wondering what had happened to the eagerness, the excitement Jo usually exhibited, unable to keep from diving into presents like these, leaving pieces scattered all around. 'The usual, you know; putting down rebellions, capturing and subduing villages, training the army. Nothing interesting.' She selected a paper cone of sugared grapes, and threw Rhapsody a packet of sulfured apricots.

Rhapsody watched Jo pop a few into her mouth, noting that she had avoided all of the sweeter confections she normally gobbled down. *Maybe she's just growing up*, she thought, trying to banish the apprehension that was making the hairs on the back of her neck tingle, and the moment the idea occurred, she relaxed. Of course. Jo was just maturing; she was human, and she was at the age of change. The thought both comforted her and made her sad.

'I was thinking that maybe you and I need a holiday,' she said, pulling the black ribbon from her hair and running her fingers through the glistening tresses. 'You know, maybe a journey to some interesting places, just the two of us. What do you think?'

Jo popped another grape into her mouth. 'Dunno. How would Ashe feel about it?'

'He's got things to do, too,' Rhapsody answered, feeling her eyes drop under Jo's intense gaze. 'I'm sure he'll keep busy. Besides, he knows I want to spend time with you.'

Jo said nothing, but stretched herself out on the bed, tucking her arms under her head.

'Would you like me to play something for you, Jo? I brought my lark's flute,' Rhapsody asked, still casting around for a comfortable conversation.

'If you want.' Jo's voice was noncommittal.

Rhapsody pulled out the tiny instrument and began a soft melody, aimless and wandering, without repetition. She caught notes from the songs of the forest and the open meadow, soothing and mellifluous. She could see Jo begin to relax, the tight expression on her face ease somewhat. Matching the movement of the shadows from the lantern light, she wove a soothing air that hovered in the room and let it lightly come to rest on her sister.

As soon as Jo seemed comfortable Rhapsody began weaving a suggestion into the song; a subtle hint that she should be forthcoming about whatever was bothering her. She loved Jo far too much to use her music to enchant her or to force her to reveal anything against her will; the tune was just a wordless encouragement.

'Rhapsody?'

'Yes?'

'Can I ask you something?'

Rhapsody sat forward on the pillows, a look of delight on her face. 'Oh, Jo, of course you can, anything,' she said earnestly. 'Haven't you always been able to? What do you want to know?'

Jo sat up on the bed and leveled a steady look at her. 'Are you going to marry Ashe?'

'No,' Rhapsody said. The lantern light flickered across her face, revealing no sadness.

'Why not?'

'We haven't even discussed it. Lots of reasons. He's royalty; I'm a peasant.'

'Peasant? I thought you were the Duchess of Elysian.'

Rhapsody lobbed a pillow at Jo's head, enjoying the return of their old camaraderie. 'All right, I'm Firbolg royalty. Which, by the way, equates to something *beneath* Cymrian peasantry.'

'Snobs,' said Jo. 'Hang them and their stuck-up pretensions.' She downed the mead in her glass, then refilled it from the jug. Rhapsody held out her own glass, and Jo poured.

'Can I ask you something else?' Jo looked at her intently.

'Of course.'

'When you lost your virginity, did it hurt?'

'No.'

'You're lucky.'

'Why, Jo?' Rhapsody asked, her stomach turning to ice suddenly. 'Are you – are you all right?'

Jo shrugged.

Rhapsody searched her face, concern washing over her like a cold ocean wave. 'What are you saying, Jo? You're not a virgin anymore?'

Jo looked at the wall. 'No. And it still hurts. I haven't really felt right since.'

Rhapsody came to her, sat on the bed and drew the taller girl into her arms. She stroked her hair and kissed her forehead tenderly, rocking slightly to comfort her and to avoid letting Jo see the look of anxiety on her own face. 'What do you mean you don't feel right? Tell me what's wrong.'

Jo said nothing. Rhapsody pulled back gingerly and looked into her face; as Jo tried to turn away she gently rested her palm on Jo's cheek and looked into her eyes.

'Tell me, Jo. I'll help you, whatever it is.'

Jo watched her for a long time, still not speaking, and Rhapsody made note of her haggard appearance, the graying of her skin, the loss of weight in her face and hands. Finally she said, 'I can't keep anything down. My stomach feels strange all the time. My whole body aches. Everything hurts.'

Rhapsody blinked back tears. She rested her hand gently on Jo's abdomen, seeing if she could feel the presence of a different soul, and she did detect a strange vibration, but there was something wrong about it, something alien. She tried to sense further, but Jo pushed her hand away.

'No, Rhapsody, I'm not pregnant. Leave me alone.'

Rhapsody made her voice as mild as she could. 'Are you sure, Jo?'

'Yes. Now stop it.' Jo rose and walked across the room, taking her mead glass with her.

'I'm sorry, Jo,' Rhapsody said. 'You know I'll do anything I can to make it better. I have lots of herbs and roots that can settle your stomach and ease your aches. Come home with me to Elysian and I'll put you in a nice warm tub.'

'It's all right,' Jo replied, taking a deep swallow of the amber liquid. 'It's probably just that my first time was a little, well, a little rough, a little violent. I'll be fine in a week or two, I'm sure.'

The words chilled Rhapsody's soul, and she felt anger, like a blush, rise to her face and choke her. She tried to keep her voice steady. 'Jo, I am so sorry,' she repeated, trying to stay calm. 'Have I been away so long? I wish I'd been here for you, you know, to talk to. I mean, I hadn't realized you were seeing anyone.'

Jo turned and looked at her for the first time from across the room. The expression in her eyes was unwavering.

'I'm not seeing anyone. Actually, you're seeing him.'

Rhapsody stared at her blankly. Jo continued on, as words tumbled over each other in their rush to spill out. 'It was Ashe, Rhaps. I'm really sorry. It was just once.'

'Jo, what are you talking about?'

'It was Ashe,' Jo repeated, her face beginning to harden. 'I had sex with Ashe. The night of the meeting, when I ran out of the council room, and he came after me – he found me on the heath. He didn't tell you, did he?'

Rhapsody said nothing, but the color drained from her face.

'I thought not,' Jo continued, watching Rhapsody turn white and avert her eyes. 'He probably told you he couldn't find me, didn't he? Scum. I tried to make him leave, but he wouldn't. And, well, we did it. Actually, although I enjoyed it a little at the time, it was pretty grisly overall. I don't think I'll ever get the image of his face as he was knobbing me out of my mind. Honestly, Rhaps, I don't know what you see in him. Don't you have anything better to do than let him rut on you?'

Her words were having their intended effect; when Rhapsody looked back up she was in tears. She stood up and, as if in a daze, pulled the covers back on the bed.

'Why don't you get some sleep?' she said, not looking at Jo. 'I'll put together some tonics for you and bring them by in the morning,' Jo watched as she gathered up her hair ribbon and the lark's flute, and left the room, closing the door silently behind her.

Ashe sat up in bed as the door to Rhapsody's chamber opened softly. He had expected that she would stay the night with Jo, and the delight he felt in her return showed immediately on his face. He pulled his hood back a bit and held his arms out to her, but she turned silently from him and went to the wardrobe where she slowly hung up her robe.

'Rhapsody?' he said, pushing himself up on his knuckles and putting his feet down onto the frigid stone floor. 'Are you all right?'

She turned to look at him and shock crossed his face as he saw the tears streaming down hers.

'Aria, what's the matter?' He started to stand, but Rhapsody held her hands out in front of her, as if to keep him at bay.

'Please, just stay there.' She crossed her arms in front of her, looking like she was fighting nausea.

'What happened? Did you have an argument with Jo?'

Rhapsody walked a few steps nearer to him, her arms still clutching her waist. 'She – said that you had sex with her the night of the meeting out on the heath above the canyon.'

Ashe's face went blank, then shock and fury roared through him like a flash flood. Rhapsody could feel the change in the electricity of the air around them as the dragon in him bristled and started to rise. She came to him and rested her fingertips on his lips as his mouth opened in protest.

'Don't say anything, please. I know it isn't true.' The tears fell like rain, and she began to tremble.

His denial cut short, Ashe put his arms around her and pulled her onto his lap. He held her tightly to his chest while his hands caressed her shining hair, caught in a chasm between uncontrollable anger at the lie and heartfelt joy at her unwavering trust in him. 'Why would she do that?' he asked incredulously. 'Why would she want to hurt us, hurt you like that? Do you think it's in retribution for us not telling her sooner?'

Rhapsody raised her face and looked directly into his eyes. For the first time since he had met her he saw fear in them.

'No,' she said, shaking. 'I think she met the Rakshas.'

45

Ashe rose slowly, like a man in shock. He savagely pulled up his hood, then walked to the other side of the room and began to gather his belongings. Rhapsody watched him in sorrow; the muscles of his body were coiled like springs, visible even beneath the ever-present mist cloak, and she knew he was struggling desperately to keep from running out the door and dragging Jo out of bed. At least he still had maintained enough common sense to know that awareness of his presence might provoke a demonic attack they were unprepared for.

'We have to go after it now, we can't delay any longer,' Rhapsody said. 'We had planned to wait until the first day of winter, but obviously that's off.' She could not see his face, but when he spoke his voice was calm, his words pragmatic.

'You understand that she may be in thrall now, Rhapsody? That she may be under the control of the F'dor?'

Rhapsody said nothing.

Ashe took her chin in his hand; his grip was gentle, but she could feel him trembling with rage.

'You *do* understand, don't you, Aria? You can't trust her now, not with *anything*. The contact may have been brief enough to only enthrall her temporarily, like the soldiers who attack their own villages, then can't remember doing it. Or the influence may be deeper, stronger; it may be using her as a spy.'

'I know.'

The grip on her chin tightened slightly, and Ashe turned her face up so that her eyes were aligned with his inside the wide hood of the mist cloak.

'She may be bound to it, Rhapsody. It may have gained access to her soul. It may own her now.' Her jaw clenched, but her eyes did not waver. 'It's not likely, though – the F'dor requires a blood contract, whether freely given or taken by force, to fully ensnare an immortal soul. Did she say that it had taken any of her blood?'

Rhapsody's face went white in his hand; Ashe loosed his grip and caressed her face gently.

'No, I don't think so,' she said after a moment's thought. 'She said the act was – violent, but she didn't mention being actually injured.'

'Was she a virgin?'

Rhapsody went numb. 'Yes.'

Ashe released her face and belted Kirsdarke. 'I think you should prepare for the worst, Aria. If she is bound to it – '

'If she is bound to it, I will secure her release as well as yours when I kill the Rakshas,' she said harshly. 'We'll leave tomorrow morning before daylight, before she knows we're gone. I'll have the guards keep an eye on her until we get back. Whatever needs to be done to save her from this, I will do, no matter what the cost. She's my sister, Ashe. She was bound to me long before she met the Rakshas. *I* have first claim on her soul, by the gods, not the F'dor.'

Ashe grasped her arm. 'Don't sacrifice yourself for her. It's not worth it.'

Rhapsody twisted away angrily. 'How dare you say that! Who are you to tell me what it is worth? Would it only be worth it if I were to make that sacrifice for you?' Ashe stood still in shock at the venom in her voice. Even without seeing his face, she knew how deeply her words had stung.

'I'm sorry,' she whispered. 'I'm sorry.'

'The answer to your question is no,' Ashe replied, bending to secure his boots. 'Nothing is worth that sacrifice. I only meant that your death would not save her.'

'I'm not going to die,' Rhapsody said, staring down at her own hands. 'Not to save her, not to save you.'

The silence between them echoed for a moment. Finally Ashe spoke. 'I should leave immediately, before it discovers I'm here.'

Rhapsody nodded numbly. 'It's for the best.'

Ashe nodded as well, then turned away. Rhapsody watched him from behind as he ran a hand through his unkempt locks, trying to regain a sense of calm, and failing miserably. He dressed in silence, never removing the mist cloak, his knotted muscles speaking volumes about his anger.

Rhapsody drew her knees up to her chest and hugged them tightly, trying to stave off the despair that was clutching at her as she watched him pack. She had known this moment was coming, known all along that he would leave, but somehow she thought it would be later, and gentler. She fought back tears as he slung his pack over his shoulder and came to the bed, crouching down beside her.

'How long do you think the hunt for it will take?'

'I don't know. It depends on how far away it is. As soon as you're away from here I will go to Achmed and tell him we have to move the plans up immediately. We'll leave tomorrow.'

'Make sure Jo doesn't hear you.'

'Of course. But she was told about our current strategy, so if she has communicated anything, we'll catch them looking.'

Beneath the hood she heard the snort of breath that always accompanied his wryest smile. 'Well, that's something to be grateful for, anyway.'

Rhapsody threw her arms around his neck. 'Please, please be careful.'

Ashe pulled her tightly to him, holding her so as to be able to recall the memory in darker times. '*You* be careful, Aria. You will be the one facing the Rakshas. I never realized how much I dread your doing this until now.'

She patted his shoulder reassuringly. 'I'll be fine. We all will. I was almost able to take him down by myself. If Grunthor and Achmed are there, too, and we have the element of surprise, we should be able to end it quickly, and forever.'

'When you fought it, you were on sacred ground on the holiest night of the year. Don't underestimate it, Aria; the gods only know what demonic powers it can draw on.'

'I won't. Don't underestimate us, either, Ashe. We know what we're doing. I need you to promise me you'll stay far enough away to be out of danger. We'll slay the damned thing, then you'll have the piece of your soul back, and the F'dor will no longer have power over you. It's probably not a good idea to call you as I did, to put your name on the wind again. How can I find you to let you know when it's over?'

He moved back and took her face in his hands again, tenderly this time. Inside his hood she could see the blue eyes gleaming intensely. 'You can't. If I could be found, I would be dead. I'll return in a month; you should be back by then, yes?'

'Gods, I hope so. Where will you go?'

'I don't know, the coast, maybe. Don't worry about me, Rhapsody. Just get through it and don't get hurt. Leave the soul fragment if you have to – it won't be worth anything if something happens to you.'

'Nothing is going to happen to me. I'll be fine.'

'I will pray every moment until I see you again that you're right.' His fingers slid into her hair as he pulled her face to him and kissed her. She could feel the rage quivering within him, and her lips trembled as well, fearing his anger would make him foolhardy. Her mouth clung to his, filling it with warmth as she tried wordlessly to console him, but it was of little use. She had never seen him so angry.

With great effort Ashe pulled away, then strode to the door and left without a word. Rhapsody sat for a moment, still stunned, then bolted to her feet. She ran to the door and looked for him in the hall, but he was already gone. He had not said good-bye. She had not told him she loved him.

For the second time that night Rhapsody crept down the hall, still watching for Bolg sentries. Seeing none, she put the basket of tonics on the floor outside Jo's door, opened the door silently, and peered in.

The girl she loved as a sister was asleep, snoring softly, curled up like a baby in the womb, or a child with a stomachache. Rhapsody watched her in sorrow, knowing how she must have suffered, how she must be suffering still.

Hatred took hold in her heart, and she felt her fingers curl into claws as she unconsciously pictured the Rakshas's smug smirk. It would take extreme force of will to prevent herself from gouging his eyes out when they met. She was not sure yet if she would avoid castrating him when they were taking him down.

As she pictured his gory death Ashe's face appeared in her mind and she started; she forgot sometimes their identical visages. Her stomach went suddenly cold with the knowledge that he had left in a tearing hurry, without the promise of staying away. Rhapsody's heart cramped in sudden fear. Perhaps he was tracking it now, seeking to spare her the danger. On a moment's further contemplation, she knew he was. She hurried back to her room, threw on her boots and cloak and ran for the gates of the Cauldron.

The darkness was thick in the Teeth, thicker than pitch. The rocky crags held the night fast, as though trying to shield themselves a little more from the prying eyes of the world, wrapping their summits in mist and anonymity. The wind was high, and cold, even as the scraggly vegetation stiffened in the rictus of autumn, bowing and bending before it with less vigor than in the supple moisture of summer. The annual death ritual of the land had begun. In the dark it held none of the promise that the colorful leaves of the forests made in daylight as to the temporary nature of summer's demise. Now it seemed as though the world might be swept forever into the cold and the dark.

Rhapsody clung to the walls of the rocky passes, trying to stay upright in the roaring wind. Her legs trembled with the chill that blasted up her nightgown, whipping it and the cloak she had hastily donned, making her feel as though tied to the mast of a ship under full sail. Only her knowledge of the terrain prevented her from plunging headlong down into the chasms that yawned around each turn. She could barely see a few feet in front of her, so pervasive was the darkness.

She called Ashe's name at each rise, the wind swallowing her voice and hurling it back into her face, blended with a wail of its own. His mist cloak would keep him from her sight, she knew, and unless he heard her she had no chance of finding him. Her heart grew tighter with each step; she was unable to shake the clutching fear that had clawed at her soul since she had seen the look in Jo's eyes earlier that night. *Soon he will have reached the steppes, and then I'll never be able to find him,* she thought, shielding her eyes from the dust and tiny shards of rock blasting against her face as she rounded the cliff face that led to the windward side of the mountain.

The wind was so fierce here that Rhapsody's cloak ripped loudly, tearing loose the stays that kept the flaps together, and nearly pulling it from her body. She cried out in pain, then made for the shelter of the pass in front of her, the last outcropping of rocks before the sheer drop to the steppes four thousand feet below. The wind had hollowed out an arch over the centuries, leaving a thin rocky refuge, open on both sides but solid in front, jutting into the middle of the pass. It seemed stable, and would afford her a few moments' rest before turning back. There was no way she could go forward and live.

Rhapsody's fingers stung where the skin had been scraped away from clinging to the rock, and when the archway was within reach she took hold, only to find her grip give way. She was vaguely aware that her hands were bleeding, and struggled to hold on, pulling herself inside the shelter. The front face of the wall seemed solid and she rested her head against it, trying to regain her breath. When she could speak she called Ashe's name one last time into the wind, hoping it would carry down the crag. Then she leaned against the wall in exhaustion, watching the wind shriek by on either side of her through the doorways of the arch. A shadow partially blocked the view on the southern side of the rock refuge.

'What's the matter? Gods, what are you doing out here? The Rakshas could be anywhere, haunting these passes, waiting for – waiting for one of us.'

Rhapsody looked up, still panting, and saw that the darkness which obscured the doorway of the arch was man-shaped. His voice had a note of panic in it. With great effort she answered him.

'I – forgot to – get – something.'

He hurried into the sheltered arch and dropped his pack, then came and took her by the shoulders. 'What?'

Rhapsody could barely see him in the inky darkness, even though he was immediately in front of her. She looked up into his hood, attempting to make eye contact. She swallowed, trying to find her voice.

'Your promise.'

She felt the muscles in his arms tighten through the grip of his hands, and he shook her slightly; she could tell he was struggling from letting the intensity of his feelings cause her harm. 'Are you insane?' he asked incredulously. 'They would never find your body if you misstepped even once. Gods, Rhapsody, what promise could have been so important?'

She coughed as he took her bare hands in his gloved ones, turning the bleeding fingers to his lips, caressing them in a rough gesture of comfort. 'I need you to swear you will not hunt it,' she answered, her throat tightening as the wind howled through the arched shelter, snapping his hood stiffly.

The dark figure remained silent, brushing her fingers with kisses that became slightly more gentle. Rhapsody's hands began to tremble, and she knew she had been right; he had set off in search of the twisted vessel that housed his soul. She thought about how desperate he must be if he would risk something so eternally awful, and realized that he was probably confronting the one prospect that was worth gambling his own damnation: the possibility of hers.

'You must stay away,' she said, her words coming out as frightened gasps. 'I told you, I will be able to kill it, and I will not be alone. Promise me, Ashe. Swear to me you will not hunt it. Let me do this. Trust me, please.'

The hood lowered, and she knew his head was bent low with the weight of her demand. 'I can't let you do this,' he said at last, his voice full of pain. 'I couldn't bear it if – '

Violently she slapped both palms on his shoulders, shoving him against the side of the mountain cliff. His head snapped back up, and she glared up into the hood again, this time catching a glimpse of blue eyes opened in shock by her blow. She took the collar of his cloak at the throat into her clenched fist.

'Listen to me,' she snarled, her voice low and deadly, but clearly audible above the howling wind. 'You will *not* do this to me! You will afford me the belief that I know what I am capable of, and you will believe in it unwaveringly. And if you can't do that, you will still yield to my request and *get out of sight*. I have already let this abomination harm the only sister I have ever had. It has ravaged her, and it's my fault. I will not lose you to it also, Ashe.' She began to shake uncontrollably, and he pulled her into a tight embrace as she succumbed to hiccoughing sobs.

His lips touched her frozen ear. 'What happened to Jo was not your fault,' he said, raw pain in his voice. 'If anyone is to blame, it's me. I could have looked harder – I didn't even check the heath.'

'Because I told you not to,' Rhapsody choked. 'I told you not to pursue her too much because I thought she was back in her room crying. I had no idea how much we had hurt her; I never thought she would go outside alone. Gods, what have I done?' The sobbing dissolved into gasps of agony, and her tears soaked his cheek. He leaned against the mountain, slipping a hand behind her neck and another behind her back, holding her with all his strength as she cried tears of deeper grief than she had ever been allowed.

The wind whined in discordant accompaniment to her weeping, and when she paused to draw breath he pulled her face up and kissed her roughly. Her own response was ungentle as well, her hands reaching under his cloak to clutch his back as her mouth sought the harsh comfort of his. He ran his hands over her flying hair, stopping long enough to pull off his gloves and throw them on the ground near his pack. Then he reached beneath her cloak, grasping her waist, pulling her closer, his mouth breaking from hers.

'You came out into the Teeth in a nightgown and a cloak? Where's your armor? Gods, what's the matter with you?'

'Promise me you won't hunt it,' she whispered, fear filling her voice. 'Please. Please, I love you. I love you. Do this for me. Please.'

She could feel him begin to tremble, his tremors matching her own. Then he nodded.

'All right,' he said, his voice cracking. 'All right, Rhapsody, I agree. I will not hunt it. But if it takes you, so help me, I'll – '

She kissed him again, her mouth seeking to silence him. 'It won't,' she said, her hands releasing his back from their grip and moving to his chest. 'Have a little faith in me.'

His hands grasped her waist more tightly. 'There is no end to the faith I have in you, Rhapsody, but you forget, I've fought this demon myself. It reached into my chest like it was an open sack of grain and dragged out a piece of my soul without breathing hard. That was the sealing of *our* blood contract. If I hadn't been able to break free then, it would have owned me, too.

'It was like a vine growing up my spine, wrapping itself around my essence, becoming part of me as gently as a breeze, spreading without hesitation until it reached through my entire chest cavity. What do you think damaged me so much? I injured myself as much as it did, ripping it out with all my strength before it consumed all of me. The piece of me that

373

it took I had to sacrifice, like an animal in a trap chewing off its foot to escape. It only took an instant, Rhapsody; I don't know if I could get away a second time. I don't know if you can, either.'

'Stop it,' she said fiercely. 'I'm not going against the F'dor yet; I'm only killing his toy. And I have far better reason to. Besides what it has done to you, it has hurt and degraded Jo. She has suffered enough in her life, she didn't need this. I have never felt this much hate before – if I don't give vent to it I will burn alive.' Her voice broke. 'Do you hear me, Ashe? I will *burn alive.*' She buried her face in his chest, her fingers drawing into claws once more.

He pulled her away and kissed her repeatedly, his mouth hard and insistent. 'Now you listen,' he said between touches of his lips, 'you sound like me. That's criminal, Rhapsody. You are the one who made me believe that love was not just a false concept in this sour world. Don't you dare turn away from it now. Don't become like the rest of us. You'll be abandoning us to our hatred forever.' His last kiss lingered; she felt all the intensity of his pain in it, and the feeling was alien to her, so unlike the gentleness she had always found in him. 'I love you. I believe in you. And I'll stay away, may the gods forgive me.' He almost spat the last words.

A crosswind blasted through the arch, pushing both of them off the mountain wall and chilling her through her flimsy clothing. He grabbed her as she fell out of the rock shelter and swung her around, pulling her back inside the arch and pushing her up against the face of the mountain.

'Are you all right?' he gasped, panic in his voice. His hands clutched her and found her skin to be cold; he began to run them over her in the attempt to warm her, and found himself lost in the throes of desperation, of fear, and he wanted her, wanted to hide her away from the danger, wanted to shelter her in his soul, to protect her with his body, with his life.

She felt the same longings; she clung to him and pulled him back into the kiss of lovers who didn't know if it was their last. Her hands ran over his upper body, then set about freeing him from the laces of the trousers that kept them apart. She trembled violently as his hands moved up under her nightgown, and she gave herself over to the darkness of fear.

There on the mountain pass, leaning against the cliff face, sheltered only by the open rock arch, they made love in panic, in desperation, cloaked in the night wind, covered only with the blanket of the misty darkness, thick as pitch, that hid the peaks of the Teeth. They found little comfort, and no joy, just the frenzy of the need for contact, perhaps for the last time. No clothes were shed, no words spoken, just the fierce need met in a way that left neither of them reassured.

When the tumult had passed they held each other, still braced against the mountain, and whispered words of promise, his oath to not pursue the Rakshas, hers to be careful. Then he kissed her, fastened her cloak for her, and ran his hand over her hair tenderly before guiding her back to the path that led to the Cauldron. She watched until the darkness swallowed him up, then made her way carefully back toward the lights in the Firbolg seat of power, buffeted by the screaming wind.

46

Morning came early. Long before the guard changed, or even had made their scheduled rounds, Rhapsody had met her Bolg partners on the heath, provisioned for a month's journey, dressed in traveling clothes and a grim expression.

The spicy scent of autumn was in the air and begged a moment's appreciation. While the men checked the gear one final time, Rhapsody closed her eyes and reflected on the last time she had experienced the odor of burning leaves in a wind that kept growing colder.

She thought back to the Island for the first time in a long while, her memories no longer as painful as the reality of the Present. Harvest had been a season of great excitement, the air alive with promise and threat; it was a heady, romantic time, far more than summer, a time when every small thing had seemed of vast importance and the blood ran close to the surface all the time. *Whatever your hopes are, catch them now*, the Earth seemed to say as it dressed in its glorious funereal finery; *time grows short. Winter is coming.*

'Ready, darlin'?' Grunthor's booming voice broke the stillness and her reverie.

Rhapsody glanced around at the fields, coming to light in the gray foredawn. Frost had come in the night, and the ground glittered in the light of Daystar Clarion. She sheathed the sword and patted her dragonscale armor.

'Yes,' she said. 'Let's go.'

The sun was just cresting the top of the tallest crag when the Three reached the summit. They had scaled the Teeth with ease and in silence, their shadows blending in with the ones cast by the peaks themselves, long and fanglike, in the growing light of the valley below.

From high above, the mighty canyon looked like a thin curved rope lying along the base of the mountains. Achmed stood among the racing clouds and cast his gaze over the range, staring out across the steppes and to the fields of Bethe Corbair beyond, unshaken in the howling wind. He turned in a slow circle, the world at his feet, as his eyes scanned the horizon. Then he sat at the highest point possible and cleared his mind.

Rhapsody had been instructed to remain silent and as still as possible. Except for Grunthor, she was the only person ever allowed to observe Achmed obtain a trail, and the significance of the trust implicit in this was not lost on her. She held her breath, watching him close his eyes and open his mouth slightly, breathing in the thin air and the moisture of the clouds. In one hand he held her shirt, encrusted with the blood of the Rakshas. The other he held open and aloft, as if testing the direction of the wind.

Achmed's breathing became measured and deep, each intake of breath becoming slower and more expansive. When he had attained the right pattern, his attention shifted to his heart. He concentrated on its rhythm, on the pressure it exerted on the vessels and pathways through which his blood flowed, and willed it to slow, lowering his pulse to a level barely able to sustain his life. He drove all stray thoughts from his mind, leaving it blank except for the color red. Everything else faded, leaving nothing but the vision of blood before his mind's eye.

There had been a time when he would have been all but deafened by the sound and feel of millions of hearts beating. Now there were but a few thousand in the world he could still hear. Those of Rhapsody and Grunthor he knew at once, but the others were far away, flickering in the distance of his bloodsense.

And then he heard it. Beating in the middle distance, not too far off. He could hear the pounding of the Rakshas's heart, feel the pulsing of its blood through the fingertips of his upheld hand. Demon's blood, blended with the blood of an animal. The blood on the shirt, the blood in those veins: they matched.

Achmed held absolutely still, remained utterly silent. He loosed the pulse of his own heart in rhythm to that of the demon's creation. Like trying to catch a flywheel in motion, he could only synchronize with one beat in every five, then every two, until each beat matched perfectly. Their hearts locked, and Achmed smiled.

Slowly he opened his eyes.

Rhapsody had been watching patiently, aware that it could be hours or days before he found the right heartbeat, if he even could. As a result, she was surprised when Grunthor suddenly seized his poleax and leapt to his feet. She could see no difference in Achmed, but the Sergeant obviously had. She had just enough time to stand when Achmed was off.

He moved like a hunting dog on the scent, racing down the mountainside. In order to avoid losing his companions he stayed in the light and crossed the paths of the wind, instead of using those things to hide as his instinct dictated. He followed the beating of his heart, heading unerringly toward the Rakshas. Grunthor had followed him on the hunt like this once or twice before, so leading the others without losing the trail was not as great an effort as it had once been. He no longer needed to work alone.

Rhapsody and Grunthor set a matched jog to follow behind him. Rhapsody was amazed at the speed at which Achmed moved, especially since he was not running. He sped down the broken path, to the steepest part of the slope, and began to descend the face of the hill like a spider. He slowed his descent when the others reached the slope so that they might keep up without falling, but once he was on the heath he traveled like the wind.

Jo waited at the bottom of an adjoining ridge. Despite the care the others had taken to slip away without her knowledge, she had wakened in the night and pursued them silently. She did not follow them to the top of the crag; to do so certainly would have revealed her presence, and they would have to come down eventually, anyway. Instead she had crossed the ridge farther down at the first slope and watched the Three as they ascended the summit, tiny black figures lost in the glare of the sun.

What are they doing? she wondered. *What am I doing?* Her actions no longer seemed to be her own; she was governed by an odd, purposeful feeling that twisted her stomach and made her light-headed and woozy when it came, making her move as if in a dream. It reminded her of the time when Cutter, one of her mentors on the street, had given her the bad toadstools, promising her happy visions and a hyperawareness of colors. Instead it had caused a nightmarish trance and paranoia that haunted her for hours. But this was much worse; the mushrooms had eventually worn off. This had not ended. She feared it never would.

Strange thoughts plagued her waking moments, thoughts of murder and violence that tormented and fascinated her at the same time. A few days before she was delighted when two Bolg children had begun to fight, and was excited by the sight of their blood. When one of the combatants screamed in pain, his arm suddenly hanging at an odd angle, instead of feeling horrified, as she had when Vling was injured, she felt aroused. *What is happening to me?* she wondered, but once again she felt the twisting in her stomach and the question was pulled from her mind. When the Three descended the slope and began to cross the steppes, she followed them.

Like a sleepwalker.

For a week the Three followed the course that curved only as the Rakshas moved. They slept without a fire at night, and ran most of the day, stopping only when its trail remained motionless for long periods of time, and only then to take a moment's rest. They hunted their prey relentlessly, across the foothills of the Teeth, over the grassy steppes and the wide plain of Bethe Corbair, onto the chalk hills of the Orlandan plateau, until Achmed stopped abruptly.

He raised his hand to the wind for a moment, then slowly closed it. He nodded to the other two, then disappeared into the high fields just behind the crest of a hill. Grunthor and Rhapsody followed him, crawling on the ground until they reached the place where Achmed lay. He pointed down into the shallow valley before them, but need not have. The sight below was clear: a cluster of nine men, three with horses, being given orders by a mounted man in gray, a man with copper-colored hair.

Rhapsody's heart skipped a beat when she saw him; it was Ashe, or at least, at this distance, it was identical to Ashe. His hair did not have the same luster, and he was clearly visible, where Ashe would not be, but otherwise this was Ashe. He gestured to the men, who rode off quickly west, then turned to the northeast and set his horse to a slow walk.

Achmed smiled as Grunthor backed away, still on his belly, and disappeared. *What a clean cwellan shot this would make*, he thought. *Oh well*. He turned to Rhapsody, and she returned his smile. Grunthor would be back with the horses of the men in a moment, and once the animals were secured and hidden they would be off again.

They followed the Rakshas for a few hours, resting from the day's run. He, and they, climbed a small hill and entered a wide wheatfield, laid low already from the harvest, the few sheaves that remained standing frozen in the remnants of the morning's frost. As he approached a small stream at the bottom of a dell, Grunthor tapped Achmed's shoulder and nodded. Achmed held up his hand and closed it into a tight fist. At once Grunthor and Rhapsody began to circle to their positions. Achmed waited until they were in place, and then disappeared into the highgrass.

The Rakshas rode slowly across the field. His eyes were set on the horizon before him, his mind wandering along the mechanical paths of torture and death that substituted for a living man's daydreams.

Dusk would come soon. He would consume this horse and use its blood to move, like a flame of night, closer to the mountain. As is the wont of those who dream vivid dreams before they are fully awake, the limited mind of the Rakshas was inventing delicious ways to see the king of the Bolg die.

He had captured a soldier in the Bolg army, and had listened with amusement to the man's horror tales of the Eye, Claw, Heel, and Stomach of the Mountain. *Fool*, he had mused while slashing the Bolg's throat, leaning closer to drink deeply from his gushing arteries. *I am the Eye, Ear, and Hand of one who has leveled mountains.*

The sun was high, and he kept his attention on the horse's footsteps in case it stumbled on one of the slick patches of frost. He was therefore somewhat surprised when the animal suddenly crumbled beneath him.

With the speed of the wolf in his blood he pitched himself from the saddle to avoid being trapped beneath his mount and rolled rapidly to his feet, sword in hand. His horse had been hit, killed with a single shot. He glanced around quickly to target the source of the missile, but instead his eyes beheld the mammoth figure with the immense poleax bearing down on him with a deadly speed. Adrenaline coursed through his artificial veins as he recognized the description the girl had given of Grunthor, and he knew instantly that it was a trap. He raised his hand in the direction of the giant, causing a wall of black fire to rise. The flames vanished instantly, quenched against his will. The shock of the fire's disappearance was excruciating. He turned to run.

'Hello, dear. It's been a long time; I've missed you.'

Rhapsody was no more than five feet away from him, the burning blade of Daystar Clarion in her grip. The Rakshas raised his arm to parry the killing blow he knew she would aim at his heart and was caught completely off guard when she slashed him across the knees instead. He could hear the pounding steps of Grunthor behind him and tried to bolt to the side, but his escape was thwarted by another slash of the firestar sword.

'Going somewhere? I told you that you wouldn't get by me.'

She stood in his way, and engaging her in combat would leave him vulnerable to the charging giant. The Rakshas tried to maneuver into a better position, but like a falcon clawing at his face, the small woman sidestepped his blows and drove him back repeatedly. His eyes widened as his back, then his chest, erupted as Grunthor impaled him on the spearlike tip of his poleax.

'Rhapsody!' he screamed as his flesh burst open, followed rapidly by the bloody point of Grunthor's spear. 'Gods, no! It's me, Ashe! I'm not the one you seek! Help me, please!'

As Rhapsody moved into closer position, he let out a moan of agony and reached out for her, driving the spike even farther through his chest. His eyes, brilliant and blue as the pinnacle of the sky, met hers, pleading for mercy. When none was forthcoming, the look in them hardened as unquenchable pain washed over his face. He took several shallow breaths, shuddering on the end of the pike.

'Gods,' he whispered. 'How can you be so stupid? It's me, Rhapsody, your own lover!' Grunthor gave the poleax a savage twist, and he gasped aloud again.

Despite everything she knew about this evil creature, Rhapsody felt her heart sink as she watched the Rakshas's features, so much like those of Ashe, contort in pain as his limbs flailed wildly on the skewer of Grunthor's pike. She could hear the hiss of acid as the blood hit the frozen ground, and the overwhelming stench she had encountered before billowed over the field, nauseating her. She looked up at Grunthor.

'Are you ready?' she asked the man who had been her first sword instructor.

Grunthor nodded. 'Ready, Your Ladyship. Make it a good clean blow, now.'

She steeled herself and lunged, driving Daystar Clarion into the Rakshas's heart, splitting it down the middle. He let loose a wild, keening wail, painful to hear, and writhed on the end of the poleax. Rhapsody wiped her blade on the ground, melting a patch of frost and leaving a deep burn in the frozen grass.

'What an unholy mess,' she said.

She torched the body with the flame from the sword, watching it go limp, then begin to melt as the ice and earth from which it was built came in contact with the purging flame of elemental power born of fire and starlight. The flame was golden and bright, Rhapsody's own fire, not the black fire of the demon, and she could feel it burning away the evil as it consumed the Rakshas's body. Great muddy rivers ran down the flaming form as it melted.

Achmed was in position, waiting for the moment of death. Grunthor swung the flaming poleax over toward him and held the enormous pike steady.

'Marshmallow, sir?' the Sergeant asked solemnly, jiggling the immense skewer slightly.

Achmed choked back a laugh and cleared his mind, breathing deeply as he began the Thrall ritual. His instinct took over immediately, and the movements came as if of their own volition. Achmed closed his eyes.

His mouth opened slightly. From deep within his throats came four separate notes, held in a monotone; a fifth was channeled through his sinuses and nose. It sounded as if five different singers had simultaneously begun a chant. Then his tongue began to click rhythmically, and the body of the Rakshas stiffened as if called.

He raised his right hand, palm open and rigid, out in front of the Rakshas's burning body, a signal of halting. His left hand moved slowly out to his side and up, his fingers pulsing gently, seeking the strands of the vibrations that he knew to be from the blood of the F'dor. Like spiderwebs floating on the wind he could feel them, strings of a nature born at the beginning of Time, fingerprints of an ancient evil that should have died with the Island, held in check by his right hand and his Dhracian blood. He could also feel the presence of another primordial spirit, one very different from the tainted nature of the demon. He slid his fingers into the metaphysical strands and drew them to his palm, then twisted his hand to wrap the strands around it. He could see the body jerk when he did, and he gave another firm pull on the invisible tether.

His eyes narrowed as the Rakshas's movements suddenly ceased. A glowing light emerged from the now-rigid body, rising from the golden flames, and Rhapsody gasped. It was the piece of Ashe's soul, drawn by death out of the melting form and preparing to dissipate into the ether. Achmed held the demon's blood in thrall, but the soul belonged to Gwydion, and, freed from its prison, it hovered for a moment, waiting for a warm wind to carry it to the light.

Rhapsody pointed Daystar Clarion at the pulsating essence and sang Ashe's name. The glowing piece of soul stopped moving. She ran to the flaming body and reached, unharmed, into the fire and grabbed the soul fragment, wresting it free from the grasp of death and clutching it to her heart.

Grunthor watched in amazement as the light dissolved into her, illuminating her upper body and making it in that instant translucent, then subsiding to a faint glow before dissipating. Rhapsody's hair gleamed red-gold for a moment, as though touched by a shaft of light from the setting sun, and then returned to its normal hue. The sergeant's eyes went from Achmed, still intensely concentrating on the strange Dhracian death dance as the ice form melted red into the earth, back to Rhapsody, whose expression had gone from a look of ecstasy when the soul entered her body to a look of horror. She was staring behind Achmed.

Grunthor's eyes caught the movement, saw the figure lunge, but he was too far away to intervene.

Rhapsody had recognized Jo immediately despite the inhuman expression locked on her sunken face, contorting it into something demonic. She knew instantly Jo's intention; the girl brandished the bronze-backed dirk that Grunthor had given her in the House of Remembrance. She was about to plunge it into the back of the Firbolg king, still in the midst of the Thrall ritual. There was no time to stop her, and Rhapsody's heart froze as she realized what she had to do.

She shouldered Achmed to the frozen ground, shattering the Thrall ritual and interposing herself between Jo and the Dhracian. Jo's course turned, following the angle of Achmed's fall; she was fast, faster than Rhapsody had imagined. The long dirk slashed through the air and drove toward Achmed's heart. With her only chance to save him Rhapsody parried with the sword, swinging the fiery blade over her head and slicing through Jo's abdomen with a sickening ease. Even before she could stand, she could see the wound was fatal.

Jo dropped her dirk. Her mouth opened and she stood up, staring down at the chasm that had opened in her abdomen. It first appeared as just a rip in her shirt, then it turned black, then dark red, then it sprawled open, her vital organs beginning to bulge out. She looked at Rhapsody and fear took hold on her face, a face now recognizable and without the demonic mask. Rhapsody's own face was whiter than death. She dropped the sword and reached out her hands to her sister.

Blood pulsed from the mortal gash, and Jo's intestines writhed, partially outside her abdomen, as her knees buckled under her. And something else; tucked among the coiled viscera Rhapsody could see a tiny green-black tendril like might be on a grape vine or a climbing bean, with what looked to be a thorn growing from it.

Suddenly all the sound around her was swallowed up in a moment of absolute focus, and in the utter silence she remembered Ashe's words: *It was like a vine growing up my spine, wrapping itself around my essence, becoming part of me as gently as a breeze, spreading without hesitation until it reached through my entire chest cavity.* The agony she was beginning to absorb – that she had surely killed Jo – gave way to an even greater horror.

'Gods! Achmed! *Achmed*! She's bound!'

The Three looked to Jo, and then to the ground. The frost from the grass was beginning to swirl into a low-lying mist, and thicken into a ropelike cloud that led from Jo's abdomen to the field beyond. The cloud darkened, and then grew substantial, knotting into a fibrous vine, shaggy with thorns and sliver-like bark. It twisted as it lifted off the ground and began to tug, dragging Jo abruptly over onto her back and nearer to its terminus.

Flecks of yellow foam spewed forth from her mouth and her skin turned rapidly gray as the blood continued in its rhythmic cascade, spraying the field and her companions with dapples of scarlet; her mouth was open in silent protest, her face contorted in the throes of death. They could see a faint glow of light emerge, wrapped in the bonds of the vine, and then her body went rigid. The physical and the metaphysical merged as body and soul prepared to separate.

Grunthor and Rhapsody fell on Jo, clutching at her stiff limbs and scrambling for purchase on the ground. With grim determination they drew their weapons, Grunthor pulling out the Friendmaker spike, Rhapsody the dragon's claw dagger. Desperately they began to hack at the snare, trying to pry it from around Jo's entrails. Pieces of flesh and viscera spattered them as they dug and slashed at what had once been her vital organs. Jo emitted one last deep gurgle. Then the only noise that came from her body was the hissing of the air escaping her bowels, the sound of ripping muscle and skin and the splash of her blood.

The vine fought back as though alive. Its tendrils flexed and banded together to form a squamous claw; it sliced at them savagely, ripping Grunthor's hide open at the wrist and drawing blood. It coiled around Rhapsody's foot in a stranglehold, and vines that had grown thorny daggers of enormous size stabbed at her back with snakelike strikes. Where it made contact it burned and smoked as though it was spattering acid.

Vines lashed out like whipcords, lacerating Grunthor's face with spiny barbs, and hundreds of small tendrils wrapped around his wrists, striking like serpents trying to pierce his hide. The two of them fought on, trying to ignore the assault. And though between them the mass they had secured Jo's body with was great, the vine appeared stronger, yanking her forward in spasmodic motions, pulling her insistently toward the middle of the field where Achmed had run.

As he crossed the fields of frost-bleached grain, Achmed could feel the air around him charged with power. There was a rip here, a tear in the fabric of the universe like the one he had seen on the Island that led to the horrors that had long ago been locked away in the Earth. When he reached the terminus of the vine Achmed stopped. Hovering in the air before him was the faint outline of a door, from behind which power was emanating and from which smoky darkness was emerging. A nauseating odor with which he was all too familiar tainted the air. It was as it had been with the Rakshas.

'F'dor!' Achmed shouted to Grunthor. The giant Bolg nodded and continued with the grisly task he had set about, trying to avoid the random lashings of the sinewy claws. Achmed pulled his hood back, took a deep breath, and seized the edges of the metaphysical door. He suspected it led to the Underworld from the reek of charnel that billowed through its ghostly cracks. The door bucked, and a great bilious roar issued forth, echoing over the meadow and into the valley below.

His blood boiled, and Achmed could feel the rhythm of his race beginning to rise up in it, humming with an insectoid noise like the scratching of cricket wings. He trembled with rage and the strain of holding the door, using the techniques he had learned ages ago to stay focused. With more force of will than physical strength he rotated his body and jammed his shoulder up against the vaporous portal. On the other side the fury of the screams he heard held a match for his own anger.

Rhapsody gasped in alarm as she saw the coils of the vine that held the formless light diverge from those that entwined Jo's body – it was taking her soul. Within moments, the sister she had loved, and had sworn to protect, would be eternally trapped within a deep earthern vault of fire, in the hands of the last remaining F'dor spirits. Her skin roared with heat at the thought.

She lunged to the right and rolled on the ground free of the vine, leaving Grunthor hacking away. Clearing her mind as best she could, she took a deep breath and began to sing. She chanted Jo's name, giving silent thanks that Jo had finally confided that she had no last name. She began a song of holding.

It started as a simple tune, repeated over and over, but with each new refrain a new element was added: a new note, a new rest, a new beat to the rhythm, so that as it became more complex it maintained its repetitive nature.

At the sound of her roundelay a tiny strand of light appeared; it billowed through the air around the formless mass glowing in the spirals of the vine, looping and weaving until it became a luminous chain hanging in the wind. As Rhapsody repeated the verses over and over it melded together, forming a circle, then a ball, of tiny light rings, like the gleaming mail of her dragon-scale armor. She directed it in the air like a net, interspersing Jo's name and her own status as her sister into the song, until she had captured the bright soul with it. Soon the chain and the vine were in opposition, with Jo's soul caught between them.

The glimmering light struggled against its musical bonds, wrenching back and forth in directionless anxiety. Rhapsody's breath was growing shorter and her notes became more staccato as the reality of what was happening began to catch up with her. With great effort not to break the tune she picked up Daystar Clarion and, raising the sword above her head, brought it down with all her remaining strength on the great arm of the vine that bound Jo's body to the door.

A hideous shriek blasted their ears, and the vine began to pulsate, its tendrils and thorns flailing wildly and slashing at whatever was nearby. Grunthor was flung out of the way as the cordage snapped and recoiled like a whip back across the meadow through the door. Only Achmed's extraordinary agility allowed him to dodge the racing vine; even so his clothes were torn by the barbs as they ripped past him. Jo's body, released from its tether, fell to the ground, and Grunthor, gaining his feet, finished gouging the remaining pieces of the vine from inside her abdominal cavity.

Achmed stumbled but maintained his balance as the rip in the fabric of the universe melted away into mist, then disappeared. He surveyed the scene around him, then returned to the spot where the Rakshas had fallen. He crouched low and touched the bloodstained ground, thinking.

Rhapsody staggered to where Jo lay as Grunthor was finishing, still singing the song of holding. She dropped to her knees on the frosty, gory earth and gathered Jo in her arms, then gave herself over to tears of deeper sorrow than she ever remembered shedding. Still she chanted, hiccoughing in between notes, unwilling to let Jo leave. Slowly, unconsciously she began to reinsert the girl's tattered entrails. The bright sun overhead stung her eyes and her world swam in a sickening haze.

Rhapsody. She barely heard the whisper above the pounding of the blood in her ears.

Rhapsody looked down at Jo's face through the waves of tears. The pallor of death had already set in, and her eyes blindly reflected the sunlight, open, as was her mouth, in frozen finality. The voice, light as air, called her name again above her faltering song.

Rhapsody, let go. It hurts.

'I'm sorry, I'm sorry. I never meant to hurt you. I can make it better, Jo.' Her sobs broke through the music. 'Hold on, hold on, Jo. A song; I can bring you back with a song. I did it with Grunthor – I'll find a way; there has to be a way. I can make it better.'

Rhapsody, let me go. My mother's waiting for me.

Rhapsody shook her head, trying to fend off the words hovering distantly on the wind. Even as they hung, lighter than the air that was pulsating in painful ripples all around her, there was a finality to them, a resoluteness that she could not deny. Deep within her soul, in the part where she and Jo were joined, she felt an impatience, a hurry to be free of the heavy air of the world.

Shaking, she let the roundelay grind to an end and drew Jo's body to her heart again. But the music continued on, soft, low tones within the earth and air responding to the heart of the Singer that did not wish to obey what she knew was right. Jo's body was beginning to stiffen in death, but she could hear the voice more clearly, though airy as before.

You were right, Rhaps. She does love me. Rhapsody began to tremble uncontrollably as her sobs grew to gasps for breath between the tears. *And happiness is waiting for me. Let me go. I want to know what it feels like.*

Grunthor's enormous hand came to rest gently on her head. 'Let her be, darlin'. Say good-bye and give her a good send-off, poor little miss.'

Somewhere inside herself Rhapsody found the strength to release her grip on Jo. Gently she laid her back on the ground, and the music ceased. With hands that shook she closed the sightless eyes. Though her head was swimming from the heat and the gore, she haltingly began the Lirin Song of Passage, the ageless tune sung under countless starry skies clouded by the smoke of funeral pyres. As she chanted the ancient lyrics she wove into them a measure of love and apology, and a clearing of the bonds of the Earth to speed the girl she loved as a sister on her way to the light.

Far off at the pinnacle of the sky she could hear the voice, one last time, soft as the falling of snow.

Rhapsody, your mother says she loves you, too.

Blind with grief, she bent her head again over the body and wept from the depths of her soul. She could feel Grunthor carefully gathering Jo in his arms and carrying her away from the site where she had fallen. Rhapsody tried to stand and follow him but the earth lurched beneath her; she swayed precariously as warm, strong hands shot forth from behind to steady her and keep her from toppling.

'Here,' said Achmed as he turned her around and looked at her. She was soaked in blood from her neck down to her knees, and pieces of the vine and fragments of Jo's viscera clung to her clothing, which was charred and still emitting smoke. He clasped her to his chest, supporting her shoulders with the embrace of one arm while the other hand ran gently over her hair and her back in a gesture meant to both comfort and bring her around. He stopped when he pulled his hand away, covered with fresh blood.

'Rhapsody?'

Achmed watched as her face turned white and her eyes rolled back. He shouted for Grunthor as he laid her on the ground, desperately examining her to find the source of the bleeding. He pulled off her dragonscale armor, tore open her shirt but found no wound. His bloodsense directed him; he followed her waning heartbeat down to her thigh and found ugly gashes, one the length of his hand, the point of a thorn still embedded in it. The wound pulsed with each beat of her heart; Achmed knew the vine had severed an artery. The ground turned crimson beneath her as bright blood seeped through her clothing and into the earth.

'Come on, Rhapsody, we've been in worse fights than this,' Achmed cajoled, trying to keep her conscious. 'I know you think you look good in red, but this is ridiculous.' Grunthor rolled her on her side, plucked out the fragment of thorn and held her stationary while Achmed ripped off the bottom of his cloak and bound her leg. Then he took out his waterskin and splashed some of its contents in her face, hoping to revive her. When there was no response he slapped her hand, then her cheek, until her eyes fluttered weakly open.

Achmed could see that her hold on wakefulness was tenuous. 'My, I enjoyed that,' he said directly into her ear. 'Please pass out one more time so I can slap you again.' Her response was still slight. 'Look, Rhapsody, sleep on your own time, will you? This is no way to get out of your share of the work breaking camp.' Her breath was no longer visible in the frosty air. He looked up at Grunthor, and the giant Firbolg shook his head.

'Here, you get Jo; I'll take her. The horses are about half a league down the grade of this hill. Let's get them out of here.'

'Right.' Grunthor rushed back to retrieve the body, the ground shaking as he ran.

They carried the two women, one dead, the other not far from it, down the windy hill to the hidden encampment where the horses waited, grimly saddled up and made for Sepulvarta.

47

The Cauldron itself was unchanged. Death was no stranger to the mountain; Canrif, and then Ylorc, had been the site of many a deathwatch after bitter retreat, as well as the planning place for many a brutal killing. For Achmed, however, it was the first time he had found himself in the semi-dark, planning for someone to live.

Unconsciously he was going about it in much the same way that he planned a demise. He went endlessly over the facts of the case, the infinitesimal details of how this could have come to pass, the hunt, the melee, the sites of her wounds, the way the blood had escaped her body. He tried to put the pieces of Rhapsody's survival into place, the way he would have arranged the sequence of an assassination.

He was not getting anywhere.

Grunthor approached the door as quietly as he could, then knocked softly. Hearing no response, he opened it and came in.

The room was dark but for the minimal light cast by a few scented candles in the corner, far from the bed, and the sporadic radiance of strangely glowing wine bottles positioned in various places about the room. Grunthor had one in his hand; he closed the door quietly behind him, looking for a moment at the flickering container before approaching Achmed who sat, as he had for the past four days and nights, in the chair beside the bed.

'Sir?'

'Hmm?'

'I brought you some fresh fireflies. Them must be gettin' tired.'

Achmed said nothing.

'Any change?'

'No.'

Grunthor looked down at her; asleep or unconscious, it was hard to tell. It was impossible, in fact, to tell at the moment if she was even still alive. Her normally rosy skin was pale like the seashell he had once found at the oceanside, and she looked very tiny in the big bed. He had teased her at every opportunity about her petite stature, but somehow in motion she gave the impression of muscular strength and vitality. Now she appeared frail, childlike.

He looked down at his oldest friend and sovereign, whose lower face was hidden by folded hands. An ancient story occurred to Grunthor, the tale of a Bolg who had placed himself at the gates between Life and Death and would allow none to pass in order to forestall the demise of a comrade. It had a messy ending.

Achmed shifted in the chair. 'Has there been any word from Ashe?'

'Not yet, sir.'

The Dhracian rested his chin on the heel of his hand and fell silent again. Grunthor assumed parade rest.

'Would you like me to stay with her for a while, sir? I'd be glad to, and you could get some sleep.'

Achmed leaned back in the chair and crossed his arms over his waist. He said nothing.

Grunthor waited a few moments more. 'Will that be all, sir?'

'Yes. Good night, Grunthor.'

Grunthor set the wine bottle down on the stone that served as a bedside table, then reached under the bed to turn over the heated rocks that functioned as the room's source of warmth. Achmed had been insistent that the room be warmed and lit without using the fireplace for fear that the smoke or the acrid fumes from the burning peat would harm her.

It was Grunthor who came up with the idea of the fireflies and ordered the Firbolg army to set about gathering them. It was a dismal task in early autumn anyway, and the sight of monsters in mail clanking through the fields with wine bottles, desperately jumping after the hovering insects would have made Rhapsody laugh if she had been able to appreciate it. Grunthor gave her a kiss on the forehead as he rose, then left the room without another word.

Achmed continued to watch her in silence. After an hour or so the Firbolg medics came in with medicinal herbs and supplies, replacement hot rocks and clean piles of the muslin rags that served as bandages. They behaved quietly and respectfully, finishing with their tasks and leaving the room as quickly as possible.

Achmed waited until they were gone, and then gently undressed Rhapsody and bathed her wounds, changing the bandages and her shirt. The irony of the situation made him grimace. He had been so annoyed with her spending time ministering to the Firbolg, soaking gauze bandages in herbs to cure infections, singing to ease their pain. Now the procedures she had taught them, and him, were quite possibly the only things keeping her alive.

He leaned forward in the chair, resting his forehead in his hands, and looked at the waves of golden hair lying around her pillow like a sunlit sea. Against his will, the memory came back to him, the first of their many exchanges about her healing efforts.

Well, that's a useful investment of your evening, he had groused. *I'm sure the Firbolg are very appreciative, and will certainly reciprocate your ministrations if you should ever need something.*

What does that mean?

I'm trying to tell you that you will never see any return for your efforts. When you are injured or in pain, who will sing for you, Rhapsody?

Why, Achmed, you will.

So many funny memories had lost their amusement value. He remembered the way her eyes had looked in the dark, how she had smiled as if she knew something. *You will.*

Achmed rested his fingers on her wrist, then her neck, sensing her pulse to see if the heartbeat had grown any stronger. It was there, fighting on, holding its own, though it still seemed weak to him.

He and Grunthor had braved the streets of Sepulvarta, the nearest place of healing to where they had fought the Rakshas, the place Rhapsody had fallen. Waves of panic had resonated through the city at the sight of the two Firbolg riders galloping up the hill to the rectory, the dying woman in the arms of the smaller one.

The priests in the manse had been unable to bring her around, and even the Patriarch, carried in from his cell in the hospice, had only been able to stabilize her. Achmed knew by the look of despair in the old man's eyes that it was absence of his ring that prevented him from being able to heal her, and he cursed Ashe silently. All the skills the Patriarch's clergyman brought to bear merely made it possible for them to take her back, still unconscious and deathly fragile, to Ylorc. The healers Achmed had sent for from the outlying areas had advised him politely to prepare for the worst, and had left hurriedly, without exception, in the face of his wrathful reaction.

'Come on, Rhapsody,' he muttered, frustration curling his face into a contorted knot. 'Show them all, the imbeciles; show them you're not the fragile harlot – show them what we both know you're really made of.'

He ran a hand over his slippery hair and brought his head to rest in the crook of his elbow. As the dim light of the room receded even more, he saw her face, bruised and bleeding from her first combat on the Root, her eyes glittering in the fire-colored darklight of the path through the Earth, as she had applied the spiced bandage to his wrist, hesitantly singing her first song of healing.

Music is nothing more than the maps through the vibrations that make up all the world. If you have the right map, it will take you wherever you want to go.

Achmed moved to the bed, sitting as close to her as he could without causing her discomfort. He leaned his head down over her chest, feeling in his skin the beating of her heart, the tides of her breath. His eyes took in her face from different angles, searching for improvement in the pallor, places where the sunken flesh might have returned to its former shape. With infinite care his fingers traced the line of the blood loss under her eyes, and came to rest on the stray lock of hair curling down the edge of her cheek.

'Rhapsody,' he said in a voice of utter solemnity, 'between two worlds I have had but two friends. I am not willing to let you alter this.'

Who will sing for you, Rhapsody?

You will.

The ritual he had used to paralyze and enthrall the Rakshas was the only song he had ever sung. It had come to him from deep within his belly, humming through the multiple chambers of his heart, throat, and sinuses until it transmitted out through his skull. The melody was not his own, but rather was written deep in the Before-Time as his race was conceived. The Grandmother had imparted to him the secrets of using it. It was not until he had done so that he had learned how it actually worked.

There was a duality to it. The ancient tune, the pattern of the notes, was the snare for the demon side of the F'dor, holding it against its will on the threshold between the Earth and the netherworld to which it sought to flee.

But the human host was vulnerable to the sounds of the song as well; the vibrations called the blood to the brain and swelled it. The Rakshas was an artificial construct, and thus not really alive. But had it been the F'dor he was enthralling, the demon-spirit in the body of a human host, it would have been different. If he were alone with such a being, and able to sustain the Thrall ritual long enough, the rush of blood would cause his foe's head to burst. This was the only song he knew, the healing act that Rhapsody needed. Achmed had no idea if it would kill her.

You know, Grunthor, you could help with the healing as well. You like to sing.

I believe you've heard the content of my songs, miss. Generally they tend to be more on the threatnin' side, if you get my drift. And I don't think anyone's ever gonna mistake me for a Singer. I certainly got no trainin' in it.

The fondness in her eyes had gleamed with an intensity that matched her smile.

Content makes no difference at all. It can be any kind of song. What matters is their belief in you. The Bolg have given you their allegiance. You're their version of 'The Last Word, to Be Obeyed at All Costs.' In a way, they've named you. It doesn't matter what you sing, just that you expect them to get well. And they will.

I've always maintained that Achmed will do the same for me one day.

Under his breath Achmed swore vile epithets in every tongue he knew. 'You set this up, didn't you? Was it really worth the risk for your entertainment? I should have left you out there to bleed to death. You deserve it for what you force me to do.' His hand trembled as he brushed the stray lock tenderly off her face.

You will.

The wilted blossom had swelled with moisture, uncurling in his palm as she sang the notes, the wordless call to its name. *It's part of what a Namer can do; there is no thing, no concept, no law as strong as the power of a given thing's name. Our identities are bound to it. It is the essence of what we are, and sometimes it can even make us what we are again, no matter how much we have been altered.*

Achmed sighed. She had bound him to it, and he hadn't even realized it when it happened. She had given him the key to help her, even as he mocked her. Like it or not, he had been named as her healer.

He glanced about the room furtively, then, reassured of their privacy, he cleared his throat and tried to summon forth a musical sound, but nothing came out. 'Bloody *hrekin*; this was brilliant of you,' he muttered, scowling at her. 'Require music of someone who has sung once in his entire life? Why not just ask the rocks to do it? You would have had better luck.' He tried to think of another song he knew.

The obscene marching song Grunthor had used to herd the new recruits came into his mind, bringing an unexpected smile to his face. Rhapsody and Jo had occasionally sung it in comic exaggerations of the Sergeant's accented bass. His smile faded as quickly as it had come at the thought of Jo, now lying, pale and lifeless, in the silent chamber that had been the only real home the street child had ever known. There was little enough difference in the way Rhapsody looked now to make his hands grow clammy.

He had seen and dispensed enough death in his lifetime to be unmoved by it. In their time together he and Grunthor had both faced the potential demise of the other without panic, each possessing an understanding of the stakes of the game they played.

This was different. As each drop of blood had left her, draining bits of her life with it, he had wanted to scream, had held Rhapsody's wounds together with his hands as they rode at full gallop toward Sepulvarta, guiding the horse with his knees alone. The terror he felt at the thought of losing her had surprised no one more than himself. A song seemed little enough to pay to keep her on this side of the gate of Life.

Achmed took a deep breath. In a halting voice that resonated with scratchy vibrato and clicked with a fricative percussion, he sang to her a song of his own making, a song that even he didn't know the genesis or the meaning of. In a world where the grinding sound of a rockslide whispered lullabyes or cracking timbers soothed the angry, it might have been a lovely song. From one man came three voices, one sharp and rapid, one low, like the shadow of a note just missed in the distance, and this time, there were words.

> Mo haale maar, my hero gone
> World of star become world of bone
> Grief and pain and loss I know
> My heart is sore, my blood-tears flow
> To end my sorrow I must roam
> My terrors old, they lead me home.

Rhapsody stirred beneath the blankets, and Achmed could hear a painful sigh escape her. Then he felt small, soft fingers with callused tips brush his hand, and heard her inhale as though undertaking something very difficult.

'Achmed?'

'Yes?'

Her voice was a weak whisper. 'Will you keep singing until I'm better?'

'Yes.'

'Achmed?'

'What?' He leaned forward to catch the soft words.

'I'm better.'

'Obviously you're not much better if that's the best you can do,' he said, smiling at the gentle insult. 'But you're still the same ungrateful brat you always were. That's nice thanks for someone who just gave you back the will to live.'

'You're right, you did,' she said slowly, and with great effort. 'Now that you – have given me – a taste of – what the Underworld – is like – '

Achmed laughed in relief. 'You deserve it. Welcome back, Rhapsody.'

When night fell the following day, Grunthor carefully lifted Rhapsody from her bed and carried her to the heath. Achmed was waiting there, the pyre built and primed. The Sergeant helped her to stand while the Firbolg king drew her sword for her and helped her hold it aloft.

Rhapsody's weak eyes came to rest for a moment on the white-shrouded figure that crowned the pile of frost-blistered wood, then searched the night sky for a star to call.

If you can find your guiding star, you will never be lost. Never.

She finally made one out that she knew, Prylla, an evening star revered by the Lirin of this land. It was named for a woodland goddess of ancient myth, the Windchild, reputed to have sung her songs into the north wind in the hope of finding the love she had lost. Only the wind had answered her; somehow Rhapsody found the legend poignantly appropriate for Jo. She cleared her mind as best she could, then pointed Daystar Clarion heavenward and spoke the name of the star.

The hillside was illuminated by a light brighter than any of them had ever seen, blinding them temporarily and radiating over the fields to the canyon. It touched the face of the mountains, making them shine with a splendor past that of the setting sun. Then with a roar, a searing flame descended, hotter than the fires of the Earth's core. It ignited the pyre, causing the wood to explode with flames that danced skyward. The fire burned quickly, sending a rolling wave of smoke into the wind and up to the starry canopy above them.

Rhapsody sang, in a voice barely above a whisper, her sister's name and the first few notes of the Lirin Song of Passage before she was too drained to continue; she had performed the rite already, she knew. Jo was already in the light.

The Three stood together, watching the flames take their friend. The ashes ascended into the air and the wind took them, whipping across the heath and over the mountains, twisting and swirling in beautiful patterns of white like rising snow in the darkness.

After that her strength returned quickly. She seemed a little more herself each day, though the light in her eyes was conspicuously absent. Grunthor sat on the edge of her bed and told her filthy jokes and bawdy stories of life among the Bolg as he had before, remembering how much they had made her laugh. The anecdotes still brought a smile, but somehow it was not the same. Her soul was not healing as quickly as her body.

Achmed worried visibly about her. His thinking was belabored and his mood worse than usual, as demonstrated by the circumspect manner that his soldiers and guards adopted when in the Cauldron. They spoke in whispers and refrained from any kind of fighting or loud arguments, having once experienced the wrath of the Warlord after their high-spirited bantering had woken the First Woman from a fitful sleep. There had been such suffering as a result that the word spread quickly throughout the Mountain, and Grunthor had many more volunteers for duty outside the Teeth than ever before.

Her two friends afforded Rhapsody her privacy, never prying into her feelings with questions about her state of well-being; they knew the source of her pain, and were at a loss to know what to do about it. Their presence was a wellspring of great comfort to her. Achmed took to reading his briefings or studying the infinite manuscripts of Gwylliam's vaults in her room at night while she sorted herbs or wrote music, comfortable in their mutual silence.

Rhapsody had come upon Grunthor, quite by accident, when walking back to her room to replenish her supply of clean clothes. She was well enough to walk alone for short periods, and was in the process of fumbling for her key when she heard a noise in Jo's room across the hall.

She went to the door and opened it quietly, peering into the darkness to find the giant Bolg sitting on Jo's bed with his chin resting on his palms, a blank look of bewilderment on his face. The crates and sacks on the floor indicated he had come to clean out her belongings, probably with a mind to sparing Rhapsody the task, but instead he had found no clutter. None of Jo's hoarded treasures were anywhere in her quarters. It was as if the street child had discarded every memento she had ever collected. He looked up at Rhapsody as she walked in and silently came into his arms, her head still barely reaching his shoulder even as he sat.

'I don't know what happened, darlin',' he said, shaking his head ruefully. 'We must have lost her a long time ago, and we didn't even know it.' Rhapsody just nodded and hugged him tighter.

Finally the awkward solitude came to an end in a queasy realization. Achmed had come in the night to check on Rhapsody to find her sitting in the corner of the room, her arms wrapped around herself, staring at the ceiling. He approached her slowly and slid down the wall next to her into a sitting position on the floor, where he waited in silence, watching her. Finally she turned to him and made eye contact. Their gaze locked, and then she closed her eyes and spoke.

'Do you think Jo was pregnant?'

Achmed shook his head. 'I saw her the day before, and she seemed vibrationally the same. Of course, I can't be sure, but I would guess not.'

Rhapsody nodded, then looked down at her drawn-up knees. 'Oelendra once said the F'dor were masters of manipulation that spent eternity trying to figure out ways to get around the limits of their own power.'

'That's accurate.'

'And the prophecy about the F'dor – the uninvited guest – says that it will "bind to no body that has borne or sired children, nor can it ever do so, lest its power be further dispersed", right?'

'Yes.'

'Elynsynos said the Firstborn, the five oldest races, which included both dragons and F'dor, have control over their own procreation.' Achmed swallowed the ugly comment about Ashe that danced on his lips. 'It's a conscious decision for them to break their essence open in order to expand their power, because having progeny makes them immortal, in a way, but it can also weaken the parent.' Achmed nodded again. 'So what if the F'dor wanted to expand its power, make itself immortal, but didn't want to lessen its own strength? How would it do so?'

Achmed saw her point immediately. 'It would find a way for its blood to reproduce without its body having to.'

Rhapsody nodded, her eyes glimmering. 'The Rakshas. It wasn't just using rape as a form of terror and a method for binding souls. It was breeding new hosts for the demon.'

'I don't think you're well enough, Duchess. You shouldn't be ridin' yet.'

Rhapsody bent down and kissed the great green-gray cheek. 'I'll be fine. Achmed is here, and if I'm feeling weak I can ride with him.' The mare danced impatiently, held in place by the reins and bridle in Grunthor's hand. The Singer spoke softly to her, gentling her down.

'We'll be back shortly,' said Achmed, mounting the horse the quarter-master had brought and provisioned for him. 'If this leads to a hunt, we'll come back here first to make arrangements.' Grunthor and Achmed exchanged a look; *keep her safe*, the Sergeant was saying. The Firbolg king nodded in assent.

'Now, where actually is this Rhonwyn person, eh?'

'In an abbey in Sepulvarta,' Rhapsody said, watching the quartermaster check her saddle and cinch the girth. 'It's about ten days' ride from here, north of Sorbold on the other side of Bethe Corbair. We should be back in three weeks easily.'

'Easy for you,' the Bolg grumbled. 'I, on the other hand, never get to go nowhere fun no more. No, I get stuck baby-sittin' the Bolglands.'

Achmed smiled. 'Try not to break any treaties while I'm gone.' He clicked to his mount, and the two travelers set off across the Orlandan plain for Sepulvarta.

48

Ashe ran through the halls of the Cauldron, his footfalls sounding on the inert stone. He had run all the way from Kraldurge after finding Elysian dark and empty, causing passing sentries to try to overtake him, only to find him gone from their vision within seconds.

One dark passageway had a light at the end. It was the council room behind the Great Hall where the downward spiral had begun, the place where things had started to go wrong. Ashe cursed under his breath as he hurried through the arched doorway.

Grunthor was sitting at the massive table, scratching away with a quill on a large field map. He was drawing terrain charts and topographical diagrams; Ashe's dragon sense innately made note of the excellent detail and accuracy. The landmarks were unlabeled, probably a function of Grunthor's limited literacy.

The giant Bolg looked up and broke into a grisly grin. 'Well, hello, Ashe,' he said, putting down his quill. He sat back in the immense chair and folded his hands over his stomach. 'I guess this means there really were two of you after all. What brings you around?'

'Where's Rhapsody? I overheard two sentries say she'd been badly injured.'

'Sorry, old boy, I'm afraid you're too late. She's gone.'

'What?' Ashe's voice trembled suddenly.

'Yeah,' Grunthor said, smiling and savoring Ashe's sudden panic. 'She and Achmed went for a ride a few days ago.' He picked up his quill again and returned to his work. 'You sure took your sweet time gettin' here.'

Ashe leaned on the table. 'What do you mean, she went for a ride with Achmed?'

Grunthor grinned but did not look up. 'Just what I said. They wanted some time alone together – if you get the gist.'

'Oh, please.' Ashe felt his face twist in disgust. He had to shake his head to drive the abhorrent picture from his mind. 'Where did they go?'

'I think they went off to find Rhonwyn, you know, your auntie.'

'I know who Rhonwyn is. Why would they go to see her?'

'Somethin' to do with Her Ladyship's grandkids. If it's any of your business.'

Ashe was growing irritated. 'What do you mean by that?'

Grunthor's head remained stationary, but his eyes looked up, and they were full of accusation. 'Well now, where was you when she was dyin', eh? After all she done, is doin' for you, where was you when she needed you?'

'I was on the coast.' Even under the hood, Grunthor would hear the self-recrimination in his voice. 'What happened? Is she all right?'

Grunthor nodded toward one of the chairs. Ashe sat and dropped his pack to the floor as the Sergeant filled a flagon from the pitcher next to him. 'She was injured while savin' the little miss's soul.'

'Jo? Jo was hurt too?'

'Yeah, you might say that. She's dead.' Grunthor's face was emotionless, his tone noncommittal, but the dragon could sense a sudden skip of his heartbeat, the increase of liquid in the giant's tear ducts, the tiny twitching of muscles in his great protruding jaw as it tightened. The silent responses said all that Ashe needed to know.

'Gods, Grunthor; I'm sorry.' Ashe's thoughts shot to Rhapsody; she must be devastated. 'What happened?'

'The bastard F'dor got to her. She must of followed us, even though we went out of our way to avoid it; we didn't even know she was there. And just as Achmed was draggin' your sorry soul out of the burning refuse, she attacked. I never in all my time with him ever seen no one get close enough to touch him, but the king was a bit, well, distracted, shall we say? He would of taken one in the heart for you, sonny. Ironic, ain't it?' Grunthor took a deep drink from his flagon.

'Of course, the Duchess couldn't let that come to pass. She was next to him, and she tried to block with her body, but Jo was too fast. So she did what she should of; she parried. And she slashed Jo open; taught her well, I must say.' He took another drink. Ashe's hands reached for the flagon Grunthor had set in front of him, trembling slightly.

'Then a bloody *tree* started growing from Jo's guts, and we was forced to cut it out, but you see, this vine-thing didn't want to be cut out, so it sort of attacked us back. It would of killed the Duchess too if it weren't for the king. You sure weren't nowhere to be found when we were trying to fix her. She still ain't gotten over killing Jo.'

Ashe stared into the immense firepit in silence. He tried to imagine what Rhapsody must be feeling, but he couldn't get past his own mountain of guilt. She was out of the range of his senses, and that bothered him more than anything else.

'I'm very sorry,' he said at last. 'I'm sorry about Jo, Grunthor. How is Rhapsody? Is she all right?'

Grunthor put his feet up on the table, the thud of the gigantic boots shaking the chairs in the room. 'Well, I suppose that depends on how you define "all right." She's alive.'

'That's a start.'

'She's awful weak, if you ask me, which nobody did; I wouldn't let her go out riding across the countryside in her current state, looking pale as a ghost. But whatever she needed to do was too important to the Duchess to get her to listen, and you can't argue with her when she's like that.'

Ashe sighed. 'I know.'

Grunthor chuckled. 'She's a little slip of a thing, but she's tough. I'd rather have her watch my back as anyone.'

'I agree. And she credits you with a lot of that, you know. She said even Oelendra admired the training you had given her.'

The giant smiled. 'Yeah, she told me. But I think it's more a matter of the fact that the Duchess's heart is bigger than her body.'

Ashe smiled to himself. 'It certainly is.'

Grunthor leaned across the table. 'And to that end, I'm warning you, waterboy, you better not do nothing to break it, 'cause if you do, I'll snap you like a twig.'

'I'll keep that in mind.' Tankards clinked together, and then were emptied.

Achmed took Rhapsody by the waist and lifted her down from the horse. He could see she was grateful to be on ground that was not moving for the first time in a while. Generally when they rode together, Achmed left her on her own to mount and dismount, but he had noticed the way her face turned white with each of these actions now, and so made an exception to his general rule of benign neglect.

They made their way through the Square of the Spire, the vast, cobbled courtyard of the walled part of the city of Sepulvarta. The courtyard stretched to the edges of the inner rim of the mercantile district.

In the center of the square stood the mammoth structure that Rhapsody had seen from the Great Basilica when she had stood with the Patriarch on the Holy Night. It was massive at the bottom, spanning the width of a city block, tapering upward a thousand feet in the air to its point, crowned by a radiant silver star. The star was visible for a hundred miles on a clear day, more at night, and was reputed to contain a piece of the Sleeping Child, the star in Seren myth that had fallen into the sea, causing the first Great Cataclysm. The impact of the star's entry into the sea, said the legend, had caused earthquakes and subsequent tidal waves that split the land and swamped the Island, leaving it half its previous size. It had lain beneath the waves for four millennia, boiling the ocean above it, until at last it had risen and claimed the rest of the Island, along with whatever had remained of Rhapsody's family and the two Bolgs' problems.

The people who traversed the streets of Sepulvarta, in addition to the same kind of travelers that were apparent in every inland city, were in many cases members of the clergy and their families. Sepulvarta was the theological seat of Roland and Sorbold, as well as the nonallied outlying states, and many priests of the religion lived there, studying in the vast library and the depositories of liturgical writings, training in the central seminaries. Holy symbols and sacred signs of the order were as apparent in the shops and homes as hex signs and runic symbols were in Gwynwood. It was, as a result, not easy to find the Abbey of the Sun, a tiny cloister in the outer ecclesiastical district, where Rhonwyn the Seer was reputed to live.

Not much was known about the middle child of Elynsynos and Merithyn. She was said to be insane, as her sisters were, bent by the knowledge that was her gift and her curse, but frail, like the realm she was given sight into. As she could only see the Present, she was considered the least useful as a Seer, for, after all, it was believed, anyone could see the

Present. Any given point in time a moment later became the Past, and was therefore beyond her sight. So Achmed and Rhapsody were not particularly surprised to find the abbey rundown and neglected, visited by none but themselves.

After passing through the wrought-iron gates and past the tiny garden, they found themselves on crumbling stone steps in front of an ancient wooden door, bound in brass, with a large ringed door knocker. Rhapsody knocked, and after some time the abbess answered. She ushered them both in rapidly and looked into the street behind them before shutting the door. Achmed recognized the behavior; he had seen people in hiding before.

After their request was made they were led to a tiny, dark parlor and left waiting for a long time. While they waited Rhapsody dropped several gold coins in the slotted box left conspicuously on a table. Finally the abbess returned and led them out through a curtained rear door into a quiet courtyard, thick with the dust of a walled city enclosure and the undisturbed passage of time. She pointed skyward.

From there they made a long and arduous climb up an external stairway hewn into the stone from which the abbey was built. The building itself, while but a few stories in height, reached up above the silent street below with a steepled tower and balcony. Inside they could see the outline of a robed figure, sitting and looking up into the sky above her.

When they reached the balcony of the tower, Rhapsody took from her pack the gift she had brought. It was the sack in which she had carried the loaf of bread that Pilam the baker had given her that afternoon, all those centuries before, in Easton. While traveling along the Root Rhapsody had blessed each meal it had made by singing the name of the bread. As a result the bread had never gone stale or grown mold, even within the dank earth. Time still seemed to have no domain within the sack; the bread within it now was as fresh as it had been the morning it was baked in Ylorc ten days before. It seemed an appropriate gift. She laid it gently in the Seer's hands.

The woman turned to her and smiled, and Rhapsody gasped. Her eyes were blind, totally without a colored iris, reflecting Rhapsody's face, like the dream she'd had in Ashe's hut. The Seer's face was smooth, in the bloom of youth, her hair red-gold like Ashe's at the crown of her head, but as it tapered down the long braid bound in leather thongs it passed into dimmer stages, darkening and turning gray until it reached the snow-white tip. She was clothed in the same robes as the abbess had worn, and in her lap rested a nautical instrument. Rhapsody had seen one before as a child; it was a compass. Rhonwyn seemed frail and lost in a dream.

'God give you good day, Grandmother,' Rhapsody said. She touched the woman's hand gently. The Seer nodded, then looked back up at the sky again. 'I am called Rhapsody.'

'Yes,' the woman answered distantly, as if considering something puzzling. She touched the compass. 'You are called Rhapsody. What do you ask?'

Achmed sighed; he knew he was going to hate this. He walked over to the corner of the tower and looked out over the street.

'Do you know the name of the F'dor?'

The woman shook her head. Rhapsody had expected this. She had once asked Ashe why consulting with this Seer would not be the easiest way to yield its name. He had told her that Rhonwyn could not even see into the Past enough to name something ancient that had originated in a land that no longer existed. Serendair had no present, so the F'dor would not be visible to Rhonwyn. Rhapsody smiled as the woman reached into the bag and drew forth some bread, raising it to her lips. She waited for Rhonwyn to swallow before asking her next question.

'Does the Rakshas have any children?'

'There is no Rakshas.'

Rhapsody sighed. 'Are there now children with the blood of the F'dor?'

The Seer nodded.

'How many are there now?'

'How many what?'

'How many children are there born of the blood of the F'dor?'

'Nine now live.'

Rhapsody nodded again. She reached back into her pack and pulled out a scrap of vellum and a piece of charcoal. 'What are their names, how old are they, and where are they today?' she asked.

'Who?'

'What are the names of the demon-spawn, how old are they, and where are they today?'

'A child named Mikita lives in the Hintervold. She has seen two summers,' said Rhonwyn.

'Where in the Hintervold?'

The Seer turned to her with blind eyes. 'What about the Hintervold?'

'Where is the child in the Hintervold?'

'What child?'

Rhapsody could feel Achmed's shoulders tense from across the tower. She lowered her voice, making it as soothing as she could to avoid upsetting the fragile Seer. 'Where is the demon-spawn, Mikita, in the Hintervold?'

'In Vindlanfia, across the Edelsak River in the town of Carle.'

Rhapsody caressed her shoulder gently. 'Is Mikita the youngest of the demon-spawn children?'

'Yes.'

'What is the name of the second-youngest demon-spawn child?'

'Jecen.'

'How old is Jecen?'

'Jecen who?'

Rhapsody sighed. 'How old is Jecen, the child of the demon?'

'Today he has seen three summers.'

Slowly Rhapsody led Rhonwyn through the agonizing ritual of

uncovering the information she needed. The Seer began to recite a litany of names, places, and ages, her voice a soft monotone droning in the wind of the tower, broken intermittently by Rhapsody's gentle questions. The list they compiled together ranged from a child of two to a gladiator in the country of Sorbold, who that day was nineteen years old. Rhapsody looked at Achmed and shuddered. That one would be difficult.

When the Seer was finished, Rhapsody thanked her and stood. She bent to give her a kiss, but stopped when she saw Achmed hold up a finger.

'Are there any unborn children with the blood of the F'dor?' he asked. Rhapsody shuddered again; this thought had not occurred to her.

'Yes.'

'Who is the mother?'

'The mother of whom?'

'Of the child about to be born?' The Seer looked blank. Rhapsody exhaled. 'I'm sorry; I suppose that she isn't a mother yet, so you can't see her. When will the baby be born, and where?' The woman stared off into the distance.

'A question for Manwyn, perhaps,' noted Achmed. Rhapsody nodded.

'Thank you, Grandmother,' she said softly, and kissed her cheek. The woman turned to her and smiled again. 'Rest now.'

'You are called Rhapsody,' Rhonwyn said dreamily. 'What do you ask?'

Eleven days later, as soon as Rhapsody set foot on the island of Elysian, Ashe knew she was there. The water had transmitted the news of her approach in the boat, but she had arrived at night, so he had been sleeping, instead of at his usual post waiting impatiently. In his half-sleep he had believed he was dreaming of her arrival, as he had each night, to wake up, alone and disappointed. He sat upright in bed, then leapt out of it, running down the stairs to greet her.

She had felt him, too, felt the worry and fear he had brought into the grotto, and came to him, letting him sweep her into his arms and carry her inside. She stroked his hair as his tears washed over her, clutching her as tightly as he dared in light of the wounds he could sense beneath her clothes. Ashe laid her down gently on the bed and sat next to her, allowing his eyes and senses to run over her, his hands following suit.

He opened his mouth to speak, but before he could she laid a finger on his lips to silence him.

'Don't,' she said gently. 'I'm fine; I'm so happy to see you. Please hold me.' He complied, drawing her back into his arms and hugging her as tightly as he dared.

After a long time had passed, he released her reluctantly and looked at her again. He began to undress her, to look at the wounds with his eyes rather than his senses, but she stopped him.

'Please, Ashe, don't.'

'Maybe I can help heal you, Aria.'

Rhapsody smiled. 'You are. And you already have.' She looked around the room. 'And you will even more if you get off your behind and get me some tea.' She laughed as he dashed down the stairs.

As she sipped her tea, Ashe sat on the edge of her bed and removed her boots.

'Where on Earth did you go?'

'I went to see Rhonwyn,' she said, her enormous eyes blinking at him from behind her cup.

'So I heard. Are you out of your mind?'

'Yes. But you knew that before you became my lover.'

'What could possibly be so important that you had to rush off there while you're still so weak? Grunthor said it had something to do with your grandchildren – are Stephen's children all right?'

'As far as I know,' she said. 'I was inquiring about some other children that I hope to be able to help, not the ones who are currently my grandchildren.'

'I see. And do you want to tell me about it?'

'No,' she said, setting down her teacup and putting her arms around his neck. 'I have a gift for you, and I want you to open it.'

'You brought me a gift? You shouldn't – '

Rhapsody glared at him in amusement. 'Shut up, dear,' she said, leaning forward to kiss him. Ashe complied, returning the kiss as gently as he could, fighting the passion that had swarmed through his soul along with overwhelming relief. She slid his nightshirt over his shoulders and gave him a sympathetic look.

'Please don't worry about hurting me, Ashe,' she said, anticipating his worries exactly. He shuddered as the memory of another woman's voice flooded his heart.

It's all right, Sam. You won't hurt me. Really. It will be all right.

Tears touched the corners of his eyes as he closed them and leaned his head against her shoulder, running his hands gently up her back. He undressed her carefully, wincing at the sight of the bandages, and drew the covers over them both.

Rhapsody reached behind her head with some difficulty and unbound the black velvet ribbon, allowing her hair to tumble over both of their shoulders. Ashe sighed and drew her onto his chest, cradling her in the crook of his arm. With some impatience she pulled free of the sleeping position, sat up and caressed his chest, her hands moving lower as his heart began to race beneath her touch. He grabbed her hands and held them in his own.

'Aria, please, perhaps we had best just sleep.'

Shock, then disappointment came over Rhapsody's face. Ashe's heart twisted as he saw the rejection he had never intended in her eyes.

'Is it the bandages? Or do you just not want me?'

Excitement was coursing through his blood, leaving his skin on fire and making his head pound. 'How can you ask me that?' he said incredulously,

400

moving her hands to the best indicator of her misjudgment. 'I don't want to hurt you, and I know you're exhausted.'

'I need you to make love to me,' she said patiently. 'Please.'

Ashe began to shake. 'Gods, you're cruel. Aria, I want to be inside you more than you could ever believe, but – '

'Ashe, you *are* inside me, and I want you to leave,' she said, exasperation entering her voice. 'Now, please, are you going to make me beg you?'

The wall of his resistance shattered. 'No,' he said, breathing deeply. 'No, and I can't believe we're having this conversation.' He pulled her to him and kissed her with all the longing in his soul.

He made love to her gently, fighting the fierce desire that had risen as a result of the overwhelming emotions of the night: fear, longing, relief, and joy in being reunited with her again. She returned his passion eagerly, moving slowly and building in him a towering pleasure that threatened to consume him. As a cold rush began to creep over him, starting at his toes and moving upward, she took his hand and put it on her heart.

'Take it back,' she urged, resting her hand over his. 'Take your soul back; it's waiting for you here.' His eyes opened in surprise, but he was too far gone to stop the rush from taking him over. He began to gasp, and as he did Rhapsody spoke the word to release the piece of his soul she had carried.

Blinding light emerged between them, shining through both of their upper bodies and making them translucent. As Ashe's body stiffened in ecstatic release, the light entered his chest and left Rhapsody's completely. She began to sigh in the throes of her own climax, and he held her until she calmed again, her face wet with happy tears.

His own tears mingled with hers as he felt the pieces of his soul knit together, the metaphysical edges sharp in places, the stains of the F'dor's dominance stinging a little when they came in contact with the rest of it. On the whole the experience of taking it back was drastically easier than he had anticipated. He had expected a struggle with an unwilling spirit, fighting to break free until he brought it under control. Instead it was sullen but subdued, and had been washed clean of much, if not all, of its past association, cleansed from the hate it had been surrounded by. It still held a few ugly memories of the Rakshas's actions, but they were closeted, held in check until he could examine them more closely and carefully, when he was in control.

Ashe looked down at the woman in his arms. She had been the vessel; that was why it had been cleansed. He was free; the evil had been burned away in the fire of Rhapsody's spirit, a spirit that believed in him completely and loved him utterly. It was in her eyes as she smiled up at him, and Ashe had to turn away, overcome with emotion. She had renamed the piece of his soul to as it had been before it was taken.

'Are you all right?' she asked, concern coloring her voice. 'Did I hurt you?'

Ashe sighed, and pulled her to his chest, burying his face in her glistening hair. 'Yes,' he murmured in her ear. 'Yes, you did. You made me love you so much that it hurts.'

He could feel her smile beneath him. 'Good,' she whispered. 'Then at least we're even.'

49

Rhapsody handed Ashe the last dish to dry and wiped the table clean as he put it away. She folded her arms and watched him in amusement, the Kirsdarkenvar, the future Lord of the united Cymrian houses, crouched in front of her cupboard as he stacked the supper plates inside it. She noticed the muscles of his back ripple and sighed deeply as she always did on those rare occasions when she allowed herself to think of the Future. Knowing her time with him was drawing to an end always made her sad.

Ashe stood up, and as he turned to her he smiled. He took her hand and kissed it, then tucked it into the crook of his arm as he led her into the parlor.

'How about a song? I haven't heard you play in a very long while.'

'I did devotions before supper. Didn't you hear me?'

'Yes. I meant a story song, a ballad of some kind. It will help me practice my Ancient Lirin so I can improve my idioms.'

'All right,' said Rhapsody, smiling. 'If you like I can sing you a Gwadd song; I know one.' She sat in one of the two chairs that faced each other before the fire.

A look of interest came over Ashe's face as he sat in the other one. 'Wonderful! I had no idea you had met Gwadd.' The tiny people, slender and almond-eyed, were legendary; most people were uncertain if they really existed.

'I saw a few of them in Serendair, actually; they rarely came to the city where I lived.' Ashe's curiosity was aroused, but he stopped himself and honored their custom of leaving the Past unquestioned. It was better to learn from the memories she offered about it, anyway.

Rhapsody went to the special cabinet where her instruments were stored and pulled out her minarello. It was a strange red instrument, sometimes called a groan-box, with many pleated folds, the whine of which sometimes reminded Ashe of sick dogs moaning, except when in her hands. He had heard many drunken sailors butcher music pitifully with one in his days at sea, but when Rhapsody played it, the instrument had a jolly sound that made his feet itch to dance. She returned to her chair and sat down again.

'Right; now, this is the Strange, Sad Tale of Simeon Blowfellow and the Concubine's Slipper.' Ashe laughed, and settled back with interest to listen to the humorous song which Rhapsody sang with great solemnity, her eyes twinkling merrily. She bewailed the fate of the title character's lost shoe; it had a comically tragic ending. Ashe applauded when she returned the minarello to its shelf, accepting his ovation with a deep, serious bow.

She returned to her chair before the fire, not acknowledging his open arms. 'I have something important I have to do,' she said, looking at him directly.

Ashe nodded. 'Can I help?' He put his hands on the arms of the chair in preparation to stand.

Rhapsody shook her head. 'Not tonight. I mean something I have to do soon, in a day or two.'

Ashe lost his smile. 'What, Aria?'

Rhapsody looked uncomfortable. 'I'm not sure of all the details, but I have to start by seeing Manwyn.'

'Why?' His voice had an edge to it.

'Because I need a piece of information I can't get from anywhere else.'

'Is this in regard to the children you talked with Rhonwyn about?'

'Yes. But I think we need to talk tonight about what you have to do, Ashe.' He stared at her, and Rhapsody dropped her eyes, trying to phrase her words so they didn't hurt him. 'The summer is gone, autumn is here now. You have your soul back; you're whole again. It's time you left to prepare for taking the Lordship.'

'You want me to leave?'

Rhapsody sighed. 'Gods, no. But we both know you have to.'

Ashe stood and came over to her. He crouched down in front of her, and Rhapsody felt her heart beat faster as it always did when he came near. 'I can't,' he said softly. 'Not yet.'

She gave him another direct look. 'Well, you're welcome to stay here in Elysian if you'd like, but I'm afraid I will be leaving soon. The Rakshas is dead, and it's time Achmed, Grunthor, and I got on with finding and killing the F'dor.

'What I have to do, among other things, is get a tool that will help Achmed locate it. There is some danger that it may switch hosts if it has a chance, especially without the Rakshas to do its repulsive bidding. Things will begin happening rapidly now; I expect to call the Cymrian Council soon after the demon is dead, assuming we can find the damned thing, and that will affect you greatly, you know.

'I think you should take this time to prepare yourself; perhaps you even want to seek out and talk with the woman you mentioned, so that you can see if she's agreeable to being your Lady.' Her voice caught a little, and Ashe felt his heart twist in sorrow for her. 'That way you can both be confirmed by the Council, and it won't have to be called a second time. Who knows, if you don't put forward your own nomination they may choose someone awful like they did the last time.' Her words ground to a halt when she realized she had just roundly insulted his grandparents.

Ashe saw her embarrassment and smiled. 'You're right. They did make a pretty poor pairing, didn't they?'

Rhapsody took his hand. 'No,' she said, looking into his eyes. 'If the two of them hadn't paired off, you wouldn't be here, so I guess wonderful things can come from even the worst of matches. But it is critical for the entire continent, not just the Cymrians, that it's right this time. You need to take the time to make sure you're ready, and that your choice of the Lady is wise. You had best go and meet her, and see if she is someone who can lead, as well as make you happy. I won't be responsible for delaying you any longer, no matter how selfishly I might like to.'

Ashe leaned forward and kissed her softly. 'Not yet,' he repeated. 'This can't end yet. We have both suffered too much to lose the one time of solace and peace we've found.' He pushed his father's nattering voice out of his mind.

'Achmed and I are leaving for Yarim the day after tomorrow,' Rhapsody said gently but firmly. 'After that I expect to be gone for the foreseeable future.' She winced as her words stripped the smile from his face and he stood, turning from her and walking over to the fireplace. With a sigh she rose and followed him, touching his arm. 'I wish I could avoid the pain this is causing you, causing both of us, but we knew it was coming. I'm sorry.'

Ashe nodded silently, lost in the shadows of the fire. When he finally looked down at her, his face was calm and his expression relaxed.

'Very well, then, if we need to move on from here, we will. I have some issues to wrestle with, foremost of which being this lovely fellow you returned to me last night.' Ashe tapped his chest; the scar he had carried in various stages of healing had vanished with the return of the soul fragment. He had examined a single memory of the Rakshas in the morning while Rhapsody was dressing in the next room. She had returned to find him shuddering in horror, curled up in the corner of the room as his mind witnessed the unspeakable acts his soul had participated in unwillingly, acts so repulsive their memory was burned into his soul.

Rhapsody shook her head. 'You shouldn't do that alone, Ashe,' she said sensibly. 'Let's deal with that before I go. I can be here to hold you and help you through it in any way I can.'

'Not much of a way to end such a beautiful summer,' he said regretfully. 'I want the memories of this time to be happy ones for you, Aria, not ones of me screaming and exorcising my demons.'

'They will be; they are,' she assured him. 'Nothing will take that away from either of us. But I have a suggestion.'

'So do I.'

'All right; tell me.'

'I'm going with you to Yarim, not Achmed,' Ashe said firmly. 'I have been there repeatedly, and I doubt he has. I don't trust him alone with you.'

Rhapsody looked puzzled. 'Why not? We have traveled alone together through much worse places. He won't let me come to any harm.'

Ashe thought about clarifying what he meant, then decided against it.

She didn't understand; she would never understand. 'Nevertheless, I'm going. That's final.'

Rhapsody's eyebrows arched at the imperious tone. 'Yes, m'lord,' she said with a touch of displeasure, but she did not pursue the point. She had avoided explaining to him about the children, knowing it would upset him. If he came to the prophetess with her, Manwyn might tell him, but Rhapsody was not prepared to deceive him if it happened. Instead she changed the subject. 'Now, would you like to hear my idea?'

'Yes,' Ashe said, sitting back down as she did. 'I'm sorry; what is it?'

'The Lord Roland is getting married in the spring, and, if you can believe this, I've been invited.'

'Tristan? No kidding. Well, I'm somewhat surprised they invited you.'

She giggled. 'Me, too. He must hate me after our various run-ins. This is why I am glad to be a peasant; you never have to invite people you hate to your wedding for reasons of state, only because they're your relatives.'

'He can't possibly hate you, that's not why I'm surprised. I would think they'd know you will outshine the bride.'

Rhapsody smiled. 'You're sweet.' Ashe sighed; he hadn't been joking. 'Anyway, perhaps we could meet up there, you know, get to see each other, if only for a little while, in the midst of a big party. It would be fun to watch the wedding. I told you a long time ago that if he invited me you could be my escort.'

He nodded. 'That you did. Perhaps being aboveboard is unwise, given that the F'dor might show up at such an important event. Its host is probably invited. It would probably be the perfect opportunity to capture it, but you're not ready.' He watched her face dim a little, her excitement wane, and he hastened to cheer her up. 'But we can still meet at the wedding if we are clandestine about it; we can be like secret lovers. I would love to go with you, Aria.'

Rhapsody looked at the fire. 'After you leave here, I think it's best if we put an end to our relationship as lovers, Ashe.' She could feel him pale in the chair across from her. 'It's going to be extraordinarily hard for me to give you up as it is, so I think it would be advisable not to confuse things. If you're off to pursue this ancient Cymrian woman whom the Council likes, I think you owe it to her to begin thinking about her in a pure way, unhindered by past – attachments.'

Ashe waited until she looked back at him. 'All right, Rhapsody,' he said casually. 'You're right. She has the right to know I'm unencumbered when I propose. If she agrees to be the Lady Cymrian, and my wife, she deserves my total fidelity and devotion, unhindered by thoughts of anyone else.' His stomach twisted when his dragon sense felt her reaction to his words; though her face was serene and betrayed no emotion, he could feel the nausea wash over her, the flush of blood circulating in the thousands of tiny veins, each counted and obsessed over by the dragon. 'You do still intend to be my ally, yes?'

'Yes, of course.'

'And my friend?'

She smiled brightly. 'And your friend.'

He stood and went to her, offering her his hands and helping her rise. He looked into her eyes and stared as directly into her soul as he could, hoping his words would resonate there. 'I love you, Aria. Nothing and no one can ever change that for me. You have said you love me as well; I know you do, I can feel it with each breath I take. Will you still? Even when we are apart?'

Rhapsody looked away. 'Yes,' she said sadly, as if ashamed to admit it. 'Always. But don't worry; I'll find a way to deal with it. I won't embarrass you, Ashe. I told you, one of my reasons for helping you is that you will one day be my sovereign, and I owe it to you to assist you in any way I can. I could never compromise your happiness or your reputation.'

Ashe laughed. 'Rhapsody, if people knew you have been my lover, it would only serve to enhance my reputation far beyond the bounds of belief. Now, two more things. First, I want you to promise me that when we get back from Manwyn's you'll let me make supper for you. We'll have a final farewell assignation of sorts; we'll dine in the garden and perhaps have a dance. Just a nice, romantic note to end on, especially if we're going to examine the Rakshas's memories tomorrow.' He shuddered involuntarily, recalling the one he had lived through that morning. 'This has been a magical summer. I want it to end the right way.'

Rhapsody grinned at him. 'That sounds wonderful. Can we dress up?'

'Certainly; I wouldn't have it any other way. Maybe I can even get something to wear in Yarim. I don't have many clothes.'

'And we can do the renaming ceremony.' Once she had returned the piece of his soul to him, she was insistent that she give him a new name, one the F'dor would not be able to find him by. He had agreed.

'Yes; that's good.'

'All right, what is the second thing?'

He took her into his arms. 'As far as you're concerned, are we still lovers tonight?'

'Yes. Do you still want to be?'

His kiss answered the question for her.

50

From a distance it was easy to see how Yarim had gotten its name. In the language of the indigenous people, long ago driven north by Gwylliam's forces, the word meant brown-red, like the color of dried blood. By and large the buildings had been constructed from the brick that bore the same name, made from the mud of this land, red clay that baked into a dark crimson in the fire as it took shape.

The capital city, officially known as Yarim Paar but often called merely by the province's name, sat at the base of a high rolling hill, and was therefore all but hidden from sight when approached from the south. Then it appeared suddenly at the traveler's feet, spreading out in all directions. The structures were the same color as the earth, and took a moment to become visible to the eye in the wind atop the hill; it was unclear whether they had sprung from the ground itself, though if they had they would have been the only things growing there. The city looked like it needed water.

A wave of heat had swept up from the east, born on a southern wind. The frost that had coated the ground for weeks was gone, leaving in its place a sense of false summer, hot and dry. In the forests to the east, the weather was undoubtedly glorious. Here it was desolate.

Yarim had once been a thriving city, but everywhere she looked Rhapsody could see the evidence of decay. The streets were lined and cobbled with stones, but between the cracks dry weeds and sun-bleached grass seemed to grow unfettered. The gutters were choked and clogged with garbage, turning the rainwater that collected in large barrels for household usage into the same muddy brown as the bricks.

On many street corners were groups of beggars, common enough that most people walked by them without notice. Rhapsody recognized some as professional lowlifes and riffraff, but many had the look of desperate hunger she remembered all too well. One young mother with an infant seemed especially in need; she reached for her hidden coin purse, only to be surprised when Ashe forestalled her by dropping some coins into the woman's lap. She handed the woman a gold piece and hurried to catch up with him.

'I'm somewhat surprised,' she said.

'At what?'

'I wouldn't have thought you the type to give alms.'

Ashe looked out from under his hood and into hers. 'Rhapsody, I've lived among these people for the past twenty years. Admittedly I've spent most of that time in the forests, but even I need to come to town now and again. I could hardly fit in with the lords and ladies, now, could I? For the most part the human contact I've had has been in the streets. It wasn't just as a result of my cloak alone that I learned how to be overlooked. It happens here and in the streets of other cities every day. It was living among these people that finally convinced me maybe there was something useful I could accomplish by becoming Lord Cymrian. We're here.'

Rhapsody turned her attention to the large building before them. In many ways the great temple-like structure reminded her of the city itself: large, majestically built, but decaying from neglect. A series of cracked marble steps led up to a wide, inlaid patio. Eight huge columns stood on this unevenly paved surface, each one marred by expanding patches of lichen. The central building was a large rotunda crowned with a circular dome with two large cracks. To either side of this central structure long annexes had been added, with smaller pillars in somewhat better condition. A tall, thin minaret crowned the central building, shining a metallic blue in the sun.

They walked up the great stair and through the large open portal that served as the entrance. The inside of the temple was dark, lit only by dim torches and candles. It took a moment for Rhapsody's eyes to adjust to the half-light.

The interior of the temple appeared to be better maintained, though Ashe had said in the course of their long journey that the rooms in the maze-like annexes were musty and neglected. Yet as she looked at the beautifully crafted foyer, it seemed hard to believe.

In the center of the vast room was a large fountain that blasted a thin stream of water twenty feet into the air, where it splashed down into a pool lined with shimmering lapis lazuli. The floor was polished marble, the walls adorned with intricately decorated tile, the sconces shining brass.

To either side of this room were small antechambers where guards stood, armed with long, thin swords. A large door of intricately carved cedar stood across from them, behind the fountain and its pool, also guarded.

Rhapsody and Ashe circled around the fountain and stopped before the guards of the great door. After they had made a substantial donation the door was opened and they were allowed to enter the inner sanctum. The fee, they were informed, was to help maintain the Oracle. Ashe wondered aloud to Rhapsody if Manwyn knew about this practice.

The room beyond the cedar door was immense, illuminated by a series of small windows in the dome of the rotunda and countless candles. In the center of the room was a dais which was suspended precariously above a large open well.

Sitting cross-legged in the center of this dais was a woman who could only have been Manwyn. She was tall and thin with rosy gold skin and fiery red hair streaked with silver. Her face bore the lines of middle age, and she wore a strange, and somewhat disturbing smile. In her left hand she held an ornate sextant, and she was dressed in green silk.

But it was the eyes of the Seer that drew Rhapsody's attention. They were even less human than Ashe's. As Rhapsody gazed up into them, she was greeted with her own reflection. The Seer's eyes were mirrors, perfect silver mirrors, with no pupil, iris, or sclera to delineate them. It was as if Rhapsody was looking into two orbs of quicksilver. She tried not to stare. Manwyn smiled.

'Gaze into the well,' she said. Her voice was a raspy croak that scratched at the edges of Rhapsody's skull. She looked to Ashe and he nodded. They began walking to the dais.

'Not you,' Manwyn snarled, glaring at Ashe. 'You must wait. The Future hides from he who is invisible to the Present.' She spat in his direction.

Rhapsody swallowed and walked to the well. She remembered what

Llauron had said about Manwyn, that she was the most unstable of the three Seers, the maddest of the group. She was unable to lie, but it was sometimes difficult to tell what were genuine prophecies and what were the ravings of an unhinged mind. In addition, the prophecies sometimes had two meanings, or hidden ones, so as to render her an unreliable source, albeit the best one, for information about the Future. Still, she was the last resort for those who came to her temple, and Rhapsody hoped, as did the others who sought her guidance, that this would be a rational and stable day for her.

When she came to the edge of the well Rhapsody steeled herself and looked down. There was no boundary to it, just a yawning hole in the floor with no apparent bottom. In the dark it was a treacherous thing to approach, its edges uneven and hard to see in the dim light. The Seer cackled wildly and pointed to the dark ceiling.

Rhapsody looked up for the first time at the dome to see it was as black as night, whether by craftsmanship or some kind of eerie magic. The dome was studded with stars, or their images, twinkling as hazy wisps of cloud passed in front of them. She could feel the wind tug at the corners of her cape, and knew somehow that she was not within the Temple, she was outside in a vast field at the loneliest point of night, with nothing and no one but the Seer present. A falling star streaked across the sky and the wind grew stronger, buffeting her cheeks.

'Rhapsody.' Ashe's voice broke the reverie; she looked behind her to see the vague outline of his cloak in the half-light of the Temple. When she turned back to Manwyn, all was as it had been when they entered, except the Prophetess now looked annoyed. She held the sextant to her eye, pointing into the dark night-dome, then gestured at the well.

'Look within to find the appointed time and place,' she said. Rhapsody took a breath; she had not even asked her question yet. She stared down into the well where a picture was forming. When it became clear she could see a Lirin woman, gray of face and in obvious pain, great with child. The woman stopped in her path for a moment to rest, her hand clutching her enormous abdomen.

A scraping noise sounded in the dome above her, and Rhapsody looked up. The stars had shifted to a different longitude and latitude; she made note of the position. Undoubtedly this was Manwyn's way of indicating the place where she would find the woman.

'When, Grandmother?' she asked the Seer deferentially. Manwyn laughed, a wild, frightening chortle that made Rhapsody's skin rise into gooseflesh.

'One soul departs as another arrives, eleven weeks hence this night,' she answered as the image in the well vanished. Manwyn stared behind her, and Rhapsody turned to see Ashe approaching, his hood down for the first time. A triumphant smile crawled over the Seer's face; it held a hint of cruelty in it. She looked directly at him, but when she spoke her words were still directed at Rhapsody.

'I see an unnatural child born of an unnatural act. Rhapsody, you should beware of childbirth: the mother shall die, but the child shall live.'

Rhapsody began to tremble. She now understood what Ashe had meant about vague prophecies. Was Manwyn referring to the Lirin woman, or to Rhapsody herself? Though the context would suggest the first, there was a clarity in the tone of her voice that indicated otherwise. She wanted to ask, but could not get her mouth to form the words.

'Exactly what does *that* mean?' demanded Ashe. He sounded angrier than she had ever heard him. 'What kind of games are you playing, Manwyn?'

Manwyn's hands went to her blazing red hair. Slowly her fingers entwined themselves into the unkempt locks, twisting them into long knotted snarls. She stared at the ceiling, smiling and crooning a wordless melody, then shot Ashe as direct a look as Rhapsody had ever seen with her monochromatic eyes.

'Gwydion ap Llauron, thy mother died in giving birth to thee, but thy children's mother shall not die giving birth to them.' She burst into insane laughter.

Ashe touched her shoulder. 'Let's get out of here,' he said in a low voice. 'Did she tell you what you need to know?'

'I'm not sure,' Rhapsody said. Her voice was shaking, even though she did not feel the fear that she could hear in it.

'Gwydion, have you bade your father farewell? He dies in the eyes of all to live in the sight of none; you are duplicitous, though you will both suffer and benefit from his living death. Woe unto him who lies for the man who taught him the value of truth, Gwydion; it is you who will pay the price for his newfound power.'

'*S!KLERIV!*' Ashe snarled in a multitoned voice she had never heard before; the word sliced through Rhapsody like a knife. Innately she knew the word meant *silence*, and in its own language it teetered close to a deplorable obscenity. She guessed the language was dragon.

Ashe had grown flushed. Rhapsody saw the vein in his forehead begin to pulse and his skin grew angry and red.

'Not another word, you wyrm-tongued maniac!' he screamed.

Rhapsody felt cold at the edges of her skin, the bristling, calculating ire of the dragon in him beginning to coil. There was a frightening calm to it, and twisted, manipulative energy that made her feet and hands turn to ice. The realization that Manwyn, too, was wyrmkin, the daughter of the dragon, made her heart begin to palpitate. She took Ashe's hand.

'Let's go,' she whispered urgently and pulled on his arm. He resisted, drawn to the edge of a ferocious battle of wills. Rhapsody felt panic wash over her at that prospect. Manwyn rose to her knees and begin to keen, a modulating wail that shook the foundations of the rotunda, causing fragments of stone and dust to fall from the ceiling above.

Ashe's hand clenched hers tighter, his eyes focused on the shrieking Oracle. Bit by bit she could feel him slip away, his concentration locked on the dais and the opponent sitting on it, now swinging wildly over the bottomless well. The air was becoming difficult to breathe, full of dust and static. The earth trembled beneath their feet, and the firmament of the dome felt as though it were about to burst into flames.

Rhapsody gave Ashe another violent tug, but his resistance was even greater this time. She took a deep breath and sang his name in a deep, low tone, punctuating it with the discordant note to Manwyn's ear-piercing screech. The sound rolled throughout the rotunda, shattering the wail and driving Manwyn momentarily into shocked silence. Ashe blinked, and in the moment that he did Rhapsody dragged him from the room, Manwyn's hysterical laughter ringing in their ears.

They were halfway to the city gates before they stopped running. Ashe was swearing to himself under his breath, weaving a vile tapestry of obscenity in a vast number of languages and dialects. Rhapsody tried to ignore him, but the imagery of his foul speech was fascinating in an offensive way.

At the edge of a large dry well they came to a halt and sat, breathing deeply in the humid heat of the last vestiges of the dying summer. Rhapsody was burning beneath her cloak, shaking from exertion. Finally she looked up and glared at him.

'Was that really necessary?'

'She began it. I didn't antagonize her.'

'No,' Rhapsody admitted, 'you really didn't. Why did she attack you like that?'

'I don't know,' said Ashe, pulling out his waterskin and offering it to her. 'Maybe she felt threatened; dragons are unpredictable like that.'

'I've noticed,' she said, and took a deep drink. She passed the skin back to him. 'Well, that's over. I have to say, the more I get to know your family, the less I like them.'

'And you haven't even met my grandmother yet,' said Ashe, smiling for the first time. 'That's an unparalleled treat. Let's hope she doesn't show up at the Cymrian Council.'

Rhapsody shuddered. 'Yes, let's hope. Well, now what?'

Ashe leaned over and kissed her, drawing an amused look from a pair of passing beggar women. 'Let's go shopping.'

'Shopping? You're joking.'

'No. Yarim has some wonderful bazaars and a spice merchant you will definitely want to see, given your proclivity for that sort of thing. I want to pick up something to wear to our farewell supper, and perhaps some interesting things to cook for it. Besides, I've never heard of you passing up the opportunity to shop.'

Rhapsody laughed. 'Well, that's true,' she admitted. 'I was hoping to find some things for my grandchildren, and perhaps a birthday gift for Grunthor. What do you think he might like?'

Ashe stood and offered her his hand, pulling her to a stand. 'I think he'd like to see you in a low-cut, backless red dress.' Rhapsody gave him a strange look. 'Oh, right, sorry; that's me. Grunthor, hmmm. Does he count coup?'

Rhapsody shuddered. She had always found the practice of saving body parts of fallen enemies disgusting. 'Sometimes.'

'Well, how about a nice receptacle to keep his trophies in?'

'I don't think so.'

'Oh, come on, be creative. What sort of cabinet shape would he need? I mean, does he save heads? Get him an armoire with hat stands.'

Rhapsody considered. 'That's not what he saves; too much work to slice off. I think a cigar box would be more the right shape.' She watched as a look of amused disgust came to rest on his face. 'Well, it was your idea.'

'That it was.' Ashe began walking toward the noisy part of town, the direction in which most of the people passing in the streets were headed. 'Rhapsody, I have to ask a favor of you.'

'Anything.'

'Don't say that yet,' he said seriously. 'You are going to hate hearing this as much as I am going to hate asking, I'll wager.'

She sighed. 'Undoubtedly. What is it?'

He stopped and faced her. 'This may not make any sense to you. Manwyn said something back there that you shouldn't have heard, not because I would want to keep it from you, but because your knowledge of it poses a threat to your own safety, as well as the safety of others.' He took her hands. 'Will you trust me to take the memory of it from you, just for a little while? Until it's safe.'

'You are blithering at me,' she said, annoyed. 'Is this more Cymrian mumbo-jumbo?'

'In a way, I'm afraid it is. But it is more for the danger it puts you in than any other reason that I ask this of you, because I don't want you to be hurt. Do you believe me?'

She sighed. 'I suppose.'

Ashe laughed sharply. 'That's a ringing endorsement.'

'Well, what do you expect, Ashe?' Rhapsody said, her irritation growing. 'First I have to face a bizarre prophetess who talks in riddles, then I have to hear you do the same? What is it you want? What do you mean, will I let you take the memory?'

'You're right,' he said, his voice softening. 'I know this has been unbearable for you, Rhapsody. Your memories are a form of treasure. As such, I can collect them, but I would only do it with your permission. They can be stored in a pure vessel, much like you stored my soul, until such a time as it is safe for you to have them.'

'Like you offered to do with my nightmare? Store it in a pearl?'

'Yes. Exactly like that. You will name the vessel, telling it to hold the memory for you, and it will leave your conscious thought and reside in the vessel until you take it back.'

Rhapsody rubbed her temples. 'How will I know to take it back, if I don't remember it in the first place?'

'I will remind you. And I will leave you a sign in case something happens to me. What I propose is this: on the night of our parting, I will explain everything to you that you don't currently understand. I will hold nothing back. We'll sit in the gazebo – we can talk freely in Elysian, and I will make sure there is a vessel there to hold the memory of that night and the one you have of this conversation with Manwyn.'

'I can't do that,' she said. 'I'm sorry. I need the information she gave me.'

'I'm referring to what she said *after* she gave you that information,' Ashe said. 'You can keep the rest. Please, Rhapsody, understand that I would not ask this of you if I didn't have to. Hear what I have to say when we get back. Then, if you choose to withdraw your permission, I will yield to your decision. But please consider it.'

'All right,' she agreed reluctantly. 'Now, let's go shopping.' She breathed deeply as the part of his face she could see relaxed into a smile. She was not sure which was worse – the prospect of him leaving after they got back, or having to live through any more of the deception that seemed to be inherent to the Cymrian people. Either way, it didn't matter. Both situations would be over soon.

51

Rhapsody finished shaking the crumbs from the linens off the table, folding them neatly and setting them on the chair she had occupied. Ashe was still inside the cottage, having cleared the table and carried the dishes in. She put the small vase of winter flowers back in the center, smiling as she caressed the stiff petals, admiring their beauty and their resolve. Long after the more fragile blossoms of summer and early autumn had withered and died, they continued to bloom, even through the first snows, defying the unrelenting grip of the whiteness of the winter, bringing fresh color to a frozen world.

She was lost in thought when Ashe returned and found her there, running one of the bloodred flowers absently along her cheek. He stopped a few yards away and watched her, his eyes reveling in the magnificence of the picture she unconsciously made.

Her golden hair had been swept up in a shining coil and fastened with tiny white dried blossoms that resembled diminutive stars, a few soft tendrils falling next to her face and at the nape of her neck. She wore a graceful gown of ivory Canderian watered silk with a high collar and a full skirt, edged with a thin band of delicate lace that brushed her wrists and her neck, and though little of her rosy skin showed save on her hands and face, the splendor of her body was made apparent by the artistry of the dress.

Ashe felt his breath return after a moment; he hadn't missed it. He thought back over their time together and realized that this was the first time he had ever seen her deliberately set about highlighting her features, adorning herself in a way that accentuated her natural beauty. The result was astonishing. As the dragon calculated the untapped power to manipulate and beguile entire populations that was lying dormant within her, the man was treasuring the understanding that she had dressed up for him, wanting his memory of her on their last night alone together in this place to be a pretty one.

After a moment her mind returned from its wanderings and she turned to him and gave him a knee-weakening smile. With an unconscious grace she lifted her sweeping skirts and stepped over the stones, coming to him eagerly with her hands outstretched. He took them both in his own and kissed them gently, then drew her into his arms, enjoying the freshness of her fragrance and the warmth of her body within the silky-stiff material of the dress. She was a treasure trove of sensations the dragon could luxuriate in, and it was no easy task to break free of the desire to do so.

'Thank you for a wonderful supper,' she said, pulling back from his embrace and smiling up at him. 'If I had known you could do such a marvelous job cooking by yourself, I would have let you do it more often.'

He laughed and ran the back of his index finger down her cheek. 'No; equal collaboration is more fun,' he said, taking her small hand and pulling it into the curve of his arm, walking her along the garden path. 'That applies to all of my favorite things to do with you. A wonderful performance in either area is not much good without a partner to appreciate it.' He watched the porcelain skin grow rosier, amazed still that someone who could be so earthy, unrattled by jokes and behavior of the most repulsive nature, would still blush so easily alone with him. He cherished the thought.

'Come back into my arms and dance with me,' he said lightly. To avoid choking up with the emotion that was swelling in his heart he swept her back into his embrace, cradling her head against his shoulder. 'We should practice, since the next time I will see you we'll be meeting clandestinely at the royal wedding in Bethany. If we're trying to dance and still remain unnoticed, it wouldn't do at all for me to step on your toes.'

Rhapsody drew back with a suddenness that jolted him. Her face drained before his eyes of its rosy glow, leaving her alabaster-pale. Her eyes searched his face, filling with an old sadness that she shook away a moment later.

'It's getting late,' she said apprehensively. 'We should talk, then get to your renaming ceremony.'

Ashe nodded, feeling bereft. The dance would have given him a chance to hold her one more moment, to feel the happiness within her sustained for just a little bit longer. 'Are you ready?' he asked, pointing to the gazebo.

414

It was where they had agreed he would reveal his secrets, then take the memory of this night from her. Her eyes dropped and he could feel her nervousness rise as she shook her head.

'Not yet,' she said, and turned toward a small bench in a secluded part of the garden. 'Can we sit there for a moment? I have something to say to you, and I want to remember having said it.'

'Certainly.' Ashe helped her step over the small rock wall, and together they strolled to the bench, hand in hand. She settled her skirts as he sat down beside her and waited to hear what she had to say.

'Before you take away the memory of the rest of this night, I just want to let you know that you were right,' she said, her dark green eyes twinkling at him in the darkness.

'Rhapsody, you are unbelievable,' Ashe said, jokingly. 'Just when I thought it wasn't possible, you have come up with yet another way to excite me sexually. Will you say that again, please?'

'You were right,' she repeated, returning his grin. 'Do I have to take my clothes off now?'

'Don't tempt me,' he said, wondering whether this was a ploy to keep from going into the gazebo. He knew that she was not happy with what was about to happen, and though she trusted him, her willingness to follow through was limited at best. 'I'm sorry; now, what were you saying?'

Her face grew serious, and her eyes darkened in the half-light cast by the paper lanterns he had strung throughout the garden. 'I want you to know that everything you said to me when you first came to Elysian was right, even though I didn't know it at the time.' She stared at her hands for a moment, then lifted her head and looked into his eyes; her own were glistening, whether from deeply held feeling or tears.

'I want you to know that I've treasured this time with you, and that it was worth having, as you said, for as long as it lasted. I'm – I'm glad we were lovers. And you were right; it was enough.' Ashe watched as a luminescent tear spilled over her lashes and rolled slowly down her face.

'I was at ease with you long before any of this, though; I think the reason we made good lovers is that first we made good friends. And since in the end that is what will be left to us, I want to still be at ease with you, if circumstances permit. I have never interfered between a man and his wife, and I'm not about to start now. So if it won't cause problems for you and – well, and the Lady Cymrian, please know that if you ever need me I'm here for you – to help, I mean.' Her words ground awkwardly to a halt, and she looked over at the gazebo for a moment.

Ashe's heart ached for her. He reached out and caught the tear as it reached her chin, then gently rested his hand on her face. She placed her own hand over it, then took his and curled it into a fist inside her own.

'I love you, Gwydion ap Llauron ap Gwylliam and so on, and I always will,' she said when she looked back at him. 'But it is a love that will never threaten your happiness; it is there to support you in any way that it can.

Thank you for giving me this time and this opportunity. It has meant more to me than you ever could know.'

Ashe couldn't stand it anymore. He took her beautiful face in his hands and kissed her, trying to extend to her whatever wordless comfort he could. Her lips were warm but they did not respond to him; she gently took his hands and removed them from her face, giving them a friendly squeeze.

'Are you ready now?' he asked, nodding toward the gazebo.

Rhapsody sighed. 'Yes, I guess so,' she said, rising to a stand. 'Just let me get my harp; I'll need it for the naming ceremony.'

'It can wait,' Ashe said. 'First, we'll talk. Then we'll do the naming ceremony. I have something I need to tell you, and something I need to ask of you.'

'Very well,' she answered. 'Interestingly enough, so have I.'

The gazebo had been positioned to provide the most breathtaking view in all of Elysian, and from its cold marble benches Rhapsody could see the whole of her gardens, preparing for the long sleep of the fast-approaching winter, the cottage, with its climbing ivy fading from verdant green to a somber brown; and in the distance the rushing waterfall, growing in strength as the late autumn rains fed the streams above it, churning the water of the lake that circled the island she loved as if in an embrace.

For the first time this year Rhapsody felt a chill in the air; winter was coming. Soon the gardens would be silent, and the flock of birds that had found their way underground to nest in her trees would be gone. The hidden paradise would lose its color, settling into hibernation. She wondered how much of the loss of warmth in the land and air around them was attributable to annual climate changes, and how much to the diminution of the fires of her own soul as she felt their love dying. Elysian would soon go dormant, settling into subsistence where there had once been glory. Just like her.

'Rhapsody?' Ashe's voice brought her back to reality.

She looked up from her reverie. 'Yes? Oh, sorry. What do I have to do?'

Ashe sat down beside her on the stone bench and held out his hand. In it was an enormous pearl, watery-white as milk with an opalescent black circumscribing it. 'This is an ancient artifact from the land of your birth, now beneath the waves,' he said, his voice reverent. 'It has held the secrets of the sea, and but one other trusted to it on the land. Name it, Rhapsody, and will it to hold the memory of this night for you until it is safe for you to take it back.'

Rhapsody took the pearl in her hands. Though it looked porous she could feel its strength, impenetrable, layer upon layer of solid tears from the ocean. She closed her eyes and began the song of naming, matching her tune to the vibrations emanating from the pearl until they were in perfect unison.

She opened her eyes again. The pearl had begun to glow with a light that filled the gazebo. It was translucent, and the most intense point of illumination was discernible in the core, shining through the layers made visible by its brilliance. Into the song she wove the command he had asked of her: that the memory of the rest of this night be contained within it.

When the song ended Rhapsody handed the glowing pearl back to Ashe. He rose from the bench and walked to the empty golden cage, placing the pearl inside it. Then he returned and sat down beside her again, taking her hands, but before he could speak she stopped him.

'Tarry a moment, please, Ashe,' Rhapsody said. 'Before you tell me anything, I want to just look at you one last time.' Her eyes studied him intently, taking in the look of his own eyes, and the line of his face, the color of his hair, and the way he looked in the handsome mariner's uniform and cape. She closed her eyes and breathed deeply, trying to capture his scent and the way he shaped the air around him, painting a picture for herself that would have to last a lifetime. Finally she lowered her gaze.

'All right,' she said. 'I'm ready.'

'Very well,' Ashe said, smiling nervously. 'Rhapsody, what I have to tell you is not pleasant, and it won't be easy for you to hear it. But before we get into it, I have one last thing to ask of you. Please hear me out.'

'Of course. What is it?'

He took a deep breath; his voice was tender. 'Aria, I know you have never refused me anything I have asked, and you have gifted me with so many favors that I haven't asked for, that it seems unbelievable I could make yet another request of you, but I have to. It's the most important thing I will ever ask of you, on behalf both of myself and, with any luck, the united Cymrian peoples. Will you consider it, please?'

Rhapsody looked into his eyes; they were gleaming intensely, and he seemed on the verge of tears. The star formations that surrounded the strange vertical pupils were glowing as she had never seen them before, and she closed her eyes, burning the image into her memory for the Future. On the loneliest nights of the rest of her life she would picture the way he looked just now. She knew that the thought would bring her comfort.

'Of course; of course I will,' she answered, squeezing his hand reassuringly. 'I've already told you, Ashe, that I will always be your friend and ally. You can ask whatever you need of me and I will do whatever I can to help you, if it's in my power.'

He smiled, then turned her hand over in his and kissed it. 'Promise?'

'Yes.'

'Good. Marry me, then.' His words were out of his mouth before his knee touched the ground in front of her.

'That's not funny, Ashe,' Rhapsody said, looking annoyed. 'Get up. What do you really want?'

'Sorry, Rhapsody, that really is what I want. It has been from the very beginning. I haven't joked about it, or argued with you about it, or even

417

brought it up until I was sure that you would listen without prejudice, because I have never been more serious about anything in my life.' He saw her begin to pale, and he took both of her hands and plunged ahead, afraid to let her answer yet.

'I know you have long been under the assumption, fed by my father, that there is a hierarchy to which you don't belong by birth, and that it somehow is a good reason to deny us both happiness and our people the best Lady Cymrian they could possibly have. Aria, it isn't true. The Cymrians may have a family right of ascendancy, but they are a free people. They can confirm or deny anyone they want at the Council that meets when a Lord is to be crowned.

'For all I know they will throw me out, and then together we will build the most beautiful goat hut you have ever seen and our days will be blessed with peace and privacy. Or perhaps you will choose to rule in the court of the Lirin, as I know well they will one day want you to. Then I will be your humble servant, massaging your neck and back after long days on that uncomfortable throne, supporting you in any way I can, acting as your consort.

'All I know is that I cannot live without you in any case. I don't mean this as a flowery endearment; I mean it literally. You are my treasure. You must know what that means to a dragon. I cannot allow myself to even contemplate the loss of you from my life, for fear my other nature will take over and lay waste to the countryside. Please, Rhapsody, please marry me. I know I don't deserve you – I am fully aware of that – but you love me, I know you do, and I trust that love. I would give anything – '

'Stop, please,' Rhapsody whispered. Tears were streaming down her face, and her hands trembled.

Ashe fell silent. The look of shock on her face was so blatant that he was stunned, and his face mirrored the hurt he felt. After what seemed an eternity, he spoke. 'Is the prospect of being my wife so onerous, Rhapsody? Have I frightened you so much that – '

'Stop,' she said again, and her voice was full of pain. 'Of course it isn't; what an awful thing to say.' She began to sob, and buried her face in her hands.

Ashe took her, still weeping, into his arms. He held her until the storm of tears had passed, and then pulled from his breast pocket a linen handkerchief and handed it to her.

'Needless to say,' he said, watching her dry her eyes, 'this is not exactly the reaction I had hoped for.' His voice was light, but his eyes watched her anxiously.

'I know how you feel,' she said, handing him back his handkerchief. 'This is not exactly the question I had expected, either.'

'I know,' he said, taking her chin in his hand and gently lifting it to look into her face. 'And I'm sorry. But I couldn't let you go on believing that I would even consider marrying anyone but you. There is a limit, even if it is a distant one, to what I am willing to do as far as my father and the responsibilities of leadership are concerned. There is a limit to my love for you. Of course it would win out. And though you will have no conscious memory of this night for a while, I hope that somewhere, deep inside you, you will remember this and stop feeling the despair we both feel now.

'Aria, none of these people, these things, matter. Be selfish, for once in your life. Make the decision that makes you happy. I can't speak for you as to what that is. All I know is that I love you beyond description, and I would make your happiness my life's purpose. It would give me the greatest joy imaginable if you would consent to be my wife. Please; forget all the rest of this; give me an answer, not as whatever else you perceive me to be, but as the man who loves you.'

There was a simplicity to his voice, a clarity that cut through the mountain of objections and laid the decision plainly at her feet.

Rhapsody looked up at him through new eyes, cleared of their blinding tears. It was as if he had shown her the trail through a dark forest, one that she had been lost in since the Three had arrived in this land, a twisted place complicated by the agendas and expectations of others, dictated by their needs and prejudices. And some of her own as well; she had assumed from the beginning there was no future for them because of their different birth classes, but Ashe had avoided the topic altogether, refusing to fight about it. She now saw that he had known all along what he wanted, and had waited until he was sure that she loved him before bringing it up.

As he caressed the paths of the tears from her face, Rhapsody thought back to a conversation she had once had with her father, not long before she ran away from home. *How did the village come to change its mind about our family?* she had asked him. *If Mama was so despised when you first married, why did you stay?*

She could see his face in her memory, wrinkles pocketing around his eyes as he smiled at her, his hands still polishing the wood carving he was making, unable to ever be idle. *When you find the one thing in your life you believe in above anything else, you owe it to yourself to stand by it – it will never come again, child. And if you believe in it unwaveringly, the world has no other choice but to see it as you do, eventually. For who knows it better than you? Don't be afraid to take a difficult stand, darling. Find the one thing that matters – everything else will resolve itself.*

Once the memory had given her wisdom about her loyalty to the Bolg. Now Rhapsody looked into Ashe's eyes, and knew again what her father had meant. It was as if heavy cloaks were falling off her shoulders; the yammering voices in her ears faded away, leaving only the song of one man, the man who had taken over her whole heart. He was offering her a handhold out of the forest, guiding her to where she wanted to go as surely as he had shown her the way to Elynsynos's lair or Tyrian. And she desperately wanted to follow him.

'Yes,' she said, and her voice was soft, barely audible, from the tears that had clogged her throat. She coughed, unhappy with the way it had sounded. 'Yes.' she said again, her tone clearer, surer; Ashe's face began to transform before her, her words bringing warmth to his cheeks and making his dragonesque eyes glisten with light. The abject fear that had been hiding beneath the calm exterior began to evaporate, and she saw happiness start to take hold.

'Yes!' she shouted, using her naming lore to add irrevocability to it. The tone rang through the gazebo and echoed off the rockwalls, swirling around the lake where it danced in the waterfall, laughing as it spilled over the brim. With the dancing echo came heat, and light; like a comet careening within the grotto her word flashed through the air, illuminating the cavern with the radiance of a thousand shooting stars. The tone picked up to other harmonics as the places it touched affirmed the rightness of her answer, and a song rang in the air around them, a song of gladness.

The fires of Elysian roared their agreement, and the grass, which had begun to dry and stiffen in sleep turned green again, as if touched by the hand of spring. The blossoms of her garden held fast to the last of their brilliance, and bloomed along with the red winter flowers that had graced their table. As the shooting light-tone touched them it absorbed their colors, and spun them skyward, exploding into shimmering fireworks as it impacted with the dome of the firmament.

Ashe watched the explosion in amazement, then looked down at her face, turned skyward as well, the reflection of the colors above them glittering in her magnificent eyes.

'My,' he laughed. 'Are you sure?'

Rhapsody laughed with him, her mirth freeing her from the clutching tightness of duty and solitude she had felt for so long. Like wind chimes in a high breeze she let it come forth, and the sound of her laughter joined the tone of her assent, filling the giant cave with music the likes of which it had never held.

Ashe took her face in his hands, studying it in the throes of joy, and burned the image into his heart. He would need this picture to get through what was to come, he knew. Then he bent and touched her lips with his, drawing her into a kiss so tender that he could feel the tears well up in her again.

They stood, lost in each other and in the passion of their kiss, until the light had begun to fade and the music slipped away, leaving a ringing tone that eventually quieted, then disappeared. As the warmth left the air she pulled back, looking up at him with eyes that had calmed, but still held a quiet contentment that made him tremble.

'I'm sure,' she said simply. He took her in his arms, holding her as tightly as he could, trying to keep the moment fast in his heart. The magic still needed to survive what he had to tell her.

52

When Ashe finally released her, Rhapsody sat back down on the bench.

'Well, that was interesting,' she said, smoothing her silken skirt. 'I can't wait for the encore. So what is it you have to tell me?'

Ashe shuddered. He knew how difficult the news he needed to break would be to hear, and he wasn't ready to give up the glow they were sharing, not yet.

'Will you sing for me, Rhapsody?' he asked, sitting down at her feet.

'You're stalling,' she scolded. 'I have a feeling this is going to be a late night; we have a lot more to discuss, plus the renaming ritual. I have to leave early in the morning, so I'll make you a offer: you tell me what it is you need to, and I'll make my request of you, and then we'll rename you and I'll sing to you afterward. Fair enough?'

Ashe sighed. 'Very well,' he said, trying not to let his disappointment show. 'Please understand I would rather die at this moment than tell you what I am about to.'

Alarm crossed Rhapsody's face. 'Why?'

Ashe rose and sat beside her again, taking her hands. 'Because I know what I am going to tell you will hurt you, and you must know by now that I seek to avoid that whenever possible.'

Calm returned to Rhapsody's expression. 'All right, Ashe. Just tell me.'

'In a little while my father will approach you and ask if you'd like to accompany him on a journey. I don't know the destination; it's insignificant anyway. You will never get there.'

'What are you talking about?'

Ashe's eyes met hers for a moment. 'Please, Rhapsody; this is far too difficult as it is. Just listen, and then I'll explain. And if, after all this, you want to revoke your permission for me to keep this memory, I will understand and yield to your decision.'

Rhapsody squeezed his hands supportively. 'Just tell me,' she said gently.

'In the midst of your travels with Llauron, the two of you will be confronted by Lark and a band of renegade followers. She will challenge my father to mortal combat, one of the rites of passage for Llauron's seat of power. Llauron will have no choice but to accept, and in the course of the combat Lark will kill him.'

Rhapsody leapt from the bench in shock. '*What*? No. That will not happen, Ashe. I will not let that happen.'

'You won't be able to prevent it, Aria. You will have been bound by an oath to my father not to intervene in any circumstance. Your choice will be between watching him die, or violating your holy word, and surrendering Daystar Clarion. I'm sorry; I'm so sorry,' he said brokenly, watching horror creep into her face, the face that only moments before had been transfixed in happiness.

Rhapsody turned away from him and wrapped her arms around her waist, ready to vomit. Ashe's senses felt the blood drain from her face and hands, leaving her pale and shaking. Finally she turned to him again, a look of disbelief in her eyes that choked his heart.

'I refuse to believe,' she said slowly, 'that you are in league with Lark, that you would plot with her to assassinate your own father.'

Ashe hung his head. 'You are half right,' he said softly. 'I am not in league with Lark.'

'Then who? Who are you in league with?'

Ashe turned away, unable to meet her gaze. 'My father.'

'Look at me,' Rhapsody commanded, her voice harsh. Ashe looked up, his face filled with shame. 'What are you talking about?'

'My father has planned, almost from the moment you arrived, to use you to help him achieve his goals. The first was flushing out the F'dor, though I think that has pretty much succumbed to the second.'

'That being?'

'Llauron has grown weary of the limits of his existence in human form,' Ashe said hollowly. 'His blood is part dragon, but that nature is dormant. He is aging, and in pain, and facing his own mortality, which is closer than you might expect. He wants to come into the fullness of his wyrm identity. If he can do that he will be almost immortal, and have the elemental power that you, and your Firbolg companions, and even I, wield now, but on a much greater scale. He will become one with the elements, Aria; where you affect or command the fire, he will *be* the fire. Or the water, or the ether; it doesn't matter.'

'Like Elynsynos?'

'Exactly. And like Elynsynos, to achieve this he needs to forswear his mortal form, and assume an elemental one, but without dying, before he can move on to the elemental existence he craves. Once he discovered that Lark was plotting against him, long ago, he has been laying plans to turn the situation to his advantage. This last part – your part – is his final manipulation in getting what he wants.'

Rhapsody's eyes broke the lock with his, and looked off over the gardens and the lake, assimilating what he was saying. 'But you just said he would be killed.'

Ashe winced. 'Everyone will believe so – even you, Rhapsody. He will bring herbs and tonics to induce a deathlike state in himself, and so when you and Lark examine his body, you will both believe he has died.'

Rhapsody walked to the edge of the gazebo and sat down on the top step leading down into the garden. She looked across the lake at the waterfall, trying to focus the thoughts that were running helter-skelter through her mind. 'And what is the point of that? So he convinces Lark, and me, that he is dead when he's not? What can that possibly accomplish?'

'Lark is in league with the F'dor, though who that is still remains hidden.

Llauron has known for quite some time that the F'dor had an accomplice among his ranks, but he wasn't certain of who it is until recently. If Lark believes Llauron is dead, she will eventually communicate this information to the F'dor, and I will be waiting to track her to it. Also, other turncoats may be with her, and then I will know who else I need to kill.'

She looked back over her shoulder, her eyes burning like a grassfire. 'But why me, Ashe? Why does Llauron need to deceive me, too? Why am I hearing this from you, under the sentence of losing the memory of it? Why didn't he just ask for my help? I've been advancing the reunification of the Cymrians until Achmed and Grunthor have threatened to hurl me from the mountain if I don't stop. Gods, haven't I proven my friendship and loyalty to this man yet?'

Ashe withered under her gaze. 'Of course you have. But there are two reasons. The first is that they will both expect you to act as the herald, as a Singer, a Namer. Both Llauron and Lark know you will only speak the truth as you know it, as you witness it. So if you believe him to be dead, then the rest of the world will, too. It will fall to you to proclaim the news. Both Lark and Llauron are counting on this, Lark to assert her right as the new head of the Filids, and Llauron to accredit his charade. Perhaps if you weren't so honest, he might have told you, hoping you would follow his plan anyway. But I'm afraid your reputation precedes you, darling.'

Acid retorts rose to Rhapsody's lips, remembering the same words in Michael's mouth long ago, but she choked them back bitterly. She looked away again, trying to spare him the fury she knew was obvious in her countenance. 'And the second reason?'

Ashe swallowed. 'Aria, if you love me, please don't ask me. Just believe that you would not participate if you knew.' He ran his hands through his metallic hair, now wet with perspiration.

Rhapsody stood slowly, crossed her arms and turned around. 'Very well, Ashe; since I do love you, I won't ask you. But I believe you will tell me anyway. Given what we just promised each other, I cannot imagine you would hold anything back from me, knowing that it will hurt me either way. You may as well just say it.'

Ashe's eyes finally met hers, and beyond the anger he saw sympathy; she understood the difficulty this was causing him. Past that, he knew she trusted him, though he certainly had given her cause not to. He closed his eyes.

'Llauron will ask you to promise, before the combat begins, that if he should die – ' His voice broke.

'Keep going,' she said impatiently. 'What will I be bound to do?'

'Believing him dead, you will have promised to light his funeral pyre by calling fire from the stars with Daystar Clarion. The flames will consume his body; it is the crucial first step in his quest for elemental immortality. He cannot go on to what he wishes to become without this happening. Llauron needs the two elements of fire and ether to begin his journey to full dragonhood. He knows you will not fail him if you promise to do it.'

He heard nothing in response, and opened his eyes. Rhapsody was staring at him, her own eyes as wide as he had ever seen them, trembling violently.

'But he won't really be dead.'

'No.'

'I will be burning him alive. I will be killing him myself.'

'Aria – '

Rhapsody bolted from the gazebo, and seconds later Ashe heard the sounds of retching in the bushes below it, followed by heartbreaking sobs. Ashe struck one of the gazebo columns with his head, his hands clenched in fury. He struggled to contain his wrath, and the rise of the dragon, knowing she needed him to be steady far more than he needed the release turning it loose would bring. He paced the gazebo, waiting for her to return, sensing the ebb and flow of the anguish that poured out of her as she wept, fighting the urge to comfort her when it would only upset her more.

Finally the tears stopped, and a moment later Rhapsody came up the stairs into the gazebo again. Her face was florid, but calm, and her dress, though wrinkled, had been smoothed into place. She met his eyes, and her gaze was without recrimination, without sympathy; he couldn't tell if she was feeling anything at all.

'So this is what Manwyn was alluding to,' she said. 'This was the information that upset you, that made you need to take that memory. You were afraid that, in my partial understanding, I might slip and reveal the plot early, or to the wrong people. This is what you are erasing from my mind; this subterfuge, and what Manwyn said about it.'

There was no point in lying. 'Yes.'

'And the memory of your proposal? Why can't I remember that you wanted me to marry you, and that I've agreed?'

'Because you will be near one of the primary minions of the F'dor. Right now they need you to give Lark legitimacy. If they thought they could get to me through you, however, that would most likely be far more important to them. If there is any chance they might discover our promise, that we are bound, one to the other, it would put you in far graver danger.' She nodded. 'Can you forgive me?'

Rhapsody's face remained passionless. 'I'm not sure there is anything to forgive you for, Ashe.'

'I could have refused. I could have put a stop to this plan.'

'How? By being disloyal to your own father, in my favor? Thank you, no. I don't want that on my head. This is Llauron's manipulation, Ashe – you're as much a puppet here as I am.'

'Albeit a knowing one. Therein lies the difference. So, Rhapsody, what will it be? Do you want to revoke your permission, keep the memory? Avoid all this? You have my wholehearted support if you want to.'

'No,' she answered shortly. 'That would be going back on my word to you, even if you give me the right to do so. And besides, what will you do then? It's too late, Ashe, much too late. We can only play our parts, and promise that, when this is all over, we will live our own lives honestly, without this kind of deception.'

He came to her, and cradled her face in his hands. 'Can there be any doubt why I love you so much?'

Rhapsody pulled away, turning her back to him. 'Doubt is not a good concept to discuss at this point, Ashe. In fact, I will allay one more doubt for you.'

His throat tightened. 'That being?'

She leaned forward on the gazebo railing, staring across the water. 'One might wonder, if Manwyn had not slipped and revealed this information, whether you would have told me like this, or whether you would have let it happen without telling me, knowing it would transpire, regardless? Being powerless to stop it? Don't answer, Ashe. Since, as Achmed says, I am the Queen of Self-Deception, I choose to believe you would have. And if I am wrong, I don't want to know anyway.'

Ashe rested his chin on her shoulder, wrapping his arms around her waist. 'One day this beautiful head may wear many crowns, Rhapsody. Certainly you are already the queen of my heart. But the open-handed, open-hearted trust that you bless this world with is by no means self-deception. Your trust hasn't been ill-placed, has it? You chose to trust Achmed, and, even though he is an obnoxious miscreant, he is a great friend to you. And you chose to trust me; I would probably be dead and eternally within the hands of the demon without that trust. Your heart is wiser than you think.'

'Then I assume you will forgive me one last offensive but necessary question that my heart needs to know the answer to?'

'Of course.' He smiled, but his eyes glittered nervously.

'Are you absolutely certain that Llauron isn't the host of the F'dor himself?'

Ashe buried his lips in her golden hair and sighed. 'One can never be absolutely certain of anything where the F'dor is concerned, Aria. I can't believe that he is, however. Llauron is very powerful, and the F'dor can only possess someone it is stronger than. In addition, he hates it with every fiber of his being, has been hunting it for a very long time. He will do anything he has to – *anything* – to find it and destroy it, including compromising you. You may not believe this, but Llauron is very fond of you.' He chuckled as she rolled her eyes. 'But that doesn't matter, of course, I'm sorry to say. He's rather fond of me, too, but that never stopped him from manipulating me, either.

'I've come to realize over time that your friendship with Achmed and Grunthor is the only thing that saved you from Llauron attempting to make you the agent of his plans long ago. When you first came to him, he knew Achmed and Grunthor were with you, but then they left for a while, and he felt you were free and clear of them. He began training you at the Circle in all the lore of the Filids. But then they came back and took you away with them. He has never really gotten over it, though he puts on a good face about it. I think you can trust that he would not do anything to harm you, but he will manipulate you in any way he can to get what he wants.'

Rhapsody sighed. 'Is that all there is to this story? There's nothing else, is there?'

'Gods, isn't that enough?'

'More than enough,' she said, turning in his arms and managing a weak smile. 'I just wanted to be sure.'

Ashe kissed her gently. 'You said you had a request to make of me. What is it? Anything you ask, it's yours. Just name it.'

Rhapsody winced. 'After all that, it seems foolish.'

'Nonsense. Tell me what I can do for you. Please, Aria, give me something to do that will prove my love to you, something to begin to make up for all this deception. What was it you were going to ask of me?'

Rhapsody looked embarrassed. 'I wanted to know if – if you would let me – keep this.' She touched his chest, indicating the white linen shirt he wore beneath his mariner's cape.

'This shirt?'

'Yes.'

Ashe let go of her and began to remove his cape. 'Of course. It's yours.'

'No, wait,' Rhapsody said, laughing. 'I don't need it now. I'm not cold, but you will be if you take it off. I just want to keep it when you leave tomorrow, if that would be all right.' She took his hand and led him down the gazebo steps, back into the house.

Ashe put his arm around her as they walked. 'One of the many benefits of being your lover – your betrothed – is that I am never cold,' he said, smiling down at her. 'You take very good care of that, Firelady.'

'Well, that wouldn't be true if you didn't have other shirts,' Rhapsody replied. 'But as I have made a few new ones for you myself to take with you, I think you will be well covered.'

Ashe opened the front door for her, and watched as the coals on the hearth leapt to life in greeting as she entered. He followed her into the parlor.

'So why, if you are making me new ones, do you want this old thing? It's really quite ratty at the cuffs – I hid them under the jacket.'

Rhapsody smiled at him. 'It has your scent. I wanted it to wear when I'm alone, to remind me of you. I was going to ask you for it, even when I thought you were off to propose to someone else. Isn't that wicked?' Tears of embarrassment glinted in her eyes.

Ashe laughed. 'Oh, just awful.' He shook his head, amazed at how she constantly surprised him.

'It's a selfish request, I know.'

Ashe stroked her hair, smiling. 'Have you ever done anything selfish in your life, Rhapsody?'

'Of course; all the time. You know that.'

'Nothing specific leaps to mind,' Ashe said. 'Can you perhaps name an example for me?'

Her face grew solemn. 'Don't joke about this, Ashe, please.'

Ashe took her hands. 'I'm not; gods, I'm really not, Rhapsody. I really do doubt that you could name anything.'

Rhapsody looked into the fire and the tears that had been brimming in her eyes overflowed. When she turned to face him again her eyes were filled with a sorrow he hadn't seen for a long time.

'I ran away from home,' she said softly, crossing her arms in front of her waist and holding her stomach as she did when she felt sick. 'I turned my back on the people who loved me to follow a boy who didn't. I never saw any of them again. I am alive today because of that selfish act, Ashe; alive, having left them to mourn me until the end of their days. I traded my life with my family for one night of meaningless sex in a pasture and a worthless copper coin.' She stopped when she saw his face go blank, and then turn white. 'What's the matter?'

'What was his name?' he asked, looking as if the world was about to come to its end.

'Who?'

'This boy,' he said, and he voice grew stronger, and more urgent. 'What was his name?'

She looked ashamed. 'I don't even know. He lied.'

'What did you call him, then? Tell me, Aria.'

Rhapsody was beginning to panic; the look on his face was turning into something frightening, and she could feel the bristling electricity signaling the return of the dragon. The air in the grotto had grown unsettlingly still, like the calm before a gathering storm, or the extreme low tide before a tidal wave.

'Tell me,' he commanded in a voice she had never heard. It was anguished and deep, and filled with alien power. She started to back away, but he seized her shoulders in a grasp that hurt. 'Tell me!'

'Sam,' she whispered, not understanding. 'I called him Sam.'

His fingers dug into her arms and a roar that shook the house issued forth, full of fury. His face went red and she watched in horror as he seemed to increase in size, muscles uncoiling in rage.

'Unholy BITCH!' he screamed, as loose items in the room began to fall and tables shook. The cords in his neck stood out as his anger increased, and the air charged with power as seething fury took hold of him. The pupils in his eyes narrowed to almost nothing. 'Whore! Rutting, miserable WHORE!'

His hands went to his head, and he began to clutch at his hair, digging his fingers into his scalp. As he released her Rhapsody backed slowly away from him, a look of heartbreak and fear written on her face. *It has finally come,* she thought ruefully. *I was wrong. He is the F'dor, and he's going to kill me now.* She thought about running, but decided against it. She either had to stand and fight, or give in and let it end now. Either way, she wouldn't run. It would be no use to do so anyway.

Ashe continued to roil in unbridled rage, swearing a stream of obscenity the likes of which Rhapsody had never heard. 'She knew,' he snarled, lashing out at the air as thunder rolled across the firmament that held the dome of Elysian in place. 'She knew, and she lied to me.'

'Knew what? What did I know?' Rhapsody gasped, struggling to maintain her balance as the earth began to tremble beneath her. 'I'm sorry – I don't know what I've done.'

His eyes narrowed to slits, blue as hottest part of a flame. ' "She did not land, she did not come" she said,' he ranted, his voice dropping to a murderous whisper. 'But she knew. She knew you had left, you just hadn't arrived yet. But she knew you were coming. And she didn't tell me.'

'She? Who? Who knew?'

'ANWYN!' the dragon shrieked. Its multitoned voice rattled the walls.

Rhapsody cast a glance at the door. Achmed. She needed to get to the gazebo and call for Achmed. Killing Ashe without the Thrall ritual would be pointless.

The instruments within the cherry cabinet rattled as tremors rumbled through the cottage. Ashe lashed out in a convulsive sweep of his arms; books leapt from the shelves and tumbled to the floor.

Rhapsody began to back up farther toward the front door. Tears were falling freely, and she glanced regretfully around, knowing that she could never reach Daystar Clarion in time. She wished for death, hoping that whatever manifestation of evil he really was would not be able to bind her soul as he snuffed out her life. The calm that normally descended when she faced danger was nowhere to be felt.

Then, as though hit by falling ice, Ashe stopped his tirade and looked across the room at her. His face crumbled as he saw her, terror in her eyes, the acceptance of death in her countenance, and the manifestations of the dragon disappeared instantly as a look of horror crossed his face. He struggled to speak, and when he did his voice was gentle, but still trembling.

'Rhapsody.' It was the only word he could form for a moment. 'Rhapsody, I'm sorry – please – forgive me, I – ' He reached out his hands to her, and took a step toward her.

Her own hands lashed out in front of her, holding him at bay. 'No, stay there,' she said, taking a concurrent step backward. 'Just stay there.'

Ashe stopped, and unspeakable pain filled his expression. He reached inside his shirt, and pulled out a tiny velvet pouch and tossed it onto the floor in front of her. 'Aria, open it, please.'

'No; don't move,' she said, taking another step away from him. She glanced around her again, and moved slowly toward the sword rack.

'Please, Rhapsody, for gods' sake, please, open it,' he begged, his face growing pale as the blood from his tantrum began to abate.

'No,' she repeated, more forcefully this time. 'Stay away from me. If you move, I'll kill you. You know I never lie. So help me, Ashe, don't test my resolve. Don't move.'

Tears began to fall from the crystalline eyes. 'Rhapsody, if you ever loved me, please – '

'Don't,' she said, her voice dissolving to a nasty whisper. 'Don't you dare throw that word at me. I don't know who you are. I don't know *what* you are.'

'Open the pouch. You'll know.'

Rhapsody straightened her shoulders and looked him in the eyes. The words that formed on her lips were the same as on the day they crossed the Tar'afel River.

'My refusal wasn't clear to you?' She had made it, inching slowly, to within reach of the sword rack. She reached for Daystar Clarion.

Ashe did not move, but he spoke once more, his voice calmer. 'Emily, please. Look in the pouch.'

Rhapsody froze. She turned back to him slowly. 'What did you call me?' she asked, choking.

'Please, Emily. You'll understand if you look in the pouch.' He took a step back, attempting to keep her fright at bay.

Rhapsody stared at him, shock on her face. After a moment, as if commanded, she went slowly to the small bag lying in the center of the living-room floor and bent to retrieve it. With hands that trembled she pulled the tiny drawstring open and shook its contents into her palm. It was a small silver button, heart-shaped, with the figure of a rose engraved on it; the song that surrounded it was of a land long gone but that lived in her blood. Her eyes returned to his face, which was beginning to relax into a look that she had never seen before.

'This is my button,' she whispered. 'Where did you get it?'

He smiled at her gently, so as not to frighten her with the joy that was beginning to creep over him. 'You gave it to me,' he said.

She did not take her eyes off him as her hand moved slowly to her throat. She drew forth the golden locket and opened it without looking at it. As the clasp opened a tiny copper coin fell out, thirteen-sided, oddly shaped and polished from years of loving caresses.

Ashe's eyes filled with tears again. 'Emily,' he said softly, and held out his hands to her once more.

The world before her eyes spun in a rapid swirl of colors and textures as Rhapsody fell to the ground in a dead faint.

53

Flickering images danced before her eyes, then disappeared, as Rhapsody struggled to regain consciousness. Through it all there were eyes, dragon eyes, gleaming down at her, their odd vertical slits spinning as her angle of perspective changed.

Finally she came around, focusing on the ceiling above her, the shadows from the firelight wafting over the heavy wooden beams. She blinked and tried to sit up, but gentle hands held her down, stroking her hair lovingly.

'Shhh,' Ashe said. As the world solidified she found she was on the sofa in the parlor, the fire burning quietly on the hearth, her head in his lap. Her shoes had fallen off, and the cool, wet arm of his jacket lay across her forehead. She blinked more rapidly.

'I fainted?'

He chuckled. 'Yes, but I won't tell anyone.'

'I had the most incredible dream,' she murmured, disorientedly touching the white sleeve of his shirt. His smile broadened, and he bent and brushed a kiss on the bridge of her nose.

'Sorry, Aria, it was no dream. It's really me; it's really you. My heart swore it the first time I saw you, but I knew it couldn't be. She said you never came through; I had believed all this time you were dead.'

'She?'

'Anwyn. After I came back from Serendair, I was desperate to find you. I went to Anwyn. I knew she would have seen if you had come from the old land, and would know if you were still alive. She told me that you never came, that when the ships landed you weren't on any of them. And, to my great sorrow, I had to believe her. When speaking of the Past, Anwyn cannot lie without losing her gift. I still don't understand how you got here.'

Rhapsody sat up, running a hand over her eyes and forehead. 'Got here? I'm not sure where I am, and I think I live here.'

Ashe wrapped a bent knee around her, giving her something to lean on. He held up the small coin, shiny copper, with an odd number of sides. 'I remember the day I was given this,' he said, musing as if to himself. 'I was three or four, and it was a Day of Convening; pompous ceremonies and long-winded speeches, and nothing interesting in any of them. They left me totally alone. I was so bored that I thought I would die, but I was expected to sit there and behave.

'I was beginning to think all my life would be just like this, that I would never be able to run or play or do anything fun like my friends did. It was the loneliest moment of my whole life to that point.

'And then he was there, this old man, leaning over me and smiling, with a gift – two threepenny pieces. "Buck up, lad," he said, and he winked – I remember that wink clearly, because I spent many days afterward imitating it – "sooner or later they'll shut up. In the meantime, you can examine these. They'll keep the loneliness away as long as you keep them together, because you can't have loneliness in a place where two things match so well."

'And he was right. I had a marvelous time studying them, trying to fit the sides into each other. It seemed like moments later when my father came to collect me, though hours had passed. I carried them with me from that day on, until I gave one to you. Because once I met you, Emily, I thought I would never be lonely again.'

Rhapsody rubbed her temples with her fingertips, trying to ease the headache that had crept behind her eyes. 'That was a different lifetime. I didn't even recognize the name when you first used it.' She looked up and caught his gaze; he looked totally happy, on the verge of giddy. 'Are you telling me that you – you're Sam?'

He sighed deeply. 'Yes. Gods, how I've longed to hear you call me that again.' He took her face in his hands and kissed her, his lips seeking hers in wonder.

Rhapsody pulled away from him and looked into his face again. 'You? It's really you?' He nodded. 'You don't look the same.'

Ashe laughed. 'I was fourteen; what do you expect? And a few things have happened since then, foremost of which was a rather reptilian transformation brought on by a near-death experience. And, by the way, you don't look the same either, Emily. You were the most beautiful thing I had ever seen, but, well, you've changed somewhat yourself.' He ran his fingers through the tendrils of hair that touched the flawless face, watching the light catch the strands, shining like burnished gold.

The emerald eyes ran over his features, trying to place the memory of his face into the one she now knew so well. Though he had changed a great deal, there was a clear resemblance; it was the denial brought on by history that made it impossible to see before. And as her eyes took him in, they began to brim with tears. She struggled to form words, but they took a moment to come out.

'Why?' she asked, her voice coming out fragmented, broken. 'Why didn't you come back?'

His hands cupped her face again. 'I couldn't,' he said, tears welling in his own eyes. 'I don't even know how I got there in the first place. I was flung back into the Past for only one day's time. One moment I was walking the road to Navarne, and then I was in Serendair. And after we met, I would have gladly stayed there forever with you, even though it meant dying, meant losing my whole world just like you did. I would have given it up in a heartbeat, because I had found the other half of my soul.

'I was incredibly excited that next morning, your birthday. I had made myself as presentable as possible, so your father would give his consent and allow me to marry you. I remember being nervous, and happy, but then, as inexplicably as before, I was back on the road to Navarne, back in this world.

'I almost went insane with grief. I looked for you endlessly, seeking out every First Generationer I could find, asking about you. And then Anwyn told me you had not come, and that made me realize it was too late, that you were dead, dead a thousand years or more, that you had not found MacQuieth, or any of the others from your time who could have saved you.

'My father lost patience, told me I had been dreaming, but I knew that wasn't true, because I had the button, and had seen three drops of your blood on my cloak, from when we made love. And from that moment on I was like the coin; odd, not fitting with anything, worth very little, permanently lonely. There has been no one in my life since you, Emily, no one – except you, the woman I know as Rhapsody. Who could have measured up? My father trotted his whores past me, hoping to shake you out of my heart, but I left and went to sea, rather than betray the memory of the only thing in my life that I had ever held holy, that had ever mattered.

'And that's all. I lived that way, even before the F'dor took my soul apart. I guess it had already been torn beyond recognition anyway by the loss of you. But now you're here; gods, you have been here all along. Where did you come over? Did you land in Manosse, with the Second Fleet? Or did you go as a refugee to one of the lands nearer to the Island?' As the questions passed his lips, he noticed her face; she was struggling to keep from bursting into tears, trembling.

He pulled her quickly into his arms, caressing her hair. 'Emily, Aria, everything is all right now. We're together; everything is all right. Finally, for the first time, everything is all right.'

Violently she pushed away, scorching pain in her eyes. 'It is most certainly *not* all right, Ashe. Nothing is all right. *Nothing*.'

His mouth opened in disbelief, then closed again. 'Talk to me, Aria. Tell me what is in your heart.'

Rhapsody couldn't speak. She looked down at her hands, clutching them until they turned white. One of Ashe's hands closed gently over hers as the other came to rest on her face.

'Tell me, Aria, whatever it is. Tell me.'

'Well, first and foremost, I won't know this tomorrow, Ashe. I won't have any idea when the sun comes up that anything is different. I will go on with my life, with the same belief that you deserted me, that I misjudged you utterly, that you died when the Island was destroyed, or before. It is something I think about every day, Ashe, even now, *every day*. It makes me doubt myself, it makes me afraid to trust. Gods, you will leave me tomorrow, and I won't know this. And I will believe that even the love I found with you here belongs to someone else now. Perhaps everything is all right for you, but for me, everything will be just as wrong as it was before, in fact, more so.'

She gave in to the tears. Ashe drew her into his arms and held her as she wept. 'You're right,' he said, kissing her ear after he spoke. 'I'm going to get the pearl.'

Rhapsody sat up, pulling out of his embrace again. 'What? Why?'

Ashe smiled at her, brushing the tears away with his knuckle. 'Nothing, nothing in this world, is worth hurting you for one more second. You have carried too much pain for too long, Emily. I'm going to give this memory back to you. You deserve it more than anyone else deserves the selfish fulfillment of their stupid goals.' He started to rise, but she stopped him.

'What will happen to Llauron?'

'I don't know. I don't care. I care what happens to you.'

Rhapsody's eyes were now dry, and radiating worry. 'Well, I do know, and I think you do, too. If I am useless to Llauron as a herald, because I know the truth, if I refuse to immolate a man I know is still alive, then the plan will fail. And it is already too late to prevent the assassination, isn't it? Lark's plans are laid; Llauron will die for nothing, and there will be no chance for immortality. He will be gone, because I was too self-serving to wait to know something I have lived without the knowledge of for more than a millennium.' She sighed heavily.

'I'm sorry, Sam,' she said, finally using the name. 'You couldn't believe I'm selfish; well, here's the proof. My whining almost caused you to let your own father die.'

'That's hardly what happened.'

'That's exactly what happened.' Rhapsody wiped the remnants of her tears out of her eyes with the hem of her dress. 'But at least we caught it in time.'

Ashe regarded her with a sharp look. 'What are you saying, Emily? You don't want to keep the memory?'

She smiled at him. 'You keep it for me, Sam. I can live without it a little longer.'

He took her in his arms and held her quietly for a moment. 'Do you want to tell me?'

'Tell you what?'

'What happened to you? When I didn't come back?'

'I don't think you really want to know, Sam.'

'Your choice, Emily. I want to know everything I missed, everything that isn't too painful for you to tell me.'

'So you wish to nullify our agreement? To talk about the Past?'

'Yes,' he said forcefully. 'Up to now we have been keeping silent not only to spare ourselves the pain, but to protect the interests of our families, our friends. Blast them. There is nothing in this world, the next, or the last, that ever was or ever will be more important to me than you are. *Nothing*. Please, Emily; I want to know what happened, whatever it won't hurt you to tell me, so that perhaps we can make sense of why it happened, and how.'

Rhapsody studied his face, lost in thought. After a few moments, he could see her eyes darken as she came to a decision. 'Very well. I need to tell you this, Sam, and you need to hear it. It may make you reconsider things you think you've decided.'

He took her face in his hands and stared at her hard, trying to emphasize his words. 'Nothing you could possibly say will make me change my mind about you, Rhapsody. Nothing.' He tried to use the tone she did when she spoke truly, as a Namer.

She recognized the attempt and smiled. 'Why don't you hear me out and then decide, Sam.'

'*Nothing*,' he repeated, almost testily.

Gently she pushed his hands away and rose, crossing the room to the corner by the fireplace. She picked up the paintings of her grandchildren and studied them, smiling after a moment. 'Do you remember my recurring dream? The one I told you about that night?'

'The one where the stars fell from the sky into your hands?'

'Yes. And then later, when I was enrolled in the marriage lottery, the dream changed, and the stars would fall through my hands, and into the water of the stream that ran through the Patchworks.

'The night you didn't come – well, let's just say it was a sad night, and when I went to sleep I had the dream again, but it was very different. I dreamt I looked into the water, and the stars had fallen in a circle around a long dark crevice, and were shining up at me. It wasn't until recently, when we fell in love again, that I understood what it was.'

'That being – ?'

'It was your eye, Sam; your serpentine-pupiled eye, so very different from what I remember and yet very much the same. That must have been what my mother meant in the vision when she said if I could find my guiding star I would never be lost. She meant it was in *you* – that you had a piece of my soul inside you, and to find it I needed to find you. That I would be complete with you. You aren't the only one who had lost a piece of his soul; now each of us has carried that piece for the other.

'Now I finally understand why I'm prescient; why I have dreams of the Future. It's because I gave you part of my soul that night in the Patchworks, and it came back here with you. That piece has been living, in the Future, all along. It has seen things that for me constituted the Future, since I was living fourteen hundred years in the Past. It has been calling to me, trying to reunite us.'

He smiled, looking down at the floor. 'Thank God for those dreams. And if I ever meet the Lady Rowan again, I'll have to remember to thank her.'

Rhapsody replaced the paintings and sighed. 'Unfortunately, I didn't understand any of this at the time. A deep despair descended on me, and I went through my days as if in a fog. My parents were very worried about me, just as your father was about you. I had told them you were Lirin, and my father was convinced you had cast a spell on me.

'He decided I needed something to salve my heart, and that marriage was the answer, so he moved up the suit interviews. That only made me more desperate and frightened, but I had to trust his judgment, because now I doubted my own. I remembered the gold coins you offered me as a gift, and decided what I had actually done was sold you my virginity.' Ashe's face constricted in pain, but she didn't seem to notice. 'It made things that happened later inevitable, I guess.'

'Then one day, about a week after you left, several soldiers rode into our village. They didn't know anything about you specifically; they were looking for anyone who had seemed unusual, who might have shown up at the same time you did. The Partches, the people whose barn you slept in, showed them the items you had left behind, and then they departed.

'I was terrified they would find you, and harm you. I knew I had to try to warn you, so I packed whatever I could carry, took one of my father's horses, and ran away, following them to Easton. I lost them after a few days once we were there.

'I had never been in a city before, and it seemed very large and very dangerous to me; my horse was stolen almost immediately. I asked everyone I met if they had seen you, but no one ever had. I even made a foray into the Wide Meadows to see the leader of the Lirin who lived there, but she didn't know any of the names you had given me, except for MacQuieth, who was a warrior of great renown that lived in the western lands past the great river. I realize now it was because, except for him, none of those other people had been born yet.

'Years later I did meet MacQuieth; it was quite by accident, really. And since he is a legendary hero in your lineage, I will spare you the details of how that occurred. I don't want to dispel any of his mythos. I guess some things run in the family.'

Ashe laughed. 'Could it be that your meeting had something in common with the way I, er, met Jo?'

She smiled sadly. 'Well, in a way, yes,' she admitted, 'but you were far nicer to Jo than he was to me. I asked him about you, and he said he had never seen you. And it was at that moment that I gave up; I knew that either you were dead, or a liar, but either way you weren't coming back for me; and I would never see you again.

'But, as I said, that was years later. After a few days, when I could find no one who had even seen you, I decided to go home. Then I realized I didn't even know where home was. The trip to Easton had taken several weeks, and I had no real knowledge of navigation then, and no horse. I always thought I would make it home someday, anyway.

'I needed money, so I sold the buttons; the silver buttons that matched the one I gave you.' He winced, remembering the excitement in her eyes, the pride on her face as she displayed them for him that night. 'They brought a decent price, and that allowed me to live, at least for a little while; the money bought me shelter and food. But then the money ran out, and I had to find another way to support myself.

'At first I found work cleaning houses. I was a farm girl, and I knew at least how to do that well. But always something would happen. Sooner or later the master of the house and his wife would begin to argue about me, and sometimes he would even – ' She turned away from him, crossing her arms and staring at the wall. The firelight reflected off the shimmering dress, casting shadows that undulated through the creases in the fabric, as though it sought to comfort her.

'Anyway, I would be out on the street again. And, unfortunately, there is a whole class of people who prey on young girls who are on the street. Then again, there are occasionally some who, while profiting from girls like me, also seek to protect them, and I was lucky enough to meet one of them, just before some of the more unsavory types moved in on me. Everyone called her Nana. She took me in, and wrapped her network of protection around me. All I had to do was – was – '

His voice was choked with pain. 'Emily – '

'I guess I don't need to spell it out for you, Sam. She sold me, often, I'm sorry to say. I wasn't exactly the easiest commodity to sell; my body wasn't womanly, my breasts small for the profession, and I didn't help things by refusing to service married men. That severely limited my clientele. Yet despite all the obstacles, she still managed to find work for me.'

Tears touched the corners of Ashe's eyes. *Easily, no doubt*, he thought bitterly.

'I thought I wouldn't care; nothing really mattered anymore, I was just marking my days. But I remember the first time,' she said, each word becoming softer. 'I was just fifteen. It had been a long time since you, and, well, Nana was able to sell me as untouched. She expected I would bleed again, and she was right. I guess she got a much better price because of it. She would always give me a treat or small gift when that would happen later on, but then it was due to violence, not inexperience. The first time there was both. I tried to be brave, but in truth I cried all the way through it. I probably would have anyway, but the kind of man who is willing to pay extra for that particular privilege – '

She stopped when she heard a deep sob from behind her. A look of alarm shot across her face; she gathered her skirts and hurried to him, throwing her arms around his neck.

'Sam, I'm sorry; gods, I shouldn't have told you. It's all right, Sam, I'm all right. Oh, Sam, please don't cry. I'm so sorry.'

He pulled her into his lap, burying his face in her shoulder as he wept. She held him to her heart until he calmed. At that moment she decided she would never again tell him anything about that time, locking the door in her memory. *That was nothing*, she thought ruefully. *He would never survive hearing about the bad stuff.*

'What is really ludicrous here,' he said when he could speak again, 'is that *you* are comforting *me*. You're the one who lived it, I'm the one who caused it.'

'That's nonsense,' she said, dabbing his eyes gently with her skirt. 'You had nothing to do with it. I'm the one who chose to run away. And it's a good thing, too – the truth is if you had not come into my world, for however short a time, I never would have followed you. I would have spent my life, married to a farmer I didn't love, never seeing the world you told me I would see, and have. I would have perished long before the Island sank; probably I would have died inside even before my body did. If you hadn't come along, I wouldn't be here now. You saved my life, Sam; think of it like that. *Ryle hira.* Life is what it is. Whatever we have suffered, at least we are together now.'

He pulled back and looked at her, sitting on his lap, holding his hands.

The perfection of the image she had made earlier was gone; the dress was rumpled, her hair beginning to come down, but in the firelight she looked as close to angelic as anything he had ever seen.

'I was wrong,' he said, his voice quiet. 'What you've told me does change the way I feel about you.' Rhapsody went pale. 'If it is possible, it makes me love you even more.'

Relief flooded her face. 'Gods, don't scare me like that,' she scolded, slapping his arm lightly. Her face grew solemn. 'But there is one more reason you might want to reconsider marrying me.'

'Impossible.'

'Sam – '

'No, Rhapsody.'

'I don't know if I can give you children,' she blurted, her face growing pale again. 'I think I'm barren.'

Ashe stroked her cheek gently. 'Why do you think that?'

Rhapsody stared into the fire. 'Nana used to give us an herb called Whore's Friend, a leaf extract that prevented pregnancy and disease. I don't know what, if anything, that has done to me inside. I have had none of that preventative in this land, but you and I have certainly made love often enough to have – '

He pulled her rapidly into this arms. 'No, Aria; I'm sorry. I thought you knew. I'm a dragon, one of the Firstborn races. In order to sire a child, it would have had to be a conscious decision on my part, and, since you didn't tell me you wanted me to – a wise choice, in my opinion, by the way – I haven't done so.' Painful memory lingered in his eyes. 'In fact, one of the greatest reasons for my despair about leaving you behind in the old world was that I never knew for certain whether you had become pregnant after our first night together.

'I had no control over it then. My dragon nature didn't come out until much later, when the piece of the star was sewn into my chest. It was my first time, too – I was utterly lost to you, even then. So for all I knew, when I left you, you were with child. The thought of it almost killed me, imagining you alone and vulnerable, probably disgraced, in pain and frightened, with my daughter or son who I would never know. It was as if, in addition to the loss of the love of my life, my soulmate, I'd lost that child, too.' The hand that caressed her cheek trembled slightly.

Rhapsody took his hand in hers and kissed it. 'There was no child. Gods, Sam, I wished for so long that there had been, but it didn't come to pass.'

His eyes sparkled sapphire-blue in the firelight. 'I'm happy to hear you say that you wished for a child, because I very much look forward to granting that wish someday, when the land is safe and the F'dor is destroyed. I dream of it, in fact, and have, even before you gifted me with your love again. And you needn't worry about your fecundity; it is I who have withheld progeny from you, not the other way around. It's not a reflection on you, or your fertility, in any way. In fact, my senses say you're fine.'

Relief broke over Rhapsody's face in the form of a heart-stealing smile. A moment later, she looked thoughtful. 'Well, I'm very glad to hear it. Do you want to hear the rest of the story?'

'If you want to tell me.'

'It gets easier from here. After a few years, a kind man took an interest in me; an older man. He seemed as interested in my mind as he was in, well, other things; probably more, really. He set me up in my own house, and encouraged my desire to learn. He made sure I had the very finest instruction in music, and art, and other scholarly pursuits.'

'All the things you told me you wanted to do that night in Merryfield.'

'Yes. He set me up with the greatest Lirin Namer in all of Serendair, a man named Heiles, to learn the ancient arts, but not long after I had finished my training as a Singer and was just about to achieve Namer status, Heiles disappeared. To my knowledge he was never found. I was close to fully trained by then. I had to study on my own for about a year. I was just beginning to figure out the science of Naming when my benefactor died.

'Soon after that, a beast who had taken a fancy to me sent one of his henchmen after me, to collect me for some private entertainment. I refused. I was rather brash about it, and it turned out to be a serious mistake. And things became, well, let's just say the situation was pretty ugly when I ran into Achmed and Grunthor. They rescued me and helped me escape. They were on the run themselves, and together we got out of Easton and made for Sagia; do you know of it?'

Ashe thought for a moment. 'Yes, the Oak of Deep Roots. It was a root-twin to the Great White Tree.'

'Yes. The Axis Mundi, the line through the center of the earth, runs along that root as well. We went in through Sagia – I'm still not exactly sure how – and crawled along the Root, forever it seems. That's when we changed, absorbing the powers of the Earth, of Fire, of Time. We passed through a great wall of flame at what must have been the center. I believe we actually were immolated, but the song of our essence went on, reforming us on the other side when our bodies burned away. And all the old scars, all the old wounds, were gone.' Gently Ashe stroked her wrist with his thumb, the place that had once borne the scar he remembered so vividly. 'We were made new; that's why when you met me your dragon sense thought I was a virgin.'

'That's not why. I told you long ago why.'

She kissed his cheek and slid out of his arms, sitting beside him on the sofa again. 'The trip seemed like it would never end. It must have taken centuries, because when finally we came out we were here, and everything, everyone we had known had vanished ages before into the sea. In fact, everyone I had loved was probably gone long before that; I didn't know how many generations had passed before the Cymrians set sail, how many it had been since they arrived.

'So, I suppose Anwyn didn't really lie to you. We didn't land; we never did set foot on any of the Cymrian ships, we never sailed. We left before those generations were born, we arrived long after the war. So, in fact, her answer to you was truthful.'

Ashe laughed bitterly, and stared into the fire. 'Technically, anyway. But Anwyn knew, Emily. She knew that you had left, that you were on your way, crawling along the Root. She chose to keep it hidden; instead all she said was that you hadn't arrived, that you never set foot on the ships that left the old world in time. It was like dying then, Aria. She watched me dissolve into anguish beyond measure, and she just stood there silently. This is my grandmother, Rhapsody, my own grandmother. Do you think my happiness, my sanity, means anything to her?'

He looked back at her. The sympathy in her eyes went straight to his heart, bringing with it warmth and consolation. 'I guess not, Sam; I'm sorry,' she said, resting her hand lightly on his face. 'Do you have any idea why? Why would she do this?'

'Power. Power over me. They are all like that; Anwyn, my father, all of them. Now can you understand why I don't care a fig for the lot of them? Why I'm willing, even now, to turn my back on them, to give you back the memory? You are the only person who has ever really cared about me, despite my illustrious lineage, the only person who ever really loved me. I owe you everything; I owe them nothing. Yet you always seem to end up with the chaff while they get the wheat.'

Rhapsody laughed, and leaned her head back against his shoulder as he put his arm around her. 'What interesting imagery. Now, which of us is the farm child? Wheat is only good if you need food, Sam. Chaff works very well to make a soft bed. Generally we spend more time there than at the table, anyway.' Her eyes sparkled humorously, and he laughed with her, hugging her tighter. 'And chaff makes a tremendous bonfire. Don't discount the value of chaff, Sam. It will be our turn for bread eventually.'

Ashe sighed deeply and stroked her hair. They watched the fire for a long time, curled around each other in comfortable familiarity, as the flames changed colors, twisting in a quiet dance. Finally, he spoke.

'I have a question.'

'Oh, good. So do I.'

'You first.'

'No, go ahead.'

'All right,' he said, enjoying the banality of their exchange, 'why did you start calling yourself Rhapsody?'

She laughed. 'Nana thought my real name was too ordinary. It was prim-sounding, not a good name for, well, for my new line of work.'

'Emily is a beautiful name.'

' "Emily" ' is only an abbreviation of my real name. It's actually my nickname.'

Interest brightened Ashe's face. 'Really? I didn't know that. What is your real name?'

Rhapsody turned red, and she looked away, although her eyes still smiled.

'Come on,' he cajoled, grabbing her around the waist, laughing as she squirmed away. 'You're going to marry me; I should at least get to know what your real name is. Gods, you know every permutation of mine.'

'I don't know why you call yourself Ashe.'

'Because "Gwydion" would get me killed. Stop stalling. What is it?'

'Be careful, Sam,' she said seriously. 'A name is very powerful. My old name has never been spoken in this world. When that happens it should be in a special ceremony, something that will surround it with power, so it won't be vulnerable to the old world demons. Like a wedding, for instance.'

He nodded, his playfulness subsiding. Rhapsody sensed his mood shift, and she climbed back into his lap.

'But,' she said, eyes sparkling with mischief, 'if I told it to you in *pieces*, it probably would be all right.'

'Only if – '

' "Rhapsody" really is my middle name,' she interrupted before he could finish. 'My mother was a skysinger; her name was Allegra.'

'Beautiful.'

'It would be a good name for a daughter, wouldn't it?'

He smiled at her tenderly. 'Yes; yes it would.'

'Anyway, my father named me after his mother, and Mama was not thrilled with the name. She thought it was staid and boring. I know because she told me once, in front of the fire, when we were alone, brushing my hair. She wanted to name me something Lirin, something with music in it, because she believed it would give me a musical soul.'

'She was a wise woman.'

'So that's where "Rhapsody" came from. Besides being a musical term, it denotes unpredictability, and passion, and wild romance. She hoped those things would counteract my first name.'

He kissed her forehead. 'It suits you perfectly.'

'Thank you – I think.'

'So,' he said, wicked mirth in his own eyes, 'what was your grandmother's name?'

'Elienne.'

'Not the Lirin one, you brat. What was your father's mother's name?'

Rhapsody's face grew rosier still, either from embarrassment or laughter. 'Amelia.'

'Amelia? I like Amelia. Emily, short for Amelia. Has a nice ring to it.'

'My family called me Emmy,' she said. 'My friends called me Emily. The only one who called me Amelia was – '

'Let me guess: your grandmother?'

Rhapsody laughed again. 'How did you know?'

'And what last name, what patronymic, did the farm families in your village generally have?'

She played along. 'Well, the one I knew best was Turner, as in Earth-turner. It signified that they were planters, and raised crops from the ground. Nice people; I was very fond of all of them. Now, if we're done with the ancient history lesson, is it my turn? Do I get to ask my question now?'

'Certainly. Ask away.'

'I want to know who this other woman was that you were going to search out and marry; the one you discovered after the ring came into full power.'

'There never was another woman, Rhapsody; I was talking about you.'

Rhapsody shook her head in disagreement. 'When you said you now knew who the right woman was, this Cymrian woman you became aware of, and certain of, to be the Lady – '

'You.'

'I see. And the woman you told me you were in love with, in the forest when we – '

'Also you.'

'What about – '

'You, Rhapsody. There is not, and never has been, anyone in my life but you. Until tonight I thought that constituted two, but, in actuality, since you and Emily are one and the same, it makes it astonishingly simple. I loved you then as Emily; I love you now, again, as Rhapsody, both very different and yet still the same. You are the only woman I have ever touched, ever kissed, ever loved. Just you.'

She wrapped her arms around his neck. 'Let's keep it that way,' she whispered, smiling with him. 'Is that selfish enough for you?'

His answer was lost in the kiss that followed; he cradled her face as their lips met, breathing her in like a spring wind, filling his soul with her essence. His hands slid up her back, his fingers caressing the crinkly silk of the dress, and carefully began to unbutton it.

Rhapsody pulled away gently. 'Sam, please don't.'

'What's the matter?'

She took a deep breath, then looked at him steadily. 'Perhaps, given that I won't have any memory of this tomorrow, it's a bad idea to become engaged tonight.'

Ashe's face fell. 'Emily – '

'Let me finish. There's no point in making a promise to marry. Those are promises easily broken, and without the knowledge that it was made, there really is no point in it. After everything you've heard, do you still want to marry me?'

His heart was in his eyes. 'More than ever.'

'And given the choice, assuming all other things are unimportant, would you rather leave here tomorrow as my fiancé – or as my husband?'

Understanding began to dawn on him, and Ashe started to smile. 'As your husband – no question.'

Her eyes mirrored his. 'Then marry me, Sam. Marry me tonight.'

Rhapsody awoke the next morning as the light began to filter through the curtains. She stretched in luxurious warmth and rolled over in her bed, coming face-to-face with the sleeping Ashe. She started, and her movement caused him to wake and open his eyes.

'Good morning,' he said softly, smiling at her. There was a happiness in his eyes the like of which she had never seen.

'Good morning,' she answered drowsily, returning his smile wanly and yawning. 'I have to say I'm surprised to see you here. I thought you planned to be gone before I awoke.' As her awareness began to return, she realized in embarrassment that they were naked beneath the sheets.

'We talked late into the night. Do you remember anything?'

Rhapsody turned the thought over in her mind. 'No,' she said, a trace of sadness in her voice. 'Not after we went into the gazebo – that's my last memory. It went well, then?'

His smile broadened, and he reached out and drew a lock of her hair across his throat. 'Very well.'

Rhapsody's face grew solemn, returning to her melancholy thoughts of the night before. 'Why did you stay, really?'

Ashe looked at her seriously. 'We wanted to spend as much time together as we could before I left. You agreed; honestly you did.'

Rhapsody sat up and saw her silk dress crumpled in a heap on the floor at the foot of the bed, his mariner's clothes scattered across the room. Color rose in her cheeks as she lay back under the blankets once more and looked at him again.

'We made love, then?' she asked quietly.

'Yes. Oh, yes.'

Rhapsody looked uncomfortable. 'You – you did want to, didn't you? I didn't make you feel guilty or beg you, did I?'

Ashe laughed. 'Not at all. As if you would ever need to.'

She turned away from him so he could not see the sorrow in her eyes. 'I wish I could remember,' she said sadly.

Ashe took her carefully by the shoulders and turned her to face him, kissing her gently. 'You will, one day,' he said. 'I am holding the memory for you, Aria. One day it will be ours to share again.'

Tears began to form in the emerald eyes. 'No,' she whispered. 'It may be mine to keep someday, but it's time for you to begin making memories with someone else.'

Ashe pulled her closer so she could not see him smile. 'Tomorrow,' he said. 'Today I am still here with you. Perhaps there is a way to make up for the loss until the memory is yours once more.' He laid her back down on the pillow and kissed her again, his hands caressing her breasts lovingly.

Fire, mingled with guilt, coursed through Rhapsody's body as his lips moved lower. She quickly gave herself over to the passion, fueled by the pain of her imminent loss, and they made love again, clinging to each other desperately, as though they thought they would never see each other again.

When it was over, neither of them looked happy. Rhapsody lay quietly in his arms, in the throes of silent guilt. The pensive sadness in Ashe's eyes was much worse; he had felt their souls touch the night before in ecstasy, and today it was gone, replaced by bitter regret, the pain of being so close to ultimate happiness and still having it elude them.

Finally, Rhapsody rose from the bed and gathered some fresh clothes. She disappeared into the bathroom, and while she was gone Ashe dressed in the clean garments she had left out for him on top of his pack. He cursed Llauron, he cursed Anwyn, he cursed himself, anyone and anything that had conspired to keep them apart and was to blame for any part of the sorrow in her eyes.

As he waited for her to come out again Ashe's senses, then his eyes, turned to the threepenny piece lying unnoticed in the rug before the fire. He bent to pick it up, smiling. He looked in the pile of hastily discarded clothes and found her locket, then carefully replaced the coin within it. He had Emily back, and she was his wife. Now if he could only keep her safe and in love with him until she knew it.

54

Meridion slammed back in his chair, his pulsing aurelay twisting red and hot with frustration. He had been trying for hours; his eyes stung from the painfully close work. Deep grooves had been worn into the flesh of his fingers from gripping the instruments so tightly, but it had been to no avail. He could not catch another dream-thread.

Rhapsody was no longer any use for such a purpose. It had been an utter fluke the first time, even less possible now; there was no give in the fabric of her dreams now that they were inextricably bound to Ashe. Despite her loss of the memory of that night, she still had given her unconscious mind over solely to thoughts of him. His attempts to pry a thread free to attach elsewhere, where it needed to be, was only causing her pain and despair; he could see it in the restless terrors and fever that haunted her sleep the night after she and Ashe parted. Meridion threw down the thin silver pick in despair.

The end was coming. And there was no way to warn them.

All his manipulation of the Past had come to nothing; the result was going to be the same, after all.

Meridion put his head down on the instrument panel of the Time Editor and wept.

Beneath his face were fragments of time, splinters and scraps of film left over from the destruction of the original strand from the Past he had tried to unmake. He brushed them away dejectedly. One stuck fast to his sweating fingers.

Meridion shook his hand, but still the scrap clung to it. He held it up to the Time Editor's lightsource.

There was nothing left of the image; the heat of the Time Editor's rending had marred the film irretrievably. The top edge was similarly rent, taking out the sensory information. The bottom edge of the film piece was the only part left intact, the piece that housed the sound from the Past. Meridion held it up to his ear.

At the edge of his hearing the Grandmother's dry, insectlike voice whispered.

The deliverance of that world is not a task for one alone. A world whose fate rests in the hands of one is a world far too simple to be worth saving.

Meridion pondered the words. *Not a task for one alone.*

Not for one alone.

The idea flashed through him so intensely, along with the heat of excitement, that he felt hot and weak, almost dizzy.

Meridion reignited the Time Editor. The machine roared to life. Bright light flashed around the glass walls of his spherical room, suspended above the dimming stars, the heat from the boiling seas churning up a blanket of mist on the world's surface below him.

There was another way, another connection that could be made with dream-thread. A path that had already been blazed, synchronicity that already existed.

A name that had already been shared.

When the machine was fully engaged, Meridion looked through the eyepiece again. Carefully he backed the film up one night, and repositioned it under the lens to another place in the dark mountains, in the night black as pitch. It took him a moment to find what he was looking for in the gathering storm, crystals of harsh snow beginning to form in the wind of the Teeth.

He caught the dream-thread easily, anchored it without difficulty. The warning was in place.

Now it was only a matter of seeing whether they heeded it.

A shaft of sunlight as golden as Rhapsody's hair broke through the morning clouds. Ashe stepped into the glow, the mist from his cloak sparking into a million tiny diamond droplets, hanging heavy in the new-winter air.

From beneath her hood Rhapsody smiled. The sight was a beautiful one, a memory she would hold on to in the sad days to come. Standing there in the sunlight, even swathed in his cloak and mantle, Ashe looked like something almost godlike, here at the crest of the first barrier peaks, on his way to the foothill rise. Soon they would part company at the pass that led to the lower rim, and he would be gone from her life.

A billowing roar echoed through the Teeth, sending shivers through her. The sound echoed off the crags and over the wide heath, frightening the wildlife that still remained in the sight of winter's coming. The sound was unmistakable.

'Grunthor!' Rhapsody spun around, searching blindly in the blaze of morning light for the source of the scream.

Ashe put his hand to his eyes, scanning the panorama of the crags bathed in the sun's brilliance. He pointed to a pass in the guardian peaks, the barracks of the mountain guard.

'There,' he said.

Rhapsody put her hand to her brow as well. From the cave door that led to the barracks hall, figures were spewing forth like ash from a rampant volcano. The Bolg soldiers of the barracks scrambled to evacuate the corridor, taking shelter behind whatever outcroppings of rocks afforded them cover. Rhapsody shook her head.

'Grunthor must be having nightmares again,' she said, watching the Bolg scatter.

A moment later, her assumption was confirmed. A much bigger figure, still dwarfed by the mountain peak, emerged from the opening. Even from a great distance, his distress was unmistakable.

Rhapsody felt for a friendly gust of wind, making certain it would carry up to the top crag. 'Here, Grunthor!' she called, wrapping her voice in the gust. A moment later the figure stopped and sighted on her, then waved frantically. Rhapsody waved back.

'I'm sorry,' she said to Ashe, who was leaning on his walking stick, his face shrouded once more by the hood of his mist cloak. 'I have to go to him.' She ran her hand down his arm.

Ashe nodded. If he was annoyed, the mist cloak shielded any sign of it. 'Of course,' he said, shifting his weight. 'I'll wait.'

Rhapsody patted his arm again, then hurried to the ledge midway up the peak. Even as she ran, she could see the wary soldiers, backs pressed against the mountain face, surreptitiously slip into the barracks corridor again once Grunthor was clearly away.

'Gods, what's the matter? You look awful.'

The Sergeant-Major was disheveled and wild-eyed, even after his sprint. The enormous chest heaved so thunderously that Rhapsody grew frightened.

'Here, calm down,' she said in her Namer's commanding tone. 'What's the matter?'

Grunthor measured his breathing, his panting diminishing somewhat. 'We gotta get down there, Duchess. She needs us.'

'The Grandmother? Or the child? How do you know?'

The Firbolg giant bent over, his hands against his knees. 'The Earthchild. I don't know how I know, I just do. I could see inside her dreams, and she's panicking. From the feel of them, I don't blame her a bit. You gotta sing to her again, Your Ladyship. She's terrified.'

'All right, Grunthor,' Rhapsody said soothingly. 'I'll go with you. I just need to see Ashe off first; he's leaving.'

Grunthor stood, eyeing her sharply. 'For good?'

'Yes.'

The sharp look mellowed into one of sympathy. 'You all right, Duchess?'

Rhapsody smiled. She remembered when she first heard him use that expression, the first of many times. It was in the tunnel of the Root; he had been trying to ascertain whether she had fallen into the endless darkness. Each time she had responded in the affirmative, knowing that the answer was only partially true; safe or not, she would never be 'all right' again. There was something sadly ironic in hearing it again now.

'I will be,' she said simply. 'Roust Achmed, and get my armor. I'll meet you on the Heath.'

Grunthor nodded, then patted her shoulder and headed back toward the Cauldron. Rhapsody watched him go, then returned to Ashe.

He was still there, as she had left him, leaning on his walking stick.

'Everything all right?' he asked.

Rhapsody shielded her eyes and looked up into the darkness of his hood. The sight tugged at her heart, but she swallowed the pain, hoping that the next time she saw him, probably from across the great Moot at his coronation, that he would be able at last to walk with his face to the sun, open to the sight of all men, without fear.

'My newest grandchild needs my help,' she said. 'I'll tend to her once we've parted at the foothills. Come; let's be off.'

55

Achmed had expected Rhapsody to be late coming back from seeing Ashe off, so he had taken his time getting to the Heath. As a result, when he came over the top of the last rise he found two figures there, one enormous, one slight, both looking grim, and both waiting for him. Achmed cursed. She was predictable in her unpredictability.

'He's gone, then?' he demanded, handing Grunthor the morning's report from the night patrol. Rhapsody nodded. 'Good.'

Grunthor shot him an ugly look, then put a hand on her shoulder. 'When'll he be back, darlin'?'

'He won't,' she said shortly. 'Perhaps I'll see him at the royal wedding in Bethany, but that will be the last time I expect to. He's off to fulfill his destiny.' She looked back into the sun rising over the crest of Grivven. 'Let's go fulfill ours.'

★

The tunnel to the Loritorium had echoed with their footsteps, and with the memory of voices.

Is she still there, sir?

Damn you, Jo, go home or I'll tie you to a stalagmite and leave you until we return.

I want to go with you. Please.

Achmed closed his eyes, his head heavy with the weight of the memories.

The torch Grunthor carried flickered uncertainly, a pale candle compared to the roaring flame that had first lighted their way into the hidden vault of magic. Achmed wondered if the weak fire was an indication that the concentrated lore, once heavy in the stale air, had begun to dissipate as the wind from the world above made its way down the ancient passages. Or perhaps it was more a sign that the fires of Rhapsody's soul were burning a little more dimly.

She said nothing, following them silently down into the belly of the mountain, her face drawn and ghostly white in the pale torchlight. All the length of the tunnel to the Loritorium she remained quiet, so unlike their travels overland or along the Root, where she and Grunthor had passed the time with songs or whistled tunes. The absence of noise was deafening.

After they had gone a thousand paces Achmed heard a slow, broken intake of breath, and she knew she was hearing voices in the echoing tunnel as well.

Do you mean to tell me that the Lord Roland sent an unarmed woman into Ylorc without the protection of the weekly armed caravan? These are unsafe times, not just in Ylorc, but everywhere.

I'm just doing my lord's bidding, m'lady.

Prudence, you must stay here tonight. Please. I fear for your safety if you were to leave now.

No. I'm sorry, but I must return to Bethany at once.

Ghosts, Achmed thought. *Everywhere ghosts.*

Finally the tunnel widened into the entrance to the marble city. The flame from the firewell was burning brightly, steadily, casting long shadows about the empty Loritorium.

'Everything seems all right here,' Achmed said, examining the fiery fountain. 'I don't feel any strange vibrations here.'

They left the Loritorium and wandered down the corridor to the Chamber of the Sleeping Child.

The Grandmother was in the entranceway, as always.

'You've come,' she said; each of her three voices was trembling. 'She's worse.'

From within the chamber the sound of moaning could be heard. They hurried past the enormous doors of soot-streaked iron, into the well of the chamber.

The Earthchild thrashed about on her catafalque, murmuring in panic.

Rhapsody ran to her, whispering soothing words, trying to gentle her down, but the child did not respond.

Achmed grasped Rhapsody's upper arm with a grip that hurt. When she looked up, he turned her toward Grunthor.

The giant stood beside the Earthchild's catafalque, his sallow skin ashen in the dim light. His broad face was pickled with beads of sweat.

'Somethin's coming,' he whispered. 'Somethin' – ' His words choked into a strangled gasp.

'Grunthor?'

The giant was trembling as he reached for his weapons.

'The Earth,' the Grandmother whispered. 'It screams. Green death. Unclean death.'

As if to mirror the Firbolg giant, the ground began to shudder all around them. Pieces of rock and granite crumbled from the walls and ceiling as dust streamed down in great rivers, blackening the air.

'What's happening? An earthquake?' Rhapsody shouted to Grunthor. The sergeant was drawing Lopper, his hand-and-a-half sword, and the Friendmaker, his expression grim. He barely had time to shake his head.

Soft popping sounds erupted around them, like sparks from wet wood in fire. From the floor, ceiling and walls, thousands of tiny roots appeared, black and spiny, poking through the dirt like new spring seedlings. Within a few moments they had grown to the size of daggers, slashing menacingly at the air. By the time they had, Achmed was across the cavern, almost within arm's reach of Rhapsody. She stifled a gasp as the roots began to hiss, and held up her hands over the head of the Sleeping Child.

Then the world exploded.

From every earthen surface massive vines, each thick as an ancient oak, broke forth, rending the air and crushing the walls. The ground below their feet buckled and reared up violently, shattering beneath the swirling wall of spiny flesh as even bigger roots ripped out of the earth, surrounding them and tossing them about like acorns.

A great wave of stench roared forth, blinding them, causing them to choke and gag. The malodor was unmistakable.

F'dor.

Achmed covered his head as a large chunk of falling debris glanced off him, sending waves of shock through his shoulder and torso. He could feel the heartbeats of the others racing in a cacophonous crescendo, pelting his skin like hard rain. Rhapsody had been thrown out of his line of sight by the violent upheaval of the earth and the lashing vines. 'Get out!' he shouted to her, coughing to clear the dust from his lungs and hoping she could hear him over the noise of the chaos.

In answer, a humming light appeared amid the falling rubble, shining through the black ash clouds that obscured all other vision. A metallic ring like a clarion call accompanied it, reaching down into Achmed's heart, sending an electric thrill coursing through him. The rippling flames hovered steady in the air for a moment, then began a furious, humming dance as the sword hacked into the thrashing vines, throwing flashes of light around the darkness of the crumbling cavern. The Iliachenva'ar was standing her ground, fighting back.

An ear-splitting roar exploded next to him. Achmed turned as a huge tendril lashed around Grunthor's foot and dragged him from the slab of ground he had fallen against, lifting him upside down into the smoky air. Dozens of whipcords wound like lightning around his neck and limbs, then simultaneously snapped with a gruesome force. Grunthor screamed again, more in fury than in agony, before the nooses tightened, choking off his roar.

With a flick of both wrists, daggers were in Achmed's hands, and he leapt to where the giant was hanging, slicing at the writhing tendrils in a flurry of gouging slashes. He grabbed for one of the weapons, hanging upside down in Grunthor's backsheath, and began to strike at the vine with both hands. He aimed first for the vines around the giant's wrists, freeing one of them before a large clawlike vine flexed and slapped him against a slab of upturned earth, pinning him beneath itself.

Achmed breathed shallowly, trying to minimize the pain from the crushing blow to his ribs. In the distance he could still hear the ringing of Daystar Clarion, the screaming of the vines as Rhapsody sawed through them, searing the ends. Her heartbeat was remarkably slow and focused, given the thunderous pounding he knew must belong to Grunthor. By the sound of it, the sergeant had wrestled himself free and was hacking ferociously at the vine above Achmed that was holding him captive. A moment later the great root snapped in two, proving him correct. He grabbed hold of Grunthor's hand, and the giant Bolg hauled him free of the morass of slithering roots that flailed beneath him, hissing and striking at his heels like serpents.

'Hrekin,' the sergeant swore, gulping for air. It was the last thing Achmed heard him say before the ground beneath his feet buckled again, hurling him back toward what had been the cavern entrance, now in ruins.

One of his daggers was wrenched from his hand and fell as he did, though he couldn't hear where it landed in the fury around him. The cold, gangrenous hand of terror clutched at his viscera as he realized the impossibility of escaping this monstrous root, this demon-vine that was devouring the cavern of the Sleeping Child. The Earthchild's catafalque was gone, blasted into the air in the initial moments of the attack. Her body was now undoubtedly buried beneath a mountain of rubble or, far worse, wrapped in the tendrils of the serpent vine, being dragged back to the clutches of the F'dor, just like Jo. He could taste his own death in his mouth.

Frozen waves of fear washed over him. It was not death itself he feared, but the hands that were delivering it. He had become used to the freedom that had been his since that humid day in the backstreets of Easton a lifetime ago when Rhapsody had changed his name, snapping the invisible collar of demonic servitude from his neck. He had almost learned to breathe again, to believe that his life, his soul, were his own once more. And now he was about to die, back once again in the demon's iron grasp.

And worse, so were his only friends.

The scratching sound of the wind filled his ears, spreading a moment later into four separate notes, held in a monotone. The ritual singing rang through his head, vibrating in his Dhracian blood. He could not see the Grandmother through the upheaval, but he could hear her clearly, the fifth note of the Thrall ritual cutting through the noise like a knife.

As the ritual clicking joined the monotonous tune, the tangled sea of roots and vines pulsed for a moment with the same rhythm as the Thrall ritual, then went rigid. For a moment Achmed was acutely aware of all the sounds around him – the throbbing of the colossal network of vines, now filling the entire cavern above and around him, dwarfing him in their titanic size; the ringing hum of Daystar Clarion, gleaming in the darkness beyond his reach; the spitting growl of the thousands of snakelike tendrils that hovered near him, threatening to strike at any moment; Rhapsody's flickering heartbeat, and the ritual cadence that was the heartbeat of the Grandmother.

He could not hear Grunthor's heartbeat.

'Achmed.' Rhapsody's voice was barely audible, and smoke was wafting from the place it originated. He pushed past a tangle of wriggling rootlets, ignoring their failed strikes, and climbed over to where he had heard her, following the sound of her heart.

He found her, wedged between two great slabs of earth, searing the end of an enormous stalk with the flames from Daystar Clarion. The tributary of the demon-vine was moaning, withering to blackness in the ethereal fire. Her eyes met his, burning green with the same intensity as the sword.

'Elemental fire cauterizes it,' she said softly when she knew he was close enough to hear her. 'Do I hear the Thrall ritual?'

Achmed nodded, wincing from the shooting pain that tore through his head with the movement. 'The vine's an extension of the demon, a construct like the Rakshas was,' he answered, taking care to avoid the ropy flesh. 'She may be able to hold the demonic essence in stasis for the moment, but she won't be able to kill the root; it's much too powerful.'

'Vingka jai,' Rhapsody said to the flame glowing on the root's edge. *Ignite and spread.* The fire leapt as if in righteous anger, and the vine shrieked in fury and pain.

'Get – out of there,' Achmed ordered, gesturing toward where the exit to the Loritorium had been. 'I don't know how long she can hold it off.'

'Where's Grunthor? The child?'

Achmed shook his head. 'Get out of there *now*,' he commanded.

'Where are they?'

'I don't know!' he snarled. The loss of Grunthor, coupled with the knowledge that the keys that would open the prison vault were on their way to the depths of the earth, was more than he could contemplate without losing his mind. The one thing he could concentrate on was getting Rhapsody out of the shards of the Colony before it collapsed. Distantly he wondered if that was doing her a favor, given what was coming. 'Damnation! Get out while you can!'

She still wasn't listening. Instead, she was staring off into the crumbled ruin of the cavern, her mouth open in astonishment. Achmed turned toward where she was looking.

There, standing amid the clouds of ash and dust hanging in the air, was the Sleeping Child. Her eyes still closed, the Earthchild was standing erect, her feet melding into the rubble that littered the Colony floor. The light from Daystar Clarion, now rigid in Rhapsody's grasp, was breaking in rippling waves over her, illuminating the smoothness of her face, the polished gray of her skin. In the firelight she seemed enormously tall, taller than she had appeared in repose, her long shadow dancing off the broken cavern walls.

'No,' Rhapsody whispered, choking. 'No, please. Stay asleep, little one.'

Slowly the child pulled first one foot, then the other, from the ground and took a step forward.

The sleepwalker.

'Please,' Rhapsody whispered again. 'Not yet, little one, it's not time now. Go back to sleep.'

The Earthchild paid her no heed. With a lumbering gait she began climbing through the hills of littered stone, gliding through the rock as if wading ankle-deep in the sea, her eyes still closed. Whipcords and tendrils of the colossal vine flexed and lashed impotently toward her, straining against the thrall caused by the strange insectoid music that the Grandmother was still making.

Achmed put his hand out to Rhapsody. 'Come on,' he said. Involuntarily she obeyed, following him over the boulders that had once been part of the ceiling.

They followed in the wake of the Earthchild, whose movements left an open passage in the rocky wasteland that the Colony had become. As they passed the great arms of the demon-root it began to tremble, causing even more dust and grit to rain down from the crushed walls and ceiling. Rhapsody coughed, trying to expel the debris from the back of her throat, as Achmed hauled her over a mound of earth and under a mammoth, hissing vine. Tiny tendrils writhed in the dark, lunging in serpentine strikes, to be reined back by the power of the Thrall ritual. Unable to reach their target, the roots spat in snakelike fury.

At the sound Rhapsody's eyes suddenly narrowed, brightened by hate and the memory of Jo's death. She let go of Achmed's hand. With a movement so sudden that he couldn't follow it with his eyes, she lashed out with a vicious sweep of the sword and struck off the tendrils, tossing them onto the floor of the cavern. The vine shrieked and shuddered, the tiny branches igniting and burning to ash on the ground.

'Not now!' Achmed hissed. 'Listen.'

The Thrall ritual was diminishing. The echo of the Grandmother's voice in the distance was thinner, rasping, as the strain of maintaining the difficult song began to take its toll.

'She's failing,' Achmed said, dragging Rhapsody out from under the quivering root and up the tunnel. 'We have to get to the Loritorium.'

'Grunthor – '

'Come,' Achmed insisted. He could barely keep the same thought from his mind. The heartbeat of the Grandmother was beginning to wane, the exertion of the ritual wearing her down rapidly. Her ancient heart would give out soon. If it did before they got to the Loritorium, there would be no chance for escape, not for them.

And not for the rest of the world, upon whom the prisoners of the ancient vault deep within the Earth were about to be loosed.

A horrific crash and the sound of falling rock rumbled through the passageway ahead, and a thick fog of dust rolled over them. Instinctively they covered their eyes and heads. When the noise abated, they looked up simultaneously and waved their arms to clear the air of the gray dust. Achmed nodded, and they hurried forward, only to stop.

A solid wall of newly fallen rock blocked the passageway ahead of them. Achmed ran his hands over it desperately, then pointed off to the side. A tiny opening beneath heavy stone slabs was the only break in the wall.

Quickly Rhapsody sheathed her sword, dropped to the ground, and crawled into the hole, breathing in the bitter dust as she did. The broken fragments of basalt ripped through the fabric of her trousers and the skin of her hands as she pulled herself through to the other side, then immediately began clearing as much of the debris as she could from around the hole.

A moment later, Achmed's head appeared, his face contorted in pain. His shoulders caught as he struggled through, wedging him in the hole. With great effort he pulled himself back again, then reached an arm through first. Rhapsody grabbed his hand and pulled, bracing herself against the rockwall with one foot. She could feel the crack of the bones in his hand and shuddered.

'Pull harder,' Achmed mumbled, his face in the gravel of the floor.

'Your ribs – '

'Pull *harder*,' he growled. Rhapsody set her teeth and repositioned her foot once more, then pulled with all her strength. A sickening popping vibrated through her hands, and she heard the intake of breath as Achmed swallowed the sound of agony. His head and shoulders emerged. Rhapsody slid her hands under his armpits and tugged again, hauling his upper body free of the hole and striping his back with streaks of blood as it grazed against the jagged rocks of the floor. A moment later he was free, clutching his broken ribs, and she helped him rise. They exchanged a quick nod, then turned and ran up the passageway again.

They scrambled over a pile of broken granite that had once been the great archway, the shattered words of the inscription now littering the ground in mute testimony to the wisdom they had once held. The

Sleeping Child was no longer within their sight. Achmed's foot slipped as he reached the summit of the mound and wedged in a crevasse. Rhapsody pulled it out before following him over the hill.

Before them yawned the tunnel opening to the Loritorium.

'Can you see the Earthchild?' Rhapsody gasped. Achmed shook his head, then rapidly descended the hill, running until he reached the smooth marble of the Loritorium floor.

The flame of the firewell was twisting brightly in its fountain, casting grim shadows around the streets and over the silent buildings. Rhapsody ran to the central square where the cases that housed the elements stood, then stopped and exhaled in relief. The Sleeping Child was standing there, near the altar of Living Stone, eyes still closed. The Sleepwalker.

Rhapsody slowed her gait and walked toward the tall figure as quietly as she could, taking care not to frighten her. The Earthchild ran her hands blindly over the altar of Living Stone, then turned slowly. She sat down on the top of the slab and then lay back, crossing her arms over her waist, resuming the position in which she had once rested on her catafalque. The shadows from the firelight illuminated her face, relaxing into a peaceful countenance, as they danced over her. She let loose a deep sigh.

Then, as Rhapsody stared in astonishment, the body of the Sleeping Child seemed to become liquid and began to shift and expand. Her chest and head glistened, then glowed with a light of their own. The flesh of her long, stone-gray body became translucent, gleaming in the flickering light from the firewell, then stretched in an absurd dance, twisting hypnotically, grotesquely, in earth-colors more intensely beautiful than Rhapsody had ever seen, a multiplicity of subtle shades of vermilion and green, brown and purple. *Like bread dough being kneaded,* she thought as the child's abdomen elongated, then distended upward. *Ethereal bread dough.*

An acrid odor shattered her reverie and snapped her to awareness. Rhapsody turned away from watching the transformation the Child of Earth was undergoing to see Achmed raking his sword through the slender channels of the Loritorium's street lamp system, as if driving a herd of small animals within the narrow arteries. The blistering odor brought water to her eyes and nose, and panic flashed through her as she recognized the smell.

He had unplugged the stone dam of the lampfuel. She looked behind him to see it was gushing from the reservoir, running in a great corpulent river from the center of the square to the tunnel into the Colony, filling the streets and pooling dangerously close to the firewell.

'Gods, what are you *doing?*' she cried. 'Get away from there! It will ignite!'

Achmed continued to drag the blade through the channels, directing the thick ooze back to the halfwall closest to the tunnel leading back to Ylorc.

'That's the idea.' He turned and stared at her as he shook the thick liquid from his sword and sheathed it again. 'How else do you propose to kill the vine? You said yourself that fire cauterizes it. It's already tapped into the power of the Axis Mundi, in case you couldn't tell. If we don't cut if off, burn it into oblivion here, now, that root will eventually reach all the way down to the *other* Sleeping Child.' He slammed the plug back into place and stared at her again. His mismatched eyes glittered ominously in the shadowlight. 'Light it.'

'We can't yet,' Rhapsody answered, feeling suddenly cold. 'Grunthor and the Grandmother are still in there.'

Achmed nodded behind her, and she whirled around. The Sleeping Child's body had become incongruously distended, swollen out of all proportion. An oblongated peninsula of earth-flesh grew large, stretching vertically, then horizontally. It surged upward in a smooth rolling motion, as if dividing itself, and rose to a monstrous height. The section made a final, twisting turn and then separated from the body of the child, now lying, significantly smaller and motionless, on the Living Stone slab.

The glowing light of the newly separated piece dimmed into the color of stone, then warmed before her eyes into gray-green skin, oily and hidelike. Instant by instant it took on a more delineated shape, taking on human lines where a moment before it had been a formless mass. Rhapsody's eyes widened.

'Grunthor!'

The giant exhaled and stumbled forward, catching himself by clutching the altar of Living Stone. *'Hrekin,'* he muttered weakly.

Rhapsody started toward her friend, only to feel a viselike grip around her upper arm. She looked up into the eyes of the Firbolg king, burning with a fury hotter than the flames of the firewell. He pointed to the trail of lampfuel, a liquid fuse from the firewell into the darkened cavern of the Colony.

'It wouldn't have mattered if he *had* been in there still. There's no other choice anymore. Now light it.'

Rhapsody shuddered at the all-consuming anger in Achmed's eyes, the hallmark of the unquenchable racial hatred his half-Dhracian nature held for the F'dor and all their minions. It was an animus that no love, no friendship, no rational thought could sway or defuse when it was in full rampage. 'The Grandmother is still in there,' she said haltingly. 'Would you leave her to die with it?'

Achmed stared down at her a moment longer, then closed his eyes and let the path lore he had gained in the belly of the Earth loose. His inner sight sped through the pale marble streets, following the flood of lampfuel through the hole in the earth-dam they had crawled under, over the broken walls and slabs of shattered stone that had once held the last colony of his kind. His mind flew over the crumbled archway and its scattered words, under the twisting vines and rootlets writhing with mounting strength. Even where he stood in the streets of the Loritorium he could smell the stench of the F'dor growing, see the clay of the Earth shuddering as it prepared to give way.

Within the ruins of the cavern of the Sleeping Child his second sight stopped. He could see the Grandmother there, surrounded by a veritable cage of hissing vines, poised to strike, one leg pinned beneath a fallen granite slab amid the buckled walls of the chamber. Her left hand was upraised, trembling with strain, her right one braced against the slab that held her captive. Rivers of poisonous lampfuel gushed over her, beginning to fill the cavern.

She seemed infinitesimal in size, dwarfed by the colossal vine that hovered menacingly above her, its massive offshoots swollen with rage, tangled within the remains of the chamber's floor. Its roots were snarling now, coated with glistening lampfuel, lashing out at her, coming nearer to reaching her as she began to fail.

Then, just as his mind was absorbing the horror of the sight, the Grandmother turned toward him, and her eyes met his vision. A tiny smile, the only one he had ever seen her indulge in, came over the ancient face, wrinkled and lined with age and so many centuries of somber guardianship. She nodded to him, and with the last of her strength turned back to face the vine that was threatening to break the Thrall.

Achmed fought back the primordial rage that was singing through his blood in the presence of the race he hated with every fiber of his being. He choked back the bile that had risen to his constricted throat as the vision disappeared. Then he squeezed Rhapsody's arm again.

'Light it,' he repeated in a low, deadly voice.

With a vicious tug Rhapsody pulled free from his grasp. 'Let go,' she snarled.

Angrily Achmed grabbed for Daystar Clarion. 'Damn you – ' He pulled back in pain and shock as she drew the sword like lightning and raked it across his open palm, singeing the skin.

'Don't *ever* attempt to wrest this sword from me unless you are prepared to draw your own,' Rhapsody shouted.

'Skychild?'

All three companions stopped, glancing around the Loritorium for the origin of the Grandmother's voice. The fricative click, the sandy sound that Rhapsody had only heard in one other voice, was unmistakable. The single word came with great effort, spoken very softly.

It was Grunthor who found the source first. He gestured to Rhapsody. 'Here, darlin'.' He was pointing to the Sleeping Child.

In a daze Rhapsody came to the altar of Living Stone where the child lay. She stared down at the smooth gray skin, the coarse brown hair so like highgrass in the heat of summer. Tenderly she ran her hand over the child's forehead, brushing the clods of fallen dirt from her brow. She could feel a surge of power, a vibration issuing forth from the stone of the altar through the body of the Earthchild, tingling across the skin of her hand and speaking directly to her heart. She had to struggle to bring herself to answer.

'Yes, Grandmother?'

The Sleeping Child's brow wrinkled with the effort of speech. Her eyes remained closed, grassy lashes wet with tears. Her lips formed the Grandmother's last words.

'*Light it.*'

The ancient Dhracian's voice had passed through the ground, as if the Earth itself had wished to serve as the stalwart guardian's final messenger. It had traveled through the slab of Living Stone and through the Earth's last living Child. The irony brought tears to Rhapsody's eyes. The Grandmother would never hear the words of wisdom she had waited a lifetime for from the Earthchild's lips. The only words the Sleeping Child would speak would be the Grandmother's own.

Rhapsody looked up into the faces of her two friends. The men watched as her sorrowful expression hardened into a resolute one.

'All right,' she said. 'I will. Get out of here.'

56

Without a word Grunthor gathered the Sleeping Child from the altar of Living Stone in his arms and nodded up the corridor that led back to Ylorc. He and Achmed ran a short distance up the tunnel.

When Grunthor was sure Rhapsody could still see him he turned toward the side wall, holding the body of the child in front of him, then stepped forward into the earth. The granite glowed for a moment as he passed through, then cooled into a rocky opening. Achmed followed Grunthor into the bunker the giant had made in the side of the corridor. He leaned back, signaled to Rhapsody, and when he saw her nod he stepped back inside. Grunthor gave the wall a strong shove, and the rock that had been cleared away to form the bunker slid liquidly back into position, sealing off their hiding place.

Slowly Rhapsody turned in a full circle, surveying for the last time the Loritorium as it had been. The pools of glistening silver memory shone, torch-bright, in the street, reflecting the flame from the firewell. She struggled not to be swallowed by the despair she felt at witnessing the end of what had once been such a noble dream, such a worthy undertaking. Scholarship and the search for knowledge, dying on the altar of greed and the lust for power.

When she was sure that her friends and the child were all the way inside the earthen bunker with the rock-seal tightly in place she drew Daystar Clarion, whispering a prayer to the unseen stars miles above her that she was doing the right thing.

In the lore-heavy air the flaming blade roared to life, singing its clarion call. It sent a silver thrill ringing through Rhapsody and the cavern around her; for an instant she was certain that the Grandmother had heard the melodic shout, and had taken heart from it. Rhapsody closed her eyes and concentrated, thinking back to another ancient woman, a warrior like the Grandmother, who had stayed, alone and unacknowledged, seeking to protect the world from the F'dor.

I have lived past my time, waiting for a guardian to come and replace me. Now that I have someone to pass my stewardship on to, I will eventually be able to find the peace that I have longed for. I will at long last be reunited with those I love. Immortality in this world is not the only kind, you know, Rhapsody.

The words of ultimate wisdom from the lips of the Sleeping Child.

Light it.

Rhapsody fought to conquer the nausea that was swelling within her. It didn't matter that she was doing as the Grandmother commanded, or how necessary the imminent act was. She was going to be the agent of the last Dhracian's death. She would be burning her alive. There was something more to it, something about the act of immolation that tugged at the edge of her memory, but she could not recall what it was, as if it had been removed from her mind. Rhapsody shook her head to clear the thought and concentrated on the sword.

Deep inside her she felt a swell of power, and strengthening of her spirit, radiating from her hands where she gripped the hilt of Daystar Clarion. The doubt and sadness of the Grandmother's impending death burned off like dew in the blaze of the morning sun. She and the sword were one.

It is you, Rhapsody; I knew it from the moment I saw you. Even if you weren't one of the Three, I believe in my heart that you are the one to do this; the true Iliachenva'ar.

Rhapsody stared at the gleaming flame of the firewell, listening to its song. Once she had passed through the fire in the Earth's heart, the same fire that was the source of this flame. The fire had not harmed her; it had seeped into her soul until it was part of her.

It was most of her.

It would not harm her now. It awaited her command.

Rhapsody pointed Daystar Clarion at the well of fire. In the rippling flame she could see her own eyes reflected, eyes burning green, blending into the fire's many hues.

Light it.

'Vingka jai,' she said, calling on her deepest lore as a Namer. Her voice rang with authority, filling the Loritorium's cavern. *Ignite and spread.*

She struggled to keep her eyes open against the fireball that ensued.

The licking flames from Daystar Clarion's blade leapt forward angrily, righteously, blazing a gleaming arc from the sword to the fountainhead. When the flame from the sword touched the Earth's fire they melded, forming a ray of light more intense than Rhapsody had ever seen, even in the starfire that had lighted Jo's funeral pyre. A commingling of the fire with the Earth, the ether of the stars, and the purest of elemental fire's flames, the burning ray blasted out of the fountainhead and torched the liquid fuse Achmed had made, sending a ferocious sheet of fire crackling to the upper reaches of the vaulted ceiling.

Then, with an earth-shattering roar, the fire and the lampfuel erupted, surging through the tunnel and into the remains of the Colony. As the mammoth fireball billowed forward, it filled the entire space, sending liquid heat and blinding light into every crevasse, expanding until it reached to the edges of the caverns and tunnels. It washed over Rhapsody, filling her with exquisite warmth and joy; in its passing she heard the song of the fire at the Earth's heart, a song she had carried with her since the first time she heard it. It was like being reborn again, cleansed of the pain and grief she had been carrying for so long.

From within the ruins of the Colony a hideous shrieking issued forth, screams of demonic intensity that tore through the Loritorium, shaking its flame-scorched walls. Rhapsody gripped the sword harder, concentrating with all her strength on directing the fire through the broken tunnels, envisioning it burning the tangled vine into obliteration.

'Cerant ori sylviat,' Rhapsody commanded. *Burn until all is consumed.* The intensity of the flames increased in the distance, raising the moan of the enormous serpent-vine to an earsplitting wail.

Above the fire's roar Rhapsody began the Lirin Song of Passage, a dirge for the Grandmother. Though she had lived her entire life within the earth, the Dhracian Matriarch was also descended from the Kith, the race of the wind. Perhaps the wind would take her ashes now and set them free to dance across the wild world, a place she had never seen from above. The song cut through the cacophony and melded in harmony with the billowing flames.

And then, suddenly, the flames grew weak and extinguished, taking with them the last of the air in the cavern. A hollow silence thundered through the Loritorium, then diminished into an ominous hiss. Rhapsody fell to her knees, breathless and gasping for air in the lifeless smoke.

The one who heals also will kill.

The enormity of what she had done to the Grandmother overwhelmed her, and, choking, she retched.

Grunthor and Achmed covered their eyes and heads, shielding the Sleeping Child as the backwash of the flame roared up the tunnel past their bunker. Their clothes grew hot from the searing heat that radiated through the solid wall of rock, and their eyes locked. Achmed smiled slightly at the gleam of fear in Grunthor's eyes.

'She's all right.'

Grunthor nodded. They waited until the noise abated, but heard nothing.

'We'll wait,' Achmed said. 'She'll be coming momentarily.'

'How can you be sure?' Grunthor asked.

Achmed leaned back against the rockwall. 'I've learned a few of her tricks myself. Believe what you want to happen, expect that it will, and somehow, miraculously, it does, at least for her. It worked with singing her back to life. It will work now.'

Grunthor nodded uncertainly and turned his focus to the Earthchild. She lay in his arms in the dark, still for the first time, sleeping so deeply that he could barely see her breathe. He watched her silently take the air in, saw it ever-so-slightly slip back out, over again, and again, utterly mesmerized by the sight.

They had shared one body for a fleeting moment, the Child of Earth and he. From the experience he had gained an understanding of many of the Earth's secrets, though he would have been at a loss to explain any of them. There was something almost holy about having felt the beating heart of the world pulsing in him, a surpassing vibrancy that left him feeling bereft now that it was gone.

He stared at the Earthchild's face, roughhewn and coarse like his own, while still strangely smooth and beautiful, visible to him even in the absence of light. He knew there were silent tears running in muddy trickles down her polished cheeks, knew that she was mourning the Grandmother, holding a silent vigil behind her eyes. Now he understood what the Dhracian Matriarch had meant when she said she had known the child's heart. Perhaps now he would know it as well.

It was not until Achmed shifted nervously and leaned closer to the rocks sealing their bunker that it dawned on him how long Rhapsody had been gone. The king put his ear to the wall, then moved back, shaking his head.

'Anything?' Grunthor inquired hopefully. Achmed shook his head again.

'Can you feel her through the earth?'

Grunthor thought for a moment. 'No. Everything's all jumbled, like the ground is still in shock. Can't tell anything.'

Achmed rose shakily. 'Perhaps I can't feel her heartbeat for the same reason.' Grunthor's eyes glinted with fear. 'We'll give her a moment more, and if she doesn't come, we'll go after her.' He leaned against the stone, trying to make out any sound he could on the other side of the rockwall. He heard nothing.

'Rhapsody!' he shouted, the sound bouncing futilely back at him, to be swallowed a moment later by the earthen bunker. He turned to Grunthor, his dark eyes glittering.

'Open it,' he ordered tersely, pointing at the rocky barrier.

Grunthor carefully shifted the Earthchild in his arms and reached one hand into the wall. A sizable piece of it fell away before him. As if in reply, he heard Rhapsody's voice calling to them from the other side of the stone wall.

'Grunthor! Achmed! Are you all right in there?'

The giant Bolg stood up and reached the rest of the way into the stone of the wall, tearing it away from the opening. When he broke through to the other side his face lit up with a tired grin.

'Well, well, Your Ladyship, you certainly took your time, now, didn't you? Had us worried, you did.'

Rhapsody smiled and offered Achmed her hand, giving him a tug out of the bunker. 'You're a fine one to talk,' she said to Grunthor. 'For the longest time I thought you were still in the Colony, buried under a mountain of rock.' Her smile faded as he stepped out of the hole in the rockwall, carrying the Sleeping Child. 'I have to admit, when I saw her walking, I thought it was over. What did you do, meld with her the way you do with stone?'

'Yep. What do you think she is, if not stone?' Grunthor answered simply. 'Didn't think I could carry her safely out through all that mess. It was the easiest way.'

Achmed gestured toward the Colony entrance. 'Come on.'

The enormous tunnel was deathly silent save for the occasional pop or hiss from the ash that blackened the entirety of the walls and floor. Around and above them, where the vine had broken violently through the cavern, nothing remained except for scorched fragments of root and the twisting ruins of the tunnel it had carved in the earth.

Achmed bent down at what had once been the arch over the Sleeping Child's catafalque and ran his sensitive fingers over the scattered letters of the words that had been carved there. Once they had warned a world that never saw them about the dangers of disturbing that which slept within it. Now they littered the floor of the cavern, broken into pieces of senseless babble.

Rhapsody's hand came to rest on his shoulder. 'Are you all right?'

Achmed nodded distantly. Somewhere here were the Grandmother's ashes, mingled inexorably with those of the demon-vine, inseparable as the intertwined fate of Dhracian and F'dor. It saddened him to think that the end of Time would find them that way. He stood and brushed the dirt from his hands. He stared down the twisting tunnel from where the vine had come.

'This goes all the way back to the House of Remembrance, two hundred leagues or more,' he said, squinting into the darkness. 'Not good. It will be a vulnerability, a passageway into the mountain for the F'dor.'

'Not for long,' Grunthor said cheerfully. He drew the Sleeping Child closer to his chest and closed his eyes, feeling the nearness of the Earth's life's blood to his heart. He reached out and laid a hand on the wall.

Rhapsody and Achmed leapt back as the tunnel swelled and collapsed, filling in the monstrous rip the vine had torn in the Earth. The Earth itself shrugged, reapportioning its mass, closing the doorway through which the F'dor had reached into the mountain.

Rhapsody looked above her. Despite the shifting of enormous amounts of earth, nothing rained down on their heads except for a little dust. She looked at Grunthor again. He was translucent, radiating the same glow that she had seen within the Earth when they were crawling along the Axis Mundi. *The Child of Earth*, she thought fondly.

When the glow diminished, Grunthor pulled his hand away from the wall, then turned and smiled.

'All closed.'

'All the way back to Navarne?' Achmed asked incredulously.

'Yep.'

'How'd you manage that?'

The Bolg Sergeant grinned down at the child in his arms. 'With help, sir.'

The cavern sealed, the three turned back toward the Loritorium. Rhapsody smiled at Grunthor and ran her fingers gently over the Sleeping Child's forehead. The Earthchild sighed in her sleep.

'What are you going to do with her now, Achmed?'

'Guard her,' he said flatly.

'Of course. I was just wondering where.'

Achmed looked around what remained of the Loritorium, its artistic carvings cracked and scarred, the beautiful frescoes and mosaics blackened with soot, the pools of silver memory gone. 'Here,' he said. 'At first I considered bringing her back to the Cauldron so that it would be easy to keep an eye on her, but it would be too disruptive to her.

'This really is the ideal place for her. It's buried deep enough that she won't be disturbed by the Bolg. She can sleep on the altar of Living Stone; she seemed peaceful there.'

Rhapsody nodded. 'Perhaps it will bring her solace.'

'Perhaps. We'll need to reseal the tunnel we made coming down here and retrap the place. There's enough lampfuel in that well to build our own volcano if we have to. Then, when he's gotten his strength back, Grunthor can open a single passageway from the Loritorium to my chambers. If the F'dor is going to make another attempt at her, I want it to have to come through me personally. It will be an engineering nightmare, but I think we can pull it off.'

Rhapsody nodded as Grunthor gently laid the child on the altar. 'It *will* try again, you know.'

'Of course. But I don't think it will try again like this. It's gathering an army to assault the Bolglands; I'm not exactly clear on how it plans to do it, but I'm certain of it. That's why Ashe was its target to begin with – he was the convergence of the royal Cymrian lines, as well as the Invoker's son. He could easily have assumed the throne of Roland, and most likely brought Manosse with him, as well as any nonaligned Cymrians from the early generations loyal to either side that might happen to still be around, like Anborn.'

'And possibly Tyrian as well,' Rhapsody added. 'His mother was Lirin.' Oelendra's words in front of the roaring fire came back to her. *If the F'dor had been able to bind him, to command the dragon, I shudder to imagine how it would have used that power to control the elements themselves.* 'The whole world is fortunate that he was strong enough to get away.'

Achmed stared at the ruin around him. 'The army Ashe could have raised might actually have been able to do what Anwyn could not – take the mountain. He would have been the perfect host for the F'dor, but he managed to get away and stay hidden from it these past two decades. Now that it knows he's alive, it will undoubtedly be looking for him again.'

'That's his problem to deal with,' Rhapsody said resolutely. 'We've given him the tools he needs to survive. His soul is his own again, he's whole once more and out of pain. He can go into hiding for a while if he needs to. He did it for twenty years. He'll be all right.'

A wry smile crawled into the corner of Achmed's mouth. 'I can't tell you how much good it does me to hear you talking like that,' he said. 'Does this mean your assignation with him is over?'

Rhapsody looked away. 'Yes.'

'What do you plan to do now?'

She stood a little straighter, and Achmed was struck by the warriorlike aspect that came over her face and posture. 'First, I want to make sure Ylorc is taken care of, and give you and Grunthor any help you need in dismantling the Loritorium and getting the Earthchild settled. After that I need a day to mourn, to sing dirges and laments for all whom we have lost.' Achmed nodded, noting that the steady look in her eyes didn't waver when she referred to her sister and the Grandmother. 'Then, if you think you can be spared from the Bolglands for a bit, I could use your assistance in locating the various children of the F'dor.'

'Only if you're planning to dispose of them,' Achmed said, a warning note entering his voice. 'Somehow given your proclivity for children, Rhapsody, I can't see you succeeding in that undertaking.'

'I have no intentions of disposing of them unless they make it necessary, and then I will do so in a heartbeat,' she replied. 'This is no different than it was with Ashe. They are people with human souls, Achmed, with demon blood in their veins. They can be helped. They need to be helped.'

'How do you know they aren't little demonic monsters like the Rakshas?' he demanded, a note of irritation creeping into his voice. He didn't like the turn the exchange had taken.

'They were born of human mothers, and Ashe's soul was present in the Rakshas. The presence of a soul in the parent bequeaths a soul to the child. They aren't monsters, Achmed, any more than the Bolg are. They're children, children with tainted blood. If somehow we can separate that blood out, they have at least some hope of avoiding an eternity of damnation.'

'No,' he said angrily. 'It isn't worth the risk. Any one of them might be bound to the F'dor already. We want to meet the F'dor on our terms, not on its own.'

Rhapsody smiled coldly. 'Exactly. Your ability to sense blood from the old world will help me find the children, Achmed. If that part of their blood which is demonic can be extracted, I will give it to you. Then you will have the blood of the F'dor, a trail of scent for the hunt.' She looked over at Grunthor, who was listening. 'We'll finally be able to find it. It has given us the means.'

Blood will be the means.

462

The king and the sergeant exchanged a glance, then Achmed looked back at her.

'All right,' he said finally. 'But make no mistake about it, Rhapsody. If there is even a split second when any of the demon-spawn pose even the slightest of threats, to any of us, I will cut its throat before it exhales, and dispatch it back to its father's realm in the Underworld. This will not be open for debate or exception. Do you agree?'

Rhapsody nodded. 'Fair enough,' she said.

57

It was eight days later when the Three finally emerged from the darkness of the crevasse that had once hidden the entrance to the Loritorium. It had taken most of that time for Grunthor to recover from the effort of sealing off all the passageways and the entire length of the tunnel he had burrowed. Without the contact he had had with the Earthchild the task had proven vastly more difficult, had taken a far greater toll on the giant, but not as much of a toll as leaving her behind in the darkness of the blackened vault, hidden away from all but Time.

The farewell itself was equally painful. Rhapsody had kissed the child's stone-gray forehead as Grunthor covered her carefully with his greatcloak in place of the soft blanket of woven spider-silk that the Grandmother had always nestled around her. Achmed extinguished the street lamps, leaving nothing but the flickering fireshadows from the flame-well dimly lighting the Loritorium, once a great undertaking devoted to the pursuit of scholarship, now only the dark cavern that served as the Sleeping Child's chamber.

As they left her to her repose, Rhapsody whispered a last lullabye, then followed her friends into the shattered entrance to the deeper realm.

> White light
> Yon comes the night
> Snow drapes the frozen world,
> *Watch and wait, watch and wait*
> Prepare for sleep
> In ice castles deep
> A promise to keep
> A year whose days left are dearth
> Remembers the Child of the Earth

Before they sealed off the charred remains of the network of tunnels that had once been the Colony, they stood one last time in the Canticle circle together. Rhapsody sang a dirge for the Dhracians who had died so long ago in the Last Night genocide, and one for the woman who had stood a lonely vigil since then, guarding the Earthchild until they had come. As she was singing the underground wind fell silent, as if finally acknowledging the death of the *Zhereditck*, the Windchildren, and the civilization they had once made to keep the Earth from destruction.

When the lament was over, Rhapsody and Grunthor went back across the crumbling bridge, leaving Achmed alone in the circle. He stood within the carved runes, the symbols disappearing from the surface of the floor with the passage of time, and watched the pendulum clock swinging endlessly back and forth through the darkness.

The Earth says it was your death, sir. That you don't know it yet, but you will.

Now he did.

Once back in the Cauldron Rhapsody checked in on her Firbolg grandchildren, then joined Achmed and Grunthor in the Great Hall to catch up on the news brought by the weekly mail caravan.

The soldiers and merchants of the convoy had sought an audience to share the report that came to them en route from Roland by avian messenger. Dual earthquakes, a great roar of heat followed by the trembling of the earth, had rumbled through the continent, the excited guards reported, disturbing the ground from the Teeth to the center of Navarne. Rhapsody cast a sidelong glance at Grunthor, who remained at unblinking attention, seemingly unfazed by the reverberations from the lampfuel fireball and his sealing of the demon-vine's passageway.

No lives had been lost, the guards reported, and no real damage had occurred, with one notable exception, Rhapsody was tremendously saddened to hear that the terminus of the tremor was the House of Remembrance, which ignited in flames and was burned to ashes, along with a goodly portion of the tainted forest that surrounded it. The only saving grace was the news that the tree in its courtyard, the sapling of Sagia brought by the Cymrians from their homeland so many centuries before, had miraculously survived the conflagration. Rhapsody secretly hoped it would thrive now that it was purged of the demon-root that had despoiled it for so long.

After the messengers left she climbed through the deepening shadows of twilight to the wide Heath, the place which had borne witness to so much hope and despair. She sat down in the high grass, blanched and dry in the grip of frost, the sword across her knees, and watched as the evening stars emerged one by one in the firmament of the heavens. The winter sky was bell-clear and cold, deepening from a cerulean blue at its apex down to the inky blackness of night at the horizon.

Hovering over the easternmost peaks of the Teeth she saw Prylla appear, the star the Lirin had named for the woodland Windchild. It was the star that had lit Jo's pyre, the marker of lost love. It twinkled in the clear air of night. Rhapsody watched it with dry eyes, listening to its song. *Do not mourn*, it seemed to whisper. *Love has not been lost; it's been found.*

She sang her evening vespers softly into the wind, letting the breeze take the last of her sadness away with it as it whistled over the mountaintops and across the rippling plain. The elements of the races that had given birth to the Lirin, the ether of the stars and the whispering wind, shone down on her, wrapped around her, cleansing her spirit, making the fire within her burn steady and bright. She was all right. She was strong, ready for whatever was to come.

She was the Iliachenva'ar.

Far away, in the ruins of the House of Remembrance at the foot of the sapling tree, a hooded figure stood in the wind as well. He gazed up into its branches, awed by the sight.

There, amid the smoldering ash blending with the mist rising from his cloak, the tree was blooming gloriously, bright blossoms gracing its boughs even in the depth of winter. A small harp was nestled in its branches, stalwartly playing a ringing roundelay.